The
MX Book
of
New
Sherlock
Holmes
Stories

Part XXXVIII – 2023 Annual
(1890-1896)

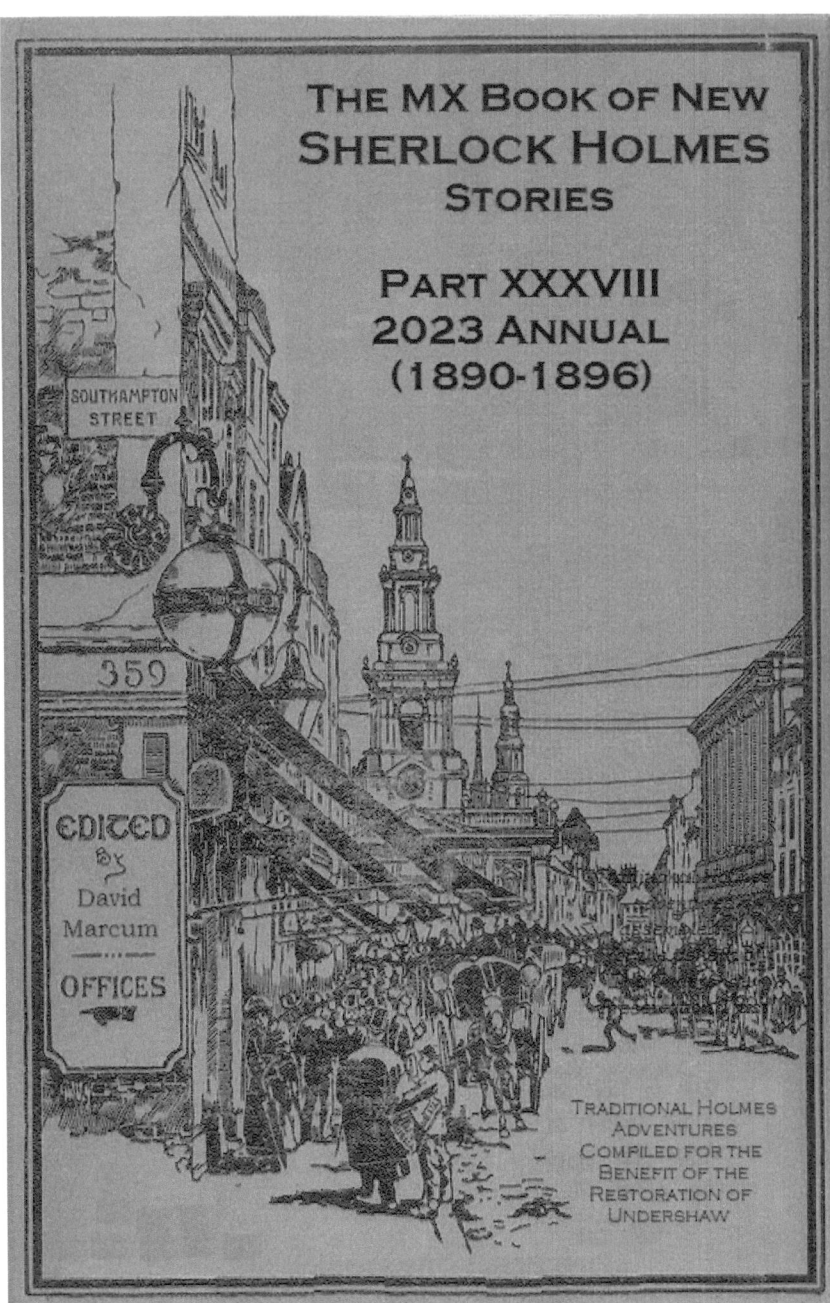

THE MX BOOK OF NEW
SHERLOCK HOLMES
STORIES

PART XXXVIII
2023 ANNUAL
(1890-1896)

SOUTHAMPTON
STREET

359

EDITED
BY
David
Marcum

OFFICES

TRADITIONAL HOLMES
ADVENTURES
COMPILED FOR THE
BENEFIT OF THE
RESTORATION OF
UNDERSHAW

ISBN Hardback 978-1-80424-225-4
ISBN Paperback 978-1-80424-226-1
AUK ePub ISBN 978-1-80424-227-8
AUK PDF ISBN 978-1-80424-228-5

Published in the UK by
MX Publishing
335 Princess Park Manor, Royal Drive,
London, N11 3GX
www.mxpublishing.co.uk

David Marcum can be reached at:
thepapersofsherlockholmes@gmail.com

Cover design by Brian Belanger
www.belangerbooks.com and *www.redbubble.com/people/zhahadun*

Internal Illustrations by Sidney Paget

CONTENTS

Forewords

Adventures

(Continued on the next page . . . .)

(Continued on the next page . . . .)

These additional adventures are contained in
Part XXXVII: 2023 Annual
(1875-1889)

Part XXXIX: 2023 Annual
(1897-1923)

(Continued on the next page . . . .)

These additional Sherlock Holmes adventures
can be found in the previous volumes of
The MX Book of New Sherlock Holmes Stories

(Continued on the next page . . . .)

PART III: 1896-1929

PART IV – 2016 Annual

(Continued on the next page . . . .)

PART V – Christmas Adventures

(Continued on the next page . . . .)

PART VI – 2017 Annual

(Continued on the next page . . . .)

The Unwelcome Client – Keith Hann
The Tempest of Lyme – David Ruffle
The Problem of the Holy Oil – David Marcum
A Scandal in Serbia – Thomas A. Turley
The Curious Case of Mr. Marconi – Jan Edwards
Mr. Holmes and Dr. Watson Learn to Fly – C. Edward Davis
Die Weisse Frau – Tim Symonds
A Case of Mistaken Identity – Daniel D. Victor

PART VII – Eliminate the Impossible: 1880-1891

Foreword – Lee Child
Foreword – Rand B. Lee
Foreword – Michael Cox
Foreword – Roger Johnson
Foreword – Melissa Farnham
Foreword – David Marcum
No Ghosts Need Apply (A Poem) – Jacquelynn Morris
The Melancholy Methodist – Mark Mower
The Curious Case of the Sweated Horse – Jan Edwards
The Adventure of the Second William Wilson – Daniel D. Victor
The Adventure of the Marchindale Stiletto – James Lovegrove
The Case of the Cursed Clock – Gayle Lange Puhl
The Tranquility of the Morning – Mike Hogan
A Ghost from Christmas Past – Thomas A. Turley
The Blank Photograph – James Moffett
The Adventure of A Rat. – Adrian Middleton
The Adventure of Vanaprastha – Hugh Ashton
The Ghost of Lincoln – Geri Schear
The Manor House Ghost – S. Subramanian
The Case of the Unquiet Grave – John Hall
The Adventure of the Mortal Combat – Jayantika Ganguly
The Last Encore of Quentin Carol – S.F. Bennett
The Case of the Petty Curses – Steven Philip Jones
The Tuttman Gallery – Jim French
The Second Life of Jabez Salt – John Linwood Grant
The Mystery of the Scarab Earrings – Thomas Fortenberry
The Adventure of the Haunted Room – Mike Chinn
The Pharaoh's Curse – Robert V. Stapleton
The Vampire of the Lyceum – Charles Veley and Anna Elliott
The Adventure of the Mind's Eye – Shane Simmons

PART VIII – Eliminate the Impossible: 1892-1905

Foreword – Lee Child
Foreword – Rand B. Lee
Foreword – Michael Cox
Foreword – Roger Johnson
Foreword – Melissa Farnham

(Continued on the next page . . . .)

Part IX – 2018 Annual (1879-1895)

(Continued on the next page . . . .)

(Continued on the next page . . . .)

Part XII: Some Untold Cases (1894-1902)

PART XIII: 2019 Annual (1881-1890)

(Continued on the next page . . . .)

PART XIV: 2019 Annual (1891 -1897)

(Continued on the next page . . . .)

(Continued on the next page . . . .)

Part XVII – Whatever Remains . . . Must Be the Truth (1891-1898)

Part XVIII – Whatever Remains . . . Must Be the Truth (1899-1925)

(Continued on the next page . . . .)

Part XIX: 2020 Annual (1882-1890)

(Continued on the next page . . . .)

(Continued on the next page . . . .)

Part XXII: Some More Untold Cases (1877-1887)

(Continued on the next page . . . .)

The Dundas Separation Case – Kevin P. Thornton
The Broken Glass – Denis O. Smith

Part XXIII: Some More Untold Cases (1888-1894)
Foreword – Otto Penzler
Foreword – Roger Johnson
Foreword – Steve Emecz
Foreword – Jacqueline Silver
Foreword – David Marcum
The Housekeeper (*A Poem*) – John Linwood Grant
The Uncanny Adventure of the Hammersmith Wonder – Will Murray
Mrs. Forrester's Domestic Complication– Tim Gambrell
The Adventure of the Abducted Bard – I.A. Watson
The Adventure of the Loring Riddle – Craig Janacek
To the Manor Bound – Jane Rubino
The Crimes of John Clay – Paul Hiscock
The Adventure of the Nonpareil Club – Hugh Ashton
The Adventure of the Singular Worm – Mike Chinn
The Adventure of the Forgotten Brolly – Shane Simmons
The Adventure of the Tired Captain – Dacre Stoker and Leverett Butts
The Rhayader Legacy – David Marcum
The Adventure of the Tired Captain – Matthew J. Elliott
The Secret of Colonel Warburton's Insanity – Paul D. Gilbert
The Adventure of Merridew of Abominable Memory – Tracy J. Revels
The Affair of the Hellingstone Rubies – Margaret Walsh
The Adventure of the Drewhampton Poisoner – Arthur Hall
The Incident of the Dual Intrusions – Barry Clay
The Case of the Un-Paralleled Adventures – Steven Philip Jones
The Affair of the Friesland – Jan van Koningsveld
The Forgetful Detective – Marcia Wilson
The Smith-Mortimer Succession – Tim Gambrell
The Repulsive Matter of the Bloodless Banker – Will Murray

Part XXIV: Some More Untold Cases (1895-1903)
Foreword – Otto Penzler
Foreword – Roger Johnson
Foreword – Steve Emecz
Foreword – Jacqueline Silver
Foreword – David Marcum
Sherlock Holmes and the Return of the Missing Rhyme (*A Poem*) – Joseph W. Svec III
The Comet Wine's Funeral – Marcia Wilson
The Case of the Accused Cook – Brenda Seabrooke
The Case of Vanderbilt and the Yeggman – Stephen Herczeg

(Continued on the next page . . . .)

Part XXV: 2021 Annual (1881-1888)

(Continued on the next page . . . .)

(Continued on the next page . . . .)

Part XXVIII: More Christmas Adventures (1869-1888)

(Continued on the next page . . . .)

Part XXIX: More Christmas Adventures (1889-1896)

Part XXX: More Christmas Adventures (1897-1928)

(Continued on the next page . . . .)

The Adventure of the Chained Phantom – J.S. Rowlinson
Santa's Little Elves – Kevin Thornton
The Case of the Holly-Sprig Pudding – Naching T. Kassa
The Canterbury Manifesto – David Marcum
The Case of the Disappearing Beaune – J. Lawrence Matthews
A Price Above Rubies – Jane Rubino
The Intrigue of the Red Christmas – Shane Simmons
The Bitter Gravestones – Chris Chan
The Midnight Mass Murder – Paul Hiscock

Part XXXI: 2022 Annual (1875-1887)

Foreword – Jeffrey Hatcher
Foreword – Roger Johnson
Foreword – Steve Emecz
Foreword – Emma West
Foreword – David Marcum
The Nemesis of Sherlock Holmes (A Poem) – Kelvin I. Jones
The Unsettling Incident of the History Professor's Wife – Sean M. Wright
The Princess Alice Tragedy – John Lawrence
The Adventure of the Amorous Balloonist – I.A. Watson
The Pilkington Case – Kevin Patrick McCann
The Adventure of the Disappointed Lover – Arthur Hall
The Case of the Impressionist Painting – Tim Symonds
The Adventure of the Old Explorer – Tracy J. Revels
Dr. Watson's Dilemma – Susan Knight
The Colonial Exhibition – Hal Glatzer
The Adventure of the Drunken Teetotaler – Thomas A. Burns, Jr.
The Curse of Hollyhock House – Geri Schear
The Sethian Messiah – David Marcum
Dead Man's Hand – Robert Stapleton
The Case of the Wary Maid – Gordon Linzner
The Adventure of the Alexandrian Scroll – David MacGregor
The Case of the Woman at Margate – Terry Golledge
A Question of Innocence – DJ Tyrer
The Grosvenor Square Furniture Van – Terry Golledge
The Adventure of the Veiled Man – Tracy J. Revels
The Disappearance of Dr. Markey – Stephen Herczeg
The Case of the Irish Demonstration – Dan Rowley

Part XXXII: 2022 Annual (1888-1895)

Foreword – Jeffrey Hatcher
Foreword – Roger Johnson
Foreword – Steve Emecz

(Continued on the next page . . . .)

Part XXXIII: 2022 Annual (1896-1919)

(Continued on the next page . . . .)

(Continued on the next page . . . .)

Part XXXVI: "However Improbable . . . ." (1897-1919)

*The following contributors appear
in the companion volumes:*
The MX Book of New Sherlock Holmes Stories
Part XXXVII – 2023 Annual (1875-1889)
Part XXXIX – 2023 Annual (1897-1823)

Editor's Foreword:
The Sherlockian Reformation
by David Marcum

We are in a Golden Age of Sherlock Holmes, and have been since 1974. The demarcation is quite defined. Before that fateful year, Holmes was known the world over, and even then he was indisputably the greatest detective of all time – despite what a few other Great Detectives might have declared about themselves – but before 1974, finding ways to enter and enjoy The World of Holmes were severely limited. There were editions of The Canon – but not nearly so many as today. There were a few pastiches, but for most people, they might as well have never existed. These might be published in some magazine that would rotate off the newsstands after a month, never to be seen or found again by the common person. A scholarly work or occasional pastiche might be written for those within the tightly controlled Sherlockian community, with no intention to ever share it outside that circle.

This went on for decades – until 1974, when the modern-day Sherlockian equivalent of Martin Luther, Nicholas Meyer, nailed a new Holmes adventure to the church door, *The Seven-Per-Cent Solution*, his version of Luther's *Ninety-five Theses*, and gave Holmes to the masses, starting the Sherlockian Reformation.

And thank God he did.

The years when The Canon initially appeared, between 1887 and 1927, seem like a long stretch of time – three whole decades – but when one considers that just a pitifully few sixty stories were published during that time, what readers were able to learn about Holmes and Watson over the course of that span was actually severely limited. Sixty stories over thirty years – that averages just two stories per year. A starvation diet! And in truth, the appearances of the original stories were even more irregular.

A Study in Scarlet was published in November 1887, and *The Sign of the Four* in 1890 – and neither made a ripple. It was only in June 1891, just a month after Holmes's supposed death at the Reichenbach Falls, that Watson – wishing to spread the word about his recently deceased friend – published "A Scandal in Bohemia" in a new magazine, *The Strand*. The results were electrifying – and one wonders if *The Strand* would have gone on to such great heights without the infusion of Holmes's adventures during its early days.

Between June 1891 and December 1893, Watson, with the assistance of the First Literary Agent, published twenty-four shorter narratives. This run of two-dozen tales came to an end for several reasons. Watson, already grief-stricken due to Holmes's death, was further rocked by the death of his wife Mary, most likely in 1893. No doubt his enthusiasm for life – and writing – was severely damaged during this bleak period. His Literary Agent, a doctor named Arthur Conan Doyle who had notions of becoming the next Sir Walter Scott with his dense historical novels, was tired of being identified with Holmes's adventures, and wanted to disassociate himself from the project. And finally, Colonel James Moriarty, the brother of Professor James Moriarty, began to attack the memory of Sherlock Holmes by way of letters, leaving Watson no choice but to respond by laying forth the true facts of Holmes's fateful Swiss encounter with the Professor. When "The Final Problem" was published in December 1893, Watson likely felt that writing other posthumous adventures was unnecessary.

At that time, much of the world was shocked to learn that Holmes had apparently died over two years earlier, on May 4th, 1891. While those who had known Holmes had been aware of it at the time, he was generally unknown to the public – particularly due to his insistence that others take the credit for his work – so his 1891 passing went largely unremarked. The announcement in 1893 rocked the world.

After Watson wrote and published "The Final Problem", his Literary Agent moved on to other things, and Watson apparently lost the will to continue producing new stories. One wonders what might have happened to him, a widower living alone in Kensington, working at a practice that likely left him quite uninspired, and eking out his days, one after another *ad infinitum*, in a dull routine of existence.

Then came a dramatic moment of fate – specifically on April 5th, 1894 – when Watson re-encountered Sherlock Holmes, not dead at all, but rather working in the shadows for nearly three years, carrying out missions in foreign lands and awaiting the opportunity to return to London and finish up the Moriarty affair. After a quick bit of business that same night in an empty house in Baker Street, Holmes was once again free to devote his life to examining those interesting little problems which the complex life of London so plentifully presented.

But this did not include allowing any more of his adventures to be published in *The Strand*.

This probably suited Watson, at least for a while. He sold his practice and returned to Baker Street, and appears to have taken a much-greater interest in Holmes's cases throughout the rest of the nineties and early 1900's – until his remarriage in Fall 1902.

For this period, The Proto-Canon consisted of twenty-six stories – two longer adventures and the twenty-four shorter tales that had appeared in *The Strand*, and later collected – with one exception – in *The Adventures of Sherlock Holmes* and *The Memoirs of Sherlock Holmes*. From August 1901 to April 1902, just one other story, another longer tale, appeared serially, *The Hound of the Baskervilles*, and when it was finished, the story count rose to twenty-seven – not very many published adventures over a fifteen-year period, and very little indeed for those early admirers of Mr. Holmes to explore and enjoy.

In Fall 1903, Holmes "retired" – ostensibly to Sussex to be a hermit apiarist, but actually to carry out various important chores for this brother Mycroft, laying the groundwork for England's defense against the ever-increasing German aggressions, and the inevitable war which was certainly coming. It was then that Watson was released to publish another set of cases – all clearly set before Holmes's publicized "retirement". These thirteen narratives, appearing from October 1903 to December 1904 and later collected as *The Return of Sherlock Holmes*, raised the Canonical count to forty.

And after that, they were published in a scattered run over the next twenty-three years. Between 1908 and 1917, Watson published eight stories, One of these, *The Valley of Fear*, was a longer case, and Watson was certainly prompted to publish it in 1915, as it told of Pinkerton agent Birdy Edwards' infiltration of The Scowrers – much like Holmes had recently done from 1912 to 1914 when, as Altamont, he infiltrated the German spy network in the years leading up to the War.

His Last Bow (including "The Cardboard Box", originally published in 1892 but not collected in *The Memoirs*) was published in 1917. And then – nothing for four more years. Eventually, another set of irregular adventures began to appear, a dozen of them from October 1921 to March 1927. There was one each for 1921, 1922, and 1923, three in 1924, four in 1926, and two in 1927. And that was it. The Canon was complete. These final twelve of sixty were collected and published in 1927 as *The Case-Book of Sherlock Holmes* – and that was the end. Sixty tales and no more.

Or so it was believed. And as so many to this day would try to enforce.

But in 1974, a pastiche was nailed to the church door, and the Sherlockian Reformation began, and there was no going back.

Thank God.

The years between 1927 and 1974 must have been bleak times for many Sherlockians. As mentioned, there were editions of The Canon, but if someone wanted to know more about Holmes beyond that, then he or she was mostly out of luck. There were some very obscure and esoteric scholarly works published, but most people probably didn't know about them and couldn't easily obtain them. A few local Sherlockian organizations were formed throughout the United States, but attendance was usually by strict invitation only (and then only if you were male and knew someone on the inside – no common Sherlockian riff-raff need apply.) And even if one was interested, most of these organizations met in locations that were far out of reach for the majority of Americans in different parts of the country. (In contrast, the much-more-welcoming and democratic Sherlock Holmes Society of London was founded in 1951, following the amazing success of the Holmes display in Baker Street during the Festival of London. American Sherlockian fellowship remained much more . . . exclusive.)

Like esoteric Sherlockian scholarship of this period between 1927 and 1974, new Holmes adventures were also a rare thing. There had been numerous parodies of Holmes since the early days of original Canonical publication, but these unsatisfying and un-clever drabs don't count. William Gillette's 1899 play, *Sherlock Holmes*, was possibly the first legitimate extra-Canonical adventure – and also the first example of someone foisting his or her own incorrect ideas onto Watson's notes. A romance with Alice Faulkner? Professor *Robert* Moriarty? *Pfui!*

In the years before and after the last Canonical story was published in 1927, a few additional new cases appeared for those who needed more – even if they weren't exactly correct. In print was Vincent Starrett's "The Unique *Hamlet*" (1920). There were a few pastiche films, such as John Barrymore's *Sherlock Holmes* (1922). Radio dramas were mightily important in the 1930's and 1940's, and Edith Meiser had the brilliant idea of adapting The Canon to radio – the two went together perfectly. But after a few years of repeating the same Canonical stories, Meiser began broadcasting extra-Canonical cases as well – and that door would never be shut again.

Further pastiche films followed starring actors who looked like Holmes – Arthur Wontner and Basil Rathbone. The occasional obscure pastiche appeared in print, such as Arthur Whitaker's curious "The Case of the Man Who Was Wanted" (1948). For a short while in the late 1920's, and then resuming in the mid-1940's, August Derleth brought forth Solar Pons adventures – *The Sherlock Holmes of Praed Street* – but like Sherlockian scholarship, these ended up being known to only a few people inside the circle, and they were almost a secret for decades – until the post-1974 world when the Sherlockian Reformation began.

1954 saw the publication of *The Exploits of Sherlock Holmes* by Adrian Conan Doyle and John Dickson Carr. This is a good set of stories, but it was viciously attacked at the time, particularly by The Baker Street

Irregulars, in part because of Adrian Conan Doyle's previous attacks on everyone else who had an interest in Holmes – for he felt that all roads to Holmes must lead through him. Ironically, there were others who felt that they were Holmes's Keepers, and that their own legitimacy was being challenged.

That all changed in 1974, when Nicholas Meyer published *The Seven-Per-Cent Solution.* It was a runaway best-seller, and made into a very successful film the following year. The pastiche had been nailed to the door of the restrictive established Church of Holmes, and people realized that they didn't have to kiss someone's ring to be a Sherlockian.

There was now a different path that bypassed this restrictive route. Numerous pastiches followed, and they have only grown exponentially.

And thank God.

As mentioned, the Solar Pons stories were published for the masses for the first time in the mid-1970's. Other mainstream pastiches followed by the likes of Nicholas Utechin and Sean Wright and John Gardner. Nicholas Meyer found more of Watson's hidden manuscripts. This was the same period when other fandoms began to exert similar influence. For example, the fires of *Star Trek*'s popularity were kept burning throughout the 1970's – from the cancellation of the original show in 1969 to the first film in 1979 – by amateurs who created fan fiction, self-publishing and distributing it by way of very amateur-looking home-made documents. The same was happening with Sherlockian pastiches. There were a number of little self-printed volumes produced during this period. Some were excellent stories (and some not-so-excellent), typed and copied by the authors, folded and assembled and stapled by the authors, and sold by the authors. These are now expensive and rare collector's items – and it's quite amusing that they are now so valued, in spite of their terrible formatting errors and typos, by the same people who treat modern Sherlockian publishing, with its same earnest sincerity, with a gibe and a sneer.

Before his unfortunate passing in 2018, Sherlockian Phil Jones had assembled and maintained a database of Sherlockian pastiches. It began to get away from him in his final years, but that was understandable, because there were so many more pastiches appearing every day. (Thank God.) Phil's Excel spreadsheet had grown to over 10,000 entries. Of course, a sizeable amount of these weren't traditional Canonical pastiches, but still, that's a lot of post-Canonical adventures. If Phil were still alive and maintaining the database, there would be many more entries, and I'm very proud that the stories in *The MX Book of New Sherlock Holmes Stories* would occupy a very sizable percentage of all known Sherlockian pastiches.

Consider: If non-traditional and non-Canonical pastiches were trimmed off of Phil's database, reducing it to an arbitrary 8,000 entries, then the MX anthologies would be over *10%* of that. With the publication of these new volumes, Parts XXXVII, XXXVIII, and XXXIX, we've now reached over *800* Sherlock Holmes adventures! In actuality, the traditional pastiches on Phil's very complete list were probably quite a bit less than 8,000, so the MX books likely occupy an even greater percentage of all the traditional Canonical pastiches that have ever been written.

The idea for these books occurred in 2015, as a push-back against the idea of a modernized broken Holmes that was infiltrating the traditional pastiches that I collect and read. Even authors who should have known better, and who were supposedly writing about the True Holmes in the correct era, were slipping in references to Holmes's *"mind palace"*, or that he was a *"high-functioning sociopath"*, and including *"Mike"* Stamford, *"Greg"* Lestrade, and Molly Hooper. It was becoming the new baseline that Watson's wound was psychosomatic, and that Mary Watson was a secret government assassin, Irene Adler a shady dominatrix, and Mrs. Hudson the widow of a drug dealer. It needed to be re-established that Holmes was a *hero*, born in the 1850's, and not a broken obnoxious creep born in the 1970's. And apparently this was appreciated, because these MX collections have since become the biggest and bestselling Holmes anthology of all time, thirty-nine massive volumes (so far) with more in the works from over 200 worldwide contributors. And along the way, the authors' generously contributed royalties have raised over *$110,000* (so far) – that's *One-Hundred-and-Ten Thousand Dollars!* – for the Undershaw school for special needs children at one of Sir Arthur Conan Doyle's former homes.

But as a Sherlockian, the best part of all of this to me is the new adventures. As a child, I discovered Holmes at age ten in 1975, one year after the Sherlockian Reformation began. (Luckily I was unaware of all of those bleak years between 1927 and 1974.) Even then, in those early days, there were very few extra-Canonical adventures once the pitifully few Sixty were read (and re-read and re-read . . . .) I *starved* for more Holmes. And now there is more, and I'm no longer going hungry . . . and thank God *. . . but there still aren't enough Holmes adventures.*

Holmes abhorred *"the dull routine of existence"*. Imagine how he would have felt to have his career defined by only sixty cases. Even adding the 140+ "Untold Cases" mentioned in the Canon only brings it to around two-hundred – which Holmes would have certainly called a *"dull routine"* if that's all there was.

Instead, new extra-Canonical adventures bring us *"the dramatic moment of fate"*, as described by Holmes, *"when you hear a step upon the stair which is walking into your life, and you know not whether for good or ill."* As the lucky editor of these books, as well as a number of similar True Holmes anthologies published by Belanger Books, I now receive new Holmes adventures *nearly every day*! Before I start to read these new submissions, each is undefined and, as Holmes once said, presents *"infinite possibilities"*. The new story might be tragic or comic. Gothic horror or police procedural. Country settings or in town. Early in Holmes and Watson's friendship, or late. The thrill of receiving and reading new Holmes stories *never gets old*. It's an addiction – and I know that it's shared by many others, the very faithful supporters of these books.

For those, like me, who need more traditional Canonical Holmes adventures, consider what it was like in a pre-1974 world, with very few Holmes adventures beyond the very-much re-read Canon. The new publishing paradigm that now immediately connects authors to readers didn't exist. Instead, getting anything published at all in those days was nearly impossible, and when (or if) it finally was, many readers would never know about it, or have the chance to read it. And except for a select few, being a Sherlockian was severely limited by those who desperately kept access restricted and the church door locked. They still would, if they could, but now it's far too late.

In 1974, a pastiche was nailed to the church door, and the Sherlockian Reformation began, and there's no going back.

Thank God.

* * * * *

"Of course, I could only stammer out my thanks."
– *The unhappy John Hector McFarlane, "The Norwood Builder"*

As always when one of these collections is finished, I want to thank with all my heart my incredible, patient, brilliant, kind, and beautiful wife of almost thirty-five years, Rebecca – Every day I'm more stunned at how lucky I am than the day before! – and our amazing, funny, creative, and wonderful son, and my friend, Dan. I love you both, and you are everything to me!

With each new set of the MX anthologies, some things get easier, and there are also new challenges. For several years, the stresses of real life have been much greater than when this series started. Through all of this, the amazing contributors have once again pulled some amazing works from the Tin Dispatch Box. I'm more grateful than I can express to every contributor who has donated both time and royalties to this ongoing project. It's amazing what we've accomplished. I also want to give special recognition to the multiple contributors of this set: Arthur Hall, Sonya Kudei, Tracy Revels, Dan Rowley and Don Baxter, Tom Turley, and Peter Coe Verbica. Finally, I cannot express how thankful I am to all of those who keep buying these books and making them the largest and most popular Sherlockian anthology ever.

I'm so glad to have gotten to know so many of you through this process. It's an undeniable fact that Sherlock Holmes authors are the *best* people!

I wish especially thank the following:

- *Michael Sims* – I'm thrilled that Mr. Sims is participating in these books. He has written a wonderful biography of the Literary Agent, *Arthur and Sherlock*, and additionally, I've enjoyed reading his posts on social media for years. I was thrilled to discover that he is originally from Crossville, Tennessee, a small town about an hour west of where I live, and where my wife and I were married. Michael: I can't thank you enough for your support and participation!

- *Steve Emecz* – From my first association with MX in 2013, I saw that MX (under Steve Emecz's leadership) was *the* fast-rising superstar of the Sherlockian publishing world. Connecting with MX and Steve Emecz was personally an amazing life-changing event for me, as it has been for countless other Sherlockian authors. It has led me to write many more stories, and then to edit books, along with unexpected additional Holmes Pilgrimages to England – none of which might have happened otherwise. By way of my first email with Steve, I've had the chance to make some incredible Sherlockian friends and play in the Holmesian Sandbox in ways that I would have never dreamed possible.

   Through it all, Steve has been one of the most positive and supportive people that I've ever known.

   From the beginning, Steve has let me explore various Sherlockian projects and open up my own personal possibilities in ways that otherwise would have never happened. Thank you, Steve, for every opportunity!

- *Roger Johnson* – From his immediate support at the time of the first volumes in this series to the present, I can't imagine Roger not being part of these books. His Sherlockian knowledge is exceptional, as is the work that he does to further the cause of The Master. But even more than that, both Roger

8

and his wife, Jean Upton, are simply the finest and best of people, and I'm very lucky to know both of them – even though I don't get to see them nearly as often as I'd like. I look forward to getting back over to the Holmesland sooner rather than later and visiting with them again, but in the meantime, many thanks for being part of this.

- *Brian Belanger* –I initially became acquainted with Brian when he took over the duties of creating the covers for MX Books, and I found him to be a great collaborator, and wonderfully creative too. I've worked with him on many projects with MX and Belanger Books, which he co-founded with his brother Derrick Belanger, also a good friend. Along with MX Publishing, Derrick and Brian have absolutely locked up the Sherlockian publishing field with a vast amount of amazing material. The old dinosaurs must be trembling to see every new and worthy Sherlockian project, one after another after another, that these two companies create. Luckily MX and Belanger Books work closely with one another, and I'm thrilled to be associated with both of them. Many thanks to Brian for all he does for both publishers, and for all he's done for me personally.

And finally, last but certainly *not* least, thanks to **Sir Arthur Conan Doyle**: Author, doctor, adventurer, and the Founder of the Sherlockian Feast. Honored, and present in spirit.

As I always note when putting together an anthology of Holmes stories, the effort has been a labor of love. These adventures are just more tiny threads woven into the ongoing Great Holmes Tapestry, continuing to grow and grow, for there can *never* be enough stories about the man whom Watson described as *"the best and wisest . . . whom I have ever known."*

David Marcum
April 5th, 2023
The 129th Anniversary of
Holmes's Return from
The Great Hiatus

Questions, comments, or story submissions
may be addressed to David Marcum at
thepapersofsherlockholmes@gmail.com

Dark Lantern
by Michael Sims

It was the day before Halloween 1993 and I was prowling the book shelves at the Nashville Goodwill store. Past a thicket of musty shirts and jeans, beyond a junkyard of orphaned kitchen utensils, I was digging for treasure at a dollar a book. I was scanning the bookshelves, left to right, top to bottom, when I felt the hair stand up on the back of my neck.

I had felt a ghost nearby – myself as a young boy.

What my eyes noticed and my instinct recognized before alerting my conscious mind was a fat textbook whose nerdy bulk shouldered aside jacketless volumes gold-stamped *Danielle Steele* and *Dean Koontz*. I saw not a grimy old book but a teenage boy in a wheelchair by a window in a ramshackle house two hours to the east, on the Cumberland Plateau. Late afternoon, with an autumn sunset gilding even the cheap, mismatched bookshelves. I was born in this house in 1958, grew up in it, learned to read in it. The window showed a rocky backyard garden. On a small hill beyond, oak-and-hickory woodland crowded the mown grass. The room held a small bed, bookcases, and a lamp on a rickety table absurdly made from the leaf of a Formica kitchen table.

That boy in memory was reading the same middle-school-level book I had just found on the Goodwill shelves – *Outlooks through Literature*, whose spine bore the names Pooley, Stuart, White, and Cline. On its cover was a drab sepia photograph of men and women silhouetted within the arches of what appeared to be a two-story bridge. Seated in a wheelchair at fourteen, standing in a thrift store at thirty-five, I turned familiar-feeling pages to a Contents list whose items inspired affection that ran like a herald before a montage of memories:

> Unit One, *The Short Story*
> Unit Two, *Biography and Autobiography*
> Unit Three, *A Book of Poetry*
> Unit Four, *Romeo and Juliet*
> Unit Five, *Classical Heritage*
> Unit Six, *A Tale of Two Cities*
> Unit Seven, *At Random*

Unit One opened with "The Adventure of the Speckled Band" by Arthur Conan Doyle, which I now know was among the first Holmes short stories after two novels. It was also the beginning of my own fascination with Victorian fiction. "'*It is fear, Mr. Holmes. It is terror,*'" I read at the top of the page. "*These words were enough to challenge the Master Detective, Sherlock Holmes, to an immediate investigation, some rapid deductions, and a brilliant solution.*" Facing it on the left, a colorful full-page illustration portrayed a woman in what appeared to be stages of collapse.

I think this was my first encounter with Sherlock Holmes as a character in a book rather than as distilled mannerisms in a TV movie. This story was the wardrobe that opened into Narnia, the tornado that whirled me to Oz. It drew me into the Holmes stories, and thence into the larger world of Dickens and Eliot, Austen and Darwin. Standing in Goodwill, I felt my cheeks tug into a smile as I perused the footnotes illuminating terms likely to baffle U.S. students: *dogcart, Waterloo, Bengal Artillery.* It was fun to see again the note for *dark lantern* – a lamp that has a movable panel to hide its light, an invention that has always struck me as confusingly metaphorical. I may have met Holmes earlier, thanks to my lepidopteran instinct to sniff every book in the garden, but if so it must have been on a page lacking the scented lure of illustrations and footnotes.

Even scanning quickly that day in 1993, I recalled this uninviting typeface, the antique illustrations, a bulk of 754 pages supposedly meant to be traversed during a school year. The endpapers bore a rubber-stamped *JOHN GLENN HIGH SCHOOL* and a Michigan address. I love about used books' archaeological clues to other lives – shards such as *Merry Christmas, David, from Aunt Iva* or a *Cats* ticket stub marking the last campsite toward the summit before a reader gave up and started back downhill.

Browsing these pages in Goodwill, I found a distinctive aspect of *Outlooks through Literature* that I had forgotten: Extra flourishes around the author bio at the end. Obsessed – almost from birth, it seems now – with how books were created, I had always read author and illustrator biographies, "*By the Same Author*" pages, acknowledgments, and source notes. In revisiting this book I found, beginning an inch below Holmes's explanation to Watson of how he had nudged Dr. Roylott to his grisly death, a section entitled "*Could This Really Have Happened?*"

There I found the results of a careful study by W.T. Williams, "*a British naturalist,*" who determined that there was no such snake as the swamp adder of the story, and that many of its antics no snake could perform. Then came questions under "*What Do You Say?*" and "*Author's Craft,*" a note about prefixes under "*Know Your Words,*" and a paragraph about Conan Doyle. These extras were like windows on the rear of a house, showing tantalizing glimpses of the building through whose back door I

11

had just emerged. It seems to me now, thirty years after rediscovering this book in Goodwill, that I spend most days peering through windows into the pantries and tool sheds of stories to see how they are made.

In late 1971, halfway through the eighth grade, I dropped out of regular school and began studying with "homebound" teachers who came to the house three afternoons a week. I suffered from increasing leg and back and joint pain, later diagnosed as juvenile rheumatic arthritis, blamed on a bout of rheumatic fever. Pain earned me my own room – in the back, overlooking garden and woods. My bed was no more than ten feet above the cellar, with its dusty Mason jars, its spider-webbed wooden shelves fitted into soil walls. Beneath my dreams, frogs declaimed from standing water. So many memories wafted from this volume.

About the same time as my original encounter with this textbook, I spent a stormy night at Erlanger Hospital in Chattanooga. I was scheduled for a spinal tap for early the next morning – the most horrific experience of my life up to then and still a milestone of agony that makes me cringe.

I was in a ward with three old men. At some point one of them was shaved with a dry scraping noise. Suddenly in the darkness after midnight, machines exclaimed and lights were on. One man had died. The only TV on that floor was in a waiting room down the hall. During a fierce thunderstorm someone pushed my wheelchair down there, where we watched *The Hound of the Baskervilles* – Stewart Granger as a pallid sixtyish Sherlock Holmes and William Shatner, of all people, as George Stapleton. Omniscient Google tells me that this version first aired on ABC in February 1972, the month I turned fourteen, but it must have run again later because my memory takes place during a summer thunderstorm. And of course you can always trust memory. Have I merged two hospital visits?

"My dear Mr. Sims," Holmes would murmur, "I must say I find you a most disappointing witness."

During the broadcast, a close flash of lightning was followed by a power outage. Soon, no doubt, the power returned, but my memory stops with the lightning and the demise of the TV screen. I don't recall getting to see the rest of the movie before going back to my room, where soon I woke to a nurse's discovery of the old man's death. I do remember lying in that bed, staring at the ceiling after they wheeled him out, feeling my own pulse ticking like a bomb, thinking about my father's heart attack at thirty-eight, when I was three.

Because I note on its flyleaf the date on which a book enters my life, I see that the year after Erlanger, on 16 December, 1973, I received the two fat volumes of William S. Baring-Gould's *The Annotated Sherlock Holmes* from the mail-order Mystery Guild that enabled me to survive my isolation. They contained the species of footnotes and sidebars found

12

in *Outlooks through Literature*, but these glosses blossomed into a tropical profusion of research and speculation: Illustrations of hansom cabs, meditations on the super-villain snake of "The Speckled Band", biographies of illustrators. Uncomfortable, as usual, in my now private room at home, I stayed up all night after these books arrived in the mail.

As I stood before those Goodwill bookshelves in 1993, I was still two years away from my first publishing deal, for a book of days called *Darwin's Orchestra: An Almanac of Nature in History and the Arts*. In its index I find nine entries on *"Holmes, Sherlock (fictional character)."* Twenty-seven years and sixteen books down the road, I see that the Sherlock Holmes stories were more important to me than I had realized even as the textbook stirred memories of their discovery. They helped enchant literature for me, and gossip about their origin opened a window into formerly opaque history. Doyle and Holmes introduced me to a number of perennial interests I found so entertaining that ultimately I built a career around them.

I have edited eight anthologies of Victorian fiction – including, to show the legacy of that textbook, *The Penguin Book of Murder Mysteries*. Again and again, as I wrote my nonfiction book *Arthur and Sherlock: Conan Doyle and the Creation of Holmes*, I found myself in the emotional terrain of that first encounter and in the nerdy landscape of literary research that the book's footnotes and illustrations inspired.

In the way that literature and life distill experience into essence, this fictional turf has become a site for discovery and adventure, not a place of pain or fear or loss. Those aspects of my childhood have seeped into its soil and perhaps nourish it, but they no longer flower. In waking my imagination and curiosity, Holmes and Watson gave me the possibility of growing up to live in a larger world – a world I first explored amid London's mythic cobblestones and fog, which could be navigated even from a wheelchair.

Michael Sims
March 2023

"What Is It That We Love in Sherlock Holmes?"

by Roger Johnson

Edgar W. Smith, as you may or may not know, was the founder and first editor of *The Baker Street Journal*. His editorial in the second issue of that august and ever-lively organ, dated April 1946, opened with the question above.

"The Implicit Holmes", as he titled it, is not a long piece – only 624 words – but the answers that Smith offers are thoughtful and remarkably comprehensive. They were certainly coloured by the writer's memories of the recent global war, but they remain valid nearly eighty years on.

"We love the times in which he lived, of course: the half-remembered, half-forgotten times of snug Victorian illusion, of gaslit comfort and contentment, of perfect dignity and grace . . . ." Many of his readers would indeed have remembered those times, and would have appreciated the way they are depicted by the detective's faithful amanuensis.

"And we love the place in which the master moved and had his being: the England of those times, fat with the fruits of her achievements, but strong and daring still with the spirit of imperial adventure . . . ." When Smith wrote that, of course, he was very conscious of the devastating changes that England – and notably London – had suffered as a result of enemy action in, not one, but *two* world wars. Since then, political shifts and the neophiliac fervour of the 1960's and '70s have caused yet more drastic and often lamentable alteration, but much of Holmes's England is still there, and the search for it can be very rewarding.

"But there is more than time and space and the yearning for things gone by to account for what we feel toward Sherlock Holmes. Not only there and then, but here and now, he stands before us as a symbol – a symbol, if you please, of all that we are not, but ever would be." One of the most appealing aspects of Sherlock Holmes, it seems to me, is that he is *not* a "super-hero": He can't fly, see through a brick wall – or punch a hole in a brick wall. He can't melt steel with heat-rays from his eyes, or move faster than a speeding bullet, nor will such a bullet bounce harmlessly off him. Sherlock Holmes is one of us – a human being, and his powers are human. You and I could never be like Superman or Captain Marvel, and the chances that we could ever rival Batman are effectively non-existent. But we *could*, perhaps, be like Sherlock Holmes.

"For it is not Sherlock Holmes who sits in Baker Street, comfortable, competent and self-assured; it is we ourselves who are there, full of a tremendous capacity for wisdom, complacent in the presence of our humble Watson, conscious of a warm wellbeing and a timeless, imperishable content." Few of us, I think – and none, I dare say, who read this – would disagree with that statement.

Brief though it is, the whole article is well worth reading, and it doesn't require access to that fabulously rare early issue of *The Baker Street Journal*. You can find it online at:

https://mseffie.com/assignments/sherlock/articles/The%20Implicit%20Holmes.pdf

Read it, and take note of the final sentence: *"That is the Sherlock Holmes we love – the Holmes implicit and eternal in ourselves."*

And, I would add, that is the Holmes we look for, and thankfully often find, in the stories that the ever-industrious David Marcum has collected and edited for our delight in this wonderful series.

Roger Johnson
BSI, ASH
Commissioning Editor: *The Sherlock Holmes Journal*
February 2023

An Ongoing Legacy
for Sherlock Holmes
by Steve Emecz

Undershaw
Circa 1900

*T*he *MX Book of New Sherlock Holmes Stories* continues to be one of the projects we are most proud of. The total raised for Undershaw school for children with learning disabilities has now passed $110,000.

There are a record 23 positive reviews from *Publishers Weekly* for the collection:

https://bit.ly/MXBookPW

In addition to Undershaw, we also support Happy Life Mission (a baby rescue project in Kenya), The World Food Programme (which won the Nobel Peace Prize in 2020), and iHeart (who support mental health in young people).

Our support for our projects is possible through the publishing of Sherlock Holmes books, which we have now been doing fifteen years. You can find links to all our projects on our website:

https://mxpublishing.com/pages/about-us

We're already looking forward to the autumn and more volumes.

Steve Emecz
March 2023
Twitter: *@mxpublishing*

The Doyle Room at Undershaw
Partially funded through royalties from
The MX Book of New Sherlock Holmes Stories

A Word from Undershaw
by Emma West

Undershaw
September 9, 2016
Grand Opening of the Stepping Stones School
(Now *Undershaw*)
(Photograph courtesy of Roger Johnson)

For this latest instalment of news from Undershaw, you find us waiting with bated breath for the first signs of Spring, but already there is life bursting through every corner of our school. Last week saw our exciting programme of events to mark National Careers Week, during which every student found themselves immersed in presentations, talks, workshops, and challenges themed around various skills and careers. As a school we have so many roles, whether it is to solidify learning, excite our students with new experiences of culture, or simply to listen, understand, and champion each young person. It's all in a day's work here. Our Careers Week was no different. We are passionate about exposing the students to the sheer wealth of possibilities before them as they begin to lay claim to their futures. The qualifications available to the students are just one part of their journey and, as we all know, it's what they choose to do with this academic landscape that will count for so much as they take the long-awaited leaps into their independent lives.

18

Undershaw is building a unique place for itself amidst a community of corporates, passionate charities, and some trailblazing organisations that all work towards a diverse, equitable, and inclusive world. Lately, we have been approached to provide insights into reports for government which will hopefully provide the bedrock of the workplaces of the future. We educate and inspire other schools on their Special Educational Needs provision, and we have more students than ever on roll and awaiting a place at Undershaw. Without a doubt, it is such a dynamic place, both inside and outside the school gates, but we continue to take each pillar of our provision and challenge ourselves to be the best we can be. Undershaw is so much more than the sum of our parts.

Our Careers Week has been such a highlight of our year so far, and it illustrates the point perfectly that in amongst our qualifications and the latest iterations of our employment record, we all started with drive, ambition, aspiration, and self-belief. This is what we do. Undershaw stands alongside students as they weave their own tapestry of interest, passion, and accomplishment. We are furnishing them with the hard and soft skills required to be successful in the workplaces of the future. What a wholesome endeavor, and one of which we shall never tire.

My heartfelt thanks as ever for joining us on our journey. Our school is something of which you can all feel very proud. It's easy to see where your generosity goes, and with friends like MX Publishing, we all feel we have a passionate band of supporters behind us. I hope you keep up with our news on our website and, if you are ever passing, please do come and see us.

Until next time…

Emma West
Headteacher
March 2023

"Undershaw," Hindhead, Conan Doyle's House.

Editor's *Caveats*

When these anthologies first began back in 2015, I noted that the authors were from all over the world – and thus, there would be British spelling and American spelling. As I explained then, I didn't want to take the responsibility of changing American spelling to British and vice-versa. I would undoubtedly miss something, leading to inconsistencies, or I'd change something incorrectly.

Some readers are bothered by this, made nervous and irate when encountering American spelling as written by Watson, and in stories set in England. However, here in America, the versions of The Canon that we read have long-ago has their spelling Americanized, so it isn't quite as shocking for us.

Additionally, I offer my apologies up front for any typographical errors that have slipped through. As a print-on-demand publisher, MX does not have squadrons of editors as some readers believe. The business consists of three part-time people who also have busy lives elsewhere – Steve Emecz, Sharon Emecz, and Timi Emecz – so the editing effort largely falls on the contributors. Some readers and consumers out there in the world are unhappy with this – apparently forgetting about all of those self-produced Holmes stories and volumes from decades ago (typed and Xeroxed) with awkward self-published formatting and loads of errors that are now prized as very expensive collector's items.

I'm personally mortified when errors slip through – ironically, there will probably be errors in these *caveats* – and I apologize now, but without a regiment of professional full-time editors looking over my shoulder, this is as good as it gets. Real life is more important than writing and editing – even in such a good cause as promoting the True and Traditional Canonical Holmes – and only so much time can be spent preparing these books before they're released into the wild. I hope that you can look past any errors, small or huge, and simply enjoy these stories, and appreciate the efforts of everyone involved, and the sincere desire to add to The Great Holmes Tapestry.

And in spite of any errors here, there are more Sherlock Holmes stories in the world than there were before, and that's a good thing.

David Marcum
Editor

Sherlock Holmes (1854-1957) was born in Yorkshire, England, on 6 January, 1854. In the mid-1870's, he moved to 24 Montague Street, London, where he established himself as the world's first Consulting Detective. After meeting Dr. John H. Watson in early 1881, he and Watson moved to rooms at 221b Baker Street, where his reputation as the world's greatest detective grew for several decades. He was presumed to have died battling noted criminal Professor James Moriarty on 4 May, 1891, but he returned to London on 5 April, 1894, resuming his consulting practice in Baker Street. Retiring to the Sussex coast near Beachy Head in October 1903, he continued to be associated in various private and government investigations while giving the impression of being a reclusive apiarist. He was very involved in the events encompassing World War I, and to a lesser degree those of World War II. He passed away peacefully upon the cliffs above his Sussex home on his 103rd birthday, 6 January, 1957.

Dr. John Hamish Watson (1852-1929) was born in Stranraer, Scotland on 7 August, 1852. In 1878, he took his Doctor of Medicine Degree from the University of London, and later joined the army as a surgeon. Wounded at the Battle of Maiwand in Afghanistan (27 July, 1880), he returned to London late that same year. On New Year's Day, 1881, he was introduced to Sherlock Holmes in the chemical laboratory at Barts. Agreeing to share rooms with Holmes in Baker Street, Watson became invaluable to Holmes's consulting detective practice. Watson was married and widowed three times, and from the late 1880's onward, in addition to his participation in Holmes's investigations and his medical practice, he chronicled Holmes's adventures, with the assistance of his literary agent, Sir Arthur Conan Doyle, in a series of popular narratives, most of which were first published in *The Strand* magazine. Watson's later years were spent preparing a vast number of his notes of Holmes's cases for future publication. Following a final important investigation with Holmes, Watson contracted pneumonia and passed away on 24 July, 1929.

Photos of Sherlock Holmes and Dr. John H. Watson courtesy of Roger Johnson

The
MX Book
of
New
Sherlock
Holmes
Stories

Part XXXIII – 2023 Annual
(1890-1896)

A Modern Detectologist
(That's "Consulting Detective")
by Joseph W. Svec III

I am the very model of a modern Detectologist
I've information useful to most any criminologist.
I know the crooks of England and I quote their deeds historical
From Ripper Jack to Twisted Lip in order categorical;

I'm very well acquainted too, with matters of all kinds of dirt
And any stain that one might find on any different kind of shirt
About footprints, you know I'm teeming with a lot o' news
With many cheerful facts about any street that I might choose

I'm very good at seeing clues, even those invisible
I know the scientific names of anything divisible
In short in matters pertinent to any criminologist
I am the very model of a modern Detectologist.
That's *"Consulting Detective"*, in fact.

I know our ancient history, that is full of every kind of crook
I can name them all without the use of any book
I quote the names of tobaccos from just the very smallest ash,
no matter where or when the thief may have chose to hide his stash

I can tell from just a single crumb, what a hoodlum had for lunch.
It is a scientific fact and not a random guess, or hunch.
Then I can tell from just a bit of chalk that you won't invest in a stock,
even if it came to you as a surprise or a great shock

Then I can write in secret code, made up of little dancing men,
about a crime in great detail, exactly where, and why, and when.
In short in matters pertinent to any criminologist
I am the very model of a modern Detectologist
That's *"Consulting Detective"*, by the way.

In fact, when I do know by sight, which house has a secret room,
it will be the downfall and the criminal's final, ending doom.
When such affairs, as tricks and traps happen to come into play

33

There is no one else who can quite hope to seize the day

When I have learnt what progress has been made in modern Chemistry
When I know more of firearms and any types of weaponry
In short, when I've a smattering of knowledge on all types of dust,
You'll say a better Detectologist has never quite been so robust.

For my logical deduction, though I'm thorough and exemplary
my conclusions are without doubt really quite peremptory
but, still in matters pertinent to any criminologist
I am the very model of a modern Detectologist.
That's *"Consulting Detective"*, of course.

The Muddled Monologue
by Ian Ableson

It sometimes occurs to me to wonder at the colossal number of people who have crossed the threshold into 221b Baker Street over the course of Holmes's long career. Surely it exceeds the number of visitors to an average London flat by several orders of magnitude. I would be willing to wager that it might even outpace the average annual visitation at some of the less-important municipal buildings. Whenever I follow this line of reasoning, I am equally struck by the variety of guests that have taken a seat to discuss some matter or another within the walls of our humble abode. If every one of them were lined up in Baker Street, their order randomized and no further context given, how many of them would I be able to recognize without the aid of my notes? How many could I sort by the correct year, correct circumstances, correct solution to their case? I have no doubt that Holmes, with the veritable research institution that he holds inside his unassuming skull, would be able to recount the details of every single client down to the smallest *minutia*. Nevertheless, despite my doubts when it comes to the complete case catalogue, I have no doubt that I would recognize either of the two visitors from this particular case without much difficulty.

It was an early March morning, and the London weather was grim and grey. The blustery winter had passed us by with a doff of its cap, and we were caught in that strange temperature where the air was too warm for snow, and yet still cold enough that rain stung the cheek as it fell. Trees and other plant life had yet to react to the beginning of spring, and so the streets of London were still missing the few spots of greenery that they normally provide.

The two clients who entered the sitting room were as different a pair as any that came to see us. One was a large man, broad of shoulder and round of belly, whose weight likely exceeded that of Holmes and me combined. He sported a bushy walrus mustache that had just started to become speckled with flecks of grey, hiding a round face that seemed prematurely lined. The mustache sat beneath a pair of hard eyes and brows crinkled into a perpetual scowl. He wore a respectable suit, likely finely tailored to accommodate his bulk. Although he seemed to have no difficulty walking on his own, he carried a metal cane in the manner of the nobility, in which the instrument in question served more as prop than aid.

His companion was likely less-than-half his age, a young man in his late teens or early twenties. His clothes were markedly less respectable than the older man's, with a few splashes of particularly bright and eye-catching colors that are typically only found amongst artists and some of the more eccentric members of the nobility. Unlike his companion, he was entirely clean-shaven, and his chestnut-brown hair was wavy and unkempt. Bright blue eyes gazed lazily around the sitting room, and his face seemed ready to break into a smile at the slightest provocation.

"Please, have a seat, gentlemen," said Holmes. "Tell me, what brings you to a detective's door on this fine . . . ." Here he stopped himself, and his eyes flickered to the grey landscape outside. He allowed himself a rueful smile. "Well, on this seasonally appropriate March day? As the two of you appear to be family, perhaps it's a family matter than has caused you to seek my services?"

At Holmes's statement the older man shot upwards, standing from the armchair that he had just lowered himself into, and cried out in surprise. The young man's eyes widened briefly, but he regained his composure quickly and adopted a relaxed posture once again.

"Mr. Holmes," the older man exclaimed. "This is unexpected. I must assume that you already know my nephew and myself, for I see no other way that you would know of our familial connection. We barely resemble each other at all. I would have you explain how you know of us, for perhaps if you have seen us before, you already know of our problem."

Holmes smiled and held up a placating hand. "My apologies. I had no desire to alarm you or to give you the impression that I knew anything about you before you and your nephew walked in not two minutes ago. It did not, however, take any longer than that to determine that the two of you share family blood. Despite your differences in age, the shape of your hairline is exactly the same, and in particular a distinctly sharp peak that rests just between your nose and your right eye.

"Furthermore, you both seem to have one thumb that is a little shorter and squatter than the other. This is a distinct trait, passed along down the family line, often referred to as 'clubbed thumb' or, less charitably, 'murderer's thumb'. For you it appears to be your left thumb, while your nephew has it on the right, but this is of no consequence when we are merely considering the presence of a family trait. But the truly telling mark of your familial resemblance is your ears. As my friend Watson here has heard me say before, the ears are one of the most anatomically unique and varied parts of the human body. While the two of you may vary widely in age, stature, and a few other relatively superficial details, your ears are nearly identical. Taken alone, any one of these traits could be a mere coincidence, but taken together the familial connection is the more likely solution."

I was reminded of a particularly gruesome case at Holmes's statement, one which I have yet to put to paper, that also involved family identification by the ears. I quickly put that matter out of my mind and hoped that the problem this pair brought before us would prove to be of a milder caliber.

The older man grunted and nodded his agreement. There was a flash of caution in his eye as he did so, and it occurred to me to wonder whether he had initially planned on sharing his relation to his younger companion with Holmes.

"Yes, well. Ears aside, it is true that this young man is indeed my brother's son. Nevertheless, the reason that I bring him before you today has less to do with family and more to do with our association in business."

"Oh? And what business might that be?"

The man puffed his chest out proudly, and said with considerable aplomb, "We are in the business of *theatre,* Mr. Holmes."

Holmes smiled. "A proud business, to be sure. Might I inquire as to where your company resides?"

It's here that I feel I must take a moment to remind you, dear readers, of my own policy regarding the anonymity of any person, living or dead, who is connected to these tales that I commit to paper. While the outcome of this particular case is, perhaps, well-known within certain circles, it is nonetheless beyond my purview as a chronicler to use the real name and location of the theater in question. To do so would undoubtedly make the names of those involved with this case simple to deduce, even without an intellect like that of my friend. Likewise, as an extra layer of precaution, the exact wording of the lines of the play will be changed within my writings, though I have done my best to preserve the spirit of the performance. Suffice to say that the show is one of many such inspired by the writings of The Bard himself. While it wasn't one of Shakespeare's plays, it nonetheless greatly resembled the style and substance.

"I am the proud owner of The Horatio, Mr. Holmes," the large man said. "My name is Eugene Porter, and this is my nephew, Ollie Porter. He is one of the actors currently employed with the theater company that performs at there."

"Ah! I don't believe I've had the pleasure of attending a performance at the theater, but I have heard it mentioned before. It's a pleasure to meet you both," said Holmes, with a gracious smile. "Now, how can I help you?"

At this moment Eugene's eyes flickered over to his nephew, and he looked over him in silence for a long moment, as though he were a jeweler appraising a finely cut stone, or perhaps a butcher assessing the best place to make a cut.

"Well . . . Perhaps I should give you a little more information. It is unusual, our arrangement, at least as far as the theater goes. Typically the owner of a theater is a businessman, pure and simple, with little connection to the company apart from that of a transactional nature. It is unusual, to say the least, to have familial connection between the owner of a theater and the company that performs there.

"I have owned The Horatio for nearly a year now, but before that it was in the possession of my brother, Edward, may God rest his soul. He was an actor – a true artist. Whether drama, comedy, history, satire – there seemed no bottom to his reservoir of talent. His portrayal of Romeo drew lovelorn sighs from every woman this side of the Thames. His Macbeth had even the most sea-worn sailing man in tears. He could turn a no-name character from an unfamiliar play into the talk of London's elite within a week. Well, Edward came into quite a sum of money – it seems his performances captured the attention of a few wealthy patrons, and after a few years of such funding he'd made quite a tidy sum for himself – and he decided to retire from acting, buy The Horatio from its previous owner, invite his old company to perform there with generous terms, and live a comfortable life for the rest of his days. And so he did, for nearly ten years or so, until an unexpected bout of the flu took him from us in the early months of last year. Alas, he had an artist's constitution along with an artist's talent.

"Young Ollie here, for his part, joined the company a few years before his father died. Now, I will not hesitate to tell you that Ollie is a chip off the old block. Indeed, as far as stagecraft goes, he has nearly the same level of talent as his father. His mother – Edward's wife – died when he was but a lad, and so he was practically raised by the theater company. The stage is in his blood, and there's nothing in this world that he's more apt to do. His star has risen considerably over the past few years, and the roles that he's been given by the company have likewise grown in prestige.

"All of this to explain, Mr. Holmes, that I haven't given young Ollie here a position in the company through some sense of obligation, nor indeed am I inclined towards nepotism of any sort. I didn't place Ollie within the company, as he was with them long before my brother's passing, and it is a place that he has rightfully earned. And yet . . . ." Here he paused, thoughtfully, and once again he gave his nephew the same appraising look.

Ollie Porter, for his part, seemed to be following the conversation with nothing but a lazy, casual concern, in the same manner that one might listen to a pair of passers-by discuss croquet scores while strolling through a park. He had shown little reaction to anything his uncle had said, apart from a quick smile in acknowledgement of the praise.

"And yet," Eugene continued, "there is something going on with the lad's head that is muddling him up. I've taken him to three doctors and two psychics already, and none of them can find anything wrong with him. I was just about to give up when I remembered you, Mr. Holmes. I've heard about you before. You are, as far as I am aware, a fixer of problems. Well, there's a problem going on here, and I am asking you to fix it."

"Really, Uncle," said Ollie with a laugh. "You make it all sound as though I'm practically on death's doorway. It's truly a minor thing. I feel perfectly fine."

The elder Porter rapped the floor with his cane. "You *feel* fine, nephew, but clearly you are *not* fine. Over the past year, I have seen you play eight roles without a breaking a sweat. You can perform dozens of sonnets word-perfect, you can substitute for other actors at a moment's notice and with barely an hour of time to prepare, and Mr. Ainsely tells me that you have the entire script of The Scottish Play contained within your wavy locks. And yet, with this *one* monologue, you are as inconsistent as an inattentive schoolboy learning his classroom recitations."

Ollie's little lazy smile didn't waver, and he fluttered his fingers as though to scare off an errant fruit fly. "The words will not stick in my brain, Uncle, that's all. I can't quite seem to get the shape of it. It isn't the most important monologue, you must admit. One of the weakest parts of an otherwise supremely crafted manuscript."

Eugene leaned forward, his weight supported by his cane. "The quality of the words shouldn't have anything to do with it! You cannot convince me that every single one of the sonnets you know is a piece of true art." He turned to Holmes. "I realize this isn't a crime, sir, nor does it fall within the usual scope of your profession. However, I am at my wit's end. The company only opened this show for a live audience a month ago, and already I fear that some enterprising theater critic will notice Ollie's inconsistencies. Mine isn't a large theater, Mr. Holmes, and I fear that one or two scathing reviews will make us the laughing-stock of the London masses."

"We would hardly be the first company to adjust a part of the script," said Ollie.

Eugene grimaced. "Adjustments are a part of theater, it is true, but this is something far stranger, and much more noticeable."

"Fascinating," said Holmes. He looked toward Ollie Porter. "Would you kindly perform the monologue in question? And Mr. Porter – do let me know when he's done whether it's correct or not."

"Certainly, Mr. Holmes," said Ollie. He stood from his chair and closed his eyes. When he opened them again, his body had changed. Gone was the lazy half-smile and the languid relaxation. In its place was a face fraught with emotions that shifted from angry to pleading to desperate, then finally settled in the end on resigned defiance. Our sitting room became his stage, and he bounded across it, making his case to invisible allies:

"What, knave? What would you have me do? Wouldst thou have me give up mine own birthright? Bend the knee to the usurpers who would rob us of our lands? Consider this, my friends, and hold it deep within thy hearts. In my place, wouldst thou heed thy own advice and suffer the same as I without recourse? Your brothers slain, your sister a prisoner in her own home? No. If I have misjudged you, friends, you must beg my forgiveness, but I believe that under similar circumstances you would act the same as I. And so my path is chosen, and it is with the certainty of Orpheus descending into Hades that I know I must follow it until its end or mine."

"He's done it right this time," grunted Eugene.

"I should think so!" I cried, impressed. I may not have much of a head for theater, but even to me the lad's talent was clear to see.

"Well done, young Master Porter," said Holmes, a theatrical twinkle in his own eye. "And what is the manner of the error in question, whenever it may happen?"

Ollie opened his mouth to answer, but the elder Porter cut him off with a grunt and a wave of his hand. "Could be anything, it seems. He forgets a line or adds one that belongs much later in the show. He gives up his homelands rather than his birthright. He follows Perseus into Hades instead of Orpheus. The errors are as erratic as the timing."

Holmes nodded contemplatively. "Well! This is an unusual problem, sir, and one that I am less-than-sure I will be able to solve. Still, it seems to me that there is little I can do until I observe the actual occurrence of the mistakes in question. If you have gained nothing else by your visit today, at least you have gained two more audience members."

Eugene nodded seriously. "I should be very grateful for that. Very grateful indeed. When you arrive at the theater, ask for Mr. Ainsley. He is my stage manager, and he would be happy to get you seated and assist with whatever you may need." With that, the Porters elder and younger left us alone once more.

"I hope you had no pressing plans for the evening, Watson," said Holmes. "If young Ollie's performance is anything to go by, I think we're about to see a marvelous show."

"I should be more than happy to attend. Still, it must be difficult for Ollie – to have so much experience and talent, and yet be unable to grasp one sequence of fifty words or so must be maddening."

"Hmm," said Holmes noncommittally. "I am not yet convinced that we understand Ollie's thoughts on the subject."

"Why is that?"

"Because Ollie Porter held that same expression – head tilted, half-smiling, eyes roaming around the room as though searching for something to distract him – during his uncle's entire tirade about his problem. When a person is being discussed with strangers, particularly against their will, it is almost inevitable to allow some thought to show on one's face. Even the most impartial of judges could never be completely unbiased when he finds himself to be the subject. To hold one expression for the entirety of the conversation is extraordinary, to say the least."

I thought about this for a moment, nodding slightly in concession to Holmes's point. "Well, he is an actor, I suppose."

Holmes smiled. "Precisely."

Mr. Ainsley proved to be easy to find. He was a man of quick eyes and quick ears, an all-seeing and immovable titan of management, shepherding the flow of audiences finding their seats with one hand and guiding the actions of the stage crew with the other. He was the eye of the storm, calm and unflappable as waves of people collided against him and were sent scuttling away to their tasks or their seats. He had a large and impressive mustache in the Imperial style, but was otherwise unremarkable in appearance. His eyes flickered to Holmes and me as we approached. He gave us both a hard look and, seeming to settle his thoughts in his head, nodded at us as we approached.

"Mr. Holmes and Dr. Watson, I presume? Eugene Porter told me that you would be joining the audience tonight. A pleasure to meet you, gentlemen."

"The pleasure is ours," said Holmes as we shook the man's hand. "Tell me, for I am intrigued: How did you know who we were? You seem to have no shortage of people approaching you, and I cannot believe that you know every member of the audience by name."

"That I do not, Mr. Holmes. But you appear to have significantly more purpose than the average audience member, gentlemen. There is a way a man holds himself when he is at work that is easily distinguished from a man engaged in leisure."

"Indeed, so I suppose there is," said Holmes. By his airy tone and sudden grin, my friend appeared to be in excellent spirits. "Might we ask you a few questions before we take our seats?"

"At your service."

"How involved are you in the rehearsal process?"

"Fairly involved sir, fairly involved. It's my job to coordinate the stagehands, the props, the costumes, and the like."

"We understand that young Master Porter has been having a difficult time with one particular monologue. Did this trouble extend to practice as well? Did he say the lines incorrectly during any of the rehearsals?"

"No sir, never. Man's mind is like a lobster trap, sir – if lobsters were words, that is. Script runs in, nothing ever escapes. I've half-a-mind that he could probably still sing the lullabies his Nan used to rock him to sleep, and she died when he was three. It's what's got Eugene so concerned, I think. Never seen an issue like this before, not with Ollie. I must admit, I'm not so worried about his misspeaking as his uncle – he portrays a major character, sure, but the monologue itself isn't so important to the story that the errors make much of a difference in the mind of an average viewer. A handful of our regulars might take note, but no more than that. Why, some productions even excise the whole scene to reduce the show's runtime. We wouldn't dream of such an alteration to the script, of course, but then we tend to be a traditionally-minded troupe." He said this last with no small amount of pride in his voice.

"Were the rehearsals all on this same stage?" asked Holmes.

"Not all of them, Mr. Holmes. We've a smaller space round the back of the building where we get most of the basics down while the main stage is still set up for the current show. But we rehearse on the main stage for two weeks or more before we open the performance to the public."

"And he said the lines correctly during every rehearsal?"

"So far as I can remember it, Mr. Holmes. The problems didn't start to show themselves until a week or so after opening night."

"Any changes in Ollie's positioning during this part of the show? Some bit of blocking that might have changed where he stands for that particular monologue? Especially any alteration that might have occurred right before the opening?"

"No sir. We changed up some of the other blocking a couple weeks beforehand, but that scene has only had superficial changes since the first day of rehearsal."

"Could you direct us to the spot where Ollie stands for the lines in question? I would like to be seated as close as possible."

"Already handled, Mr. Holmes. He delivers the monologue far stage left. I've saved you a pair of seats close enough that you ought to be able

42

to look him right in the eye." Ainsely hesitated for a moment. "However, it is my duty as a stage manager to ask that you not do anything that may affect the young master's performance. Watch all you want, Mr. Holmes, but please don't disrupt the show."

"I wouldn't even dream of it," said Holmes cheerfully. "Thank you, Mr. Ainsely. That will be all for the moment. I'm sure you have plenty of work to do to get ready for the show." Ainsely nodded in gratitude and waved over one of his ushers to take us to our seats. We settled in. Holmes spent most of the overture with his neck craned to scan the audience behind us, but before long the first actor made his way past the curtains, and we settled in to watch the show.

"Well," said Holmes after the last of the applause died down and most people were standing from their seats. "What did you think?"

"I must say, I enjoyed it. I have been an infrequent visitor to the theater of late. I must seek rectify that in the future."

"And what of the monologue? Did you catch any mistakes?"

"No, Master Porter's performance seemed indistinguishable from his demonstration at Baker Street."

"I agree. I didn't catch any noticeable differences," said Holmes. "Did you happen to notice that during that particular monologue, Ollie Porter is standing in a unique spot? Extreme stage left, and far enough downstage that he could practically spit in an audience member's eye? At first I thought perhaps there was something in the environment in that spot that might influence Ollie's psyche. Some chemical, perhaps, that was making him a little lightheaded. However, in such a case I would have expected to detect it as well, as close as we were to him. On top of that, it would be reasonable to expect that he would make the same mistakes during any rehearsals that took place in the same location.

"There is a simple explanation for all of this, Watson, much simpler than some complex interaction of man and environment, but it will be difficult to prove. I'm glad you enjoyed the show, because we'll need to return to The Horatio for at least a few nights more."

"How many performances do you intend to see?"

Holmes smiled. "As many as it takes for young Mister Ollie to get the monologue wrong."

We attended the performance at The Horatio three more times before Holmes got his wish. On that evening, he arranged for Mr. Ainsely to let us enter through a rear door, where the cast and crew entered the theater, rather than the main door. He also requested that we be given different seats, in the far back of the theater. When we entered, I expected him to question the crew or other cast members, but instead Holmes avoided eye contact with everyone and hurried us to the back of the theater, seemingly content to mingle with the crowd of audience members until the time came to take our seats.

Ollie's monologue came approximately two-thirds of the way through the show, after the intermission. I listened attentively, as I had every night previously. It was strange to be so distant from Ollie during this, the key part of the evening for the both of us, but I trusted that Holmes had his reasons.

> *"What, knave? What would you have me do? Wouldst thou have me give up mine own birthright? Bow thy head to the usurpers who would turn our lands to ash? Consider this, my friends, and hold it deep within thy hearts. In my place, wouldst thou heed thy own advice and suffer the same as I without recourse? Your brothers slain, your sister a prisoner in her own home? No. If I have misjudged you, friends, you must beg my forgiveness, but I believe that under similar circumstances you would act the same as I. And so my path is chosen, and it is with the certainty of Orpheus descending into Hades that I know I must follow it until its end or mine."*

I didn't need to see Holmes's satisfied expression to know that our night had come. The changes to the fourth sentence – bowing the head rather than bending the knee, turning the lands to ash rather than robbing him of them – were just as noticeable to me after our repeated viewings. Just as with the other changes that Eugene Porter had mentioned in our office, the overall meaning of the monologue didn't appear to have changed, only the exact words that were used.

Although I could sense that Holmes was eager to continue his investigation, we couldn't very well stand and cause a commotion in the middle of the performance. We watched to the end of the show – which I had now seen often enough to appreciate differences between individual performances, ranging from small, improvisatory changes in inflection or tone to some more noticeable changes to cover the occasional error – and barely had the applause begun when Holmes sprang to his feet. To my surprise, he didn't walk towards the stage, but made straight for Mr. Ainsely. The beleaguered stage manager was talking with one of his ushers, his quick eyes already darting towards his next task.

"Mr. Ainsely, a moment, if you please."

"Certainly, Mr. Holmes, certainly."

"I fully agree with you that the young Master Porter's errors in his monologue are minor at best. However, you mentioned that only a handful of people would notice the mistakes. Do you happen to see any of that handful in the audience today?"

"Well, certainly, Mr. Holmes. Always have a few of the regulars stopping by to spend their evening at the shows."

"Might you point them out to me as they prepare to depart?"

Ainsely arched an eyebrow, but he didn't question any further. He scanned the seats.

"Well, there's Mrs. Gainsborough – the elderly lady with the larger hat – row D, just to the right of center. You see her? She's been coming to this theater for longer than I've been the stage manager, and there aren't many who can claim that, no sir. The couple two rows behind her – see the tall, blond woman and the man with the red hair? Mr. and Mrs. Evans, come here every Thursday and the occasional Tuesday as well. And then this man here, closer to us with the top hat and the salt-and-pepper beard – that would be Mr. Huxley. Any of the four of them have seen the show often enough to know when Mr. Porter's had one of his slip-ups and changed the monologue."

"And were any others here beforehand who may have left during intermission?"

"No, sir. None of the regulars would leave before the show's out. We have a difficult enough time making some of them leave when the curtains have closed."

"Thank you, Mr. Ainsely. You've been most helpful. I won't keep you any longer, as I'm sure several dozen pressing matters have developed that require your attention in the short span of time that I have monopolized it."

Ainsely loosed a barking laugh. "You understand theater, Mr. Holmes, I'll grant you that." He scurried away, a small flock of ushers and stagehands following behind him as though caught in his wake.

"Is it your intention to question the regulars?" I asked. "They all seem about ready to depart, but I could perhaps waylay one or two of them while you speak to the others."

"No need for that, Watson, though I appreciate your offer of support, as always. While it is possible that the Evanses or old Mrs. Gainsborough are involved in some way, I would be willing to place a rather large wager that Mr. Huxley is the one we want. I've had my eye on him for a while, in fact. His seat of choice is very close to our own on the other nights when we were here – which, if you'll recall, were chosen for us specifically for the purpose of hearing Ollie's monologue." He turned and waved at the man in the top hat, who looked a little startled at the greeting. Holmes

45

darted over to him and was shaking the man's hand before he had the time to react.

"Mr. Huxley, I presume! Fine to meet you sir, fine to meet you indeed! Forgive my intrusion, sir, but I have a very urgent matter that I wish to discuss with you. Sensitive issue, sir, sensitive issue indeed. I was reassured by someone I trust very much that you were the man for the job, yes sir."

The expression on Huxley's lined face morphed from astonished bemusement to sudden understanding. He shook Holmes's hand in turn.

"Indeed? Do you find yourself in need of legal assistance? I will be happy to provide you with my card and directions to my office."

"No, sir, shan't take but a moment, it's only a quick question. What is the meaning behind the errors in young Master Porter's monologue, and why does he look directly at you while he delivers them?"

The lawyer's lined face shifted again, this time going from incredulous shock to cold dismissal in a matter of moments. "I'm afraid," said Huxley stiffly, "that I am rather busy this evening. Good day, sirs." He left without another word. Holmes chuckled.

"Well! I'd hoped to catch him off guard, but I suppose that would be a rather astounding stroke of luck. Nevertheless, I think we've gathered the information that we need."

"Have we? From such a short interaction?"

"Never underestimate the power of speaking with intention rather than clarity, Watson! It seemed likely to me that our top-hatted friend here was observing Master Porter in his professional capacity as either a doctor or a lawyer. My initial statement could have applied to either profession, and his response revealed the truth. To my second question, he turned cold rather than baffled. Between those two points of data, I believe a more-or-less clear picture has begun to emerge. Come, we must find our client."

Eugene Porter was in the midst of a group of wealthy-looking audience members, apparently greatly enjoying the company. However, he quickly made his way to Holmes and me once he saw us.

"Well, Mr. Holmes?" he rumbled. "You saw him. It's just as I said! For whatever reason, the lad can't keep his head on straight during that one part of the show. I am certain that people will begin to take notice soon. I pray you come to me with a solution."

"There may be a solution, but I am not yet sure," said Holmes evasively. "Might I speak to your nephew alone? Dr. Watson and I have some questions for him, but I must insist that we have the opportunity to speak to him without any others present."

Eugene hummed. "Can you wait until a little later in the evening? After the rest of the cast has cleared out, I can guarantee you privacy in the Green Room."

Holmes and I agreed to his request, and Eugene set off to make the arrangements. We talked idly about varied topics for perhaps half-an-hour or so until the theater was empty of occupants and most of the cast and crew had departed as well. Afterwards, Mr. Ainsely escorted us to the Green Room, a small but functional room used by the cast and crew alike as a staging area before they made their way onto the stage. Ollie Porter was already in the room, sitting casually on a chair without a care in the world.

"Well, Mr. Holmes?" he said breezily. "My uncle asked me to meet you here. Have you developed a theory? Some strange foreign affliction that alters my brain patterns, or perhaps a chemical effect that changes my speech? Or is it stars and spirits that twist my tongue? The doctors and the psychics have such a colorful variety of hypotheses. I do wonder what yours will be."

Holmes spoke softly, but firmly, apparently intent on not being overheard. "I'm sorry to disappoint, but my theory is likely much simpler than theirs. There is absolutely nothing wrong with you, Ollie Porter. There is no affliction, no environmental factor, and indeed no outside influence of any sort that is altering your words. When you change the monologue, you do so entirely of your own volition. By so altering the play, you are communicating something to a certain Mr. Huxley, who sits in the perfect location to hear your monologue clearly, despite his failing hearing, no matter the rowdiness of the crowd. The communication in question regards a legal matter, at whose nature I can guess, but haven't confirmed. Despite your relaxed demeanor, I think you were rather worried that I might see through your act, for you recited the monologue perfectly every night that you knew we were in the audience. Only tonight, when Watson and I entered through a different door and didn't sit in our usual spots, did you feel safe to change the monologue and thereby give Mr. Huxley another message."

Ollie Porter froze. Façade forgotten, he sat in slack-jawed astonishment, staring at my friend. Slowly he slunk down in his chair and placed his head in his hands, the very image of defeat.

Holmes's expression softened. "It seems a strange thing," he said casually. "Edward Porter dies suddenly of disease. He has a son with a great talent for all things theatrical, with a well-known attachment to the theater itself. And yet, for some unknown reason, upon his demise the theater goes to his brother, rather than the son."

Ollie Porter's head rose, ever so slowly, from the hands that held it, and he stared hard at Holmes. I cannot be certain what was going through his mind, but if the young actor was trying to discern my friend's thoughts from his expression, I believe he was likely sorely disappointed. Holmes may not have been a thespian, but to him every case was like its own stage, upon which he played a variety of roles. Just as every problem was different, so too did the method of Holmes's assistance change drastically from case to case, and the part that he played one day could be vastly different from the rest. On rare occasions, it wasn't his part to solve the case at all.

"Indeed," Holmes continued, as though he hadn't noticed Ollie's reaction, "should I have been placed in a similar situation, I may have felt the need to pursue legal counsel. Perhaps I would have reason to believe that my uncle hadn't acted in good faith. Perhaps my father's will was discovered, but I had some reason to question its authenticity. Or perhaps no will was found at all, and yet my uncle convinced the executor of my father's estate that I was too young to inherit such an important establishment. And perhaps I had good reason to fear that my uncle, who may or may not be involved in the mystery surrounding my father's will, was paying very close attention to me, justifying a rather obscure method of communication with the legal counsel in question."

Ollie Porter shook his head in disbelief as he listened to Holmes. "You've the right of it, Mr. Holmes, though I can't for a moment imagine how you got there. I suppose I may as well tell you the whole of it now, seeing as I have so little left to hide.

"From the onset, allow me to correct an impression that you may have gotten from my uncle during our introduction. When he told you the story of my father and myself, he told it as though he was in close contact with his brother for the entirety of his life, and that he has known me – as an uncle might – for many years before he owned The Horatio. This isn't the case. I didn't even know that I had an uncle until the age of ten, when I met him at my grandmother's funeral. He and my father had a falling out many years ago, long before my birth. Their relationship was even strained at the funeral, though they refrained from any public displays of disunity for the sake of the family. I can only assume it was there that my uncle learned of my father's success, and of the theater he now owned.

"When my father passed away, my uncle and I were called up for the execution of his will. Young and blinded by grief as I was, it didn't occur to me to ask where such a document had been found, nor why the lawyer who executed it was a man my father had never once mentioned. I was shocked into speechlessness when the lawyer announced that my father had left The Horatio to his brother. Ownership of the theater hadn't yet crossed my mind, but the idea that he had left it to his estranged brother, for whom he had a clear (if mostly unspoken) distaste, was baffling to me. My uncle tried to explain it away, saying that my father must have wished for the theater to be in more experienced hands, but I was never convinced.

"Thankfully, I wasn't the only one who noticed the discrepancy. Mr. Huxley has been a blessing, an angel on earth. He has been a regular at The Horatio for over a decade now, and he knew my father exceedingly well. When I was young, I would sometimes catch them having wine together in the rafters, laughing like schoolchildren. He came to me not long after my father's death, just after the property transfer had been completed. He told me that my father had once revealed to him that he had made a will stating that I was to receive ownership of The Horatio upon his death. Together, he and I hatched a plan to build a case against my uncle.

"At first I searched through my father's old things, looking for any sign of the original will, but that swiftly turned into a dead end. Now I have instead been searching through my uncle's office when he isn't looking, trying to find evidence of this and other crimes. Progress has been slow, but I have found a few clues. Mr. Huxley, meanwhile, has been trying to locate the clerk who originally recorded my father's will, as well as trying to pin down the executor. In my grief, I'm afraid I missed the man's name. However, the sight of us talking seems to have spooked my uncle. He forbade me from talking to Huxley, muttering some nonsense about not listening to a senile old man. We had to find a creative way to communicate.

"Our first plan was that I would leave him messages in some hidden spot in the theater, but we quickly discarded that idea. I don't believe there is a square inch in the theater that's hidden from Mr. Ainsley, and while I believe the man might sympathize with my plight, I don't wish to take the chance unless I must. Instead, I sneak from my room at one o'clock in the morning and meet Mr. Huxley on the street when I have some new piece of information or evidence. In order to let him know when to meet, I wait for a night that he's in the audience – he comes whenever he can, generally three or four nights a week – and I change something about the monologue. At first I tried to be subtle with my changes – a misplaced word, a different emotional pattern, something that might escape notice. But we had a low success rate, as Mr. Huxley would often miss my changes, or think I'd intended to send him a message when I didn't. Thus, I began to make drastic changes. It works wonderfully well as a method of communication, but it had the unintended side effect of catching my uncle's attention. He may not have been a presence in my childhood, but I cannot deny that he's taken a very keen interest in my abilities as an actor. Whether due to some

49

lingering sense of familial obligation or simply for business reasons, he does seem to care for my success. Thus all of the doctors, the psychics, and finally, you.

"I find myself rather at your mercy, Mr. Holmes. If you choose to report everything I've just told you to my uncle, I imagine he will come down on me with every restriction he can think of, until I am monitored more closely than a prisoner. Furthermore, I am sure Huxley will be banned from the theater, and the case we have built will collapse without any further communication between us."

Holmes smiled, a twinkle in his eye. "Well, young Master Porter, answer me this question: What do you remember about the man who executed your father's will?"

` As I previously implied, I feel I may have overplayed my hand in committing this particular story to paper. There is no doubt in my mind that a handful of people, especially those well-versed in the peculiar politics of our local London theaters, will find the answer to a few of their own burning questions buried in the text of this story. It is unlikely that I will ever write of Holmes's part in the ensuing legal drama between Porter and Porter, and he would be the first to insist that his role was a small one given the complexity of the case. I will say only that many of the assumptions of Ollie Porter and Mr. Huxley proved to be correct, that Holmes's further assistance to the injured party was completely effective, and leave it at that. For the rest, I suppose you will need to rely on your own theater of the mind.

Bad Timing
by Gordon Linzner

The Devil's Acre, they called it.

A London slum that lay in the shadow of Westminster Alley and the Houses of Parliament. In the 1870's, much of the area had been cleared away, displacing hundreds of impoverished families. Still, more than a decade later, some unpleasant, foul-smelling, dangerous pockets remained, to be avoided the city's better-off residents, if possible.

In the wee hours of a humid evening in late August of 1890, ten-year-old Ginger Collins could be heard racing through this neighborhood. She stumbled over rough cobblestones along Old Pye Street, her reddish locks flapping, struggling to stifle screams of fear. The child had become an orphan only moments earlier, but could not yet afford to mourn. This was not a good time for a young girl, dressed in little more than a thin cotton shirt and ragged pants, to be overwhelmed with shock.

She had only one practical action:

Run.

Given the darkened sky of a waning moon and the sporadic glare of a lantern bobbing somewhere behind her, the child could barely make out the figure chasing her. He was a man, that much was certain. The coarse voice that initially demanded the youngster to halt, followed by the heavy tread of his thick leather boots as they splashed through the muddy, stench-filled street, confirmed as much.

Ginger turned down one twisting alley after another. All to no avail. The stranger seemed as familiar with the squalid neighborhood as herself, who had lived there all her short life. There seemed little hope of escape.

Then, as she turned a final corner, her teary eyes spotted a cesspool cover inadvertently left ajar. Without hesitation, the child bent, slid the metal plate further aside, wide enough for her small, sobbing figure to climb down into the foulness below.

Huddling in that dark, fetid atmosphere beneath the street, Ginger shivered, arms wrapped tightly around her chest. She held her breath, struggling to remain quiet, to not panic further, listening with increasing dread as the footsteps grew nearer.

Then they hurried past.

Ginger let loose that deep breath, took in another. Once the tread above completely vanished, she reached up with trembling fingers to leave that hiding place.

She froze halfway.

The footsteps returned, more plodding, more determined, but assuredly belonging to the same man. Her pursuer had doubled back.

Ginger choked back a sob, fearful lest the slightest sound attract his attention.

Once again, the footsteps slowly, much too slowly, faded away, this time in the direction from which they had initially come.

Several more minutes passed before Ginger, exerting every fiber of her ten-year-old being, worked up enough nerve to crawl out of the cesspool.

She shuddered with relief, taking in the apparently deserted alley and the empty street beyond. The child had no idea where to head next, only that it must be as far from the Devil's Acre as possible.

A firm hand gripped Ginger's shoulder from behind, pulling the child back into the shadows.

Constable Winston Fulbright knelt over the woman's body, lantern in hand. His face twisted with frustration and disgust.

The victim would later be officially identified as Marion Collins, one of the neighborhood's more familiar faces.

Mrs. Collins lay face-up in a corner of the little-traveled alleyway. Streaks of mud and blood showed where it had been dragged out of range of the streetlamp's glow. Her skull's left side was deeply indented. The eye near the wound protruded, looking ready to fall free. A narrow stream of blood continued dribbling from there, mixing with the mud of the cobblestones.

That was how the pale-faced, flaxen-haired Inspector Tobias Gregson found Winston Fulbright when he and his men approached.

"Constable?" Gregson addressed the subordinate.

Fulbright looked up. The inspector towered over him, face impassive. The constable hastily rose, brushing at the mud and bloodstains at his knees, to acknowledge a superior who still stood a half-foot taller than himself. The rest of Gregson's squad was already dispersing, in what would likely prove a futile search for evidence or witnesses.

"Yes, Inspector?" the constable asked.

"I need details." Gregson pulled a notebook from his side pocket. "Your name?"

Fulbright spelled it out while pointing to his badge number.

"What happened here?" Gregson continued.

"I have no idea, Inspector. I just now came across the body."

Gregson nodded. "That explains why we received the call from an anonymous source. Go on."

"I was about to look for her murderer, seeing that this poor woman was beyond help. You can see several fresh sets of footprints. The killer likely doubled back."

Gregson snorted. "It's a good thing my men and I arrived when we did, then. You only have one job now, Constable, and that is to remain on the scene. My men and I will carry on with our investigation."

"But if the killer is nearby – "

"There are more than a few varied sets of footprints surrounding us, Constable Fulbright." Gregson scribbled in his notepad. "A few of these tracks do look fresher than others, but all in all they're a jumble. Some were obviously made by children, women – even yourself. I doubt they will prove of much help."

"I should at least like to try."

Gregson shook his head. "No. I need you to secure the site while my men spread out and I attempt, at least, to make inquiries."

"But – "

"No arguments, Constable. You arrived at the scene before any of us, though according to your statement not much sooner. You are therefore in the best position to determine should anything on the scene be subsequently disturbed, as well as preventing any such activity."

"If you'll excuse my saying so, Inspector, I know the Devil's Acre better than most of your men," Fulbright protested. "I've been working here the last six months and more."

"Nonetheless." The inspector's eyes narrowed as he stared down at the constable. "You may not be aware there was a similar case in Soho last year. There might well be a connection."

The constable lowered his eyes, glancing again at the woman's body. "That seems unlikely. The business these women are in makes them a target for anyone."

Gregson closed his notebook shut. "You seem a bit over-concerned about this particular murder, Constable."

"It's just that . . . ." The constable paused. "The victim, this woman – she looks so innocent. Of course, in this slum, she could hardly be so, yet . . . ."

"Did you know her personally? If so, I shall have to order you to withdraw from this investigation altogether. It's never a good idea to participate in a case when you're involved with the victim."

Fulbright's lips twitched in a brief, nervous grin. "Me? Her? No. I've seen her around the Acre, of course, but in my current assignment I've seen most, if not all, of the slum's inhabitants." He leaned closer to Gregson. "The fact is, Inspector, I've been wanting to move up the ranks to the detective squad for a while now. Extra pay, more interesting work.

This case could provide me with valuable hands-on experience. If I can provide any assistance at all – "

"Are you asking me to mentor you?" Gregson offered a tight smile.

The constable shrugged. "Guilty as charged, Inspector. Throw the book at me."

"We'll see," Gregson replied. "For now, however, the most important contribution you can make is to keep this scene safe from intruders."

Constable Fulbright let loose a sigh of resignation. "As you say, Inspector."

"Don't scream," whispered Ginger's assailant. The lad slowly removed the hand covering her mouth. His voice maintained a non-threatening tone, even as he dodged several vicious kicks to his knees and higher. "He's gone now, but any odd sound might bring him back."

Ginger's struggles eased but did not entirely stop. "Who?" she demanded, in an equally low whisper.

"The man chasing you." Her captor loosened his grip further, allowing Ginger to pull free. She turned to glare defiantly into the cool brown eyes of a wiry boy not more than half-again her own age. The girl felt confident she could flee from him, if necessary.

"You saw him?" the redhead asked. "Do you know what he looks like? Because I don't."

The boy shook his head. "I couldn't get a clear look. Too far away. He'd moved on before I could close the gap. My apologies for not reaching you sooner. What's a lad like you doing on these streets anyway, at this hour? Was that man trying to kidnap you?"

"I could ask you a similar question. You don't look much older than me."

"Ah, well, you see, my mates and I are used to keeping irregular hours. It's how we earn a few extra pence. Honestly, too. You can call me Wiggins."

The girl relaxed a tad more. "Collins. Ginger, to my friends."

"I could be your friend, if you like."

Ginger gave a suspicious side-eye. "Maybe."

"Let me see you home," Wiggins offered. "Your family must be worried."

"I only have my mother." Ginger shivered as memory of the evening's events came flooded back. "Had." The child leaned into Wiggins' arms and began to sob.

"Are you all right?" Wiggins asked.

Ginger sobbed again. "That man. The one chasing me."

"Yes?"

"He killed my mother."

Winston Fulbright raised his left hand to shield his eyes against the rising sun.

"Go home, Constable," Gregson had growled at him a few hours earlier, over Fulbright's protests. "Get some rest. Clean the dirt and blood from your uniform. There's nothing more for you to do here at the moment. When you return for your next shift, tomorrow night, check in with me. I'll know by then if we still need you."

Instead, Fulbright was back on the street at dawn, dressed in his own plain clothing. He'd been unable to sleep. The dead woman, he knew, had been mother to a child of nine or ten. He'd often seen the pair while patrolling the Devil's Acre. The constable imagined the child wandering London's unfamiliar streets, lost, frightened, grief-stricken.

A child who might be able to identify her mother's murderer.

A child whom Fulbright was determined to locate on his own, even out of uniform, not only to preserve his rightful position in the Metropolitan Police, but to possibly earn him a promotion. He could use the extra income to make up for recent losses in other areas.

"A red-headed youth, you say?" repeated the newsstand owner. "Not too common, those. I did notice one such lad while I was setting up this morning. He was accompanied by another urchin, who I did recognize: The infamous Wiggins."

"Infamous? A criminal?"

The newsstand owner chuckled. "My little joke. The lad I speak of could be famous or infamous. Depends upon which side of the law you're on. Wiggins is a member of the Irregulars. You've heard of them, right?"

Fulbright's eyes widened. Everyone in the Metropolitan Police knew of the Baker Street Irregulars, though few on the force had ever encountered one personally. "You mean those pesky street Arabs that Sherlock Holmes uses as his eyes and ears?"

"Ah, you have heard of them." The vendor suddenly narrowed his eyes. "Who did you say you were?"

Fulbright turned away from the vendor to scurry down the increasingly busy street. If the late Marion Collins' offspring was under the scrutiny of London's most famous consulting detective, he had little hope of making and keeping a solid name for himself on the Force.

If, on the other hand, the connection was mere coincidence, the constable still had a chance. Assuming the stories his colleagues at Scotland Yard told him were true, the Irregulars could come off as an arrogant, self-serving lot. This Wiggins lad might be toying with the idea of rivaling his sometime-employer, and that possibility would give Fulbright his opportunity to save the day.

To insure the lad's cooperation, impress him with an official appearance, Fulbright decided he would best be served by slipping back into uniform.

Ginger blinked awake. The tiny room held only one other occupant, the boy she'd met the night before, on a nearby chair. "Where are we?" she asked.

Wiggins was pleased to see the rescued child stretch out arms and legs, then slowly roll into a sitting position on the hard couch cushions. His younger companion was showing further signs of trust.

"This is one of Mr. Holmes's secret apartments. He has several scattered about London, uses them when he hasn't time to return to Baker Street to change his disguises, or simply needs to lie low a while. I brought you breakfast." He handed over a bag of sweet rolls.

Hunger and curiosity temporarily overcame Ginger's depression. As she eagerly tore into the bag, she asked, "You know Sherlock Holmes?" Who hadn't heard of London's famous consulting detective? "He lets you use his rooms?"

"I work for him, yes. My friends and me. Sometimes. Eat – I finished my own while sitting here, waiting for you to wake."

Ginger looked around again, more attentively, as she took her first huge bite. "The room looks, um, empty."

"He mostly uses it as a dressing room. You should freshen up. I'll step out into the hall, give you some privacy. Call out when you're done."

Ginger paused before taking her next bite. "I don't think your boss will like me staying here."

"Only one way to find out. Once you're ready, we'll head over to Baker Street and formally consult with the man you called my 'boss'. If anyone can solve your mother's murder, and have her killer brought to justice, it is he."

"What about the man who followed me? What if he's lurking outside?"

Wiggins confidently folded his arms across his chest. "We can evade him easily enough. I've learned more than a few tricks from my association with Mr. Holmes."

Mrs. Hudson couldn't help but notice that, even allegedly cleaned up, the red-haired visitor gave off a fouler odor than the usual Irregulars. Nonetheless, once she led the pair upstairs and announced their presence, Sherlock Holmes seemed to have no problem with the child's hygiene. He didn't even appear upset at being called out of bed before noon, though the detective usually roused himself much later, except when on a case.

Mr. Holmes allowed his Irregulars too much freedom, as far as the landlady was concerned. Still, the good he did for the world at large made up for these minor eccentricities. At least he'd stopped using the rooms for target practice.

"Good morning, Wiggins," Holmes greeted, tightening the cord of his dressing gown. The landlady had already retreated downstairs. "And who, may I ask, is this young lady?"

"What did you say?" the boy replied.

"I'd meant to correct you," Ginger apologized to the Irregular.

Wiggins stared at her, wide-eyed, then looked to Holmes. "How did you know he – I mean *she* – was a girl, Mr. Holmes? And how did I not know?"

"You are one of the brightest of my Irregulars, Wiggins. Like my friend Watson, however, you often fail to observe what you see. The way she looks about the room, more cautious than any of you boys. The fact that her ring finger is slightly shorter than the index, opposite of most males, is something of an indicator. I could go on, but I see this discussion is making your friend uncomfortable." He offered her an uncharacteristically warm smile. "As Wiggins here is still considering my observations, perhaps you could introduce yourself?"

The girl instinctively nodded. The detective's matter-of-fact tone had an oddly reassuring effect, undercutting her usual reluctance to share personal information with any adult she'd never before met.

"My name is Ginger Collins. Wiggins brought me here because, last night – "

She paused, her throat tightening.

"Perhaps you should take a seat," Holmes suggested, pointing at the padded visitor's chair behind her.

"My mother," Ginger managed to squeeze out. "Murdered." Her lips trembled. "In front of me."

Her hands quivered. Her body swayed. Wiggins hurried to the girl's side, gently grasped her right arm, and led her to the chair.

"I am deeply sorry to hear of your loss." Holmes gave a sympathetic bow. "I'll ask Mrs. Hudson to bring us some tea and biscuits. Then you can fill me in on the details. At your own pace."

Ginger sniffed to clear her throat. "I don't know if I can tell you anything useful."

"You'd be surprised at what you may know."

"It can wait until you've had your tea," Wiggins put in. "Isn't that right, Mr. Holmes?"

The consulting detective nodded, moved to the door, and called down to Mrs. Hudson. She, knowing the detective all too well, had been expecting the request.

Ginger, however, couldn't wait. "My mother and I live – *lived* – alone in a room on Old Pye Street," she began as Holmes turned back to her.

"Lucky you," Wiggins interrupted. "Most people in the Devil's Acre have to share space with other families."

A raised finger from Holmes caused the boy to fall silent again.

"I woke in the middle of the night," Ginger went on. "My mother's bed was empty. She often took late-night walks. To clear her head, she said."

Holmes rubbed his chin. This wasn't a point, at her age, upon which the girl would benefit from further clarification. "Go on."

"The window was open. I heard shouting from the street below. That's what woke me. I looked out, saw my mother arguing with a dark figure standing outside of the streetlamp's glow. I had never heard her that angry, not even when I did something wrong. I quickly got dressed, ran downstairs to help."

Ginger paused, taking deep breaths. Holmes waited patiently until she calmed enough to continue.

"My mother lay on her back, in the street, eyes wide open. I ran toward her. The shadowy figure blocked me, swinging a truncheon. 'Bad timing,' he growled.

"I dodged him, raced through streets and alleys. He seemed to know the neighborhood as well as I do. I finally ducked into a partly open cesspool."

Wiggins spoke up. "That's when I found him – I mean *her*. I mean Ginger, Mr. Holmes. The hour was late – too late to disturb you. I took her to one of your side cribs to recover. My apologies if I overstepped."

"You did so in a good cause," Holmes replied with a shrug. "However, I would appreciate it if you didn't do so again without first consulting me. Why were you yourself out so late, by the way?"

Wiggins looked away, uneasily.

Holmes fixed him with a hard stare.

The boy gave in. "I wasn't doing anything illegal, I promise you. Mostly not. I was doing a bit of research, is all."

Holmes raised a finger to his lips. "Very well. You've already said too much, Wiggins. Even your new friend here could likely guess your secret." Holmes turned his attention back to the girl. "My sympathies are fully with you, Miss Collins, but from what I've heard so far, this is hardly a case requiring my talents. It sounds more within the purview of the Metropolitan Force."

Ginger inhaled sharply.

"I take it you disagree?"

"My mother had some bad experiences with the police. More than once I had to spend time in a nearby orphanage, waiting for her release."

"And more than once," Holmes guessed, "you escaped from those homes before she officially returned. I understand. The British public in general continues to mistrust our police and, I fear, not without some justification. Nonetheless, I have several trustworthy contacts within the department to whom I may reach out."

"Would I know any of them?"

"Possibly. I can summon one of them now, if you like."

The girl curled her legs up onto the chair, wrapped her arms tightly about her torso, and rocked back and forth. "Could I stay here? With you? For a few days? I feel safer here than on the streets."

Holmes frowned. The only person with whom he'd ever felt comfortable sharing his rooms was his friend and sometimes-colleague, Doctor John Watson, who had married and moved out over a year ago. And they, too, had suffered their share of disagreements. Given his moods and indulgences, Holmes hardly considered himself a good role model for a girl of ten. What if she stumbled across his cocaine supply? Suppose she decided to play with his revolver?

"Wiggins!" he called to his Irregular, who stood in a far corner of the sitting room.

"Mr. Holmes?"

"I have a job for you. You know which detectives at the Yard I have the most respect for, but I'll make a short list anyway. Find out who is handling this case. Should it be Lestrade, or Gregson, or any of a dozen names I give you, ask the detective to visit me for a consultation. Tell them I may have information they lack. Don't mention Miss Collins."

"Yes, sir!" Wiggins then added, with a wink, "When shall I be reimbursed for my efforts?"

The red-headed girl stared at her rescuer in disbelief as his audacity.

"Cheeky devil, isn't he?" Holmes said to Ginger, before turning back to his Irregular. "You came to Baker Street to consult with me, Wiggins, remember? Is it not enough that I waived your fee?" Holmes finished his list, then opened a side drawer of his desk.

"Well," Wiggins explained, "since you mention it, Miss Collins is sort of a friend now. I would be happy to attend to her needs without recompense, but my reputation . . . ."

Holmes tossed a coin at the lad, who caught it deftly. "Naturally I shall reimburse you for your trouble. Another coin awaits you, should you accomplish your errand within the hour. Starting – *now*!"

Holmes raised his pocket watch.

Wiggins saluted briskly, winked at Ginger, and dashed down the stairs. Mrs. Hudson gave a stern cry as the boy nearly crashed into her. She managed nonetheless to not spill her tea tray.

"And now, Miss Collins," Holmes addressed his young guest, "while we await the arrival of the cream of Scotland Yard, perhaps we should we turn our conversation to less-distressing topics."

"I don't want to talk any more, Mr. Holmes."

"Understood. Some music to calm your nerves, then. Yes? Excellent! Allow me a moment to tune my Stradivarius."

Not long after Mrs. Hudson had left the tea, a coarse voice echoed in the stairwell leading up to the detective's first-floor rooms. It was loud enough to penetrate the closed doors, interrupting the otherwise soothing tones of Holmes's violin.

"I must talk to Sherlock Holmes now! It is my obligation, my right, my *duty* as an officer of the law!"

Mrs. Hudson responded in an equally loud, equally stern tone. "And it is my duty to announce your presence first, constable or no."

Ginger Collins cringed. "Is that one of your police friends?" she asked nervously.

"Not that I know of."

"He sounds scary."

"Not pleasant, I agree. I suggest you climb those stairs leading up from the landing, just outside the door, and enter the room above. Close the door. Turn the lock, if you like. That was my friend Watson's bedroom before he married and moved out. It should be comfortable enough, although I have moved some of my bulkier equipment in there over the past year."

"What does he want?"

"That's what I intend to discover."

"I need to know."

"Listen, if you must. But keep silent, for your own safety."

Ginger gave a shiver. Holmes immediately regretted the intensity of his warning, but too late to soften it.

Once the red-headed girl disappeared up the stairs, Holmes moved to the door of his flat. He stepped down from the landing far enough to peer around toward the front door.

The situation between his landlady and the officer was heating up. It needed to be defused.

"It's all right, Mrs. Hudson," he called down. "You may send the caller up to me."

"And you promised today would be a quiet one," the landlady muttered.

The newcomer pushed past her, storming up the stairs.

"I never claimed to be infallible, Mrs. Hudson," Holmes assured her. "Only less fallible than most people."

Holmes didn't recognize the visitor, to his annoyance. He'd specifically ordered Wiggins only to speak with one of the trustworthy names on his list. The uniform told him this man was a mere constable, not even a detective.

Of course, Holmes had also said he hoped to see the investigator within the hour, if Wiggins was to earn his extra coin. The lad might have decided one restriction cancelled the other.

Holmes would have to have a long discussion with his Irregular.

"Thank you for seeing me, Mr. Holmes," said the constable in a calmer voice as he entered the sitting room. He extended his right hand.

Holmes pretended not to notice the greeting. "You didn't leave me much choice, to judge from your tone with my landlady. Your name, Constable?"

"Fulbright. Winston Fulbright. I've been with Scotland Yard for a little under a year. I apologize if I came across a bit heavy-handed. This case is very important to me. It could affect my standing with the Yard."

"Understood." Holmes moved to his usual seat and then pointed a long finger at the basket chair opposite his own. "Have a seat, Constable Fulbright. Proceed."

The constable took his place, then leaned forward, clasping his hands beneath his chin, as if ready to unveil some deep, dark secret.

"Last night – well, more like very early this morning – while on patrol in the Devil's Acre, I discovered the body of a woman near Old Pye Street. She had been viciously attacked, murdered, her skull bashed in and partially crushed by some blunt object. I later learned a child was seen running from the site. I believe this youngster may be responsible for the death. The injuries may have been accidental, although the nature of the blows seem to indicate deliberate intent. In any case, I need to locate this child."

Through the partially open door to the landing, Holmes heard a faint sob from the stairs leading up to Watson's old room. Fortunately, the constable seemed not to notice, being occupied with presenting his story.

"This sounds far too straightforward a case for me," Holmes replied. "One the police could easily handle without my intervention."

"I quite agree. My point is, one of the witnesses I interviewed claimed he later saw this child wander off in the company of one of your Irregulars, a boy named Wiggins. I only require an address where I might find this lad, and I will be on my way."

Holmes leaned back in his chair and crossed his fingers. "For what purpose?"

"I only wish to ask him a few questions. Help me track down the killer."

"What makes you so certain a child could commit so brutal a crime?"

"Why else would you run off, unless you yourself were responsible for the death of your own mother? Why would you not immediately go to the police?"

"Then you know the identity of the victim, as well as her alleged murderer?"

"Marion Collins, yes. The child's name is Ginger."

"Since we're being hypothetical," Holmes suggested, "let us presume you, or someone you know, has had more than one unpleasant experience with the police. Regrettably, such things are common in our poorer neighborhoods."

Fulbright stiffened. "Are you accusing me of harassing a ten-year-old child?"

Holmes thumbed his right forefinger knuckle against his chin. "Your tone indicates you believe I am targeting you. What reason would I have to do so? Should I make some inquiries of my own among your associates, might I discover complaints made against you?"

Fulbright leapt to his feet, glaring at Holmes. "How dare you speak to me this way, sir? I am a full member of the Metropolitan Police. Your sterling reputation and so-called expertise are no excuse for such insolence!"

Holmes didn't care for this abrupt turn in the constable's attitude. He rose, moving to the fireplace, ostensibly in search of a cigarette. His actual goal was to keep within range of the iron poker, should its use prove necessary.

Constable Fulbright followed him.

The tension in the air was broken by Mrs. Hudson's sudden appearance at the open door of the flat. "You have another visitor, Mr. Holmes. A more familiar one. I'm told it's the gentleman you were expecting."

"Please, let him in, Mrs. Hudson," Holmes replied, keeping a cautious eye on Fulbright.

A moment later, Inspector Tobias Gregson marched into the sitting room, followed by the excited Wiggins.

"Good day, Mr. Holmes," the Inspector greeted. "I'm told you have some vital information for – Constable Fulbright? What the devil are you doing here? And in uniform! You should still be off duty. On my orders!"

The constable's eyes widened in the presence of his taller superior.

"I, er, discovered some information that might be useful in this case. Purely by chance. I thought a man of Mr. Holmes's reputation could best point me in the right direction for following up."

"And you didn't seek to inform me first?" Gregson's tone made that question a statement.

"I didn't want to waste your time, Inspector, in case it proved a dead end."

"That is my decision to make, not yours." The inspector looked toward the consulting detective. "Has this man been harassing you, Mr. Holmes? He asked me if might help him upgrade to detective. I'm having doubts about that right now."

"Everything is under control, Inspector, thanks to your timely arrival," Holmes responded. "Constable Fulbright here asked me if I might direct him toward one of my Irregulars, to interrogate the boy. Such is obviously unnecessary now, for I see you're already in touch with Wiggins. Or, rather, he's been in touch with you." Holmes nodded toward the lad who stood to the left of Tobias Gregson.

"You're Wiggins?" Fulbright snapped.

The boy gave a defiant grin.

Fulbright angrily turned to Gregson. "Marion Collins' killer was seen in the company of this boy!"

"Her *alleged* killer, to be precise, Constable," Holmes responded.

Wiggins rolled his eyes. "I came across a frightened little girl, Inspector, ten years old, running through the streets at an ungodly hour," he admitted. "I took her somewhere safe. We chatted a bit. If that child is a murderer, I'm next in line for the throne."

Gregson nodded, then addressed the constable. "You're telling me, Fulbright, that a ten-year-old girl would savagely bash in her own mother's skull?"

"It wouldn't been the first time it might happen."

Gregson turned back to the Irregular. "Where is this child now, Wiggins?"

The boy glanced at Holmes.

"I have made already temporary arrangements for her," the detective explained. "The girl felt terrified, threatened, and justifiably so. She just lost her mother. Wiggins here is in no position to tell you her exact location."

The Irregular opened his mouth to contradict Holmes, then shut it again. The detective's side glance was all he needed to remain silent.

"That child is a murderer!" the constable shouted. "She killed her own mother! You're nothing more than a conspirator, Holmes!" He turned to Gregson. "You mustn't believe a word she says, Inspector!"

Gregson eyed Fulbright coolly. "Tell me honestly, Constable: Had you found her on your own, you would have brought her to me at Scotland Yard for questioning?"

"I would have . . . ." Fulbright lowered his voice. "She might have resisted. You know what children are like. I would do what was necessary."

"'What was necessary'," Gregson replied, lips tightening, "would have been to inform me of this situation so that I might dispatch a proper squad for a search."

"The red-headed girl ran off when I found that body. I couldn't follow her immediately – not until I made certain the woman was dead."

"Which you assuredly did," Holmes interjected.

"Yes. No! I didn't mean it in the way you imply!"

Gregson grew increasingly annoyed. "And this was moments before my men and I arrived on the scene?"

"Um. Yes. I just said as much."

"Why did you not mention the child then?"

The constable looked from Gregson, to Holmes, to the boy, then back to his superior. "I'd been distracted. By all the blood."

"Distracted by the sight of blood. Yet you want to be a detective."

"It was simply bad timing."

Holmes raised an eyebrow. "What kind of timing?" he asked. "I didn't quite hear you."

"Bad timing!" Fulbright shouted, peeved.

Gregson could hardly miss the shriek that came from the open door to the landing.

"I think I know where Ginger Collins is," Wiggins whispered.

"I believe you do," Holmes replied. "Go upstairs, Wiggins. Talk to the girl. Convince her it is now safe for her to come down, that she'll find herself among people who have only her best interests at heart." He looked toward Fulbright. "All but one."

"This is absurd, Inspector!" the constable complained.

"We shall see," the inspector countered.

It took Wiggins several minutes before Ginger Collins was persuaded to climb down the stairs from Doctor Watson's former bedroom. She remained partially hidden behind the Irregular, eyeing Gregson suspiciously, taking in Holmes's confident stance.

"I didn't see his face," she managed at last, "but I know the voice that spat those words over my mother's body. I will never forget them." Her trembling finger focused on Fulbright. "That man killed my mother!"

"*Your mother!*" snarled Fulbright. "A woman of ill repute. Trying to cheat me out of my fee! Threatening to turn me in! She hardly deserved to raise an offspring. Yet she acted as if I were unworthy of her attention and employment." He glared at Ginger Collins. "This child is no better! I did her a favor!"

Ginger half-leaned, half-collapsed in shock against Wiggins' side. The boy supported her erect, wrapping an arm about her waist.

Gregson clasped the constable's shoulder. "Anything else you'd like to say in front of these witnesses?"

The constable fell silent. Too late, he realized his temper had doomed him.

Holmes laid a gentler hand on his Irregular's shoulder. "Wiggins, lead Miss Collins down to the ground floor. Perhaps Mrs. Hudson could use some help cleaning up." In a softer voice, he added, "Also advise her the child will be spending the night in Watson's room. Come morning, we shall seek more suitable accommodations."

Wiggins shot a wary eye at the constable, who looked away.

"Mr. Holmes and I shall finish sorting things out here," Gregson told the youth.

Once the youngsters left, Holmes faced the constable, his tone cold as ice. "What kind of favor?"

"Well. You know. Help her escape that horrid life. Arrange a bit of work for her. I deserved a share. I didn't kill her! We just had a connection."

"Those bloodstains on your uniform," Holmes taunted. "That's the mother's blood, is it not?"

"I did bend over her body, after all," Fulbright protested. "Checking for a pulse." He turned to Gregson. "I didn't have time to do laundry."

"That explains some stains, but not the faint splatter pattern on the upper chest. That appears more likely the result of blood being spewed at an even level – let us say before the unfortunate woman fell to the ground. Would you agree, Gregson?"

The inspector nodded grimly. "It's more obvious in the daylight."

"You can't seriously believe this nonsense, Inspector!" said Fulbright, hoping his newest attempt to sound calm would compensate for his earlier outburst.

"I'd suggest conducting a close examination of his truncheon, as well." Holmes held out the weapon. "It shows severe signs of recent heavy use."

"How did you get that?" Fulbright reached out.

The inspector quickly clamped his handcuffs on Marion Collins' killer. Fulbright dropped to his knees, silent, resigned, refusing to meet either detective's eyes or say another word.

"The man is too easily distracted," Holmes explained.

"So he is," Gregson affirmed. "If I could borrow your telephone to call for a wagon . . . ?"

"Of course." Holmes stepped away from the fireplace. "It's downstairs. In the meantime, I'll keep an eye on our guest."

Fulbright continued kneeling in place, in a deep, morose silence. A silence he wished he'd been in better control of earlier.

"That went more smoothly than expected, Inspector," Holmes observed, while they waited for the police van to arrive. "Our perpetrator appears drained of all resistance."

"It happens, sometimes," Gregson acknowledged, keeping an eye on his captive. "Constable Winston Fulbright – well, soon to be ex-constable – seems to have expended most of his energy on that ill-advised outburst."

Fulbright leaned forward slightly, continuing to kneel on the floor Holmes's flat at 221b Baker Street, features taut, struggling to not listen.

"Bad timing, indeed, on his part," Holmes affirmed.

The Adventure of the Living Terror
by Craig Janacek

O_{ne} morning late in August of 1890, I found myself unbusied by my typical duties. My wife had decided to take a little trip to Brighton with Mrs. Whitney, and the bank holiday had left me without any patients for the day. I therefore resolved to stop in at Baker Street and inquire into the recent activities of my friend, Mr. Sherlock Holmes.

He was in rather excellent spirits, and he welcomed me into my old armchair with a sweep of his hand. I gave him an account of some of the sorry tribulations that I had recently encountered in my practice, while gazing fondly about the suite that once had been my home for a number of years.

"I see you admiring the new plaque in the corner, Watson."

I had noted a large blue-and-white plate standing on the shelf above my former desk where I had once kept my medical books. "Indeed. It is new since my last visit, is it not?"

"Your powers of observation progress," said he, with a smile. "You are correct. It once belonged to Mrs. Quinlan. I recently helped her determine the location of her missing daughter, even though it was obvious that the poor woman could not afford my fee. Her son, who is presently somewhere in the South Atlantic and therefore unable to assist, was once a young able-bodied seaman on the *Inflexible* at the bombardment of Alexandria. [1] A cannon shot made a hole in the Khedive's palace and – when the lad landed – he located this new ingress. The intrepid midshipman Quinlan crawled through, whereat he found himself in the Khedive's kitchen. With an unfortunate eye to loot, he seized this plate, and crawled out again. He gave it to his mother, and it was the most treasured thing the old lady possessed – or so she said. In lieu of a fee, Mrs. Quinlan begged me to take it, and I thought much of the action." [2]

"Oh?" said I, raising an eyebrow. "I have only seen you waive your professional charges for cases of extraordinary interest."

"Well, the suspect was obvious, and it was an exceptional opportunity to observe the influence of a trade upon the form of the hand. At first, I wasn't quite sure whether the man was a cork-cutter or a slater. I observed a slight callus, or hardening, upon one side of his forefinger, as well as a little thickening on the outside of his thumb. Those are, of course, a sure sign that he was either one or the other. I shall have to tell you of it someday, Watson, for a record of it might be rather more educational than your most recent brochure, which I am afraid was veritably drenched in romanticism. Poisoned blowpipes and exotic treasures are hardly a fit subject for a treatise on the science of deduction." [3]

"But the adventure was there," I remonstrated. "I couldn't fail to relate the facts as they occurred. And why not tell me the story of the slater now?"

"Because within the next minute, a gentleman will be sitting in the settee across from me, relating the details of a new case."

"Surely you are joking!" I protested. "No, wait," said I, glancing over at the mantel clock. "It is almost nine o'clock. Someone must have sent a note that they would call at this time."

"An excellent guess, Watson, but I am afraid that the answer is simpler. You must not forget to utilize all your senses. Just now, I heard the distinctive noise of a pair of hooves and grating wheels against the curb outside. The horses aren't winded, suggestive that they aren't ordinary nags from a cab-yard. Therefore, these are the sounds of a fancy brougham, which can only signal the appearance of a well-to-do client. Yes, there is the sharp pull at the bell as I speak."

"Yes, I see now," said I, while waiting for the visitor to climb the steps up from the pavement. "But why a gentleman? Why not a lady?"

"Ha!" said Holmes, with a laugh. "You have me there. This was merely a playing of the odds. You may have observed that my clientele to date has been predominantly male. While there have been some remarkable examples of the fairer sex who have graced our sitting room – your wife first among them – I have found that, by-and-large, the female of our species is less likely to seek out my assistance than their counterparts. And from the sound of the shoes upon Mrs. Hudson's steps, it appears that my guess is correct."

A knock upon the door heralded the appearance of a gentleman who – based upon the silver in his hair and the lines on his face – was about three or four years shy of sixty. His dress was quiet and sombre – a black frockcoat, dark trousers, and a grey necktie. He held out his card for Holmes's inspection.

"Good morning, Mr. Summers," said Holmes. "Pray take a seat. What might I do for a lawyer of the Inner Temple?"

Too well-mannered to say it out-loud, Mr. Summers's eyes briefly glanced in my direction.

"Oh, don't mind Dr. Watson, here," said Holmes, with a smile. "He is the soul of discretion, and I have found that his skills are often essential for the successful conclusion of a case. A personage no less august than Sir Henry Baskerville will attest to that."

"Yes, well, I suppose that the opinion of a medical man might come in handy regarding this matter," said Mr. Summers. "You may have read in the papers, Mr. Holmes, of the death of Lord Southerton six weeks ago?" [4]

"Of course. He was one of the richest peers in England. In fact, I recently investigated a case that took place quite near his estate of Otwell House, in the vicinity of Winchester. [5] However, I understood from the papers that Lord Southerton was an elderly gentleman who passed on from natural causes?"

"That is true. His Lordship was nearing seventy-five and had been in poor health for some time. At the end, he was in a fairly critical condition."

"Then I fail to see how I may be of use to you."

"The question, Mr. Holmes," said Summers, "is whether his heir, Mr. Marshall King, is fit to succeed him to the title."

"Surely that is a matter for the Chancery court, not a detective?" [6]

Summers shook his head. "The legitimacy of Mr. King's inheritance is undeniable. His father was the younger brother of Lord Southerton, who was a bachelor. Furthermore, the terms of his Lordship's will are quite plain."

"Then what has Mr. King done to call into doubt his windfall?"

"He has possibly murdered – or at least caused the death of – his cousin, Mr. Everard King."

"That is a serious accusation, Mr. Summers," said Holmes. "And what does Mr. Marshall King have to say about such a charge?"

"Mr. King was gravely wounded in the same apparent misadventure which claimed the life of his cousin. He has been delirious, drifting between life and death for the last six weeks since the event."

"Tell me about Mr. Marshall King."

"He is young fellow, thirty years of age, a bachelor and man about town. He lived in a suite of apartments in Grosvenor Mansions, with no known occupation, save that of pigeon-shooting and polo-playing at Hurlingham. [7] Like many such individuals, Mr. King had expensive tastes, great expectations, and aristocratic connections, but no actual money in his pocket, and no profession by which he may earn any. I was a friend and confidant of Mr. King's late father, Richard, who was a good, sanguine, easy-going man. Mr. King's father had such confidence in the wealth and benevolence of his bachelor elder brother, Lord Southerton, that he took it for granted that his only son would never be called upon to earn a living for himself. Mr. Richard King imagined that if there weren't a vacancy for his son upon the great Southerton Estates, at least there would be found some post in the diplomatic service, which still remains the special preserve of our privileged classes."

"But neither such position manifested itself?" asked Holmes.

Mr. Summers shook his head. "As is common with men of great wealth, Lord Southerton was something of a notorious miser. Sadly, Richard died eight years ago, too early to realize how false his calculations had been. Neither his brother nor the State took the slightest notice of Mr. Marshall King or showed any interest in his career. An occasional brace of pheasants, or basket of hares, was all that ever reached him to remind him that he was heir to Otwell House and one of the richest estates in the country."

"It is challenging to subsist on the occasional pluckings of a hunt."

"You are correct, Mr. Holmes. While Mr. Marshall King waited month by month for the passing of his uncle, and therefore the great wealth of his inheritance to devolve upon him, he found himself in a position where his lack of an allowance was making it was more and more difficult to get the brokers to renew his bills, or to cash any further *post-obits* upon an unentailed property. [8] In short, ruin lay right across his path, and every day I imagine that Mr. King must have seen it clearer, nearer, and more absolutely unavoidable. I believe that he was expecting a rather long visit to Bankruptcy Court."

"It sounds like Mr. Marshall King was in rather dire straits," I interjected. "I suppose that Lord Southerton would have hardly looked sympathetically upon his heir residing in a debtor's gaol." [9]

"Quite so, Doctor," agreed Mr. Summers. "Such a disgrace could easily have led Lord Southerton to enact the legal proceedings required to skip over Mr. Marshall King in favour of the next individual in line."

"Which was Mr. Everard King," said Holmes.

"Precisely!" agreed the lawyer. "This is one of the difficulties. Mr. Everard King was the sole other direct heir, being the son of Lord Southerton's youngest brother. He was also fifteen years older than Mr. Marshall King, his father siring him at a much younger age. After him, there are numerous well-to-do distant cousins, but it would be much more problematic for the estate to devolve upon one of them. With his cousin, Mr. Everard King, out of the picture, Mr. Marshall King's inheritance would be suddenly on much firmer grounds."

"And were the cousins close?"

"Not at all. In fact, up until about a week prior to Mr. Everard King's death, I don't believe that they had ever met."

Holmes's eyebrows rose. "Surely that is unusual?"

"It is my understanding that – many years ago – Mr. Everard King's father had taken his family to the Brazils. Mr. Everard King had spent an adventurous life in South America, where he had prospered and married. He had recently returned to this country to settle down on his fortune. It seems that he might have been attempting to distance himself from some of the political turbulence wracking his adopted country." [10]

"Do you know how he made his money?"

"No, but he appeared to have plenty of it, for he bought the ancient estate of Greylands Court, near Clipton-on-the-Marsh, in Suffolk." [11]

"How recently did Mr. Everard King return to England?" asked Holmes.

"About one year hence."

"But the cousins only met a few weeks ago?"

"That is correct."

"Interesting," said Holmes. "And what changed?"

"From speaking to Burrows, Mr. Marshall King's valet, Mr. Everard King sent his cousin a letter asking him to come down and spend a short visit at Greylands. As I understand it, the penniless Marshall was overcome by a very great relief and joy by this potentially providential invitation, for he thought that he might be able to borrow some money from his cousin. He ordered Burrows to pack his valise and set off that same evening for Suffolk."

"Where a misadventure resulted in the death of Mr. Everard King and the grievous injury to Mr. Marshall King," said Holmes.

"Correct."

"Was it a shooting accident?" I asked.

The lawyer shook his head. "No, it is rather more peculiar than that, Doctor. In fact, if I hadn't personally spoken to Mr. King's physician, Sir Jasper Meek, and confirmed the nature of his injury, I would scarcely credit it. It is like something out of Baker."

Holmes leaned forward, plainly intrigued. "An exotic animal?"

"Just so, Mr. Holmes. It seems that Mr. Everard King had brought with him from the Brazils a large menagerie of foreign creatures, which he was endeavouring to rear in England. The acclimatization of these beasts was one of his hobbies. Some of these animals were allowed to roam freely in the grounds of Greylands Park, though one was deemed too dangerous to ever be uncaged. This was a large cat of some sort."

"And this Brazilian cat somehow got free?" asked Holmes.

"Yes," said he. "Not entirely, of course, or there would have been a much larger uproar. However, by some means, the beast got into the same room as the two cousins, resulting in the death of one and the near-death of the other. The local constable considered it to be a tragic accident."

Holmes shook his head. "Then I fail to see how I may be of use, Mr. Summers. While I consider myself an expert of sorts regarding the affairs of man, the realm of the great beasts is rather beyond the ken of this agency."

"I understand. Nevertheless, I wish for you to go up to Clipton, Mr. Holmes, where you might look over the scene and speak to the witnesses. Surely your talents can determine whether this was simple mischance, or whether there was a more nefarious design at work. I assure you that your professional charges shall be promptly paid in full."

Holmes considered this proposition for a moment, drumming his long fingers upon the arm of his chair. "Very well," said he. "I suppose that it may prove interesting. It isn't every day that an animal is the instrument of an individual's death, though certain villains with a flair for the macabre have employed them in such a fashion. [12] What say you to a trip up to Suffolk, Watson?"

After seeing off Mr. Summers, Holmes glanced at his pocket watch and consulted *Bradshaw's*. Assuming my interest in joining him, he instructed me to proceed to Liverpool Street Station and purchase return tickets upon the next train to Ipswich.

"What about a valise?"

"No need," said he, with a shake of his head. "I trust that we shall be back by nightfall."

"What about you?"

"I must quickly attend to an errand."

Forty minutes later, I was pacing up and down the platform, worried that the train would depart without us, when Holmes's tall, gaunt figure came racing up. We jumped aboard just as the conductor sounded his whistle and soon settled into a pair of window seats for the hour-and-a-quarter run up to Suffolk.

"Where have you been?"

"My apologies," said he. "I didn't intend to cut it so short, but my inquiries took a bit longer than I expected. I first sent a telegram to Greylands Court, informing them of our visit. I then went 'round to Grosvenor Mansions to speak with Mr. King's valet. Despite what appear to be good intentions, Burrows proved to be not terribly helpful, for he remained in London while Mr. King went up to Suffolk alone to visit his cousin. Burrows didn't hear from his master again until word came of the attack. A surgeon had been sent for from Clipton, and Burrows arranged for a nurse to go up from London. Mr. King recuperated at Greylands for several weeks until his health was sufficient for him to be carried to the closest train station, and he was thus conveyed back to Grosvenor Mansions."

"Does he have a private physician?"

"Capital, Watson," said Holmes, approvingly. "My first thought exactly. I learned that Sir Jasper Meek has taken over his care. Therefore, I called upon Sir Jasper, who was most laudatory of the local surgeon's work upon Mr. King's wounded thigh and calf. Even the man's fingers were terribly lacerated in the attack. While he remains delirious from fever and the terrible loss of blood, Sir Jasper is certain that Mr. King shall eventually pull through, though he is likely to require a cane for remainder of his days."

"Did you learn anything else?"

"Mr. Summers's impressions of Mr. King's finances were quite accurate. Burrows allowed me to glance through the notes in the man's pocketbook, which was somewhat bloodied during the attack. From my inspection of the figures within, it is clear that Mr. King's unbusinesslike ways had left him in a rather lamentable position. The list of tradesmen and creditors – from his landlord to his valet – is extraordinarily long."

After changing at Ipswich, a little local train deposited us at a small, deserted station lying amidst a rolling grassy country. A sluggish and winding river curved in and out amidst the valleys, between high, silted banks, which showed that we were within reach of the tide. Despite Holmes having wired ahead, no carriage awaited us, so we hired a dogcart at the local inn. The driver, an excellent fellow, was full of praises for the recently deceased Mr. Everard King. We learned from him that his had been a name to conjure with in that part of the country.

"Mr. Everard regularly entertained the local school-children," said the driver. "He threw his grounds open to visitors, and he subscribed to all of the local charities."

"He sounds universally benevolent," murmured Holmes.

"Indeed!" said the driver. "I can only account for it by supposing that Mr. Everard had Parliamentary ambitions. It is a right shame that he will never see the inside of the Commons Chamber now."

My attention was drawn away from our driver's panegyric by the appearance of an exceptionally beautiful bird, which settled on a telegraph-post beside the road. At first, I thought that it was a jay, but it was larger, with a brighter plumage.

When I spoke this thought aloud, the driver nodded. "That bird once belonged to the very man of whom we were speaking. He brought with him from the Brazils several of that land's birds and beasts."

When once we had passed the gates of Greylands Park, we had ample evidence of this peculiar taste of Mr. King. Some small spotted deer, a curious wild pig known – I believe – as a peccary, a gorgeously feathered oriole, some sort of armadillo, and a singular lumbering in-toed beast like a very fat badger, were among the creatures which I observed as we drove along the winding avenue. [13] Despite the exotic inhabitants of its park, Greylands was a typical broad, stone English mansion, with solid wings and Palladio pillars before the doorway. Jefferson, the butler, met us as our dogcart pulled up.

Holmes explained that we had come at the behest of Mr. Summers, the lawyer for Mr. Marshall King, and the butler nodded, as if expecting such a visit.

"Is Mrs. King in?" asked Holmes.

"No, sir. Mrs. King departed the day before Mr. Marshall King was removed to London."

"To where?"

"I cannot say, sir."

"Surely she left a forwarding address?"

"Well, sir, I only know that she purchased a ticket to London."

"And did she say when she planned to return?"

"She did not."

"Is Mrs. King usually so cryptic regarding her intentions?"

"Well, sir, Mrs. King is from the Americas," said Jefferson, hesitantly. "Although she speaks excellent English, her customs are – of course – somewhat different than those of a lady raised in England."

"How so?"

The butler paused and licked his lips. "It isn't my place to say, sir."

Holmes frowned. "Need I remind you, Mr. Jefferson, that your master is dead? I have been retained to get to the truth of the affair. Every detail, no matter how indecorous, might be of critical importance."

The man shook his head obstinately. "Constable Murray said it was simply a terrible accident."

"Tell me, Mr. Jefferson," said Holmes, "did you regard Mr. Everard King to be a careless man?"

"No, sir. Quite the opposite."

"And yet, somehow, he found himself and his cousin in a room with an uncaged, murderous beast. Does that not strike you as strange?"

"I suppose so."

"Then we must consider the possibility that this was something other than an accident."

"What do you mean?" asked the butler, his brow furrowed in confusion.

"It has been proposed that someone meant to kill Mr. King."

Jefferson shook his head vigorously. "I cannot believe that, sir."

"Why not?"

"Those sorts of things only happen in stories. No one around these parts would ever do such a thing. There might be a brawl or two down at the local tavern, but you will not find many cold-blooded murderers hanging about Suffolk."

"But Mrs. King wasn't from Suffolk, was she? She and Mr. King only came here a year ago."

"That is true," said the butler, slowly.

"Then you see, Mr. Jefferson, why it is imperative that you explain to me precisely the situation of Mr. and Mrs. King, as well as that of their recent guest."

The man considered this argument and then nodded. "Very well, what would you know?"

"Let us start at the beginning?" said Holmes, reasonably. "Tell me what happened when Mr. Marshall King first arrived at Greylands."

"Mr. Everard welcomed him warmly. I recall him saying that he was delighted to make his cousin's acquaintance, and that it was a great compliment that Mr. Marshall would honour our sleepy little country place with his presence."

"And was Mrs. King as cordial as her husband?"

"No, sir."

"How would you describe her attitude?"

"Well, sir, truth be told, I would say that she was rather frigid towards him. Even somewhat rude."

"And you excused her manners on the score of her ignorance of our customs? Was she so rude to all the visitors to Greylands Court?"

"No, sir, though Mr. Everard didn't have a great many visitors. I should say, sir, that her actual words to Mr. Marshall were, as a rule, courteous, but the general impression was noticeably clear from the first that she heartily wished him back in London once more."

"And what did Mr. Marshall think of this ill-temper on the part of Mrs. King?"

"I believe that he attempted to disregard her coldness. He certainly reciprocated the extreme cordiality of Mr. Everard's welcome, who had spared no pains to make his cousin comfortable. His room was a charming one – I will show it to you, should you so desire – and I often heard Mr. Everard ask his cousin to tell him anything that could add to his happiness."

"It seems that Mr. Everard was a quite large-hearted and hospitable man," said Holmes.

"Indeed, sir."

"So Mr. Everard and his cousin got on well?"

"Yes, sir. After dinner they would smoke Havanas and drink coffee, which Mr. Everard had specially grown upon his own plantation in the Brazils."

"And what was the state of the relationship between Mr. Everard and his wife?"

"Mr. Everard had a strong will and a somewhat fiery temper when Mrs. King behaved poorly towards his guest. Upon occasion, I heard him talking in a low voice of concentrated passion to his wife."

"And what was the reason for Mrs. King's curious aversion towards Mr. Marshall?"

"I heard Mr. Everard say that his poor dear wife was incredibly jealous. That she hated that anyone – male or female – should for an instant come between them. That her ideal was a desert island and an eternal *tête-à-tête*. He confessed to Mr. Marshall that his wife's actions, upon this particular point, weren't very far removed from mania."

"Fascinating," said Holmes. "Such manias are always challenging to predict what form they might take. I wonder if I might look over Mr. King's desk?"

"Very good, sir."

The butler led us to a study. Bookcases lined the room on three sides, while large windows looking over the grounds of the park dominated the fourth wall. A desk was situated in such a way to fully enjoy this view. Upon this was a framed picture of a man and a woman.

"Mr. and Mrs. Everard King?" asked Holmes, picking this up.

"Yes, sir," agreed the butler.

The gentleman's appearance was very homely and benevolent. He was short and chubby, some forty-five years old perhaps, with a round, good-humoured face, and shot with a thousand wrinkles. Although the sepia tones made it impossible to say for certain, I imagine that his skin was burned brown with the tropical sun. He wore white linen clothes, in true planter style, with a cigar between his lips, and a large Panama hat upon the back of his head. It was such a figure as one associates with a veranda bungalow in some far away land. At his side was a tall, haggard woman with a sallow face, which a shadow largely obscured. It was difficult to make out much regarding her features, but she was undoubtedly the possessor of a pair of particularly expressive dark and forbidding eyes.

Setting down the picture, Holmes glanced over the stationary-covered desk. "This is most interesting," said he.

I frowned in confusion. "What is?"

"Note, Watson, that Mr. Everard King's desk contains a considerable number of telegram envelopes, all of them from the days leading up to his death. Look at the dates. It seems that he received at least three or four telegrams a day, and sometimes as many as seven or eight."

"That's right, sir," added the butler. "They arrived at all hours, and were always opened by Mr. Everard with the utmost eagerness and anxiety upon his face."

"And yet, of the telegrams themselves, there is no sign," noted Holmes. He picked up a letter opener and poked through some ashes in a tray. "I see that cigars are not all that Mr. King set alight. Do you know the contents of these missives, Mr. Jefferson?"

The butler shook his head. "I am afraid not, sir. Sometimes I imagined that it must be the turf, and sometimes the Stock Exchange."

"Well, from the Hampshire stamps on these envelopes, it is apparent that whatever this very urgent business was, it was something not transacted upon the Downs of Suffolk," said Holmes, musingly. "Now, then, Mr. Jefferson, I should like to see the cage of the great cat that killed your master."

"Very good, sir. If you would follow me."

The butler led us through one wing of the house. A fine collection of South American utensils and weapons, which had been brought, no doubt, by the gentlemen from his adopted home, occupied much of this wing. I noted that amongst these were some empty cages.

"Tell me, Jefferson," said Holmes. "Did Mr. King keep certain of his animals in the house itself?"

"Yes, sir. You may have noted a few of the beasties roaming free in the grounds, such as some of the birds who are trained not to fly away, and some of the beasts that cannot climb the surrounding wall. But others would be a risk for getting out into the countryside, so he kept those in these cages. He was so enthusiastic about them – so happy when one gave birth and so despondent when one died. I often heard him cry out in delight, like a schoolboy."

"And where are the caged animals now? I note that all these cages are empty."

"Yes, sir. After Mr. Everard's death, Mrs. King ordered the beasts sent away to some place in Lambeth that dealt in such exotica." [14]

"She disposed of her husband's life passion?" I interjected.

"I suppose that she couldn't bear to be so reminded of him," said the butler, circumspectly.

"Indeed," murmured Holmes, noncommittally.

Finally, the butler led us down a lamp-lit, Persian-rugged corridor that extended from one wing of the house. We came to a plain door, which opened into a stone-lined passage, some one-hundred feet long. Near the end of the passage, a wooden cupboard lay against one wall. At the furthest end of this lay a heavy door with a sliding shutter in it. Beside it, an iron handle attached to a wheel and a drum projected from the wall. A line of stout bars some fifteen feet in length extended along the passage.

"If you draw that shutter, sir," said Jefferson, "you may look through."

Holmes did so, and I found that we were gazing into a large, empty, whitewashed room, with stone flags, and small, barred windows upon the farther wall. A golden patch of sunlight shone through these and illuminated the floor of this outlying-house.

"That is where the cat used to lay," said Jefferson, nodding towards the yellow pool of light. "Just like any other house-cat, cuddled up and basking in the warmth."

"Shall we go in?" asked Holmes.

The butler shot back the spring lock with a sharp metallic click and opened the door, allowing us into the room. I noted that a pungent, musty smell peculiar to the great *carnivora* still lingered. A horizontal grating about two or three feet from the ceiling covered one side of the room. Mr. Jefferson explained that if one turned the iron handle from the passage outside the door, it would slide the line of bars in the corridor along wheels through a slot in the wall. This would close in front of the horizontal grating, thereby creating an effective cage of about fifteen feet in length.

Here is a rough chart of the place that I sketched at the time:

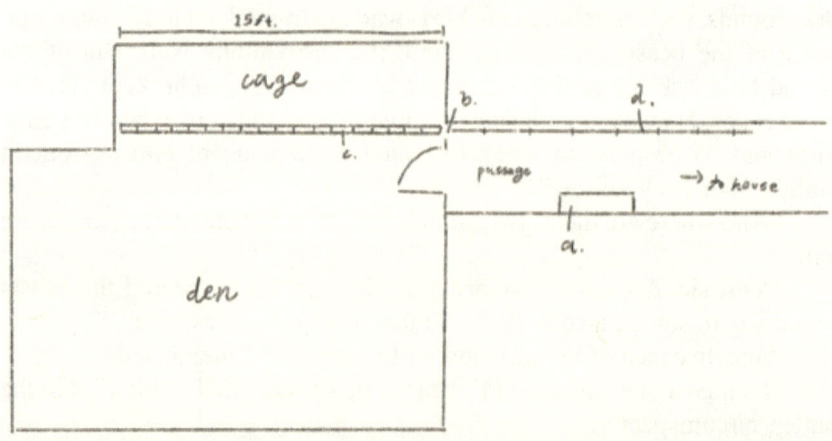

For further explanation, I note that the letter "*a*" represents the cupboard in the passage, "*b*" is the slot in the wall through which the line of bars slide, "*c*" is the line of bars fully extended into the den, and "*d*" is the track upon which the bars would slide when retracted into the corridor.

"Once the grating is fully extended into the room, it automatically locks into place," continued Jefferson. "It can only be opened again from the passage. That is how Mr. King and Mr. Baldwin, the groom, worked it. They gave the beast the run of the room for exercise, and then at night they put him in his cage, which used to be lined with straw. You could let him out by turning the handle from the passage, or you could coop him up in the same way."

"An ingenious system," said Holmes, approvingly. "One might tell that the cage was closed simply by noting that there was no grating visible in the passage, and this fact could be confirmed via the use of the viewing shutter. There is even a handy hook upon which to hang a stable lantern, to ensure that one does not miss the cat in the shadows."

"Just so, sir."

"And how long was Mr. Marshall King with you at Greylands before the night of the accident?"

"Six days, sir."

"And how did the cousins get on during this time?"

"Most cordially, sir. Every night after dinner, they would sit up late in the billiard room. Mr. Marshall shared some reminiscences of London life, which interested Mr. Everard so much that he vowed he would come up to Grosvenor Mansions and stay with his cousin. I heard him say that he was anxious to see the faster side of city life – Certainly, it would have seemed quite the change from the quiet downs of Suffolk or the jungles of the Brazils. For his part, Mr. Everard was an exceptional storyteller, and he told his cousin some desperate and reckless tales of his adventures in the Americas."

Holmes's eyebrows rose with interest. "I did not realize that Mr. Everard was such an adventurer."

"You wouldn't have thought so to look at him, sir," laughed the butler. "In truth, Mr. Everard was short and rather stout. He certainly didn't appear like one's conception of an Allan Quatermain." [15]

"Tell me about the last day – the day of the accident."

"Very well, sir. By then, Mrs. King's jealously had progressed to the point where she completely ignored Mr. Marshall's existence, as if her goal were to make his stay at Greylands as uncomfortable as she could. So offensive was her manner during the fateful day that it is a wonder that he didn't depart at once."

"But he could not," said Holmes.

"Sir?" asked Jefferson, his brow contracting in confusion.

"Mr. Marshall King hoped to borrow a sum of money from your master. He had rather severe pecuniary difficulties, and his ruin was imminent."

"Ah, yes, that makes sense now, sir – why Mr. Marshall would stick it out. Well, on the night of Mr. King's death, it was extremely late when the accident occurred. Mr. Everard had been receiving even more telegrams than usual during the day. He went off to his study after dinner, and only emerged when the rest of household had retired to bed. I heard him go round locking the doors, as was his custom every night, and finally he joined his cousin in the billiard room."

"What was Mr. Everard wearing when his body was found?"

The butler considered this. "His dressing-gown and his favourite pair of red Turkish slippers, the kind without any heels."

"A strange thing to wear to have a drink, even if just with family. Did you attend on them in the billiard room?"

"No, sir," said the butler, shaking his head. "Mr. Everard didn't mind making his own drinks, and he often dismissed me early."

"And was he drinking that night?"

Jefferson nodded. "We found a half-full glass of grog – his customary whisky-and-water – by his usual armchair. And the maid found the unsmoked end of his cigar in the grate."

Holmes appeared to find this of interest. "How long was the remaining cigar?"

"About two-and-a-half or three inches."

"Was Mr. Everard in the habit of not finishing his Havanas?"

"No, sir. He savoured them mightily. He said that they reminded him of his home in the Brazils."

"Very good," said Holmes, with a nod. "And how was the weather that night?"

"There was a fearsome storm, sir. The wind was howling and screaming round the house, and the latticed windows rattled and shook as if a horde of Vikings was trying to come in. Eventually, I managed to drift off, but the cries of my master awakened me."

"What time was this?"

"Sometime after four o'clock in the morning. I distinctly recall hearing the tinging of the chiming hall clock break through the deep roar of the gale. The wind was sweeping past with the rush of a great river."

"But you could still make out the cries of Mr. King?"

The butler's face drew into a grimace. "I have never heard such screams before, Mr. Holmes, and I hope never to hear such a thing again. It was the sound of death itself."

"What did you do next?"

"As soon as I could manage to shrug on my gown and slippers, I roused the groom, Mr. Baldwin, and some of the others, then we went looking for our master."

"And you found him here in the cat's room?"

"That is correct, sir. It was the first place we looked. I knew that only that terrible beast could have provoked such screams. I always thought that having such a savage creature about the place was a dreadful risk."

"Tell me the situation of the room when you arrived."

The man pondered this for a moment. "The door was closed, and there was no grating visible in the passage, so it seemed that the beast must be in its cage. But we checked the little window to be certain, and what we saw inside was like something out of a nightmare. Mr. Everard King was plainly dead – his tattered, blood-soaked figure lying just here." Jefferson pointed to a spot in the middle of the floor and shuddered. "The beast lay contentedly beside him, ripping hunks of flesh from his leg."

"And Mr. Marshall King?"

"We thought him dead too, at first, for his trousers were torn to ribbons and a great pool of blood lay all around him. After Baldwin stalled off the cat with hot irons, we were amazed to find him still alive. We carried him to the bedroom and called in Dr. Tuttle to minister to him."

"He was found next to his cousin?"

"No, sir. Only his coat was in the main part of the room. Mr. Marshall himself was in the beast's cage."

"What!" I cried. "He was in the cage?"

"That is correct, sir," said Jefferson, plainly.

"Most interesting," said Holmes. "The importance of his coat's location cannot be overstated. And what happened to the cat after this attack?"

"Well, we could hardly leave such a murderous creature alive. And we couldn't get in to retrieve the bodies. Mrs. King ordered it shot at once. Baldwin carried out the task through the loophole of the door."

Holmes nodded. "What transpired with its remains?"

"Mrs. King had the cat skinned and the rest of the body burned out in the park."

"Of course," said Holmes, with a wry smile. "It must have made a terrific rug. May we see it?"

"Indeed, sir, the rug was magnificent. However, I am afraid that Mrs. King had it packed in a trunk to take on her trip."

"Ah, yes," said Holmes, reasonably. "Now then, I shall take a look around."

The butler shook his head. "There isn't much to see, sir. Baldwin cleaned the place up. The floor was so covered in blood that it looked like an abattoir."

Holmes first stepped to the door, which I noted had no handle on the inner side. In the passage, he turned the winch-handle. With a creak and a whine, the grating rattled through the slot and into the former.

He paused halfway through this operation. "That moves quite easily," he noted.

He then went back over to the partial cage and pointed out to me to some obviously fresh scuffmarks upon the floor immediately outside it. He stepped into the smaller space and looked all about him. I have said that the cage had a top as well as a front, and this top was left in place when the front was wound out through the slot in the wall. It consisted of bars at an interval of a few inches, with stout wire netting between, and it rested upon a strong stanchion at each end. It seemed like a great barred canopy over the creature's former lair.

The space between this iron shelf, and the roof may have been only two to three feet, but it was here that Holmes turned his attention. Both Jefferson and I were rather surprised when Holmes suddenly sprang up, seized the iron edge of the top, and swung himself onto the canopy. He then writhed in, face downwards, to the far back of the space nearest the wall.

"Holmes!" I exclaimed. "Whatever are you doing?"

"Looking at the spot where Mr. Baldwin would haven't thought to clean."

"But why would he need to clean up there?" I asked.

For a minute, Holmes didn't answer me, and then he pushed himself back off this iron couch and dropped back to the floor. "Because, Watson, that is where this rag was situated."

He held out a small swath of black fabric, crusted with the distinctive rust of dried blood.

"What is it?" I asked.

"It is an exceptionally fine wool, such as is used by the tailors of Savile Row in the making of summer-weight evening wear for gentlemen. Unless I am much mistaken, I believe that it is a piece of Mr. Marshall King's dress trousers." He turned to the butler. "I suppose they were burnt after the attack?"

Jefferson nodded. "I am afraid so, sir. No amount of scrubbing could get out all the blood."

"Pity," said Holmes. "Still, we may take this as the most probable source of the fabric."

"But how did it get up there?" I asked.

"That is an excellent question, Watson, and one that I am most desirous of asking Mr. King when he awakens from his delirium."

"I don't understand," said I, with a shake of my head. "How did you think to look up there?"

He smiled. "Look here, Watson," said he, as he pointed to various scratching upon the bars on the inside of the cage. "What do you see?"

"Just the marks of the beast's claws, as might be expected from any bored cat."

"But note the rust of the iron. The degree of it provides an estimate of the age of the mark. The rustier, the longer ago it transpired. Do you agree?"

"I suppose so."

"Now then, with this postulate in hand, look here." He indicated the marks on the inside of the cage about waist high. "These are all quite old. And in a locale at which the cat would typically paw. But these ones," said he, motioning to scratches on the roof of the cage, "are both newer and far fewer in number. For what reason would the cat have to reach above itself and paw the top bars? I propose that it is only if an individual was situated in that spot. The spots of blood that you can just make out upon the bars confirm this. Now, come here, Watson." He led me outside the caged area. "Do you see the deep marks at the spot where I sprang onto the canopy? The cat also tried to jump up there, but found it a challenging perch upon which to find a grip."

"If Mr. Marshall King was lying atop the canopy, how did he get into the cage?"

"This is the problem, Watson. Can we re-construct the chain of events that transpired on that fatal night? To do so, I believe it would be an immense help to speak to a few more individuals." He turned to the butler. "Where is Mr. Baldwin now?"

The man shook his head. "I can hardly say, sir. After he shot the cat, Mrs. King dismissed him."

"Was Mr. Baldwin from around these parts?"

"No, sir. He came to Greylands with Mr. King. I believe that he is an American."

"And did he have any vices?"

"The usual," said the butler, with a shrug. "He liked a good tobacco, a fine brandy, and followed quite closely the runnings of the turf. He was also always chasing the girls in the village – rarely with any success."

"Very good, Jefferson. You have been of inestimable assistance."

Holmes led us out of the manor and was silent during the entire ride back to the station. I knew better than to interrupt him while he was lost in thought and refrained from questioning him until we were settled into our seats on the train. Meanwhile, I attempted to work things out for myself – though this effort proved to be in vain. Eventually, I decided to admit defeat.

"Do you have a theory," I finally asked, "as to what transpired in that chamber of death?

He pulled out his travelling pipe and took a moment to light it. After blowing a smoke ring into the air, he smiled. "The beginnings of one."

"I presume that you believe it was not a tragic misadventure."

"No, Watson, it was most certainly not an accident."

"Then surely Mrs. King must be responsible."

His eyebrows rose into the air. "Why do you say that?"

"She plainly hated Mr. Marshall King. Some would call her a creature of the tropics – with a nature to match. She is certainly a woman of great passion and jealousy. Unable to drive Mr. Marshall away, she decided to lure him into the cat's den, after which she opened the cage."

He nodded slowly. "That is possible. And her husband? Surely you don't think that she meant to kill him too?"

"Of course not. She loved him desperately. When he realized what his wife had done, Mr. Everard must have rushed in to try to save his cousin. The cat turned on him and he was unable to defend himself. But this heroic sacrifice gave Mr. Marshall sufficient time to crawl into the cage and pull the bars closed, so that he could be safe from further attacks of the cat."

Holmes smiled. "I think you are onto something there, Watson."

I was pleased by this praise for my detective skills. It was plain that I had picked up a thing or two during my years of studying Holmes's methods. "Then Mr. Marshall King is innocent! He is free and clear to inherit his uncle's estate."

"I believe so. Still, I wonder if we would benefit from a conversation with the groom. He might be able to confirm your theory. So, how do we go about tracking down Mr. Baldwin?"

I shook my head. "I hardly know where to start. It could be anywhere!"

"I think not. In fact, I suspect that we will find about a mile from Baker Street."

"You must be joking!" I cried.

"Not at all. Shall I explain my train of reasoning?"

"Please. I am most eager to hear it."

"Very well. First, Baldwin is hardly a typical country groom. Such an individual is most unlikely to possess the skills required to handle an exotic Brazilian cat. And he came with Mr. King from the Americas. He is likely hoping to return home, but the state of his pocketbook – drained by losses on the turf – would require him to first restore his capital. There are two probable places where someone like Mr. Baldwin might find employment. Beyond Mr. Everard King and the late Dr. Roylott, very few country gentlemen have great cats situated upon their estates. Therefore, we must look to more typical locales. The first are the circuses. Now, if

Mr. Baldwin has taken refuge in one of the wandering circuses, then we shall have a more challenging task ahead of us, for their caravans could be located at any small country village. Wombwell, Sanger, and Ronder may have all passed on to the proverbial big-top tent in the sky, but there are many others of their ilk wandering about the Home Counties – such as Vittoria's Menagerie. [16] Not all of them have an exhibit holding a lion or tiger, of course, given the obvious dangers involved, and if Baldwin were with one of them, an advertisement might eventually pin him down."

"But you said that you believe him to be in London?"

"Indeed. Most such circuses already have their own lion tamer. Unless one has recently been mauled or killed – an event that would most certainly have found its way into the papers – they would have little need for Mr. Baldwin's services. However, the Regent's Park Zoo might just find a use for him. [17] Furthermore, Jefferson noted that Baldwin expressed a strong interest – often rebuffed – in the affections of the village girls. Would he not naturally think that London offers more options in that arena, even if he need pay for such services?"

I shook my head in disapproval. "I suppose that is possible."

He smiled. "I expect that I am correct – you shall see. Did you not once write that all the loungers and idlers of the Empire irresistibly drain to that great cesspool? There is a reason that I practice my profession in our metropolis – it affords more possibilities for study of the criminal mind than any other locale on the globe."

Once we arrived back at Liverpool Street Station, Holmes engaged a hansom cab to take us around to Regent's Park. A few conversations with various zoological officials later, we found ourselves standing outside the lion cage in the presence of a bull-necked man with coarse features, but keen blue eyes.

"Yes, I am Jack Baldwin," said he, in response to Holmes's question. "Who wants to know?"

Holmes introduced us and the purpose for our visit. "You have a most unusual accent, Mr. Baldwin. I have made a habit of collecting various lilts and have only encountered one such as yours – in people hailing from the Floridas."

"That's right, Mr. Holmes," said the man, grudgingly. "I lived a great deal of my youth in Biscayne Bay, in the far south of Florida. Do you know it?"

"I do. In fact, Watson and I recently visited St. Augustine and Tallahassee." [18]

The trainer smiled. "Then you know Florida is rough place. That is where I learned to wrangle cats, for there is a panther that stalks Florida's swamplands." [19]

"And how did you come into the employ of Mr. Everard King?"

"I heard through the grapevine that a gentleman at Pernambuco was willing to pay top dollar for a person with my skills. I hopped aboard the first steamer heading that way and soon was employed caring for Tommy."

"Tommy?"

"That was what Mr. King called his Brazilian cat. Tommy was the jewel of Mr. King's collection," said he, sadly. "There is only one other specimen in Europe, now that Tommy and the Rotterdam cub are dead. [20] The people at the Zoo here were dying to have him, but Mr. King always refused to part with him. Tommy was more than a hobby to Mr. King – he was more like family."

"Tell me about this Brazilian cat. How did he differ from any other cat?"

"Well, some people call it a black puma, but really it isn't a puma at all. The proper term is American panther, or jaguar. That fellow was a magnificent beast, nearly eleven feet from tail to tip. [21] Four years ago, he was a little ball of black fluff, with two yellow eyes staring out of it. He was sold to Mr. King as a new-born cub up in the wild country at the headwaters of the Rio Negro. [22] I understand that they speared his mother to death after she had killed a dozen of the natives."

"They are ferocious, then?" I asked.

"The most absolutely treacherous and blood-thirsty creatures upon Earth, Doctor. You talk about a Brazilian cat to an up-country native and see him get the jumps. They prefer humans to game. When we got him, Tommy had never yet tasted living blood, but when he did, I knew that he would become a living terror. He wouldn't stand anyone but Mr. King in his den, who was like the cat's mother and father in one. Even when he was a baby, you would risk your hand if you thought to pat Tommy's glossy flank. Even I dared not go near him except when it came time for his feeding – he liked a rough joint of mutton, which I brought to him on a fine silver tray. Mr. King was peculiar like that. Imagine serving a beast a bloody mass on a silver platter!" he concluded, with a barking laugh.

"I understand that, after the accident, Mrs. King ordered the cat destroyed?" asked Holmes.

Mr. Baldwin's face fell. "A sad day, for I helped rear Tommy from a little cub. But the right thing to do, of course. After that, Tommy wasn't fit to keep in captivity any longer, and it would have been too great a risk to try to transport him back to the jungles. Even when he was little, it was no joke bringing him over from the centre of South America, and once he was full grown, it would have been nigh impossible. I carried out the grim task myself, I did." He paused and shook his head. "A tragic end to a noble creature."

"Mr. King took precautions to avert an accident, did he not?" asked Holmes.

"Oh, yes. If you have been up to Greylands, then you must have seen how the room was constructed – just to his specifications. And he took very few individuals in to see Tommy, warning each of them about taking liberties with the cat. In fact, on the day of his arrival, I saw Mr. Everard pull back his cousin's arm when Mr. Marshall tried to reach through the bars and pet him. I recall that Mr. Everard's face was quite serious, and he assured Mr. Marshall that Tommy wasn't safe."

"Then what do you believe happened on the night of Mr. King's death?"

Baldwin shrugged. "Tommy didn't much care for the Suffolk storms. A high wind excited him. Somehow the two cousins opened the door to the room when the bars were still retracted into the corridor."

"But the entire system was designed to prevent just such an accident, was it not?" asked Holmes. "One would know that the bars weren't in place because they would be visible outside the door."

"I can hardly say. Perhaps it was dark? And now that you mention it, Mr. Holmes, I don't recall seeing a lantern hanging on the peg when we went to investigate the source of the cries."

"So the two gentlemen went to look in on the cat in the middle of the night, during a storm, in the dark, and then opened the door without confirming that the beast was secured in its cage?"

"Maybe they were three sheets to the wind?" said Baldwin, with a shrug. "Men do foolish things when deep in their cups. What other explanation can there be?"

"What other explanation indeed?" said Holmes, plainly not expecting an answer to this final question.

We took our leave of Mr. Baldwin, and my friend looked over at me as we emerged from the zoo. "There is one last person with whom we should speak – Mrs. King."

"Then you agree that she is responsible?" said I, happily.

"Not at all, Watson. Your theory is absurd."

"What do you mean?" said I, somewhat dismayed by this brusque dismissal.

"Mr. Jefferson told us that Mrs. King was exceptionally rude to Mr. Marshall King. Unless the man is singularly obtuse, surely, he would have noticed such unusual behaviour. Marshall must have known that she disliked him. Do you agree?"

"Yes, that seems logical."

"And tell me, would you follow a woman whom you thought hated you down an unlit corridor during darkest part of the night – In the middle of a storm, no less! – to a place you knew to be the den of a living terror?"

"Well, when you put it like that, I suppose not. Still, surely there is another way that she could have lured him to the cat's lair."

He shook his head. "No, no, Watson. While such convoluted plans are always possible, you should look for the simplest explanation. You are ignoring the most obvious suspect of them all."

I searched my brain. "Not Jefferson!" I exclaimed.

"No, Watson," said Holmes, with a small sigh. "The butler did not do it. I speak of Mr. Everard King."

"But he died trying to save his cousin from the cat!"

"Did he? What, precisely, makes you think that? We have no evidence to that effect. Only the speculation of Mr. Jefferson. No, I think Mrs. King shall be a more reliable witness to the workings of her husband's mind."

"But she hasn't been seen since the day before Mr. Marshall returned to London."

"Yes, we must hope that her ship has not yet departed."

"Her ship?"

"Surely, Watson, it must be obvious that there is nothing keeping her in England. She would return to her people in the Brazils."

"But how are you to locate which ship she will take?"

"We must trust that the lady would wish for a direct route, which rules out the more frequent departures of the Guion Company or Cunard Line to New York. Nor would she have any reason to quietly slip aboard a ship at Gravesend, as our friend Mr. Small once intended, or one near Plymouth, as was being arranged by Mr. Barrymore for his troubled brother-in-law. No, Mrs. King would take the most obvious route, aboard the South American line operated by Lamport and Holt from Liverpool. You may recall, Watson, that Mr. Browner once sailed that line, but left it for a position on the Liverpool and London boats after meeting Mary Cushing. [23] It might be a waste of three hours each way, but if we hurry, I expect that we may catch the next train from Euston."

Fortunately, I had a book in my pocket, and I spent this voyage alternating between lines of Hafiz's poetry and the land of Nod. [24] Upon our arrival at Lime Street Station, Holmes inquired about impending departures to South America and discovered that the S.S. *Amadeo* was due to depart on the evening tide.

"We must be swift, Watson," said Holmes, glancing at his pocket watch, "if we wish to avoid taking an unexpected voyage across the Atlantic. We have less than two hours to speak to our final witness."

We raced to the Canada Half-Tide Dock, where the *Amadeo* was tied up. Holmes confirmed that Mrs. Paloma King was listed as a passenger aboard. With a small emollient applied to the man's palm, Holmes convinced a purser to allow us to climb the ramp and speak with her. The man agreed to carry Holmes's card to Mrs. King and, a few minutes later, we were knocking upon the door to her cabin.

I had expected to find the haggard, sallow-faced woman of her picture, her lines of worry magnified by the tragic passing of her husband and her head covered with a mourning veil. Instead, we were faced with a lady whose face wore a fresh expression, as if the years had melted away and her charms were blossoming under a warm sun. Her cabin was surely one of the largest and most well-apportioned of the ship's staterooms. Besides the furniture typical of such ocean liners, her berth had one object of décor that I thought was certainly unique: Her feet rested on an enormous rug made from the skin of a black cat. The ebony hairs were so sleek and so absorbent of the light shining in from the portholes that it seemed more diabolical than something of this world.

She followed our gaze. "Isn't he splendid?" said she, enthusiastically.

"Glorious!" agreed Holmes. After introducing us, he continued. "Do you know why we are here, Mrs. King?"

She shrugged. "I expect that it has something to do with the matter at Greylands."

"Indeed. I was retained to investigate how Mr. Marshall King acquired his life-threatening injuries. I understand that you developed a curious aversion to your husband's cousin, and your manners towards him were almost offensive."

"The fool!" said she, the vehemence plain in her voice. She shook her head. "I did my best to warn him! When my husband was not within earshot, I told him the best train back to London for him to catch. Still, I am glad to hear that he will survive. I wouldn't have wished Mr. Marshall's death on my conscience."

"So you admit that there was a method to your behaviour?"

"Of course! Mr. Marshall King has only himself to blame. Did I not do all I could for him? From the beginning, I tried to drive him from the house. By every means, short of betraying my husband, I tried to save Mr. Marshall from him. I knew that my husband had a reason for bringing his cousin to Suffolk. I knew that he would never let Mr. Marshall get away again. No one knew my husband as I knew him, who had suffered from him so often. I didn't dare tell Mr. Marshall all of this. My husband would have killed me. If you don't believe me, Mr. Holmes, I will permit the doctor here to inspect my back. I am certain that he will agree that only the lashings of whip would leave such scars."

Holmes shook his head gravely. "That will not be necessary, Madam. I have no doubts regarding the true nature of Mr. Everard King. I merely wished for you to confirm it."

"Then you know that I did my best for Mr. Marshall. As things have turned out," said she, with an ironical smile, "he has been the best friend that I have ever had, for he set me free, and I once fancied that nothing but death would do that. I am sorry if he was hurt that night, but I cannot reproach myself. I told him that he was a fool – and a fool he proved to be – but at least he was sufficiently clever to escape my husband's cruel trap."

"So you didn't love your husband?" I asked, trying to catch up to the twists in the conversation.

"Love?" said she, sharply. "The women of my family do not marry for love, Doctor. We are sold like chattel to the highest bidder. My cousin married a German sugar king, who was generous enough to move on to Paradise within the year, leaving her both rich and free. [25] But I was not so fortunate. My husband had sufficient wealth, of course, though it was never enough for him. And he was too young to die of natural causes any time soon. No, my sweet release has only come through the workings of his own madness."

"And now you return home?" asked Holmes.

She smiled sadly. "I have already put Greylands Court up for sale. There is nothing else tying me to this gloomy land."

"And what shall you do in the Brazils?"

"My people have been leaders in Pernambuco for generations, but I am no longer of any use to them. And I have seen enough of the sorrows of this world, Mr. Holmes. I intend to take the veil. [26] My only regret is that I doubt that they will permit me take old Tommy here with me into the convent. I shall have to treasure him while I have the time," she concluded, with a sardonic smile.

"Then I leave you to your mission, Mrs. King. Or should I say, Senorita Paloma? For surely you have no intention of keeping a name that is hated by you?"

A gleam entered her dark eyes. "Then you understand me well, Mr. Holmes. *Adios.*"

"A complex woman," said I as we settled into our seats for the return trip on the last train of the evening.

"I find that most of them are, Watson," Holmes replied. "Their hearts and minds are insoluble puzzles."

It was late when we finally returned to Baker Street. Holmes suggested that I bunk down in my old room rather than return to my empty house, and I gladly took him up on this offer. For her part, Mrs. Hudson seemed rather pleased to see me, and quickly arranged things so that I had a spot to rest my head – for Holmes had turned it into a sort of extension of his lumber room, and the place was already half-filled with old daily papers and tin boxes presumably containing various souvenirs of his concluded cases.

While Mrs. Hudson departed to carry out this task, Holmes proceeded to slice open the day's mail with the jack-knife from the mantel. One in particular caught his attention, and he turned to me after reading it.

"This is a note, Watson, from Mr. Summers relating that Sir Jasper has pronounced Mr. Marshall King well enough to do business. He proposes that we meet him at Grosvenor Mansions at nine o'clock tomorrow morning. Will you come?"

"Of course. I would hardly miss the conclusion of such a case."

The following morn found us outside Mr. Marshall King's Victoria Street mansion flat. The lawyer was waiting for us when we arrived. He promptly had the valet, Burrows, show us into his master's sick room.

Although Mr. Summers had previously told us that Mr. King was only thirty years of age, the events of the past weeks had caused him to appear far older. Any roundness that his face had once possessed had been burned away by the fires of delirium, his pale blue eyes were still rather dull, and his untrimmed brown hair and beard were already shot with new strands of grey.

"Hallo, Summers," said he, weakly, after the lawyer introduced us. "I am glad to see that you are the first to take advantage of the end of my convalescence. I must admit that Sir Jasper's recent permission for visitors wasn't very welcome to me, as I am anticipating a rather large inrush. Though, I fear, Mr. Holmes and Dr. Watson, that I don't recall either of you gentlemen being on my list of creditors."

"We are not," said Holmes. "We are here on other matters. I must say that I am most glad to see that your Lordship is so much better. Mr. Summers here has been waiting a long time to offer his congratulations."

"What do you mean, Mr. Holmes?" asked Mr. King, his brow contracted in a massive frown. "This is no time for joking."

"I mean what I say," my friend answered. "According to Mr. Summers, you have been Lord Southerton for the last six weeks, but Sir Jasper feared that it would retard your recovery if you were to learn it."

"I can hardly believe my ears," said the new Lord Southerton. And then he paused, as if doing figures in his head regarding the amount of time that had elapsed, and how it coincided with his injuries. "Then Lord Southerton must have died about the same time that I was hurt?"

"His death occurred upon that very day," said Holmes, looking hard at his Lordship. "Yes, a very curious coincidence," he continued, "Of course, you are aware that, after you, your cousin Everard King was the next heir to the estates. Now, if it had been you instead of him who had been torn to pieces by the Brazilian cat then, of course, he would now be Lord Southerton."

"No doubt," said the former Mr. Marshall King, weakly.

"Your discretion is quite appropriate, your Lordship," said Holmes. "You cannot see what there is to be gained by exposing such a family scandal, and I concur with your assessment. Fortunately, Mr. Summers here is bound by his oath of confidentiality to you, his client. Mrs. King has already sailed from these shores, and neither the butler, Mr. Jefferson, nor the groom, Mr. Baldwin, are very shrewd fellows. They haven't guessed the true state of the case. On the other hand, while I know all, I assure you that Watson and I shall remain silent." [27]

"I hardly know what you mean, Mr. Holmes," said the new Lord Southerton, cagily.

"I know that you went up to Suffolk with the hopes that you might induce him to advance you a sufficient enough sum to ward off the most pressing of your creditors."

"Guilty as charged. I freely admit that – from the moment that I met my cousin – it was on the tip of my tongue to inform him that a blank cheque would materially help towards the achievement of my happiness, but at least for the first few days I felt that it might be premature in the present state of our acquaintance."

Holmes smiled at this witticism. "On the night of the attack, you and your cousin stayed up late discussing the sorry state of your fiscal affairs. I presume that he gave you some assurance of his promptly forthcoming assistance. He then invited you to inspect Tommy once more, for the cat had been excited by the storm. After opening the door to the den, you both went inside. However, Mr. Everard soon invented some excuse for stepping back into the passage – probably by remarking that he needed to fetch the cat some food from the larder outside to put it in a better humour. He then shut and locked the door, trapping you in the den. Unless you are made of firmer stuff than most men, you must have been terrified when you heard the bars being retracted and grasped that your cousin was letting loose the beast."

"Hmm," murmured the new Lord Southerton.

"From the lacerations that Dr. Tuttle found on your fingers," continued Holmes, "I wager that your first thought was to try to pull the bars back into place. While your strength likely would have been buoyed by something akin to rage and horror, and your cousin was somewhat older than you, you were disadvantaged by the fact that you were wearing smooth bottomed evening shoes, which would have slid upon the slick flagstones. Eventually you realized that you couldn't possibly hold out against the force magnified by the cranking winch and gave up the hopeless struggle. Fortunately for you, the cat was unused to live prey, and had remained motionless throughout your efforts to maintain the barrier between you. You quickly appreciated that the barred windows were too narrow to afford a passage, and there was only the one door leading from the room. Your sole hope was to last through the night and trust that your cousin was alone in his villainy. With the break of dawn, perhaps you might be rescued, you reasoned.

"Therefore, casting your eyes about the chamber, you realized that there was one spot that might offer a small refuge – or at least a spot of less-immediate danger than standing in the middle of the open floor. You jumped onto the barred canopy – you should be most thankful, Lord Southerton, that your cousin overlooked this flaw in his nefarious design – and attempted to minimize the number of directions from which the beast could attack. Of course, the cat would have first attempted to get at you from below, and one of his claws dug a nasty furrow in your knee. I suppose that the cat would have then begun to pace about in the larger space of its den. At one point, it tried to leap into the crawl space that you occupied. It must have misjudged its jump, but such a jungle beast would have been more than ready for another attempt. I suspect that this is when you began to doubt the continuing safety of your current position.

"Then you had a stroke of something that I might be tempted to call genius. You grasped that the cat's cage could work both ways. If it could keep him in, it could also keep him out. If you could somehow transition from your current perch into the beast's cage and tug the bars into place, you might be safe. Of course, the difficulty lay in the window of time when you were making your move, for surely you would be horribly exposed. Therefore, you distracted your attacker for a moment by pulling off your dress-coat and throwing it over the cat's head. At the same moment, you dropped over the side and carried out your plan. This worked almost perfectly, if not for the fact that the cat extracted itself from your coat rather quicker than you hoped and managed to swipe off most of your calf with a stroke of its huge paw.

"I have no doubt that you subsequently succumbed to blessed oblivion from the pain of this wound, and would have eventually bled to death, if not for the fact that your cousin eventually returned to learn the results of his monstrous handiwork. When he looked through the door, he was likely amazed to find that you and his cat had somehow switched places. However, your insensible form – and the large pool of blood around it – were probably sufficient to convince him that you were dead. Foolishly, in his glee to confirm this fact, he opened the door and stepped inside, trusting that his bond with old Tommy would protect him.

"What Mr. Everard King then learned – to his eternal sorrow – was that his old prediction was finally proven correct. The taste of fresh blood had turned the cat into a fiend. And the frustrations of the night, when the cat failed to get more than a few licks of blood from the floor and a small hunk of your leg, were sufficient to put it into a mad hunger. It turned on its master and ripped him into shreds. Fortunately for the rest of the household, Mr. Baldwin got there before the cat had finished consuming its meal and went in search of new prey. He managed to slam the door closed, while planning to mount a rescue operation of your Lordship. And the rest is known to all."

"That is quite the tale, Mr. Holmes," said the former Mr. Marshall King, coolly.

"It is no story," said Holmes, with a shake of his head. "It is the only explanation that accounts for all of the facts."

"If you say so," said King, with an eloquent smile. "If such a thing were true – which I am not saying is the case – I wonder what might keep a man alive through such an ordeal? Perhaps the contemplation of a man's villainy and monstrous treachery, his unparalleled hypocrisy, his malignant hatred? Still, it is almost enough to make a man believe in the *karmic* wheel."[28]

"Upon occasion, perhaps the mills of the gods grind swiftly," agreed Holmes. [29] "I shall give you one final piece of advice, Lord Southerton: I recommend that you immediately sack your late uncle's former valet without references."

"Whatever for?" he exclaimed.

"When we returned to London last night, I made some inquiries as to the identity of the individual who was sending so many telegrams from Otwell House. That scoundrel was in the pay of your cousin, and he was keeping Mr. Everard King abreast every few hours of the state of his Lordship's failing health. That would have been about the time when you were down at Greylands. Is it not strange that your cousin should wish to be so well informed, since he knew that he wasn't the direct heir?"

"Very strange," agreed the new Lord Southerton. "And now, Summers, if you will bring me my bills and a new cheque-book, we shall begin to get things into order."

As we strode down through the back streets of Westminster, making our way in the direction of St. James's Park, I shook my head in wonderment at the thought of how the new Lord Southerton had survived the attack of that inhuman monster and said so aloud.

"As I think of it, Holmes, I see clearly how cunningly the thing had been arranged. Mr. Everard King had apparently gone to bed with the others. No doubt he had his witnesses to prove it – at least his unfortunate and thoroughly-cowed wife would so testify. Then, unbeknownst to the servants, he slipped downstairs, lured Mr. Marshall King into the beast's den, and abandoned his cousin to what he thought would be a most grisly end. His story for the police would be so simple. Everard had left his cousin to finish his cigar in the billiard room. Marshall had gone round on his own account – on some whim perhaps – to have a last look at the cat. Not being adequately familiar with the security precautions, Marshall had entered the room without observing that the cage was open, and the cat ravaged him. How could such a crime possibly be brought home to Everard? Suspicion, perhaps – but proof? Never!"

"I wouldn't say that, Watson," said Holmes, mildly. "Had Mr. Marshall King perished up at Greylands and his cousin inherited the vast estate of their uncle, I am fairly certain that the reports in the papers would have eventually caught my attention. The coincidence of the two deaths was really too much. If I were Mr. Everard King, I would have done away with my cousin a week or two earlier, when it would have appeared much more like a tragic accident, and less like a Jacobean stage-play. [30] No, in the end, it was badly managed on his part, and he paid the ultimate price for his overly theatrical taste for a dramatic ending."

"Well, no matter how poorly staged, it was still a rather narrow escape for Marshall King," said I. "He almost didn't survive his encounter with that living terror. What a horrible beast."

Holmes shook his head. "Not at all. Tommy – stripped from its natural jungle surroundings – was merely acting according to its nature. The true monster here was the man beneath whose cheerful face lurked the spirit of a mediaeval assassin. In fact, I feel rather bad for the poor cat."

NOTES

1. The Bombardment of Alexandria (11-13 July, 1882) was the precursor to a full-blown invasion of Egypt in support of the Khedive, Tewfik Pasha, whose reign was being threatened by the nationalist uprising of Ahmed 'Urabi.

2. Sir Arthur Conan Doyle, Watson's first literary editor, also came into possession of one of the Khedive's plates under similar circumstances, as recounted to the journalist Harry How in an 1892 interview entitled "A Day with Dr. Conan Doyle", published in *The Strand Magazine*.

3. Holmes is plainly referring to *The Sign of the Four,* published in February 1890.

4. Additional details regarding the details surrounding the death of Lord Southerton eventually were published in *The Strand Magazine* by Sir Arthur Conan Doyle in the form of a supposedly fictional short story entitled "The Story of the Brazilian Cat" (1898). The astute reader will note that many of the elements of that tale can also be found in the present adventure, suggesting that Sir Arthur got the whole story from Watson and chose to omit Holmes's involvement in the case. It is unclear why he didn't see fit to change the names of the various individuals involved in the matter that transpired at Greylands Court.

5. Mr. and Mrs. Jephro Rucastle, their children, and Miss Violet Hunter briefly occupied the Hampshire estate near Winchester known as the Copper Beeches. Woods that were part of Lord Southerton's preserves surrounded this estate ("The Adventure of the Copper Beeches").

6. The medieval Court of Chancery – responsible for determining the legal validity of wills and dispositions of estates – was dissolved in 1873, but these powers were absorbed by the newly-created Chancery Division of the High Court of Justice.

7. Lord Robert St. Simon also had rooms at Grosvenor Mansions on Victoria Street in Westminster ("The Adventure of the Noble Bachelor"). Hurlingham, a social and athletic club located in Fulham founded in 1869, would later be where Baron Adelbert Gruner likewise played polo ("The Adventure of the Illustrious Client").

8. A "*post-obit*" was a bond securing a loan of money against a future sum expected to be inherited upon the death of a relative, while an "unentailed" property was one which could be sold off by its possessor rather than being required to remain part of a familial succession.

9. The Debtor's Act of 1869 mainly abolished the notorious practice of debtor's prisons, though some defaulting individuals still were sentenced to prison during the era of Holmes's active practice.

10. On 15 July, 1889, Pedro II of Brazil (1825-1891) survived an assassination attempt by a young republican named Adriano do Valle. Four months later, a *coup d'état* overthrew his government, and he was sent into exile. This timing appears to coincide well with the date when Mr. Everard King departed Pernambuco (approximately one year prior to July 1890).

11. This editor has been unable to place a village named "Clipton-on-the-Marsh" in Suffolk, nor a manor by the name of Greylands Court. We may presume that Watson obscured the names to protect the reputation of those involved.

12. Holmes is plainly referring to both the terrible "swamp adder" (the precise species of this serpent has yet to be conclusively identified) employed by Dr Grimesby Roylott ("The Adventure of the Speckled Band") and the Gila monster set loose by Dr. Ulysses Goode, as recounted in the non-Canonical tale "The Adventure of the Monstrous Blood", collected in *The First of Criminals* (2016).

13. All of these are South America animals – including the so-called "badger", which may have been a capybara, the largest living rodent. Mr. Everard King shared this interest in the native animals of his adopted home with Dr. Grimesby Roylott, who had both a cheetah and a baboon from India wandering freely over his grounds at Stoke Moran ("The Adventure of the Speckled Band"). Such a passion may suggest the workings of a nefarious mind.

14. It is tempting to identify this as the establishment of Mr. Zebulon Eastland on Old Paradise Street, as depicted in the non-Canonical tale "The Adventure of the Monstrous Blood", collected in *The First of Criminals* (2016).

15. Allen Quatermain was the great adventurer in H. Rider Haggard's massively popular novel *King Solomon's Mines* (1885) and its various sequels.

16. George Wombwell (1778-1850), John Sanger (1816-1889), and Ronder (d. c.1889) were all famous circus showmen. Holmes once had a case – the details of which have yet to be divulged – involving Vittoria, the circus-belle.

17. Sir Stamford Raffles and Sir Humphry Davy established the Zoological Society of London in 1826, and the zoo was built on the northern edge of Regent's Park two years later. It opened to the public in 1847.

18. The details of this trip, which is dated to June 1890, can be found in the non-Canonical tale "The Oak-Leaf Sprig", which is a sequel of sorts to "The Five Orange Pips". It is included in the collection *Round the World* (2020).

19. Technically a cougar, the Florida panther can grow to over seven feet in length, but lacks the ability to roar.

20. Rotterdam has one of the oldest zoos on the Continent, having opened in 1857.

21. The jaguar is the only panther native to the Americas. Rare specimens have black coats, but none are recorded as being eleven feet long from tail to tip of the nose – six feet is more typical. Jaguars rarely attack humans unless cornered or wounded, suggesting that Mr. Everard King might have purposely trained Tommy to do so.

22. The Rio Negro is the largest left tributary of the Amazon and the largest black-water river in the world. Its highly descriptive name comes from the slow-moving water's distinctive "black tea" colour caused by tannins produced by decaying vegetation.

23. The adventures involving Jonathan Small (*The Sign of Four*), Selden (*The Hound of the Baskervilles*), and Jim Browner ("The Cardboard Box") all took place in 1888-1889, shortly before the events of this case.

24. Hafiz, more commonly spelled "Hafez", was the penname of a Persian lyric poet. Portions of his collection of poems called the "Divan" (or "Diwan") were first translated into English in 1875. We have evidence that – despite his general disdain for poetry – Holmes was familiar with the work, citing it when referring to Miss Mary Sutherland ("A Case of Identity"). The "Land of Nod" was a pun invented by Jonathan Swift in his Gulliver's Travels (1726) – derived from a place mentioned in *The Book of Genesis*, but instead intending to mean a mythical land of sleep.

25. It has been speculated that Mrs. King's cousin was none other than the notorious Isadora Klein, whose people "have been leaders in Pernambuco for generations" ("The Adventure of the Three Gables").

26. Pernambuco appears to be a popular place to disappear – Dr. Octavius Gaster is known to have fled to the Brazils in 1882. Pursuing that villain, Jack Daseby perished when *HMS Shark* was lost off Pernambuco in 1890 – as depicted in the non-Canonical tale "The Adventure of the Most Dangerous Man"*,* collected in *Their Dark Crisis* (2021).

27. By relating the details to his first literary editor, Watson appears to have broken this promise spoken by Holmes. Although he was only thirty years of age in 1890, it is possible that – by 1898 – Lord Southerton had passed on though some accident or sudden illness, such that any concerns regarding a family scandal were no longer a barrier to publication.

28. The Hindu-Buddhist principal of *karma* – wherein intent and actions of an individual (cause) influence the future of that individual (effect) – were popularized in the West by the works of The Theosophical Society, founded in 1875 by Madame Helena Blavatsky.

29. The Proverb *"The mills of God grind slowly"* – referring to the notion of slow but certain divine retribution – comes from the Roman philosopher Plutarch. A section of his treatise *Moralia* (c.100 CE) entitled *"De sera numinis vindicta"* (*On the Delay of Divine Vengeance*) runs: *"Thus, I do not see what use there is in those mills of the gods said to grind so late as to render punishment hard to be recognized, and to make wickedness fearless."*

30. Jacobean tragedies – such as John Webster's *The Duchess of Malfi* (1613) – were known for continuing and amplifying the trend of stage violence and horror set by some Elizabethan tragedies.

The Adventure of the Predatory Philanthropist
by I.A. Watson

The wizened down-at-heel fellow in the nicotine-stained basement apartment had brown teeth, a drooping eye, lank long greasy hair, and a hand that trembled from palsy. He faced Mr. Denham Sparrowhawk, clutching a tattered copy of a two-day old newspaper, as if that might help him to ward off the man to whom he owed the vast sum of five pounds and interest.

Mr. Sparrowhawk regarded the pathetic pauper with a sympathetic eye. "Your make-up is excellent," he said at last. "You have neglected no detail in your impersonation – *Mr. Sherlock Holmes.*"

The seedy tenant of the Brixton slum looked suspiciously at his visitor. Sparrowhawk laughed out loud.

"Oh, perfect! Just the right amount of baffled surprise. I should have liked to see you perform on the boards during your theatrical days. Come, Mr. Holmes! Your charade has failed." Sparrowhawk pointed to the closed closet door behind which I hid. "Perhaps you should let Dr. Watson out of his confinement. He will be able to overhear and bear witness to our conversation better without an inch of wood between us."

It was clear that our trap had misfired. Holmes drew himself to his full height and began to eschew the false hair, stuffed cheeks, and stained teeth-guard that altered his appearance entirely. I emerged from the adjacent walk-in closet where I had been hidden.

It is difficult not to look sheepish when one's cunning concealment is so thoroughly penetrated.

"Few men see through Holmes's disguises," I commented.

"You seem almost outraged at it," Sparrowhawk replied. "A man in the detective line of work must expect to be detected occasionally."

"And so I have been," my friend acknowledged. "Might I enquire what part of the scenario failed to capture your imagination?"

"I doubt that any note I give could improve such a performance," the financier responded. "It really was a treat to see your portrayal of Old Joe Kepple, former schoolteacher of much reduced circumstance, now forced to eke out his diminishing days on a meagre pension insufficient for his survival. The character, his background, the hovel in which he is placed – Excellent! Quite excellent!"

"Evidently not excellent enough," Holmes admitted. I know that he had hoped for better from his trap for Denham Sparrowhawk.

"That's so." The financier looked about the sparse grim single-roomed dwelling where the supposed Joseph Kepple was meant to reside. "Do you think that those chairs might survive us sitting on them? Perhaps we should test them and meet at table to talk about why you fabricated this elaborate charade?"

I took Holmes's lead and we all carefully placed our weight on the rickety furniture, occupying the only three seats in the flat.

"I don't suppose Kepple keeps a decent brandy about?" Sparrowhawk breezed. "Not even a bottle of rotgut since he signed the Salvationist's Pledge? Ah well, we shall have to have our chat without the lubrication of spirits to ease the awkwardness, I suppose."

Holmes was now mostly himself again. The wig, teeth, and faked nose lay on the dirty table before him. "There are certain questions about you and your business that I have been retained to answer, Mr. Sparrowhawk," he admitted.

"Retained by one or more of the outraged family of one or more of my clients, I suppose."

Holmes did not reveal who had engaged him, but the financier's guess was near to accurate. "I fancy that I could summarise the main part of your business."

Sparrowhawk leaned back on his stick-chair causing it to creak alarmingly. "Likewise," he responded. "Which of us shall go first?"

"You are very confident for a criminal," I commented.

"A criminal must commit a crime, Dr. Watson. Which law do you believe that I have broken? You should be careful making such statements. Slander is also against the law."

I was about to respond hotly when Holmes intervened. "Since you seem to have penetrated my ruse, you might as well continue your streak by outlining what you believe has brought us to this."

"The better to offer you material for your analysis and conclusions? Very well, Mr. Holmes. Let us play the game."

Sparrowhawk laid his cultured hands upon the table, first palm up and then down, allowing Holmes a good look at them, cuffs and all. Then he closed them into relaxed fists as he spoke.

"I am a professional philanthropist," the financier began. "When some wealthy individual wishes to salve his conscience, to do good for his soul's sake, to increase the benefit of mankind, I am he to whom such persons apply for advice how best to disburse their riches.

"After all, the grant of charity isn't that simple. Who is a genuine case, and who seeks to defraud a generous patron? Which support might change a life, and what sums will simply enable destructive habits to become even worse?

"That is my special role. I advise those who wish to alleviate the poor about which paupers are worthy of relief. I identify men and women whose reduced circumstances are no fault of their own, or else are due to some tragedy or failure that makes them sympathetic of pity. My clients then disburse a generous sum of money to support these cases.

"Of course, this doesn't always suit those relations of my clients who had looked to inherit. If a rich uncle gives away his fortune to a stranger rather than to his expectant nieces and nephews, if a dead man's will leaves a family estate to the deserving poor rather than a complacent and debauched grandson, then there will *always* be objections. And legal challenges, of course, but as you must be aware, the Last Wills and Testaments that I facilitate are all quite proper and ironclad.

"I imagine, therefore, Mr. Holmes, that some outraged and disinherited individual, disappointed at being excluded from the resource they anticipated was their due, has resorted to you to demonstrate some wrongdoing that would allow them to recover the wealth that they have failed to receive.

"You, being by all accounts a logician and observer of significant capacity, might at once suspect a clever fraud. Suppose that I recruit needy individuals, groom them to be appropriate recipients of my clients' charity, and extract from them some percentage of the beneficence they receive? Suppose it is I who have enmeshed these paupers in debt, and am therefore well-rewarded from the disbursements they are given? In convincing those who wish to bestow their wealth to place it on specific individuals, I might line my own pockets with a proportion of every bequest. That would be the basis for undertaking your fantastic ruse.

"Clearly mine is no ordinary deceit. You therefore determined an extraordinary snare to overcome it. You created for yourself the persona of Old Joe Kepple, a sad figure who is exactly the kind of fellow that I might recruit for my schemes. In fact, there may actually be a Joseph Kepple whose background and actual existence offer verisimilitude, and who has simply been sent off to some spa resort to recuperate while Sherlock Holmes takes the stage.

"The idea was that I should approach Kepple, incorporate him in my schemes, and make my offer to defraud some knight of the realm or leader of industry. The whole plot would be revealed out loud with Dr. Watson concealed behind a door to offer corroborating testimony. If the witness of the great Sherlock Holmes and his estimable companion proved insufficient against the word of a prominent and respectable financier, then you would at least have achieved a better understanding of the means by which I perpetrated my deeds. More likely, my confession would have closed your case.

Sparrowhawk smiled, pleased at his cleverness. "Is that close to the chain that led us here, sir?" he enquired.

"It is a reasonable summary," Holmes allowed. "I might add, though, that there is additionally the matter of your methodology in convincing your 'clients' to consider such philanthropic donations. That detail is of interest to me. Of course, since your clients are all deceased at the time your involvement becomes known, it isn't possible to interview them."

"One must recognise the limits of the deductive process," the financier sympathised.

"You make yourself sound like an honest broker," I confessed to Sparrowhawk, "There are many reasons to suspect you are anything but."

He looked at me sympathetically. "Ah, Doctor. I see why Mr. Holmes keeps you around. You are a wonderful diversion. While I address your splenetic outrage, your friend is at liberty to read my expressions and to assess my voice, to discern myriad clues – they are termed *clues*, are they not, in the deduction trade? I trust that you are gathering plenty of material, Mr. Holmes?"

"I am quite content with my harvest, Mr. Sparrowhawk," Holmes assured the garrulous fellow.

"What a delight to engage your intellect! I am an avid follower of your work. I deem being the object of one of your investigations to be a highlight of my life. Of course, you may discover that you have been wasting your time, but I suppose that assembling and performing this Kepple charade may have been its own reward for a creative and artistic temperament."

"You are preying upon vulnerable men and women who near the ends of their lives and exploiting the destitute to further your own ends!" I accused the financier.

"Then prove it," Denham Sparrowhawk challenged us. "I say that I am a philanthropist – a consulting philanthropist if you will. My endeavours should be lauded, not reviled. My efforts are legal and by the book."

"And those who are dispossessed by such efforts, sir?"

"It is a truth of law that one party or other is almost always dissatisfied by the outcome of due process, Doctor." Sparrowhawk rose from table and looked about him. "As for you, Mr. Holmes: Unless you are prepared to bear false witness, there is nothing in your trap here that profits you. Indeed, unless you will perjure yourself, you would have to admit in court to fabricating a bizarre scenario to attempt to enmesh me in your elaborate and fantastical theories. It is you who have perpetrated a fraud. But I am,

102

as is evidenced, a charitable man, and shall say no more about it – unless you decide to press matters further. Shall we shake hands and part amicably?"

"We may shake hands and part," Holmes agreed. "It is likely that we shall meet again."

"Until such time then, I shall bid you good day." Sparrowhawk accepted the proffered palm and shook it firmly like an honest man.

Sparrowhawk compounded his arrogance by sending around to Baker Street a complimentary box of Fortnum's thin mints with his calling card and a brief note of thanks for an amusing afternoon.

"The bounder is mocking us!" I objected as I nibbled on the confectionary. "He believes himself able to withstand an investigation by Sherlock Holmes!"

"He does," my friend agreed. "However, if you could refrain from eating all the evidence, I should like to examine the business card."

I passed the deckle-edged cardboard rectangle to Holmes for him to consider. "There is Sparrowhawk's office address upon it," I pointed out. "We already knew that."

"We also know that Declan Sparrowhawk is the sort that enjoys proving himself superior to those whom he encounters. He is a gloater, Watson, and that is always helpful. He likes to feel superior. Our encounter yesterday helped to establish that."

"Did you expect him to see through your disguise? Was it part of your plan?"

"I would like to confirm your belief of my omniscience, Doctor, but I have cautioned you before that my foresight has practical limits. In truth, I underestimated my opponent and was dealt a resounding rebuke for it. I shall eat my mints with humility. However, our encounter with Sparrowhawk offered much useful material to further our discoveries."

"And the calling card?"

Holmes reversed the object, pointing to the minute font on the back that indicated the printer's address. "One shall visit this establishment later to determine what other stationary the effervescent Mr. Sparrowhawk has ordered."

I regarded the piles of newspapers that threatened to engulf the whole of our dining table. Holmes often copes with chagrin by resorting to his clipping scissors. Now there were perhaps four or five score of neatly cut rectangles spiked upon different piles. The discarded broadsheets occupied the upright chairs. "I take it that you have discovered something of use from your reading?"

"Oh, my background research was completed before I attempted the guise of Old Kepple. It comprises that wad of cuttings stuffed into the jam-jars yonder. Those in the blackcurrant pot are all notices of bequests made, legal announcements from executors seeking some individual to whom a sum has been left. Sparrowhawk uses those advertisements to guide him to people who have recently been endowed with legacies and who might therefore need to make wills and testaments of their own. The collection in the strawberry jar is a sample of those charitable institutions who advertise offering donations for the poor, which helps our quarry towards those requiring philanthropy against whom he will set his traps. The cuttings of those loan-men who will venture unsecured sums to people in poverty are, perhaps fittingly, rolled up in the honey jar."

"There must be hundreds of such notices," I objected. "How can you be confident that the ones you have collected are the correct cuttings?"

Holmes snorted amusement. "An inspection of Mr. Sparrowhawk's dust-bin rendered up his discarded newspapers with their absent rectangles where notices have been extracted. Tracking down copies of the same publications and snipping out the same advertisements was hardly a difficulty."

"Thus you can trace how Sparrowhawk discovers those who he might force to change their will, and those he might suborn to receive charity, only to pass it on to him."

"You might say so. These additional cuttings that I am presently assembling aren't from the notices columns, save for those in the Acknowledgements section, thanking well-wishers for flowers and sympathy after accidents and bereavements, but are rather from the news pages, covering the events that required such melancholy responses."

"You believe that Sparrowhawk has harmed people?"

"I am quite certain of it. For all his civilised veneer, Denham Sparrowhawk is as ruthless a predator as his namesake, as vicious as any foe we have encountered. It is how he is able to convince his wealthy 'clients' to make their wills out to total strangers. He threatens the well-being of the testator or testatrix's loved ones, warning of accidents and misfortunes. There is often a convincing event – a fire, a burglary, a supposed accident that leaves a child or wife in hospital. On two occasions, I have found reports of 'carriage injuries' that have left people dead, a woman and a boy of nine. It is likely that such coercion is followed with the assurance that even worse can follow to other family members."

"The fellow has his rich men in a grip of terror for those they care about," I realised. "Why have none gone to the constabulary?"

"As you said, Watson: For *fear*. But one such victim did come to me instead, and hence we have our case."

"I suppose that having used such cruel intimidation upon the wealthy, Sparrowhawk would have no scruples in using force to bend his impoverished pawns to his will. They would sign over whatever bequest they receive, simply to escape the debt in which he has them ensnared."

Holmes nodded. It was to gain evidence of such behaviour that he had attempted his ploy in the guise of Joseph Kepple. With that gambit thwarted, my detective friend would need another method of bringing his adversary to justice.

Holmes heaved his pile of newspapers aside to reveal a more modest stack of telegrams and postal correspondence. "I have also been looking into our predatory philanthropist's past," he informed me. "I am interested to discover that Mr. Sparrowhawk didn't exist until seven years ago – at least he had no address, no bank, no tax record. Nor does he seem to have a birth certificate, school report, or any other paper evidence of his identity until that time."

"Then surely we can expose him as a fraud!" I expected.

"It isn't a crime for a man to change his name or leave his past behind. Sparrowhawk is now meeting all the legal requirements of a respectable citizen, and has an Englishman's right to privacy in his financial and personal affairs within the law. On the other hand, his former anonymity does suggest a history which he would prefer not come to light. My investigations continue."

"What can we do, though?" I fretted. "This fellow plays a long and wicked game. He spins his webs over years, capturing his victims by threats and violence, profiting from the misery of the poor he uses as tools. And yet there is no fact or proof than can be brought against him."

Holmes reached into his drawer and produced a pocket-book, the sort issued by banks, pre-printed for notes of hand – exchequer slips where one need only write in the sum to cash and append one's mark. "My client is of a pragmatic bent," he revealed to me. "Hence, I am in a position to fight back against Mr. Sparrowhawk."

"You intend to purchase something?"

"These cheques draw upon the case account that our client has established. He sees that it is better to spend some portion of his wealth to thwart our enemy than to lose all of it to brutal coercion."

Holmes now filled out no less than sixteen cheques, completing them with a flourish.

I looked over the bank drafts, not recognising the names of the creditors.

Holmes supplied the answer. "They are poor folks whose debts are insurmountable, who owe sums which seem impossibly large to them, that place them in Mr. Sparrowhawk's power. I am paying off all their accounts."

"They will all go free? You will give Sparrowhawk his money?"

"I shall rob him of his groomed recipients of wills and testaments which he has already caused to be written. If these folk are no longer indentured to a moneylender, how can he force them to pass the greater part of their legacies to him?"

"His former coercions will not profit him!"

"Indeed. Even if these are greedy, grasping folk, why should they now disburse a vast percentage of their new gains to a dubious third party? Yes, Sparrowhawk might threaten force. Freshly-rich individuals have new resources with which to simply up and vanish."

"In short, terminating these debts will inconvenience Sparrowhawk immensely," I summarized, "and provoke him to action."

Holmes reached for his pipe and Persian slipper pouch. "I trust that it shall, Watson," he replied, also allowing himself a thin mint.

"Your friend has displeased me," Denham Sparrowhawk told me in a low angry voice.

I was surprised by his appearance. A fellow doesn't expect to see an errant villain in one's own medical consulting room, come in from the waiting room as the next patient in a queue. I confess that the incongruity of it caused my heart to quicken with a splash of fear.

"I am displeased," Sparrowhawk repeated. "I would speak about it to Holmes himself, but he has too many loiterers about your Baker Street residence to make it easy to go there unnoticed. I thought it might be better to refer the matter to you and allow you to convey my message."

The fellow spoke lightly, but there was a deadly wrath in his eyes.

"This is a medical practice, sir," I cautioned the fellow. "There are deserving people in need of my attention. Kindly be brief so that I can get on with my surgery."

"Stay in your chair, Doctor Watson. If you rise from it, I promise I shall beat you down. Don't think I can't. For that matter, my colleagues in your waiting room might decide to take a hand also, where there are any number of sick and elderly patients awaiting your attentions. A ruckus would become very ungentlemanly."

"I might have expected a bully to also be a coward," I sneered.

"Spare me your public school judgements, Doctor. I might enjoy sparring verbally with Sherlock Holmes, to be able to say that I once did it, and overcame him. I have no interest whatsoever in you, except as a convenient messenger. Be glad that you are presently unimportant enough not to rate my attention."

"I would be pleased to occupy your full attention in any fight you hadn't rigged, in any place that isn't filled with sick and vulnerable people – Sirrah."

Sparrowhawk snorted disdainfully. "That isn't the way. I don't fight 'fair', Doctor. I fight to win. I do what is necessary, and no matter the cost."

"You said you had some message. Deliver it."

The financier smiled thinly. "Mr. Sherlock Holmes's life is very fragile. Most people's existences are. They depend for their contentment upon certain things: A person, a home, a position, possessions – treasured things which define one. Things that would destroy them to lose. My entire business is based upon it."

"Upon extortion by threats? A thug may prosper for a time, but not forever. Especially when he encounters Sherlock Holmes."

"What things do you think comprise the elements of Sherlock Holmes's fragile life? You, most certainly, Doctor Watson. He would be devastated if aught became of you. And you have family, of course, Doctor, whom you would struggle to protect.

Sparrowhawk went on. "Holmes has lodgings at Baker Street, where he keeps all his precious files and case-notes, his reference books and resource materials. The loss of that home and its contents would certainly injure the great detective, as would the deaths of your landlady and junior staff."

I half-rose from my chair, despite Sparrowhawk's former caution, but he gestured me back. "For that matter, there are all those curious people who keep watch upon Baker Street and who poke into places where they shouldn't take an interest. Many of those are very young – urchins of the street who rely upon their youth and anonymity for survival. Once their presence is exposed, they are perhaps the least protected of all. I imagine that your logical, clinical friend might be touched all the same if misfortunes occurred to his beggar boys and girls."

"That's your threat, is it?" I snarled back. "Do you think no other criminal has tried to curtail Holmes's investigations by menaces and coercion? The gallows were full of such men."

"Your friend isn't immortal," the blackguard promised. "Be glad of this final warning. If Holmes continues to interfere in my work, he shall suffer loss – grievous loss. Or perhaps you shall."

He turned and departed my consulting room, calling to my patients, "Next!"

* * * * *

107

"I am sorry for your unpleasant afternoon," Holmes told me. "In compensation, I spent the time that you were distracting Sparrowhawk well."

"You discovered the other business cards and letterheads that Sparrowhawk commissioned from his printer?" I surmised. "His aliases and holding companies?"

"Indeed. His brio in sending me a little gift has proven to be costly to him. From such links, I have identified the solicitors' firm whom he prefers to remake wills on his behalf. I paid them a call at much the same time as you were encountering your unpleasant patient."

"Solicitors aren't known for their forthcoming behaviour regarding their clients' business."

"But neither are they happy to be referred to the Law Society or to Scotland Yard for their participation – however unwittingly – in crimes up to and including murder. Goldall and Prace is a seedy little practice in Soho, but they quickly saw the benefit in offering some co-operation in exchange for my forbearance. I suspect that they have other business dealings that they might prefer didn't come under the lens of my scrutiny."

"They were willing to sacrifice Sparrowhawk if it kept their other clients away from the dock."

"Indeed. I now have a comprehensive list of some thirty-three men and women who have been frightened into remaking their wills. I have sent off letters to each of them explaining what I have discovered and urging them to rescind their former documents in favour of their genuine dispositions."

"That will surely drive Sparrowhawk to a rage, and to fresh violence."

"So it might, Watson. For that reason, we must act tonight to end this sordid case. Sparrowhawk's villainy offers only limited intellectual diversion, but he must be curtailed in the public interest before he can do further harm – and before he bores me too greatly."

Sparrowhawk's registered business address was around Temple and Bar. Holmes and I were presently in a two-wheeler heading along towards Limehouse. "Might I venture to enquire where we are going now?"

"As you might imagine, Watson, Mister Sparrowhawk prefers to operate his actual proceedings from a more anonymous location than his official site."

"The letterheads," I supposed.

"The invoice paperwork held by Goldall and Prace, along with some observations made by those street urchins whom Sparrowhawk chose to threaten. Those who might spy out such spies shouldn't presume they have found them all. My Irregulars have a home-ground advantage about Baker Street."

We trotted into the seamy docklands east of The Tower, where the streets were narrower and the gas lamps were fewer. The first wisps of a night river-mist drifted over the cobbles.

I felt for my service revolver beneath my coat. I was following Holmes into an unknown stronghold of a proven violent menace.

Holmes saw my gesture and nodded approvingly. We were both armed, with stout canes in addition to our police and army-model firearms. Holmes's cane concealed a small sword blade.

We paid off our cabbie at some grimy street corner that had no name plate. Behind us wound the labyrinth of arches and courtyards that comprised the warren of Limehouse, that melting pot of foreigners and paupers that has perhaps replaced St. Giles and Old Mint as the rookery of London. [1]

I didn't like the look of the down-at-heel huddle of layabouts who were clustered together under one gateway. I was surprised when Holmes approached them and we were greeted and recognised, albeit in a muted whisper. "Evening, Mister 'Olmes, Doctor Watson!"

I looked again at the flat-capped figure who had saluted me. I added ten years and twelve inches and came to a conclusion. "Butcher? Nobby Butcher?" I hadn't seen the fellow since he had been a grazed-kneed lad running with Wiggins and the other grubby urchins in my first days at Baker Street.

Butcher grinned. "Tole you 'e'd be surprised," he remarked to his fellow, whom I now remembered as being a spot-faced youngster called Narrow, but who had also bulked out in manhood.

Narrow had evidently also acquired some nautical experience, judging by his tattoos, of which Holmes could doubtless specify the provenance. "Good evening, Doctor Watson," he welcomed me. "I'll never forget 'ow you 'elped out wi' me old mam's last months. I 'opes I finds you well?"

Nor were these two only known to Holmes and me. The whole knot of ruffians proved to be alumni of that ever-changing band of street-brothers upon whom my friend often relied for his best intelligence.

"Mr. 'Olmes said as some lairy cove is threatening to go after the little-uns," Butcher explained to me. "We 'as come to explain to the fellow as 'ow that is a very poor idea."

These chaps were now all brawny or strappy fellows in their early twenties, experienced in the world and at surviving in it, and they each seemed equipped with some cudgel or baton with which to protect themselves and their younger replacements.

"Mr. Sparrowhawk has made a miscalculation," Holmes explained to me. "He assumes that I am a policeman, subject to judge's rules and the process of the courts. Whereas I am actually a private individual, entitled to take my own actions within the confines of our nation's regulations."

I looked at the mob of rogues – our rogues, but still rogues – who lounged under the archway ready for trouble. "Within the law?"

"Of course, Watson. As always, if required to give statements to the police or in the witness stand, our testimony will be the truth. Come and see."

Sparrowhawk owned an entire building, a four-storey brick-built lading house that backed onto the Thames, its rear supported by groynes piled into the riverbed. The whole edifice was run down, lower windows boarded and upper ones filthy. A scruffy peeling sign of three hanging brass balls signified a pawnbroker. The only light came from the shop windows on the ground floor, signalling that even at this late hour the usurer's emporium was open for business.

There was a burly fellow positioned outside the door. Holmes and I approached him without our escort. Holmes tipped his hat to the man. "Good evening," my friend bade the sentry. "I am come to do business."

The guard was confused. Holmes and I didn't resemble the regular shabby clientele of this sad place. As he tried to decide what to do, Butcher and his fellows emerged from the shadows and surrounded him.

"No point making a fuss, Squire," the ex-Irregular murmured into the guard's ear. "Stand over there and no 'arm done, eh? Or make a noise and it *will* be 'arm done. You decide."

The sentinel determined the better course of valour and was escorted away. Holmes and I entered the establishment unmolested.

The first detail that struck me was the odour. The moneylender's shop was foul with stale sweat, sour alcohol, wet rot, and the stench of desperation. Some part of the room was sectioned off with packing shelves, the better to hold items left in pawn, and doubtless contributing to the overall bouquet of the establishment.

By night the interior was dim, illuminated by a mere pair of lanterns near the dingy windows and another at the counter. A tired-looking junior clerk sat behind the desk, labouring amidst a pile of legers. Another brute like the one outside, similar enough to be his brother, lounged by an interior door to a shadowed stairwell.

"Good evening," Holmes called out again. "I am here to make a payment."

The clerk regarded us suspiciously. "A payment?" he parroted, surprised.

"In the name of Kepple," Holmes clarified. "It was under that pseudonym that I contracted the obligation. Mr. Kepple presently owes the sum of five pounds, nine-shillings-and-ninepence, including compound interest at the barbarous rate of sixty-five percent." He held up five shillings. "Here is some payment on account."

The sight of the crown arrested the clerk's attention and stayed the response of the shop guard, who by now should really have been wondering where his fellow outside had gone.

"The name of Kepple," Holmes repeated. "You will find it under '*K*'."

"Who are you?" the clerk recovered somewhat.

"I am a man who requires a receipt for five shillings, sir. Upon being given written acknowledgement of the partial discharge of an incurred debt, I shall move on to other enquiries. I am already aware, of course, of the details of your life and employment. You were born and yet live in Rotherhithe, residing with a sick father for whom you care. You have recently suffered from the shortages that poverty inflicts, probably so as to afford the medication that your father needs. You have taken work that you find distasteful in order to manage your growing burden of debt."

"I'm not – "

Holmes tapped the paperwork on the clerk's desk. "You have even taken to watering the ink in your pot, since an unfeeling employer doesn't provide such material. So much and more is obvious at a first glance, but since you already know it and you aren't of any particular interest to my enquiry, we may take my deductions as read."

I tried to observe the clerk by Holmes's methods, but the frayed cuffs, mud-spotted boots, and ill-trimmed fingernails meant nothing to me. Sometimes I simply had to allow my colleague's acumen.

I could tell, however, when the security man became alarmed. Just as he summoned more fellows from upstairs, the shop door opened again.

Nobby Butcher entered the premises, hand raised in the air, proffering a shilling. "I 'as come to make a payment, I 'ave," he announced loudly to all. "I am 'ere to 'ave this on account of Mr. Joe Kepple!"

A second and third large ruffian emerged from the building's interior to support their comrade. "What's all this then?" one of them demanded, a heavy-set bushy-bearded brute who peppered even that short sentence with profanities.

"It's quite simple," Sherlock Holmes instructed him. "My companion and I are here to render due payment to Mr. Sparrowhawk. I believe this chap behind us in the queue has announced a similar intention." He glanced at me. "All quite legal."

The door rattled again as Alfie Narrow made an entrance. "Got a bob to pay 'is nibs for Sparrow'awk," he called out on arrival. He held up a clenched fist with Holmes's shilling pressed under his thumb. "See?"

"Get out!" Bushy-beard demanded. "I don't know what your game is, but – "

As he advanced on Holmes, Nobby Butcher got in his way. "Game? Don't know what you're on about, Mister. I'm 'ere to 'elp out me old mate Kepple with a donation to 'is tally."

Narrow also intervened. "Aye, me 'an all."

Another of the old Irregulars came in, proffering a pair of sixpences, announcing his intention to credit them to Old Kepple's account.

The growing numbers of supposed customers alarmed Bushy-beard. "Now look 'ere," he warned. "If you don't get out, you won't like what 'appens next."

"And what would that be?" Holmes enquired as a fourth and fifth well-wisher joined the rest in proffering small coins on behalf of the fictional debtor.

"You can't just come in here like this!" the clerk protested. "This is a place of business."

"We're here to do business," I pointed out, getting into the spirit of the thing and fishing out a thrupenny bit. "Either get on with it, or call the manager."

"An excellent point, Watson," Holmes chimed in. "I am a very dissatisfied customer, and that large fellow's language leaves much to be desired. I insist upon seeing the owner."

Three more ex-Irregulars clustered through the door, completing the roster that Holmes had assembled, too excited to come in one by one in case they missed a fight. They each held out their sixpences like talismans, except for the one who had wedged it between his knuckles like a boxing cheat.

Bushy-beard retreated to the stairway, calling for more aid.

"What did you just call me?" Butcher asked him in unfriendly tones, advancing on the doorway.

Holmes addressed the clerk. "As you can see, your customers are becoming unhappy. Before anything unpleasant occurs, I shall require you to note down my contribution to my indenture. *Now*, if you please."

"Best do as he says," I advised the chap. "Holmes believes that you're just trying to earn a crust and support your father, eh? Don't blame you, even if it means working for a worm like Sparrowhawk. Best you just do your job and give us a receipt. There's a good lad."

The clerk tried to ignore the growing tempers at the interior door, and the conflict that might erupt into violence at any moment. He dipped his ailing quill into his watered ink and opened a ledger to make the proper annotations.

"A moment," Holmes said, after the payment was recorded. "I wish to check that you have spelled my name correctly." He swooped up the heavy financial tome and inspected its contents.

"That is . . . those are private," the clerk attempted.

Holmes held up a hand to deter him from interrupting. He flicked through the account book with his usual rapidity. "Yes, I see how the trick is done now," he commented. "Nothing remarkable. Prosaic villainy, and disappointing."

I was watching Holmes make his way through Sparrowhawk's financial records, so I didn't observe the moment when Nobby Butcher head-butted the thug with the bushy beard and the fellow went down like a felled tree.

There was a brief melee in the stairwell. Sparrowhawk employed brutes, but they were more used to being the outnumbering bravos than facing an organised and tough resistance. Moreover, the former Irregulars were outraged at the possible threat to their junior counterparts and weren't above using illegal fighting methods to express their ire.

By the time Holmes returned the clerk's book, peace reigned again at the base of the stairs.

"'E started it, Mr. 'Olmes," Butcher insisted.

"Yes, his nose struck your forehead," Holmes observed from the available evidence of groaning guards. "Well, if these men are alleged to have committed assault, you had best secure them until the constabulary might be informed. How fortunate that you brought rope along on your philanthropic visit."

With these ruffians confined, *our* ruffians accompanied us further inside, exploring the warehouse section on the ground floor where the contents of several inherited estates were stored for sale and shipping, and then venturing upstairs in search of Denham Sparrowhawk.

"We are complaining to the manager, I suppose?"

"Quite so, Watson. If Mr. Sparrowhawk can call upon you at your place of work, it seems only fair that you should return the compliment."

There were a couple of additional bullies lurking about. Nobby Butcher and his pals restrained them as they had the others, with the same lack of delicacy.

"Point of 'onour," Butcher explained. "We wants word o' this to get out, see? We wants to make it clear as 'ow some kinds o' threats is a bad thing, an' bad things 'appen to them as makes 'em." His florid face wrinkled into a frown as he strove to make clear his position. "I dun't mean threats to Mr. 'Olmes or you, sir, since as you two goes looking for trouble. But them as looks wrong at Mrs. 'Udson or the young-uns, well . . . that ain't gonna stand."

113

"Quite so," I agreed. "Carry on."

Denham Sparrowhawk was in his office despite the hour, as Holmes had known he would be. He had received news earlier about Holmes's visit to Goldall and Prace and had suspected to what use an implacable detective might put the details he had obtained. Perhaps he had even discovered the content and tenor of Holmes's correspondence with the testators who had formerly bent to Sparrowhawk's will.

Nor could the financier be unawares of the fracas below, for the sound of brawling men must have echoed up that stairwell to his second-floor office suite.

Sparrowhawk sat behind an impressive mahogany desk, apparently at ease. I noted that he kept one hand below the table, out of sight, and concluded that he might be armed. He was certainly dangerous.

Holmes and I entered alone, while our compatriots secured the building and its other occupants.

"This is trespass, Mr. Holmes," Sparrowhawk warned us.

"On the contrary, this is a business call," my friend contradicted him. "I am here to make a complaint. I came to render a payment to Mr. Kepple's account and was treated without the courtesy one might wish for a British establishment in the capital of the Empire. We aren't in Cape Colony [2] now."

Sparrowhawk's confidence wavered as Holmes named the South African state. "Why would you mention that?"

"You grew up there," Holmes replied. "I have seen your hands. They bear the tell-tale callosities of one who spent his youth mining. The mild jaundice in your eye suggests childhood tropical disease. Your English, though very good and well-trained, betrays when you are jubilant and gloating a trace of a colonial accent. I'd venture that you were brought up in the vicinity of Mount Kurrie and its Dutch diamond fields, that territory which were annexed in '77 when you were a schoolboy."

Sparrowhawk flushed. "If you have a point to make, make it, Mr. Holmes."

"My point is that you might be good at winkling out useful facts to discover and exploit your victims, but I am just as suited to discovering hidden truths. You will discover that whenever you feel inclined to rely upon vicious threats and brute force to overawe your prey, decent men will combine to suppress your criminal efforts."

"It isn't me who trespasses here!" the financier cried.

"By all means, summon a constable," I offered, in the spirit of the confrontation. "I've no doubt that a look over those ledgers downstairs, interviews with the bullies who have been used to enforce your word, and

114

a precise investigation by the greatest detective alive will give the attending officers plenty to do. You hide like a spider in the shadows. Holmes will turn over your rock and expose you to the light."

Holmes had a worse threat. "A bright enough light might shine all the way to Africa, to the circumstances of a young man fleeing his homeland and taking ship for England under a different name. I have correspondents in the Cape Colony Police Department who have assisted me before. Doubtless there will be people in Cape Town who are interested in the present whereabouts of a man named 'Sparrowhawk'. Before long I should be able to provide them with an older name."

As Holmes spoke his adversary went red, then white. There was anger in the extortionist's expression, but also a bitter dollop of fear. "You come here by night, mob-handed, using violence, and you threaten me!" the financier pointed out. Now he displayed his gun openly. "I am a man defending his property, and perhaps his life, from a known troublemaker who has finally gone too far."

The thought of our murder apparently restored his garrulity. "You wasted your time as well as your life in coming here, Mr. Holmes. I daresay your Scotland Yard cronies will want to search this place, but they will find nothing illegal. Every stick of furniture, every heirloom, is properly acquired, with verifying paperwork. Every debt is certified by full documentation, signed and sealed. As for evidence of any assaults that you believe may have occurred to convince my clients to accept my advice, alas Mr. Sherlock Holmes will have no opportunity to undertake such researches."

Holmes looked disappointed. "You believe you have seen through my efforts once more, and have thwarted me again? No, I have come to finish this matter because you have become tedious, Mr. Sparrowhawk."

The blackguard scowled, offended to be so dismissed.

Holmes sniffed at the scheming financier. "Having captured the ruffians that you employ, I am certain that under proper questioning one or more will prove to know about and have been involved in the 'accidents' that befell your victims. Having identified the rat's nest of business endeavours through which you channel earnings from your extortion operation, I am confident I can bring proof of that also."

"And by threatening us with a firearm, you have guaranteed yourself the long drop," [3] I added. "The law doesn't forgive the criminal use of guns."

Sparrowhawk was about to retort – Holmes had identified him as an habitual and compulsive gloater who had to have the last word – but my friend extended his cane to point directly at the fellow as if in warning.

"You are an unpleasant and brutal murderer who has taken up too much of my time. Now you threaten to kill again. I say enough!"

I knew that Holmes's cane was a sword-stick. I was ready as he levelled it at Sparrowhawk. Holmes thumbed the spring-release button on the handle, which frees the blade from the casing by sending the cover flying off with some speed. The wooden length was propelled over the eight feet to the villain like a blunt spear, and might have caught him a nasty rap had it hit him instead of scattering the contents of his desk.

That did not matter. The sword-cover wasn't the point, and neither on this occasion was the bared blade. It was distraction.

I had promised myself a crack at Sparrowhawk ever since his visit to my medical practice.

I caught up a file-box larger than a bread-bin and hurled it at the blighter's gun-hand. The weapon discharged as it was knocked aside, burying a round through that expensive office desk. Holmes swept the firearm away with a swipe of his sword-cane.

Sparrowhawk rose up, brutally and lethally. As he reached for Holmes, those savage instincts from survival on the diamond fields, from whatever savage youth he had escaped to reach England, burst out in a killing temper.

I was disappointed. *I* had hoped to deliver the drubbing to Denham Sparrowhawk.

Holmes is a precise boxer and an elegant wrestler. I have seen him before shame heavy powerful brutes who rely upon their strength and ferocity to overwhelm their opponents. Holmes could wax lyrical for hours on "The Sweet Science", which he had studied with the same application as any of the arts required of the modern detective.

Sparrowhawk had evidently mistaken and overestimated his own physical skills. Holmes tutored him on his deficiencies. The financier tumbled back, toppling his chair, scrambling up while Holmes waited. Then Sparrowhawk made the mistake of drawing a knife.

Holmes displaced his adversary's radius, a distal fracture that probably broke some of the smaller hand-bones as well. Sparrowhawk's blade tumbled to the floor to join his gun.

Holmes's *ennui* lifted briefly as he demonstrated his pugilistic skills. It was for him a purely intellectual exercise, as calculated a piece of mathematics as any scientific formula. He read his opponent, anticipating assaults with ridiculous ease, countering with easy deflections, until he was in a position to deliver a full-force uppercut to Sparrowhawk's jaw – a knockout blow!

"Bravo!" I applauded, pleased to see the fellow fold up and fall with a broken mandible and less teeth. I threw away a pang of regret that it wasn't me who had delivered the thrashing. "I believe the blackguard is down for the count."

Holmes massaged his knuckles, which he had undoubtedly bruised. "We have no time to waste, Watson. Sparrowhawk was right that we have assaulted him in his own premises. He has a strong legal defence for his actions. We, on the other hand, have a window of opportunity to do what he sought to prevent us from doing, which is to search his chambers for evidence."

"He said that there was no proof of illegal activity in this sorry grime-hole."

"He never said we would not find data suggestive of his original identity, or the reasons for his flight from Africa. Alas for Denham Sparrowhawk, he is in no position to refuse our searches."

Sherlock Holmes can be as inexorable as an act of God, a natural disaster that rolls over men to their misfortune with no way of preventing it. While I convinced a desk sergeant to venture a pair of constables into the Limehouse docks on a cold foggy night, it took my friend less than the thirty minutes to uncover what he needed.

"Sparrowhawk has a distinctive scar concealed under his collar and onto his shoulder, badly stitched long ago, which should help with his identification in Cape Town," Holmes instructed me. "Given his reaction to my discerning his origin, I am confident that there are crimes for which he is wanted in the colony before ever he began his predations here. However, the best evidence I can offer is this little pocket-book of payments made to people noted only by their initials. These entries match to the names of several of the crestfallen guards that Butcher and his comrades are now handing over to the police. I have already procured the first admission of arson from one of the bullies, who was paid nine shillings on the 19th November last for the deed. Even a detective inspector will be able to derive other such confessions from this little treasure-store."

The suspicious constabulary were unconvinced that all the rich goods warehoused in his premises weren't the stolen store of some criminal middle-man. All the paperwork proof in the world cannot easily offset a policeman who has made up his mind. It looked like a receiver's den, and that was sufficient to hold the financier.

Moreover, the word of Sherlock Holmes was enough for Sparrowhawk to be taken into custody.

It took less than the twenty-four hours of "arrest upon suspicion" for the Limehouse police to drag confessions from Sparrowhawk's minions. In under a week the suspect's original identity and violent crimes were reported back from Cape Town. Mere days later, Holmes's client and other victims of the predatory philanthropist were willing to come forward with statements. The work of untangling the legalities and ownership of properties would fill up the courts for years.

Holmes took no further interest in the case.

"That fellow was done with as soon as 'e came up across Mr. 'Olmes," Nobby Butcher assured me. "Soon as 'e started talking large about 'urting the little-uns. That was it for 'im!"

"I believe that it was," I congratulated the beefy young man. I shook hands with the grown-up Street-Arabs – a very different kind of Irregular, but quite effective.

As for boastful gloating Sparrowhawk, he had nothing to say to us given that his jaw was wired shut while the fracture healed. And then, after his appointment with the hangman, he said nothing at all.

NOTES

1. The rook was characterised as a dishonest and thieving bird, and the rooks' collective nests, the rookery, became a synonym for a thieves' den and a thieves' quarter. The slums about St. Giles' Church and the Old Mint were the worst parts of mid-nineteenth century London, described often in fiction, shunned by police and honest citizens in fact. Charles Dickens wrote much about the places in stories and articles, based upon first-hand inspection in 1850 when he accompanied Inspector Field, "*the formidable chief detective of Scotland Yard*", an assistant commissioner, and three other officers on an all-night excursion through the Rat's Castle [Ratcliff Highway and Petticoat Lane], backed by a squad of local police within whistling distance.

    St. Giles, Bermondsey's Jacob's Island, and the East End's Old Nichol Street Rookery were demolished in the late nineteenth century as part of London slum clearance and urban redevelopment projects, but this merely displaced gambling, prostitution, and extreme poverty to other locations, such as the Limehouse docklands.

2. Cape Colony, the African territory around the Cape of Good Hope, was captured by the British from the Dutch in 1795 and was held with one interruption until it was combined with three other colonies in 1910 to form the Union of South Africa.

3. Capital punishment by hanging. British courts of the nineteenth century were exceptionally and deliberately hard on gun crimes.

119

The Affair of the
Addleton Giant
by Margaret Walsh

The year 1894 was a busy one for Mr. Sherlock Holmes and myself. One of the strangest cases that we dealt with was one that Holmes almost refused to take. Indeed, looking back, I truly wish we had not taken it. I have spent years trying to forget what I saw. Even now, I write this down in the hope, most likely vain, that the act of doing so will exorcise the memory.

It was a late summer evening when Freddie Taverner, a Member of Parliament whom we knew reasonably well, and who had been involved, albeit somewhat tangentially, to several other cases of ours, arrived at 221b Baker Street.

I showed Taverner into a seat, and he gratefully accepted the glass of whisky that I offered him.

"My thanks, Dr. Watson," he said with a small smile.

"What brings you to our door on this fine summer evening?" Holmes asked.

Taverner took a sip. "I have been asked by a friend, whom I know through my work as an MP for Dorset, to approach you for assistance."

"And what is it that means this friend cannot come himself? Or herself?" I added.

"The friend in question is the Bishop of Salisbury. The diocese of Salisbury covers Dorset, where my seat is, and most of Wiltshire."

"Why does the Bishop of Salisbury wish to consult me?" Holmes asked.

"Bishop Wordsworth has concerns about one of his vicars."

"What is the vicar doing?" I asked. I was unsure as what a vicar could do to worry his bishop, apart from possibly taking advantage of women of the parish or stealing the church plate.

"From my understanding, the Reverend Solomon Jenkins was considered to be going far in the clergy. He is highly intelligent and a dedicated theologian. Until January last year, he had the benefice of a parish in Salisbury itself. The bishop had been having problems finding a vicar for the small village of Addleton, and Jenkins offered to go. Within

120

a short time of Reverend Jenkins moving to Addleton, his personality began to change."

"How so?" Holmes asked, leaning forward in his chair.

"You have heard of the Cerne Abbas Giant?" Taverner asked.

Holmes shook his head, but I frowned slightly. "It is a large figure of a man carved into the chalk of a hill, is it not?"

"It is, Dr. Watson. Addleton is quite close to the figure, but you cannot view it from there. Jenkins has, according to Bishop Wordsworth, become obsessed with the giant. He would like you to go to Addleton and look around."

Holmes raised his eyebrows. "I am a consulting detective, Mr. Taverner, not a Commissioner of Lunacy. And to be quite blunt, from what you have told me, it seems that this is most likely a case for the latter."

"Bishop Wordsworth would much rather avoid that scenario, if at all possible. Reverend Jenkins behaviour is only the latest in a long line of odd occurrences in Addleton. In fact, the bishop confided in me that he is beginning to wonder if this predecessor should have listened to the villagers and not built the new manse where they did."

"New manse?" I asked.

Taverner shrugged. "Apparently there was a flood quite a few years ago that virtually destroyed the old manse. The manse had been flooded before, and the church was sick of making repairs, so they demolished it and built a new one on the hill behind the church. The villagers were unhappy, as they consider the hill to be – well, maybe not sacred, but definitely *not* a place you would wish to build."

"Interesting," Holmes murmured. He was silent for a moment. "Very well, Taverner, Watson and I will go to Addleton and have a look around. Is there someplace we can stay?

"There is a pub called 'The Sleeping Giant'. It has rooms and does good meals. I've stayed there myself when touring my constituency." Taverner paused. "The village is quite difficult to reach. You will need to get the train to Dorchester, but if David Miller – that is, the publican of The Sleeping Giant – knows you are coming, he will send the pub's pony and trap for you."

Holmes nodded. After a few more pleasantries were exchanged, Freddie Taverner took his leave.

"Kindly look up Addleton in the Dorset *Gazetteer* for me, my dear Watson."

Obligingly I took the volume down from the shelf and opened the book. The entry for the village wasn't large. I read aloud: "'*Addleton: Village of little historical interest apart from a few ancient barrows. The name is believed to have derived from the Saxon name "Aethelstan" who was possibly a landowner in the area prior to the Norman Conquest. Addleton is situated close by the River Piddle, between Cerne Abbas and Buckland Newton.'"*

"Not very enlightening," Holmes observed.

"Taverner did say it was a small village."

"True."

I frowned as I put the book away. "There is no mention of a hill in the village."

"I suspect the hill in question is an ancient barrow. We have seen for ourselves how large then can be." Holmes was referring to our sojourn in the Wiltshire village of Barrow-upon Kennet, that I have recorded as *The Case of the Perplexed Politician.*

"That is true," I replied after a moment's thought. "They can look like natural hills."

"It would also explain the reluctance of the villagers to see anything built upon it. They may not know exactly what it is, but local folklore would ensure that they remembered that it was special." Holmes got to his feet. "Come, Watson, pack your things for a few days. I shall let Mrs. Hudson know that we will be away and send a telegram to the pub to reserve us two rooms. Oh, and do make sure you put your walking staff aside to take with you."

"What on earth for?"

"What could be more natural than two friends heading to Dorset to hike around the barrows and the view the famous chalk giant?"

I nodded and went to my room to pack, as Holmes headed downstairs.

The journey to Addleton was long and mostly tedious. The train was, unfortunately, not an express, meaning that the trip took much longer than I had anticipated. When we got to Dorchester, the pony and trap from The Sleeping Giant was waiting for us, and although it was a long ride from Dorchester to Addleton, at least I had the pleasant Dorset countryside to soothe me. We passed by many farms and barrows, and through picturesque villages, until we finally arrived in Addleton.

The village was very small. Except for the presence of a church, one would have called it a hamlet. The church in question appeared to be of late Norman construction, though its name, St. Eadwold of Cerne, was clearly of Saxon origin.

A hill rose up behind the church. I could see a house was built on top of it. When Holmes had suggested that it might be a barrow, I had naturally thought of the smaller constructions that we had seen in Wiltshire. If the hill was indeed a barrow, it was quite the largest I had ever seen, and I wondered at the engineering skills of the ancient Britons who had raised it.

We were met at the door of the pub by the owner, Mr. David Miller. He was the antithesis of the image of a jolly publican. The man was tall and spare with chestnut hair touched at the temples with silver. He regarded us with sharp green eyes, but his voice was warm as he said, "Welcome to Addleton, gentlemen. My wife had prepared two rooms for you. We've put you at the back overlooking the churchyard. Those are the quietest rooms we have. Not everyone cares to view graves from their window, but I figured that men of science and medicine, like your good selves, wouldn't be troubled."

"It will certainly make for an interesting view," Holmes responded, as he introduced us. Though I felt it was probably unnecessary. It seemed that David Miller knew exactly who we were.

Miller turned to me. "I am a regular reader of *The Strand*, Dr. Watson. It's a pleasure to have yourself and Mr. Holmes as guests." He turned to Holmes. "You are here because of the vicar, aren't you?"

"What makes you say that?" Holmes asked.

"Mr. Taverner was here last week. He was inordinately interested in the church and the manse. And now, you are here. Dr. Watson has made the point many times that you are a creature of the city, Mr. Holmes. I don't believe for one moment that you are here to view the Cerne Abbas Giant. For one thing, there are hostelries much close to it than here."

Holmes chuckled. "There are few men as observant as publicans. If you decide to become a detective, Mr. Miller, then I'm afraid I may need to retire."

"There is no fear of that, Mr. Holmes. I like what I do well enough. My father owned this pub. As did his father, and his before him. In fact, my family has had the pub here in Addleton since the days of Charles II. Come, I shall show you to your rooms. My man has taken your bags up."

We followed David Miller through the comfortable bar and up a flight of stairs at the end of the room. A further flight took us up another level, to where the better rooms were. Those allocated to us were side by side. Both were laid out identically with a large bed, a bedside table, a large mahogany wardrobe against one wall, and a small table with a fine china ewer and bowl for washing, as well as a small mirror set beside them. Next to the window sat a well-upholstered armchair. In all, the rooms were pleasant and comfortable. It would be a pleasure to stay here.

Holmes was looking out of the window. "The church is a fine specimen. Is it possible to view it?"

"Aye, if you can catch the vicar there. He gives his sermons on Sunday and spends the rest of the time prowling around the churchyard or on the hill at the back."

"Well, the latter is understandable if that if the manse on top of it," I said.

Miller shook his head. "You misunderstand me, Doctor. Reverend Jenkins walks 'round and 'round the hill. If you ask him what he is doing, he says he is looking for the way in."

"I understand that the manse is relatively recent," Holmes said.

"It is," Miller replied. "If you want to know the history of it, I suggest you talk to Professor Giles. He knows all the dates."

"Professor Giles?" Holmes asked.

"Professor Rutherford Giles," Miller replied. "He is a local. Went to Oxford. He retired back here several years ago. He is an antiquarian with a deep interest in local folklore and history. He'll tell you anything you want to know about the area, and everything you don't want to know as well. Get him started and he will not shut up."

"Thank you, Mr. Miller. Where can we meet this Professor Giles?"

David Miller consulted his fob watch. "He'll be in the bar shortly for his daily glass of sherry. If you gentlemen would like to get settled in, I shall send someone up to fetch you when he arrives."

"Thank you, Mr. Miller," Holmes replied. "You have been most helpful."

I left Holmes in his room and went to mine, busying myself with unpacking the small bag that I had brought with me.

It was perhaps fifteen minutes later when a young boy came upstairs to tell us that Professor Giles had arrived.

When we went downstairs, I spotted a tallish older man, with a head of bright white curls, seated at a small table near the back of the bar. He was leaning back contentedly in his chair, surveying the room with bright, interested eyes. Every so often he would take a sip from the glass of sherry that rested on the table before him.

Mr. Miller took us across the room to the gentleman's table. "Professor Giles, I have two gentlemen here who would like to meet you."

The professor gave us both a sharp, somewhat quizzical look. "Are you sure, David? It seems to me that Mr. Sherlock Holmes and Dr. John Watson would find little that I would have to say to be of interest."

Holmes pulled out a chair and sat down unasked. "This village seems to have uncommonly observant residents," he said dryly.

A brief smile flittered across the professor's face. "I wouldn't say that I am uncommonly observant. I have a friend who lectures at King's College in London. He pointed you both out to me once when we

124

happened to dine at Simpson's on the Strand, and you were also there. It is less a case of observation, and more a matter of having a prodigious memory for faces."

Professor Giles waved for me to be seated beside my friend. He nodded to Miller, who went back to the bar.

"So what is it that I can assist you with, Mr. Holmes?"

"Mr. Miller tells us that you know all that there is to know about the history and folklore of this village."

"I do. What do you wish to know?"

"Whatever you can tell us about the church, and the manse. And the hill upon which the manse sits."

The professor took a meditative sip of his sherry before placing the glass on the table and getting to his feet. "Come, gentlemen, let us have tea at my house. I can tell you what I know there in comfort, without the possibility of being overheard."

I looked around and noticed that more than a few men were trying to eavesdrop while pretending that they were doing no such thing.

We walked from the pub to a well-maintained little house at the edge of the village. Giles let us in the front door and showed us into a cosy parlour with a view that looked away towards hills. The professor headed further back into the house, and I heard him talking to someone. He rejoined us a few moments later. "Mrs. Fleming, my housekeeper, will bring us tea in a few minutes."

By the time we were comfortably seated, and a small table fetched from a corner, the lady in question wheeled a trolley into the room. A pot of tea in a plain knitted tea-cosy was placed on the table, followed by cups, saucers, a bowl of sugar lumps, and a small jug of milk. These were followed by a plate of egg sandwiches, some shortbread biscuits, as well as a plate of savoury biscuits to go with some rather good local cheese, which Professor Giles told us was called Dorset Blue Vinny. It was comparable to a particularly fine Stilton.

After Mrs. Fleming had left the room, and we each had a small plate of comestibles and a cup of tea, the professor regaled us with a smile. "I am assuming that this is about the vicar?"

"Does everyone in Addleton know our business?" Holmes asked, somewhat testily.

"More that everyone is concerned about the vicar," Giles replied. "He seemed pleasant enough, and sane enough, when he and his family arrived. But he has gone very strange."

"Mr. Miller told us about his continual walking around the hill that the manse is on, muttering about finding the way in," I said.

125

The professor nodded. "Reverend Jenkins was much appreciated when he arrived, as the village had been without a clergyman for three years."

"That is a long time for a benefice to remain vacant," Holmes observed. "Admittedly this is a small village with little scope for a family, but I should have thought it would have been excellent for a cleric just starting his career – or ending it."

"You would think so," the professor agreed. "But by 1890, people had begun to believe that the manse was cursed."

"Cursed? In this modern age?" I was aghast.

"Let me tell you the sequence of events," Giles said.

We both nodded our acceptance and sat back to listen.

"Both the church and the manse were built quite close to the River Piddle. The river, like many in Dorset, is exceptionally prone to flooding during heavy rain. The church has never flooded, something that the superstitious put down to the blessing of St. Eadwold of Cerne's protection. The manse, however, used to flood regularly. After a particularly bad flood in 1857, that deposited dead livestock inside the lower floor, the church decided to demolish the building and build on higher ground."

"The hill behind the churchyard," I said.

The professor nodded. "Exactly. The locals were against the idea. There is a local legend that says that the hill is the home to a sleeping giant, and if he is disturbed, he will wreak vengeance upon those who awaken him."

Holmes snorted. "Does this giant have a name?"

"Some versions of the legend say that it is the giant whose image is at Cerne Abbas. Others call him *Aethelstan* or *Addle*. The only constant in the various versions is that it's a giant that sleeps inside the hill."

"Hence the name of the local pub," Holmes said.

"Indeed," Professor Giles replied. "The architect William Butterfield designed the new manse. The man was quite well regarded, having designed Keble College in Oxford, and several churches in London. It was built by builders from Dorchester and wasn't completed until 1860, when a new vicar was installed just in time for Christmas."

"Three years seems a long time to build a house," Holmes said.

"I was still in Oxford at the time," Giles replied, "but I understand from other people that the project was beset with problems from the start. Workers kept quitting, materials were delayed or lost, that kind of thing."

Holmes hummed an interested sound. "What happened then?"

"In March of 1863, the incumbent fell down the internal staircase in the manse and broke his neck. Died instantly. The next vicar was killed in

126

July 1870 when he was thrown from his horse and hit his head on a rock. The man who was vicar in 1882 died from a heart attack, and then in May 1890 the last vicar, Reverend Wallingsworth, dropped dead from apoplexy while preaching his Sunday sermon. In between the deaths there were other instances of scandal and misery."

"Such as?" Holmes asked.

"One vicar stole church plate to fund his gambling debts. Another caused a scandal with a local girl that resulted in a hasty marriage, and yet another became involved with several married women in the area."

"Not a good record for such a small parish," I said.

"The relocation of the manse was swiftly viewed as being the cause of the problem. Good men appeared to become corrupted by simply being there, and those who were too hard to corrupt by whatever force was doing the corrupting ended up dead."

"And your own thoughts on the matter?" Holmes asked.

Professor Giles shook his head. "Even though I have an interest in folklore, I am a rational man, Mr. Holmes. I don't believe in supernatural creatures affecting humans. And I am not given to flights of fancy. However, I must say that I don't like the atmosphere in the manse. The building is heavy and brooding with an almost palpable aura of menace. You must see for yourselves. Tomorrow morning, I shall call for you and take you up to the manse to meet Reverend Jenkins."

Holmes got to his feet. "Thank you, Professor Giles. That would be most appreciated."

We took our leave of the professor and walked back towards the pub. "Well," I asked, "what do you make of it?"

Holmes stopped walking and stood, staring thoughtfully, at the manse where it squatted above the church. "The sequence of events shared by the professor are certainly interesting. I can see why the locals would believe that the site is cursed."

"But what do you think?"

Holmes shook his head. "I don't know, my friend. I'm loathe to speculate before I meet the vicar. Like Professor Giles, I'm a rational man. The idea of a curse in this enlightened age doesn't sit well with me."

I nodded my understanding and we returned to the pub.

Mrs. Miller served us an excellent dinner comprising of roast Dorset lamb with mint sauce and gravy, roasted broccoli and potatoes, and followed by an excellent bread-and-butter pudding with delicious homemade blackberry jam.

Holmes and I returned to the bar after dining and mingled with the locals who had come to drink. We asked polite questions about the vicar, but all we received were assertations that he had seemed a good fellow when he first arrived, but the giant had driven him barmy. Eventually Holmes retired to bed, while I sat for another hour idly chatting with anyone who came near before I, too, went up to my room.

Professor Giles was true to his word and arrived at ten o'clock the next morning to escort us to the manse.

A rather care-worn woman answered the door. She was of middling height, with soft chestnut curls and deep brown eyes that were troubled. Worry lines were visible on her forehead and around her eyes. "Professor Giles, what a pleasant surprise."

"Good morning, Mrs. Jenkins," the man said as he removed his hat. "I have brought two gentlemen to meet the vicar."

Mrs. Jenkins turned her attention to us. "Do come in. My husband is in his study."

She let us into the house, and we followed her down a hallway to a small room with windows that looked out towards the church. I briefly glimpsed the pub from the window before my attention was drawn to the man seated at the desk beneath the window.

If Mrs. Jenkins was worried and worn, the Reverend Solomon Jenkins was the exact opposite. The man almost fizzled with energy. He looked up from the book he had been studying. "Ah, Giles. Do come in! I am making marvellous progress."

"Good morning, Reverend. I have brought two gentlemen from London to meet you. They are interested in the giant."

Reverend Jenkins got to his feet and came towards us with his hand outstretched to shake ours. He pumped Holmes's hand vigorously and then mine as Professor Giles made the introductions.

"Splendid! Splendid! So, you are interested in our giant, eh?" The man fairly beamed at us.

"It is a fascinating subject," I replied, not completely untruthfully.

"Of course," Jenkins said. "It is not a common giant."

"Is it not?" Holmes asked, eyebrows raised.

"Most definitely not," Jenkins replied firmly. "The first clue was the reluctance to build on the barrow. Other barrows have been built upon or even levelled without fear of the consequences."

We nodded.

"At first, I thought that it wasn't a barrow at all, but simply a place of pagan worship. *Deuteronomy* Chapter 12, Verse 2: '*Thou shalt utterly destroy all the places where the nations whom thou shall dispossess serve their gods, on the high mountains and on the hills and under every green tree.*'" Reverend Jenkins's eyes were gleaming with excitement. "But the local legends tell of a giant sleeping beneath the hill. And I thought: What if it isn't a merely legend, but a *folk memory*?"

128

"Folk memory?" I asked.

It was Professor Giles who answered. "A folk memory is a myth or legend that is believed to be a memory of a past event that has been passed down orally from generation to generation."

I nodded my understanding. I remembered what Holmes had said about the hill after Taverner had visited us. Holmes made no comment. I turned back to the vicar. "But what exactly is it a folk memory of?" I asked.

The Reverend Jenkins gave me a look of approval. "I believe that what lies beneath this house is something so amazing, so singular, so terrifying, that the locals have given it wide berth even up until today. Gentlemen, I believe that in the barrow beneath this house lies a *Nephilim*."

I blinked at him. I wasn't familiar with the word.

"'*There were giants in the earth in those days, and also after that, when the sons of God came in unto the daughters of men, and they bare children to them, the same became mighty men which were of old, men of renown,*'" the Reverend intoned.

"The book of *Genesis*, I believe," Holmes said.

"*Genesis*, Chapter 6, Verse 4, to be exact," Reverend Jenkins replied.

I frowned. "What does it mean by '*the sons of God*'?"

"Some authorities believe that it means angels," Professor Giles explained. "Others that it was angels who had already fallen, such as Lucifer."

"So a Nephilim was the child of a human woman and an angel?" I asked, trying to get it clear in my mind.

"Essentially," Revered Jenkins replied. "They were most prevalent in the antediluvian period, but according to Biblical sources, many did survive the Great Flood. Goliath of Gath, who was slain by David, may very well have been the descendant of one. Some of these sources claim that they spread out all over the world. Legend has it that when Brutus, the grandson of Aeneas, came to Britain, he discovered that England, which was then known as Albion, was inhabited by giants." He beamed at us. "So it isn't too much of a stretch of the imagination to believe one may be buried in Dorset."

I was rapidly coming to the opinion that the good vicar was suffering from dementia, given his level of delusion. His wild-eyed excitement also made mania a good solid bet.

Reverend Jenkins moved out into the hallway and gestured for us to follow him. "Come, gentlemen. There is something you must see."

We followed him through the house, into the kitchen, and then down into the cellar. It was cold and damp there. The floor was a simple one of beaten earth. Stacked in one of the corners were lengths of wood. A spade, a mattock, a pick, and a shovel leaned against the pile of wood. The vicar, holding a lantern that had been hanging from the cellar wall, moved to stand about three feet away from the woodpile. He pointed at the floor. "Below here, gentlemen, is, I believe, the exact last resting place of the Nephilim. I intend to begin digging down this very day. Do you wish to assist me?"

Holmes shook his head, "Alas no. My friend and I didn't bring clothing suitable for such manual labour. I will, however, be most interested in whatever you discover."

We took our leave of Reverend Jenkins. As we climbed the stairs, I looked back to see that the man had hung the lantern back up, doffed his waistcoat, rolled up his sleeves, and commenced digging.

Outside of the manse, the professor wished us a good day and walked away, leaving us to walk back to the pub.

"What do we do now?" I asked.

"I think that we need to send a message to the Bishop of Salisbury."

"And ask him to send a Commissioner of Lunacy after all?"

"It may come to that. Come, we shall send a message and then wait to see what the good Bishop replies."

Holmes arranged for Miller's man to take him to the nearest village with a telegraph office. I amused myself by exploring Addleton. The church was locked, but the churchyard was interesting, if somewhat melancholy, with faded gravestones encrusted with lichen and moss.

Holmes returned quite late in the evening. He had waited for a reply to his telegram. "Bishop Wordsworth has asked that we wait here until he can arrive."

"What on earth for?"

"I suspect that he wants impartial witnesses. It is no minor thing to remove a vicar from his benefice at the same time that one declares him mad."

I sighed but nodded my acceptance. To be honest, I really wished to return to London. Something about the manse, sitting and seeming to brood over the village, made me uncomfortable. Whether I had been influenced by Professor Giles's opinion or not, I really wished to be gone from Addleton.

It was a matter of three days before everything came to a dramatic and terrifying head.

Holmes and I were breakfasting on bacon, eggs, and sausages, with good strong cups of tea. Holmes preferred coffee in the mornings, but this wasn't available. He had taken to staring morosely into his cup most mornings, as if an act of sheer will could transmogrify the beverage.

Two children, a lad of about twelve and a girl several years younger, came running into the pub. The boy caught at Mrs. Miller's apron. "Please, Mrs. Miller, father says can you send the gentlemen from London over right away."

I looked at Holmes. He put his cup down and turned towards the children.

"We are the gentlemen from London, lad. Who is your father?"

"Please sir, I am Rehoboam Jenkins, and this is my sister, Taphath. Our father is – "

"Reverend Solomon Jenkins," Holmes said with a slight smile. "He gave you both names of children of King Solomon."

The boy sighed. "At least I don't have to explain to you, sir, as I have to do to most people. Will you come now?"

"Of course. I have finished my breakfast." He turned to me. "Watson?"

I took a last sip of my tea and rose from the table. "As have I."

We accompanied the children to the manse where the vicar's wife was waiting at the door for us. "Thank you for coming, gentlemen." She twisted her hands together in anxiety. "He is in such a foment that I fear for his sanity."

I reached out and patted her hands. "We shall do what we can. Do you know why he has sent for us."

The lady shook her head. "He came up the ladder from where he has been digging in the cellar and yelled for me to fetch you. He looked demented. I didn't dare leave, so I sent Reb and Tappy to you."

"You did the right thing," Holmes said softly. "He is in the cellar, you say?"

"Yes, sir."

"Have you any spare lanterns? I suspect that my friend and I will have to go down to where your husband has been digging."

Rehoboam was dispatched to the scullery to collect two small paraffin lanterns, which we took from him carefully. After suggesting that the lady and the children retire to the kitchen or some other place that they felt safe, we headed downstairs to the cellar.

It was a mess. The wood that had been stacked in the corner was gone, and the tools that had been there laid scattered around, rather than neatly stacked. Most obvious of all was a gaping hole in the middle of the earthen floor. There was no sign of the vicar.

Holmes went to the edge of the hole and called down, "Reverend Jenkins!"

A voice floated up from below. "Ah, the London men! You are here! Come down! Come down!"

"How on earth shall we do that?" I muttered.

Holmes bent and lifted something out of the hole. "By means of this rope ladder."

We fastened the lanterns to our belts and gingerly made our way down the rope ladder that, though securely affixed, swayed dangerously. I was glad when we reached the bottom.

I had been expecting the floor to be like that of the cellar but was surprised to discover that the ground beneath my feet was smooth stone. It was pitch dark. Small pockets of light came from lanterns that were attached to timbers that buttressed the walls, but it wasn't enough light to chase away the pervasive, almost malevolent, dark that surrounded us. And it was cold. So very cold. The old expression "*As cold as the grave*" came to mind. I shivered involuntarily. Around us, the timbers creaked and groaned like something from a nightmare. A figure lurched out of the darkness at us. It was all I could do not to scream. Holmes detached his lantern and held it up.

The figure proved to be the Reverend Solomon Jenkins. Gone was the respectable man of the cloth. He was still dressed in the clothes he had been wearing when we visited the manse with Professor Giles. Now, however, they were stained with dirt and sweat, and he stank abominably. There was an unnatural light in his eyes. They were fever bright, almost crazed. And he was waving something in the air.

With the lack of light, and the frenzied movement, it took me a moment to realise that what the vicar was waving around with a human femur. At least, it looked like a human femur. But it couldn't be. The bone was huge. At least three times the size of that of the average man.

"I was right," Jenkins cried. "It is a Nephilim. Look at the bones!"

Holmes walked to where a jumble of bones lay on the floor. I joined him, dodging to avoid the femur being swung like a flail by the obviously deranged vicar. Holmes knelt beside the bones, and I crouched opposite him. We studied the disarticulated skeleton on the floor.

"It cannot be," I whispered. "It looks human. But the size . . . ."

"Could it be some form of ape?" Holmes mused aloud. "But if so, why would ancient people have given it such a burial?" He raised his head as if to call to the vicar, and then froze. "Watson," he whispered, getting to his feet, his voice hoarse, "Behind you."

I slowly got to my feet and turned around to see what it was that had provoked such a response from Holmes. When I saw it, I too froze. It was a skull. A clearly human skull, and of a size that matched with the outsized skeleton on the floor. Reluctantly, we approached the shelf on which it sat. I leaned forward to examine it. It seemed to me, in the flickering light of the lantern, that dark eyes watched us balefully from within the empty

132

sockets. I swallowed hard. Nothing would induce me to touch it. Holmes, it appeared, was of the same mind. We both lifted our lanterns to get a better look. What I saw was enough to have me backing away.

I moved back to the rope ladder. I could hear Holmes behind me. Behind him, Reverend Jenkins was alternating between crooning at the skull and laughing wildly.

Once in the house, I settled my shaken nerves enough to recommend to Mrs. Jenkins that she and the children find some other accommodation. It was my concern that, with the vicar's deteriorating state, she and the children might not be safe.

Mrs. Jenkins thanked me for my kindness but said firmly, "I swore to cleave to him in sickness and in health, Doctor. I will not abandon him now, not when he needs me." I nodded my head sadly.

We hastened back to the pub, where upon Holmes organised for Mr. Miller to send his lad to send another telegram to Bishop Wordsworth, advising him that it was now imperative that he come to Addleton immediately.

While Holmes was doing that, I procured two large glasses of brandy from Mrs. Miller and took them up to our rooms. I was waiting in Holmes's room when he returned and handed him one of the glasses.

"For shock," I told him.

"*Physician, heal thyself*, hmm?"

I shuddered. "Please don't quote the Bible at me, Holmes. I am not sure that I can stand it."

Holmes nodded.

"Is what we sure genuine?" I asked. I was hoping Holmes would tell me it was a hoax.

Holmes took a sip of his brandy, which brought a little colour back to his cheeks, which had gone pasty white. "I rather fear that it was."

I shuddered.

"Consider this: Only three days ago we were in that cellar. The floor was smooth, beaten down, earth. If it had been dug up previously, then there would have been signs. Not to mention that, given the size of this village, someone would have seen the skeleton being brought in."

I nodded sadly.

"And even if the skeleton was fake," Holmes continued, "the skull clearly was not."

I shuddered again, almost spilling my brandy. Holmes took the glass from my hand and seated me in the chair by the window.

"It is definitely genuine," I admitted. "I have seen fake skulls, and there is one thing that the fakers always forget."

Holmes nodded. "The sutures."

"Yes. All three main sutures were present on the skull."

"I noticed that," Holmes said. "They appeared to be mostly closed."

Feeling more sure of myself now that we were talking about something I knew, I took a deep breath. "Going by the sutures, the individual was somewhere between twenty and thirty years old when he died. The coronial suture between the frontal and the two parietal bones was almost completely closed. The sagittal connecting the two parietal bones was more open. I never got a good look at the lambdoid at the back of the skull connecting the occipital bone to the parietals, but nothing would have induced me to touch that skull!"

"It was a human skull," Holmes said. "Not an ape. There are obvious differences."

I nodded. "Regardless of size, that skeleton was of a human."

"Mostly human," Holmes murmured. "'*The sons of God came in unto the daughters of men, and they bare children to them.*'"

My shudders returned. "Holmes! What on earth do we do?"

Holmes placed his hands on my shoulders. "We do nothing. This, Watson, is not our problem. This one belongs firmly to the Bishop of Wordsworth."

"But – "

"No. We have done a favour for the bishop. We have investigated the vicar. Whether he is truly insane, or possessed by the spirit of the Nephilim, or Widow Twankey for that matter, that is for the bishop and the Dorset Commissioner of Lunacy to decide. No crime has been committed. Come, let us take a walk in the fresh country air. We shall remain here tonight, and tomorrow we shall return to London, regardless of whether Bishop Wordsworth has put in an appearance or not."

My friend helped me from the chair and led me downstairs. We spent the rest of the day strolling along country lanes, stopping to admire the scenery and to chat with the locals.

When we returned to the pub, we packed up our luggage and elected to have an early night, as Holmes had inveigled Mr. Miller into getting his man to take us into Dorchester at first light so that we might get the earliest possible train back to London.

I awoke in the dark. Something had awakened me, but I couldn't say what. As I settled down to go back to sleep, I heard it. A deep, grinding, creaking noise, that turned into a tortured shriek, followed by an unholy crash. I threw back the covers and leaped from my bad.

I rushed into Holmes's room. He was already out of bed and standing at the window. I joined him. I stared in horror at the sight before me. The manse had collapsed. The building had crashed down, no doubt undermined by the vicar's excavations. I rushed to my room to dress, and Holmes and I hurried downstairs.

As we hastened towards the manse, with Mr. Miller, and his man, other men of the village joined us. The barrow that the manse had been built upon was shaking.

"Stay back!" Holmes shouted.

Everyone froze as, with one enormous shudder, the barrow collapsed in on itself, swallowing the remains of the manse whole.

I swallowed hard. "No one could have survived that."

Holmes nodded. "It happened swiftly. Mercifully, I don't believe that anyone would have been aware what was happening."

When the sun rose, it was indeed obvious that there had been no survivors. Holmes and I returned to London in a very subdued state of mind. It was maybe four days later that Freddie Taverner, M.P., called on us, this time bringing Bishop Wordsworth with him.

We told them both, as succinctly as possible, what we had seen that day inside the barrow.

Bishop Wordsworth sat silently for a few moments, his head bowed in thought. "I do not think it serves any purpose to try and recover the remains," he said finally. "It would be too hard on the people. What I shall do is consecrate the area as part of the graveyard. They may rest in peace where they lay. There will, however, be a service for them in the church, if you gentlemen would like to attend?"

I looked at Holmes. He shook his head, answering for both us. "We thank you for the offer, but neither of us is inclined to return to Addleton."

Taverner and the bishop took their leave. Holmes stood at the window, watching them go. Then he shook himself and turned to me. "Well, what about a spot of supper at Simpson's?"

"Sounds good to me," I replied.

We gathered out coats and walked out into the gentle summer twilight.

The Adventure of the
Faithful Wolfhound
by Tracy J. Revels

"Here's the thing, Mr. Holmes: Do I have the killer already locked away in a cell? Or should I be looking for the villain among the thousands of people who might have rejoiced in such an act? Is my job difficult, or absurdly easy?"

My friend offered our travelling companion, Inspector Winston Holly, a comforting smile. "Most criminal cases are quite simple, but it is human nature to create a great mystery where only the blandly obvious exists."

The inspector – stout and tall, with ginger hair and a ruddy complexion that indicated his love of the sporting life – briskly nodded. He was one of the legions of young men, professional detectives scattered across the nation, who would willingly take the earliest train to London to seek my friend's advice.

"Occam's Razor indeed. And yet . . . I feel a nagging doubt that something has eluded me, and that a missing piece of the puzzle may be the most essential element."

"Then let us have it again," Holmes commanded, his sharp gaze studying the scenery from the train window. "I think we have just enough time for a retelling – especially as Watson was a slugabed and did not hear it over coffee."

I recognized the cue to take out my notebook. However, I was not willing to let the friendly insult pass.

"Not every man is a cold, thinking machine, Holmes. Some of us enjoy a long evening at the opera, seated beside a charming companion. I didn't return to Baker Street until after one!"

Holmes gave an arch chuckle. "Inspector, if your problem can spare me from losing Watson to yet another wife, I shall be forever in your debt. Now let us have the problem from the beginning."

"That would be almost a year-and-a-half-ago, with the tragedy at the duck pond. It is a body of water on the edge of the village, perhaps a quarter-of-a-mile in diameter. Mrs. Barton's father, Sir Lewis Tidwell, was the country squire, and quite a wealthy man who left many properties to his daughter, who was his only child. Luckily for the villagers, however, the jolly old man, God rest his soul, gave his duck pond freely to the common folk for public recreation. In the summer months, it is a popular place with the younger set for boating parties and picnics. On the fifth of June of last year, Sir Lewis's grandson, Andrew Barton, took a young lady out upon the surface, with tragic results.

"A word on Master Andrew – the lad had a terrible reputation. He was a first-rate rotter as a boy and showed little promise as he grew to young manhood. Last summer, he had been sent down from Oxford in a cloud of disgrace for his misdeeds. His only interests were fishing, hunting, and carousing with a group of like-minded rowdies. No amount of correction or discipline could affect a change in him. I once saw his mother remonstrating with him in the High Street, begging him to amend his ways. He pushed her away so roughly she nearly fell in front of a carriage. It made my blood boil to witness such a thing, especially as Mrs. Barton was a kind and decent woman, a consistent friend to the poor and forgotten, who never deserved such caddish treatment.

"But back to that fateful afternoon when young Barton took Miss Lizzie Wyatt out on a rowboat. It was a hot day, and a half-dozen couples were gathered on the shore. I spoke with each boy and girl, and all were consistent in their testimony. Andrew was dangerously intoxicated, and so was Miss Lizzie. They were waving about bottles of champagne, laughing loudly. Andrew began cutting capers – balancing on boat's rails, performing handstands in the craft, twirling the oar above his head. Then, with a cry, he lost his footing, and both passengers were flipped into the water, in the deepest part of the pond.

"The lads on the shore rallied, many of them diving in fully clad to try and rescue the pair. They pulled Andrew out easily enough, but the girl had sunk to the bottom, weighed down by all her skirts. It was almost an hour before they found her body tangled in the weeds."

"How awful," I said.

"Was Andrew Barton charged?" Holmes asked.

"No. It seems unjust to me, but the judge ruled that since the lady was also rather in her cups, the boy could not be blamed. The incident was dismissed as a tragic accident."

"I take it the village has found this verdict hard to accept?"

"You have it, Mr. Holmes. The girl was a sweet lass, never known to be intoxicated before – everyone felt that Andrew was taking advantage of her naivety that afternoon. To make matters worse, Andrew Barton expressed no remorse. He was overheard in the pub saying things like she was a silly girl and not a great loss to the village. Even the toughs who had been his friends rejected him out of disgust. More than once, he was pelted with filth by schoolboys, or had chamber pots dumped upon his head by otherwise-sedate matrons. Three months ago, his parents did the wisest thing they could and packed him off for adventures in South Africa. Mr. Henry Barton has a small import business in the colonies, and while I cannot imagine that his son will improve his profits, at least in Cape Town, Andrew is safe from those who might wish revenge for the girl's death.

"Since that time, Mrs. Barton had largely retired to Atwell, the family's hunting lodge some ten miles from the village. It is a small, rustic home of only a few rooms, hardly fit for a woman of her status, but a place she had loved since childhood. Most importantly, it is the site of her wolfhound kennels. Her great passion was the breeding and exhibition of champion dogs, and she was one of the founders of the Wolfhound Society of Britain. Since Andrew's departure, she had devoted even more time and energy to her animals."

"Did Mr. Barton reside there as well?"

"Only during the weekends. Otherwise, he divided his time between the rather elaborate house they have in the village and his London offices."

"And what was Mr. Barton's reaction to his son's misdeeds?"

"That is difficult to say. Barton is a quiet, morose-looking man, a native of Manchester who has never particularly taken to village society. He rarely mingles with any of us, to be honest, so I know little about him. But the servants, both in their village home and at the lodge, describe the pair as very devoted to each other, with no quarrels between them."

"Intriguing. And surely this brings us to the heart of the matter – the events of two evenings ago."

"It does indeed. Barton returned to the village on the afternoon train and was driven out to the lodge by a local boy, once he completed a bit of marketing. The lad said they reached the house at seven, and that Barton seemed to be in good spirits, despite the horrid weather which left them quite drenched. Indeed, it was a wild night, with driving rain and howling winds, the true witch of November, I suppose. According to the statements given by Barton and his two lodge servants – a married pair, an elderly housekeeper, and an even more antique butler – Barton went up to his room and changed his sodden clothing, then joined his wife for supper. Jenkins – the kennel master – stepped in just as the coffee was being served and updated Mrs. Barton on the dogs. A short time later, the lady expressed concern about her animals and, despite her husband's entreaties not to go out in such a storm, she donned her waterproof and prepared to walk the quarter-mile from the lodge to the kennels. Barton felt he had no choice but to accompany her and did so. There they found that one of the bitches was almost ready to whelp, and Mrs. Barton was loathe to leave her. After about fifteen minutes, Barton left his spouse to her canine midwifery and returned to the house. He went to his study, drank a sniffer of brandy, and was almost dozing when the housekeeper stuck her head in, asking where her mistress might be.

"'Off with those d----d beasts, I suppose. Get Jenkins to fetch her.'"

Holmes raised a hand. "I take it by this statement that Mr. Barton does not share his wife's passion for prized canines."

The inspector nodded. "That is putting it succinctly. In fact, the only thing the servants mentioned as being a 'bone of contention' between the pair – " Here Holly grimaced at his bad pun. " – was her dedication to the dogs."

"Ah. Please continue."

"Jenkins had already retired, and the butler roused him from bed. You can imagine he was in something of a foul humor, to be told to get dressed, shove his feet back into his boots, and walk down to the kennels. The weather had grown even wilder, and naturally the storm had set the dogs to braying. But when he opened the door to the kennels, he claims he found the body of his mistress on the floor, her brains blown away by a shotgun blast. The animals were all incensed, and he ran back to the house. A doctor was summoned, but of course he was far too late to be of any assistance. The poor lady had surely died instantly."

"So who have you arrested?"

"The kennel master."

Holmes scowled. "And why?"

"Well, there were no tracks except those of Jenkins and Mr. Barton, despite the ground being a veritable soup. The lady was slain with one of the shotguns from a rack inside the kennels – it was found dropped not five paces from her corpse. The doctor's best estimate for the time of her death was between eight and ten – and he favored the later time, just before she was found, which would rule out Mr. Barton. Plus, there was no reason for Barton to slay his wife, while Jenkins is the uncle of Miss Lizzie Wyatt. This relationship must have been unknown to the Bartons, but several of the man's friends have since told me that he was fond of the girl and had vowed to avenge her. Still . . . ."

"Something doesn't make sense. A piece does not properly fit in the puzzle."

The inspector nodded. "Maybe it is just a hunch. I have seen the body, and the kennels. I have spoken with everyone concerned, and yet . . . I am not satisfied. I feel the true solution dangling, just out of reach."

"Then we shall see if we can help you to snare it," Holmes replied. "I believe the next stop is your village."

"Yes. You'll wish to speak with Jenkins, I'm sure. And the lady's body is at the local undertakers'."

At Holmes's request, we stopped first at the mortuary, where it was clear that no amount of funerary art could repair the horrific damage. Mrs. Barton had clearly been a tall woman, with long hands and a beautiful figure, but the shot had obliterated her skull, and so horrifically distorted her face that the casket would, of course, remain closed throughout her burial service.

"The shot came from behind?" Holmes asked, as he gently laid a silk cloth back across her features.

"Yes."

"Describe where the body was positioned."

"The kennels were once the stables. The old horse stalls have been converted into pens. She was stretched out toward the enclosure of her favorite animal, a magnificent dog named King. Her right hand seemed to be reaching toward him."

Holmes nodded and signaled that he was ready to meet with the prisoner. When we arrived at the gaol, we saw that Jenkins was a small man, with a twisted spine, knobby much-scarred hands, and bloodshot eyes. His wild beard and unkempt hair gave him the look of a tramp, but he nodded with dignity as Inspector Holly explained the reason for our visit.

"You are under no obligation to speak with these gentlemen, of course," Holly reminded him.

"That may be true, sir, but if this famous detective might in any way help me, why should I hesitate? I swear upon my life, and on my mother's soul, that I would never hurt dear Mrs. Barton. You cannot imagine how it feels, to be locked away in this cold and dark cell, knowing that I only discovered the tragedy. I will see her poor dead body until the end of my days."

"But you made threats against the family," Holmes said sternly, "for the death of your niece."

"Aye, I will not deny it. I was drunk, and stupid, and blind with grief, for I had known sweet little Lizzie since her birth, and I loved her as if she were my own daughter! In the days after she died, and when the judge refused to hold the young man accountable, I confess I contemplated revenge. But I quickly realized that there was no good in carrying hatred in my heart. It is for God to judge Andrew Barton, not me. I never mentioned my sharp and ill-considered words to my employers, though somehow they must have learned of them. One day, just a month after poor Lizzie's funeral, Mrs. Barton came to me and begged me, upon her knees, to forgive her for having failed to raise a better son. What could I say to that? We wept together, she and I, and I promised to always be a good servant to her."

140

"And Mr. Barton? Was he also as forgiving?"

"He was a man of few words, sir. He said nothing to me of it, and so I let matters lie."

Holmes asked him to recount the evening of the tragedy. Jenkins settled onto his bunk, rubbing his rough hands together as he spoke.

"I had seen to the dogs, fed them and got them all bedded down. But it was a wild night, and I knew the animals wouldn't rest easy. They are sensitive. The lightning and the rain causes them to howl and be restless. Still, I did my best, then took a lantern and walked back to the house."

"You spoke with both Bartons when you returned to the lodge?"

"I did. They were finishing supper."

"Did you mention that the arrival of puppies was eminent?"

The man blinked. "You mean Duchess? Oh, she's far gone, should whelp next week, and this is only her second litter. She lost the first pups, so we were worried about her. But no, I don't believe I mentioned anything special about Duchess that night . . . at least not that I can recall."

"And when you went down to the kennels after the butler dispatched you – ?"

Jenkins scrubbed one hand on his face and tugged roughly at his beard. "I fear I spoke sharply to Cutter, and he was just doing as Mr. Barton had told him, but my rheumatism had been giving me the devil, and I had just dropped off to sleep when he shook me back awake. I may have said something . . . unkind to him, or of the master."

Holmes fought back a little smile. "No one shall judge you for that. Just tell us of how it was when you returned to the kennels."

"Sir, I – I knew something was wrong. Don't ask me how, I just felt it in my bones. The dogs were barking something terrible, even worse than they normally do in a storm. I stopped with my hand upon the door, and for a moment I hesitated. I nearly went back to the house, to demand that someone come with me. Then I thought about poor Mrs. Barton, alone in that place, and I pushed open the door. And there she was."

Holmes had settled on the narrow cot beside the prisoner. He held out one hand, almost like a mesmerist.

"Mr. Jenkins, clearly you have been the kennel master with the Bartons for some time."

"Almost ten years," he answered, with a touch of pride.

"Then the inside of the kennels is a familiar place to you. I wish you to close your eyes, place yourself back inside at the moment of your horrific discovery. Besides the tragedy, what was different? Was anything out of place?"

"The shotgun was on the floor. It had been taken down from the rack, to do the horrible thing." The man swallowed tightly. "It was Mrs.

Barton's own gun. She went on a trip to America, back when Andrew was just a lad, and did some hunting, somewhere in that place they call Wyoming. It was a souvenir of that trip."

I glanced toward the inspector, who was furiously scribbling notes. This was clearly new information.

"What else?"

"The dogs were all wild, of course. They knew what had happened. They had smelled the blood. King was there, and I was startled to see him . . . ."

"What do you mean?" I asked.

"Why, sir, King was her favorite. He was her guardian and protector. She rarely went anywhere without him by her side. Unlike the others, he slept in the house, at the foot of her bed. There was a stall for him, of course – the nicest in the kennels, as befitted his status, I reckon. But it was rare for him to be put there and . . . ." The man sobbed. "He was chained."

"Chained within his enclosure?" Holmes asked.

"Yes. This was rarely necessary, but King was the biggest and by far the cleverest of the dogs. The gates are high, but if King wished to get out, he could manage. I've seen him stretch his long legs, dig in his nails, and scale the walls like a cat, then fly across the bars! That's why there was a chain, but Mrs. Barton rarely used it. She loved that dog, and couldn't bear to see him restrained, as long as he was behaving himself."

Holmes nodded, as if some private theory had been confirmed. "Anything else?"

"Just one, sir, though I doubt it is worth mentioning: There was a dead rabbit on a shelf."

We all stared at him. Jenkins shrugged.

"I couldn't tell you how it got there. Sometimes the dogs will yap at rabbits, but a wolfhound isn't a spaniel or a terrier, and it is rare for them to go after such meager prey."

Holmes thanked Jenkins and assured him his case wasn't hopeless, for which the poor fellow rung my friend's hand and offered him a thousand blessings. As we emerged from the cell and took our places in a landau to ride out to the hunting lodge, Inspector Holly's face was red with embarrassment.

"I cannot believe that I didn't notice the rabbit. Nor did Jenkins call it to my attention!"

"It may mean nothing, and yet . . . You have spoken with the lad who drove Mr. Barton home after he did his marketing. Did the boy say what the gentleman purchased?"

"No. He merely assumed, based on the wrappings, that it was items for his dinner." The inspector frowned. "You think it is significant?"

"I think it is potentially instructive. But for now, let us simply enjoy the drive."

We reached the hunting lodge in the afternoon, just as the winter sun was beginning to lose its battle against darkness. Holmes asked that we be taken immediately to the kennels, so that he could walk through them before his interview with Mr. Barton.

The building was large and spacious, a converted stable with gated stalls and plenty of room for the dozen animals who lounged about in pairs and trios. Morris pointed out where the body and the gun had been found. I paused to admire the substantial rack of weaponry just opposite of the pens, which held shotguns and rifles of various calibers. Holmes gestured toward the largest enclosure, where a bronze plaque spelled out *King*.

"I do hope His Majesty hasn't been assassinated."

"I fear it is possible his master did away with him for safety's sake. The dog was quite ferocious that evening, worked up into a frothing frenzy by the lady's blood. We will have to make inquiries." Holly shook his head. "But it will be a pity if Barton has killed him. King was a magnificent creature."

"Indeed. Ah, and here is the unnoticed corpse. I suppose Mr. Barton has had enough on his plate without adding the chore of cleaning up his kennels. At least the poor dogs appear to have been fed."

Holmes removed the dead rabbit from the shelf and subjected it to scrutiny with his lens, much to Inspector Holly's disgust.

"What on earth can that dead thing reveal to you?"

"Everything I need to know. Come, let us visit the widower."

Mr. Henry Barton was a man of slender physique and medium height, with dark hair heavily slicked back and a look of perpetual persecution about his features. He brushed aside our condolences with a weary wave, led us into his study, and offered us whisky. Neither Holmes, the inspector, nor I partook, but Barton poured himself a liberal amount from a decanter that rested inside a half-globe.

"I am surprised that you are not at home in the village," Holly said. "Surely it would be more convenient for you?"

Barton shook his head briskly. "No, I would rather remain here to mourn my beloved Diane privately. The funeral will be tomorrow, of course, but I plan to return here immediately afterward." He gave a heavy sigh, wiping his hand absently across his thin lips. I noticed that his shaky grasp on his libation had already caused him to spill some of it onto his shirt. "Perhaps it is difficult to understand, but I simply cannot bear either of the looks I know that people will give me."

"Either?" Holmes asked.

"Yes . . . the look of sadness, or the look that implies justice was somehow done. I fear behind every comforting smile lurks a smirk of cruelty. So many people hated us – blamed us for what Andrew did – and for the tragic loss of that poor girl. To be very frank with you gentlemen, I am no longer convinced that Jenkins is our only villain."

Holmes was slowly walking around the room, admiring the many trophies, ribbons, and photographs of Mrs. Barton with her dogs. "Oh? And what has changed your mind?"

"A hunch. A premonition. It is well for you as a professional detective to dismiss such things, but I believe in them, as did my wife."

"She foresaw her murder?"

"The more I brood upon the thing, I believe she did. Diane was a strong-willed woman, fearless in the saddle, competent in the show ring, unconventional in many ways, but she also had a woman's heart, with all its terrors. She told me, on the very night she died, that she knew Andrew's sin would come back to haunt us. It was why she rarely went into town, and why she had stopped attending church. She couldn't tolerate the sensation that people were plotting her death, even as they sat in the pews behind her."

"Yet she was willing to go to the kennels in the midst of a howling storm, and to remain there alone."

Barton harrumphed. "Have you ever known a consistent woman, sir? It isn't in their nature. And besides, she cherished the delusion that here, at the lodge, so far removed from the village, we were safe."

"Tell me why she insisted on going out at that hour."

"Why, Jenkins had mentioned that one of the girls – Duchess, I believe – was about to have her puppies. Diane was quite assertive that, if possible, she should be there when the litter was delivered."

"Wouldn't it have made more sense to have taken Jenkins with her? Forgive me, Mr. Barton, but you aren't overly fond of dogs."

The man looked stunned. His face turned white. "How on earth could you know such a thing? I have never said to you – "

"You didn't have to. Your housekeeper's testimony made it clear." Holmes offered a charming, reassuring smile as he gestured towards the array of awards. "And it requires no great deduction to see that you are in none of these photographs. Of course, there is no crime in disliking dogs."

Barton burst into a high-pitched laugh. "Well, you have hit upon a truth, sir. I was badly bitten on the hand by a bull terrier as a lad – See, here are the scars! – and thus I cannot abide the filthy creatures. I could have sent Jenkins back out, but he needed his dinner and to warm up, so I assumed my company would be equally welcome. I promise you, if we had arrived to find the dog in labor, I would have run back to fetch Jenkins, *post haste*."

"Clearly, there were no puppies that night. But what, pray tell, did King do to so offend his mistress that she restrained him?"

Barton twisted in his chair, settling his arms like a man getting comfortable for a night of winter storytelling.

"He was a very bad dog! Diane went into Duchess's enclosure, and I took King outside – Inspector Holly has probably told you that King was my late wife's great pet, an almost nine-stone baby that she insisted share our domicile instead of residing full time where he belonged, in that cage. Anyway, he darted off in the rain, and when he returned, he had a rabbit in his massive jaws. I was able to tear the poor thing away, at substantial risk to my fingers I might add, but it was already dead. I took it inside and showed it to Diane. She was upset by this brutal murder, and she disciplined King by chaining him inside his enclosure. A night of missing the warmth of our bedroom fireplace would, she hoped, teach him some manners. I tossed the hare's carcass upon a shelf and, when Diane wasn't inclined to leave Duchess's side, I came back to the house. It had been an exhausting week in London, and I was nodding over my brandy within moments."

Holmes had listened to this saga without commentary. Now he held up a hand.

"What did you buy at the market on Friday afternoon?"

"A cut of pork and some potatoes . . . but I hardly see what that has to do with my wife's murder."

"You might be surprised, Mr. Barton, at how the mundane often leads to the fantastical. I have but one more question for you: Since your wife's murder, what has happened to King?"

Barton's face turned red. "I am ashamed to admit it, Mr. Holmes, but I nearly executed him. After all, he had failed in his duty, to protect his mistress with his life. Yesterday I stood in front of his enclosure with my pistol in my hand, but I could feel my wife's spirit nearby, begging me to spare the poor fellow. He couldn't escape being chained, and she was the one who had locked him away for his misdeeds. I summoned my neighbor, Mr. Curtis, who has always admired my wife's animals, and made a gift of King. The old gentleman was truly grateful."

"As am I," Holmes said.

Holmes's behavior for the next two hours seemed nothing short of bizarre. After making inquiries as to when the funeral for Mrs. Barton would be conducted, and dispatching a half-dozen telegrams, Holmes informed Inspector Holly, before we left his company, that we would spend the evening in the village. I was annoyed, as I hadn't so much as a toothbrush with me, but as always, my army training saw me through yet another unexpected campaign. We found rooms in the local inn, and – just as I was about to suggest we adjourn to the pub for a pint – Holmes stepped out, hired a rig, and instructed the lad to drive us to the home of Mr. Curtis.

"Holmes, perhaps you can exist on nothing more nourishing than air and cigarettes, but I will require sustenance!"

"Which we will receive unless I miss my mark badly," Holmes said with a wink. "While you were in the washroom, I quizzed the innkeeper as to the nature of Mr. Curtis, and learned that he is lonesome widower who enjoys nothing so much as good libations and convivial company."

"It is rather late to call."

"Country folks aren't such sticklers for city etiquette. Still, you must be on your best behavior, my dear Watson, and be prepared to be charming! I shall count on you to edify the gentleman with detailed reminiscences of our great adventures."

I folded my arms and pretended offense. "And why is that?"

"Because I need his dog."

The innkeeper's assessment of Mr. Curtis's personality hardly conveyed the man himself. He appeared to have stepped directly from the pages of one of Mr. Dickens's novels, complete with a crown of wiry white hair, a stubby nose, and glowing cheeks. He was clad in the fashion of almost fifty years past, complete with silk stockings and down-at-the-heel slippers, as well as a Turkish-style dressing gown that flapped about him like red satin wings with every dramatic gesticulation. He had, of course, read several of my stories and was thrilled to meet my friend. Luckily for us, along with his great enthusiasm for our cases, Curtis was also blessed with an excellent cook and an even finer wine cellar. We spent a long evening in his company, regaling him with tales of adventures and chases and nearly fatal encounters with desperate villains. A few of the stories were even true, though some of the tales that Holmes spun were so fantastical I wondered if he had consulted with both the American author, Edgar Allan Poe, and the Frenchman, Jules Verne.

As a result, the next morning found me rather bleary-eyed, with an aching head, drinking my third cup of strong coffee and nibbling gently on a stale muffin in the inn-keeper's parlor. Holmes, as always, seemed not to suffer for his offenses. In fact, he had already run out to the telegraph office, read several newspapers, and passed the most outrageous

146

compliments to the landlord on a room that I was convinced had been infected with bedbugs.

"At least you got the dog," I said, staring down at the massive animal which was sleeping beside us on the rug. He was clearly an elder of his species, his muzzle nearly white while the rest of his fur was a mixture of black and grey. He had seemed rather indifferent to our host, and to us as well, though his tail began happily thumping on the floorboards when Holmes offered him one of the antiquated pastries. "What in Heaven's name will Mrs. Hudson say when we arrive with him?"

"She will say nothing, for he will remain here with Mr. Curtis, who I believe will be a kind and gentle master to him in his declining years. But he does have one task to perform – one final duty to discharge."

I winced. Holmes's voice was rather loud. "And what is that?"

Holmes checked his watch. "It is time. Come, Watson – let us test a theory."

Much to my chagrin, Holmes gathered up the dog's leash and led us out into the oddly bright sun and brisk winter wind. We strolled down the High Street and turned a corner.

"I see the lady's body will be making its way to the church very soon," Holmes said.

An elegant hearse, drawn by two shiny black horses, stood outside the mortuary establishment. A small crowd of loiterers had gathered, the black coats of several men announcing their intention to attend the funeral and burial. A knot of veiled and crepe-clad women waited as well, huddled together, weeping quietly into their handkerchiefs. Holmes led us across the street and mounted the two steps of the opposite building, so that we would have a view of the cortege's departure.

We had barely taken our place when the pallbearers emerged from the doorway, bearing the mahogany coffin. They moved in a steady, stately tread to the back of the hearse and slid the ornate casket inside. At just that moment, Mr. Barton, clad in the finest black mourning clothes, with a high hat wrapped in a long weeper, stepped through the doorway. He turned briefly to shake hands with the sad-faced undertaker, then started down to the cobblestones.

I was aware of a sudden, low growl. King's fangs were bared. His fur was standing on end.

"Holmes, perhaps we should – "

Before I could finish the thought, King bolted. The loop of his leash slipped from Holmes's grip, which was fortunate, for as strong as my friend was, I doubt his willow-like frame would have stood fast against the dog's impulsive, violent charge. King bayed like a demon and bounded across the street in two great leaps. The ladies shrieked. The men in the crowd either flew to place themselves between the beast and the members of the fair sex, or shamefully took to their heels.

But King had eyes – and teeth and claws – for only one victim.

The undertaker had, out of instinct, drawn inside and slammed the door. This left Barton pinned, and in an instant the dog was upon him. Fortunately, the man threw up his arms, and the wolfhound latched to his wrist instead of his throat. Holmes was immediately in pursuit and, much to my surprise, Inspector Holly also came flying from the doorway of an adjacent shop. Together, the two strong men seized upon the dog and pulled him off Barton.

"Watson, your assistance may be necessary," Holmes called, and I realized that it had all happened so quickly I had never moved from my post. I hurried over, my bag in my hand. Barton's arm was clearly lacerated, but it seemed minor in comparison to his shock. His face was white, his eyes wide, his entire body was trembling, almost convulsing in his pitiful terror.

"My God! My God – forgive me. Forgive me! Diane, I . . . *I killed her*! I confess – Only forgive me! Save me from the dog! Save me!"

Holmes looked down at the thrashing animal, then to his professional colleague. "Dogs do not make mistakes. Inspector, I suggest we remove Mr. Barton and allow his late wife to be decently laid to rest in peace and, I trust, in justice."

"He will protest," Holly said to us, an hour later as we sat inside the inspector's neat little office. The prisoner was now installed in a locked, windowless room, and liberally sedated after stitches had been necessary to close the wounds along his arms. "He will claim the dog was set upon him. When you sent me that note and said you would allow the dog to view Barton, I hardly thought – "

"If Barton revokes his confession, you may present him with these." Holmes opened his coat and removed a sheet of paper along with several telegrams. "When you arrived at my doorstep on Baker Street and told me of Mrs. Barton's murder, it raised a memory of another, earlier investigation into some nefarious doings in the business sector of London. While my prey was a different gentleman, one who had defrauded numerous clients via an insurance bubble, the name 'Henry Barton' had surfaced on several occasions. I believe the man's finances are completely depleted, and his world was shortly about to crash down about his ears. Your revelation that both the village home and the hunting lodge were his wife's properties made it clear: With his spouse in the grave, Barton could liquidate the homes and depart – perhaps to South Africa to join his son." Holmes tapped sharply on the papers. "These are the notes I made upon

Barton's involvement in the improper affairs of one of his business partners, and the telegrams are replies from other specialists I have consulted, including some who specialize in financial investigations. They may be rather persuasive in encouraging Barton to throw himself upon the Queen's mercy, as they speak directly to his motive in doing away with his wife."

"And if he is unmoved?"

"Then I would suggest that you present the evidence of the dead rabbit. Barton claimed that he took the beast from King's jaws on that fatal night. Indeed, it served as an explanation as to why the dog – who certainly otherwise would either have protected or immediately avenged his mistress – was unable to act. Barton told us that his wife willingly chained the dog up at the evidence of its misdeed in killing the little animal. However, I subjected the rabbit's corpse to a close inspection with my lens. There are no teeth marks upon it. This wasn't a resident rabbit, which fell afoul of an over-excited dog, but a rabbit bred for the slaughter and purchased in the village, along with the other 'items for dinner'. Do speak with the man or woman who sells hares at your local market, and you will learn the truth."

Holly rubbed his chin. "He needed the dog chained, but only she could do it."

"Precisely. Dogs are extremely intelligent animals, and fiercely loyal to those who love and care for them. Barton despises dogs. I'm certain that King here felt, even if he couldn't logically understand, Barton's contempt. Barton had to trick his wife into restraining the animal, for otherwise it would have escaped the pen and killed him, just as it would have done in the street, had we not readily come to Barton's rescue. Jenkins told us that King could, with enough motivation, clear the gate of his pen. The murder of the woman who had raised and cherished him since a pup would have been just such motivation – and Barton knew it."

"He also knew about the threat that Jenkins made."

"And was willing to use it to shift any hint of blame from himself. That is textbook enough . . . yet I find Mr. Barton to be a very curious kind of killer."

"What do you mean?" Holly asked.

Holmes leaned back in his seat and gave the dog, who had been glaring at the closed doorway, occasionally emitting a low, rumbling growl, a calming pat to his head.

"In some ways, Barton is cold and calculating. He had no difficulty in dispatching his wife – a woman he wasn't known to quarrel with – in a brutal manner. The deed was clearly not an act committed in a moment or rage or passion. The purchase of the dead rabbit speaks to the cunning, the

149

premeditation of the thing." Here, Holmes allowed the aged wolfhound to lift itself up and place its gigantic head across his lap. "And yet, when given the opportunity to slay the one witness to the deed, a creature he clearly detested, and whom he could have dispatched without anyone questioning him, he stayed his hand. He didn't hesitate to shoot his wife, but in the end, he could not kill her dog. Perhaps his conscience was simply pricked too deeply. A very strange man, and an even more bizarre murderer."

We returned to London via the mid-afternoon train, our last sight of the village being Inspector Holly, Mr. Curtis, and the liberated Jenkins waving goodbye to us from the station platform. King sat obediently at his new master's feet.

We sped along for half-an-hour before I gathered up the courage to speak my mind.

"Holmes."

He had pulled his flap-eared travelling cap down over his eyes. Now, he lifted it.

"Yes, Watson?"

"You set the dog upon him."

"I did no such thing. That would have implied a *command*. I merely didn't hold the leash as tightly as I should."

"But still – had you not been so fast, and Holly so strong – Barton could have been killed."

My friend favored me with an unwavering gaze. "That is true."

"Holmes!" I protested. "At times, you take great liberties with the law, and with justice!"

Sherlock Holmes sat up straighter in his seat and removed his hat. At that instant, he seemed to age a dozen years, and I recognized that far more thought, and emotion, stirred inside him than I often realized. I had viewed him as almost mechanical in his resolve. But now, in that one second, I saw how difficult and weighed his decisions had been. He spoke calmly, but his eyes blazed.

"Guilty as charged, Watson. But the evidence of Barton's perfidy was clear, and an innocent man was imprisoned, with the noose dangling before him. I had a sense that Barton was unravelling – did you not notice how his hands shook with his liquor, and how the tone of his voice flitted back and forth while he spoke with us? The octave of a man's laugh can give him away, and Barton's skittered along the scale. I knew that one simple move, daring and dangerous, would end the game and probably bring about a confession even before the lady was placed in her grave. It was indeed a gamble, but the odds were in my favor.

150

"And I couldn't banish from my mind the image of that beautiful, noble woman, lured down to the kennels and betrayed in the most intimate and savage manner. Note that Barton lied to us about Jenkin's words on the impending motherhood of Duchess – Jenkins stated that he never mentioned the impending birth of the pups during his report to the Bartons at dinner. Barton must have concocted some other means of getting his lady to the kennels on that wild night, so he could murder her with a shotgun blast. In the last instant of her life, she saw her husband take down the weapon, and in a moment of unbearable horror, she knew his intention. She spun and ran for her only protector, who she had just been deceived into restraining. Her last act of life was to reach for her beloved dog.

"It seemed only fair to let him avenge her."

The Texas Legation Business
by David Marcum

Chapter I

"It is," said Mycroft Holmes with a frown, "something of a pesterment."

"I didn't suppose," countered his brother, Sherlock, "that you invited us to catch up on the latest gossip from Baker Street, or to ask Watson his opinion about the Merseyside Derby."

Our conversation was interrupted by a soft knock at the door, followed by the entrance of one of the silent servants who roamed the halls of the Diogenes Club, slipping in and bearing a tray with tea and various comestibles that had been excellently prepared in the basement kitchen. Sherlock Holmes didn't appear interested, but due to an unexpected medical call I had missed my lunch, and was glad for the opportunity. It had been a number of years since I was in the Army, but I hadn't forgotten the basic maxim to eat when given the opportunity, as one never knew what might happen to prevent the next meal. Having known Sherlock Holmes for nearly as long as I'd been away from the military, I'd found this lesson to still be especially relevant.

Holmes took out his pipe, stating, "You needn't worry, Mycroft. The plans for the *Canopus* have been secured. Carpenter is buttoned up from every direction, and his meeting with Carrington on Sunday is a *fait accompli.*"

Mycroft held up a hand. "You make assumptions without facts, Sherlock. You should know better than that. I didn't call you here for an update on the missing clerk. Colonel Boothroyd has kept me informed of your progress. It has been satisfactory." His lips pursed. "No, there is another more-recent matter to which I'd like you to attend – and you, too, Doctor, if you don't mind."

I nodded my tentative willingness. I owed payment for the quantity of debt I was contracting, based on the amount of magnificent smoked salmon that I was greedily consuming.

"What," asked Mycroft, pinching the bridge of his nose, "do either of you know about the Texas Legation?"

I glanced toward Holmes, who for once didn't give any indication that he had some knowledge of the topic. I wiped my lips and cleared my throat. "I've heard of it," I said, almost timidly, as if I was an uncertain boy offering an answer in the classroom. "It was located somewhere near here, in the 1840's, before – " I did a quick calculation. Yes, I believed it was even before Mycroft was born in 1847. " – before any of us were born."

"That is correct," said Mycroft, nodding. "It was in Pickering Place, just around the corner in St. James's Street, from 1842 to 1845. Texas was still an independent nation then, and had similar legations in Paris and Washington, D.C."

Holmes was looking at me curiously.

"When I was recovering at Peshawar," I explained, "I got to know a fellow named Jefferson Brody. His mother was from Cornwall. She had moved to London in the early 1840's, and not long after met and married one of the Texans who was associated with the Legation. After the Legation closed and the other Texans returned to America, Brody's father remained here. Brody told me a little bit about it. I believe," I added, asking Mycroft to confirm, "that they established their little embassy in the years following their independence from Mexico, before obtaining American statehood. As I recall, it was set in place in order for them to have leverage as a way to negotiate favorably as an independent nation."

"Rather," explained Mycroft, "it was more of a ploy to maneuver for better terms when they finally became an American state. After they won their independence from Mexico in 1836 and formed a Republic, there was a great internal divide of opinion about whether to remain a separate country or immediately request American statehood. However, it didn't matter, as the United States wasn't immediately willing to accept Texas into the fold, as they would have entered as a slave-holding state, which upset the abolitionist-minded northern states, while also disrupting the delicate voting balance of free and slave states within the Congress.

"The Texas president, a fellow named Houston, argued for statehood, but he was also uncertain as to whether it would ever happen, so he initiated discussions with England regarding our support – financial and otherwise – should the new nation remain its own country. Britain very much wanted Texas to remain an independent country, and we offered to support them militarily by helping to defend their borders with Mexico *and* the United States. But it turned out that the Texans' overtures to Britain were less-than-sincere, and were instead used as a stick to goad the United States government into finally admitting them, rather than allow a further British influence to be established in their hemisphere – and in fact right at their back door. They didn't wish to be bracketed between British Texas and Canada – especially with their expansion to the Pacific already becoming a popular idea.

"With the election of James K. Polk as President in 1845, the path was finally clear for Texas to join the Union. Polk and Houston were both from Tennessee, and had served in the Congress together representing that state in the 1820's – even sharing lodgings when they resided in Washington. Based on their arrangements, the Texans agreed to annexation in June of '45, and statehood was accomplished in December. Of course, this immediately set the country on a course toward war with Mexico the following year – the same war that became a training ground for all of the future American generals – Unionists and traitors – who served on each side of their Civil War."

Sherlock Holmes wasn't restless yet, but I knew – as his brother certainly did – that he wasn't concerned with the events of half-a-century earlier without knowing why they related to our summons to the Diogenes Club.

"Enough with the history lesson," he said. "What has happened *now*?"

"Indeed," agreed Mycroft. "But you know as well as I how history is always relevant. Here, then, is what has happened *now*: Late this morning, work was being done at the building which once housed the Legation. As I mentioned, it's within Pickering Place, a small square, but the address is No. 4, St. James's Street. There have been any number of residents – both business and domestic – within the location since the Legation departed in 1845. Workmen were pulling off the old wainscoting and found a small wall safe, about one cubic foot in volume, covered over and hidden. The safe's door was decorated with a flamboyant enameled painting of an American steamboat, and wording identifying the manufacturer as the '*Texas Lock and Vault Corporation*'. The workmen alerted their supervisor, Bessemer, who in turn notified the lease-holder of the building, one Amos Berry, whose father-in-law, Clive Loughborough, is the estate agent for Claude Jermyn. Loughborough then informed Jermyn – who was just up the street at Boodles.

"Jermyn walked down and was on site when the safe was broken open to reveal several bundles of Republic of Texas currency – a few thousand of their old money in packets of three, five, and fifty dollar bills – and a most-curious document. Jermyn, who as you know did a favor for us in '90 when his son's body was found in the wall of the Battersea Bridge, thought that the document might be something of interest to the Government. However, while walking around here to put it into my hands, he was followed and accosted in the street by one of the laborers who had been working on the building's renovation. The worker pushed Jermyn down and pulled the document from out of his coat pocket before the older man could defend himself. Passersby did nothing to help – apparently it happened too quickly – and the thief then dashed east toward Waterloo Place, where he vanished."

154

"Was Jermyn injured?" I asked. I recalled the man from when we'd initially encountered him, a little over four years earlier. He was a small fellow, in his mid-fifties, and very earnest and serious. From meeting with him then, one had the impression that he had no sense of humor at all. That was, however, possibly an unfair assessment, as we'd only had dealings with him in connection with the brutal murder of his son, and the revelation that it had been committed by his favored daughter.

"Not at all," replied Mycroft. "He was quite angry, actually, both at the assault and the perceived betrayal by one of his employees, and also the fact that he couldn't persuade anyone walking along the pavement to assist him. He gave chase, but it was futile."

Holmes then asked the obvious question. "And what was this document that generated such an unplanned and violent assault?"

Mycroft's quiet answer seemed to explode into the room: "For one-million pounds, to be paid to the government for the citizens living there at the time, Great Britain purchased The Republic of Texas."

We were quite silent for a moment as we examined that idea in our heads. Mycroft looked from one to the other of us as we pondered the implications, patiently sipping his port. Finally I was the first to speak.

"But surely that is impossible. It's been fifty years – and so much water under the bridge. Texas is no longer an independent country. The United States had their Civil War to preserve the Union. The idea that we could now show a document proving that one of their states was never legitimately a part of their country to begin with . . . ." I shifted my gaze back from the distant view I'd been imagining. "It *is* impossible, isn't it?"

Mycroft nodded. "Yes, Doctor, it is indeed impossible."

"I take it," interrupted Holmes, "that no record of payment has been discovered that would have solemnified the arrangement."

"That is correct. But that isn't the problem. The idea of pursuing such an agreement at this point in time is ludicrous. There is no legal enforceability. And in any case, the global disruptions that it would cause – even I find it difficult to see how such events would progress. The United States would not take it well, to say the least, if such a thing were to go forward. I'm certain that the Texans, despite being on the losing and traitorous side of the Civil War, would not react well to suddenly being told that they were now British citizens – and a million pounds wouldn't go nearly as far in the present day when spread among the current population, should payment be made. Mexico would certainly have something to say about it, and suddenly Canada would be at risk if the United States decided to reciprocate and annex parts of that country, based on old ties, treaties, claims, territory gained in battles, and varying and contested borderlines."

155

"Then I don't understand the difficulty," I said. "This is nothing more than a curious historical anomaly."

"I suspect," said Holmes, "that the issue isn't enforceability, but how such a document might be used to further some other agenda – either as a distraction, or perhaps to pour fuel on another fire that's already burning."

"Both," said Mycroft. "Our relations with the United States are generally cordial, but you may not realize that there is nevertheless some tension. After their Civil War, they rebounded into a great deal of wealth and influence – and with that has come a certain level of jealousy regarding our mastery of the seas. Oh, not to the level that the Germans have carried it. As you know, surpassing us in that sphere has become a rather dangerous *idée fixe* in the Kaiser's head. The Americans haven't carried things to that degree – but it is on their minds."

He shifted in his chair "I doubt if either of you are aware of the publication in America of *Influence of Sea Power Upon History*." He looked from one to the other of us, and we both shook our heads.

"It was written 1890 by Alfred Thayer Mahan. It came about this way: Ten years or so ago, he was appointed a lecturer in naval history and tactics at the American's Naval War College. While there, he developed a series of lectures regarding the importance of powerful navies in world affairs – leading directly to the subject of his book. Around that same time, he was tasked with devising a war plan to match his strategic outline, and he determined that the American fleet was too weak and limited to be effective in a real war. Their navy had very few vessels that would be of any use at all. In order to demonstrate this, he devised a theoretical war between Britain and the United States – and he showed that we would win under current conditions, and what they would need to do to prevent that outcome.

"It was Mahan's belief that their insufficient navy wouldn't be able to cross the sea and attack us here at all, and that all of the battles would be fought alongside the American coast. We would be unable to land our forces, but instead we could bomb the harbors and shoreline, and blockade their ports – and particularly their economic centers.

"Mahan proposed that the American response would then be to overrun Nova Scotia by land and occupy our coalfield there – our only one on the Atlantic coast – thus denying a way to refuel our warships. He further advocated for a massive buildup of American naval ships – particularly battleships and torpedo vessels.

"Of course, this was all theoretical to some extent. Every nation has such contingency plans, but it's no surprise that Mahan's study received a good bit of attention, and in the four years since the book was published, their navy has since begun to modernize and expand in earnest. Not initially seeing it as a matter of security, Mahan freely shared his lectures with a good many other academics – including our own John Knox Laughton at King's College. Laughton in turn made our Government aware of the situation, and we've kept our eye on it ever since."

"And some in our Government," extrapolated Holmes, "see this as a legitimate threat – or at least they plan to present it that way as an excuse to escalate the situation into something more hostile."

"Indeed – or at least as something that they can use as a distraction while they further their own ambitions in the shadows. If the Texas document were to become public just now, on top of this recent American tension, it could be used to fan their flames."

"You wish us to retrieve the document," said Holmes. "It seems to me that you have a hundred foot-soldiers at your disposal already. Why us?"

"Because you are discreet, and so far this situation is known to just a very few. I have agents that I could redirect along these lines, but they are blunt instruments, and every one that learns the secret exponentially increases the risk of its being accidentally shared in the wrong place."

"Are you certain that the document is legitimate?" I asked. "Did Claude Jermyn have the chance to thoroughly examine it before it was stolen?"

Mycroft nodded. "Direct evidence is always best." He leaned toward the small table to his right and pressed a button, which I knew connected with a small and very discreet bell somewhere deeper in the building. In a moment, the door opened to reveal one of the Club's servants, a fellow named Jernigan. "Please bring Mr. Jermyn now," Mycroft instructed.

We hadn't seen Claude Jermyn since early July 1890, just before the opening of the Battersea Bridge. He had been on the Board of Directors for the Mowlem Company charged with constructing the bridge, and had been unaware – as was proven later at the trial – of his childrens' financial chicanery. The resulting murder of his son, and the bizarre way in which it was hidden in the final construction of the bridgeworks by Jermyn's daughter, would have been enough to break most men, but he was made of sterner stuff than that. Still, four years had aged him terribly. He had already been a fellow of small stature, but he'd since lost a great deal of weight, and his hair had thinned to a few wispy whitish fluffs.

The reserved and polite way in which he greeted us showed that we would always be associated in his mind with the great tragedy of his life, but he was still courteous as he took a seat and accepted a brandy from the servant. When the latter had departed, he began to speak.

"I knew as soon as I saw that document that it might be important. I said so to Loughborough, and this laborer must have overheard me. I learned later that the fellow had only worked there for a week – hired for the lifting and carrying. The last tenant was some sort of Italian hair stylist, and he did things with steam and oils that nearly ruined the walls. We have to get it repaired before the rooms can be re-rented. I generally let Loughborough take care of all that, but when the safe was found, he knew that it was beyond him."

Holmes leaned forward. "What can you tell us of the worker who assaulted you and stole the document?"

Jermyn shifted to face Holmes and pulled a sheet of paper from within his coat. "I understand from Mycroft that the less this is stirred up, the better. Here is the man's name – Stephen Newbold." He handed Holmes the sheet. "You can see that his address is in Limehouse."

"Hmm," responded Holmes, folding the sheet and putting it into his pocket. "Probably false, but we'll see."

"From what I could learn about him by asking questions of the other workers when I returned to the building," Jermyn continued, "he's something of a quiet one – didn't mix with the others very much, and I doubt that he would have lasted another week, even if he hadn't assaulted me or stolen the document. Clearly he had the idea he could get something for it."

"Describe him."

Jermyn closed his eyes, and after a moment he said, "He is his early forties, I suppose. Tall with broad shoulders, and oddly long arms with big hands. For his height, he has a longish torso with short legs, and blonde hair sitting on a rather flat head. Additionally, he had a reddish scar horizontally across his left cheek – it's quite curious, dropping from his left eye, and then making a sharp turn across his cheek toward his ear. I'm told that he'd said it was a badly healed wound received in a knife fight when he was young."

Holmes nodded. "For the short time you saw him, you have recalled a great deal."

Jermyn grimaced. "After . . . after the events of four years ago, when your observations and methods were so . . . so useful, I was impressed. I've since made an effort to notice more – details of my surroundings, and the people I encounter. Practice has only made it more effective."

"You have learned a lesson then that many will not undertake," Holmes replied. I was grateful that he had the courtesy not to pointedly look in my direction for emphasis.

"Do you think you can find the man?" asked Jermyn. "Track him down?"

"Your description is quite clear," responded Holmes. "In fact, I believe I already had an idea of his true identity and where to locate him."

"True identity?"

"Yes. The unique characteristics you've listed sound remarkably like a known thug-for-hire named Isa Ulford. I should be most surprised if he isn't the same man. I should have him by day's end."

Jermyn seemed quite impressed, but before he could comment, Holmes continued. "What can you tell us of the document itself?"

"It was parchment – about sixteen inches high and twelve wide. Folded in half each way – into quarters so that it was about eight-inches-by-six. The writing was faded but legible, and I got the gist of it right away – there wasn't any fancy legal *fol-de-rol* or Latin nonsense. Fortunately, none of the others in the room were close enough to see it – even Loughborough stepped back while I opened and read it to myself. The text was centered in the middle, with a few unmarked inches bordered on all sides. It was quite clear: For one-million pounds, Texas sold itself to England. It was all done up right and with a bow on it. There were two signatures. For the British was Richard Pakenham – "

"Envoy Extraordinary and Minister Plenipotentiary for Great Britain to the United States from 1843 to 1847," Mycroft interrupted. "He successfully carried our end during the Treaty of Oregon, but he was considered something of a failure in regard to the Texas question as the United States, despite our best efforts at the time, and with offers of financial aid and troops, nevertheless instead chose annexation to statehood in December 1845."

Jermyn nodded and continued. "For the Texans, the document was boldly signed by Sam Houston, their President."

He glanced at Mycroft, as if to see whether he should stop, but when he wasn't prevented, he continued. "There was a provision in the main text that seemed especially important – it was the last item before the signatures. In addition to defining the sale and describing the area to be purchased, there was a *caveat*, stating that the terms of the sale could be enforced for up to fifty years beyond the date of the signing."

"And that date being – ?" asked Holmes.

"The twenty-third of December, 1844."

"Good Lord," I said. "The fifty years is up in within days!"

"It doesn't matter, Doctor," assured Mycroft. "Fear not. As I've explained, the terms are unenforceable. For us to try and exercise the agreement now would cause worldwide turmoil."

"And yet," I said, "you indicated that there are those just now who *could* happily make use of such turmoil."

Mycroft didn't respond. Perhaps I was being indiscreet by discussing that aspect with Jermyn still present.

159

Jermyn cleared his throat and continued. "Beneath the formal signatures and dates was another smaller note, apparently added by President Houston as well. The faded ink had the same shade as his official signature, and it looked to be the same handwriting. It consisted of but a single word – maybe in Latin – and his signature again, this time dated the sixth of March, 1845."

"Do you recall the word?" asked Holmes, but Jermyn shook his head.

"Foreign languages were never my strong suit, and I didn't recognize this one."

"Presumably," Holmes continued, "there were two copies of the treaty – one for the Texans, and one for us. Apparently the Texans' copy was kept in the safe – and then left behind when the Legation closed in 1845, upon the acceptance of Texas into the Union, there being no further need for an embassy."

Mycroft nodded, and Jermyn added, "The story goes that when they packed up and departed, the Texans also neglected to pay £160 in overdue rent."

"What about the stacks of Texas currency?" I asked. "Were those taken from you as well?"

Jermyn reached into his pocket and pulled forth three packets, laying them on a small table. "He left it. Of course, anyone would realize that it's worthless now, except possibly to a collector."

Holmes picked up the old cash, looked it over, and then handed it to me. There were three bundles, each about an inch thick, with a paper band centered around the middle, labeled *National Bank of Texas.*

"It isn't much," said Jermyn. "Slightly more than eight-hundred of their dollars."

"Is there any sign of our copy of the treaty?" Holmes asked his brother, as if Jermyn hadn't spoken.

Mycroft shook his head. "As I said, there is no record of any payment being made."

Holmes raised an eyebrow, and said, "You've been busy, Mycroft. What time did the theft occur?"

"Around ten this morning," answered Jermyn.

"And it's two o'clock now."

"For whatever reason," Mycroft continued as if he hadn't been interrupted, "the arrangement was never consummated. It's likely that the Texans never truly wanted to be part of the Empire, and this was just a ploy to obtain some leverage in their quest to become a State. They fixed up the treaty to see which way the wind would blow. And as for our side of things? It would have been in accordance with our policy at that time to take ownership of Texas, which we didn't want to be part of the United

States, so I'm not sure what happened or why the payment wasn't made. Perhaps Pakenham muffed it somehow. His career, after all, wasn't noted for its brilliance."

We all fell silent, considering our own thoughts. Holmes's expression seemed the most distant as he was examining the problem. Finally, he seemed to reach a decision. "I don't suppose," he asked Jermyn, "that there would be any difficulty with Watson and me dropping by the old Legation office in Pickering Place."

Jermyn shook his head. "Not at all. I rather thought that you might. Shall I join you?"

"No need. I doubt that we'll be there long, or find anything of interest, but I would be remiss not to examine it, especially as it's so close."

With that, seemingly sensing that he had no more to contribute, Jermyn nodded and rose. Then he turned and departed. Sadly, it was the last we'd see of him. It will be recalled by many that he was found on Christmas morning, just a few days later, alone by the dying fire in his bedroom, the victim of a massive coronary failure that occurred sometime during the night. His loss to the country was tremendous, but I knew that he'd never been a happy man after the deaths of his son and daughter.

"Surely tracing this Isa Ulford should be your top priority," said Mycroft when Jermyn was gone.

"I'll set that in motion immediately," Holmes replied. "However, I should first like to examine the safe for myself."

Mycroft waved a hand. "Handle it as you see fit. In the meantime, I'll learn more about who would make use of such a distraction."

With that, Holmes and I departed. The convention that the two brothers might actually say goodbye to one another seemed to be, by common agreement, an unnecessary waste of time.

Chapter II

Outside, a cold wind blew along Pall Mall with just a few leaves from the previous autumn still skittering along the pavement. We stood just outside the door of No. 78 to don our gloves, and I glanced across the street to No. 48, the building where Mycroft resided when he wasn't in the Diogenes Club behind us, or at his office in Whitehall. I could see that we'd been observed by Keeton, the longtime doorman of the residential building. He clearly recognized us, for Holmes was unmistakable in his Inverness and fore-and-aft cap, worn year-round, with indifference to whether he was in town or the country, and regardless of societal demands. It had only been a month since Keeton had been in our Baker Street sitting room, having worked up the courage to approach Holmes in the matter of his missing daughter. What was nearly a tragedy had been narrowly averted, and now the doorman was one of those countless grateful individuals who would do anything to repay Holmes for the salvation of his family's happiness.

I nodded, and Keeton returned it, and then we turned left and walked west into the wind.

As we passed the nearby Oxford and Cambridge Club, I commented, "It's difficult to comprehend the problems that the revelation of this document could cause. And yet, as Mycroft stated, the document itself isn't enforceable – and would not be enforced."

Holmes was silent for a moment, not speaking until we reached the corner, with St. James's Palace on our left. We turned right, up St. James's Street toward Piccadilly.

"There's obviously more to this than simply getting the document back before the instigator releases it," he finally said. "Wheels within wheels – that is the world in which Mycroft lives. In spite of his statement that he'll find out who is behind this, I'm sure that he already knows, and has probably taken steps to head off any revelations."

"Then why are we following along after Isa Ulford? Why weren't we sent directly to the document's final destination – the man who will use it?"

"We're here to obtain evidence – the links in the chain that Mycroft can use to maintain his omniscience when he confronts the master plotter. The facts that we gather now will be documentation and evidence later. But I wonder . . . ."

"What?" I asked as we neared our destination.

"Why did Ulford steal the document? How did he even know what it was, or that it was important? Jermyn pointed out that he alone looked at it. Even his man Loughborough stepped back. One would think that if Ulford were motivated to leave his job and follow Jermyn with theft in mind, he'd take the bundles of cash, not realizing they were worthless – Ah, but here we are."

The entrance to Pickering Place, No. 4 St. James's Street, was a dark and narrow passage stretching back, tunnel-like, through the center of No 3, the long-standing and successful Berry Brothers and Rudd, Wine Merchants. It was only seventy or eighty feet up from the Pall Mall corner. The narrow pathway, just a couple-dozen darkened feet in length, brought us into the actual court, said to be the smallest in London. I'd heard that it was the site of the last duel fought in the capital, but the location seemed much too small. Perhaps with swords – ? But no – surely the last duel would have occurred long after firearms became the preferred weapon of choice.

The site of the former legation was easily determined, as there was a great deal of construction material – lumber, casks of nails, sacks of plaster, Portland cement, and such – stacked nearby. We wended our way up the narrow dark stairs and into a room where the sound of hammering let us know we'd accurately arrived. There we were met by a stout fellow in his fifties who introduced himself as Bessemer, the foreman.

He was the type who, after nearly every sentence spoken, touched two fingers to his brow, as if to tug at the spot where his forelock might have been a long quarter-century earlier. He knew that Jermyn had stepped around to seek help regarding the stolen document, so he'd been expecting someone to drop by. But he hadn't been expecting Sherlock Holmes.

"But I thought you were dead, sir," he added in a puzzled tone, as if inviting an explanation.

Those latter months of 1894 had been curiously strange. After May 1891, it had been widely believed that Holmes had died at the Reichenbach Falls. It was reported in the press at the time, although it turned out to be a less well-known fact than I'd initially thought. In mid-1891, I had set about recording and publishing a series of sketches of some of Holmes's cases – not necessarily the most exciting or important, but rather those which would illustrate both his methods and his personality. In late 1893, a combination of several events brought those recollections to a close. My poor wife, Mary, had passed away earlier that year, and my enthusiasm for the project – and indeed, life in general – had waned to a dramatic and grim degree. Next, the fellow who had served as my literary agent, arranging for placement of the narratives in a relatively new monthly periodical, had lost interest too, as he wanted to focus more on writing his own historical novels. But most of all, the recent slanders in the press by Colonel Moriarty, the Professor's corrupt brother, had prompted me to write and reveal the true account of the events leading to Holmes's death – and after that was published in December 1893, it seemed rather anti-climactic to continue providing additional posthumous tales.

Holmes miraculously reappeared just months later, on the fifth of April, 1894, having spent three years wandering the world, carrying out various tasks for Mycroft in all corners of the Empire and beyond, and also tying up many of the loose ends related to the eradication of the Professor's criminal organization. Upon his public return to his old life, Holmes was rather amazed – and vexed – to discover that many didn't want to believe that he had ever actually been alive in the first place. In fact, much of the populace had fallen under the impression that the accounts I'd written were fiction, and as such, Holmes was merely a character in a recurring series of stories. When "The Final Problem" was published just a few months before Holmes reappeared in London, I had been amazed to see the public reaction upon learning of his "death". There was a period of great national mourning that had been completely absent when Holmes actually "died" in the spring of '91. Only when "The Final Problem" appeared in print did the great masses seem to acknowledge Holmes's supposed passing. That feeling and belief was still fresh in their minds when he returned, and many people initially seemed to think that he was merely an imposter, someone with the peculiar imitative mania to wear a deerstalker cap.

Holmes, who was already rather unhappy that two-dozen stories of his investigations had been published between 1891 and 1893, was further displeased at having to regularly verify his true identity on a number of occasions. On the other hand, he was often unwilling to admit that the publication of the stories had increased awareness of his abilities to a much greater degree than before his disappearance, leading to a regular surge of clients needing his help – much more than the old days when we'd first begun sharing rooms and had each commonly worried about making our shares of the rent.

Now, faced with someone he'd thought dead for over three years, Bessemer looked back and forth from one to the other of us, his unasked question about Holmes's reappearance remaining unanswered – for Holmes wasn't inclined to waste time explaining it, and it must be recalled that I wouldn't publish the account of how Holmes survived at Reichenbach for nearly another decade.

As Bessemer tried to form a query, Holmes looked around until he saw a noticeable hole in the wall. "The safe was there," he declared.

Bessemer swallowed and nodded. "Underneath that mildewy wainscoting we tossed over there. The Italian barber who was up here before had machines to make steam, and he'd mix it with olive oil and it has soaked the plaster something terrible – "

But Holmes had already walked over to the hole in the wall, where he was kneeling and feeling with his fingers, picking out crumbles of material where the safe had been located."

"This isn't plaster," he said. "It's cement."

"That's right," answered Bessemer. "The safe rested on a base of it, set just there onto that cross-brace, and then the cement had been slathered in around it."

"Did you have any trouble getting the safe loose?"

"Not particularly. It pulled right out."

Holmes broke off some of the cement and put it into one of the envelopes he always carried to retain bits of evidence. Then he obtained another piece and held it up. "See how it crumbles?" He proceeded to mash it until it disintegrated into bits that fell to the cluttered floor.

"Is that relevant?" I asked.

He nodded and stood. "The safe, please."

It was lying on a work-table near a window, a metal box, thick-walled, and about one-foot square. The front consisted of the open door, black iron with a colorful steamboat and logo brightly enameled above the combination dial. The other sides were dull and dusty metal with fragments of irregular cement clinging to them. Holmes pulled out his magnifying glass, using it to look at the object from all angles, including the scratch marks and distortions around the door. "You used a hammer and wedge to open it," he commented to Bessemer.

"We did. We thought about drilling, but that would take too long, and the wedge opened it fairly easy."

Holmes leaned forward and sniffed around the door. Then he pulled his handkerchief from his pocket and dabbed along the hinge. Then he held it up for us to see.

"Oil," I said. I looked at Bessemer. "Did you oil it before cracking it open?"

The foreman looked puzzled. "Not at all. It opened fairly easy," he repeated.

"Of course it did," Holmes said softly. Then he stood upright. "This renovation – when did it begin?"

"Two weeks ago, although we discussed it another week before that."

"Any particular reason that it began now?"

Bessemer nodded. "It seems that someone has expressed an interest in renting the place, quick-like."

"And the new tenants didn't like the previous arrangement."

"Well, as I said, that Italian barber had some strange ideas, and he'd done a lot of damage. If you'd seen – "

"Tell us about Stephen Newbold," Holmes directed, using Isa Ulford's false name.

Bessemer proceeded to give us a description that matched that provided by Jermyn. "He walked in nearly a week ago," he added, "seeking work. Quiet – kept to himself. Worked hard."

"We heard that he'd told how he received his scar," I said.

"That's right – in a fight when he was a lad. He offered the story one day as we ate our lunch. People were talking about their old injuries – construction can be a dangerous business. No one asked him about it beforehand, of course. It's a bad scar, and one doesn't just mention things that."

"Did he have any friends here?" asked Holmes. "Did anyone hire on at the same time?"

Bessemer shook his head. "No. He kept to himself, and he left alone at the end of the day. He didn't go to the pub with the rest of us when we left each evening. I had the sense that he wanted to get home."

"And the attack on Mr. Jermyn," Holmes continued. "Did he show any unusual interest in the document when it was first removed from the safe?"

"Not that I recall, but I wasn't watching him. I was the one who used the wedge and hammer, so my attention was on the safe. When it was open, we all backed away and let Mr. Jermyn look at what was inside – a bit piece of folded parchment, and some money. Later, after Mr. Jermyn left, I didn't notice that Newbold was missing. He could have been downstairs with the supplies, or smoking outside. It was only after Mr. Jermyn returned and told me what had happened that I realized that Newbold had left and followed him without any of us realizing it."

Holmes glanced around, and I saw that the other workers who happened to be in the room were surreptitiously watching and listening while half-heartedly pursuing their tasks. They seemed very still, wondering what would occur next. I thought that Holmes might question one or more of them, but instead he simply thanked the foreman and we departed, returning down to the small court, and thence out to the street. The afternoon was moving on, and clouds were beginning to drift in, giving the street a darkened feel.

"You saw the cement?" Holmes asked.

I nodded.

"Further tests on the sample I obtained would confirm it," he explained, "but it's fresh cement of modern origins – it's barely had time to cure, and certainly wasn't up to its full compressive strength."

I comprehended his thoughts. "So the safe was recently set into the wall – it hasn't been there for fifty years?"

"That's right. And for that matter, the Texas decoration upon the safe door, although somewhat scuffed and aged to appear otherwise, is of recent origin as well."

"Then the document is also forged!" I concluded. "This is all a tempest in a teapot."

Holmes didn't speak, although he shook his head slightly. I pulled my coat tighter, asking, "Is it time to find the Irregulars and have them locate Ulford?"

Holmes shook his head. "I fancy that I can lay my hands on him at any time. He isn't unknown to me. Rather than hie off in that direction, I'd first like to have a better understanding of the puppeteer who has set these events in motion. And if Mycroft isn't ready to reveal his name . . . ."

166

As I started to ask if this was drifting too far from Mycroft's request, Holmes glanced across the St. James's Street to No. 86, where a bow window on the first floor, facing east, looked down upon us, and with a limited view back along Pall Mall as well. Suddenly I felt as if I were being spied upon, and I realized we'd likely been observed as we turned the corner a quarter-hour before and entered Pickering Place. Observed, and easily recognized. Unless he was in disguise, Holmes made himself known wherever he went.

Looking up at the first floor of the building across the street, I knew what the view upon where we were standing would look like, as I'd gazed down from that bow window on a number of previous occasions. I knew then who Holmes intended to consult in order to find more about the man behind these recent events.

Chapter III

In those days, I was quite disapproving of Holmes's friend, Langdale Pike, who then spent – and continues to do so as of this writing – his days sitting in that bow window of his St. James's Street club, a spider in the center of his own uniquely contrived web, and a great clearing-house of facts both important and subtle: Those that are immediately relevant, and others percolating for years until they might become significant. At that time, it was several years before I became aware of the infamous society blackmailer, Charles Augustus Milverton, but when I met the latter, who Holmes had described to me as being similar to the "slithery, gliding, venomous creatures, with their deadly eyes and wicked, flattened faces," I recalled my early impressions of Langdale Pike.

I had no use then for such parasites, trading on gossip and misery. It was only in later years that I became aware of the other hidden side of Pike's existence – how just as often he suppressed dangerous or damaging secrets instead of using them to expand his own income. How he manipulated events when possible to provide good outcomes for unfortunates that would have otherwise been impossible. And how he funded a number of charities and supported many a sad cause, all in the shadows without a single thought of receiving credit, privately storing up his treasures in Heaven rather than publicly here on earth. When I began to perceive the truth about him, I was ashamed. He was still a strange and languid creature, but not the vile reptile I had so long imagined.

At some later point, I asked Holmes why he hadn't corrected my earlier perception. "You knew what I was thinking," I said, the burden of my guilt heavy upon me.

"It wasn't my story to tell," he replied simply.

167

But upon that day in December 1894, I still thought of Pike as a distasteful sponge and acted accordingly, sitting aloof and judgmental while he and Holmes conversed.

After their usual greetings, sharing of news and recollections regarding those they had known many years before, and sly unspecific references to matters which were implied but not directly discussed, Holmes got down to business, frankly relating the events that had occurred just across the street in Pickering Place, and holding back nothing regarding the documented sale of the Texas Republic to England and its implications. I thought it quite indiscreet, but I also trusted Holmes.

Pike nodded. "It's almost certain to be Ronald Warrington, you know."

Holmes nodded grimly. "I must admit, he hadn't occurred to me."

"Wait," I added, speaking for the first time. "Ronald Warrington?"

Pike nodded. "His mother was a Knutsford," he added, as if that explained all, or at least that it was some kind of explanation – or excuse.

I turned my palms up and tilted my head, indicating that he'd told me nothing.

Holmes smiled grimly. "That possibility reveals a great deal, and why Mycroft chose not to tell us the other end of the story."

"Ronald Warrington?" I repeated, relaxing my upright posture to lean forward a bit.

"Indeed," confirmed Holmes. "The coal and steel magnate who has suddenly been teasing a business relationship with Alfred Krupp of Germany, at the expense of supplying our own naval shipbuilding efforts."

"But . . . I don't understand." Both Holmes and Pike stared at me as if I'd indicated that I didn't know how to add two plus two.

Then Pike explained. "It's rather simple. This document, outlining the sale of one of the American states to Britain, though unenforceable, would be a nine-days' wonder in the press. That would allow Warrington to complete whatever arrangement he has made with the Krupps while national attention is diverted elsewhere."

"The distraction could have been anything," said Holmes. "Any event would have served. We're lucky that he didn't arrange for the assassination of some minor nobleman to start a war on the Continent." He looked at Pike. "The old magician's trick: Do something flashy with one hand – in this case rile the Americans – while using the other to surreptitiously carry out the hidden agenda with the Germans. But where did he get the idea of involving the Texas Legation? That is truly obscure. Do you suppose that the treaty is real?"

"I expect that it is," responded Pike. "Warrington probably obtained is as a curiosity – Through some dealer, perhaps? – and then the idea

168

suggested itself. A bit of research would probably show that the document has been floating around for years, although known only to collectors and historians."

"Possibly," said Holmes, pondering.

"Then," Pike continued to theorize, "with document in hand, Warrington could have learned where the former Legation was located and arranged to have it 'found' by workmen who were themselves likely set in motion by his own false intention to suddenly rent the place. But somehow – and this part doesn't sense – the document was stolen before it could be publicly revealed."

Holmes nodded in agreement, and I asked, "Then what should we do? Holmes, you've indicated that Mycroft likely already knows about all this – about Warrington. What is our purpose then? Do we continue chasing along the path of the stolen document?"

Holmes nodded. "I believe so. As I mentioned earlier, we are gathering a portion of whatever Mycroft requires for his overall plan – whatever that may be. He involved us for a reason. He knows that I will follow my own lines. Possibly along the way, we shall see something of additional value that we can provide that he doesn't expect."

I thought his use of "we" was generous, but I was happy to provide what help I could.

"There isn't much that Mycroft doesn't 'expect'," added Pike wryly – and it seemed to me how similar in some ways Pike was to Mycroft, each of them motionless in the center of their quivering webs, feeling every pull and vibration, and physically separated from one another by just a few hundred feet along Pall Mall. "I doubt if he thinks you'll limit yourself solely to pursuing this one low-level thief."

A question occurred to me, and I voiced it, despite my reluctance to appear ignorant: "If Warrington went to the trouble to fabricate a false Texans' safe, put the document in it, install it in the building, and then arrange for the rooms to be rented, requiring renovation leading to the discovery – I am understanding that correctly?"

Holmes and Pike nodded, and I continued. "He did all that so the document could be discovered there, in the old Texas Legation, giving it an extra legitimacy. Therefore, the document being stolen and removed by Ulford before it could be publicly revealed has seriously hampered his elaborate plans. Therefore, isn't Ulford, who probably still has the document, in serious danger, should Warrington find him?"

Both of them nodded again, and Holmes added as he stood, "That's why our next stop is Ulford's modest home in Lambeth, where we will find him first."

I thought then that Holmes should remind Pike to keep this confidential, but apparently he didn't see the need, instead thanking him for providing a short-cut to understanding. I stood and joined Holmes as we said goodbye, and Pike nodded in return, a wry smile upon his face as he read the judgment in my expression, before turning his gaze back toward the bow window and its view of the darkening December day, and the gaslights that were now lit along the bit of Pall Mall that we could see in front of the Palace.

Chapter IV

Holmes thought that it would be easier to find a cab in Piccadilly, so we walked north to the main thoroughfare and then east, finally intersecting with a hansom discharging its passengers outside Fortnum and Mason. My stomach rumbled with the thought of the various items for sale so close by, and I wished that I'd taken on a bit more at the Diogenes, but I'd be able to eat again soon enough.

Holmes gave the cabbie an address in Lambeth, and soon we were working our way east and south toward the Westminster Bridge. Throughout, Holmes was silent as he considered the problem at hand. Finally, however, I felt compelled to voice my uppermost thought.

"It seems to me that whoever came up with such an ambitious plot – a deal with the mightiest of the German munitions kings, to the cost of our own national interests – would have planned something a bit more effective than relying on an unenforceable fifty-year old treaty."

"Watson, you underestimate the ways in which the public and the press can be sent baying after a shiny object. Consider what's occurring as we speak to the unfortunate Captain Dreyfus in France. It's been less than two months since his arrest for high treason. I've heard strong indications that he is innocent, but you've seen how France has ignited since then. It fills their press. Their coffee shops and drinking spots and meeting places seethe with discussions and arguments and threats of violence. Dreyfus is likely to be convicted any day – and can you imagine what reaction that will cause? And I guarantee that in the shadows, there are those who are taking complete and orchestrated advantage of this chaos in very calculated ways – either those who are simply riding this wave for their own personal advantage, or others, more sinister, who are deliberately manipulating it and, most hidden of all, those who are responsible for it.

"No, something like the Texas purchase agreement, adroitly maneuvered and directed, could cover a multitude of sins. What's more worthy of consideration is the fact that this certainly isn't the only arrow in Warrington's quiver."

170

The idea left me aghast. "Surely – " I began, and then spoke again. "You mentioned assassination. Someone high in the Government? Or the Royal Family?"

"Not just our own," replied Holmes. "As I mentioned, Warrington, with the help of the Krupps, could have something planned on the Continent. Such an action elsewhere could serve to light the same fuse as here. But we are fortunate," he concluded before returning to his pondering, "that this affair has been discovered so early. Assembling the details will provide Mycroft a wedge to open this door, and knowing one plot will certainly lead to the exposure of the next, and the next after that."

As we crossed the bridge, a gust of wind rocked the hansom, and I pulled my coat closer. A glance at the sky showed the dark clouds were rolling constantly, and now there was a wet feeling in the air, as if rain was not far away. If the temperature continued to drop, there would be ice tonight instead of rain or snow.

Not long after leaving the river behind, we crossed under the tracks leading south out of Waterloo, near the Necropolis Station. Then we turned left onto Lower Marsh Street before making a sharp right. We were almost to Oakley Street, just past the school, when the cabbie stopped before a shabby little tailor's shop. Climbing down, Holmes paid and dismissed our driver. I expressed surprise, as we'd need a way back – particularly if the weather continued to turn bad.

"I expect," was Holmes's reply, "that we'll need something bigger than a hansom if we compel Ulford to depart with us."

Holmes led me along the front of the shop before turning through a narrow alley, arriving at a set of rear stairs that climbed to the second floor. There, upon a shaky landing with two adjacent doors, he firmly knocked upon the left. Then, after just a few seconds, he checked the knob. Finding it unlocked, he led me inside.

It was surprisingly tidy compared to what I'd expected for the residence of a man who was recently involved in assault and theft.

"Behold," said Holmes softly, gesturing to the snoring focus of our trip to the Surrey side: "Isa Ulford."

And indeed it was the curiously structured and scarred man described by Jermyn and Bessemer. But now there was no threat to him, for he'd been tamed by the contents of the nearly empty brandy bottle standing on the floor beside the sofa where he was sprawled.

He showed no reaction to our voices as we softly exclaimed upon observing, lying on a nearby table, a folded yellowed document, about eight inches by six. A quick examination showed that it was the stolen purchase agreement.

171

Holmes turned up the overhead lamp, pulled out a chair, spread the document upon the table, and began a minute examination. From nearby, I could see that it was as described – a concisely structured agreement, with signatures of both the British Envoy and the Texan President. Below the main body of the text, in brownish and faded ink, was an additional notation – the curious word *asesvda*, followed by the Texan president's signature and a date, *March 6, 1845.*

Before I could ask what Holmes thought it meant, Isa Ulford stirred and sat up. "Here, what's this?" he mumbled, rubbing his face briskly and trying to focus. Then, as Holmes – who was still in his fore-and-aft cap – turned and stood, Ulford recognized him and sagged back onto the sofa.

Then he swallowed and his eyes dropped. "Ah, Mr. Holmes," he rumbled. "I shouldn't be surprised, should I?"

Holmes folded the document and slid it into his pocket. "There isn't be much time, Ulford," he said. "You are in danger. Tell us the truth, and we can help you."

"Danger? What danger?"

"The man who arranged for this document to be found in Pickering Place went to a lot of effort. You carried it off before it could be put to its intended use, and if I could find you so easy, it won't be any harder for him."

"No, Mr. Holmes, you don't understand. When it all went wrong, I helped salvage what I could."

"What? You knew about this document beforehand?"

Ulford nodded.

"Watson, watch the rear court. Someone could arrive at any moment."

I moved to the window, beginning to understand that there was more risk than I'd first perceived. The financial arrangement between the very-rich coal and steel owner and the Krupps would be massive, and a group that might consider assassination to further their plans wouldn't hesitate to remove a small-time criminal – or a detective and a doctor.

The rear court was empty, but it was also getting darker, and I tried to keep my focus there, instead of continually glancing back into the poorly lit room, thus ruining what limited night vision that I'd achieved. Behind me, I heard Holmes and Ulford converse.

"Who hired you? Ronald Warrington?"

"Who? No, Mr. Holmes, it was a fellow named Shields."

I could imagine Holmes nodding. "Roland Shields – Warrington's man of business," he said softly. "Much is suspected of him." Then, louder, he continued. "Tell us about the document, and the safe."

"I was hired a few weeks ago – by Mr. Shields. He said that they had an old agreement – the one that you put in your pocket – and that they wanted it found in such a way as to gain a great deal of attention, in order to help a business deal. It had been signed by the Texas government years ago, and they wanted it discovered in the old Texas Embassy in Pickering Place. They found an old safe and fixed it up to look like something the Texans would have had. They put the sheet and some old Texas money inside and gave it to me. Then I got into the old Embassy at night – it was closed up and deserted after the last tenant had moved out – and found a place where the safe could be hidden. I took off the nasty old wainscoting, hollowed out a hole in the wall, and cemented in the safe. Then I fixed the wall so that the safe would be found later.

"Then I took a job there with the construction crew and helped out as needed, waiting until today, as arranged, to pull off the wainscoting and find the safe. Then, after it was pulled clear, I hinted to Bessemer how we could open it. But then it started to go wrong. There were people hired to wait outside. They were supposed to hear about the safe – to come in and make a big deal about finding it, so that it would be reported in the press. Instead, when Bessemer saw the safe, he sent for the rich man who has the lease, just up the street at his club. He came, looked at the sheet, and put it in his pocket to go and show someone else nearby. That's when I knew things were getting off-track – all that trouble to find and fix up the safe, and arrange for the sheet to be found, and now, before the news could be spread as planned, some other man was carrying it away, maybe never to be seen again.

"Without thinking about it, I took after him. It was easy to catch up and get the sheet back – it was just inside his coat pocket – and then I came here, to wait and find out what to do next."

"And of course, knowing the importance of the document, you ignored the old money."

He nodded. "It was worthless – why grab it?"

"Did you notify Shields that you'd retrieved the document?"

"I did. I sent a message to him on my way back here."

I glanced around and Holmes was checking his watch. "Get your coat, Ulford. We have to leave – *now!*"

The man may have settled down to get drunk upon his return, but it didn't affect his reflexes. He seemed to have some keen animal awareness of danger, for he was in his coat and with me by the time I was out the door. Holmes was right behind us, and we wasted no time reaching the ground. Instead of turning back toward the main street, Holmes led us deeper into the shadows, toward a rear alley – and not a moment too soon. Hearing steps coming down the passage from the street, we hid behind the stairs to another building and watched as three men, all dressed in black and moving like quick-shifting shadows, crossed the distance to the bottom of the stairs leading up to Ulford's rooms.

Ulford watched, wide-eyed, while Holmes tugged at my sleeve. "This way," he murmured, barely heard. We slipped away into the darkness.

We emerged from the alleyways along Waterloo Road, where we had no trouble finding an empty growler to take us back across the river to Scotland Yard. Ulford seemed resigned to being carried to the police, but he was full of questions regarding who we'd seen climbing the stairs in such a silent and threatening manner. I didn't want to provide him any more knowledge than he already had – beyond suspecting that they were Warrington's men, I really knew nothing – and Holmes was silent, cogitating upon something with great intensity.

At the Yard, we had the cab wait while we went inside. Ulford was expecting to be arrested, and was surprised when Holmes instead summoned Inspector Stanley Hopkins, explaining that our companion was an important witness who needed protection before his testimony could be taken in full, no questions asked. Without comment, Hopkins understood and took Ulford in charge, leading him away to a hot meal.

Chapter V

Outside and back in the cab, Holmes directed that we should return the short distance to Pall Mall. "Mycroft will be pleased," I said. "In just a few hours, you're back with the lost document, the thief under lock and key, and his testimony as well."

"I'm not so sure," said Holmes cryptically. "And we have a stop to make before reporting to Mycroft." He pulled out his watch. "Is your friend Lomax still as diligent as always?"

"More so, I expect," I said. "As the years pass, he becomes ever-more serious about his work."

"Good. Then he'll still be there. It always saves time to have someone knowledgeable point the way and save a few steps."

Knowing that we were going to see my old friend, the librarian, I wasn't surprised when Holmes knocked the head of his stick upon the cab roof halfway down Pall Mall, a hundred feet or before we reached the Diogenes. Paying and dismissing the man, we crossed the street and entered the western side of St. James's Square, walking to the far northwestern corner and the London Library.

In spite of the early darkness outside and the imminent threat of bad weather, Lomax was where we expected to find him, at his desk deep within the surrounding protection of countless books. He was quite absorbed in some ancient text, taking the time finish what he was reading before looking up. Then he did so with a raised eyebrow, the closest he ever came to surprise.

"What?" he said. "Both here at the same time?" He smiled. "This is a rare treat indeed." He stood and offered his hand to each of us. "It's been too long. What can I do for you?"

Holmes pulled the document from his pocket, unfolded it, and laid it facing Lomax on the desk. "We are researching the background of this item."

Lomax adjusted his glasses, leaned forward, and gave it a short look before standing upright again, saying, "An agreement to sell Texas to the Empire." He displayed no shock. "It looks to be half-a-century old."

"I'm more interested in the later notation at the bottom," replied Holmes. "What can you tell us about how it came to be added?"

Lomax gave a half-smile. "Ah, Mr. Holmes – Librarians are like priests. We believe in confidentiality, and the right of our patrons to privacy, and to keep their secrets."

Holmes nodded and raised an eyebrow. "I understand – indicating that you're protecting a secret indicates that you have prior knowledge of that secret. But you'll notice a very slight indentation beside the second signature of the Texas president – as if a sharpened pencil point had rested there for just a moment. That mark led me to consider just how that signature came to be there, and just what that curious word – *asesvda* – might mean. From there, I determined that three people might be able to explain it to me. One is my brother, whom we will visit shortly. The second is the forger who most likely and so skillfully added the second signature, probably within the last week or so, despite the apparent age of the ink and the March 1845 date. That talented fellow lives in Islington – too far to travel tonight when there are better and quicker options. The third man – and this was a bit more of a long shot – is much closer: *You*, Mr. Lomax, who probably helped locate the word *asesvda* in the first place so that it could be added onto the original fifty-year-old document."

Now Lomax smiled fully and his face looked suddenly young, as if he were a boy seeing a magic trick performed. "Again, Mr. Holmes, confidentiality is our watch-word here. But perhaps I could direct you to a few specific volumes that might give you some insight?"

"That would be most acceptable," replied Holmes, picking up and refolding the agreement.

As Lomax led us away from his desk and into the ranges of shelves, I wanted to ask Holmes just what was going on, but I knew – or hoped, in any case – that enough of an explanation would follow that I'd be able to catch up soon enough.

A moment later, we were standing at a chest-high table while Lomax pulled a couple of old books from different but nearby shelves. He returned, placed them before us, and stepped back, as if willing to help if asked, but allowing Holmes to first find what he needed for himself.

The first book was a biography of the first Texas president, Sam Houston. Holmes glanced through it quickly, and then more slowly, with purpose, as it seemed to provide some information that he needed. As he did so, I picked up the second, a smaller volume, and saw that it was a dictionary of the Cherokee language.

While I tried to recall the little I'd heard of the Cherokee: An American Indian tribe originally from the southeast who had been forced to migrate west in the late 1830's, resulting in massive deaths – almost an extermination. This had been done so that American settlers in that region could take possession of the Indian lands, regardless of the unimaginable pain and suffering that the relocation had caused.

As I considered what I remembered, Holmes was reading rapidly through a number of pages in the front of the first book. I opened the dictionary and quickly found the mysterious word: *asesvda*. There was a note that it this was the phonetic pronunciation, while the written form looked something like *D4RL*. It translated as "*cancelled*".

"Holmes," I said, holding the book out to him and pointing toward a small mark beside the word – as would have been left by the sharply pointed end of a pencil. It was the same sort of mark beside that word on the old document.

Holmes took the dictionary and handed me the biography in return, opened near the front to the early life of Sam Houston, former President of Texas. He was born in Virginia in 1793, and in 1806, moved with his family to Maryville, Tennessee, on the extreme eastern edge of the state, and at the western edge of the Smoky Mountains, a part of the greater Appalachian range, and not far over the border from North Carolina. There he led a rather carefree existence, refusing to help with his family's farm and store, and instead spending several years living with the nearby Cherokee Indians.

The biography went on to relate how he'd returned to Maryville in 1812 to open a school, and he later recalled that he had "*experienced a higher feeling of dignity and self-satisfaction than from any other office or honor which I have held.*" A year later, he joined the United States Army, fighting in the War of 1812 under the leadership of General Andrew Jackson, also a Tennessean (and the man later responsible for the Cherokee relocation, known as "The Trail of Tears".) After the war, Houston returned to Tennessee, becoming a lawyer, working with the Cherokee tribe, and also involving himself with the Jackson presidency.

176

In the early 1830's, he was convinced to settle in Texas, then a part of Mexico. He was subsequently involved in the struggle for Texas independence. The battle of the Alamo in February and March of 1836 served as a rallying cry for the Texans, and Houston was leading the Texas army that brilliantly defeated the Mexican president, Santa Anna, in April 1836 at San Jacinto. The Mexican president, captured as he fled while dressed as a woman, surrendered, and soon Texas became an independent nation, with Houston elected its first president. Later, when Texas became a state, he was one of its first two U.S. Senators. The city of Houston was named for him.

But what was important here was Houston's connection with the Cherokee, and the inclusion of the Cherokee word, along with his signature – apparently forged – upon the document.

Holmes and I closed the two books at the same time. "You may borrow those if necessary," said Lomax, still with a smile upon his face.

"Thank you, but no," replied Holmes. "We've seen what we needed. Your assistance was most useful."

"Simply doing my job, gentlemen." He replaced the books upon their shelves and led us back to the front of the building. Glancing through the door, we could see that a mixture of sleet and rain had begun to fall. "I wish you luck," he said as we departed. "Always a pleasure to assist the Holmes brothers in their work." Then he added, "And you too, Doctor."

It was a short but unpleasant walk to the Diogenes. We could have run, I suppose, but the street was already becoming slick.

Mycroft was waiting in the Stranger's Room by the time we'd removed our coats and were led through the building. Wasting no time, Holmes immediately handed his brother the half-century-old document, which Mycroft laid aside after a single glance.

"Ulford is in protective custody at the Yard," explained Holmes. "We spirited him away from his rooms just moments before three men in black arrived – presumably from Warrington, or the Krupps, or both of them."

Mycroft nodded, showing no surprise at Holmes's additional knowledge of the situation.

"I'm afraid," Holmes continued, "that it was Jermyn's involvement that derailed the plan. Of course you know that. Ulford indicated that there were men waiting nearby for the document to be discovered, so that it could be publicly paraded and generate attention, but before they could become involved, Jermyn was summoned and, recognizing the importance of what was found, he chose to leave and bring it to you. Ulford, mistakenly trying to help his employer, followed him and took it back."

Mycroft pursed his lips. "As I thought. Nevertheless, despite my plan being in disarray, it may be salvageable."

"*Your plan?*" I had to speak. "Excuse me, but I feel the need to understand. We have been to the London Library – " I realized then that Holmes might not want that aspect revealed, but he nodded, and I continued. "The meaning of the word written at the bottom – *asesvda* – is known – *canceled* – as well as its Cherokee origin. Apparently it was forged, as was the second signature of the Texas president, Sam Houston. But I don't understand why."

"Wheels within wheels, Watson," murmured Holmes.

Mycroft glanced at him with something like a smile, and then back toward me. "Doctor, when the Government – and by 'Government' I mean me – became aware of Warrington's inclinations to form an alliance with the Krupps at the expense of his own country, it was also soon apparent that to do so, he would need distractions. Not knowing what he intended, we – by which I mean I – devised a plan to provide him with another distraction, a tempting one which would be known to us, and which we could control to some extent."

"You already knew of the British copy of the document," said Holmes. "That's what you used – not the Texans' copy. You altered it, by way of the second forged signature and a later date, to make it seem as if it were the Texans' document, still in their possession a year after it was signed in 1844."

Mycroft nodded, and I said, "So the document itself was real – as was the sale."

"Apparently so – although no money was ever transferred. It seems that Houston never really planned for the sale to actually occur, but rather he did want a legal document to use as a cudgel, forcing the United States government to go ahead and annex Texas into Statehood. Somehow, Houston convinced Richard Pakenham, the British Envoy, that having such a document in existence would be effective if Texas ever needed to assert a rejection of attempts by the American government to take Texas under terms that they didn't like."

"And," I continued, "adding the world '*canceled*', written in Cherokee – a language with deep associations to Houston's background – gave both veracity to the document's authenticity, and also a legal method, as part of your plan, of proving the agreement was void if needed, but in a subtle way that wouldn't be easily or initially understood."

"That's correct," replied Mycroft. "It seemed unlikely that anyone would do the research necessary in the bowels of the London Library to find that the word *asesvda* was Cherokee." He looked at his brother. "That was an astute leap."

Holmes shook his head. "You were careless, Mycroft. I've seen how you rest your sharpened pencil beside what you're studying. You made such a mark on the document beside the second signature. I knew when I saw it that you were involved, and I'd already seen that the second signature was forged – the ink and the fading, while good, don't look as if it was written fifty years ago. Knowing that *asesvda* would have some obscure meaning, I pondered where to determine it – and where *you* would have determined it. Of course, it could have been something already in your brain attic, but I decided to see how it might relate specifically to Sam Houston. The London Library is nearby – right on your way to and from your office in Whitehall, as a matter of fact. Stopping there and seeking Lomax's help would have been very easy. And checking there was easier than tracking down the forger, Blaine, who added the second signature. Your additional pencil mark in the Cherokee dictionary was simply additional confirmation."

"So what happens now?" I asked. "All of your efforts to manipulate the events – finding and altering the document, getting it to Warrington's attention so that he'd be tempted to use it, and then waiting for him to find a clever way to do so just so you could pull the rug out from underneath him – it's all been for nothing."

"Fear not, Doctor. This wasn't the only plan afoot to outmaneuver and manipulate our straying industrialist. There are half-a-dozen other shiny objects in play to tempt him. While he flounders about, trying to salvage this scheme, the nets are tightening. There are several parallel strategems in the works. He'll soon be brought to heel one way or another."

I wanted to know more. Why hadn't Mycroft just told us the whole story to begin with, instead of setting us along one strand, to find our own way to the center of the web. And if the plan that we knew about, concerning a lost and apparently real treaty to sell Texas to the British, was so curiously interesting, what else had Mycroft's agile mind conceived? But I knew that he wouldn't tell us, and Sherlock Holmes had known the same thing for much longer. Our work that night was done, and our parts played. Instead of pursuing it further, we said our goodbyes and departed with Mycroft's thanks. Finding a cab was more difficult as the weather worsened, but it wasn't too long before we were safely ensconced in our Baker Street rooms, and with a topic to spend the evening discussing.

Not too many weeks later, I was surprised to see a newspaper report that Ronald Warrington had negotiated a number of very lucrative arrangements with the Royal Navy, and that he would be on the Queen's next New Year's Honors list. I threw down the paper in disgust.

"They're rewarding that traitor with a knighthood!" I exclaimed.

Holmes simply shook his head, stating, "Mycroft did indicate that he had several other plans to bring Warrington back into the fold. I try not to worry too deeply about the machinations of Government. I fear that as the world becomes more tangled, we'll be drawn into them at some point, whether we want to be or not. For right now, let us leave it for another day."

And with that, he returned to the intense study of an old palimpsest, related to some ancient English Charter, that had absorbed him off-and-on for the past couple of months.

Death at Simpson's
by David MacGregor

I will confess, dear reader, that in an effort to tell this tale, I have endeavoured to begin it no less than a dozen times, but on each occasion found myself giving up less than a page into the narrative. I realise now that the hurdle I was unable to overcome was somehow finding the proper tone and moral stance, but if the story is to be told I shall simply have to make a clean breast of it and not concern myself with the wagging tongues of the public at large. The simple fact is that this case was easily the most enjoyable murder investigation that Holmes and I had ever embarked upon. I will go further to say that the murder itself wasn't nearly as gruesome as I anticipated, and the sheer tidiness of the affair made it easier to focus on the considerable charms of the location of the crime and the benefit rendered to the community. Finally, I should note that any persons whose reputations might potentially be sullied by the telling of this tale have passed into the Great Beyond.

But I fear that I am getting ahead of myself. Suffice to say, that on this chilly evening in early December, Holmes and I were quite happily ensconced at 221b Baker Street, with a gentle snow falling outside and a well-tended fire casting flickering shadows on the walls of our rooms. Holmes was utterly immersed in a chemical experiment of some kind, and I had sat down with the full intention of making some headway into Gibbon's *The Decline and Fall of the Roman Empire*. With a snifter of brandy at my elbow, I soon found my attention to the follies and foibles of the Roman emperors waning, as I descended into a not-at-all unpleasant fog reminiscing about a truly remarkable gingerbread cake that a grateful client of Holmes's had delivered only the day before.

How long I would have persisted in this reverie before dropping off into gentle slumber will have to remain a subject for speculation, as I dimly realized that Holmes had turned his attention from his flasks and tubes to our front door. Listening more closely now, I heard the gentle tread of footsteps on the stairs, and a moment later Mrs. Hudson had ushered Inspector Lestrade into our presence. Shaking the snowflakes from his hat and coat, he removed his gloves to hold his hands out to the fire as Holmes regarded him expectantly.

"Do help yourself to some brandy, Lestrade," began Holmes.

"You are very kind, Mr. Holmes," returned Lestrade, opening the decanter and pouring himself a healthy glass.

"It's scarcely the kind of weather in which one expects the criminal class to be unduly vigorous in their activities," continued Holmes. "In fact, I have often thought of devoting myself to a small monograph on the relationship between weather and crime. May I take it, then, that your visit is related to some crime of passion committed indoors?"

"Quite so," answered Lestrade. "And if you don't mind, I will relate the scant details of the case as I enjoy your quite exceptional brandy. After all, the body isn't going anywhere soon."

Holmes shot me an amused glance as I brought out my notebook. "Jot that down, Watson. Apparently, we are dealing with a non-migratory corpse."

Lestrade remained planted in front of the fire, but turned his back to it as he began recounting the events of the evening that had brought him to us. "Would either of you happen to be familiar with the gentleman known as Lord Percival Chesterfield?"

Holmes raised an eyebrow as I looked up from my notebook. "Watson may correct me if I'm mistaken," replied Holmes, "but neither of us has had occasion to make Lord Chesterfield's personal acquaintance. We are, however, familiar with the gentleman, and have had the misfortune of observing his public displays of poor behavior on more than one occasion. Do you happen to recall his temper tantrum at the British Museum regarding the general public disturbing his viewing of the Elgin Marbles?"

"Vividly," I muttered. "Absolutely disgraceful."

"Dr. Watson?" Lestrade turned in my direction. "I would be grateful for your candid impression." As I hesitated, Lestrade continued, "And you have my word that anything you say will never leave this room."

"Very well," I began. "To say that the man is an insufferable scoundrel scarcely scratches the surface of his utterly depraved nature. He is infamous for heaping abuse and the most vile language on almost anyone who crosses his path. He seems to thrive on the loathing of his fellow man, has sued more than one merchant into bankruptcy, and my understanding is that his wife killed herself rather than be forced to spend another night under the same roof as him."

"It was murder," interrupted Lestrade. "As sure as I'm standing here, he killed that poor woman in cold blood. Poisoned her with strychnine. The man killed his own wife with rat poison . . . ." Lestrade's voice quavered and he took a moment to regain control of his emotions. "But Lord Chesterfield has influential friends in high places, and I was pointedly told by the Commissioner to drop my investigation."

"Didn't I read just last week that Lord Chesterfield is newly engaged?" I asked.

Lestrade nodded. "To the recently widowed Lady Pemberton, who inherited her husband's sizable estate. Presumably, Lord Chesterfield has found himself low on funds in order to support his various debaucheries, and so . . . ." Lestrade trailed off, letting Holmes and me fill in for ourselves what dire fate might await the innocent Lady Pemberton.

"To put it bluntly," I said, "he's a madman whose title shields him from the consequences of his own actions. Why, Holmes and I once observed him spewing torrents of obscenities towards the staff at Simpson's simply because he noted a smudge on his water glass and because a napkin wasn't folded to his liking."

"You have captured the essence of the gentleman quite nicely," nodded Lestrade. "And, in fact, it was at Simpson's that Lord Chesterfield partook of his Last Supper, so to speak."

"You mean to say it's Lord Chesterfield who is dead?" I asked. "I assumed his temper had finally got the better of him and he took his rage out on some innocent bystander."

"Not at all," answered Lestrade. "The Lord himself was rapidly cooling to the touch when I left him."

"Dear, dear," muttered Holmes. "So it would appear that Lord Chesterfield has finally received his just desserts, as it were."

"He never made it as far as dessert," answered Lestrade with a puckish attempt at humour. "In fact, he never made it to his main course. And between us, good riddance. I'm heartily glad that the old curmudgeon is dead, because he has been a pain in my side on more than one occasion. If not for his title and money, he would have been rotting behind bars for the past decade. Still, murder is murder, so if you and Dr. Watson would care to accompany me, I would be happy to take you to the location of the crime."

"May I take it that his killer has not been apprehended?" enquired Holmes.

"Not yet."

"Do you have a suspect in mind?"

"None."

"You mean to tell us," I interrupted, "that a member of the British peerage can be murdered in the middle of a popular restaurant with no one the wiser?"

"It would appear so," answered Lestrade.

"And for this you propose to take Watson and me on a three-mile trek across London on a snowy evening? As you can see, we are perfectly happy where we are, and if the atmosphere of London is improved by Lord Chesterfield's untimely demise, why on earth should we stir ourselves?"

183

"An excellent point," returned Lestrade, "and one that I did consider, but there are other factors to be taken into consideration."

"Such as?" asked Holmes.

"For that, I'm afraid I must lay the blame at Dr. Watson's feet," answered Lestrade as he turned to me.

"Me?" I expostulated. "What on earth did I do?"

"Let's just say," continued Lestrade, "that if you had confined your interests to your medical duties, I wouldn't be here right now."

As my brow furrowed in thought, I caught the shadow of a smile crossing Holmes's face. "If I'm not mistaken, Watson, I believe our good friend Lestrade is referring to your literary efforts."

"What about them?" I answered, immediately on the defensive. "I poured my heart and soul into those stories, and if I don't say so myself, managed to build up a substantial and loyal readership."

"And there is the problem, Dr. Watson," said Lestrade. "Your readers came to include several members of the Metropolitan Police. Most of them take the stories for what they are – amusing, and perhaps occasionally instructive, tales of mystery and intrigue. However . . . ."

As Lestrade refilled his glass, I saw a look of apprehension cross Holmes's face.

"Oh no. You don't mean to say – ?"

"I'm afraid I do, Mr. Holmes."

"What?" I asked. "What's happened? What's going on?"

"Thanks to your dubious influence, Dr. Watson," Lestrade paused for a healthy swallow of brandy, "I now have two constables on the force who fancy themselves as new Sherlock Holmes-es: Constables Boswell and MacDuff by name. When I left them at the restaurant, I told them not to touch or move anything, and they were both crawling along the carpet looking for clues. They are determined to find the culprit by any means necessary, but I fear that any number of bystanders will suffer from their attentions."

Holmes shook his head. "So that in addition to defacing the scene, they are likely to charge some innocent soul with murder."

"I shudder to think who we will find clapped into darbies upon our arrival," said Lestrade, "but if I could impose upon you gentlemen to abandon your cosy abode, perhaps we can clarify matters as soon as possible."

"Well, well," Holmes pushed himself away from his chemical experiment. "Needs must, eh Watson? Let's make the best of it and enjoy a scenic drive through snowy London."

Five minutes later, Holmes, Lestrade, and I were headed in the direction of Covent Garden, and the drive was very pleasant indeed. The

184

snow on the ground served to mute the harsh sound of horseshoes on cobblestones, and the luminous reach of the gas lamps was generously extended by the reflective qualities of the light snow that settled on every surface. Both carriages and pedestrians, mindful of slipping on slick surfaces, proceeded at a more cautious pace than normal, producing a kind of dreamlike vignette of a metropolis where time had slowed its inexorable pace. It was all rather beautiful, truth be told, and by the time we pulled up outside of Simpson's, all thoughts of a violent murder had drifted out of my mind.

As we descended from the carriage, I was swiftly brought back to reality by the cordon of constables holding back a sizable crowd that had somehow smelled the scent of noble blood being spilled the way vultures detect carrion from a distance. Better yet, a murder at Simpson's promised to be front page news because it was likely that some toff or other member of the so-called 'Upper Ten-Thousand' had met his demise. Holmes, Lestrade, and I entered the restaurant only to be met by more policemen, as well as a tall and rapier-thin *maître d'* whose typical air of sangfroid had utterly deserted him, given the events of the evening. He looked beseechingly at Lestrade, and then his gaze shifted to a seated waiter, who had the expression of a man already on the gallows, with his manacled hands twisting fitfully in his lap. He was middle-aged, with a swarthy complexion, and even at a distance I could see a fresh wound above his left eye.

"There's our man, sir." A large, bull-necked constable with piercing blue eyes had materialized next to Lestrade. He was immediately joined by a much-shorter constable, whose thick black mustache served to almost completely obscure his thin lips. From this mustache came confirmation of the first constable's claim. "He done it, all right. Cold as ice, he was."

Swallowing down whatever his initial response might have been, Lestrade indicated Holmes and me. "Constable Boswell, Constable MacDuff. Allow me to introduce you to Sherlock Holmes and Dr. Watson."

I don't think either constable actually heard my name, as at the mention of Holmes their eyes had widened and both jaws had dropped. There then followed a stream of unintelligible gibberish from both that I could scarcely make out, although I believe the general gist of it was that they both revered and worshipped Holmes as if he were a living deity. Tempted as I was to point out that I was the person who had actually made Holmes famous, I kept my tongue as Holmes inclined his head at the two constables and then turned to Lestrade.

"If I might see the body, Inspector," said Holmes.

"Of course," answered Lestrade. "This way."

Exiting the lobby of the restaurant, we made our way to the gentleman's dining room, where tables draped with white tablecloths were ringed with light-brown wooden chairs, and comfortable booths upholstered in green leather lined the walls. Most of the tables were strewn with the remains of meals in various degrees of completion, as the well-heeled crowd had presumably fled for the exits at the discovery of the murder, and the management of Simpson's quite sensibly elected to leave the entire scene untouched until the arrival of the authorities. Near the entrance to the kitchen sat a spacious booth with curved seating, and slumped over the table was the form of a man with a large carving knife protruding from his back. This, then, was the late and unlamented Lord Chesterfield. I hasten to add that the highly distinctive handle of the carving knife was in the shape of a horse's head – or rather, a knight in chess, as Simpson's was the very epicentre of London's chess scene.

It was here that Englishman Howard Staunton had laid claim to being the greatest chess player in the world, and over the years such luminaries as the Austrian Wilhelm Steinitz, the German Emanuel Lasker, and the American prodigy Paul Morphy had crossed pawns. Upon the occasions when Holmes and I ventured to Simpson's for a meal, we would often see two grizzled heads ensconced in a booth and bent over a board. Speaking for myself, the appeal of the game paled in comparison to the sumptuous fare on offer at Simpson's, most especially their delicious roasts of meat that were carved tableside. I was chagrined to see that one of those roasts sat entirely untouched on a serving trolley next to Lord Chesterfield's table. Protruding from the roast was a large fork, whose handle was in the shape of a rook, thus complementing the knife lodged just to the right of His Lordship's spine. A single slice of beef had been cut halfway through, but then the carving knife had been used to much more deadly effect on Lord Chesterfield.

With his hands clasped behind his back, Holmes took in the scene of the murder from every angle, with Constables Boswell and MacDuff holding their breath to see if the great man himself might spy some clue that had somehow evaded them. Holmes inspected the body and the portion of the carving knife that could be seen, and then brought out his magnifying lens for a more detailed examination of the table itself and the serving trolley. The wooden ledge behind the booth received particularly close scrutiny, with both his nostrils flaring as he bent over to smell the wood. Diving beneath the table, Holmes emerged with a heavy glass pot which I recognized as the typical vessel used by Simpson's to hold their signature concoction of horseradish, and it was only then that I looked around to see that splashes of horseradish were on the serving trolley and the carpet as well. Holmes then beckoned towards me, and I was instantly by his side.

"What do you make of it, Watson?" he asked. "With a carving knife driven up to its handle into the back of the victim at that angle, what would be the cause of death?"

"Well, we can only be certain once a *post mortem* is conducted," I answered, "but were I to hazard a guess, I imagine that the blade sliced clean through the aorta. If you consider the position of the body, it would appear that death was almost instantaneous, and the absence of any blood emanating from the mouth or nose suggests that the blow didn't pass through the lungs."

"Excellent," nodded Holmes. "I concur completely. Whether the fatal blow was aided by sheer chance or a familiarity with human anatomy remains to be seen."

Holmes turned his gaze to the dining room and his eyes swept across it like the human panopticon that he was.

"Clearly, there were many diners here when the murder took place, but I will assume there were no witnesses."

"Quite right, Mr. Holmes," Lestrade looked suitably impressed. "How ever did you know that?"

"Given my knowledge of Lord Chesterfield and the condition of the roast next to his table, I suspect there was something that displeased him."

"Yes, yes!" It was the *maître d'* who now elbowed his way forward. "The kitchen had mistakenly included a pot of horseradish with his meal, which Lord Chesterfield positively loathed. He preferred a special tomato-based sauce, which our Chef prepared for him personally."

"And presumably," Holmes continued, "Lord Chesterfield let his displeasure be known at considerable volume."

"Yes, that is exactly what he did!" confirmed the *maître d'*. "In fact, he threw the horseradish at poor Georgios, his waiter, striking him just above the eye. Georgios, to his credit, immediately ran to the kitchen to correct this mistake. I accompanied him because Georgios has only been with us for a week, and I wanted to impress upon the Chef the importance of creating his signature sauce immediately."

"And how did Lord Chesterfield react to the disappearance of his server?"

The *maître d'* winced at the memory. "Not well. His shouts and curses were audible to everyone in the kitchen. He was furious – practically out of his mind with rage."

"Thus explaining the lack of witnesses to his murder," murmured Holmes.

"I'm not sure I understand," I said. "The *maître d'* and the waiter may have left the room, but there were still other guests seated at their tables."

"Indeed," nodded Holmes, "but I would impress upon you the importance of taking into account the habits of Londoners of a certain class. Had Lord Chesterfield been whispering something to a companion, almost every eye in the room would have been upon him. However, since he was bellowing his lungs out, every eye would have been studiously averted. The upper and middle-classes of England are a curious breed of *savants* when it comes to ignoring things they don't wish to see or acknowledge."

It was at this point that Constables Boswell and MacDuff, who had barely been able to contain themselves, interrupted Holmes's train of thought.

"And with no one watching him, that is precisely when Georgios came back into the dining room undetected and stabbed Lord Chesterfield!" announced Boswell.

"Why should he do such a thing?" asked Holmes.

Boswell and MacDuff looked at one another in mystification, recalculating their high opinion of Holmes.

"Surely it's obvious," began MacDuff. "He had been humiliated in front of everyone in the room – "

"And had just been violently struck with a heavy glass pot of horseradish – " continued Boswell.

"And his temperament simply couldn't take it," concluded MacDuff.

Holmes looked from MacDuff to Boswell with a bland smile.

"I see. And what is this 'temperament' of which you speak?"

"Well, he's a foreigner, sir," began MacDuff. "Fresh off the boat from Greece."

"It's the Mediterranean background," added Boswell helpfully. "They're a very hot-blooded people."

"Ah," Holmes nodded in comprehension. "Hot-blooded in the manner of Socrates, Plato, and Aristotle, you mean?"

Boswell and MacDuff exchanged an uncertain glance, giving Holmes an opportunity to deliver a short lecture.

"Gentlemen, if you wish to advance in your chosen profession, you would do well to clear your minds of any and all prejudices you may have concerning any race, ethnicity, profession, or gender. Human beings, each and every one of us, are capable of anything. Let the facts and the facts alone lead you where they may. In this case, Georgios, being newly arrived on these shores, would have been largely immune to Lord Chesterfield's colorful tirade due to his unfamiliarity with the language. Furthermore, were he of a homicidal disposition, he would most likely have killed Lord

Chesterfield immediately after being hit by the pot of horseradish, because he quite literally had the knife in his hand at the moment he was struck. Instead, he put the knife down and accompanied the *maître d'* to the kitchen. Lestrade, you may release the prisoner. The poor man is no more guilty than you and I."

Here I will confess that while I had my notebook out, my attention has strayed to the untouched roast still sitting only feet away from the deceased Lord Chesterfield. It was a gorgeous thing as it sat on its silver platter, medium rare, with roasted potatoes nearby in a separate dish, and a flagon of brown gravy just waiting to be poured over them. The ever-vigilant Holmes took all this in with a single glance and turned to the profoundly grateful *maître d'*, whose colleague had just been cleared of all charges.

"I wouldn't wish to inconvenience you or any of the staff, but my friend Dr. Watson and I were just about to enjoy a late supper when we were called upon by Inspector Lestrade to come here to investigate the crime. I don't suppose – "

The effect of Holmes's words on the *maître d'* was absolutely electric. He thrust his chin into the air and cleared his throat. "Not another word, sir! It would be an honour to serve Mr. Sherlock Holmes and Dr. Watson as they consider the case. Please make yourselves comfortable!"

Holmes cast a bemused look my way, then turned to Lestrade. "Would you care to join us, Inspector? One can hardly do one's best work on an empty stomach."

"Capital idea!" enthused Lestrade. "Let me just clear the room so that we may focus on the case."

As Lestrade set about his task, Holmes strolled among the tables and booths, looking at each of them in turn before waving me towards him as he stood beside a booth not more than ten feet away from Lord Chesterfield's corpse.

"Let us convene here, Watson. This booth is free of any half-eaten meals which might distract you."

I was able to take Holmes's gentle jibe in good stride thanks to the knowledge that we were in the more than capable hands of the *maître d'* and his staff, who would no doubt exert themselves in an effort to keep Holmes and Lestrade happy and to somehow preserve the good name of Simpson's. As Holmes and I sat down opposite one another, the only object on the table was a chessboard with a game in progress, along with a single glass of red liquid. The chessboard and glass were closer to Holmes's side of the table than mine, and he proceeded to wave his hand over the glass and pronounced his verdict.

"Claret."

A moment later Lestrade had joined us, squeezing in next to me as Holmes took in the position on the board.

"Do either of you gentlemen play chess?" Holmes enquired.

"I'm afraid not," answered Lestrade. "A good game of chequers is enough to keep me happy. Although if it's a Christmas party, I must say I enjoy a round of Charades or Blind Man's Bluff."

"Watson?" Holmes flickered a glance at me.

"I know the rules," I answered, "but not much more than that. I certainly wouldn't be a challenge for any of the gentlemen who play here. What about you, Holmes?"

"My brother Mycroft and I played when we were children. Being older, he trounced me repeatedly, which gave him no end of pleasure. Until the day came when I decided that I didn't want to lose anymore."

"So you stopped playing?" I asked.

"On the contrary," replied Holmes. "Quite in secret and without Mycroft's knowledge, I studied up on the game for a solid month. In fact, a number of the games that I used to hone my skills were played right here at Simpson's. I became familiar with such strategies as The Queen's Gambit, The English Opening, and The King's Indian Defence, but I was especially drawn to the Ruy Lopez. It was developed by the Spanish priest Ruy López de Segura in the sixteenth century, fell into disrepute, then was rediscovered by the Russian Carl Jaenisch just a few decades ago. At the next opportunity I employed it against Mycroft, and with great satisfaction was soon able to pronounce '*Checkmate!*' – much to Mycroft's chagrin."

"And did you continue to beat him after that?" enquired Lestrade.

"Oh no," Holmes looked up as he noticed two serving trays being wheeled our way. "After that loss, I found that the chess set had been deposited into the rubbish bin. Mycroft refused to play me again. He accused me of cheating."

"How on earth were you cheating?" I asked.

"I was *trying*, my dear Watson. Trying harder than Mycroft was willing to try, and in his mind that constituted cheating. But enough talk of chess. I believe our food had arrived."

Sure enough, the *maître d'* and Georgios materialized pushing not one, but *two* serving carts, their contents covered by large silver lids concealing the salvers beneath them. Up close, I got a better look at the nasty wound sustained by Georgios, courtesy of Lord Chesterfield's pot of horseradish, but he had clearly insisted on staying on to serve the man who had just cleared him of all charges. In unison, they removed the silver lids from the salvers to reveal not one, but three different roasts, along with a dazzling array of side dishes. Close behind the *maître d'* and Georgios came the Chef himself, carrying two bottles of their best claret and three

190

glasses. As he set the glasses down and began pouring the claret, he nodded to each of us in turn.

"Gentlemen, please accept this small offering on the house. What has happened here is absolutely dreadful and unprecedented in the history of the restaurant. You will have, of course, our full cooperation, and we would be grateful for any gestures that you might be able to extend to us, by way of preserving our reputation and clientele. Now then – " He turned his attention to the serving carts. " – what we have prepared for you are three different meats: A roast fore-quarter of lamb with mint sauce, roast sirloin of beef with Yorkshire pudding, and roast saddle of mutton with red currant jelly. We also have new roasted potatoes, baked beans, and vegetable marrow. Could I possibly interest you in some boiled neck of lamb with caper sauce or chicken Marengo? Perhaps some anchovies on toast or macaroñi tomato? Our entire menu is yours for the asking."

"This is . . . ." I found myself lost for words. "This is . . . *wonderful!*" Were those tears welling up in my eyes? I couldn't recall the last time that I was this blissfully happy.

"It looks absolutely splendid and is most gracious of you, Chef," said Holmes. "We will quite happily sample all of this fine fare as we discuss the case. Many thanks."

The Chef offered us a curt nod. "Then I will wish you *bon appétit.*" As he Chef made his way back to the kitchen, the *maître d'* and Georgios proceeded to pile our plates high with samples of everything from the serving carts. With no hesitation, Lestrade and I tucked in, while Holmes picked up a small piece of mutton, dabbed it with red currant jelly, and chewed thoughtfully as he analyzed the position on the chessboard.

I will freely avow that I am a man with a good appetite, but it was everything I could do to keep up with Lestrade, who appeared to be absolutely ravenous. I suspected his visits to Simpson's were far and few between on a policeman's salary, and he was determined to take advantage of the serendipitous circumstances surrounding this particular murder to their full extent. After doing significant damage to all three roasts, we proceeded to lay waste to a lemon jelly, a St. Clair pudding, and a truly magnificent chocolate *blanc mange* and cream. Holmes, I was interested to observe, ordered only the *meringues glacé* and a cup of coffee for dessert. As he sipped it, he glanced across the table at Lestrade and me, who were both, admittedly, in a bit of a daze thanks to a surfeit of food and claret.

"Well, gentlemen," Holmes began. "You have dined as well as two Englishmen could ever hope to dine. Have you solved the crime?"

Gathering our muddled senses as best we could, Lestrade and I came back to the fact that we were seated just a few feet away from the corpse of Lord Chesterfield. As I turned in my seat, I could still see the gleaming silver knight at the end of the carving knife in his back.

"Suicide?" offered Lestrade, and for a brief moment I thought he was serious. Then I saw the smile on his face and began to laugh, which caused Lestrade to break out into laughter as well. This, in turn, caused my own amusement to increase, and within moments both Lestrade and I were quite helpless with mirth, tears running down our respective cheeks. Slowly, I became aware that the Chef, the *maître d'*, and Georgios had crept back into the dining room, but kept their distance. Across from us Holmes was simply shaking his head, although I could see that he was doing his best to suppress a smile.

"Elementary, my dear Lestrade!" I managed as I spooned the last morsel of pudding into my mouth. Toasting one another with the dregs in our claret glasses, Lestrade and I emptied them and turned our attention to Holmes.

"What do you make of it, Holmes?" I asked. "If it wasn't Georgios, who is our murderer? Where did he come from? And where did he go?"

"As to his identity, I confess myself at a temporary loss, although that will soon change. Where did he go? Out the front door. Where did he come from? Right here."

"Right where?" asked Lestrade. "We know he was in the restaurant."

"I mean right here," continued Holmes. "Where I'm sitting."

Lestrade and I looked at Holmes in bewilderment.

"How so?" asked Lestrade.

"The only evidence I can offer is circumstantial," began Holmes, "but I would ask you to consider the following. This wasn't a premeditated murder, as one would hardly choose Simpson's as the ideal location for such a crime. In addition, the choice of murder weapon, a carving knife, suggests the crime was of a spontaneous nature, with our murderer simply utilizing the best weapon within reach. Then there are the other tables as compared to this booth. Each and every one of them show evidence of at least two diners. There was only one diner in this booth. Indeed, he had not yet begun to dine. He had only a glass of claret and had pulled the board from the middle of the table towards him so that he could regard it more closely as he waited for his opponent and dining companion to arrive."

"That's all very well, Mr. Holmes," said Lestrade, "but how does that add up to murder?"

"Perhaps it doesn't," answered Holmes, "but let us continue our journey down this particular path." Holmes indicated the chessboard in front of us. "What we are looking at is a game in progress. Two gentlemen began the game, presumably earlier today, this week, or this month, but realized they wouldn't be able to finish it. Simpson's very kindly set the game aside until their return, so we can assume both gentlemen are regular customers. Our murderer sat where I'm sitting, playing the white pieces and puzzling over his next move."

"How do you know it was his move?" asked Lestrade.

"Because he is in check, Lestrade. His position isn't fatal, but it is dire. It would only be through the most delicate and sophisticated strategy that he would be able to extricate himself from this situation to try and manage a draw. Further, I would suggest to you that he is playing an opponent superior to himself, so that he is almost certain to lose."

"What makes you say his opponent is superior?" I asked.

"Our murderer is playing the white pieces, which afforded him the first move of the game. This could be mere chance, but you will note the missing black pawn in front of the queenside rook. This wasn't taken in the course of the game. No gentlemen, our murderer's opponent, confident in his ability, offered him pawn and first move to make the game more competitive. However, any advantage our murderer had was swiftly overwhelmed as white endeavored to play the Ruy Lopez, but then was confounded by what has come to be recognized as the Morphy Defence, played by black. Not knowing what to do, white blundered and fell into what is known as the Noah's Ark Trap, in which the white bishop is rendered helpless by the black pawns, thus leading to the position we see before us."

"That still doesn't add up to murder, Mr. Holmes," offered Lestrade.

"Doesn't it?" answered Holmes. "If I cast my mind back to my early games with Mycroft, all I remember is the anger and humiliation I felt after each thrashing. I knew that I was intelligent enough, but somehow the game negated any natural advantages I felt that I had. Time and again, it was like being wrapped in the coils of a constrictor until the very life was squeezed out of me. I was helpless, utterly incapable of eluding my grim ending. And here we have our murderer playing the white pieces, staring at what he realises is an almost inevitable fate. He considers one strategy after another, sips his claret, and feels the coils tightening. His pulse begins to increase as he grinds his teeth in frustration. He needs to focus every ounce of his concentration on the task at hand to have even the glimmer of a hope of success, and then . . . ."

Holmes looked at Lestrade and I expectantly.

"Lord Chesterfield went off on one of his rants," I nodded.

"He flings the horseradish at Georgios," added Lestrade, "and when Georgios runs into the kitchen, His Lordship begins screaming and cursing at the top of his lungs, according to the *maître d'*."

"Everyone has their breaking point," offered Holmes. "Even the most respectable among us. I suspect the roots of this behaviour lie somewhere in our distant past, as outlined by Charles Darwin's evolutionary theories. When we are threatened or feel impossibly trapped, like a mother crocodile defending her nest of eggs against some predator, we lash out violently and murderously, with no thought of the possible consequences to ourselves. Simply put, the gossamer-thin thread of humanity in our chess-playing gentleman snapped, as it might snap in any of us given proper provocation. And there, only a few feet away, was a carving knife positively beckoning to him, for Georgios hadn't left it on the serving tray."

"No?" asked Lestrade. "Then where was it?"

"On the wooden ledge directly behind Lord Chesterfield, where Georgios had dropped it in his panic as he ran to the kitchen. If you would care to look, Lestrade, you will observe small drops of grease from the roast, as Georgios had already begun to carve it when he was assaulted by Lord Chesterfield. The knife was thus left behind, in full sight of our mystery diner who was sitting right here. It was a simple enough matter to stand up, take hold of the knife, plunge it between Lord Chesterfield's shoulder blades, then make his way out of the restaurant, with every eye averted."

"But . . . but . . . ." Lestrade stammered, "If that's true, if there were no witnesses, then we can't prove anything."

"And it's here," began Holmes, "that we need to ask ourselves, do we really *want* to prove anything?"

Lestrade's eyes went wide. "Hold on now. Are you saying – ?"

"I'm saying that as a consulting detective, I am at perfect liberty to decide which cases I wish to pursue to their end. You, on the other hand, are an official representative of the police. I will leave it up to you to decide what your duties and conscience require."

A worried look entered Lestrade's eye as he considered what to do next. When the *maître d'* materialized beside us to enquire if we needed anything else, Lestrade straightened his shoulders and looked the *maître d'* in the eye.

"There is one thing I would appreciate knowing," began Lestrade. "Do you happen to recall who was sitting in this booth prior to the attack on Lord Chesterfield?"

"Of course!" the *maître d'* nodded. "It was Dr. Saxonhouse, waiting for his opponent, Dr. Halley. They both practice at Charing Cross Hospital and often stop here for some dinner and chess."

Holmes turned to me, "You're our resident physician, Watson. Are you by chance familiar with either of those gentlemen?"

"I consulted with Dr. Saxonhouse on one occasion and found him remarkably erudite and helpful," I answered. "I believe he also teaches anatomy courses at King's College. He's a tremendously accomplished surgeon, and is known for offering his services free of charge to the indigent. In fact, I believe he is on the short list for a knighthood next year."

"I believe I know the man," interrupted Lestrade. "Remember that bad business at Bisset's jewelry shop a few years back, Mr. Holmes? Two of our constables were badly wounded, and it was Dr. Saxonhouse who somehow managed to save both their lives. Do you know he slept in the same room at the hospital as the two constables for three nights until he was sure they would recover? I asked him if he didn't have a wife or family to go home to, and all he said was, 'Humanity is my family.'"

"He is the kindest, most thoughtful gentleman you could ever hope to meet," added the *maître d'*. "Although I will say I did see another side of him on one occasion."

Lestrade's interested was instantly piqued. "What side was that?"

"It was last year," answered the *maître d'*, "in the middle of summer, a dreadfully hot day, and I had stepped outside to get a breath of fresh air. The road was crowded with people and carriages, when one of the horses suddenly collapsed to the ground not twenty feet in front of me. No doubt it was overcome with the heat, and my heart went out to the poor creature as people gathered around to try and help. But the carter jumped down from his seat and began beating the poor beast unmercifully with a stick. It was horrible to witness, and my voice joined many others in beseeching the man to stop, but he was relentless as the horse began to scream in agony. It was then that I saw Dr. Saxonhouse forcing his way through the crowd, with a wild look in his eye that I remember to this day. He didn't say a word, but when he reached the carter he swung his walking stick at his head with such violence that the heartless villain collapsed to the ground senseless. When Dr. Saxonhouse turned and saw me, he came towards me, and in a voice trembling with emotion said, 'Get a veterinarian for that poor horse, but leave that swine where he lays.'"

As the *maître d'* gathered up some of our empty plates, a blanket of silence descended over us, and it was Lestrade who found his voice first. "If I could possibly have a small glass of port?" he enquired. I seconded this request, and was surprised when Holmes deigned to join us. The *maître d'* quickly made his way back into the kitchen, and only moments later we had three crystal glasses of ruby red port in our hands as we looked at one another.

"Good God," began Lestrade. "What now?"

"It would seem," I offered, searching for the right words, "that on the one hand Dr. Saxonhouse is almost a saint in human form, but on the other hand he doesn't respond well to witnessing innocent creatures or people being violently abused."

Holmes's gazed was fixed on the fluid in his glass. "And is that a crime?" he asked rhetorically. "Perhaps more importantly, has Dr. Saxonhouse spared Lord Chesterfield's new fiancée the grisly fate of his first wife?"

"Mr. Holmes," began Lestrade, "my sympathies are entirely with yours, but the fact of the matter is that there was a murder here, a murder that is our duty to solve."

"Quite right," agreed Holmes. "Let me see if I can solve it to the satisfaction of the local constabulary."

Holmes looked across the dining room, beckoned with his hand, and a moment later Constables Boswell and MacDuff were headed our way, like greyhounds who had just been released from the slips. Having observed our lack of conversation and activity, they had deduced that some conclusion had been reached and were anxious to be apprised of the news. Both men were bright-eyed and almost breathless as they arrived at our table and looked at Holmes.

"Have you done it, Mr. Holmes?" asked Boswell.

"You solved the murder?" added MacDuff.

"Well, of course he has!" enthused Boswell. "He's Sherlock Holmes!"

"Of course he has!" agreed MacDuff.

Holmes's sombre gaze drifted from me to Lestrade, but when he lifted his face to the two constables, somehow he had conjured up a pleasant smile.

"You are very kind, gentlemen," he began, "and I deeply appreciate your faith in my meagre abilities. Yes, I believe I have solved the murder, but I would impress upon you that it is only a theory. Would you care to hear it?"

Holmes may as well have asked a pair of terriers if they would like a rasher of bacon, as both constables were fairly jumping out of their skin with excitement. Slowly, Holmes extricated himself from the booth and pulled himself up to his full height.

"Quite a remarkable case," he began, "and one that I believe is unique in the annals of crime."

Holmes moved closer to the corpse of Lord Chesterfield, and as Constables MacDuff and Boswell practically danced around him, Lestrade and I both exited the booth and exchanged glances of apprehension.

196

Dedicated readers of these tales will recall that I have on occasion remarked upon Holmes's abilities as an actor, and it was now that he may as well have strolled onto the stage at the Lyceum Theatre to play the role for which he was born. Pointing to the scene of the crime, he began to lecture Boswell and MacDuff.

"I will keep this brief and to the point. Consider the scenario before us, gentlemen. The serving trolley has just arrived, the lids are lifted off the salvers, and our waiter Georgios drives the fork into the roast, then picks up the carving knife with the intention of cutting off pieces of the roast for our noble diner. However, our diner spies an item that causes him to fly into a paroxysm of rage: Namely, the pot of horseradish that I found on the floor beneath the table. His fury is such that he wishes to strike out at the unfortunate waiter standing before him. The waiter is out of reach, and so our diner grabs the pot of horseradish with the intent of using it as a weapon. Being seated doesn't give him proper leverage, as he wishes to hurl the pot with maximum force, so he gets to his feet, using one hand to balance himself on the table. The other hand grasps the pot of horseradish, which is then thrown with sufficient force to cause a considerable contusion on the forehead of Georgios."

Holmes paused in his recitation to take in the reaction of Boswell and MacDuff, who I believe had both stopped breathing. Encouraged, Holmes continued with a flourish of his right arm that would have done Sir Henry Irving proud.

"Stunned by the blow, but still wishing to accommodate Lord Chesterfield's wishes, Georgios rushes for the kitchen and drops the carving knife down on this small shelf here at the back of the booth, not being mindful of the danger of the manner in which it is placed, with the point of the blade projecting towards the booth, and the end of the handle being jammed against this small lip of wood. Observe, gentlemen, these small drops of still moist grease from where the knife was laid."

Both Boswell and MacDuff instantly scrutinized the wooden shelf, before Boswell turned his face to Holmes in awe. "How did you find that, Mr. Holmes?"

"By looking for it, my dear Boswell. Shall I continue?"

Boswell and MacDuff nodded in unison as Holmes cleared his throat for his grand finale.

"The pot of horseradish, meanwhile, had rolled beneath the table, and when Lord Chesterfield attempted to adjust his position to hurl further abuse upon Georgios on his way to the kitchen, he inadvertently stepped on the pot of horseradish and lost his balance. Being somewhat elderly and not particularly athletic, he was unable to brace himself as he fell back heavily into the booth, thereby impaling himself on the blade of the knife through the weight and force of his own body. He then collapsed face first onto the table as we see him now, dying almost instantly due to a severed aorta. Providence, with a keen sense of poetic justice, had determined that the final victim of Lord Chesterfield's violent temper would be none other than himself. *Quod erat demonstrandum*."

Constables Boswell and MacDuff stared at Holmes in something approaching rapture, and I believe would have broken out into applause had Inspector Lestrade not been standing right there. It was to Lestrade that Holmes now turned.

"Unless you happen to have a different theory, Lestrade?"

It was difficult to read the cascading thoughts and emotions clearly enveloping the Inspector, but after a moment he held out his hand. "By George, Mr. Holmes, you've done it again!"

As the two men shook hands, Boswell and MacDuff scampered off to inform their colleagues of the successful conclusion to the case. I looked at Holmes.

"With all due respect, Holmes," I began, "it's slightly terrifying that you can come up with something so ridiculous and so plausible at the same time."

"Indeed," agreed Lestrade.

"I could give you half-a-dozen other plausible explanations should you wish," replied Holmes. "The mark of any good investigator is an imagination that seeks out multiple solutions before choosing the best one."

As we made our way back to the lobby of the restaurant, Lestrade was clearly deep in thought, but kept nodding to himself as he dismissed one objection after another. Seeing us to the door, he shook both of our hands.

"I'll handle the rest of this affair along the lines suggested by Mr. Holmes. I can't say that my mind is entirely easy, but I know that London is a better place than it was earlier today, and that's good enough for me."

Moments later, as Holmes and I were in a carriage on our way back to Baker Street, I felt compelled to ask him a single question.

"Do you have any misgivings at all regarding this evening's events?"

"Just one," answered Holmes as he looked out the carriage window. "I fear that Dr. Saxonhouse may suffer a bout of conscience tomorrow and turn himself in to the police. I therefore propose to make any early morning call on him to explain how the matter stands, and to assure him that he can continue to provide the estimable services of his profession to Londoners of all stripes."

"And your conscience?" I asked.

"Perfectly clear," answered Holmes. "The horse being beaten in the street by Lord Chesterfield would have defended itself if it could.

Similarly, Georgios would have defended himself against Lord Chesterfield's assault were he not a newly arrived immigrant in need of a job. Self-defence isn't a crime. Nor, I would argue, is self-defence by proxy, which is the service that Dr. Saxonhouse exercised in both instances. Those of us who have the ability to act upon behalf of the downtrodden and persecuted have a sacred responsibility to do. That is the banner beneath which we march, Watson, and I'm very glad to have Dr. Saxonhouse in our ranks."

Holmes paused to gaze out the window at the passing images of London, still gleaming under a white blanket of newly fallen snow.

"It's a beautiful world, Watson. And the truth of the matter is that it becomes even more beautiful when some people leave it."

"Hear, hear," I nodded, and we rode the rest of the way back to our rooms in silence.

The Adventure of the Reluctant Executioner
by Arthur Hall

During the years of my association with my friend, the consulting detective Mr. Sherlock Holmes, I was privileged to assist him on behalf of clients from many walks of life. Many times a case would be brought to his attention as a result of a visit to our lodgings in Baker Street by pawnbrokers, factory owners, retired soldiers, servants, members of British or foreign aristocracy, and others – even kings. There was also the singular occasion when his help was sought by one who proclaimed himself to be, or to have been, an executioner.

The early summer rain that had beset London for the past week had ceased quite suddenly. The stormy conditions of our journey to the Old Bailey were replaced by weak sunshine by the hour of our return.

"I must congratulate you, Holmes," I said as I poured brandy for both of us. "Benningham is a skilled defence lawyer, but his best efforts failed to alter your testimony."

"I confess to being absolutely determined to do my utmost to assist Melhuish to obtain a conviction." He accepted the offered glass and lowered his thin form into his usual armchair before the unlit fire. "Martha Fellstoke has caused more than enough misery to the citizens of our capital. When the evidence came into my possession, I could not in good conscience allow her activities to continue."

I sat opposite him, before the fireplace, as we drank.

"Ah," I said then. "I hear Mrs. Hudson below. The hour for luncheon is almost upon us."

"It doesn't surprise me that you are conscious of that. You have displayed symptoms of a need for sustenance since before we left the court."

"Really, Holmes, I – "

But my reply was interrupted by the chimes of the doorbell. Almost immediately, I heard our good landlady answer.

"It may be," my friend smiled, "that we are to be denied an early meal. New clients have been rather scant of late, and the inactivity has made me rather restless. For a moment, I feared that our caller was a delivery boy, or someone here to converse with Mrs. Hudson, but he follows her up the stairs now and we shall soon learn his purpose."

I made to ask how he could be certain that our visitor was a man, but realised that he had deduced it from the heaviness of the tread. Before now, I had received a rebuke for failing to reach such an elementary conclusion.

A knock, and our door opened. Our landlady announced a tall young man who appeared somewhat bewildered as he entered with her as "Mr. Amos Haddrell," indicating that his intention was to see Holmes. I noticed that his clothes were of good quality, but badly in need of pressing.

We both rose and Mrs. Hudson withdrew as my friend went to welcome our visitor, who regarded us with uncertainty.

"Come in, sir. I am Sherlock Holmes." He hesitated and I saw a look of concern appear on his face. "But I see that you are unwell. A restorative may help, I think. Watson, pray pour a brandy for Mr. Haddrell."

I complied at once and Holmes guided him to the basket chair. Once seated, he took the glass from me with a shaking hand and drank it in two swallows before setting it down.

"Thank you, sir, thank you. No, I will not take more, for I must keep a clear head in order to make my explanation concise." He glanced at my friend. "It is true, I take it sir, that you accept cases that appear impossible, or to have no explanation?"

Holmes inclined his head. "There have been a number of circumstances surrounding some of my investigations that could be described as such, but the truth that comes out is invariably little out of the ordinary."

"I pray that it may be so in my case."

"Well then, if you are quite yourself again, perhaps you could tell us of your difficulty. Oh, but I have been remiss. Permit me to introduce Doctor John Watson, my friend and colleague, before whom you make speak as you would to me. You have my assurance that he is the soul of discretion."

Our visitor leaned forward in his chair. His face was pale as he spoke.

"Yes, I know of the good doctor sir, as I do of you from the newspapers. I must apologise for my appearance and my demeanour. Of late, my heart has caused me some trouble, and the pains affect me now and then. I have made enquiries, but nothing can be done."

We expressed our regrets of his condition, and he nodded his acknowledgement.

"I see from the ink stain on your cuff that you occupy a clerical position," Holmes observed. "But your hands tell me that you haven't always done so. Is the problem that evidently worries you so connected with your work?"

"In a way, Mr. Holmes, or at least it started with the work I did then. It was six months ago, when I was working as the assistant to the executioner at Newgate Prison. I have no doubt that you have heard of Jake Dent."

"I have indeed. One of Inspector Lestrade's most notable successes of late. Dent preyed on rich women that he chanced to meet at society gatherings, killing his victims after robbing them to prevent their identification of him afterwards. It was you then, who dispatched him?"

"It was, because the official executioner was down with influenza at the appointed time. Dent's was my first job alone, and even after all that training I felt nervous and sick. I never really wanted the job in the first place, but the opportunity arose, and my wife and I have to eat. It went off all right, but it was what he said to me as I placed the rope around his neck that was so upsetting."

"He threatened revenge by means of his friends or relatives?" I ventured.

"No, gentlemen, it wasn't like that at all. Dent refused the hood over his head, as if he wanted to see the effect of his words on me. He said, and I noticed that his voice didn't tremble as they usually do, that I would know the answer to something that many have wondered about for centuries, if I took his life. He swore that, if I failed to smuggle him out of the prison, I would suffer more than he."

"I have heard such statements from condemned men before," recalled Holmes. "It is a wild last gamble to effect release."

"Did he elaborate as to the nature of his threat?" I enquired.

"Indeed he did. I asked him, there on the scaffold, what he meant by that. He leered at me in that unnerving way of his and told me that I would discover that the dead can haunt the living."

"Come now, Mr. Haddrell," Holmes responded sympathetically. "In your former profession, you must have learned that this is quite impossible. The dead go to their rest and remain there. They don't return."

"So I always believed, sir, but that was before things began to happen to me. I have been attacked in the street by a masked man who I beat off with my stick, narrowly missed being knocked down by a coach on two occasions, and once – and this was a terrifying experience – I awoke in the early hours to find Dent standing over me."

"You actually saw him? Alive?"

"He stood before me in the darkness, but his voice was clear to me. He said he had come to fulfil his promise, which meant my painful death. I had seen him before that though, or at least it seemed I had. When I was attacked, I could see his red hair sticking out from beneath my assailant's hat. The mask hid his face, but not his identity."

Holmes paused, a thoughtful look upon his face.

"Did your wife also witness this?"

202

He shook his head. "Margaret is an unusually sound sleeper, and I couldn't see her terrified, in any case."

"Were there other instances?" I asked then.

"There were, sometime later. Twice I arrived at my house after a day's work to be told by my wife that a visitor had called in my absence. On both occasions it was the same man, who she described as red-haired and sharp-featured."

"Is that the appearance of Jake Dent?"

"If you had seen him, Doctor, those are the things that would have struck you immediately."

In the moment's silence that followed, I heard the cry of a woman outside. It was repeated less audibly as she progressed along Baker Street, but without variation. A flower seller, I concluded.

"Surely," Holmes said then, "there were other witnesses to Dent's threat?"

"Apart from the two warders who made no response, there was but one other in the chamber. Dent spurned the minister as he was read to from the Scriptures – the Twenty-third Psalm, I think. I believe his name was Reverend Simon Moldacre, from the nearby All Saints Church."

"You have indicated that you are a married man, Mr. Haddrell," my friend recalled unexpectedly.

Our client's face brightened momentarily. "Oh yes, sir. One year and three months now it has been, since my Margaret and I were joined together."

Holmes smiled. "And where do you reside?"

"In Gravesend, now. At first we rented rooms above a tailor's shop, but my wife came into some money from an aunt who emigrated to the Americas and died there. Shortly after, Margaret saw this place for sale, an old Tudor building called Gormley Manor. It isn't as grand as you would think from the name, but she was taken with it and said we could now afford it. I suppose it needs some repair, but I will see to that if these infernal chest pains cease for a while."

"Thank you Mr. Haddrell. Now pray tell me, if you will, of your financial standing. Please don't view this as an impertinence for, I assure you, it is probable that it has a great bearing on the solution to your problem."

"Since my health began to fail, the Governor of Newgate gave me a position as a clerk in the prison office. It's little more than booking people in and out and making tea, but it feeds us and we get by. It was a piece of luck, my wife getting the money to buy our house like that. There's no rent to pay now, you see."

"Quite." Holmes rose and we did also. "Thank you, Mr. Haddrell, for bringing this most interesting set of circumstances to my attention. Doubtless you will be hearing from us in the near future, but let me assure you now of two things: First, that however convincing this apparition may have been, it wasn't Jake Dent. Second, that we will discover the true nature of these events, and your mind will be put at rest. Now, other than to prevail upon you to furnish your address and any other details that you think might assist our investigation to Doctor Watson, I think we need detain you no further."

As I took up my notebook our client thanked us effusively, and seemed surprised at the answer when he enquired about Holmes's fees.

"My fees are set upon a fixed rate. Good day to you, sir."

Our most welcome luncheon was Mrs. Hudson's pork pie. Not unusually, Holmes declined dessert.

"I can see that you have been pondering continually about Mr. Haddrell's problem," I remarked as I finished my stewed apple. "Am I to take it that we are to begin our investigation this afternoon?"

He nodded absently. "A visit to Reverend Moldacre wouldn't be amiss, I think."

Within the hour, a hansom deposited us near the corner of Old Bailey Street. Holmes examined our surroundings for a moment before pointing with his stick towards a narrow passage near the law courts. "I believe All Saints to be near the opposite end."

We emerged into a quiet street. Several solicitors' offices and an anonymous square building surrounded the church, and we made our way to the stout double doors. They opened easily and we entered into a poorly-lit and silent interior. We glanced towards the altar and saw no one, but an instant later, a bespectacled man in clerical attire who appeared nearly as wide as he was tall approached us from a cloister.

"Good afternoon, gentleman." His voice echoed faintly from the walls. "How can I be of assistance?" He paused and appeared greatly surprised. "Good Heavens! Are you not Mr. Sherlock Holmes, sir, the consulting detective about whom I have read?"

"Indeed I am," my friend replied, "and this is my friend and colleague, Doctor John Watson."

We shook the priest's hand, he participating enthusiastically while regarding us almost in awe. "But what brings you here, gentlemen? Do you require guidance?"

"On this occasion that isn't our purpose, Reverend, but we would be grateful for some clarification."

At this, the cleric appeared puzzled. "Of what, pray? I will assist you if I can, of course, but I fail to see how I can be of help with secular matters."

"This concerns a man to whom you ministered in Newgate," I volunteered. "His name was Jake Dent."

He peered at us, owl-like, through the spectacles at the end of his nose. "But the man is dead."

"You are quite certain of that?" Holmes enquired.

"Absolutely. I saw him hanged and his body removed for burial in the prison yard."

"There is no possibility that there may have been some sort of deception, so that he still lives?"

The Reverend shook his head. "I know a dead man when I see one, Mr. Holmes. The Lord knows that I have seen many."

"What is it that you recall most, about Dent?"

After a moment's consideration. "His hair, of course. It was of an unusually vivid red. Then there was his disposition. He refused to acknowledge God, or to allow me to read from the Scriptures for his benefit as he was led to his death. Also, the succession of oaths he spat at his executioner might well have issued from the mouth of the Devil. I pray that he finds mercy from his Maker."

"Did he attempt to induce the hangman to allow his escape?"

"I believe that was mentioned, but quickly disregarded."

Holmes regarded the priest carefully. "Tell me, Reverend: Did you at any time encounter the wife of the hangman?"

"Why, yes. Mr. Haddrell and I left Newgate together that day, and his wife awaited him nearby. Despite his profession, he was visibly upset at ending a man's life which may be, as I understand it, why he now pursues a different employment." He shook his head slowly, and in a slightly puzzled manner. "Yet she in no way acknowledged his obvious anguish. She spoke only of a house that she had discovered to be for sale, and with great enthusiasm."

"Was it Gormley Manor?" I ventured.

"I believe that was indeed the name."

"Did the lady mention how she came to know of the place?" Holmes asked.

"Now that you ask, I do recall the name of the agents that Mrs. Haddrell consulted. Quentin and Rourke is a long-established concern. She seemed most satisfied with their service."

Holmes nodded. "My thanks to you, Reverend. You have aided my investigation considerably. We will, I think, leave you to your devotions now."

From the priest's expression, I deduced that he was puzzled as to how the interview could have assisted us. His bulk restricting his movements, he accompanied us from the church. Outside the building, he bade us farewell, remaining there as a passing hansom bore us away.

I wasn't surprised when Holmes was silent throughout dinner. When we had settled ourselves in our usual chairs, I could contain my curiosity no longer.

"I believe you have formed a theory."

He smiled briefly. "You know me well. I cannot, however, enlighten you until I have my suppositions confirmed. Tomorrow, we will pay a visit to Quentin and Rourke, the house agents, to see what can be learned there."

He spoke little during the evening. Each time I looked up from my book, it was to see him staring before him, his position unvarying. I felt some embarrassment, but knew better than to interrupt his thoughts, and was relieved when he announced that it was time for him to retire.

The next morning, we consumed an early breakfast. I had hardly followed my bacon and eggs with the last of the coffee when Holmes, already wearing his outer garments, handed me my coat and ushered me from the room before him.

The offices of Quentin and Rourke stood in Hammersmith High Street and appeared to have known better days. As we entered, I noticed the peeling paint and tarnished brasswork, and the general atmosphere of neglect was unmistakable.

We stood in a short corridor with two doors leading off. From the first the sounds of a typewriting machine, operated at considerable speed, were audible. Holmes knocked upon the second door, and we were bade to enter.

The room was bare of decoration except for a portrait of our Queen. Below it, behind a well-worn desk, rose an elderly gentlemen who couldn't have seen less than seventy years. His morning suit, in contrast to his surroundings, was immaculate, his grey moustache and beard carefully trimmed. His eyes, I noticed, were bright, suggesting that age hadn't robbed him of his awareness or intelligence. I wasn't surprised, however, to hear a slight tremble in his voice.

"Good morning, gentlemen. How can I be of assistance?"

We returned his greeting.

"Have I the pleasure of addressing Mr. Quentin, or Mr. Rourke?" Holmes enquired.

A faint smile appeared on the house agent's lips. "I am Arthur Quentin, at your service. Ernest Rourke passed away four years ago, sir, but I decided to leave his name with the company for old time's sake. Since then, as you see, business has declined, but we still have some desirable properties on our books."

"Of that I am quite certain, but I regret that a sale isn't our purpose here today. My name is Sherlock Holmes. I am a consulting detective, and this is my associate Doctor John Watson."

"Surely I have read of you in *The Standard*?"

"They have reported my trifling assistance to Scotland Yard, from time to time."

I reflected that my friend's reputation was spreading favourably.

Mr. Quentin bade us sit, then leaned across his desk towards us. His face appeared alight with interest, so that I wondered if this interview was a relief for him from the tedium of the long waits between customers.

"If I can aid your enquiries, for certainly that is why you are here, then pray tell me how."

"In the course of our current investigation, mention of your former client, Mrs. Margaret Haddrell, and the property known as Gormley Manor, has recurred frequently. Our enquiries are on behalf of her husband, Mr. Amos Haddrell, but it is important that we are able to view the matter from a different perspective. If you would be good enough to relate to us the circumstances surrounding the sale, it would assist us considerably."

After a moment's thought, Mr. Quentin agreed. "I will tell you all that I can recall, Mr. Holmes, but my assistant, Mr. Edward Sharp, who dealt with this, seems to have deserted me. I am no longer able to get out to view the properties, nor to accompany prospective buyers, so I was left with little choice but to hire someone younger. Mr. Sharp was given the task of arranging a meeting with Mrs. Haddrell, prior to accompanying her to the old Tudor property, Gormley Manor. Apparently she was quite taken with the place, since the visit was repeated several times before she finally decided on the purchase.

She explained that she was acting on behalf of her husband also, since illness had made it impossible for him to attend. It was therefore with some surprise that I completed the transaction, since the house stands amid the Kentish farmlands and was once itself used for that purpose. Shortly after the property passed to the Haddrells, Mr. Sharp ceased to continue to present himself. I have taken on his duties as best I can, but if he wished to leave my employment, I would have appreciated notification. As it is, I don't know if he is alive or dead, or if I should hire another to replace him."

"Most puzzling," said Holmes. "But what of the house itself? Is there any aspect of it that appears unusual? It's condition, perhaps?"

The house agent considered briefly. "I saw the place but once, when it was originally left with us by the estate of the previous owner. It had been reasonably well-maintained for a building of such an age, although some restoration would have to take place in the foreseeable future." He paused, appearing to retrieve some thought. "Ah, I have it! What struck me as strange was the size of the rooms, which were much smaller than the outward appearance of the house suggested. According to Mr. Sharp, Mrs. Haddrell noticed this at once and, far from seeing it as an obstacle to the sale, found the unusual feature quite charming."

"It's likely she saw that the cleaning of the place would be a lesser task than she had anticipated," I ventured.

"That is probably so, Doctor," he laughed shortly. Then, after considering for an instant, he added, "Well, I can bring to mind nothing more that might assist you, but I hope what I have explained may serve that purpose to some small extent."

We rose together.

"We are indebted to you," Holmes assured him. "for you have thrown considerable light on the problem before us. I see that you have a map opened out upon your desk. Would it be possible for you to point out where Gormley Manor is situated?"

"Most certainly." Mr. Quentin unrolled the map further and weighted down the edges with a paper weight and an earthenware ash tray. We leaned across the desk to see clearly. "It is here, you see – about two miles from the extremity of Gravesend."

Holmes nodded. "Thank you. If I may prevail upon you for one more time, can you describe Mr. Sharp to us?"

Mr. Quentin looked at him curiously. "Why? Do you believe you are acquainted with him?"

"Not at all. It is simply that a fellow I know slightly complained that one of his workers left without explanation in much the same circumstances a short time ago. He wished to employ me to trace the man and, unlikely as it is, it occurred to me that the two missing men might be one and the same."

"Highly improbable I should think, but Mr. Sharp is of no more than average height, black-haired and clean-shaven. His dress is conventional, except that he wears a large-coloured handkerchief about his neck instead of the usual collar and formal tie. This is in the manner of the gypsy and I asked him about it once. He replied that his throat is scarred from birth and abnormally sensitive, and indeed I noticed that his speech was sometimes reduced to a croak. The pressure of customary attire about his neck, he said, quickly becomes uncomfortable to him."

"It cannot be the same fellow then," Holmes concluded. "Thank you once more for your assistance, Mr. Quentin. No, pray don't rise again. Good morning to you, sir."

Holmes said little during the journey back to our lodgings. Over the years I have come to recognise this as an almost certain sign that he has seen something of significance in whatever problem currently occupies his mind, and is in the process of devising a solution. As for me, I was unable to define any connection between the threat of an executed man and my friend's apparent interest in the purchase of a house by his executioner's wife. I consoled myself with the expectation that Holmes, as always, would reveal his suspicions and deductions to me in his own time.

The partridge served by Mrs. Hudson for luncheon was cooked to perfection. It didn't surprise me that Holmes hurriedly consumed the portion of it that he deemed as sufficient, nor that he excused himself while I still enjoyed my dessert of strawberries and cream. He seized volume after volume of his index, rapidly turning the pages until his search suddenly ceased. A look of satisfaction crossed his face as I left the table to join him.

"As I thought," he muttered.

"What is it that you have discovered?"

"I have found Vernon West."

"Is he someone connected to our enquiries?"

He nodded. "Mr. Quentin identified him as Edward Sharp, but I felt there was a similarity with someone I knew from before."

"Ah! The scarf worn about his neck stirred a memory."

"Precisely. That peculiarity came about as a result of his past activities. The man is a professional seducer, Watson! During my years in Montague Street, I was consulted by a man whose daughter had been bewitched by West. My client, being a rich man, suspected the intentions of his prospective son-in-law, and I was able to confirm that West has a history of marrying and then absconding with his bride's share of the family wealth shortly afterwards. On this occasion, however, he failed, since I reported to my client before the marriage. His response was to confront West before hanging him from a lamppost. He was cut down in time by a constable, but bears the livid scar about his neck to this day."

"Was your client prosecuted?"

"I believe he was on friendly terms with the local magistrate, for the case never came to court. It was West who received a warning that imprisonment for fraud would follow if he continued his activities, but he appears to have paid it no heed."

"I suspect that we are to continue our investigation this afternoon," I said as he returned his index books to their place.

"Definitely, since I feel we may be in deeper waters than I at first thought. Pray be so good as to find the time of the next train to Gravesend from my *Bradshaw*. I have a mind to be there by mid-afternoon."

I plucked the volume from the shelf at once. "If we can be at St. Pancras in half-an-hour, we can meet the early connection."

"Excellent."

Holmes promised the cabbie an extra half-sovereign if he could deliver us on time, and the horse was young and willing, so it was that we caught the train with minutes to spare. During the journey, I attempted to learn from my friend how he had deduced that the answer to our client's problem lay close to his home – for why else would we now be on our way to Kent? My efforts were to no avail of course, but he made a single response as we neared Gravesend Station.

"Only the cause – the *motive* – eludes me, but I expect to have it within my grasp soon."

There were few people on the platform, but Holmes quickly espied an elderly man who was loading empty milk churns onto a cart. A few minutes conversation secured us transportation to a lane that passed not far from Gormley Manor, and the fellow left us to walk amid trees that showed the first signs of their summer splendour.

Presently we strolled around a curve and a panorama opened up to us. Amid the wide expanse of farmland stood a single house. Holmes agreed that it was as our client had described it.

"That is undoubtedly his recently acquired home. It seems to be surrounded by a considerable tract of land, though Mr. Haddrell made no mention of taking to farming."

"Perhaps it was the remoteness of the place that attracted him and made him agree to his wife's suggestion that they should purchase the place. That narrow track that stretches almost out of sight appears to be the division between his property and that of the adjacent farm."

Holmes nodded. "And there, further along this lane, is a man at the plough near the edge of the field. He is within shouting distance and appears to have paused to adjust the horse's harness. If we're quick, we may catch him. Come, Watson."

We broke into a run and Holmes hailed the fellow as we approached. He was a big, burly man, with a tattered hat upon his head and a wide smile animating his broad features as he trod across the furrowed ground to speak to us.

"Good afternoon, sirs. What can I do for you?"

We returned his greeting. Holmes asked, "Are you the owner of this farm?"

"I am that, sir, and my father before me. My name is John Birtle. Are you a stranger in these parts? Have you lost your way?"

"No, but I believe an acquaintance of mine is your neighbour. Is that Gormley Manor at the edge of your land?"

Mr. Birtle raised his hand to shade his eyes from the afternoon sun. "It is, sir. A fine old place – Tudor, I think. My family has been trying to buy it for years, to make all this land one farm, but until recently it was impossible."

"Has your offer now been accepted, then?"

"That was the strangest thing. After all our efforts failed over the years, a young chap came to our place – you can't see it from here, it's just over the hill – and offered to sell it to me. He said he was acting on behalf of the family, but I've never met them. They must have changed their minds about the place, because they haven't owned it for long"

I saw Holmes's expression change to one of satisfaction. Whatever supposition he had formed was proven.

"And you haven't encountered Mr. Amos Haddrell or his wife?" he asked the farmer.

"I would have called before now to become acquainted, had I not been short-handed in the fields. I'm familiar with their name only because of the fellow who made me the offer, but I must put that to rights soon. In any case, we will certainly meet at the lawyer's offices when they sell me the land."

"Quite so. I am obliged to you for the information. As it is getting rather late, I think it best that we visit on another occasion. Good day to you, sir."

Mr. Birtle touched the brim of his hat in recognition, and we retraced our steps along the lane. We hadn't gone far when Holmes turned to me with his eyes glittering. I knew, as I had known many times before, that the thrill of the chase was upon him.

"We'll return here tomorrow, Watson, but first I have some small preparation to make. After that, I can safely say my case will be complete."

I couldn't imagine how long it would be before we reached a main road where we were likely to encounter a hansom or coach. Holmes strode along in a jaunty fashion – excited, I supposed, by his anticipated conclusion to this affair. I grew more weary with every step and could have cried out with delight when we emerged into a wider road where a coachman struggled to replace a lost wheel. We assisted him, Holmes and I with our shoulders beneath the coach, while its driver pushed the wheel back into position and secured it. Then, in appreciation, he was quite willing to convey us to Gravesend Station without charge, although Holmes wouldn't hear of it. We paused once, at my friend's request, at a Post Office into which he disappeared briefly.

"I presume that you have untangled this puzzle." I said as he resumed his seat, and the horse broke into a trot. "I was surprised to learn that Gormley Manor is to be sold, so soon."

"I have said that the purpose had escaped me, but now I have Mr. Birtle's explanation."

"Then the telegram, if there is a crime here, was to Scotland Yard?"

"One of them." He interrupted his observations of the passing scene. "The other was to Gormley Manor on behalf of Mr. Quentin. I fear that I have of necessity caused that gentleman some inconvenience."

Again I recognised his mood. Further questioning, I knew, would be pointless. I therefore resigned myself to sitting in silence until we reached the station but, not for the first time, Holmes surprised me by demonstrating an extraordinary knowledge of a variety of obscure topics. This he continued until our train was nearing St. Pancras, after which he abandoned his narrative to hail a waiting hansom, which conveyed us to our lodgings.

Mrs. Hudson's poached salmon was most welcome, and Holmes surprised me once again by consuming his dinner with relish. He ate little of his dessert, however, but watched as I finished mine before pouring coffee for both of us.

"What was the purpose of the telegram to Gormley Manor?" I asked him when we had settled comfortably in our chairs and finished our first pipes. "Will you confide in me at least to that extent?"

"It was to the effect that a difficulty has arisen in its sale to Mr. Birtle."

"Since you sent it as if from Mr. Quentin, I assume your purpose was to cause Mr. Haddrell and his wife to visit his offices. Do you propose to enter their home in their absence?"

"Indeed. The only question is whether we will find our client there, or if he will have accompanied his wife to Hammersmith. If he does, she will have a considerable amount of explaining ahead of her."

"Do you believe that she has sold Gormley Manor to Mr. Birtle without her husband's knowledge?"

"Is she hasn't, her intention is to do so shortly. When Mr. Birtle confirmed that an intermediary was used to arrange the sale with him, I became certain. I suppose, if the purchase money belonged to Mrs. Haddrell alone, then no law has been broken, but there is more to this, as we will find tomorrow."

"But by all accounts, she was eager for the purchase of the place, more so than our client."

"Not until she actually set foot inside the building and Mr. Edward Sharp, otherwise Vernon West, entered this little drama."

"Is there, then, any actual crime in all this?"

212

Holmes leaned back in his chair and retrieved his clay pipe. When he had blown a smoke ring into the air above him, he answered.

"Oh yes, Watson. The crime, if it is allowed to occur, will be murder. I believe we can prevent it, but we shall see."

"And you intend that we will frustrate their plans tomorrow?

"If all goes well, we will have done so before Lestrade arrives, and his role will be simply to take charge of the wrongdoers." He glanced at his pocket watch. "But I have already revealed more than enough for tonight. Your curiosity will be satisfied in the morning. As for now, I suggest that you return to the book that lies neglected by your side, while I read the late edition of *The London Evening News* which appears to have a singularly interesting headline."

I wasn't surprised when Holmes refused his early breakfast, save for a pot of strong coffee. He had no appetite when a case was close to its conclusion. In that, he was predictable.

We left Baker Street soon after. Although the repeated journey was passed mostly in silence, there was a constant air of good humour about him. On this occasion we were fortunate enough to procure a hansom at Gravesend Station, shortly after leaving the train. When we again found ourselves near the track that led to Gormley Manor. He dismissed the cab and drew me into the concealment of a large beech festooned with thick leaves.

"I don't think they will have left for Hammersmith before now. It is imperative that we aren't seen, and also that we are able to determine whether Mrs. Haddrell is alone, before we approach the house."

"I don't think that Inspector Lestrade would approve of this."

"Nor do I, but we aren't bound by the same constraints as Scotland Yard. This isn't the first time that we have briefly stepped outside the law in order to affect its greater fulfilment, and I doubt that it will be the last. Hopefully, the good inspector will neglect to enquire how we came to be in the house. Otherwise I suppose I will have to invent some excuse."

As he finished speaking, I became aware of the approach of horses. Moments later, an open trap pulled by two young mares came into view and quickly vanished along the lane by which we had arrived.

"Did you see?" he asked.

"Clearly." I had caught a glimpse of an overly rouged face surrounded by rich auburn hair. "Our client sat beside his wife as he drove."

"I imagine the conversation will become quite heated before they reach Hammersmith. Although, as I recall, Mr. Haddrell gave the impression that he loves his wife dearly, which may mean that he will forgive her for selling their home."

"But why has she done this in secret?"

"Because she doesn't return her husband's feelings. She is taking advantage of an opportunity to leave him, taking with her a considerable amount of money."

"Can you be certain?"

"I believe so. You will recall that Mr. Quentin mentioned that Mrs. Haddrell visited the house several times with Edward Sharp. Even had I not known that Sharp is in actuality Vernon West, I would have suspected that the reason for the repeated meetings was because an attraction had sprung up between them. Knowing also that Mrs. Haddrell was selling the house without consulting her husband caused me to wonder if she was contemplating desertion. In any case, what wife who loved her husband would do that, or allow him abroad with his clothes in such a creased and untidy state?"

I conceded that his reasoning, as always, was sound as far as I could see. We left the shade of the tree and made our way down the track that was barely wide enough to accommodate a coach until we stood before the house. It was a square building with tall chimneys and a foreboding appearance. As we approached the studded door, I heard movement nearby. Both Holmes and I stood still for a moment, until we realised that the sound was from the stable where another horse was shifting in its stall.

Holmes produced his pick-lock, and we were soon standing in a high-ceilinged foyer. Other rooms led off it with doors ajar and I peered into several where furniture was hidden under heavy covers. I remembered that Mr. Haddrell had indicated that there was work for him to do here, after his hoped-for recuperation.

We walked straight ahead into a wide room with a long table at its centre. Portraits, doubtless of ancestral figures of the family of the former owners, adorned the walls, but Holmes ignored them. He took a measuring tape from his pocket and applied it to various places in this and the surrounding rooms. Finally, he nodded in satisfaction.

"As I suspected," he said, "from the moment that Mr. Quentin spoke of the rooms being smaller than one would expect."

"What have you discovered, and how is it connected to our client's problem?"

"Soon that will become abundantly clear to you. For now, it would be best if we waited outside, I think, as if we had never entered."

At that, we left the house to stand in the warm sunshine after Holmes had relocked the door. A swarm of birds circled overhead, and he began a lecture on their breeding and feeding habits that was unfinished when Mr. and Mrs. Haddrell returned. Our client's eyes widened in surprise as he saw us, but his wife, I noticed, showed only a stern curiosity. She whispered something to her husband which was undoubtedly an enquiry as to our identities, and on receiving an answer her expression changed to one of fearful anticipation.

They alighted and Mr. Haddrell, looking to be in better health than I remembered, approached us directly.

"Mr. Holmes, Doctor Watson! I am surprised to see you here. Does this mean that you have discovered something?"

Holmes nodded. "You may take it that all is known. The man you hanged, Jake Dent, is dead and has remained so. You have been the victim of deceit and trickery."

He was visibly relieved. "Thank Heavens! Come, gentlemen, and meet my wife. I didn't inform her that I had consulted you for fear of causing her alarm, but I have just explained your presence and she is eager to meet you."

I saw at once, as Holmes certainly did, that she didn't appear to be anticipating our introduction favourably. After the pleasantries, her husband led the horses to a nearby brook where they drank thirstily, and the conversation was stilted until his return.

He appeared not to notice his wife's reticence and bade us enter the house at once. He led us to a room that was clearly in use since the furniture was uncovered, and we were quickly settled in armchairs near the fireplace. Mr. Haddrell and his wife sat facing us on a *chaise-longue*, with him clearly excited at the prospect of learning the explanation of his experiences.

We refused his offer of refreshments. I sensed that Holmes didn't wish to linger here.

"First," he began, "I must ask you a question that will seem to you to be without connection to the circumstances that caused you to consult me."

Our host appeared slightly confused. "Very well."

"Have you, in recent weeks, found it necessary to purchase more food than before?"

"I really couldn't say. Our supplies are delivered by a concern in the village. As we have yet to employ a servant, Margaret places orders in accordance with our needs."

He turned to speak to her and was abruptly still, for she had blushed a deep red. She knew that all was lost.

"I think your wife has given us the answer," Holmes said. "I will now relate the reason for the increased consumption which has surely occurred, and the true nature of the events that brought you to Baker Street. I regret, Mr. Haddrell, that you will not find my explanation to be pleasant."

Our host glanced at his wife uncomprehendingly. Although obviously puzzled, he answered, "Pray proceed, nevertheless."

"Very well," said Holmes. "This is what transpired after Dent's execution. Do you recall recounting to your wife his threat and remarks regarding his return from the grave?"

"Of course. She questioned me regarding the incident that same day. I was reluctant to disclose the details for fear of causing her anxiety, but she insisted."

All eyes were on her. Still red-faced, she stammered. "We have always confided all things to each other."

"Not quite." Holmes resumed. "It may have been that she formed the scheme to ruin you then, or the circumstances may have been opportune to a previously concocted plan. Only she can be certain."

"Mr. Holmes!" The outrage written on Mr. Haddrell's face appeared so intense that I feared for an instant that he would strike my friend, but he continued after a moment in a much calmer voice. "Surely, Margaret cannot in any way be responsible for this. Could it be that there is some error in your investigation?"

"Your reluctance to believe is natural, but I am much afraid that the evidence is overwhelming. It gives me no pleasure to impart such findings, but all too often they are revealed by scrutiny. As you are aware, your wife enlisted the services of Quentin and Rourke, the Hammersmith house agents, because she had somehow heard that this house, a former Tudor mansion, had been placed on sale. The agent who was given the task of guiding her through the property was one Edward Sharp, who is actually Vernon West, a notorious swindler long known to Scotland Yard. This liaison was repeated on several occasions and at some point, I have no means of telling when, an attachment was formed."

Mrs. Haddrell responded to this with shame and embarrassment, and quickly produced a handkerchief in an attempt to conceal her tears from her husband. I saw his expression change, his brow darkening as he moved away from her.

"Is this true, Margaret?"

She made no reply, but turned her face away.

A short silence descended on the room, broken only by her sobbing. Her husband, I could see, was struggling to collect himself until he raised his head to face us once more.

"Pray continue, Mr. Holmes."

"No doubt at Sharp's suggestion and instigation, she formed the intention of leaving you. Using knowledge gained by way of his current profession, he explained to her that the purchase and subsequent re-sale of this property could make them both rich, since the owner of the adjacent farm, seemingly ignorant of the value of the land, was prepared to offer a sum several times larger than that which she was about to pay. If Sharp, or

216

West as he really is, conformed to his usual strategy, then his plan was to abscond with the entire amount which, of course, would have left your wife and possibly you, sir, almost penniless. Nor did your wife's misdeeds end there. Her reports of a red-haired man calling to see you were false, as you will already have realised, and the identity of your attacker is now obvious, but you will doubtless be wondering how the appearance of 'Dent' was achieved."

"A simple disguise, aided by the darkness?" I ventured.

"Precisely. But what explanation is there for West's presence in your house in the early hours, apparently so easily achieved?"

Mr. Haddrell shook his head. "I have none."

"Here we come to the other reason that your wife sought so eagerly to own this house." Holmes glanced at her, but she couldn't meet his eyes. "It was, as you know, constructed in Tudor times. In those days there was great religious unrest in England, the victims being those of a different religion to the present reigning monarch. It thus became necessary to conceal visiting priests from the frequent military patrols whose objective was to capture those not of the current faith as heretics, for torture or execution. Consequently, many homes of rich families were built to include a hiding place or network of passages, able to conceal such clerics until the danger had passed. Now you will perceive the reason for my enquiry regarding your purchases of food."

Our client sprang to his feet, fury written upon his face.

"Are you saying, Mr. Holmes, that this man West is concealed under my roof, with my wife's compliance? I know of no such 'priest holes' such as you describe."

"They are here, nevertheless. It may not have occurred to you to seek them out, but I can demonstrate at least two of their entrances. I have taken the liberty of informing Inspector Lestrade of Scotland Yard of the situation, and he will doubtless arrive with others who will make a thorough examination of all concealed spaces in the course of arresting West, if he is there."

At this he turned suddenly to Mrs. Haddrell. She had now ceased to cry, but the fear in her eyes told that she did indeed fear the exposure of her lover.

"We shouldn't have to wait for long" Holmes concluded.

Less than an hour later, Lestrade arrived with two burly men who he introduced as Sergeants Powell and Howard. Mrs. Haddrell attempted to leave us for the seclusion of her room, but her husband restrained her. Holmes glared at her with unusual ferocity, and I formed the impression that she understood his meaning when he spoke. "Madam, there is still more to come. All is known to me."

There was an instant when her eyes went wide with fear, but at that moment Sergeant Howard, who had entered the concealed place that Holmes had revealed, reappeared with a handsome but furtive-looking man in his grasp. I noticed that a scarf was knotted about the man's neck, and that the official detectives recognised him at once.

"Come on, m'lad," Lestrade said as Sergeant Powell snapped police handcuffs on the prisoner's wrists. "We'd like a word with you, down at the Yard."

"I've done nothing!" West cried, indicating Mrs. Haddrell. "It was all her doing! She persuaded me, until I didn't know what I was doing!"

The inspector gave him a knowing look. "And did she force you to hide in this house? It wasn't to keep Mr. Haddrell company, I'll be bound." He gestured to the sergeants. "Take him away."

West was led out, still protesting.

"Well, Mr. Holmes," said Lestrade, "we seem to have cleared this little matter up without any trouble. We have two coaches outside, if you and the Good Doctor would care to accompany us."

"Indeed we would, Inspector, but neither you nor I are finished here yet."

I remembered, at that moment, that Holmes had mentioned murder in this affair.

"How is that?" Lestrade asked.

Throughout the search and subsequent discovery of West in his house, Mr. Haddrell had watched in anger and amazement, saying little. His expression was that of total disbelief as Holmes addressed him.

"Mr. Haddrell, you have been married one year and three months, as I recall."

I saw his wife, denied escape, shrink into a corner as he answered.

"That is so. Our courtship was short, but we felt the time was right."

"Had you been acquainted for long beforehand?"

He shook his head, miserably. "We met at a *soiree*, at the house of a mutual friend – only weeks before I began to call on her. She seemed to have great enthusiasm for our blossoming friendship."

"Undoubtedly. The prospect of a change of name and circumstances must have been most attractive and a useful disguise, since she had been pursued for some time by the official force."

I saw Lestrade's posture stiffen at this.

"She features strongly in my records," Holmes continued, "so that I recognised her at once when you both set out for Hammersmith earlier this morning."

I glanced at the inspector and at Mr. Haddrell. Their expressions were of astonishment, while Mrs. Haddrell bowed her head.

"Allow me to introduce Mrs. Ada Pollock, who has now added bigamy to her crimes. I would wager that her 'inheritance' was actually the proceeds of her previous wrongdoings. She is better known to you, Lestrade, as the Highgate poisoner who has eluded the Yard for years."

"Is she, by Heaven?" Lestrade produced a pair of handcuffs and secured her amidst a succession of oaths – most unexpected from a lady – that became hysterical pleadings as one of the sergeants was recalled to remove her.

"Is there no end to the horrors of this day?" our client muttered sadly.

We left him not long after, a broken man. Holmes, I knew, was invariably saddened, despite his reputation as a cold reasoner, on occasions when a case was concluded in a way such as this. I, also, felt pity for Mr. Haddrell.

"We had ourselves a good haul today, Mr. Holmes," the official detective observed during the journey to the local police station. "Two for the price of one, you might say."

"The credit is all yours, Lestrade," my friend answered.

Later, installed again in our lodgings, I recalled Holmes's previous remark.

"Did you not mention that we might prevent a murder?" I asked him.

He lowered the mid-day edition of *The Standard*. "You are correct, Watson, and that was indeed accomplished, as I had hoped."

The half-smile that crept across his hawk-like features told me that he was enjoying my confusion. After a moment, he enlightened me.

"Had you been aware of the criminal history of Ada Pollock, you would be in no doubt that, when his usefulness was ended, she intended to dispose of West as she has of so many other unfortunate souls. He is alive today because we exposed their scheme."

"But he will probably never know it."

"That is of little consequence now. Be so good as to pour us both a glass of porter. The decanter is no more than a foot from where you are sitting."

That was the extent of our involvement in the affair. Sadly, although neither Holmes nor I were surprised, Mr. Haddrell died shortly after the woman who he had regarded as his wife was hanged. The attacks she had conspired to effect on him had been enough to cause his weakened heart to give out. Absconding with West would have been made easier, but the irony was that her husband's death had occurred after her own demise. At his trial, the long criminal career of Vernon West, also known as Edward

219

Sharp and many other names, was read out to the court. He received a long prison sentence which, as I write, is still unfinished.

Apart from that short discussion on our return to Baker Street, Holmes never mentioned the case again. I suspect that it was because no one emerged from it happier, richer, or wiser.

The Norwegian Shipping Agent
by Sonya Kudei

During the first week of July in the year 1895, at the behest of Inspector Stanley Hopkins, my friend Sherlock Holmes took part in the investigation of the death of Captain Peter Carey, a retired seal and whale fisher who had been murdered in his Sussex residence under unusual circumstances. The murder weapon, a harpoon that had pinned Carey to a wall, was one of the strange details pertaining to the case. Stranger still, at least on second glance, was the matter of an obscure 1883 maritime incident that was revealed to be at the bottom of the Sussex tragedy. For, as we learned during the course of the investigation, in August of '83, a failed banker attempted to sail to Norway in his yacht with a box of securities, only to be intercepted during the crossing by Carey's steam sealer *Sea Unicorn*. Carey killed the banker and stole the securities, the subsequent sale of which financed his retirement in the Sussex countryside.

John Hopley Neligan, the missing banker's twenty-year-old son, had been discovered in the act of going through Carey's records in the latter's cabin the night after the murder. When confronted by Holmes and Hopkins, who had been lying in ambush nearby, he proclaimed that his sole intention of breaking in had been to obtain records which would show that it had not been his father but Carey who had sold the securities, thus clearing his father's name. Despite the young man's earnest appeals, he was treated as the prime suspect by Scotland Yard until Holmes demonstrated, with his characteristic flair, who it was that had really murdered Peter Carey – one Patrick Cairns, the *Sea Unicorn*'s spare harpooner who had attempted to use his knowledge of Carey's murder of the banker back in 1883 to blackmail the retired captain.

This case, which had every appearance of having been concluded upon the completion of my friend's dramatic and artfully staged revelation, ended up with an unexpected epilogue that saw the two of us travelling all the way to Norway at the beginning of the third week of that eventful month of July. The decision to continue investigating the case overseas was one Holmes had made no prior mention of, nor had he told me the precise reason for the journey or what it was exactly that he was after. And so it was that when he announced our coming Nordic journey to Hopkins on the day of Cairns's arrest, this was as much news to me as it had been to the inspector.

I acquiesced, however, in my long-suffering way, to accompany him on this surprise journey without trying to force an explanation out of him before he was ready to offer one freely. Experience had taught me that whenever Holmes acted reticent, it was never without a reason. In this case, I sensed that the reason was uncertainty. Whatever it was that he was truly after, he was still unsure as to whether he would find it in Norway or, if he did, what conclusions this might lead to. So I gave him the unquestioning support that I knew he had come to expect of me.

Holmes, to his credit, was at least willing to acknowledge the irony of the situation. The day before our departure, as Holmes sat smoking contentedly in his armchair, having apparently put his thoughts in order, I was still trying to decide what to bring with me to the journey by writing endless versions of a theoretical Scandinavian packing list in my journal. When I looked up, Holmes was regarding me with an amused look.

"My dear Watson," he said, "I dare say that you are over-thinking this little expedition. Why not treat it as a summer holiday excursion? After all, we are long overdue one."

"Holmes," said I, snapping shut my journal, "I am perfectly happy to go on this speculative journey with you without knowing your true reasons for undertaking it. There is, however, one detail that I feel I have every right to know in advance. I need not remind you that my experience in India has trained me to stand heat better than cold. So if your itinerary includes the two of us climbing an iceberg or venturing into subarctic regions – "

Holmes brushed off my argument with a wave of a hand before I could finish. "Fear not. You will not be made to suffer the elements. We are only going as far as Bergen in the southwest of the country. The climate there is much milder than the latitude would suggest. You will find that summer temperatures in that region are very much like those in London."

And so I made no amendments to the items I had already set aside for the journey, although I couldn't help noticing that some of the garments that Holmes had packed seemed more suitable for one of his naval disguises than for a gentleman consulting detective.

The overland leg of the journey brought us first to Lincoln, and then, after a change of trains, to Grimsby. At Grimsby harbour we boarded the Wilson Line steamer *Stavanger*, which would be our home for the following six days. The voyage was a pleasantly uneventful one, and the sea was calm as we reached the Norwegian shore on the 22nd of July. As our boat approached its destination, Holmes and I went out onto the deck and were treated to the serene sight of a town nestled within a range of mountains that towered in the background and braced the city on either side like a large green horseshoe.

The busy Bergen harbour formed a contrast against the town's verdant surroundings. Hundreds of fishing boats were crowded along the docks, and small traditional sailboats moored side-by-side next to larger steam-powered vessels. A particularly large steamship with an oddly sullen air that stood slightly apart from the rest of the boats caught my eye. Holmes, who had clearly been to Bergen before and seemed to have more than a passing knowledge of the place, explained that this was an emigration ship that ran regular routes between Norway and America, and was often used as a last resort for locals who struggled to make a living and sought to make a fresh start in the New World.

Holmes had emerged from his cabin wearing the coarse weathered attire of an outdoorsman. It was only then that he told me, somewhat offhandedly, that throughout the duration of our stay in Norway he wouldn't be Sherlock Holmes, consulting detective, but rather Axel Sigerson, Norwegian seafarer and Arctic explorer, one of his many disguises. Meanwhile, I would be Dr. John McAlister Ray, ship's surgeon and Sigerson's colleague. The announcement came as a bit of a shock to me, for although I found great enjoyment in writing in my records about the masked exploits of my friend, I was myself a very poor actor. It was probably for this reason that Holmes chose to impart this piece of information to me just as we were about to disembark at Bergen harbour, as the general bustle that ensued shortly after prevented me from making any kind of protest concerning this *ad hoc* update.

At the dock, we were met by a man who had clearly been expecting us. He was a sturdy ruddy-faced fellow with flaxen hair who didn't differ in dress or manner from the many local fishermen that could be seen going about their business in the harbour. Upon seeing Holmes, the man greeted him cordially, and the two immediately fell into a vernacular conversation. My friend's narrative of his various adventures during his three years' absence when he was presumed dead had indeed featured a brief reference to the remarkable explorations of a Norwegian named Sigerson, and I had naturally assumed that he must have acquired some knowledge of the Norwegian language during that time to lend at least a superficial verisimilitude to that persona. Nothing, however, could have prepared me for the level of proficiency that my friend presently displayed while conversing with his Norwegian acquaintance. The fluency with which he uttered words in the strangely archaic-sounding dialect unintelligible to my ears could have made him pass as a native of that land.

"Let us switch to English, if you don't mind, for the sake of my colleague, Dr. Ray," said Holmes before introducing the Norwegian fellow as Sigurd Eriksen, Bergen fisherman and ship owner. The latter had no difficulties in conversing in English for, as he explained, he had worked for some time in America, where he had evidently developed a solid grasp of the English language.

"Have you accompanied Sigerson in many Arctic expeditions, Dr. Ray?" asked the Norwegian with a certain dose of naiveté.

"Indeed he has," answered Holmes on my behalf. "We took part in twelve voyages on the *Pole-Star* prior to Captain Craigie's tragic end. Dr. Ray was the ship surgeon."

Holmes conveyed this entirely fabricated tale with the sort of ease that would have been disconcerting but for his brilliance. Eriksen looked duly impressed by his account, while I made the wise decision to let my friend do all of the talking.

At length our guide led us to the Torvet, the spacious yet oddly deserted main square. Only a handful of pedestrians were to be seen, most of them sombrely-dressed people conversing in small groups or strolling at a leisurely pace. There wasn't much traffic either, only a few open carts here and there, as well as the occasional horse-drawn tram, which to someone as accustomed to heavy London traffic as I was, presented a startling sight. However, as I would soon learn, most of the action in this town took place in the harbour area, and empty streets were a phenomenon that one soon got used to.

Eriksen directed us to a hotel, where he had arranged for us to be lodged. The hotel was located in one of the many three-storey buildings that lined Torvet on each side, its name, Fjell, sounding charmingly quaint to my ears. It was quickly pointed out to me, however, that *fjell* was a very common word in Norwegian, meaning "mountain".

Before bidding us farewell, Eriksen remarked in a jocular manner that we had chosen just the right moment to come to Bergen, "because for once something was happening in this town."

"Indeed?" asked Holmes.

"Oh, yes." The fisherman could barely contain his excitement. "You see, there has been a murder. A dead body was discovered near Bryggen a few days ago. An unknown man. From what I've heard, his skull was smashed."

Holmes thanked him, his brow wrinkling, but he volunteered no opinion on the unexpected Bergen murder at that time.

The two of us checked in at the hotel, where I gratefully settled into my room, whereas my friend, after taking some refreshments, immediately went out again and didn't return until the following evening, during which time I learned that summer nights in this part of the world were almost as bright as day. Indeed, I spent most of my first night in Norway sitting by the window, watching the silver disk of the sun as it hovered just above the horizon without setting and feeling as if I were inside a dream.

224

When Holmes finally returned, he had the appearance of a man who had just attended a business interview. As it happened, this did indeed turn out to have been the case.

"Holmes," said I as we sat smoking in the sitting room of our suite after my friend's brief description of what he had been up to, "I have already gathered that our Norway trip has something to do with that wretched Peter Carey case and the stolen bank securities, but I fail to see how your attempt to lease a boat from a Bergen shipping company under the assumed name of Sigerson can have a bearing on that affair."

"My dear Watson," he said, "I would very much prefer to be able to proceed in a less indirect fashion, just as I would be glad to tell you more about the hypothesis that has brought us here. Alas, a hypothesis is all I have got to work with at the moment, for I lack sufficient data to form a theory. It would be a capital mistake in a matter as abstruse as this one to theorise ahead of data. And data, for the time being, continues to evade me. This time tomorrow, however, I should be able to tell you more. Until then, I should hope that you will be able to find some form of entertainment that will keep you occupied. I hear that the hiking trails in this region are particularly scenic. Eriksen has offered to give you a tour of the fjords tomorrow, if you feel so inclined."

The midnight sun brought with it yet another sleepless night, but even though I was up by six o'clock, my friend had already gone out on yet another mysterious errand. Nevertheless, that day didn't want for diversions, for Sigurd Eriksen dropped by the hotel just after breakfast and, just as Holmes had hinted, proved to be more than happy to act as my tour guide for the day. The Norwegian gave me a lift in his boat up the nearby Osterfjord, whence we enjoyed a scenic hike among green meadows down to the charming village of Hosanger, before returning to Bergen in the early afternoon. Holmes had just arrived back at the hotel around the same time, and I briefly wondered whether the two of them had pre-arranged the duration of our excursion.

After Eriksen had departed, my friend took out his grey clay pipe and lit it with luxuriant unhurriedness while standing by the sitting room window and gazing out at the Torvet. I could tell by his relaxed manner that whatever adventure he had been on that morning, it hadn't been a fruitless one. Gone was the closed, brooding look of uncertainty from his face. Whatever clue he had been after, it was evident that he had found it.

"Well, Watson," said Holmes, "I hope the quiet start of our Norwegian sojourn hasn't misled you into thinking that we are here on a mere holiday, for I assure you that this whole time I have been on a hot scent."

"Does this mean that you have succeeded in tracking down the missing Neligan securities?"

"Ha!" Holmes made a theatrical half-turn, the outline of his figure appearing radiant against the bright halo of Nordic sunlight coming in through the window. "You underestimate the scope of this affair. No, I have tracked down Neligan himself."

I was so startled by this that for a few moments all I could do was gape. "Surely you don't mean John Hopley Neligan's father, the deceased banker?"

"That is precisely who I mean. The gentleman's full name is Gerard Winslow Neligan, and he is presently residing in Bergen." Holmes took a long satisfied drag from his pipe.

"But Holmes! Neligan died at sea twelve years ago. He was murdered by Peter Carey."

"Indeed, that is what we have been led to believe." Holmes went up to the small table at which I sat with a cup of oddly salty-tasting tea and took a seat opposite me. I had no doubt that in that moment he missed the comforts of our Baker Street rooms as much as I did.

"Our assumptions," he continued, "as to Neligan's alleged death have been based on verbal accounts of two people: One was made by young John Hopley Neligan, who was only ten years old at the time of his father's disappearance and who knows nothing of the actual circumstances, and another by Patrick Cairns, the man currently on trial for the murder of the very man he claims to have killed Neligan."

"But Cairns had nothing to gain by fabricating a story of Neligan's murder. He is going to stand trial for Carey's death nevertheless."

"He may be covering someone's tracks."

"What do you mean?"

"I mean that there is more to this affair than it appears. The events that we have witnessed thus far are only the tip of the iceberg. It is my intention to uncover what lies beneath. And I am very happy to inform you, Watson, that the little fictitious venture supposedly being laid out by Captain Sigerson has brought me to the threshold of unravelling the various threads of this obscure mystery."

We ordered for more refreshments to be brought to our apartment and, once a traditional lunch of *fårikål*, which is a kind of lamb-and-cabbage stew, rye bread rolls, and slices of some curious brown cheese had been laid out on the table, Holmes went on with his narrative.

"I followed the Dawson and Neligan affair," said he, "with some interest around the time of the bank's collapse. It was in all the newspapers. The coverage included a wealth of data on the missing banker. It appears that Gerard Winslow Neligan, whose wife was

226

Norwegian, had considerable connections with the Norwegian shipping industry through his father-in-law, a successful shipping agent. Neligan was also a stakeholder in a number of companies specialising in the transport of goods between Norway and Britain. So when his son told us on the night we found him in Carey's cabin that it was to Norway that his father had attempted to flee, I was instantly struck by the idea that his escape may not have been a desperate flight of a disgraced, persecuted man, but rather a calculated, pre-planned move. A scheme devised to sever all his ties to a foundering bank in England without suffering the consequences of its failure. One that, at the same time, looked to the future by capitalising on his extensive Norwegian resources, while allowing him to avail himself of the stolen bank funds to procure any prerequisites that such an undertaking would require."

"Holmes! You don't seriously think any single person would be capable of such a complicated scheme?"

"It's a hypothesis, my dear fellow. A working hypothesis. One that I have come here to test. Assuming, then, that Neligan didn't die in 1883, and that he is in fact alive and well in Norway, the next logical step would be to locate his present whereabouts. The impression I had formed as to Neligan's character told me that he wasn't the type to sit idly on top of a nest egg, however large that nest egg may be. I had no doubt that sooner or later he would be back in business, and that his choice of business would almost certainly be shipping, a thriving industry in Norway, and one that he was singularly well equipped to enter.

"Shortly after our encounter with Neligan's son, I wired my contacts in each major Norwegian port, requesting information on any shipping companies that may have been founded around the year 1884, particularly if that company were headed by a foreigner. The result of this search was a list of about a dozen shipping companies, six of them in Kristiania, two in Tønsberg and Haugesund, and four in Bergen. Upon further research, the majority of those companies could be traced to established shipping agents that had been active in Norway prior to 1884. Two, however, contained all the suspicious elements I had been looking for, and both were based in Bergen.

"Once the search had been narrowed down, the next step of the investigation had to be done in person, and I am very much in your debt, Watson, for your agreeing to accompany me on this quest, as I may still need your invaluable aid. In order, however, to be able to identify our missing banker-turned-shipping agent without arousing suspicion, I had to approach him in his natural environment, and this is where my Sigerson disguise proved to be remarkably useful, for obtaining a ship in order to undertake an Arctic expedition is precisely the kind of high-risk business transaction that would necessitate the attendance of the most senior agent in a shipping company.

"Yesterday, I – that is to say *Sigerson* – had an appointment with the first company on my list, Marberg Dampskibsselskab, and I can safely say that Marberg isn't our man for he, as well as the rest of the staff down to the bellboy, is clearly and very blatantly German. That leaves us with Haraldsen Dampskibsselskab, the shipping company where I had an appointment earlier today."

"And?" I could no longer bear the suspense. "Have you reason to believe that this company might be harbouring Neligan?"

"I certainly have. The man posing as the manager, Magnus Haraldsen, is no other than Gerard Winslow Neligan."

"Good Lord! Are you sure of it?"

"Without a shadow of a doubt. In preparing for this investigative journey, I had examined all available photographs of Neligan taken throughout the course of his erstwhile career in banking. And, allowing for some minor differences caused by aging and coiffure, there is no doubt that Haraldsen and he are one and the same person.

"I must say, Watson, Neligan is bolder than I had suspected. I was expecting him to impersonate a foreigner, if for no other reason than to avoid the strain of having to pass as a Norwegian amongst Norwegians all the time, but I must admit that Neligan's talents for the art of Thespis surpass my own. His Norwegian persona is suffused with an admirable degree of realism, and his Norwegian pronunciation is impeccable. Of course, for someone who has seen through his disguise, the clues are everywhere. He wears the latest London fashion, he smokes British-imported Indian cigars, his secretary is British, and there is even a replica Constable on the wall. The secretary, Dolby, does a good impression of speaking Norwegian in the presence of clients, but as soon as I was out of the office, I could hear the two of them speaking English to each other behind closed doors.

"From what I've heard, Neligan has profited handsomely from his Norwegian sleight of hand. It appears that he has entered the shipping business at the right place and just at the right moment. Around the time that he was starting his Haraldsen venture, the Norwegian shipping industry was on the cusp of taking the leap from sail to steam. For the most part, it hasn't been an easy transition, but Neligan has been among the first shipping agents to specialise in steam exclusively, investing heavily in steamboats, and this approach has made him one of the wealthiest ship-owners in the country. In fact, the city of Bergen now has the largest steam fleet in all of Norway."

"But how could Neligan have found the capital to finance such a costly venture as a shipping company if Carey had stolen all of the bank securities Neligan had brought with him?"

"Obviously the story Patrick Cairns told us upon his arrest was a lie. The alleged murder never happened, and neither did the theft of the securities, at least not as described. What is more likely is that the two of them, Carey and Neligan, made some sort of deal after the latter's boat had been intercepted by the *Sea Unicorn* in the North Sea. As to what the precise terms of that deal might have been, I'm awaiting further information that should give us a more complete picture of the affair. In the meantime, we may yet get a chance to obtain more data on Neligan in ways that I hadn't foreseen for, as a result of a chance encounter, I was presented with this."

Holmes produced a crumpled piece of paper from his inner pocket and tossed it over to me. I folded the paper open and smoothed it over the table. The word '*Haraldsen*' and that date caught my eye immediately, but the rest of the Norwegian text was unintelligible. The print had the crude, urgent quality of a political pamphlet.

"What is this?" I asked.

"An advertisement for a meeting scheduled to take place tonight at seven in the Sandviken neighbourhood of Bergen. I got it from a most informative lady named Ingrid Nilsen, who is a passionate critic of Haraldsen's business practices. It appears that while I was busy conversing with the gentleman formerly known as Neligan, Mrs. Nilsen had held a brief impromptu demonstration outside the Haralsen building before being asked by Dolby to leave. As I was coming out of the building, the lady accosted me in the street and began to preach her anti-Haraldsen gospel at me. She is so compelling, Watson! I don't see how anyone could resist becoming converted to her cause. Apparently the lady is well known to the staff, as she frequently haunts the Haraldsen building demanding to speak to Haraldsen. He, however, staunchly refuses to see her."

"How extraordinary!" said I. "What sort of grudge does this lady hold against him?"

"Oh, Mrs. Nilsen has a number of them, and has been kind enough to give me an overview of each one, but not before advising me against entering into any form of agreement with him. That woman is remarkably knowledgeable about the Norwegian shipping industry. Apparently the success of Haraldsen Dampskibsselskab is founded on the strategy of buying large quantities of steamboats at the lowest possible price and putting them into commission on a contractual basis. The company's biggest clients are the local timber and paper industries, but they're happy to offer their ships to anyone willing to pay their fees.

"Smaller local ship-owners, who still rely on sailboats, have been lagging behind with the change-over to steam, and are unable to compete with large companies such as Haraldsen. Many of them have gone out of business. You see, prior to the appearance of steam and the emergence of large companies such as Neligan's, ship owning used to be a small enterprise in Norway. Joint ownership of individual ships was the norm. People from all walks of life would take part in this type of investment, as it was just as easy for a craftsman or shop owner to buy shares in a ship as it was for a government clerk or a wealthy merchant. Indeed, this was a source of livelihood for some people. Many of these small ship-owners, however, have now been pushed out of the shipping business by Neligan's steam fleet, and as a result some of them have been reduced to being wage laborers on Neligan's own steamboats. "

I was amazed at my friend's newfound area of expertise. "Are you saying that you learned all this from a lady while standing with her outside Neligan's office?"

"Data, Watson, has a way of travelling down mysterious avenues before it reaches its destination. In this instance, Mrs. Nilsen has indeed been an invaluable channel. And that wasn't all the good lady had to say."

"Let us hear it, then."

"Mrs. Nilsen has also hinted that small ship-owners haven't been the only victims of Neligan's business tactics, for it is no secret in business circles that to maximise profits, Neligan buys only the cheapest second-hand steamboats. The working conditions on these ships are very poor, often hazardous. As a consequence of all this, his fleet has had an astonishingly high incidence of shipwrecks. Mrs. Nilsen has recently lost her husband, a sea captain, to one such shipwreck, and this tragedy has inspired her to speak out against Neligan with particular vehemence. The lady wants him to be held accountable, and is apparently not alone in her view as, according to her estimate, there should be at least a dozen like-minded people in attendance at tonight's gathering. Neligan has thus far refused to have any dealings with them, acting as if he were above the law. It is their hope that by coming together, they might put pressure on him. These are just some of the main points I've been able to gather from our lady's most excellent exposition. I have no doubt that more data will be forthcoming at the meeting. I hope you haven't made any sight-seeing plans for this evening, for I expect you to come along."

"What you have learned today may very well be the case, but I honestly cannot see what you could possibly hope to achieve by attending this event or, indeed, continuing to be in Norway. If Neligan has managed to orchestrate a complete reinvention of himself with such surety, and to succeed in running a thriving business for a decade without arousing the slightest suspicion of authorities on either the British or Norwegian side, what hope do we have of uncovering some evidence against him during out brief stay?"

"Watson, I am wading in murky waters here. I can only move one step at a time. If I make a false move, such as doing anything at all that might alert our friend Neligan to the fact that there is a London detective in town investigating his disappearance, he will no doubt escape as quickly as he did last time. Attending this meeting is the next small step I can take until I'm able to do something more decisive. Fortunately, I should have the opportunity to do just this in three days' time, for today's appointment with Neligan, also known as Haraldsen, was only the first. In three days, I'm scheduled to meet with him again, ostensibly to formally close the Sigerson deal. The more data I gather until then, the more effective my visit will be."

As Holmes finished his exposition, a far-away look came over his face that told me there was something else on his mind. Had we been in our sitting room in Baker Street, this would normally have been a cue for him to reach for his violin and begin playing some meditative tune while ignoring any remarks I might make. However, our fairly Spartan Nordic apartment afforded him few of the distractions to which he was typically accustomed, so I thought there would be no harm in attempting to coax the matter out of him.

"That isn't all," said I. "There is something else about the Neligan affair that has occurred to you earlier today, possibly while you were in his office."

"By Jove, Watson, you're a mind-reader!" The far-away look disappeared for an instant. "It is just a small detail I observed during my interview with Neligan, something that may not have any bearing on the matter at hand. Our friend Neligan has a heavy walking stick that he keeps propped up by his desk. The metal handle is of a very peculiar design: Bulky, heavy-looking, and shaped like a serpent's head. The ornament is set with some gemstones that form a pattern around the eyes. I couldn't help noticing that there were what appeared to be dried blood stains around some of the finer gems. In view of what Eriksen told us about the unsolved murder, this struck me as suggestive."

"What have you inferred from this?"

"As with all things connected with this confounding Neligan affair, I once again lack sufficient data to form a theory. Nevertheless, it is something worth mentally filing away for later."

That evening, before Holmes and I set out for Sandviken, Sigurd Eriksen stopped by to check in on us, offering to procure a horse and a trap for the occasion. My friend, however, politely declined the offer, explaining, once Eriksen had left, that driving such a short distance might have struck any onlookers as unusual, and as he had been careful to maintain the believability of his Sigerson disguise, doing anything so out of place would have been imprudent. And so the two of us went on foot.

Sandviken was a borough just two miles to the north of the centre, and getting there made for a pleasant stroll with excellent views of the bay. At the address indicated on the leaflet, we found a wooden church that had been converted into a community hall for the evening. We were greeted at the door by Ingrid Nilsen, a tall stately woman with a wide angular face and steel-grey eyes. About twenty people were gathered inside, and most of them were already seated at the wooden pews. Holmes and I took our seats at the back row.

The meeting began shortly without ceremony. Mrs. Nilsen came up to the podium to give an emphatic introductory speech, and was followed by half-a-dozen other speakers. Holmes acted as my personal interpreter, discreetly summarising the gist of each talk for me during the gaps between the speeches.

Several speakers offered their perspectives on the poor conditions on Neligan's ships and the dangers they frequently encountered as a result of insufficient maintenance. One of them, an angry young man with a scarred face that was partly concealed by the high collar of a woolen jacket, claimed to have confronted Neligan in person after having a serious accident during his term of service on an old steamboat with faulty equipment. To stress his point, the youth lowered his collar, revealing his injuries to be far worse than they appeared at first glance. The lower half of his face was severely disfigured, and one of his earlobes had been blown off in an explosion of a ship's dilapidated boiler. It was evident that he held Neligan personally responsible for what had happened to him, and that it had been in the spirit of an honest labourer wronged that he had approached the ruthless shipping agent. Neligan's response had been an aggressive verbal outburst that may have escalated into physical violence – the magnate had allegedly raised his stick at him – if a third party had not intervened. As he spoke of these events, the young man's voice rose with barely suppressed rage, and there were more than a few answering interjections from the audience. The hostility of their tone left no doubt that Neligan was not a popular figure in these parts. Indeed, some of the younger men in attendance, their station as uncertain as the scarred youth's, sounded as if they wished the former banker dead. It took a few minutes for the commotion to die down.

The atmosphere did not mellow down again until the commencement of the last address, given by a gaunt elderly man with watery eyes who was apparently one of the many former small ship-owners that had been ruined by Neligan's company. Despite my inability to understand the language, I could feel the man's pain during that part of his narrative which, as Holmes explained to me afterwards, told the tale of how the ruin of his family business had driven two of his sons to emigrate to America, while his youngest son was on the verge of emigrating as well.

On our way back, Holmes was walking more briskly, as if stirred up by some detail of the meeting. His tone of voice reflected this sudden change of mood.

"I have been a fool," he said. "A fool to dismiss the recent Bergen murder out of hand. Not even the sight of Neligan's walking stick could persuade me that he might have had a hand in it. But after hearing these accounts of his conduct, I no longer have any doubts as to Neligan's capability to commit such an act."

"What will you do? If you truly suspect him of murder, we must alert the police."

He was silent for a long time, and we were back in our quarters at Torvet Square before he finally answered.

"You may be right," said he as we sat to the cold supper that had been laid out for us in our sitting room before our return, "but I fear that the police would be no match for the deviousness of our friend Neligan, who would no doubt find a way to outmanoeuvre them were we to bring the official channels into this business. This would almost certainly be just the prompt he would need to slip out of reach. He has done it before, and would no doubt be able to do it again. No, I do believe that this is a case that must be handled with the lightest possible touch until the very last moment."

I couldn't get much more out of Holmes that evening. The following morning he had gone out before I had risen, and didn't return until the evening of the following day, looking like a person who had done a hard day's work after a sleepless night. As he was tired and famished, we first had dinner at the ground floor bar before retreating back to our apartment, out of earshot of any potential eavesdroppers. My friend lit his pipe and began to tell me what he had discovered since I had last seen him.

"Before I say a single word about my adventures," said Holmes, "I must commend our friend Hopkins, who hasn't been sitting idly in his London office since we went away. Indeed, he has succeeded in procuring information on Dawson and Neligan's stolen South American securities, which has been one of the key missing links in this case. This he has duly forwarded to the Bergen address I gave him when we last spoke.

"The information shows that substantial quantities of these securities appeared on the Rio de Janeiro Stock Exchange, first in 1884 and then in

1887. The original seller of a smaller portion of these securities was Peter Carey, whereas the majority of them were sold by an obscure Nordic company which, upon further investigation, was traced to 'Magnus Haraldsen'. This tells us that, first of all, Carey and Neligan did indeed make a deal that involved splitting the securities and, second, that Neligan, who was the seller of all the shares that appeared on the market in 1884, had used the stolen securities to raise the capital for his Norwegian shipping venture. Before, however, you commend Hopkins for doing all the work, I should add that I have myself done some stock market investigation as well, and discovered that Neligan has sold another batch of securities formerly owned by Dawson and Neligan – this time, however. at the Bergense *børse* in the year 1892. In the months leading up to this sale, his company had suffered a particularly high incidence of shipwrecks, and it is highly probable that he had sold the securities to make up for the resulting financial loss, or else he wouldn't have risked exposing his past connections with the bank. So much for the matter of the securities."

"Holmes," said I, "this is splendid! You have solved the stock enigma."

"It was a collaborative effort. Nevertheless, that was only one part of the puzzle. My next step was to examine the body of the murdered man at the morgue. The Bergen police had no objection to an out-of-town seaman viewing the corpse, as they are clearly at a complete loss as to how to conduct the investigation. They had made no inferences whatsoever as to the man's identity, despite its being perfectly obvious that he is a former sailor, originally from Scotland, who had done at least three voyages in the far North before undertaking commissions in Australia and China. The tattoos on his forearms indicate as much. That he had been retired for some years is also plain enough to see. As for the cause of death, this was no doubt due to severe head trauma caused by repeated blows with a blunt instrument. There are, however, some fine cuts around the edges of the wounds indicating that the surface of the instrument was covered with tiny sharp points."

"Could these markings have been made with the ornaments on Neligan's walking stick?"

"Quite possibly. My investigation, however, didn't end at the morgue. The next step was to obtain and peruse all the shipping lists printed in the regional papers over the last month. This search yielded the clue I was looking for. One of the local publications, the *Bergens Tidende*, the July 18th edition, lists one Hugh MacGregor among the passengers that arrived in Bergen on the steamboat the *Göteborg* the previous day. This name is known to me, for Hugh MacGregor was one of the original crew members of the *Sea Unicorn* around the time Peter Carey was captain. MacGregor's most recent whereabouts in Bergen cannot be traced, nor are there any records of his leaving town. From this, it can be inferred that it is his dead body that lies in the morgue, where it continues to mystify the police. That is, it did until this morning, when I sent an anonymous telegram to the Bergen police headquarters, advising them to ask the *Göteborg*'s captain, who is still in Bergen, to come and identify the body. The captain has kindly done so, confirming my inference that the dead man is indeed Hugh MacGregor and that it had been he who had made the passage on the *Göteborg*."

"By George, Holmes! What could this mean?"

"I suspect it means that it was Carey who had sent MacGregor here to see Neligan, presumably to convey a message or make a point through him. Given the manner of MacGregor's untimely end, we can infer that a likely purpose of this message may have been blackmail. Evidently Carey hadn't been satisfied with what he had already got out of the banker, or had perhaps found an additional means to squeeze him. I am, however, hoping to get the explanation directly from Neligan at our second interview tomorrow. I would be very grateful if you would attend this appointment with me, as my colleague, Dr. McAlister Ray."

"By all means, although I cannot think what purpose my presence could possibly serve."

"Oh, it would serve multiple purposes. For one thing, having a colleague at my side would add credibility to the Sigerson venture. Secondly, the presence of an additional person may forestall Neligan's violent tendencies, should they be triggered by such contingencies as unanticipated references to his past."

"In that case, I will certainly come along, but I must say that I am still at a loss as to where you are heading with this investigation. Without the involvement of the regular force, what do you hope to achieve by confronting Neligan tomorrow?"

"My dear Watson, you're very right in your observations as to the irregular nature of this investigation. Unlike the official business of the Peter Carey murder which initiated my involvement in the Neligan affair, there is neither money nor credit in this unofficial postscript to the case. And yet, there is something about this dark, hidden underside of the public Peter Carey drama that intrigues me more than the official case ever did. I simply cannot rest until I have unravelled the whole of this mystery, if for no other reason than to be able to admire it from all angles. Call it *l'art pour l'art*, if you will. For just as I was starting to fear that the criminal mind has become devoid of all resourcefulness and imagination, here we are, faced with a case whose repercussions may yet prove to offer a beacon of hope for the continued survival of intellect in the realms of the criminal – a case that, while failing to reach the achievements or the range of the late Professor Moriarty, may yet hold some interesting surprises in store."

Having concluded all he had to say on the subject of Neligan for that evening, Holmes became silent and meditative once again, while I retreated to my room, wondering whether the coming day would bring us any closer to a resolution of this strange mystery.

The second appointment was scheduled for eleven o'clock next morning. Holmes and I headed out after breakfast disguised as two hardened seafarers dressed up for a formal occasion. As to how he had procured the wardrobe that did a truly marvellous job of creating this impression, he didn't say. Perhaps he had brought it with the rest of our baggage all the way from London. I didn't typically take part in any of my friend's adventures that involved pretending to be a different person – this was his area of expertise, one that he enacted with no small degree of panache – and the idea that I would be required to play a part filled me with some apprehension. My friend assured me, however, that my role would be largely a silent one. And, as my invented persona was a doctor like myself, the part wouldn't be entirely out of character.

Neligan's office was in an area of Bergen harbour called the Bryggen. This array of wooden buildings lining the east side of the dock had once been used as the offices of the Hanseatic League, and the legacy of that historic organisation was still evident in the architectural style. These were all handsome, nearly identical three-story wooden buildings, and nothing about the one Holmes led us to singled it out as the head office of one of the most successful companies in the region.

A uniformed bellboy let us into a tasteful reception area, where the secretary, Mr. Dolby, greeted us in a Norwegian that sounded stilted even to my untrained ears. Within a few minutes we were shown into the main office, where the man who called himself Magnus Haraldsen sat behind a massive oak desk.

He was a neat, compact fellow with a meticulously trimmed grizzled beard and a slight stature that instantly called to mind the fragile form of John Hopley Neligan. This was, however, where the resemblance ended, for the two shrewd dark eyes that glared up from under deeply lined brows spoke of a habitual watchfulness and even a hidden fierceness. The walking stick propped against his desk where Holmes had said it would be was clearly not a mobility aid, for the man rose without any apparent difficulty to greet us.

Apart from the handful of small tell-tale signs that Holmes had already mentioned, there was nothing about the man to suggest that he was anything other than the prosperous businessman that he purported to be, and I must admit that at that point, in spite of my complete confidence in my friend's judgment, a part of me was still not entirely convinced that this man really was the long-vanished banker. There was simply something about the whole idea that made it seem to outlandish to be true.

My friend's confidence, however, was in no way shaken, as I would soon find out. The two of them exchanged a few words in Norwegian, Holmes giving an excellent impression of introducing me as a ship's surgeon and his closest colleague. Then the shipping magnate motioned us to take our seats, and turned to go back to his desk, when he was stopped in his tracks by my friend's sudden switch to English.

"I suggest we end the pretense," said Holmes, "as my colleague and I both know you aren't who you claim to be."

"How can you – ?" Turning around, the former banker stopped mid-sentence after realising that his instinctive retort in his native tongue had given him away.

"Know? We can know this because it is a fact. For it is true that you are none other than Gerard Winslow Neligan, of the Dawson and Neligan fame."

At the mention of his real name, the banker's face turned livid. My friend's tactics of taking Neligan by surprise were evidently working, for at present the latter just stood there, appearing to have temporarily lost the ability of speech.

"We also know," continued Holmes undeterred, "about your daring escape to Norway back in 1883 with a substantial amount of stolen securities that you subsequently sold for a large sum of money. And we know that you used those funds to reinvent yourself as Magnus Haraldsen, Norwegian shipping magnate. So we may as well move on to the most recent chapter of the story – the death of Hugh MacGregor. What was your motive for murdering him? Was it because he had been sent to blackmail you by Captain Peter Carey, a former adversary whose death at the hands of Patrick Cairns you were still unaware of at the time, or was it because you were afraid that, after all these years, you would be exposed?"

"Who are you?" Neligan's voice had a quiet, menacing ring. "And how do you know these things?"

"Allow me to introduce myself – my name is Sherlock Holmes, and this is my colleague, Dr. Watson. Perhaps some word of my reputation as London's only consulting detective may have reached these shores?"

Neligan didn't respond, but the hard stare in his eyes suggested that he may well have heard of my friend before.

"If your answer is silence," said Holmes, "then I shall provide a brief overview of the events leading up to MacGregor's death. I suspect that

237

Peter Carey sent MacGregor here to add muscle to his most recent attempt to blackmail you. Although Carey had obviously known that you didn't die in 1883, he did not know where you had gone in hiding until recently. It must have been his old network of naval contacts that informed him about your new identity and your current whereabouts. In a way, this was always inevitable, for the more your business expanded overseas, the more likely it was that some of Carey's old shipmates would encounter Haraldsen Dampskibsselskab in their business transactions and recognize you.

"When Carey got wind of Magnus Haraldsen, this must have seemed like a godsend to him, for he had been low on cash for some time, and his usual method for raising funds, selling the stolen securities, no longer looked as appealing to him as before. Recent reports from the London Stock Exchange confirmed that the value of the remaining securities in his possession had fallen in recent years, suggesting that he would have got far less money for them than he expected had he attempted to sell them. This was bad news indeed, for he needed ready cash to run his Sussex estate. Besides, the whole business of selling shares had never been to his liking anyway. He was a pirate at heart, and like a true pirate he preferred real, solid things such as cash over abstract bank documents. When he discovered your current whereabouts and your lucrative business venture, this gave him the idea of getting more money out of you without the hassle of selling the remaining securities.

"Carey's scheme rested upon the existence of the August 1883 ship log, specifically those pages detailing the *Sea Unicorn*'s encounter with your yacht. These records were surely the perfect basis for blackmail, for we can now guess their true contents – namely, that after crossing paths with the *Sea Unicorn*, a banker called Neligan sailed safely on to Norway on his yacht, presumably because his own boat had never been damaged in the first place.

"As to what truly happened to the yacht's crew, this is anyone's guess, although, as the crew of the *Sea Unicorn* had acted as an unusually tight, reticent bunch since then, we can only guess that the crew's fate must have been a sinister one. In fact, this may well have been what made you strike a deal with Carey in the first place. A chance encounter with a violent, readily-bribed pirate in a stormy sea was just the opportunity you were looking for to get rid of anyone who knew of your past life and to start over as someone new.

"Carey had been prudent enough to remove the relevant pages from the sea log and place them somewhere out of reach, so we will never know the finer details – that is, if he ever recorded them in the first place. It's ironic, however, is it not, that almost at the same time that Patrick Cairns was said to have attempted to blackmail Carey, Carey himself attempted to blackmail you through his agent MacGregor, who must have given you quite a scare when he came up to you in a back alley by the docks. Was this why you killed him?"

Throughout the duration of my friend's astounding exposition, Neligan had been able to hold his obvious fury in check, but this last remark of my friend's, and the bluntness of its delivery, shattered the veneer of the latter's composure.

"I care not what you know, sir," growled the banker, "or whether you indeed are who you claim to be. I shall not attempt to refute any of your theories as regards my boat's encounter with the *Sea Unicorn*, as no one can prove what happened that night. The missing ship's log pages cannot be found. And as to whatever other evidence may once have existed, the sea has long claimed it. But I am well within my rights to defend myself from being attacked by miscreants at my own doorstep – especially if they have been sent to blackmail me by that devil, Carey!

"I don't know how that blackguard found out about me, but somehow he did learn about my business in Norway and, as if taking half of my securities wasn't enough, the villain decided to go after the rest of my money too. He began threatening me with exposure, saying that he would make public what happened that night in 1883 and how I had feigned my death. But I refused to acquiesce to his demands, and so he decided to send one of his former underlings to intimidate me. That ruffian accosted me in a dark alley behind the Bryggen, while I was making my way to the office early one morning. I acted in self-defense, I tell you!" Neligan's voice rose abruptly. "So if you are here to accuse me – !"

At the sound of the angry voice, a side door opened, and a young man rushed into the office from an unseen inner study. I was more than a bit startled when I realised this was John Hopley Neligan, the banker's son. The feeling was undoubtedly mutual, for at the sight of us, a look of dread appeared upon young Neligan's pale, delicate face.

"A-ha!" Holmes sounded triumphant. "At last, the final piece of the puzzle."

"What is the meaning of this?" The banker's fury had become mixed with confusion. "John, do you know these men?"

"Father, be careful what you tell them. That man is the London detective I told you about. He has got all of Scotland Yard at his beck and call."

"I don't understand. How can he know so much?" The elder Neligan, apparently exhausted by his own reaction, leaned against the edge of his desk.

"I must commend you," said Holmes to the younger Neligan, "on the excellent little exposition you treated us to on the night we caught you red-handed in Peter Carey's cabin. It was a fine performance indeed, and I must admit I was myself moved. It did have just one flaw, however, in that it was perfectly false. Would you care to fill us in as to your true role in this affair, or should I do the honours?"

John Hopley Neligan launched into a series of feeble protestations in a nervous, quivering voice, but Holmes silenced him with cool efficiency before proceeding with the rest of his narrative, this time addressing the younger Neligan.

"I was immediately struck by the strange timing of your nocturnal visit to Peter Carey's cabin. What a singular coincidence that both you and Patrick Cairns should decide to speak to Carey over something that happened twelve years ago practically on the same night. From this, I came to the inevitable conclusion that this wasn't a coincidence, but a carefully thought-out plan, and that you and Cairns had been acting in collusion. This inference, however, left me with a major conundrum: Namely, what strange common cause could possibly bring together such disparate personalities as yourself and the seasoned harpooner, Patrick Cairns? There had to be a third party acting in the background that could bring about such a collaboration. From this, I deduced that, however improbable the odds, the third party had to be no other than your father, Gerard Winslow Neligan.

"Once I had established the main players in this affair, it was a fairly simple matter to reconstruct your role in the recent events. As soon as he had started receiving blackmail notes from Carey, your father instructed you to go to Carey's Sussex residence and retrieve the incriminating ship's logs. There was no other person he could entrust with such a delicate task. Remembering Carey to be an ill-tempered violent man, your father also tracked down Patrick Cairns, whom he may well have remembered as one of the more sympathetic members of the *Sea Unicorn* crew, and who may have played some part in his escape to Norway of which we are unaware. Having found Cairns, he then hired him to act as your bodyguard for the occasion. Cairns was also given the additional task of ensuring that you obtained the correct ship log records, as he had seen them before and would therefore know what to look for.

"After you and Cairns met near Woodman's Lee, a night's surveillance of Carey's cabin, where he was in the habit of spending his evenings by himself, showed you that he was in a dangerous mood. Therefore you decided that Cairns would approach Carey by himself. This, however, led to a violent fight between the two, as a result of which Cairns killed the latter in self-defense using the singular method of harpoonimpalement. This didn't stop him from going through the ship's log afterwards, but he found the relevant pages to have been already torn out. After Cairns had informed you of the unsuccessful result of his mission, you went back to Carey's cabin by yourself to verify the truth of Cairns's claim. And it was while you were so engaged that Dr. Watson and myself first saw you.

"That leaves only the matter of the missing box of the securities to be explained. Whereas I have no doubt that Cairns stole the box with the remainder of Carey's securities on the night of the murder, I also do not doubt that he had been instructed to hand the box over to *you*, and that it is yourself who hold these securities now."

The younger Neligan was now looking nauseous with anxiety.

"That is a fine theory, Mr. Holmes," he stammered, licking his lips, "but you cannot prove any of it."

"On the contrary," said Holmes, "I have already proved it."

"That is enough!" exclaimed the elder Neligan. "I will not have some stranger come in here and treat my son and myself as criminals on my own property. What will you do now – set the Bergen police on me?" With this, he reached for his ornate walking stick with one quick movement and raised it at Holmes with startling vehemence. My friend, however, snatched the weapon out of his hand in mid-air and snapped it in half as easily as if it had been a twig, before tossing the two halves onto the floor. The elder Neligan stared at the broken fragments with an expression that would have been comic under different circumstances.

"You need not worry," said Holmes, "for I am done my investigation here. I may have no jurisdiction over you, but I am confident that justice will find a way."

The following Friday was our last day in Bergen, and Sigurd Eriksen had come to the harbour to bid us farewell.

"Have you heard?" he asked just as our ship's siren had announced its imminent departure, "that there has been an arson attack in town? Someone set fire to the Haraldsen office building at the Bryggen last night." The building in question was just on the other side of the harbour, and one could just about glimpse a cloud of soot hanging over the area above the tops of the many sailboats that were lined along that side of the dock.

"The building burnt down to the ground," continued Eriksen, "and the old man who was head of the company died in the fire."

This startling news and the abruptness of its delivery struck me with a force that felt almost physical, and it took conscious effort on my part not to betray shock. My friend, however, did not skip a beat.

"Magnus Haraldsen?" he asked.

The Norwegian nodded.

"Have the police been called in?"

"They were at the site last night," said Eriksen, "but now they are gone. Nothing left to be seen but ashes."

"And they are certain it was he who died?" Perhaps it was the fact that the two of us were the last two passengers who had not yet boarded the ship, or perhaps it was simply a case of my friend no longer being able to hold his natural impatience in check, but Holmes was no longer making a great deal of effort to conceal his professional interest in the affair. "How can the police be certain that the remains found in the ruins are truly Haraldsen's?"

"Ah, but they weren't." The big Norwegian looked momentarily sheepish as both of us shot him an inquisitive look at the same time.

"What I mean to say," he explained, "is that his remains were not found in the ruins. It seems that as the fire was raging, the old man somehow found his way out of the burning building. Once outside, he raised the alarm before collapsing onto the pavement. A local constable, who was walking home after a late shift not far from the Bryggen, heard the cry and rushed to help. But he was too late – the old man was already dead of heart failure. In spite of his singed hair and charred clothes, there was no doubt that the dead man was Magnus Haraldsen. Fortunately no one else died in the fire, as the old man was in the habit of staying in the office by himself after closing time on most nights and working long hours, sometimes all night."

"I see," said Holmes, sounding bafflingly unsurprised. "And have the police identified any suspects? Have any witnesses come forward?"

Eriksen shook his head. "Not that I have heard of."

It was then that I noticed that someone was watching us. At the back of the scattered crowd of onlookers that lingered around at the dock, chatting animatedly as they awaited the moment of the ship's departure, there was a silent unmoving figure of a man who stood apart from the others. Despite his unseasonably heavy jacket and muffler, I instantly recognized him as the young man with the mutilated face who had made an emphatic speech against Neligan at the workers' meeting. Holmes too had caught his eye and, although I might have imagined this, the two of them seemed to exchange a quick enigmatic look.

As the ship's siren let out one final impatient blare, Eriksen wished us a pleasant voyage, and then my friend and I finally boarded the steamer that would take us back to England.

"Holmes, what is the meaning of all this?" I asked as we stepped onto the deck.

"Your guess is as good as mine, my dear Watson." Holmes had changed into his regular travel clothes for the return journey. I briefly wondered, not for the first time, how he managed stow away so many different items of clothing in a single ordinary-sized suitcase. On this occasion, however, any further musings on the subject of wardrobe were cut short by a rising sense of vexation that had been brewing inside me throughout our stay in Bergen and which now threatened to burst onto the surface.

If any of this annoyance was showing on my face, my friend seemed to be oblivious to it. "If the Sandviken meeting has taught us anything," he said with an abstracted air, "it is that Neligan had many enemies."

"Holmes," said I, with more than a modicum of acrimony in my tone, "I may not be the keenest of observers, but one would have to be very dull indeed to fail to notice that there is something going on here that you are not letting on. You speak of Neligan's enemies as if they were a theoretical idea, when only a few days ago both you and I were in a room full of people who had been terribly wronged by him and who appeared to wish for nothing more than to see him gone. Are we now, in the wake of his sudden death, to sail serenely away without staying on for the murder investigation, especially when it is obvious even to someone as slow as myself that practically half of the people who were at the workers' meeting that night may well be potential suspects. One of them was right there at the dock a minute ago, looking like a man who had just completed some daring mission, and I know that you saw him too. Surely you of all people should be interested in staying on and making sure that the murderer is caught – that is, unless you already know who he is and are content to do nothing about it for some reason beyond my comprehension."

My friend looked taken aback by my uncharacteristic display of mental acuity, but his amazement quickly dissolved into a mischievous smile.

"My dear Watson," he said, taking a slim cigarette case out of his inner pocket. "I do believe I owe you an apology." He lit a cigarette, and smoked in silence for a few moments while gazing at the azure summer sky before turning his gaze back to me. "It pains me to admit that the role I assigned to you for this trip was one that scarcely extended beyond the capacity of a tourist, whereas you once again have shown yourself to be in possession of abilities far more deserving than that. The sharpness of your intellect dazzles!"

"Does this mean that I am right in assuming that the workers are in some way responsible for Neligan's death?"

"Oh, I have no doubt that one or more of them had a hand in the fire. My Sigerson disguise has got me into more than a few workers' meetings, some of them less-official than the one we attended the other day. I have suspected all along that there was a small faction among them, the most misused of the outcasts, whose demands for justice went beyond the merely social and political, and that it was only a matter of time before they made their move."

"And yet you stood by and did nothing!" I could not keep the righteous indignation out of my voice. "Holmes, that is unlike you."

"Your reaction is understandable on the face of it, but it lacks context. If you had a more in-depth understanding of the circumstances, you would see that your moral outrage is misplaced."

"Enlighten me then."

Holmes lit another cigarette. There was cheering from the crowd as our ship finally pulled out of her berth.

"The course of justice," he said, "which is driven by an unstoppable force, can at times, if obstructed, be compelled to use unconventional outlets. Neligan was too slippery for official channels. Therefore justice was impelled to find alternative means to achieve its end. We must see these desperate men, who are no criminals, in this light. They are merely the hands of justice that could find no other way to assert itself. The police, of course, are perfectly free to make their own inferences as to the circumstances leading up to the arson and to take whatever measures they see fit. For my part, however, I have no wish to further interfere with the workings of the law, either worldly or divine, in this matter, nor do I have any objections as to the latter's chosen methods."

"By Jove, Holmes! You sound positively philosophical."

"Perhaps you would too, my dear fellow, if you had spent as many long nights by yourself under the Arctic sky as I did during my exile."

"Let us hope we never find out."

My friend's startling exegesis had mollified my temper, and my thoughts now turned to the other member of the former banking family.

"What about John Hopley Neligan?" I asked. "What do you think will become of him now?"

"The Younger Neligan has no doubt fled already. It is unlikely that he will be implicated in any crimes if this affair ever becomes public, which is improbable. It is too complex and far-reaching for official channels to handle. I doubt, however, that he will choose to return to England. Indeed, it would not surprise me if young Neligan discovered he had his father's talent for starting over under an alias."

Our steamer left the harbour with another long toot of its siren. As it passed the outer docks, we caught sight of the big emigration ship, which too was scheduled to set sail later that day. The elderly man who had spoken at the Sandviken meeting was there, saying goodbye to his

244

youngest son. The familial resemblance was striking, as was the old man's grief.

When Inspector Stanley Hopkins of Scotland Yard called on Holmes at Baker Street shortly after our return to London, my friend limited the discussion of our Norway trip to the topics of sightseeing and the numerous merits of *kjøttkaker*, omitting any reference to his investigation into Gerard Winslow Neligan. His attempt to avoid any discussion of the Neligans was only partly successful, for Hopkins himself brought up the topic of John Hopley Neligan.

Apparently the Younger Neligan had been found dead off the coast of Ireland. The shipping mogul's son had been trying to sail there from Norway in one of his late father's private yachts when the vessel got caught in a storm and capsized. It appeared that he survived the sinking of the ship by getting into a lifeboat but, as he had no practical knowledge of navigation, ended up drifting aimlessly for several days before perishing of exposure to the elements. He had to be identified by his papers, of which he had a good deal in a metal strongbox. In fact, this seems to have been the only item he had salvaged from the shipwreck.

Hopkins also informed us about the outcome of the Cairns trial. The old harpooner had been acquitted, as it had been found that he had killed Carey in self-defense.

"Justice," said Holmes after Hopkins had left, "is at times as swift as it is sardonic."

Then he picked up his violin and played a sorrowful tune for the rest of the evening.

Lucky Star
by Jen Matteis

Those who follow the reports of my extraordinary friend Sherlock Holmes may recall a case involving a racehorse, Silver Blaze. Less known is the case of Lucky Star, a racehorse equally gifted at the track and no less embroiled in the type of fantastic circumstances upon which Holmes thrives.

The case fell upon our doorstep on an otherwise languid afternoon in late May. Holmes had spent much of the day cataloging and dissecting a novel assortment of smokeless ammunition, and now he stood by the window puffing away at his worn black pipe, idly watching the traffic.

"I believe we are about to receive a client, Watson."

"Oh?"

"There is a young woman with a slight hesitation in her step that says she dreads the process. Yet here she comes, determined."

Soon enough there came a light tread on the stairwell. I opened the door and admitted a woman in her late twenties, lithe and lean and dressed in a stylish grey riding habit. She eyed us both keenly and then addressed Holmes.

"Mr. Sherlock Holmes, my name is Miss Marion Caswell. I've heard much about your abilities and how you have helped those left with no other recourse once the police have tried their all. I am in one such quandary."

"Please, sit and tell us everything," said Holmes. "I believe you'd feel most at ease upon a saddled horse. Alas, we have none here. Pray, try this old armchair there for comfort instead. This is my associate, Dr. Watson. You can speak freely before him. The two of us maintain the utmost confidentiality, and he has assisted with no small number of cases."

"You are in the very best of hands with Holmes," I said. I poured her a cup of tea from the pot Mrs. Hudson had left us. She took it gratefully and smiled at me, but there was a sadness in her expression that I knew all too well.

"Thank you." Miss Caswell sipped her tea, her hands unsteady on the cup. It clattered loudly on the saucer when she put it down. "Four days ago, I lost my older brother, Thomas Caswell. Someone came into our house in the middle of the night and killed him." Her voice shook. "I was the one who found him."

"Were the police of no use at all?" asked Holmes.

246

She shook her head in frustration. "The police are ruling it a simple robbery gone wrong. They haven't found the person responsible, nor anyone who even wished him harm. Thomas was well loved by all."

"What was the manner of his death?"

Her voice wavered but her eyes burned with a fevered intensity. "He was bludgeoned in the head. The police said the wound matches a blow from a heavy object, likely a painting that was on display in the study. Of the painting, there is no sign."

"Is there any significance to the painting?"

She shrugged. "To anyone outside of my family? No. It was a portrait of Lucky Star."

Holmes raised an eyebrow.

"I've heard the name," I said. "It was a horse that met with great success on the track, I believe."

"Lucky is the foundation of my family's wealth. Though his racing days are behind him, our stable continues to perform well thanks to his bloodline."

"I've encountered countless dangerous weapons – including racehorses, believe it or not – yet never before a painting." Holmes frowned. "I wouldn't have believed a horse's image as perilous as the beast itself." "How did your family come by this painting?"

"It was a gift from dear friends and neighbors of ours: My fiancé, William Wright, and his brother, Nathan Wright, who painted it."

"Do you know how someone might have gained access to your home?"

"The police are uncertain. They found no broken windows or forced locks. They suspect a servant or one of the stable hands let someone in, though I tell you in my heart I trust them all."

"I find it hard to imagine that the perpetrator of a crime of this magnitude would leave no clues, regardless of what the police have concluded." Holmes tapped out the ashes of his pipe in the fireplace. "May we visit your home?"

"I would like nothing more," Miss Caswell said with evident relief. She handed us a card with the name and address of a horse farm: *Lucky Star Stables*. "Would it be possible for you to stop by tomorrow, on the three o'clock train? My younger brother James will be there, as will my fiancé."

"We would be happy to come at that time."

"Thank you. By the way, it was Inspector Lestrade who recommended you to us."

"We know him well, and we have worked together often in the past."

A luxuriously cushioned landau cab met us at the station the following afternoon, sent by the Caswells. The driver was a garrulous sort and filled us in on the family history during the ride to the manor. The family had come into wealth a dozen years back after the acquisition of Lucky Star from an auction. The horse had performed well in most of his races and came within a hair's breadth of winning the English Triple Crown. Since then, his stud fees had kept the family comfortable, in addition to winnings earned by his progeny at Alexandra Park Racecourse.

The manor stood on a slight hill on the very edge of London, not far from the track which sustained it. Surrounding it on three sides were paddocks dotted with horses. To the east was a low flat-roofed stable and a track where an exercise boy was putting a well-built bay thoroughbred through its paces.

"I see they are deeply invested in their horses," said I.

"Indeed," said Holmes. "The olfactory evidence was ripe upon Miss Caswell, but I determined for once that the observation wouldn't benefit our conversation."

A rider on a blue roan cantered over to meet our cab. Miss Caswell dismounted and handed the horse to a stable boy who followed at a slight distance on a fat lead pony.

"Thank you for coming so quickly." She took a letter out of her pocket and handed it to Holmes. "Here is a note from Inspector Lestrade. Excepting my poor brother's body, of course, they left the room as they found it. Please, come."

Miss Caswell led us into the house and across a broad foyer lined with horse racing trophies. Holmes examined them as we passed. The largest was a golden first-place trophy for Lucky Star in the London Cup. She brought us to the sitting room, where a tall and lanky man with a trim mustache and the swagger of a horse rider stood to greet us. He had a tousled mop of brown hair and the same striking blue eyes as Miss Caswell, even down to the touch of sadness.

"This is my brother, James Caswell."

He shook our hands firmly. "Mr. Holmes, Dr. Watson, thank you for coming." He turned to Miss Caswell and spoke to her softly. "Please, Marion. You have done enough bringing them here. Leave this to me."

She hesitated for only the slightest moment. "Thank you." She kissed him on the cheek.

"I'm certain we are in capable hands," said Holmes, nodding to her as she left.

Caswell shook his head. "She has barely slept since Thomas's death. You should have seen her hounding the police when they made no arrest. I hope you can bring her some peace."

248

"Please, tell us everything so that we might solve this puzzle."

He motioned for us to follow him down the hall. "Thomas was murdered in the study, which belonged to our father, George Caswell III. He passed away not three months ago, God rest his soul. My family has seen more than its share of death lately."

The study was a tidy and comfortable area, if one of the smaller rooms we'd seen so far. An enormous mahogany desk and a padded leather desk chair took up most of the space. Bookshelves and paintings, both strongly racing-themed, lined the walls. A heavy bronze paperweight, also in the form of a horse, sat on the desk. A bare spot behind the chair drew Holmes's gaze immediately. He touched the wall where the painting had hung, then glanced at the clean floor disapprovingly. "I see everything was tidied up nicely. Let us see what Lestrade had to say about it." He took out the note and read it quickly. "Succinct and as uninformative as I would have expected. Still, there are some useful details. It must have been a man of uncommon skill, or uncommon luck, to deal a deadly blow to the head with the point of the frame. Your brother was armed, but he didn't draw his weapon, despite what must have been a shock at finding an intruder in his house in the middle of the night. When was his body discovered?"

"Marion found him in the morning, just before breakfast."

"She also said there was no sign of the painting. Now I see she wasn't exaggerating." Holmes knelt on the wooden floor below where the painting had hung and traced a finger along one board. He examined the dust in the light from the window, then placed it into a small vial that he returned to his coat pocket. James Caswell watched him with skepticism.

"What do you think to find that the police would have overlooked?"

"Almost anything. One must open oneself to any possibility when collecting evidence, and let the findings speak louder than one's assumptions. So far, I find this a very strange case. How often does a man murder another in a midnight act of desperation, yet have the wherewithal to make off with every shred of evidence afterward? There isn't a scrap of the painting left behind, despite the likelihood of it having broken upon impact."

"Well, I suppose one runs off with the gun or knife used on a victim, for fear that it would reveal something. Perhaps the painting would have revealed something?" I felt foolish even as I said it.

"Perhaps," said Holmes dismissively. He turned to Caswell. "Did Thomas often sit up late in the study, or do you think he heard a noise and went to investigate it?"

"Thomas was exceptionally close to our father, and it fell to him to manage the household accounts upon his passing. I don't doubt he spent many long hours here while the rest of us slept."

"What can you tell us of your staff?"

"We employ seven total. I trust all of them. Emma, our maid, is the closest to us. Most work in the stables, and none are new to the household."

"Did any of them see anything?"

"Nothing out of the ordinary. The police interviewed all of them extensively." He hesitated. "Inspector Lestrade did talk to one of the grooms for longer than the others, but I don't know if it means much. We have absolute trust in him. Joe Irving has been here a decade or more."

"Yes, Lestrade mentioned that name in his note. I would certainly be interested in speaking with him."

"He is usually in the east stable, if you wish to find him later."

"Thank you." Holmes examined the sole window, which looked out over the southern paddock. "Can you please show us the ways an intruder might have gained entrance?"

"That is one of the few facts we know." Caswell led us out of the study and down the hall. "The house is always locked at night. However, the back door was unlocked that morning, which must be where he made his exit – perhaps his entrance as well. It's a wonder we all slept through the incident, but it is a large house. Our bedrooms are on the other side of the house, on the upper story."

Holmes knelt to examine the lock. "The police were correct in this, at least: The door hasn't been forced. Are there many who have keys to your home?"

"Unfortunately, yes. In addition to myself, my sister, and our servants, the Wrights have access. That has been the case for many years. Our families are closer than most. Their home is only a short distance away, and the two of them are practically brothers to me." He smiled. "And they will truly join the family, as soon as the wedding takes place between my sister and William."

"Did anyone in either family object to the engagement?"

"Not a one. My father may have had some misgivings, but the engagement didn't take place until after he had passed."

"I should very much like to meet the Wrights," said Holmes.

At that moment, the front door opened and we heard Miss Caswell's voice in conversation with a gentleman.

"You shall not have to wait long. There is William right now, if I'm not mistaken. He is here more often than not, sometimes with his brother as well."

We joined Mr. Wright and Miss Caswell in the dining room, where Emma had set out a late afternoon tea. Wright stood and came over to greet us. "Mr. Holmes, how is your investigation proceeding?" He was a well-built young man with dark eyes and a serious expression, dressed neatly but not richly.

"I expect it to proceed quickly, if I am unhindered."

"Anything is yours if you believe it will assist you," Mr. Wright said sincerely.

"Is your brother at home today? I'm curious to speak with the painter."

"Certainly, though I doubt he can aid you. We can be there in a moment. It's but a short walk across the southern field."

After our tea, during which Miss Caswell shared recollections of her late father, Wright led us out the back door and down a dirt path along a paddock. An old swayback thoroughbred came over to us and thrust his grizzled head between the railings. "If you had seen the painting, you might recognize Lucky Star." Wright scratched him behind the ears and the horse whickered softly. "He isn't the specimen he was in his youth, but he still has his charms. Don't tell Marion, but I sneak him some sugar cubes every now and then – hence his sweet demeanor toward me. He has come a long way since his temperamental youth."

"What was your opinion of the horse's portrait?" asked Holmes, his keen eyes taking in every detail of the paddock. "Did it have any special significance?"

"Only the obvious, it being a symbol of the Caswells' success," said Wright. "It was a magnificent painting. It didn't deserve to be hidden away in George Caswell's study, even if that's where Nathan recommended it for display. I told him I would move it to the parlor for everyone to see once Marion and I are married."

The path took us through light woods downhill to the country road and another house, less sumptuous by far. "This is our family home, and also Nathan's studio," Wright said. He pointed to a little outbuilding, no more than a shed. "He does all of his painting there, except for Lucky Star, which he did *en plein air* at the paddock you saw."

"Is it only you and your brother who live here?" asked Holmes.

"Yes." His face darkened slightly. "Life hasn't always been kind to Nathan, so please excuse any rudeness on his part. Our parents passed away when we were very young, and our aunt raised us here until we came of age. I have two sisters as well, though they both live in the city now. You can speak with Nathan at least, who is home, and we can arrange for you to speak with anyone else in my family if you wish it."

We crossed a rickety porch that creaked underneath our boots. Inside, a bearded man who shared his brother's dark eyes and somber demeanor sat at the table with a chipped mug in his hands.

"Nate, this is Mr. Sherlock Holmes. He is a private detective who is helping the Caswells find Thomas's murderer."

"Yes, I remember Marion mentioned him the other day. Please, sit. Join us for coffee if you like."

"How did you hurt your arm?" asked Holmes. Now that he mentioned it, I saw Nathan Wright was holding one arm at an odd angle.

"An old injury from my youth, I'm afraid. Horse riding agrees with some of us more than others."

"He was thrown by Lucky Star. He was only five at the time. It's fortunate the injury wasn't more severe."

Nathan smiled bleakly. "You don't have to tell him our whole family history." He stood and served us coffee, though it didn't look an easy task for him. The tabletop was splintered and marked with rings. Though it was tidy, the whole house looked worn down, especially when compared to the opulence of the Caswell estate.

"I apologize for our poor accommodations," said Nathan, as if my thoughts were clear to him. "We aren't all as fortunate as the Caswells or my brother here." He clapped his brother on the back.

"The Caswells have modest roots." William addressed this to his brother, as if it were an old argument. "It was only their luck at the track that changed their situation."

"Indeed."

"What can you tell us about the painting?" asked Holmes. "I've been told that it wasn't particularly valuable, which lands us hard against the problem of why someone would wish to make off with it."

Nathan shifted uncomfortably. "There isn't much to say about it. I simply wanted to give them something in return for all they have done for us. Art has always been my gift, in more ways than one."

"Our families have exchanged presents for as long as I can remember," said William. "That silver pitcher is from Mary Caswell, their late mother. So is the platter on the shelf beneath it. If someone wanted to make off with valuable items belonging to the Caswells, they would do as well to steal from this house as from their own."

"They even helped with our medical bills after my fall," continued Nathan, "though Mr. Caswell had barely more to his name than our father did back then. Thomas was like a brother to us both." He paused. "I wish I could help you, but I cannot think of anyone who had an argument with Thomas, or any other of the Caswells. In any case, I hope you find who did this."

"That is my sincere hope as well," said Holmes. "Thank you for your time. I should like to return to the manor and speak with some of the others there. I hope to come back tomorrow and continue our investigation."

The older Wright led us back to the manor and pointed us to the eastern stable, the smaller of the two. Then he left us. It was a long, dimly lit building filled with the soft sounds of horses shuffling over straw and whickering to each other as the sun began to set. Far in the back, an old white-haired groom sat on a stool, polishing the silver buckles on a saddle with an old rag. "Joe Irving?" asked Holmes.

The groom put aside the saddle and stood to shake our hands. "You must be Mr. Holmes, the detective. I spoke with Inspector Lestrade. He said you might come by and have a word. I appreciate you trying to find Mr. Caswell's murderer." He shook his head mournfully. "That's a horrible business."

Holmes appraised him a moment in the failing light. "You have seen something that has made these recent events less of a surprise to you than to everyone else at this horse farm. Yet for some reason, Lestrade didn't share the details of his conversation with you."

"Well, it hasn't anything to do with Thomas." Irving stood and picked up a pitchfork, then began to clean a stall with a sort of nervous energy. "But that Lestrade, he asked me about anything funny I might have seen, and this is what came to mind straight away. No one wants to hear it, but I think someone tried to off old George Caswell. He was riding out in the paddock and the saddle slipped off, tumbling him onto the ground. He could have been seriously hurt, but he got right back up. He led that horse back to the stable here and had me look it over. One of the straps was cut mostly through, neat as you please." He stopped cleaning and looked at Holmes meaningfully, resting on the pitchfork. "Like it was deliberate. I said as much to Mr. Caswell and to anyone else who would hear me, but they didn't pay no mind. They said these things happen. I take care of the tack for this house, so I know it was in good shape the night before, because I check every night before I leave."

"When was this?" asked Holmes.

"Three years back, that summer after Lucky's son Rising Star won the races at the Frying Pan. Alexandra Track, as you might know it. Everyone went on with life as usual, but that shook me to the bone."

"Was there any chance Thomas could have gotten on that horse instead of George Caswell?"

"Not a one. Thomas wasn't much of a rider, not like James and his da. Happy to mind the books and manage the races at the track, but he didn't like to get his boots dirty. Not like the other Caswells – now they are all real riders, not ones to let the jockeys have all the fun."

"Did the older Caswell have any enemies that you're aware of?"

"Everyone'll tell you the Caswells don't have enemies, but the fact is, if you race, you make enemies, even if you done nothin' to deserve it.

253

Every win you take, that's a loss for someone else who wanted that purse, and you never know how badly. Now, I can't give you no names, but there's a long list of owners that have seen their darlings place second or third to a Caswell horse, and if someone needed that race money bad enough, or lost a bid on the wrong day, that's an enemy right there, no two ways about it. Might take a bump, a bit of elbow, or a fall to make an enemy even then. But those things happen. Intended or not – who can say?"

"I see. Thank you."

Holmes fell into a thoughtful mood in the carriage to the station, having silenced the garrulous driver with a curt retort early in the trip. A light rain had begun to fall by the time we arrived back in Baker Street. Despite the late hour of our return, he set aside his collection of bullets and busied himself at the microscope with the samples that he had collected throughout our visit to the Caswells' home.

"Mud and manure, Watson," he finally pronounced. "Neither are in short supply in these samples. There must be something we have overlooked."

"Could there be something hidden on the painting – a more valuable drawing on the back or a map? If you recall the Musgrave Ritual, the possibility of a family treasure is a real one."

"Running into that twice would be an exercise in improbability, but we mustn't rule it out." Holmes began to pace. "You're correct in the line of reasoning, at least. The painting is without doubt the key. But it also cannot be valuable to the thief, which is the real puzzle."

"Why do you say that?"

Holmes halted his pacing and looked at me with an amused smile. "Were it truly valuable, I doubt he would have used it to deal such an unconstrained blow to poor Thomas."

"If he were surprised by him, he might have."

He waved away my objection. "The study had no shortage of more suitable items – the paperweight on the desk for one. No, he didn't hold back from using it as a weapon. It may as well have been a club to him, given how he wielded it. Yet he cleaned up every shard and took it away with him! That does suggest another value to the painting, and even fits your treasure map theory, though it's a supposition brought by a previous case and not very well matched with our present circumstances."

Holmes resumed his pacing while I tried to figure out if I had been dealt a compliment or a well-meaning insult. A moment later he looked at me and said, "I didn't mean to insult you, my dear fellow! I appreciate your insights, even those that point in the wrong direction, as they often place me more firmly upon the correct path." He collapsed onto the sofa and stretched out his long legs. To anyone else, it would have appeared he had decided to take a sudden nap. Finally, he shook his head as if coming out of a daze. "We have been focused on the wrong thing entirely, Watson."

"Is that so?"

"There is more to this incident than appears on the surface. Would you mind paying a visit to the Coroner's Office tomorrow morning, while I return to the Caswells' manor to look into another matter?"

"Of course. I assume you wish to see the coroner's notes on Mr. Caswell's death?"

"Yes." He smiled in a self-satisfied manner. "But the elder Caswell, not the younger."

"George Caswell? But he died alone in his study. You aren't interested in the report regarding his son's death?"

"That cannot hurt. However, any items of interest will be found in the father's report and not in the son's. In any case, meet me at the manor tomorrow afternoon and we'll compare our findings. I believe I shall have recovered the painting by then."

The following afternoon I found Holmes in the back of Lucky Star's paddock, with his boots and pants drenched in mud and worse. To my astonishment, I had interrupted him in the middle of shoveling out a compost pile. The horse stood far off on the other side of the paddock, which made me wonder if Holmes had admonished him for disturbing his work.

"Holmes! You're a sight. Did they take you on as a stable-hand? Here, I have the papers you wanted."

"At least one of us met with success." Holmes glanced at the papers, and then pocketed them with a look of satisfaction. "There is no shortage of muck around here where one could dispose of a painting. Come, lend me a hand. I've brought gloves and pitchforks for both of us. Between the two of us we'll make short work of it."

"You think the painting is here?" Holmes had already moved a veritable mountain of manure out of one pile and into another. "Why would someone throw it here, after going through the trouble of stealing it?"

"The answer to that lies in the painting. Let us find it first. Then it will surely tell us all we wish to know."

Though my recollections often tell of the thrilling and the fantastic, in truth much of detective work is a slog. For how could Holmes come to his extreme knowledge of the minutest fact without hours of tedious study? That afternoon passed in some of the most dreary detective work I have known, and I will not belabor the point. I was beyond relieved when my pitchfork finally brought up a canvas impaled on its tines: Filthy, sodden from the rain of the night before, but still very much recognizable as the missing painting of Lucky Star.

"How did you know to look here?" I presented it to Holmes on the tines, feeling relief and curiosity in equal measure. The horse stood gleaming in the grassy paddock, muscles standing out under a glossy white coat. I'm no connoisseur of art, but I could tell it was painted by a talented hand.

"Careful with it! Don't touch it without the gloves."

"Holmes, I have absolutely no intention of touching this with my bare hands."

"As for how I knew to look here, I believe someone was thinking it would be exactly the last place anyone would want to look." Holmes held open a bag and I inserted the item. He closed it thoroughly and tucked it in his jacket. "Let us bring this back to Baker Street where we can study it at our leisure."

Back in our rooms, Holmes cut away a piece of the painting with a scalpel and examined it under the microscope. He then performed a series of chemical experiments that yielded vile fumes, at which point I decided to take a short walk for my health. I returned to find a dog-cart and its driver patiently waiting outside and rightly supposed it would soon take us back to the Caswells'.

Upon my entrance, Holmes's eyes gleamed with satisfaction and he sat on the couch with the demeanor of a cream-sated cat. But he sprung to his feet at once and grabbed his coat and hat. "Come, Watson! I knew your curiosity wouldn't let you roam too far, so I waited for you. Let us return and settle this matter once and for all. I've taken the liberty of hiring a driver – there is no time to wait for a train. I trust you have your revolver." He fairly raced down the stairs, and I did my best to match his long-legged stride.

We boarded the carriage and set off quickly for the Caswell estate. The sun sank as we rode across the bumpy cobblestones, lending a yellow hue to the slate-topped roofs and shining windows. Holmes caught my glance at the picturesque scene. "The city puts on such a bright display, but what horrors lie behind these windows? For each case you record, Watson, I wager a thousand more go undiscovered." Holmes sank into a melancholy mood for the rest of the trip and ignored the questions I asked him.

When the carriage pulled up to the manor, Holmes jumped out with renewed enthusiasm, having set aside whatever grim thoughts had plagued him. "Now to find James Caswell. He should witness this."

We collected Caswell, and Holmes set out in a determined trot for the Wrights' home, both of us trailing him. The hour had grown late, and William Wright met us at the door blinking wearily. "What is it? Have you found Thomas's killer?" He noticed my revolver with alarm. "Should I fetch my gun?"

"No need. Please, wait outside," said Holmes smoothly, stepping into the house. Nathan sat at the table in the same worn seat as before. He looked up as we entered.

"Mr. Holmes."

"I found something of yours." Holmes took from his coat a section of the canvas we had recovered and held it out to Nathan, who drew back from it, his eyes wide.

"Where did you find that?"

"I see you aren't as delighted to see it as someone unfamiliar with its secrets might suppose. I found it in Lucky Star's paddock, exactly where you left it." He unrolled the painting and placed it in front of Nathan, who stood and moved away from it. Holmes's eyes gleamed with satisfaction. "What would you say, Watson, were I to tell you that this painting was absolutely dripping with poison?"

"I might say that was the less offensive of two things it was covered in. There are several pigments that contain toxins, are there not?"

"That is true, but never to this degree. It is as I thought. The painting is a murder weapon twice over – the second a botched effort to conceal the first. In a close room like that study, with the warmth of the fireplace above which it was mounted, its poisonous properties would have some opportunity to fill the environs. It might have taken months or even years to work its evil, but I believe it matches the symptoms in the coroner's report. It also explains why Wright chose to work on this painting outside, instead of in his studio."

"Good Heavens!" I cried.

"Yes, he decided to take a more subtle approach, after his attempt to harm him by cutting the saddle strap didn't work."

Nathan glanced at the back door, then at Holmes.

"Inspector Lestrade will arrive imminently with several of London's so-called best," said Holmes. "Fleeing will only compound your guilt."

William had overheard our conversation and came in to confront his brother. "Is it true? You killed good old George Caswell? For God's sake, why?"

Nathan spat on the floor angrily. "'Good ol' George Caswell' is the source of our family's ills far more than any gain. As you may recall, if you think for half a moment, that he placed me on the back of an ill-tempered thoroughbred when I was five, then thought we should love him for it when he paid for part of what it took to put my shoulder and my arm back together, though they never healed right."

"What about the gifts they gave us? They cared for us like their own – George and Mary both."

"What good did those gifts do us? There they sit, collecting dust and looking pretty, but could we sell them for the money we need? No, curse our pride as well, for there they had to sit so every time a Caswell visited they could look upon them and see what good they had done our family, when in fact they had done no good at all."

"Did you kill Thomas as well?" asked William. Holmes motioned to me, and I went to stand near William, whose fists were clenched with rage. "You cannot say he ever did you any harm, regardless of what mad imaginings you have invented for his father."

Nathan sighed and all the anger drained from him in a moment, replaced by abject misery. "No, Thomas didn't deserve that. He surprised me in the study." He looked up at William. "It was an accident. I panicked and hit him a tremendous blow, not knowing how to explain myself. I had to get rid of that painting before you moved in. It could have killed you if you had hung it in the parlor. We never needed the Caswells, William. We lost our parents, but we had each other. You didn't have to try so hard to replace them by abandoning me and spending all your time there. I didn't want the Caswells' love and I couldn't abide their charity. All I wanted was a brother, and now they have taken that for good as well."

William turned away in grief and anger. James went to him and placed a hand on his shoulder, but he shrugged it off and pushed his way out the door.

"Let him go," said Holmes. "He will go to Miss Caswell, and it is for the best that she hears about this from him directly."

Nathan sat down and sank his head into his arms on the table. "The Caswells took my health, my brother, and now my freedom. I hope you at least understand my motives now, sad as they are."

"The world takes from all men," said Holmes. "It is how they respond to loss that best defines them."

Lestrade arrived shortly and took the despondent Nathan Wright away. It left a sour note in my stomach seeing him leave with our sharp-faced detective friend.

"Will the courts take mercy on him?" I asked Holmes later that night in our flat. A fire burned merrily on the hearth, but my thoughts were with the young artist. "He seems a sorry specimen for a murderer, as he let that accident as a youth define him."

"Perhaps. In a different world, Watson, men would be resilient and not be driven to such acts. But then I would be out of work, so I cannot truly wish for what might otherwise seem a utopia. More than anyone else, you have seen what idleness does to me."

I shrugged. "Your work is akin to mine. My medical duties are filled with the tawdry and grim, and yet it brings fascination and satisfaction as well." I poured us each a shot of whisky. "But let us not curse the world for our own sakes. May the human body one day gain unmitigated resilience as well as the soul. I would be happy to see us both unemployed."

Holmes smiled at me. "I suppose so. The delight of the surefooted hunt ends with prey in hand, which is always the least satisfying aspect of the process. Still, as man is tied to the accident of his birth, we will continue to act as our nature directs us. But a moment's reflection brings satisfaction, for the tangled plots we have unwound and the evil we have brought to its end."

A Matter of Convenience
by Geri Schear

As I have said elsewhere, my friend Mr. Sherlock Holmes considered the year 1895 a high water time for his business as a consulting detective. Despite his almost constant activity, I never saw him look better. He thrived on his cases and the mental stimulation they provided.

One of the most unusual matters to engage his attention that year was the curious death of Mr. Rupert Ellison, the Cornish mine owner. I say one, but in truth, this presented two cases in one following, as it did, the peculiar disappearance of Ellison's daughter two months earlier.

For all the peculiarities of the case, I could not persuade *The Strand* to publish my account, thanks to the mention of the ladies' convenience in Piccadilly. Perhaps one day when mores are less stringent, it may come to light.

That Tuesday morning in late October, we were pleased and surprised when Inspector Stanley Hopkins called upon us as we were finishing breakfast. I felt particularly happy to have a distraction from the raging toothache that had kept me awake all night.

"Inspector Hopkins," Holmes greeted the policeman, not even trying to hide his delight. The young inspector was a favourite of my friend's and had brought him several of his more interesting cases. "It is always a pleasure to see you. From the Kentish mud on your shoes and trousers, I gather you have brought me another intriguing puzzle."

"You are almost right, Mr. Holmes," Hopkins replied, "But I have brought you two cases – or one case in two halves, if you prefer."

"Even better! Please sit down and help yourself to the coffee, then tell me how I can help you."

Cup in hand, and settled in his seat, Hopkins said, "If you will indulge me, Mr. Holmes, it is difficult to know where to begin. But I believe I must start ten weeks ago, in August. Miss Ysella Ellison, daughter of Rupert Ellison, was brought into the city by her father to purchase a trousseau for her upcoming nuptials. She needed to use the ladies' – ah – *convenience* in Piccadilly. She went down the stairs to the facility and never returned."

"Wha'?" I exclaimed.

"This was in August?" Holmes said. "And since?"

"She hasn't been seen since that day. We would have consulted you on the case, Mr. Holmes, but you were in France at the time.

"Part two of the tale occurred last night, Mr. Rupert Ellison either flung himself or was flung from his bedroom window and met his death in the forecourt beneath."

"Death by defenestration!" Holmes exclaimed, and chuckled. "Splendid! Rupert Ellison? Do you mean the infamous Cornish mine-owner?"

"The same. I thought you would like it," Hopkins said drily.

"I don't think I've ever heard of him," I said. Though it came out sounding like, "*I own fick I ver errd v'im.*"

For some reason, Holmes seemed perfectly able to understand me and he translated for Hopkins before explaining, "Ellison owned a tin mine not far from Lamorick – it must be twenty years ago now. The miners told him many times that the mine was unsafe, but he ignored the warnings. Eventually the mine collapsed, and it was only thanks to Providence that no more than three men lost their lives."

"He should have served time," Hopkins said, pursing his lips in disdain.

"While I am eager to hear about Ellison's misfortune, we ought to begin with his daughter's disappearance. Pray tell me, Hopkins: What are the facts?"

"Ellison never achieved the riches he felt entitled to and he blamed the miners for this lack. Eventually, he met and married Jennifer Dalrymple, the only child of Sir James Dalrymple. What the young woman's father made of the match we can only imagine. Still, the marriage went ahead, and Ellison left Cornwall to live with his wife in Sevenoaks. Sir James had given the couple a limited lease on Stag Hall.

"About a year later, Mrs. Ellison was delivered of a baby girl, Ysella. However, the mother unfortunately died in childbirth.

"The child grew into a handsome young woman and was very popular with everyone she met. Earlier this year, she became engaged to a fine young man named Stephens. They had known each other for several years, and everyone was very excited about their union.

"Ellison arranged for his daughter to spend a few days in the city to purchase her trousseau. She was to travel with her governess, Miss Gertrude Lilly. Unfortunately, the governess was urgently summoned home to Bristol a couple of days before the outing was scheduled. Miss Ysella was willing to wait until she returned to go shopping, but Mr. Ellison decided that he would take her.

"It was supposed to be quite the adventure for her and her father. Tea at Claridge's, shopping at Harrods, then dinner at the Savoy where they planned to stay. Mr. Ellison also promised Ysella some visits to the theatre.

"Miss Ellison had felt poorly the day before with an upset stomach – nervous excitement, they thought – but when they reached the city, she needed to use the – ah – *facilities*."

He paused and I could see Holmes becoming impatient. "The ladies' convenience in Piccadilly was close at hand," Hopkins continued, "and Mr. Ellison had the coach wait while the lady went down the steps."

"Mr. Ellison waited several minutes, but there was no sign of the lady returning. After some fifteen minutes or so, he asked a police constable to check if his daughter was all right. He was afraid she might have taken ill. However, when the officer investigated, Miss Ellison was nowhere to be seen. There were several ladies in the convenience along with the attendant, but no one had paid any heed to Miss Ellison in all the confusion. At this point, the policeman suggested perhaps they had missed the lady – either while he and Mr. Ellison were talking, or prior to his arrival. However, as the gentleman observed, their coach was standing hard by, and she would surely have returned to it."

"Curious," Holmes said.

"'Ow is 'at posh'ble?" I asked.

"How indeed?" Holmes agreed. "As I recall, there is only one means of egress in the public facilities. If the father stood watching the steps, he surely couldn't have missed her."

"Quite the mystery," Hopkins said in his usual deadpan way.

"And the girl hasn't been seen since?"

"No, Mr. Holmes, not a hair of her."

"What efforts were made to find her?"

"We conducted an exhaustive search. Every woman in the convenience was questioned, but nothing."

"Curious." Holmes remained silent for several minutes. Hopkins and I remained quiet, allowing him to think. At length, he seemed to shake off her reverie and said, "I gather the girl had no wealth of her own. Who benefitted from her death?"

"With respect, Mr. Holmes, we don't know she is dead, but to answer the question, no one really. The girl receives a monthly stipend from Sir James and was likely to receive a generous wedding gift upon her nuptials. Her fiancé, Edgar Stephens, is one of five sons, and his family, though well respected, are not wealthy. However, he is a fine engineer and has already begun to make his name."

"I take it Ellison has no wealth of his own to pass on?"

"Not a *sou*. He inherited his wife's fortune but that's gone, for the most part. The Hall and its upkeep are paid for by Sir James."

"Sh'pr'd 'esh sh'll 'ere," I mumbled.

"Yes," Holmes agreed. "I confess I share your surprise, Watson. That Ellison was allowed to remain in the Hall after his wife's death," he added to Hopkins.

"The lease permitted Ellison to remain as long as his children were unmarried. It should have passed to any male heirs once they reached their majority to be theirs in perpetuity. Should Ellison and his wife have only females, their first-born grandson would then inherit."

"And upon Ysella's marriage?"

"The lease transfers to her and her husband."

I emitted a string of what I'm sure were incomprehensible vowels. Holmes nodded.

"As the doctor says, it seems unlikely that Ysella would evict her father, though I suppose her husband might. At any rate, the Hall wouldn't be Ellison's to do with as he wished."

"True enough," Hopkins said.

"What happens if his daughter dies before him?"

"Ellison loses all rights of tenancy, and the Hall reverts back to Sir James and his line – he has three living brothers. But, of course, she hasn't been declared dead, just missing."

"'Ow 'id 'ey ge' on?" I mumbled.

A confused Hopkins looked at Holmes. "How did they get on?" Holmes translated. "Father and daughter, I assume." I nodded.

"Very well, by all accounts. Though Ellison wasn't what you'd call doting, he seemed very proud of the young woman. That said, according to the housekeeper, Ysella, though dutiful to her father, adored her grandfather Sir James and he was equally fond of her. I gather she bore – or bears – a marked resemblance to her mother."

"Curious," Holmes said. "Well, let us move on to Ellison's death."

"About eight weeks ago – that is, approximately two weeks after Ysella's disappearance – Ellison awoke from a sound sleep in a state of terror. He claimed his daughter's spirit had appeared to him and told him he would soon die. With some considerable effort, the butler, Bates, managed to calm him, and he went back to sleep, but a few days later, it happened again.

"He spoke to the local minister, Reverend Franklin, saying that the room suddenly became very cold, and he awoke to see the flames in the fireplace glowing green. The smoke began billowing out and his daughter's face appeared in the midst. She cried, 'Papa, why?'

"For the next several weeks this continued. Ellison would waken screaming, convinced that his daughter was haunting him. It got so he was afraid to go to sleep. He was seen by his physician and told that his nerves were getting the better of him. His physician told him that his distress over

263

his daughter's disappearance was the reason for his 'nightmares', and suggested he go to a sanatorium for some rest, but this he refused to do so.

"His housekeeper, a Miss Malvern-Pitt – "

"Agnetha Malvern-Pitt?" Holmes interrupted.

Hopkins checked his notebook. "That's right. Do you know her, Mr. Holmes?"

"I've never met her," he replied with a smile. "Forgive my interruption and pray continue."

"The housekeeper suggested he go away on holiday for a time. He still owned a small estate in Cornwall, though he hadn't been back since his marriage. He refused, saying, 'I must be here waiting for Ysella when she returns. What would she think if she came home and found I wasn't here?'

"Finally, last evening, Ellison retired early complaining of a headache. At around two o'clock, he awoke screaming. The butler ran into the room, but it was hard to see with all the smoke. Then he heard a crash and realised Ellison had fallen through the window. He landed on the forecourt below and died moments later."

"Fallen or was flung," Holmes commented. "What do you make of it, Hopkins?"

"I think there's something fishy going on, and I'd like to find out what it is. There's nothing I can put my finger on, Mr. Holmes. That's why I've come to you. You've never steered me wrong yet."

Holmes nodded in acknowledgement.

"There is one other point, Mr. Holmes. Before I left Sevenoaks, I spoke with Reverend Franklin. He confirmed that Ellison had been to see him and had claimed that he was being haunted.

"Franklin scoffed at the notion, but Ellison was so distraught that he offered to bless the Hall. This he did, but with no good effect."

Holmes rubbed his hands together, unable to hide his glee. "Well, quite a double-headed problem," he said.

"Will you come to Sevenoaks?" Hopkins asked. "I confess I'm a bit at a loss with this one."

"Perhaps in the morning," my friend replied, yawning and stretching on the chair.

"Could you not come this afternoon?"

Holmes sighed. "I do have a rather busy morning," he said, though I knew for a fact nothing could be further from the truth. "I suppose I can come later today. Say, five o'clock?"

"Thank you, Mr. Holmes," Hopkins said, rising. "I appreciate it. Doctor." And donning his hat, he left.

I said something that I hoped sounded like, "You don't mean to go there at once, Holmes? I would have thought time is of the essence."

"How so?" he said, lighting his pipe. "The man is already dead, and the body will be in the morgue by now. Besides, there are some things I need to investigate here in London before I leave. I shall endeavour to return here by, let's say half-past three. If I'm not here by then, go ahead to the Charing Cross Station and I shall meet you on the platform at four o'clock."

I had intended to see my dentist that afternoon, but I convinced myself that I would be likely to miss my train that afternoon if I kept my appointment.

My overnight bag was already packed, so I allowed myself to doze off in the armchair to make up for my wretched night.

I jerked awake at three o'clock thanks to Mrs. Hudson bringing up a pot of coffee. When it was sufficiently cool, I drank it, and nibbled on the egg sandwich she had been kind enough to make for me. Feeling fortified, though still in pain, I took a hansom to the railway station.

With less than a minute to spare, Sherlock Holmes joined me on the platform. Not until our train was on the way did he greet me.

"Oh dear," he said. "I'm not sure you should have joined me, old friend. I can see you are in some discomfort. Did you see the dentist?"

"Uh, no," I mumbled.

"Tsk. If you would prefer to return to Baker Street, I will quite understand."

"Nosh if I cam helph."

"Oh, I'm sure you can be of enormous help," he said. All the same, I worried about the mischief I saw in his eyes.

As we travelled, he told me about his morning.

"I visited the ladies' – ah – *facilities* in Piccadilly," he said. "As Hopkins said, there is but one means of entrance and egress. As you may recall, the convenience is below ground, with the sole entrance on an island in the middle of the thoroughfare. Inside, there is a central area of washbasins, with the facilities on either side of the room. Privacy is maintained by curtains."

"Waip," I muttered. "You wenf in?"

"Of course I went in. How else could I examine the premises? Oh, relax, Watson, I disguised myself as an old lady. No one looked twice at me."

I shook my head, unconvinced.

"The room was quite busy, at least half-a-dozen ladies were tending to female matters. Two women sat on a bench nursing infants. No, of course I didn't more than glance at them. Really, Watson, what do you take me for? An attendant was on duty, a rather dour woman who accepted payment from the ladies without a comment but was quick enough to assist any lady who needed it, fastening buttons and approving the manner of dress met with societal standards. I asked her in a husky voice of the very old about the young lady who'd gone missing two months earlier. She'd been on duty that day, she said, and she had no recollection of ever seeing the lady in question."

"Truf?" I asked, trying to limit my speech as much as possible.

"Yes, I believe she spoke the truth. She demonstrated excellent recall for who was present and so forth."

"So whaf 'appen?"

"There are only three ways a person can vanish, Watson. Either she finds a previously unknown means of egress. She disguises herself and so leaves in plain sight, but not recognised. Or . . . ."

"Or?"

"Or she was never there to begin with. I have satisfied myself that there is only one way in and out of the ladies' convenience, and that is via the staircase that leads down from the street. That leaves the other two possibilities. I will need further information before I can narrow it down."

Sevenoaks is roughly twenty-eight miles from Baker Street, and the journey took less than an hour. Hopkins met us at the station and, at Holmes request, drove us in a cart directly to the morgue. Holmes sat back in his seat with his eyes half-closed. I didn't dare speak thanks to the condition of my jaw. It was, therefore, a silent journey.

The morgue was, like every other such facility I've been in, cold, gloomy, and poorly lit. The surgeon, had he not been standing when we entered, might easily have been mistaken for one of his cadavers: Tall, thin to the point of emaciation, a head as hairless as a billiard ball, and that look of one who is more at home among the dead than the living.

The remains of the late Mr. Rupert Ellison lay waxen and cold on a slab. My friend immediately got to work, examining the body.

The dead man had been fifty-eight when he died. He was about five-foot-eight and of a sturdy build. His thinning hair was grey, and his face suggested a strong character. The bones were fine and well-developed. The fingers long and thin.

After several minutes of close examination leaning over the corpse, Holmes straightened his back. "A non-smoker," he declared, "but a whisky drinker, particularly at bedtime. He used to walk a great deal, but hasn't done so in recent weeks. He was a keen fisherman, but hasn't held a rod in some months."

He studied the face of the dead man and said, "Was his bedroom door to the left or right of his bed?"

Hopkins blinked at the question and said, "To the left, Mr. Holmes, if you were standing at the foot of the bed."

"And the fire was to the right?"

"Yes, that is so."

"Ah. So, the fellow didn't like to confront the unpleasant." At our bewildered expressions he chuckled. "The line down the left side of his face indicates he habitually slept on his left side, facing the fire. However, in recent weeks, he has been sleeping on the other side, facing in the other direction."

"Remarkable!" Hopkins declared. "But I confess I am baffled."

"Yes?" he seemed surprised. "Well, the condition of his teeth reveals him to be a non-smoker and the odour of his mouth tells us clearly that he was a drinker. That the scent is so strong suggests he drank not long before retiring. His feet have no less than five callouses on the right, and three on the left. However, these have started to fade in recent weeks. Ergo, he was a walker formerly, but less so of late. His fingers give eloquent testimony to his interest in angling.

"Now, gentlemen, if you would be so kind as to help me turn him."

With some grunting exertion, we three rolled the body onto its side.

"He landed on his back, I see," Holmes said. "There is considerable bruising here. From the lividity, I gather he remained *in situ* for some time before he was moved."

"Yes, he was already dead. The staff covered the body with a sheet but didn't move him until I gave them permission."

Holmes responded with a distracted smile before saying, "I suspect there are a number of spinal fractures, but the neck and head seem to have escaped serious injury."

Hopkins noted everything in his book. "Splendid. Thank you, Mr. Holmes. Anything else?"

"The breaks all lie to the posterior part of the body, likewise the various cuts and bruises. It appears that he fell backwards out of the window, rather than flinging himself through it face-first. This was an unexpected nocturnal flight." He smirked at his phrasing.

"Odd," Hopkins said. "What about cause of death?"

"As you undoubtedly observed, Inspector, the various injuries don't seem life-threatening. There may, of course, be internal injuries that we cannot perceive. Watson?"

"Pwobably a hath adack," I mumbled.

"Indeed," Holmes said. "A heart attack seems most likely. We will not know for sure until after the autopsy."

Dr. Updike listened to our comments and agreed. "I should have the results available in an hour or two," he said. "I shall send them directly to the station."

"Ah, send them to the Hall, if you would be so kind," Hopkins said. "You will find us there."

As we turned to leave, the surgeon smiled in an unsettling manner and added, "I'd be happy to take care of that tooth for you, Doctor. No need to suffer."

"Oh, it'sh not sho bad," I said. I thanked him and hurried up the steps.

The Hall dominated eight acres of magnificent Kent countryside, including a small lake to the north. The building, a magnificent Tudor structure, left me speechless. Even on a bitterly cold October evening framed against the icy grey sky, it looked majestic.

Bates, the butler, welcomed us with an offer of coffee in the library. Holmes would have demurred, but Hopkins and I overruled him. The library felt warm and comfortable thanks to a roaring fire in the ancient hearth. The coffee helped remove the chill, though I confess I couldn't drink mine until it was almost cold.

As we drank, Holmes engaged Bates in conversation. The butler seemed to me a bull in human form, with broad shoulders and a habit of tilting his head forward, like a beast about to charge. Though in height he could be no more than five-nine, his no-nonsense air made him seem far taller. I put him in his forties and thought he must be a Celt thanks to his thick black hair, dark eyes, and fair complexion. When he spoke, however, he sounded as refined as any fellow educated in Eton or Harrow.

"How long have you worked here?" Holmes asked.

"A little over thirty years, sir," the man replied. "I arrived no more than a lad."

"So you were here before Mr. Ellison came?" Holmes pressed.

"Yes, sir. I served old Lady Dalrymple to her death, then when Sir James gave the house to his daughter and her husband as a wedding gift, they asked me to stay on."

"So you know the family well?"

"I do indeed, sir. I knew Miss Jennifer – Mrs. Ellison, I should say – since she was a babe. From the day she was born she was a big favourite with all the servants. No one ever had a bad word to say against her. No kinder or sweeter maid ever walked the earth, and her daughter just like her."

"And Mr. Ellison? What was he like?"

For a moment he hesitated. When he replied, however, his tone was forthright.

268

"Most thought him a hard man when first he came here, used to running a mine, and as tough as they come. He mellowed, though, when he married the mistress, and they both were so happy to know they had a babe on the way. Then the mistress died, and he turned back into that hard man."

"Would you describe him as a good father to his daughter?"

"Well, I'm sure he tried, sir. I don't think he knew much about young ladies, or how to be a father, but he did try. He hired Miss Gertrude Lilly as governess, and she became like a mother to the girl. When Miss Ysella became engaged, Miss Lilly arranged to take her to the city to buy her trousseau. Unfortunately, she received word the night before that her mother had been taken ill and she had to leave suddenly. Mr. Ellison didn't want the girl to be disappointed, so he said he would take her instead."

"A fair solution," Holmes said in an airy tone. His eyes, however, told me he was uneasy about this development.

"I don't think the lady was keen on the idea, frankly. She loved her father, but as she often said, what man knows anything about women's clothes? He insisted, however, and said they could stay at the Savoy and he would take her to a show – Miss Ysella loved the theatre – and make a holiday out of it."

"They travelled by coach?" Holmes continued.

"Yes, sir. Miss Ysella hoped to take a train, but Mr. Ellison said the coach would be more convenient with them going around the shops and so on."

"Had Miss Ellison been to the city before?"

"Once or twice, but not for a year or so at least. The last time was when Miss Lilly took her to a show that she really wanted to see, but that was about five years before . . . before she disappeared, sir."

"And the coachman who took them into town that day – the day Miss Ellison went missing. May we speak with him?"

"That would be Mr. Evans, sir, but I'm afraid he left not long after Miss Ellison vanished, sir. Just up and left in the middle of the night. Left a note for Mr. Ellison saying he was sick at heart about the lady going missing and had decided to go to America and try his fortune."

"One last question, Mr. Bates: Had Miss Ellison made any purchases on the day she disappeared?"

He blinked. "I don't believe so, sir."

To our surprise, Holmes chuckled. He downed the last of his coffee and set down his cup. "We would like to see Mr. Ellison's bedroom," he said.

Bates merely nodded and said, "Certainly, sir," and led us up a staircase to the first floor.

269

We found Ellison's chamber in the centre of a long hallway. A pair of demilune tables containing large bowls of golden chrysanthemums flanked the intricately carved walnut door. This was guarded by a pair of uniformed policemen.

Inside, the wooden floor was highly polished and partially covered by a large Persian rug in shades of sapphire and ruby. Another, smaller rug in similar style lay near the door facing the window. Its puckered and untidy state seemed hazardous and I bent down to straighten it, but Holmes caught my arm and shook his head. I realised then that he wished to examine it and the rest of the room first.

The enormous bed, an Elizabethan four-poster, dominated the centre of the room. The mattress sat high, about four or five feet from the floor. A small set of steps sat beside the bed on the side away from the door to enable the occupant to climb in. The bed faced three diamond-paned windows, each flanked by drapes of heavy silk in pale gold. The mullioned windows, much larger than I would have expected from the era, were set deep into the thick stone walls. The window facing the door remained open allowing a bitter wind to swirl round the room. Hopkins and I stood by the – thankfully – hearty fire and hugged our arms around ourselves.

"Has this room been cleaned since Mr. Ellison's death?" Holmes asked the butler.

The butler shook his head. "No sir. The inspector told us not to touch it."

Holmes nodded in appreciation. "What time did Mr. Ellison fall to his death?"

"Around two a.m., sir."

"And you arrived when, Inspector?"

"A little after six, Mr. Holmes. The local constables were on the scene not long after the man's death, however."

Holmes stood facing the window. "Very well. Thank you, Bates. I think we can manage from here. We'll ring if we need anything further."

Hopkins and I stood by the roaring fire and watched as Holmes began his examination. He started with the open window. "The sill and the floor beneath were soaked very recently. Do you know what time it rained here last night, Hopkins?"

"It rained all evening, Mr. Holmes, but stopped shortly before Mr. Ellison's death." At Holmes's quizzical look, he added, "The ground on which he lay was wet, but the top of his body was only slightly damp. Besides, one of the footmen mentioned the rain to me when I arrived." He grinned.

"Ah, how else can one identify an Englishman if not by his fascination with the weather?" Holmes said, then added, "Did Ellison usually sleep with an open window?"

"On occasion, according to the housekeeper."

"I' wash co'd," I said.

"Yes," Holmes agreed, "It was bitterly cold last night. But I perceive there was a substantial fire in the hearth."

"Perhaps the room felt too stuffy," Hopkins suggested. I nodded in agreement.

"Perhaps."

"This is the window through which our unfortunate victim fell?"

"Yes."

Holmes turned and his keen eyes scanned every inch of the room, though he didn't move.

"Everything in the room seems well-ordered," he commented, "with the exception of this floor rug."

He bent down and studied the rumpled rug that lay between the window and the door. He measured angles and distances, and made some quick calculations. This done, he lay down and began to crawl around the floor, examining every speck and thread he found. He lifted the valance and the upper half of his body vanished beneath the bed. I heard a dull chuckle.

"You all right there, Mr. Holmes?" Hopkins said.

"Excellent," Holmes said, and re-emerged from beneath the bed.

"Did you find anything interesting?"

"Interesting, yes. Inculpatory, no. Still, early days."

"Mr. Holmes – " Hopkins began.

Holmes dusted down his coat and replied, "Someone has been lying under the bed very recently. A woman." He produced a long silver hair.

"Bu' wy?" I asked.

"It's an old performer's trick, gentlemen. With a magic lantern and some chemicals on the fire, a clever person can produce an excellent and very convincing effect, particularly for a man who has taken more whisky than he might at bedtime."

He turned his attention to the fireplace.

"This is a fine example of an Elizabethan hearth, is it not? What tales this could tell."

He knelt down and studied every aspect of the fireplace. "Did you notice this, Inspector?" he asked.

"The damper? Yes, Mr. Holmes. Not original to the house, of course. I gather it was added about ten years ago."

Holmes waved a dismissive hand. "You saw that it was closed? And you will perceive a thin layer of smut upon the mantel and some of the furniture."

He then dug in the ash and chuckled. "Ah, yes, just as I expected."

Hopkins and I knelt down beside him and observed he had taken some remnants of candle wax from the front of the hearth. It had an odd colour. "Copper sulphate, I believe. It will turn flame to a very pretty shade of green. Tell me, Hopkins, has this always been Ellison's bed chamber?"

"As far as I know."

"Well, then, let us go downstairs and talk to Miss Agnetha Malvern-Pitt," Holmes said.

We went downstairs to the library, and after a few moments, Miss Malvern-Pitt joined us. She stood about five-feet-six and wore her silver hair in a coil at the back of her head. I estimated her to be in her mid-fifties, but she was still a handsome woman. Despite her pallor, there was something exotic about her. I wondered if she hailed from Eastern Europe or some such place.

She sat before us, as sedate as a queen, her hands folded on her lap.

"A great pleasure to meet you, Miss Malvern-Pitt," Holmes said in his most genial voice.

She bowed her head slightly in acknowledgement.

"How long have you been employed here as housekeeper?"

"I was hired as a personal maid to Miss Dalrymple when she was about sixteen. After her death, I remained as an attendant to her daughter. I have been here for twenty-five years."

"And before you came here, where did you work?"

"In many different places."

"Theatres," Holmes said.

A flash of surprise crossed her face. "Yes," she said.

To Hopkins and me, Holmes said, "Miss Malvern-Pitt is well known in theatrical circles as a remarkable artist. She designed many sets and costumes for dozens of prestigious productions. Your *Macbeth* was a particular success, as I recall."

She bowed slightly. "I am flattered you remember. It was a long time ago."

"How could anyone who has seen your work forget it? Those witches bathed in green light set a standard for all who followed, not to mention your use of the magic lantern."

The woman smiled briefly and said, "You are very kind."

"Why did you leave? You were at the height of your talents, by all accounts."

"Jennifer Dalrymple, Ysella's mother, was a dear friend. I had known her for many years. I happened to run into her one afternoon in the city. I was having problems with my hands. I knew I couldn't last much longer at my profession. An artist must have strong hands. Jennifer told me her governess had left, feeling that she, Jennifer, had learned everything she could teach. While my old friend agreed, she also felt she needed a companion. Her father, Sir James, had always been inclined to indulge her, and so it was on this occasion. I became something of a ladies' maid, companion, and whatever else she needed. When she married, I continued to serve her here."

"You must have been very close," Holmes said.

"We were."

Her blue eyes were indecipherable. I found her impossible to read. Holmes, however, seemed delighted with her answers. "Her death must have been hard."

"It was, for everyone who loved her, and that was everyone who knew her."

"And her daughter too?"

"Ysella was very much her mother's child. They looked uncannily alike, and the younger had the older's temperament. It was an honour to serve both of them."

"And after Miss Ysella's disappearance," Holmes persisted, "you decided to stay here?"

"It was where I felt close to them. Sir James asked me to stay on as housekeeper, and I agreed."

"Sir James?" Holmes said. "Not Mr. Ellison?"

She hesitated, but only for a moment. "The house still belongs to Sir James."

"Did you speak to Miss Lilly before she went home to her mother?"

A noticeable hesitation. Then she replied, "No. I gather there was some urgency and she left in the middle of the night."

"Then she had received a telegram?"

Again, that curious hesitancy. "That is what Mr. Ellison said."

"Have you heard from her since she left?"

"No."

"No? Not to say when she might return, or to ask for her things?" Holmes persisted.

"I do not know, Mr. Holmes. If she wrote to Mr. Ellison, he didn't say so."

Holmes remained silent while she seemed to be pondering. After several moments, she added, "I wrote to Miss Lilly at her mother's address saying I hoped her mother was on the road to recovery and that she,

Gertrude, would come back soon. The old woman sent a letter back saying her health was excellent and that she hadn't seen her daughter in months."

"Did you ask Mr. Ellison about it?"

"Yes."

"Describe the conversation to me, if you would be so kind."

He leaned back in his seat and, with his eyes half-closed, listened as Miss Malvern-Pitt explained how she had confronted Mr. Ellison one morning a few weeks earlier.

"He refused to discuss the matter with me," she said. "He stood there staring off in the distance, and he said that he was too worried about Ysella to be troubled about a governess. No doubt she would return in due course."

"The bedroom where Mr. Ellison slept last night – has that been his chamber since he first moved into the house?"

"No. His room was initially on the other side of the house. He decided to move into the room facing the drive about two months ago. He said the original room reminded him too much of Ysella and her fondness for the lake."

"He hasn't gone fishing in the lake in some time, I think."

"No, he says it brings back too many memories."

"Ch'd be a co'ort." I muttered. The woman stared at me in bewilderment.

"I agree with the Good Doctor," Holmes said. "Most men would consider it a comfort. Still, it is our differences that make us unique, is it not? Tell me about the morning Mr. Ellison left for London with his daughter."

"They left very early. Mr. Ellison said there was no need to trouble the staff and we should all have a relaxing morning. He asked cook to make some packed breakfasts for himself and Ysella and Evans, the coachman. I saw them leave from the front hall window."

"Did you see them clearly?"

"No, they were in the carriage."

"When was the last time you spoke with Ysella?"

"About two days before," Miss Malvern-Pitt replied. "We were told she was unwell and had decided to remain in her bed sleeping. We were asked not to disturb her."

"Wha'?" I exclaimed and rubbed my tender jaw as it protested the sudden jerk of my head.

"Yes, it does seem odd," Holmes said, "to leave the girl unattended all day. But I assume Mr. Ellison felt he would rather take care of her himself."

"So he said." The woman's voice was flat.

274

"Was this his usual custom?"

"No."

I shook my head in disgust. Leaving a sick girl unattended all day? Monstrous!

"Tell me, Miss Malvern-Pitt: When did you first suspect Mr. Ellison had murdered his daughter?" Holmes spoke in a level tone.

The woman took a sharp breath, but her expression never changed. "When he returned from the city without her. All the peculiar events of the previous week started to make sense. Miss Lilly having to go home, keeping Ysella in her room with no one allowed to visit her, and leaving so early. Then, telling the staff to have a relaxing morning. He's never thought of the staff even once in all the years I've known him."

"How often have we seen it that a killer thinks himself far cleverer than the people around him?" Holmes said. "You planned to force him to confess?"

"That was our intent, yes."

"Yours and Mr. Bates?"

"Yes."

"And you arranged a little performance for him," Holmes continued. "Some copper sulphate in balls of candle wax that you could easily toss onto his fire and turn the flames green, closing the damper of the chimney so the smoke would billow out – a perfect background for you to project an image of Ysella from a magic lantern."

"You seem to have worked it all out," she said with a wry smile. "The entire thing was clumsy, but we had to make do with what was available."

Holmes bowed slightly, as one master to another. "How did you project your voice?"

"When I worked in the theatre, one of our shows featured Leonard Baines, the ventriloquist. He taught me some of his techniques. One never knows when such things will prove useful."

"Indeed. And, mimicking his daughter's voice, you asked him why?"

"Yes. It is simple and to the point. I didn't want to say too much lest he begin to recognise my voice. We thought asking why might demand an answer."

"And when that failed, you pushed him out of the window?" Hopkins said.

"No, indeed! We wanted a confession, that is all. I encouraged him to drink some whisky before retiring, then Bates and I made it our business to confront him with our 'performance' two or three times a week. We were sure he would confess eventually. Unfortunately, last night he became hysterical. He leapt from his bed and began to run wildly around the room. He slipped on the rug near the window and fell through."

"You had left the window open in order to make the room cold," Holmes said.

"That, and to make sure the smoke didn't build up too much. Yes."

The surgeon, Dr. Updike, arrived a few minutes later. As I had surmised, Ellison had died of a heart attack. With some small persuasion from Holmes, Hopkins agreed to mark the death as accidental.

Holmes and Hopkins went outside to explore the grounds, but my friend urged me to remain with the surgeon who had kindly brought several of his surgical tools with him.

Later, Holmes told me he and Hopkins discovered a wheelbarrow had been moved from the garden shed. They found it hidden behind some trees near the lake.

"This is how he transported the bodies," Holmes said.

"Bodies?" Hopkins had asked.

"Oh yes. Ysella, Miss Lilly, and, unless I miss my guess, the coachman. He would never have permitted Evans to leave and run the risk of blackmail. No, no. They are in the lake, the three of them."

"So Ysella never went to the city?"

"No indeed. I suspect it was merely the coachman and Ellison. Initially, I thought he might have made Miss Lilly dress as Ysella in order to fool the staff, but the way things worked out, that was unnecessary. She had been dead for two days, unless I miss my mark."

"But why kill the governess?" Hopkins asked.

"She would have insisted on seeing Ysella when the girl was supposedly sick," Holmes replied, "and she would have expected to travel with the Ellisons into the city. At a minimum, she'd have wanted to see her charge before they left. No, he had to get rid of her."

"But why? What did he gain?"

"The house. I read the terms of the lease this afternoon, Hopkins. It said clearly that Ellison could remain in the house as long as his daughter lived and was unmarried. With her declared missing, and not dead, he could remain here, living the life to which he had become accustomed, and without the bother of having to work for it. It was no more than a matter of convenience."

Back in Baker Street, minus one offending tooth thanks to a determined Dr. Updike, I sat by the fire with Holmes, a glass of brandy in my hand.

"A thorny problem," Holmes said, "and one for your annals, I think."

"I'm glad Miss Malvern-Pitt and Bates didn't kill Ellison. Though no one could have blamed them if they had."

276

"You think them innocent, then?"

"Of course! I know their silly performance was partly responsible for his death, but when it came down to it, he died of a heart attack. That's what Dr. Updike said." I rubbed my jaw, thankful that I had surrendered to the man's surprisingly gentle ministrations.

"Perhaps," Holmes said. "It cannot be proved either way, but I suspect Ellison refused to confess and Bates or Malvern-Pitt, or possibly both, pushed him through the window. I found it odd that though they endeavoured to remove every trace of their mischief, and so on, they made some mistakes. They opened the fire damper but didn't remove all the traces of smoke from the furnishings. They also left some scraps of the copper sulphate wax balls around the fireplace. They left the window open, but they couldn't explain why that was the case. Finally, they moved the rug into disarray so it would support their contention that Ellison slipped on it and fell through that one, conveniently-open window. However, the rug was aslant, and more than six feet from the window. If Ellison had slipped on it as it was, I believe he would have landed on the floor. Furthermore, there should have been some mark on the floor showing evidence of his skid. There was none."

I pondered this unassailable argument and finished the last of my brandy. "It doesn't bother you to mislead Hopkins?" I asked.

"The fellow died of a heart attack and, given the full story, I cannot imagine any English jury would convict. Besides, Ellison was himself a killer and deserved his fate." He downed his drink and rose. "It bothers me not a whit. Goodnight, my dear Watson."

The Spectral Centurion
by Charles Veley and Anna Elliott

Chapter I

My story begins early in the evening of a dreary Thursday, the nineteenth of December, 1895, when, after a long afternoon seeing patients, I arrived home at Baker Street. I had felt stagnated of late, and in need of exercise, so I had walked the twenty minutes along the darkened streets, becoming progressively colder and colder from the raw northern wind. I looked forward to the warmth of a blazing fire in the rooms I shared with Sherlock Holmes.

I opened our outside door with my latchkey.

Mrs. Hudson was coming down our stairs as I entered. She appeared more excited than usual.

"He's just had a parcel," she said. "From a Lord Winstrom, no less. Do you think it's a Christmas gift?"

"We have six days until Christmas, so this would be a bit early," I said. "And I don't recollect any Lord Winstrom."

"Then it's a new case," she said, with satisfaction. "Just what he needs, poor thing. He's been sulking all week." She gave me a maternal look. "Good for you, too, I imagine. You've been trudging around as well. Best to occupy your mind and not think about what you're missing this time of the year."

I nodded inwardly, in rueful acknowledgment. I had found it difficult to maintain a genial attitude appropriate to the holiday season since the passing of Mary, my dear wife. For the first time I felt an emotional appreciation of what Holmes confronted on a regular basis, needing his work to ward off the gloom which invariably arrived when he no longer had a challenge with which to occupy himself. Following his example, I had determinedly busied myself with my routines and my patients and, so far, had succeeded in maintaining my professional manner with my patients. Coming home, however, was another matter.

But if Holmes had a new case . . . .

"We shall soon find out," I said.

I hung up my overcoat and mounted the steps to our sitting room.

Holmes, in his dressing-gown and slippers, was standing at the table he reserves for chemical experiments, holding an uncorked glass bottle at eye level, as if examining its contents. An empty glass beaker was positioned atop his unlit Bunsen burner stand. On the floor was a cardboard box and an untidy heap of string and brown wrapping paper, on which I observed a large red-wax seal.

He saw me and set down the bottle. "No, I shall not accept," he said. "Without further data on which to build, the assignment is a meaningless one."

"I had hoped for an adventure," I said.

In reply, he handed over a note, written on high-quality paper and bearing an embossed emblematic crest at the top. The handwriting was round and precise. I read:

> *Gates Court, Corsham*
> *18 December*
>
> *Mr. Holmes:*
>
> *You will kindly commence at once to determine the presence of hallucinatory toxins in the enclosed sample of Royal Spa mineral water. The contents were taken from a carafe given to the foreman of a major restoration project in the City of Bath, in which I have a controlling financial interest. We must ascertain why the man would have the illusion that he was attacked by a spectral body. It is most essential that the restoration work continue and that the spa's reputation not be compromised. You may name your fee. A special messenger will call this afternoon for your reply.*
>
> *Winstrom*

Holmes was scribbling on a telegraph pad. He stood and read aloud: "'*Returning bottle and contents by separate post. Will explain more fully if and when your messenger arrives.*'"

My spirits fell. Here was a case from a wealthy client, the very thing Holmes needed, and yet he was spurning the opportunity. I asked, "Holmes, is this wise?"

"It is always wise to make one's position clear from the outset, particularly with someone as presumptuous as this particular aristocrat. I shall post this and return forthwith. Meanwhile, you might see what you can learn about this Winstrom from *Burke's* and my index books."

He dressed rapidly and left to post the reply.

I was encouraged. He had not rejected the opportunity after all. I went to the bookshelves and took down the current *Burke's* as well as the "*W*" volume of his case indexes. By the time Holmes returned, I had *Burke's* open to the Winstrom entry, and had determined that the full name of the current baron was Gerald Gates, Lord Winstrom. I also had the "*W*" and "*G*" volumes of Holmes's indexes open to the pages that would have included Winstrom and Gates, had there been any such entry.

He glanced at the entry in *Burke's*. "Not much to go on," he said. "Gates is the fifth baron. Resides in Gates Court, Corsham. Town residence in Grosvenor Square. His club is the Carlton. Served in the 9th Lancers. A widower. No offspring. Ah, well. We may learn something useful from the messenger."

Chapter II

The messenger arrived shortly afterwards. Her name was Sarah Brandt, and she was a strikingly attractive woman of perhaps thirty years of age. She wore a fur-trimmed hat, gloves, and a tailored black wool overcoat with a matching fur collar. Entering our sitting room, she handed me the hat and gloves as if I were the butler at a home which she visited frequently. Then she turned, shedding her coat, clearly expecting me to take it from her and hang it up. I did, of course. Her green eyes sparkled with anticipation, but also with what I felt to be some underlying distress. "Thank you, Dr. Watson," she said.

She then addressed Holmes, who stood in his frockcoat at our mantel, his back to the hearth, which he had freshly stoked with coals.

"I am Sarah Brandt, Mr. Holmes. Thank you for seeing me."

He nodded. "Pray, take the chair here by the fire, Miss Brandt. May we offer you refreshment?"

She shook her head. From her hair, a dark red-brown, and her ruddy complexion, I had the momentary impression that she might be Scottish.

"My mission is twofold, Mr. Holmes. I have, of course, instructions from my employer, Lord Winstrom. But also, I have a strong personal stake in the matter, which I need to impart to you as well in hopes that you will interest yourself in our local drama." She paused. "And you, no doubt, are busy, so I should very much like to get on."

"Proceed, then."

"You may well be aware that the City of Bath has a strong association with the Roman Empire going back very nearly two-thousand years. There are artifacts continually coming to light, more with each new building that is constructed, it seems. You may also be aware that the Romans once celebrated with a festival at this very time of the year."

She looked at Holmes as though inviting him to show his knowledge of ancient history. I couldn't entirely suppress a smile as, stone-faced, he turned up an empty palm. "The subject is of no interest to me," he said.

"Not as yet, Mr. Holmes." She leaned forwards, her chin outthrust, her wide shoulders squared off to face him.

She went on, "The Saturnalia, for such is the name of the Roman festival, was a period of the most heathen and debauched excesses, in honour of Saturn, the Roman god of the harvest. Precisely sixteen-hundred years ago, in the year 395 AD, that festival was held in Bath for the last time."

"Why?" Holmes asked.

"For reasons which I am about to make plain, Mr. Holmes, I assure you."

Holmes took his pocket watch from his waistcoat. "You have five more minutes, Miss Brandt."

"I shall make the most of them then. There is a chemist and historian in Bath named Farnsworth who has done extensive research into the Saturnalia and the libations consumed. His principal interest is in the healing powers of some of the libations, since, as you know, many of the visitors to Bath come for the promise of renewed youth and vigour. He gave a lecture on the ancient Romans the day before yesterday."

"Why that day?"

"December 17 was the traditional beginning of the Saturnalia. The lecture described an illuminated manuscript he had recently come upon in a forgotten storage room of a local monastery. The manuscript described a drink consumed by a local Roman centurion that evidently gave him unnatural powers."

"What powers?"

"I shall come to that. The Roman was in love with one of the local women, who was what we would call nowadays a witch. She had nursed him back to health with her heathen potions after he was wounded while on duty. And during that convalescence, the two fell in love. Or at least the Roman did. He thought his love was reciprocated, for she continued to treat him and live with him, without expectations of pay."

"Why did he not pay her?" I asked.

"Because his wages had been delayed. These were the waning days of the Empire, so the transmission of payroll gold from Rome to our remote island took some time and was long and involved. At any rate, the two married. Then, on the first day of the Saturnalia, the supply caravan with the wages for the garrison arrived. The centurion now had all the back pay due him for three years, in gold. He celebrated with his wife. She drugged him. That night she cut off his head, took the gold, and fled the region."

"An evil enchantress indeed," I said.

Miss Brandt nodded. "In retribution, the remaining centurions from the local garrison slaughtered all of her relatives and burned their dwelling places to the ground. The Saturnalia was never celebrated in Bath again."

"A cautionary tale," I said.

Holmes asked, "She took the recipe for her special drink with her as well?"

"She did. All that remains is the record in the illuminated manuscript stating that there was a drink, and that it gave extraordinary powers."

"Nonetheless," Holmes said, "the centurion couldn't survive without his head."

"However," Miss Brandt said, "the spirit of the centurion survived. The manuscript records its appearance at night during the period of the no-longer-celebrated Saturnalia."

"Doing what?"

"The spectre walks the darker streets of Bath, the manuscript says, in search of his faithless wife. He carries his sword in one hand and his severed head in the other. He holds the head up like a lantern."

The way she intoned the words had an other-worldly quality, such that a chill passed over me.

Holmes, on the other hand, sat forward and put away his pocket watch. "I believe you have come to the subject of your employer's message to me," he said. "The spirit of the centurion, I take it, is the hallucination to which Lord Winstrom refers?"

"It is, Mr. Holmes."

"And have many residents and visitors witnessed this horrific illusion? No? Then the hallucinatory substance isn't in the water itself."

"But it may have been placed in a carafe given to my brother, Frank. He is the construction foreman to whom Lord Winstrom's note refers."

"And he saw the apparition."

"He did. And lest you think Frank is the sort to imagine things, let me tell you that he is quite practical and level-headed, as well as highly energetic, as is necessary for his work. He is also powerfully built."

"You believe he was drugged."

"He believes it as well. He will tell you all about it if you will make the journey to Bath with me."

"Did he describe his experience to you and Winstrom?"

"Quite vividly. He was attacked by a headless creature carrying a disembodied head that wore a centurion's helmet. The creature struck him down with a sword." She paused for emphasis, and then added, slowly, "Frank has the mark of the sword on his neck to prove it."

"You have seen the mark?" I asked.

"I have. A red welt, as though he had been lashed with a whip."

"But not a cut," I said.

She nodded.

"After two-thousand years," Holmes said, "the spectral sword has evidently grown dull."

"Please do not jest with me, Mr. Holmes," she implored. "I believe my brother to be in danger. If someone attacked him once, they may do so again. Also, if the public becomes alarmed, we may lose funding for the restoration project."

"Ah. We come now to Lord Winstrom's concern."

"My brother and I both have invested in the project as well. If it fails, we lose everything. And my brother and I cannot afford that. Please help us, Mr. Holmes."

"Perhaps. Where can we find the Bath chemist and historian?"

"Frederick Farnsworth. He has a shop on the Pulteney Bridge – Farnsworth's Antiquities. A modest shop, as they all are in that area, so Farnsworth gave the lecture at the parish church to accommodate a crowd. The rector allowed it. He preached a homily regarding the ancient roots of our holiday festivals."

"Did your brother attend the lecture?"

"We both did. So did Lord Winstrom. He thought it wise for us to know all we can, since we are involved in restoring and enhancing an important Roman artifact. Our excavations might unearth something priceless, after all."

"Is there another lecture planned – for later on in the Saturnalia calendar? Perhaps the 24th – the anniversary of the crime, so to speak?"

"Not that I know of. We might ask Mr. Farnsworth. Now, Mr. Holmes, will you analyse the water sample as Lord Winstrom requested?"

Holmes shook his head. "I have no chemical test for hallucinatory substances. Short of drinking the water, which I will not do, I know of no other way to proceed."

"Perhaps Dr. Watson would drink some of the water as a medical experiment?"

Noting Holmes's warning look, I shook my head.

"You are afraid?" she asked.

Holmes raised his hand to prevent my reply. "The issue of bravery is immaterial, Miss Brandt, and your challenge to male vanity is a transparent one. I have already wired your employer that I shall return the sample he

283

sent. It is in that glass bottle on my table, unchanged by me. You may take it with you."

To my surprise, she crossed over to the table, picked up the bottle, and drank its contents.

Chapter III

"Are you expecting me to collapse at any moment?" she asked, calmly returning to her seat by the fireplace.

Holmes's tone was equally calm. "My expectations are immaterial, Miss Brandt. I take it you were the person who prepared the sample?"

"I was."

"And, contrary to the statement from your employer. Lord Winstrom, the sample didn't come from your brother's container?"

"You are right again, Mr. Holmes. But how did you know?"

"It is a question of probabilities. Hallucinatory effects of a drug would take some time to appear. It is plain that you weren't with him when the apparition came upon him, for otherwise you would have been more knowledgeable on the point of how his neck obtained the welt-like lesion."

"I had gone to the office to take care of some letters. We have a great deal of correspondence."

"Do you know whether he had drunk anything in particular?"

"We had dined together at The Royal Arms, in town. He had spa water only, as usual, when he was with me. He was fine when I left him."

"Spa water only," Holmes said.

"That was why Lord Winstrom wished to have the spa water investigated."

"Did he remain at The Royal Arms after you left?"

A guarded expression crossed her face. "He may have done."

"And you didn't report the attack to the police."

"Lord Winstrom is concerned about the public image of the spa. He believes that attackers, ghostly or otherwise, would discourage visitors and be bad for business. He wanted discretion, and your name came to mind."

"So to signal that you wished me to pursue an inquiry grounded in scientific fact, you sent a sample of the spa water."

"I have read some of Dr. Watson's accounts," she said. "I was sure you wouldn't agree to investigate a disembodied spirit."

He gave one of his tight, momentary smiles. "Then we are agreed in principle. You wish me to ascertain who drugged your brother, and for what purpose."

"Yes. And to protect the integrity of the restoration project. It is valuable. It will be good for Bath, good for history, and good for England."

I nodded. I had heard of the project, which seemed likely to attract large numbers of visitors and become as popular with the public as The Tower of London.

"If you say so," Holmes said.

"About your fee – "

Holmes interrupted. "I shall name it after the investigation has concluded with a positive result. I choose my own cases. Your case has its points of interest."

"What do you need from me, Mr. Holmes?"

"I shall need to know who was at the parish lecture regarding the centurion. I shall need to interview the antiquarian, and to view the manuscript providing details to the remarkable story of the unfortunate and grievously wronged centurion. I shall also need to interview your brother."

"I can arrange all of that. Can you be in Bath tomorrow morning?"

Holmes's face fell. "Alas," he said, "I have a prior commitment tomorrow."

"Then when?"

Holmes's expression brightened. "But it is possible that Dr. Watson may be able to assist."

I was surprised, for I knew of no prior commitment Holmes had made for the following day. I had the feeling that Holmes had his own reasons for wishing me to attend in his place.

"I shall make myself available," I said.

"Excellent!" Holmes rubbed his hands together. "You can wire me of further developments as they occur. Also, Miss Brandt, I should like Dr. Watson to see the construction site, and to interview your employer."

"I shall arrange that as well," she said, "at His Lordship's earliest opportunity."

Chapter IV

The following morning, I boarded a train at Paddington. Less than two hours later, I found Miss Brandt waiting for me on the platform at the Bath station.

She was dressed in the same furs, bundled up against the cold, and I noticed that her boots, black and also with brown fur trimming above the ankles, were newly polished. "We have a busy day ahead of us," she said. Her smile had a worried air about it. I wondered why. "We'll start with the construction project."

I walked beside her, feeling a momentary pleasure when she took my arm. She went on, "We need to hurry, if we're to catch Lord Winstrom before he sets off for London at the end of the day."

As we walked, I suggested, "Perhaps I could return on the train with him. Share a compartment."

"He travels on his own train. But I'll suggest that you join him, if we need the time. Meanwhile, we will begin at the construction site. My brother is working there."

We walked side by side on a pavement wide enough for two carriages, let alone pedestrians. In the distance, above the rooftops, the surrounding hills were visible beneath grey clouds. The air was clearer than London's, and the stone facades of the Georgian-style buildings around me had a pleasant, warm colour. I admired the classical columns. The place seemed refreshing and clean, busy, but not too crowded. No wonder, I thought, that people came here for a relaxing, therapeutic holiday.

"The River Avon is over there," Sarah said. "Our project isn't far away, near the city center. The Romans built a bath here to take advantage of the hot springs. Over the many centuries, the bath filled up with silt and all but vanished. Now it's being excavated and we're going to make it Bath's central attraction, with enormous new pillars in the Roman style. A proper monument to the grandeur of the ancients."

We reached our first destination, which proved to be a large fenced-off area nearly the size of a lawn tennis court. Peering through one of many viewing panels in the wooden slats, I could see a rectangular pit had been dug deep into the street, extending far downwards. The bottom was possibly fifty feet below street level. Workmen down there were digging with shovels and filling wheelbarrows, which they then maneuvered to a great dirt pile at the base of a tall network of scaffolding and ladders and pulleys. The surface looked dark and damp and muddy, like a gigantic grave.

"The men down there are shovelling out nearly two-thousand years of silt and dirt. Soon the hot spring will flow freely to make a huge pool. Then the men will line the pool with lead, and the pool will be ready for bathers."

I stepped back and surveyed the scene around me. Close by were pedestrians and shoppers, entering and exiting a variety of shops. One building proclaimed itself to be The Royal Arms Hotel.

"All these buildings will be gone soon," Miss Brandt said. "This will be a gigantic plaza surrounding and overlooking the public bath below us. There will be pillars of polished granite all around the bath, tall and majestic, rising up to high above where we stand here on the street. Enormous, like the pillars of the acropolis or the Lyceum Theatre."

"What will the pillars support?"

"They'll hold up a decorative frieze all around us and thirty feet above our heads. It will bring the area here together like a gigantic picture frame.

The view from down below will be breathtaking." She paused, looking through one of the observation windows. "Oh, look, there's Frank now. Down there with the excavating crew."

Chapter V

Frank Brandt had soon climbed the ladders and scaffolding to join us. He was ruddy and red-haired, much resembling his sister, though nearly six inches taller and with a powerful musculature that was evident even beneath his thick wool overcoat. He also wore a bowler hat, which he doffed briefly, prior to giving his sister a perfunctory hug.

"Is there a quieter place where we could talk?" I asked.

"Sally Lunn's is nearby," Sarah said. "We can have tea and rolls there."

"I can spare a few minutes," Frank said, "but before we go, just notice what we're doing here and think about it for a moment." He swept his gaze and one of his brawny arms in a wide arc. "Someone's raising trouble. That's why you're here, correct?"

"About the spirit you saw," I said.

"There's no spirit. Someone put something in my food or my drink and then whacked me on the neck. And what was the purpose of that, I ask you? What do I matter to anyone?"

"You matter to me, Frank," Sarah said.

"Don't talk rubbish, though I do appreciate your caring, sister dear." He gave her a tight, momentary smile and turned to face me. His expression was earnest. "No, the only thing achieved by putting me out of commission is to hold up the construction we're doing. And that construction means that this lot – these buildings right here – have to be torn down. And some of the owners don't want to let them go."

He pointed again to the buildings that surrounded the fence and the yawning black chasm beneath. "Some of them have complained, and I think they're the ones causing the trouble here."

He pulled a folded paper from his coat pocket and handed it to me. "I went to the guildhall and wrote down the names of complainers. I was going to try to match these with the owners of the buildings we're trying to take down. Now that you're here, you lot can do that."

Sarah took the paper. "I don't recognise any of these names," she said. "I'll check the property records."

"Good. Then we'll know who doctored my drink last night."

I was glad Holmes wasn't there, for he would certainly have disagreed with the man's rapid leap to a conclusion. I decided to take a middle ground. "Let us continue our conversation over tea at this Sally Lunn's," I said.

Chapter VI

We entered the tea shop, a charming little affair doing a brisk business on a cold morning. We were soon seated and served our tea, with some delicious baked sweet rolls of very generous proportions.

I asked Frank, "Could you tell me what happened the day you were attacked?"

"It was at night. I was walking home from the architect's. Going over the plans for the next day. You see, there's a building we want to take down first – "

"Could we go back further?" I asked. "I understand you saw a lecture about a beheaded centurion at the Abbey earlier that afternoon."

"Yes, I did. But I didn't think much of it."

"Nothing at all?"

"Well, I did imagine how the old boy must have felt when he realised he was about to be done in. When the poison from that wife of his took effect."

"How did he feel?"

"Betrayed. Angry. Wanting to get even."

"But when you were attacked, were you afraid of this spirit?"

"Why should I be afraid? It was the wife who hurt him. He's out for revenge on her, the story said. He doesn't have anything against me. Besides, the Romans were good men. I admired them. Brave soldiers, they were. Any real Roman spirit would sense that and leave me alone. If there were such a thing as a real spirit."

"You think your attacker was an actual living person?"

"Of course I do. Come see where the attack happened, and I'll show you why."

Chapter VII

We walked through town for perhaps five minutes, until we were at the edge of the Circus, a ring of beautiful honey-coloured limestone townhouses. We stopped beneath a tree.

Frank pointed to one of the townhouses, a three-story affair at the centre of the ring. "My sister and I own that," he said. "Built more than one-hundred years ago, when this area was booming with the wool trade."

"You purchased it together?" I asked.

"It belonged to our parents," Sarah said.

"They're both gone these past four years," Frank added. "I was on my way there when I was attacked. Feeling a bit groggy, I was, so I was eager to get home and get to bed. We'd been dining out, Sarah and me."

"Where?"

A light seemed to dawn in Frank's green eyes. "The Royal Arms. It's on the top of that list I gave you. I thought at the time I might have eaten a bit too much. But they could have had someone slip something into my food or my water."

"Did the two of you leave together?"

"Sarah went to the office."

"I told you, I needed to finish some letters," Sarah said.

"Did you stay on after Sarah had gone?"

"Not long. Then I stopped in at the architect's, as I said."

"What time did you leave there?"

"About half-eight."

I turned to Frank. "So when you were attacked, you were here?"

"Passing beneath this very tree. A heavy weight hit me around the head and shoulders. Everything went black."

"Someone dropped down on you?"

"I'm sure of that. When I came to, I saw this creature standing over me. Just like the story I heard earlier at the Abbey."

"Did you see the severed head as well?"

"Oh yes, he was holding it by the hair. Eyes, flickering like flames, staring at me."

"And the creature was headless?"

"I've thought about that. Could have been a costume padded upward from the shoulders, with the man looking through eyeholes in the chest."

"Did you have that impression at the time, or only later, after thinking about it?"

"At the time, I saw only those bright flickering eyes. But then I came back in the morning – that was yesterday– and I looked upwards. Then I got a ladder, and I looked more closely to make sure."

"What did you see?"

He crouched down and locked his hands together between his knees. "See for yourself. I'll give you a boost. You can put your hand on my shoulder."

Feeling my age, I hesitated. Then I imagined reporting this incident to Holmes, and the pitying look he would have given me had I remained on the ground.

I stepped one foot up onto Frank's clasped hands and hauled myself upright, my hands grasping out for the tree. My fingers connected with the rough bark. I kept my balance as Frank pushed me upwards. Above me, a stout limb protruded.

"Reach up for that limb and I'll lift you further."

I got both hands on the top of the limb and pulled as he pushed from below, and soon I was standing on his shoulders. "What am I looking for?" I asked.

"A worn spot. A straight line crossing the limb, near where it joins the trunk. The bark has been sloughed off."

"I see it."

"Now, see if you can find any fibres from a rope."

Up so close, with my eyes such a short distance away from the surface of the limb, it was difficult to discern. But I managed to locate a small tuft lodged at the edge of the bark, which I dislodged with my thumb and plucked away, putting it into my vest pocket. "I have the fibres," I said. "Lower away."

A moment later I was safely on the ground.

"Now you have evidence to prove the incident wasn't supernatural," Frank said. "Ghosts don't need ropes. Someone climbed up. Couldn't afford to use a ladder, because I'd have seen it, so he used a rope. He waited up there until I came near. Then he swung down and clouted me from behind. He took the time I was unconscious to slide the rope off the tree limb and light up his effigy of a head. Probably put candles inside some hollowed-out mask. When he saw I was awake, he made sure to dangle the thing before my eyes. Then he hefted what might have been a sword and hit me again."

"Where did he hit you?"

"On the side of my head. Might not have put me out, if I hadn't felt woozy to begin with. But I noticed this afterwards." He opened his coat and loosened his necktie. Then he unbuttoned his collar and pulled it back. "I expect that while I was unconscious, he rubbed the rope back and forth to make this mark. Then he scarpered."

I saw a brownish welt, possibly the width of a finger, along the side of his neck.

"I looked for footprints," Frank said, "But the ground was frozen. Still is, you'll notice. We can't even see our own."

As I looked downwards at the frozen grass, I pictured Holmes, magnifying glass in hand, down on his knees.

I crouched down and did the best I could to examine the surface of the lawn in the immediate area beneath the tree. Then I saw a whitish substance.

"There," I said. "Candle wax." I scraped it up with my fingers. Wishing I had brought along a paper envelope, I tucked the shapeless mass into my other waistcoat pocket. "This explains the burning eyes in the disembodied head."

"Like I told you, just a man," Frank said, turning to go. "Not a spirit. Now I've got to get back to work."

Sarah said, "And now we must go to the Pulteney Bridge to meet Farnsworth."

Frank turned back to his sister. "You're barking up the wrong tree," he said. "Farnsworth's sweet on you, you know that. He'd never do anything to harm you or me either."

"He may be able to provide useful information, nevertheless," I said.

"Suit yourself, but don't forget my list of building owners."

"We'll bear it in mind," she said.

A different idea was dawning. "Is there anyone among your men who would want to be the project foreman?" I asked.

Frank's eyes narrowed. "Someone wants to frighten me off so they can take my job? Hadn't thought of that. Well, bring 'em on."

"Best be careful, Frank," Sarah said. "Someone might try to do more than just frighten you."

Chapter VIII

"We should go inside," Sarah said.

We were walking on the Pulteney Bridge, a large stone structure across the River Avon, linking the eastern and western halves of the city. On our right I could see the gilt letters over a storefront that read "*Farnsworth's Antiquities*". The storefront was one of a dozen or so that lined the bridge on either side, blocking the view of the river so that someone walking on the bridge saw only an ordinary street with a collection of shops.

A cold gust of wind pelted our faces with a spatter of rain and sleet. The afternoon sky above us was black with storm clouds. Sarah made a grimace and took my arm, propelling us towards a black-painted door immediately to the right of Farnsworth's. A modest brass plaque alongside the door read "*Gates Construction*".

"It's our office. We can dry off before we see Farnsworth."

The interior room was sparsely furnished with a worn Oriental rug, two tables, and a few wooden chairs. "We meet clients in here," she said, stepping inside.

On the floor in front of the doorway was an envelope bearing a red seal – similar, I thought, to the note Holmes had received the afternoon before.

"From Lord Winstrom?" I asked as she picked it up.

She nodded, broke the seal, and read the note inside without comment, though a hint of worry tinged the otherwise business-like expression she had maintained since my arrival.

She moved quickly to an interior door at the back wall. "Here's where I work. It has a better view."

She opened the door, and I saw a plain flat wooden desk and some file cabinets, another table with stacks of documents and rolled-up papers, and another door along one side of the room. The back of the desk nearly touched the sill of a large bare window overlooking the river that flowed beneath the office. Outside, on the water's edge, a few chunks of white ice drifted leisurely downstream on choppy water, speeding up as they reached a smoother area about twenty yards away. There, the ice tumbled over a kind of waterfall and reappeared further downstream. I watched for a moment, catching my breath and gathering my thoughts.

"It's called a weir," Sarah said. "A kind of rock wall that acts like a dam. Been here for centuries. Keeps the river from flooding the city – or at least gives people more time to evacuate their homes if the water really becomes unmanageable. In the summer, people use the weir for swimming."

I imagined myself in a rowboat with Mary below the weir, drifting down a tranquil river in summer with a full picnic hamper on board, to be opened when we landed. There would be champagne in the hamper, and two shining goblets . . . .

I pulled myself out of my futile daydream. "What do you keep in these cabinets?" I asked.

"Oh, the contracts and correspondence and bills and receipts. All the dull records that must be kept by any business. When the afternoon mail comes, I'll have another great stack of letters to go through and sort out. Those rolled-up papers on the table are blueprints of the buildings near the site that must be demolished. And we keep a map of any Roman graves we encounter in our excavations, with a record of the artifacts we recover. We give the artifacts to a small museum that Farnsworth manages."

She sat on her desk and leaned back. "Now, let's prepare. What do you expect to learn from Farnsworth? We're now convinced Frank was attacked by a real human, so what do we care about Farnsworth's ancient history research?"

"You're thinking about what your brother said – that Farnsworth is sweet on you."

She flushed slightly. "I suppose."

"I plan to avoid that topic altogether. We want information from Farnsworth, and we want him to have a clear mind."

"Good. What information, exactly?"

292

"He can tell us who else would know about the centurion."

"Everyone who attended the lecture in the Abbey knew about it."

"But who knew before then? It's more likely a person would need some time to create the kind of disguise your brother described."

She pursed her lips, nodding in acknowledgment. "Good point."

"Also, we should learn where Farnsworth was when your brother was attacked."

"Farnsworth was here. I saw him when I came in to work on my letters, and he was still here when I left. I got home after Frank had been struck down."

"Let's just have him tell us about it, shall we?"

"You don't trust me?"

I shrugged. "Irrelevant," I said. Outside, the rain was coming down in earnest, droplets spattering the window and dancing on the slow-moving surface of the river. "Shall we make a quick exit and nip into Farnsworth's?"

"No need," she said, and moved to the interior door along the side of the room. "We'll use the connecting door. He never locks it."

Chapter IX

Farnsworth was in his back room, standing on tiptoe to lift a wooden box up onto one of perhaps a dozen shelves that lined the walls. Beneath his rear window was a stone counter and a sink, with a number of bottles and chemical equipment that resembled the array familiar to me from Holmes's experiments. Farnsworth, a chubby little man with pomaded black hair and beady black eyes, turned when he saw us. His face creased in an excited smile.

"Sarah! You honour me with your presence! So delighted! Who is this gentleman friend of yours?"

"Dr. Watson works with Sherlock Holmes. He's here because someone actually saw that centurion you told us all about."

"There's been a sighting?" Farnsworth's small dark eyes lit up. "That's wonderful! People are believing in the legend!"

"Not so wonderful," I said. "Someone dressed to look like the centurion attacked Frank Brandt."

"Oh dear. When was that?"

"Thursday night."

"I'm terribly sorry. Was Frank hurt at all?"

I shook my head. "He's fine. Where were you at the time?"

"Oh, I can tell you that readily enough. And by the way, I completely understand your asking. I was the one who introduced the centurion story,

293

after all. Well, Thursday night I was here until midnight. Sarah can vouch for me for some of that time. I was catching up on my cataloguing. She said hello when she came in and goodbye when she left."

Sarah nodded, appearing satisfied to have had her story confirmed.

I asked, "Can you think of anyone who would wish to impersonate this ancient Roman?"

"Only a madman would do such a thing," he said. "And I don't associate with any of those."

"What about someone with an economic motive?" I asked.

"What do you mean?"

"Someone might see the restoration project as a threat to their business. Attacking the construction foreman might slow the progress and postpone the loss of profit."

Sarah spoke up. "For that matter, attacking me would slow the progress as well."

"Heaven forbid!" Farnsworth shook his head and reached out a hand, as though to comfort her.

Sarah turned away.

"I really am sorry," Farnsworth said. "It hurts me deeply to think that I may have inadvertently caused you pain."

"You hadn't told anyone else of your discovery?" I asked.

"Oh, certainly not. No one knew about the unfortunate centurion. I never thought of the implications."

"Other than the commercial benefits?" Sarah asked. I caught a twinkle in her eye. Farnsworth caught it as well, and returned it with an eager wink.

"Oh, you know as well as I that we all want more business here in Bath. This ghost story seemed made to order. Too good not to share. After all, people love to hear about the ghosts at The Tower of London and all those haunted castles. They pay good money for tickets, and even more to hotels and restaurants and gift shops. Why shouldn't we use our own history to bring in some tourists?"

"Why not indeed?" Sarah said. "But I don't want Frank to be harmed."

Farnsworth gave a solemn nod.

"Do you plan another lecture?" I asked.

"Oh, certainly not. Not this year, anyway. It's Christmas time. A most inappropriate time for proper Christians to dwell on the Romans and their Saturnalian excesses."

"But your sources for the centurion legend were monks, were they not? Didn't they disapprove?"

294

"They were acting as historians, not passing judgment. They were simply recording the legend as it had been orally communicated to them."

"Can we see the manuscript?"

"Of course. It's in the museum at The Royal Arms, along with the replica helmet and centurion's armour I used in the lecture. And the centurion's sword."

"Is there a list of those who attended?"

"I never saw one. The rector would know."

Sarah consulted her pocket watch. "We are to meet Rector Archer in fifteen minutes. He may have a record. At least he may recall greeting the attendees as they entered or departed."

I could see the river outside Farnsworth's window, which had a view identical to the one from Sarah's office. The rain had abated, the clouds had broken, and the late afternoon sunlight cast long shadows across the river. "We had best be going, then," I said.

"I could meet you later at The Royal Arms," Farnsworth said, with a hopeful look at Sarah. "Show you the manuscript there."

Sarah gave a polite nod. "Shall we say four o'clock then?"

Chapter X

Sarah and I walked to the Abbey, which was, thankfully, only a short distance away. The rain had given way to blue skies, and a brisk chill wind from the north pressed at our backs. I clapped my hat down on my head. Before us, the long rays of late afternoon sunlight shone on the golden sandstone of the Abbey, a strikingly beautiful Gothic structure, lighting it up like a gem.

We entered through the vestry. For a moment I stood transfixed, watching the light stream though the enormous stained-glass windows. I felt I was inside a fairy-tale treasure cave, albeit one that had grown to an enormous height and airy spaciousness.

"A joyful place," I said.

"I suppose it is," Sarah said. "I don't get in here very often. The rector's office is inside."

Sarah introduced me to Rector Robert Archer, a kindly, vigorous man of perhaps fifty years, with a ruddy complexion and a closely trimmed white beard. He motioned us to chairs before his desk and then sat behind it, hands clasped. "What can I do for you, Dr. Watson?"

"There's been an attack on my brother," Sarah said, pre-empting my reply. "Someone dressed up as the ghostly centurion Farnsworth told us about in his lecture here. Frank isn't hurt, thank goodness."

"Very sorry to hear that he was attacked at all." He sat forward. "And you want to catch the attacker?"

"We want to understand who would know enough about the centurion to use that disguise," I said. "We hoped you'd recall a bit about Farnsworth's audience and the way they responded."

"Happy to try. What, specifically?"

"Did you have a list of people who attended?"

"No. Admission was free. No tickets."

"Was there anyone who seemed especially interested?"

He bit his lower lip, considering. "No one stood out. Not that I can recall."

"How would you describe the audience?"

"Hopeful, I'd say. The tale, of course, was a sad one, but hopeful because of the way Mr. Farnsworth presented it. He said it was an opportunity the town might use to their advantage if the Roman bath were successfully restored and the museum successfully expanded. He compared our town centre with The Tower of London. He said half-a-million visitors go there every year, eager to hear about the ghost of Anne Boleyn, the unfortunate wife of King Henry the Eighth. Quite a remarkable fellow, Mr. Farnsworth. Gave the entire talk from memory."

"Did he mention the elixir that the centurion's wife had supposedly given him?"

"Indeed, he did. He thought it tied in nicely with our situation here in Bath, where visitors come to obtain renewed health and vitality. He said he hoped to replicate it one day, based on the records he had found."

"Did anyone in the audience claim to have seen the centurion?"

"Not at all. People were mainly interested in the renovation project and the museum expansion."

Dead end, I thought.

"However," the Rector continued, "I plan to use the story of the centurion as a homily on the subject of revenge being the province of the Almighty. After all, the centurion's spirit – if indeed it is a real spirit – has endured a fruitless quest for two-thousand years because he couldn't control his thirst for revenge."

"Very helpful advice, I'm sure," Sarah said.

"Have you called in the police?" the Rector asked.

"My brother doesn't want to press charges for assault," Sarah said. "Publicity for the restoration project should all be favourable and hopeful. No mention of any danger in any form."

I added, "But of course we want to prevent another occurrence."

"So of course you're considering why someone might attack Frank Brandt. It would be the first question a policeman would ask, I expect."

Fair point, I thought. "Do you know anyone who might wish to hurt Mr. Brandt?"

"No one who'd fit the description of a centurion. But you know what they say about a woman scorned."

"A woman?" Sarah looked surprised. "What woman?"

"I believe Frank has broken off the relationship."

"Is it that little baggage from The Royal Arms? Judith Anne Hart?"

"You know of her, then?"

"I saw her that night at The Royal Arms. She kept her distance. She knows I don't approve." Sarah shook her head. "I'm sure Frank let her know there was no future for her with him. I think he stayed after I left, to tell her that."

"Why don't you approve of her?" I asked.

"She has no family. She works daytimes in The Royal Arms spa and evenings in their tavern."

"Oh." Class distinctions were a part of life that made me uncomfortable. "I suppose that makes her unsuitable socially?"

"More than that. Visitors to the spa complained of valuables taken. They'd go back to wherever they were staying and find things missing from their rooms. Miss Hart always had an alibi, because all the thefts occurred away from The Royal Arms, but the police interviews showed the victims all had previous conversations with her and recalled telling her where they were staying. So that started the rumours that she had an accomplice who did the actual robberies."

"Did the police investigate?"

"Police did arrest a man. Brad Harwood. But he wasn't convicted, and he never implicated Judith Anne."

"Did she attend Farnsworth's lecture here?" I asked Rector Allen.

"I don't recall," he replied.

"Is she one of your parishioners?"

"I don't believe she's a parishioner anywhere," he shrugged. "Charming, though. Has a lovely voice. I'd love to have her in the choir, but alas, I fear circumstances will prevent."

"This Harwood, though," I said. "If he were an accomplice for robbery, he could be an accomplice for the attack on Frank Brandt."

Sarah shook her head. "I believe he went away to London. After the court proceedings."

Another dead end, I thought. There was no way Miss Hart could have left The Royal Arms, taken a rope, dressed as a Roman centurion, and arrived at Frank Brandt's home before he did in order to attack him. And her only known accomplice was in London.

But possibly her accomplice had returned to Bath?

We took our leave from the Rector. Outside the Abbey, Sarah said, "Shall we keep our appointment with Mr. Farnsworth?"

Chapter XI

The Royal Arms was a large Victorian brick building on a street corner only a few hundred feet away from the Abbey. Sarah led us to the side entrance, where Farnsworth stood beside a small door, waiting for us. A well-crafted sign above the door read, *"Roman Museum. By Appointment Only."*

"A modest affair," Farnsworth said. His smile and manner were effusive, mainly directed at Sarah. "But the rent is low. Someday there will be a bigger museum, a place to display all the artifacts that have been preserved over the centuries. You may not know it, Dr. Watson, but the citizens of Bath have been excavating and uncovering artifacts for many, many years. I have so many fascinating examples – "

Sarah interrupted. "The illuminated manuscript, if you please, Mr. Farnsworth. We are on a busy schedule."

"Of course."

He led us down a short dusty corridor, reminiscent of a small, old library. We turned a corner and found ourselves in a narrow aisle, between more shelves on either side. There was dust on all the volumes and the shelves beneath them.

"It's just here," said Farnsworth, turning around to look at Sarah. "A folio volume, on the next shelf. I've brought gloves so you can examine it. Our fingers leave traces of oil that can be quite corrosive – "

She interrupted. "Where is the manuscript?"

"Why, it's – "

Farnsworth broke off. The space on the shelf he had pointed to was vacant. A large book-shaped area was free of the dust that covered the remaining surface of the shelf.

"I put it here – right here!" The little man clenched his fists. "Thursday morning, before I walked over to the Abbey to check on the arrangements for my lecture. I didn't like to keep it in my own office, you see." He shook his head and then patted his hair into place with trembling fingertips. "I can't think what could have happened!"

"Evidently someone moved it," Sarah said.

"But only recently," I said. "Just look at the place where the book rested. It is clean, right up to each of the four edges. No dust."

"Think back," Sarah said. "Where did you last see the book?"

"I had it here. But let me think for a minute. I was going to take some armour and a helmet with me to the Abbey to show people at my lecture.

Then I decided I wouldn't. Too much of a distraction. I decided to give the talk entirely from memory."

"Perhaps you left the volume with the armour and the helmet," I said.

Farnsworth didn't look hopeful. "Then it would be on this shelf up here."

Above us was a box, with a freshly made paper label: "*Sword and Armor, Centurion. Replica.*"

"Replica?" asked Sarah.

"We don't have the leather materials. Those would have long ago decayed. But these are very well crafted."

He stood on tiptoe, pulled the box off the shelf, and set it down on the floor.

The box was empty.

"Oh, dear," Sarah said. "Now you've lost your proof of the legend."

"And the recipe for the elixir as well," he said. "Though fortunately I have made my own progress in that regard – what I hope to be a useful treatment for the common cold. I believe the formula is based on an Oriental remedy, derived from a shrub native to China. The Romans, as you know, did trade with the Orientals and the local Druids would – "

"It's getting late," Sarah interrupted. "Will you report the theft to the police?"

"I don't know that I want the police roaming about. But I have had some other things go missing, from my laboratory. And the book was my father's. He was the one who acquired it from the monastery, I must confess, and that was years before he died. I really would like to get it back." He paused. "Yes, I definitely will consider the police."

He moved to go.

"One more question," I said, gesturing towards the long line of boxes and shelves. "Where will you store all these materials when this building is demolished?"

"Oh, I've already made the arrangements. The building owner here has a similar facility, and he's willing to rent me temporary space at a storage rate. Then of course when the Bath restoration is completed, I'll have a proper museum to display them."

Farnsworth then took his leave, and with a final, wistful glance at Sarah, he departed.

Sarah said, "Well, he doesn't seem to have any motive to stop our project. Another dead end for our investigation, I'm afraid." She looked at her watch. "It's nearly six o'clock. You're to meet Lord Winstrom in The Royal Arms dining room."

"I am?"

She took the note from her pocketbook and showed it to me. It read: "*Reserve table for two at Royal Arms. Quiet corner. Have Dr. Watson at the table at six.*"

"Puzzling," I said.

"A bit distressing," she said. "You would think he would want me to be there. I don't know why I'm to be excluded." She gave a tight smile. "But one dare not question orders from His Lordship. Come with me. I'll show you where you're dining this evening,"

Chapter XII

We left through the museum entrance and went around to the front of the building to enter through the hotel lobby. The dining room hadn't yet opened. We heard music coming from the other side of the room: A lute, and someone singing. Coming closer, we saw a venerable wood-panelled tavern with a few patrons at the bar.

"Would you like to try the spa water in the tavern?" Sarah asked. "You have fifteen minutes until the dining room opens."

"Perhaps I'll have an ale."

There was no hostess, only a man behind the bar. The room was lined with ornately carved varnished wooden booths, some of which were occupied. There were also several unoccupied tables. A blonde-haired young woman holding a lute sat on a tall wooden stool in the corner, singing a sweet melody.

Sarah stiffened when she saw the young woman.

She turned away. "That's the Hart girl," she said. "I won't be going in."

"You don't want to wait for Lord Winstrom?"

"I'll be at the office in case he needs me. He can telephone me from here. You can do the same, if you want anything further. I expect Lord Winstrom will send you back to London in his private train."

She turned and walked away.

I took the table closest to Miss Hart.

The Rector had been quite right about Miss Hart's singing voice. It was lovely. She had completed one song and was beginning another, a sad verse set to the familiar folk melody:

> *Alas my love you do me wrong*
> *To cast me off discourteously;*
> *And I have loved you, oh, so long,*
> *Delighting in your company.*

300

She put such feeling into the lyric that I wondered if her thoughts were on Frank Brandt.

When she had concluded, there was a smattering of applause. She rose from her stool and bowed. She saw me holding a five-pound note folded between my fingertips, the way Holmes does on occasion when he wishes to attract the attention of a potential informant. She smiled at me. A slender woman of perhaps twenty-five, she had a lovely face and a smooth complexion. For some reason, I thought of a stained-glass Madonna in the Abbey window. I reminded myself that Miss Hart may have been mixed up in a criminal ring, obtaining information from clients to be used to rob them later.

She sat at my table, her wide blue eyes on the five-pound note.

"What can I do for you?" she asked.

"I'm looking for information," I said. "It concerns Mr. Frank Brandt."

Her eyes narrowed. "What about him?"

"Someone attacked him two nights ago."

"Are you from the police?"

"Nothing of the sort. I'm a private investigator. I need to determine if the attack was connected to the project Mr. Brandt is working on."

"The big restoration? What can I tell you? Did you speak with him?"

"He seemed to think that someone attacked him in order to slow down the project."

She shrugged. "I don't know anyone who would do that. Everyone I know wishes it were already completed."

"Including the owner here?"

"Why would he be different?"

"This place will close down when they start construction, won't it?"

"He won't bat an eye. He owns four more hotels like this one. Duke's Arms, Earl's Arms, Baron's Arms, Viscount's Arms. All doing well, and they'll do even better after the restoration, when the crowds get bigger. Besides, he was paid handsomely for this building and land, just after the construction was approved."

"What about you?" I asked.

"Me? I'll be working at the Duke's Arms. I'll be fine."

"I'm happy to hear that."

And yet another dead end, I thought.

Then I realised she had said something else. "Sorry? I didn't catch that."

"I said, 'Besides, it won't be too long.'"

"It won't?"

"If the restoration's a big success, Frank will get a lot of the credit, getting it built on time and at the right price. He'll be able to take on more projects, and not just as an employee."

"Good for him."

"And then, knock on wood – " She rapped the table lightly with her bare knuckles. " – Frank and I might just be together. If I don't find someone better in the meantime. And if everything goes well."

I tried not to show my surprise. I didn't want to explain what I knew of her reputation and her recent legal trouble. "What might not go well?"

"That sister of his. She hates me, for some reason. But I'm hoping he'll stand up to her."

At that moment the dining room gong sounded, indicating that the six-o'clock opening hour had arrived. "That's my cue, I'm afraid," I said. "Meeting someone."

She pocketed my five-pound note. "It was quite lovely talking with you, sir. Come back after your dinner if you like. I'll be here until nine."

I made my way into the dining room and told the hostess my name. She consulted her book.

"Oh yes. Lord Winstrom's table. The other gentleman's already here."

She led me to a small table at the far end of the room.

At the table sat Sherlock Holmes.

Chapter XIII

"You aren't in London!" I said.

"Indeed so, old friend," Holmes said. "After your departure this morning, I thought it would be well to confirm the identify of our client. There is now a competent telephone service from London to Bath, though a somewhat circuitous one. I eventually reached Lord Winstrom and spoke with him personally."

"What did he say?"

"He sent the water sample at the behest of Miss Brandt, as we had surmised. He considers her a valuable employee. He also said the danger to his enterprise is rather a remote one. Gossip about spectral phenomena tends to increase interest in a tourist attraction rather than the reverse. Contamination of the water supply, however, is a more serious matter, as would be the loss of his restoration project foreman. When Miss Brandt convinced him that she was fearful of her brother's safety, he took action and sent his note to me, accompanied by the water sample for the reason Miss Brandt indicated. He agreed with my conclusion not to test it."

"What did you do then?"

"Knowing your propensities for taking regular nutrition, even during an investigation, I asked him to arrange a meeting here at the dining room. I placed another telephone call, to Inspector Lestrade, and asked him to arrange with the Bath Municipal Police to have a report awaiting me upon my arrival. I then took the next train. Upon my arrival I stopped at the police office, picked up the report, and then had time to make a call at the Bath Registry."

"Getting the lay of the land, so to speak," I said.

The waitress arrived at our table. "Take your orders, gentlemen? The cod is very fresh. Will you be having our special mineral water? Directly from the natural spring it is, and very highly praised – "

"Porter for me," Holmes said, "and a cut of the beef roast. Medium rare."

I ordered the same, adding rolls, potatoes, and carrots, for I was hungry after the long day.

Holmes said, "Now, about your investigation. Perhaps it would be wise for you to start at the beginning. Where have you been and what have you learned?"

I told him, starting with my arrival at the station and my meeting with Miss Brandt, and ending with my recent interview with Miss Hart, the singer, and potential suspect in the affair of the Brad Harwood robberies.

"So that's it, I'm afraid," I concluded. "A number of potential suspects, but each has proven to be a dead end. Plus, I spent five pounds on Miss Hart and all I have to show for it is the memory of a lovely song."

"You were entitled to some holiday diversion," Holmes said.

He sat back, musing with his fingertips together beneath his chin, as he often does.

Then he sat up straight. "Have you another five-pound note?"

I took one from my wallet and handed it to him.

He placed it on the table. Then he stood up. "We must go."

"But Holmes – our supper!"

"The five pounds will cover it," he said. Then he was striding to the exit, pausing only to collect his coat and hat from the cloak room.

Tugging on my own coat, I caught up with him as we reached the street.

"Where are we going?" I asked.

"To Pulteney Bridge," he said.

Chapter XIV

We walked unimpeded for perhaps three minutes along a darkened street, and then the bridge was within our sight. The band of rushing white

303

water above the weir had grown larger and the sound of it was louder than it had been earlier that afternoon. Fortunately, the rain hadn't resumed. We had a clear view of the bridge shops and their windows. All were dark, except for a single window at the centre. Light from within showed the outline of a figure, a woman, seated and picking up a paper from what appeared to be a substantial stack. I saw another stack on the other side of the desk.

"Miss Brandt," I said. "She told me she would be working on some letters."

As we drew closer, I saw her place the paper on the desk and lean forward.

Holmes said nothing.

We reached the roadway and walked onto the bridge. Streetlamps cast pools of yellow light at either end, but the bridge itself was deeply cloaked in shadow, as were the storefronts.

I led Holmes to the door of Sarah's office, but he turned instead to the one next door, beneath the sign that read "*Farnsworth's Antiquities*".

"Stand watch, old friend," Holmes said. He took something from his coat pocket and crouched over the door lock. A moment later I heard a soft click, and the door swung open.

Holmes held his index finger to his lips. "Keep silent. We are stalking our prey."

Once inside, he closed the door behind us and turned the bolt.

The two of us made our way among Farnsworth's shadowy relics and shelves to his back-room doorway. The door was open. Entering, Holmes stopped before the worktable where Farnsworth kept his chemicals. He spent several minutes hovering over the equipment.

Then he glided soundlessly along the side wall to the door that connected with Miss Brandt's office.

Slowly he turned the doorknob. After an interval that seemed interminable, he eased the door open. I saw a gleam of dim light through the narrow opening. Holmes held the door motionless. The gap was less than one inch.

He motioned for me to look inside.

Miss Brandt, still at her desk, faced the window and away from us, her sturdy back bent, a pencil in her right hand, writing. An electric reading lamp stood on the far side of her desk, alongside one of the stacks of papers I had seen through the window. The other stack lay on the near side. I could see Miss Brandt's face in the window reflection. She appeared calm, concentrating on her work. She put down her pencil, placing the paper before her one stack, and then taking another paper from the other stack.

Holmes murmured. "Now we watch and wait." To my surprise, he moved to the far side of the door, a position which, due to the angle, cut off his view of Miss Brandt and nearly everything else. He pressed his ear to the door frame and held his finger to his lips.

I heard no sound, other than the muffled sound of rushing waters beneath the bridge.

An interminable hour passed. I shifted uncomfortably, wishing I had a chair but glad that I did not, for I didn't want to doze off. As it was, I slumped against the wall and my attention wavered. I came fully awake with a start. Though the narrow doorway opening I could see Miss Brandt's stack of letters on the near side had grown, while the stack on the far side had dwindled to only two or three remaining. "She will be finished soon," I whispered.

Holmes nodded. He had his pocket watch open and tapped it, significantly. In the light from the office, I saw the time was half-an-hour past eight.

Then, reflected in the window, I saw a shadowy, helmeted figure. A large man. The image loomed above the reflection of Miss Brandt. A dark metal band from the helmet obscured the man's features, adding a sinister effect.

My heart pounded in my chest as the reflected figure grew larger. "Holmes – !" I whispered.

Miss Brandt looked up and saw the figure looming behind her in the window. She turned and screamed.

At the same instant, Holmes threw open the door and sprang through, colliding with the intruder. I followed him.

With an enraged bellow, the man flung Holmes aside and continued towards me. His vicious, scything elbow struck me before I could even put up my fists. I staggered back, trying to catch my breath and get my feet under me. The room spun.

As if from a great distance, I saw the intruder club Sarah on the side of her head. She fell across her desk. The man leaped over the desk and flung up the window, letting in the chill air and the sound of the rushing waters directly below.

To my horror, I saw the helmeted man was gripping a short, sharp sword like those once carried by the Roman centurions. With his free hand, he grasped the unconscious Miss Brandt by her jacket collar. He lifted her across the desk and drew her up to the open window, moving her unconscious body as if she weighed no more than a bag of feathers.

He raised the sword above Miss Brandt's bare neck.

At the same moment came the sharp crack of a revolver.

The man's arm fell, dangling at the man's side below his wounded shoulder, but still holding the sword. He clutched at his wound with his free hand. Raging eyes, like those of a mad dog, glared at Holmes from beneath the helmet.

"Drop your sword, or my next shot will kill you," Holmes said. "You should surrender while you can. The crime you intend cannot possibly succeed, and to attempt it will make your penalty far more severe." He paused, and added, to my shock and surprise, "Mr. Brandt."

The man let go of his wound and tore off his helmet.

I recognised Frank Brandt. The foreman's eyes were wide and oscillating wildly, like those of a madman, looking for an escape.

Then he threw the helmet at Holmes and, in one swift motion, transferred the sword to his good hand. He leaped at Holmes.

Instinctively I jumped forward to intervene, colliding painfully and knocking him off balance. He staggered back against the desk.

Then he turned to charge again, sword in hand, heading straight for Holmes.

But Sarah had pulled herself upright, kneeling on the desk. She cried out, her words loud and shrill. "Frank! What have you done?"

Frank Brandt froze. Then he spun around towards his sister, the blade of his sword still upraised. For an interminable moment he stood, staring, eyes blinking, as if waking from a trance.

"It isn't too late, Mr. Brandt," Holmes said. "Put down your sword."

"Please, Frank!" Sarah cried. "For my sake!"

The Roman sword made a metallic clatter as it hit the wooden floorboards.

Chapter XV

Frank Brandt sat exhausted on the floor, head down, arms folded, eyes shut, weeping. Sarah sat beside him, holding his hand.

"You have saved yourself, Mr. Brandt," Holmes said. "Now you must defeat the drug that has become your own mortal enemy."

Brandt shuddered. Then he raised his gaze to Sarah, as if to beg forgiveness. He tried to speak, but could only utter great sobs.

The three of us got him to his feet and walked him to the local infirmary, which was fortunately only a short distance away. There a doctor extracted the spent bullet and bandaged the wound.

The doctor also provided a sedative injection. I administered it after we had brought Frank home to the Circus in a cab and placed him in his own bed.

He soon slept.

306

We sat briefly in the parlour with Miss Brandt.

"Clearly, you need rest after a most difficult shock," I said.

She shook her head, "This is my fault."

Holmes said, "Hardly that, Miss Brandt. Your brother has been under the influence of a powerful vegetable alkaloid derived from the Asian plant – *ma huang*, if I'm not mistaken, judging from the prevalent scent of it on Mr. Farnsworth's chemical workbench. Farnsworth introduced him to the substance and soon he became addicted, to the point that he was entering Farnsworth's workroom to steal it. Your brother was partly driven by his ambition to excel at his work, and partly because he thought success would enable him to be seriously considered as a husband by Miss Hart. None of that was your fault."

"He wanted to win over Miss Hart," she said. "He wanted to sell his ownership in our family home to bolster his chances with her. I flatly refused."

Holmes shrugged. "You may reconsider at any time. Also, in future, you might allow your brother to pursue his own course when he seeks feminine companionship. He may decide on Miss Hart, or he may not, after he becomes better acquainted with her outside her domain as a performer."

"I hoped that he'd see through her, but I realise now that he must make up his own mind. I ought not to have been so harsh."

"I gather you thought Miss Hart's criminal reputation would threaten your rapport with Lord Winstrom?"

She blushed. "Something of the sort."

"I doubt Lord Winstrom would be influenced by Frank's choice of feminine company. From the way he spoke of you, however, he does value your ability and your companionship. You might take that into account when considering your own future."

We agreed that Holmes would tell Lord Winstrom his conclusion, namely that Frank had become addicted to Farnsworth's drug in his zeal to perform more effectively in his job, that the drug had caused him to hallucinate, and that the hallucination had resulted in an unfortunate gunshot wound. I strongly recommended that Frank receive medical supervision to guard against relapse.

"I'll see to it," Sarah said.

Holmes added, "And I will ensure that Farnsworth destroys his supply of the drug and never produces more."

"How can you do that?" Miss Brandt asked.

"He will agree, or I will expose his fraudulent story of the centurion. It is entirely fabricated. The manuscript in which he claimed to have found the monks' annotation doesn't exist."

She gave a great sigh of relief. "Thank you, Mr. Holmes and Dr. Watson. You have saved us."

"And now you will save one another," Holmes replied.

Chapter XVI

Holmes and I took a late supper at The Royal Arms.

"How did you know?" I asked.

"From your report, the conclusion was inescapable."

"How so?"

"As you said, there were numerous suspects, but investigation of each one resulted in a dead end.

"Could Farnsworth have been Frank's attacker? No. Sarah had been with him at the time, and he stood to benefit from the project, with a new museum to contain and better display his artifacts.

"Was someone jealous of Frank and hoping to replace him as project foreman? No. Frank would have known if that were the case, as would Lord Winstrom, who would have been approached by the competitor.

"Did the owners of the surrounding properties plot against the project, as suggested by Frank? Again, no. As the good Rector reported, the general feeling of the crowd was enthusiastic, and those gentlemen had every reason to support the restoration of the Roman Bath.

"Last, as hinted at by the good Rector, we come to Judith Ann Hart. If feeling unfairly rejected by Frank, might she have hired someone to avenge herself on him? Possibly, but as you determined, she didn't feel she had been a woman scorned. She still entertained hopes of an alliance with Frank, as she mentioned to you at the tavern.

"There remained one other possibility, however improbable: Frank Brant had insisted from the beginning that he had been drugged and attacked. But what if this hadn't been the case? He was the only witness to the attack on him, after all, and it is an elementary precaution to investigate the credibility of any witness. When I visited the Bath Registry today, I examined the deed to the Brandt property. It is a deed of joint tenancy, with full title to the property going to the surviving tenant. Incidentally, the Registry clerk remarked that I was the second man to ask for that deed this week. His description of the first man fits that of Frank Brandt.

"If no one attacked Frank, then the question became, what would Frank have to gain by fabricating the story? The answer is this: He would have planted the suspicion that there was a madman on the loose, brandishing a sword, hoping to damage him, or possibly harm the restoration project. What would he gain by that? He would provide a scapegoat for the elimination of his sister, since she is known to be essential to restoration. With Sarah gone, he would inherit full ownership of their jointly owned townhouse.

"His frustration at his sister's opposition to his courtship of Miss Hart, magnified and distorted in his drug-addled mind, overwhelmed all his moral sense and judgment.

"Tonight, he planned to kill his sister with the Roman sword. As was obvious from his opening the window, he would have dropped her body into the river. The rain-swollen waters would have washed it downstream, making the time and place of her death very difficult to determine. He would have gone from the office to The Royal Arms, met Miss Judith Hart when she came off duty at nine o'clock, and she would have given him an alibi for the remainder of the evening. He would have dropped the sword and the armour and the helmet into the river at a later time, at a place further downstream. To appease his conscience, he might blame the spirit of the vengeful centurion. He wouldn't be the first murderer to claim that a devil had forced him to commit his crime."

"Horrible," I said.

"Fortunately, you delivered your very complete and helpful report, and we were able to prevent a tragedy."

I paused. "I have one more question. You came to Bath, so clearly you didn't have to remain in London today. Why, then, did you send me to investigate?"

"I thought the diversion would do you good, old friend," he replied. "You have seemed out of sorts recently."

Then he took two green tickets from his coat pocket. "I propose another diversion as well. Upon our return to London, we shall repair tomorrow evening to The Royal Albert Hall, and immerse ourselves in the powers of a spirit far more benevolent and restorative than that of a Roman centurion."

He handed me the tickets. They were for Her Majesty's Opera, performing Handel's *Messiah*.

NOTES

This a work of fiction, and the authors make no claim that any of the historical locations or characters appearing in this story had even the remotest connection with the events recounted herein. However . . . .

1. The restoration of the central Roman bath was completed in 1897 and opened to considerable acclaim and success. Today, thermal springs still provide hot water to the central structure, although swimming or drinking there isn't permitted due to sanitary considerations. The Roman Bath is the primary attraction of the City of Bath, which draws more than six-million visitors annually.
2. The Bath Abbey underwent major restoration in 1870. Its stained-glass windows occupy more than three-fourths of its wall space. It is listed by Historic England, a branch of the British Government, in the highest category of structures of particular historic interest requiring special protection.
3. The *ma huang* shrub, native to China, has been used to treat symptoms of cold and flu for nearly five-thousand years. The alkaloid stimulant *ephedra* was first extracted from *ma huang* in 1885. More powerful derivatives include *methamphetamine*, the detrimental effects of which are widely known and, at the present time, recognised as a public danger. Hitler is said to have given the drug to storm troopers to enable them to stay awake and fight for days on end during a *blitzkrieg*.
4. The Pulteney Bridge is still fully tenanted with shops. The Pulteney Weir, rebuilt in 1970, still offers some protection to the city against floods along the River Avon. In summer, swimmers do use it as a jumping off point, though officially cautioned against doing so, particularly during times of high water.
5. One can still enjoy an oversize sweet roll at Sally Lunn's Historic Eating House and Museum, Bath's oldest dwelling, built in 1483. The Sally Lunn roll was also immortalised in one of Gilbert and Sullivan's early operettas, *The Sorcerer*.
6. Handel's 1741 oratorio *Messiah* is one of the world's best-known and frequently performed choral works. It has been performed at The Royal Albert Hall every year (except 1940) since the opening of the Hall in 1871.

The Hyde Park Blackmailer
by Peter Coe Verbica

"Life is full of surprises to the unobservant."

Chapter I – Six Gold Sovereigns

A morning fog hid flower beds in St. James's Park, gravestones in Highgate, and doorsteps in Baker Street. It cloaked the Thames and muted light from our flat's window despite the mid-morning hour. Coals glowed in the hearth and radiated the room with a pleasant warmth. Gas lamps danced upon the wall, adding to the overall comfort. A plaster bust of Napoleon and a Persian slipper rested upon their familiar perches.

The consulting detective set down his newspaper abruptly, looked over his aquiline nose, and eyed my empty teacup. He retrieved an ornate Chinese teapot which I hadn't seen before and refilled the cup. He returned the pot to its stand on the table. I was surprised by his hospitality. His contemplative nature normally left him absent from such civilities. I was about to thank him, but I noticed the liquid was a deep green rather than the amber one would expect.

"Holmes – What on earth did you serve me?"

"Eh? Why, how very odd," he replied, alternating quizzical looks at the pot and cup. Holmes clasped the teapot and deftly poured into his own cup which was in front of him.

"Well! Look here, Watson," he responded. "My tea seems perfectly normal."

I leaned forward and could see that, unlike the dark mixture in my cup, Holmes's tea looked very much as one would expect.

"I don't know what to make of this," I said holding up my cup and saucer. "It was perfectly fine before the second pour."

"Life is full of surprises to the unobservant. Take this teapot. What do you notice?"

"It appears to originate from the Far East. Round with a generous handle. Perhaps an antiquity. It's in the crude shape of a seated, older man. It has a surfeit of colors baked into the porcelain."

"A good start, but do you discern anything else unusual about it?"

"Not really, I confess. Perhaps it's the hour of the day."

"We should be freshest in the morning," Holmes reproached. "Very well. What do you notice upon closer examination of the spout?"

"It has a subtle split inside it."

"Pick it up and turn it about carefully if you would."

"I can see a small hole on the top of the handle, and – " Then I paused. " – another small hole is strangely located at the bottom of the handle."

"Precisely. This novelty is what some call an 'assassin's teapot'. It has two compartments for liquids – controlled by plugging or unplugging the respective holes in the handle with one's thumb. Vacuum between the air and the liquids determines which batch lands in the cup. Simple physics."

Slightly maddened by the parlor trick, I withheld further comment when we were suddenly interrupted by a knock at the door. Holmes rose, walked over, and turned the knob.

Into the sitting room stepped a trimly dressed gentleman of medium height with a full head of grey hair. He had a well-groomed mustache which met muttonchops beneath his ears. His face, bright and narrow, appeared to be colored and lined by time spent outdoors. His blue eyes were alert and he looked at us directly. He carried a Miller-style bowler with a wide band and extended a gloved hand to both of us. He shook firmly, and with the enthusiasm and energy one might associate with a younger man.

"Mr. Holmes!" the man belted with good cheer. "A pleasure meeting you in person! And Dr. Watson. I've read of you both. I'm Everett Wutton."

"Originally of Lincolnshire," Holmes replied. "Please, come in and be seated. Would you like a cup of tea or a cigar?"

"Nothing for me, thank you. Forgive me if I smell of horse, but I've been out for a brisk ride, and the groom was ill. I saddled and unsaddled our newest gelding myself. A spirited animal with a wonderful gallop." He moved a hand and made the motion of flowing water.

"Let us be seated and explain the purpose of your visit."

We each took a chair. Holmes crossed his long legs and studied our visitor.

"Watson, Sir Everett is one of the three largest landowners in the East Midlands."

"Well, Mr. Holmes, we know our place under the Dome of Heaven. You have those in Norfolk, Cambridgeshire, and Rutland who are certainly men of means. But I am here to ask for both of your assistance with a rascal who is quietly simply – *mean*."

"To whom are you referring," Holmes inquired.

312

"That's the crux of it, gentlemen. I'm dealing with a blackmailer. As you would undoubtedly anticipate, the scoundrel is faceless. Hidden in the shadows. I want you to flush our quarry out into the open. He's chosen the wrong adversary to cross!"

Sir Everett's face muscles tensed and he clenched his fists. "It is time, gentlemen, to release the hounds!" he announced dramatically.

"Well, I suppose we've been called worse," said Holmes. "We'll take the description as a compliment. We are dogged in our pursuit. Do you have a blackmail letter?"

"I do. But it's obvious to me that the man doesn't know me from Adam."

"Why do you say that?" I asked.

"He claims to have been watching me, knowing where I go, implying that I visited a house of ill repute. He threatens to provide the information to my wife and children. Says that he has witnesses and other tell-tale evidence, including a surreptitiously taken flashlight photograph. There are a couple of problems, however, with his threats."

"What would those be?" I continued.

"I am a God-fearing, and most-happily married Anglican who walks the straight and narrow for one. I don't frequent those types of places. They waste both time and money, both of which I hold in the highest regard. There's another more verifiable discrepancy."

"You have no issue," Holmes said, his chin set upon the tips of his fingers.

"No issue?" I asked.

"No children, Dr. Watson," Sir Everett replied.

"May we see the letter?" Holmes inquired, holding out his hand.

"Of course, Mr. Holmes," he answered, pulling a torn envelope from his jacket pocket. "I received it yesterday."

Holmes extracted the dispatch with his slender fingers, set it before us, and pressed upon the folds. It was written in neat rows with a tremulous hand and read as follows:

> *We all have our secrets and I have been studying yours with utmost care.*
>
> *There are many modern marvels, but few fascinate me as much as the camera. Thanks to the electric battery cell, flashlight photographs are remarkably detailed. I have a number catching you* in flagrante delicto.
>
> *What would your wife, neighbors, and children say if they knew that you have been whiling away your hours with fallen women?*

*I am a reasonable person and perfectly willing to keep
your despicable habits quiet for a modest sum.*

*If you would like both the photographs and the negative
plates, I urge you to follow my instructions with the greatest
of care. I will place them under your front doorstep once you
have paid me the sum I request.*

*Two days from receipt of this letter, you shall place six
British gold sovereigns, exactly a dozen cloves, a goose
feather, and one four-holed button into a leather coin pouch.*

*Hide the pouch under the bench which faces Piccadilly
Street at the northeast corner of Hyde Park across from the
Marble Arch.*

*Any deviation from these instructions will result in my
turning this information over to the newspaper, which would
result in your profound embarrassment.*

"Mr. Holmes, I took this to a handwriting expert who tells me it's written by an older or sick person who is left-handed," Sir Everett said, patting his own forearm. I took it to be the man congratulating his own resourcefulness.

"You've wasted your money," Holmes responded. "The writer is neither."

"But the smudging of the ink shows that it was written by someone who is left-handed! And the shakiness of the writing reveals the person as aged or sick!"

"No to both, I'm afraid," Holmes answered, holding up the paper for closer inspection. "Granted, it is written with a left hand, but the tremors are the result of a right-handed person trying to disguise the cursive. It's also clear that this letter was written very slowly, with extraordinary determination, and pressed with firmness upon the paper. These elements further lend to my conviction that the author is inexperienced in regularly using the left hand for cursive writing. The individual is normally right-handed and, given the force of the pen on the paper, I would say a male, and, rather than infirmed, he is in vital health. He is also, based on my experience, most likely to be less than sixty years of age."

"Well, Mr. Holmes and Dr. Watson," Sir Everett declared, leaning forward in his chair, "I see that I've placed this caper into the best of care!"

"One more thing, Sir Everett: Can you give us a general sense of your circle of friends and acquaintances? Perhaps there's a link. For example, your church, immediate neighbors, your clubs – that sort of thing."

"Saint Andrews Church. Neighbors? I guess my biggest are Blake, Chastnam, and Withers. As to clubs, only one – The Elivas. Why?"

"Just a curiosity at present. I advise that for now you follow the blackmailer's instructions. I'll have some of my agents keep watch over the park bench."

"Understood, Mr. Holmes. Kindly keep me abreast of any developments. Let's catch this rascal."

The gentleman shook my hand vigorously but refrained from disturbing Holmes, who continued to examine the letter with a magnifying glass. Sir Everett saw himself out with the same assuredness with which he had arrived.

"You're putting your 'Irregulars' on this?" I asked.

"My invisible army, Watson. Seen but unseen."

"The Baker Street Irregulars", as Holmes liked to call them, were a band of street urchins who served as his informal eyes, ears, and messengers. Because of their youth and lower station, the orphans attracted less attention and disappeared into London's surroundings, whether in Piccadilly or Devil's Acre. Holmes avoided praise, but his employment of the waifs kept many away from more unsavory pastimes, such as pickpocketing and robbery to name just two.

Chapter II – The Queen's Drawing

Holmes stuffed the bowl of his pipe with some of my ship's tobacco, lit it with a match, and took several puffs.

"What can we deduce from the letter, Watson?"

"He's worried that he'll get caught, I suppose. Thus the use of altered handwriting. He seems to have a command of the King's English, and so must be educated."

"Agreed as to the education. This isn't the work of a barkeeper or chambermaid. But perhaps we can deduce more about this individual." He then listed some points which I recorded:

1. *Doesn't know the victim well.*
2. *Enjoys playing games.*
3. *Settles for a relatively modest sum, given the damage he claims that he could inflict.*
4. *Has an interest in science and keeps up on the latest inventions.*
5. *Is a person with some financial wherewithal. The note was written slowly and by someone who has the luxury of leisure.*
6. *Is well-traveled. A less-traveled person would simply request "gold sovereigns" rather than "British" ones.*
7. *Has at least a modest acquaintance with Latin.*

8. *Is artistic.*
9. *Doesn't like authority and looks at things differently.*
10. *A male under the age of sixty.*
11. *The ink and paper are of common nature and easily sourced.*
12. *Eccentric, given the request for cloves and a button.*

"Artistic? Doesn't like authority? I understand that he's a lawbreaker, but how do you determine these attributes?"

"The man is nearly ambidextrous. Let us reasonably infer that he was corrected in school to use his right hand, despite his natural predilection. We can surmise that he has a reflexive resentment towards authority. This was imprinted upon him when he was a schoolboy."

"And what makes you think that he is artistic?"

"The artistic nature of his personality is simply based on my awareness that DaVinci, Michelangelo, and Mozart were left-handed. Did you know that Queen Victoria is a bit of an artist as well? She bestowed upon me one of her sketches of Buckingham Garden."

"A drawing by Her Majesty? You forever surprise me. I take it she's also left-handed?"

"Her eminence writes with her right hand, but paints with her left."

"I'll confess to not having that sort of intimacy with the royals."

"I mention it not out of sentimentality, but rather as confirming my thesis."

"I would expect nothing less," I replied.

Chapter III – The Prince of St. Giles

For reasons obvious to the reader, it is rare that I write of Holmes's use of cocaine. Like a high-strung racehorse, his mind took umbrage to any confined stall or pen of idleness. His intellect, to tease the analogy further, preferred to lope at a full gait. His use of the stimulant was infrequent enough that I was largely spared any role as his medical counsellor. And while he willingly communicated about the topic, even as to his rations and the preferred percentage of solution, his headstrong tendencies made him the least preferable of patients. It was therefore with some concern that I returned to find Holmes with his arms folded, in recline, with a syringe and colored vial at the table beside him.

"What gives here?" I inquired.

Holmes opened his eyes, and his look was alert and free of any opaque languidness.

"Ah, the syringe and vial. You're jumping to conclusions, Watson. I've extracted a particular poison from a stock of the *atropa belladonna*, or Deadly Nightshade, made famous in *Macbeth*. I've been ruminating over rats – in particular, how they breed, infest, and the best ways to kill them."

"I see."

"Knowing my methods, you can assume that I've been researching aspects of Sir Everett's routine. His church, Saint Andrews, has its intrigues – God forbid you cross the Alter Guild ladies! Sir Everett's neighbor, Blake, is in financial straits due to his underwriting a merchant vessel which was lost at sea. Another of his neighbors has a mistress, an ambitious actress with atrocious grammar. But it's Sir Everett's club which attracts my attention."

"The Elivas," I added. "But I don't know what that has to do with rats. It's safe speculation that they aren't permitted there."

"One would think. It's one of London's most exclusive organizations. Over the past months, its management and board have been doing their utmost to keep a perplexing issue secret from their members."

"I take it they have a rat problem. Can't they just trap or poison the creatures?"

"They've used every traditional means at their disposal, including hiring the prince of all rat catchers, Jack Black, Jr." *

"A prince? I didn't know that rat catchers have their own aristocracy."

"Men tend to form pecking orders, and the rat catching business is no different than high society. Jack Jr.'s father was a bit of an impresario who wore a self-made uniform, including iron rat pendants affixed to his sash. He was often seen carrying a favorite rat in a portable cage."

"Undoubtedly popular with the ladies, I suppose."

"I'd like to pay him a visit. I'd like you to join me."

"It wouldn't top the list of choices, but I will oblige you."

"Bring your Webley. We'll be traipsing near St. Giles."

"Even if Dante's Virgil was our driver, we'll be lucky to get him to drop us off a few blocks from that destination."

"All the better to observe our quarry unawares. I'll bring a weighted walking stick for good measure."

We departed later in the day than I would prefer as the afternoon dimmed. Clips from our horse's hooves echoed in the alleyways. Atop a slate roof, I made out the silhouette of ravens against the grey cloud cover.

Holmes exited the hansom first and began a brisk pace. I hopped out onto the cobblestones and was instantly greeted by the fetid smell of squalor. Hats and scraps of blankets had been stuffed into broken windows to fend against the cold. A one-legged man leaned against a lodging house. Two women with headscarves bowed their heads and hid their faces as they walked past us.

I endeavored to keep up with my determined friend. We passed a series of workhouses and rookeries and arrived at a narrow passageway. Holmes beckoned for me to follow him and descended into the darkness.

We surprised a hulking figure who suddenly spun and lunged at us like a wrestler. The man was enormous and had a protruding, low forehead. Despite the close quarters, I withdrew my revolver quickly. With the inherent danger of our surroundings, my reflexes had been a coiled spring from the onset. The blackguard's eyes narrowed as he raised his hands above his misshaped head. More beast than human, he backed away slowly, growling through an uneven row of teeth. He seemed more accustomed to being the predator rather than the prey.

Cordially grinning at the ruffian, Holmes leaned on his walking stick as if he was ready to have a casual chat with a shopkeeper.

"You're making an excellent decision, sir," Holmes said, as the man receded out of our sight.

I placed the revolver back in my pocket with some reluctance.

"Thank you for efficiently expressing your convictions," Holmes said. "May I draw your attention to the sign above this door?"

A wood placard hung above us, attached to two rusted chains. In its center was a crude carving of a rat, including the bulbous body and long tail. The image had oxidized downwards as if someone had used bootblack, printer's ink, or some other impermanent substitute for paint.

"No need to use letters on your sign when many of your customers can't read," Holmes commented as he rapped the top of his walking cane on the small door. After some moments of no response, he repeated the exercise. The door opened narrowly and we were greeted with a partial view of a pale, round-faced man wearing a chin-curtain beard. He blinked at us.

"We've come to seek your counsel on a matter involving rats," Holmes said. "I'm here to see the Prince."

"He isn't presently here, but give me your card," the man responded gruffly. "He visits customers. Customers don't often visit him."

"Are you familiar with The Elivas? It seems to be having an ongoing infestation of rats, and I thought you might know something about the club's odious problem."

"Hand me your card and I will ask that you get a call next week," the greeter responded, extending his palm.

Holmes grabbed the man's hand and flipped it to a position which induced the man to yelp, "What ho, now!"

My friend inserted his walking stick in between the door and threshold and leaned in with his shoulder. We made our way into the hovel, which stank of eye-watering urea.

318

"Watson, would you be kind enough to shut the door behind you?"

I closed it and acclimated to the uninsulated, wood-slat interior. Row after row of rat cages lined the walls filled with blinking red eyes. A rush-light burned in the room next to a pair elbow stick chairs. In front of the crude light was a pile of spare, greased rushes. A string of jam jars filled with tallow and wicks sat upon makeshift shelves. Hung upon a dressmaker's dummy was a full-length velvet coat which looked to be from a different century.

The scowling proprietor had deep-set coal black eyes and the translucent skin of a cadaver which seemed to glow above his beard. I assessed him further: Potbelly, prominent Adam's apple, and thin, bird-like arms. He wore a dirty nightshirt, a pair of ballooned gypsy pants, and a pair of unlaced boots.

"Well, Jack Black, Jr. I recognized you instantly. The Rat-catching Prince looks very much like his famous father, the Rat-catching King. Please, sir, take a seat."

"What do you want?" he asked, sitting down slowly. "Who are you?"

"No need to worry about who we are, Mr. Black. As I suspected, the rat *catcher* is also a rat *breeder*. A rat needs less than thirty days to litter more of these varmints."

"I catch and breed for the rat pits. It's perfectly legal."

"Rat pits?" I repeated, finding the activity vile.

"As you know, Watson, a blood sport," Holmes replied. "A specially-bred terrier is placed into a pit filled with rats. It's timed, and the number of rats killed are counted."

"Can't they just watch a tennis or rugby match for entertainment?" I asked, knowing that such was wishful thinking.

"The activity does attract a peculiar lot, I must say," Holmes responded. "I see you also make tallow candles, Mr. Black. I suppose you boil the tallow from the dead rats? You're an enterprising one, I see."

"It makes for a living," Black responded grimly.

Tapping the top of his walking cane to his palm, Holmes surveyed the rat catcher. After a long pause, he said, "Mr. Black, we came to find out who is bribing you to infest The Elivas with rats. I'm inclined to give you the business end of my walking stick. Instead, let me ask how much you're paid to do your skullduggery and I'll double it. If I find out that you've given me a false amount by so much as a farthing, I will come back to retrieve my stipend and leave more than a few marks of violence upon your personage."

"I've received a total of five pounds," he admitted.

"If I'm satisfied with your information, Mr. Black, I have ten pounds in my pocket for you. Who hired you for your rat releases at The Elivas?"

"I couldn't tell you because I've never seen the man. Only his money."

"How does he pay you?"

"I have to visit Hyde Park and retrieve a coin pouch under a bench."

"Under a bench? Where is it located?"

"The corner of Palace Avenue and Kensington Road," he responded, clearing his throat. "May I take a pull of whisky? I suffer from terrible headaches."

"When we leave," Holmes responded. "How quickly we leave is up to you."

On a nearby table, Holmes placed two five-pound coins, which Black eyed longingly.

"Mr. Black."

"What is it?" he mumbled, transfixed by the coins.

"I also expect you to ensure The Elivas is free of rats from now on."

"Yes, yes, of course," he replied, his eyes watering.

We left the rat catcher and, after walking several blocks, were able to hail a cab. Inside the carriage, I wondered about Holmes's generosity towards Black.

"Justice doesn't always come full circle, but in Black's case, he will pay for his misdeeds. His headaches are but a precursor of what is to come."

"The headaches are from the poisons he encounters in his profession! The man must be exposed a thousand-fold to what one would normally encounter."

"Precisely."

"I will need to have my shoes cleaned and clothes boiled after that visit," I said ruefully.

"Be sure that they add some lemon juice, baking soda, or vinegar to the laundry."

"Just one of those three?"

"Salt of sorrel, furocoumarins, pearlash, turpentine, sulfuric acid, oxgall, or milk acid concoctions would be too harsh," the detective said, offhandedly. "Dealing with criminal cases does require an understanding of stains and their removal."

"Thank you," I responded with mild irritation.

Chapter IV – The Infinite Corridor

Drawing upon a pipe, Holmes had surrounded himself with a stratum of grey smoke. He looked through it, as if he were trying to call forward an apparition from the very miasma. I speculated that he was weaving together threads of the disparate facts before him, no matter how thin or subtle they might be. I had seen him extract a man's entire biography from the examination of a simple felt hat. Some of London's cleverest criminals had mistakenly underestimated the great detective, to their detriment and incarceration.

"I have been turning over another curiosity in my mind."

"What might that be?"

"Why didn't Sir Everett ever remove his gloves during his visit with us?"

I took a moment to ponder Holmes's observation.

"Poor circulation? His coloring would indicate the contrary. Perhaps he wanted to hide that his left hand had dragged through some ink."

"One must consider all of the possibilities."

Holmes clapped his hands and rose.

"Let us sally forth once again. I think it's time we visited Sir Everett's club and discreetly interview a few of its members and staff. If the blackmailer is using The Elivas as his favorite pond, there may be other fish there that he's baited and hooked. Sir Everett has arranged for our visit."

In short order, we and our hansom made our stop in Brooke Street in front of the club's neoclassical terrace. Once inside, we walked over a series of black-and-white tiles. Holmes announced our visit at the greeter's desk, and we quickly made our way up the carpeted staircase. A pattern of swirling vines decorated its wrought-iron railing.

We sat a green felt table in the club's bar, next to a richly paneled wall and fireplace. But for us, the room was unoccupied. Holmes ordered a claret, and I requested a whisky-and-soda. The liveried waiter, an athletic man in his thirties, returned with our drinks. Holmes asked him to stay for a moment.

"Thank you for the speed of your attentiveness. I am Sherlock Holmes, and this is my colleague, Dr. Watson. We are guests of Sir Everett Wutton."

"A good man, indeed, sir. It's said that a man should protect himself by friends rather than fences," said the waiter with an Irish accent. "You've chosen well, in my opinion."

"Donegal County," Holmes said. "Part of the O'Donnell clan?"

"A great guess, sir. You are correct. I come from a long line of Patrick O'Donnells."

"I've been to Donegal Castle," Holmes said. "In fact, I helped the Fifth Earl of Arran negotiate the castle's stewardship under the Office of Public Works."

"No doubt the O.P.W. will own every brick and turret by the time they're done," O'Donnell replied, sorrowfully. "I've read about you in the paper. What brings you here, sir?"

"I recently advised one of London's most-prominent clubs on its problem with scurrying, long-tailed creatures. The club to which I'm referred should find the issue eradicated."

"As someone who might work for said club, I shall then thank you, Mr. Holmes."

"I know that you mind your own business as a matter of course, but have you had any observations regarding the staff or members who have been acting out of their normal character?"

"You're right about me minding my own business. I make it a practice to avoid intrigue."

"Understood. I'm going to give you my calling card. We're going to have a bite to eat in the main dining room. When we leave, I plan on coming by the bar. Write down a few names on the back with a word or two, even if they seem senseless. You have my assurances that the discloser will be kept confidential. And that my objective is to be of help to Sir Everett and the club itself."

O'Donnell took the card and placed it in his vest pocket.

"Put your thinking cap on, if you would," Holmes said, slipping the man the calling card. "*Mutuam habeatis caritatem*."

The man raised an eyebrow, bowed, and left.

"'*Have love for one another*'?"

"Charity. It is the county's motto in Latin."

Holmes and I proceeded to the dining room upstairs. It was a large, well-lit room with white walls and gilded ornamentations. Four club members were seated at a six-chaired round table covered in white linen. They leaned towards center and spoke in hushed tones. One looked up and seemed entranced by Holmes. The others noticed their friend's distraction and ceased talking. The man who had first seen Holmes beckoned us to join the table.

"The well-known Mr. Holmes," the club member said.

Holmes looked mildly embarrassed.

"We're reluctant to interrupt your private conversation," Holmes responded.

My friend then proceeded to sit in one of the two empty seats and beckoned me to take the other.

"Nonsense," the man exclaimed. I learned that the bald, garrulous man was a banker. He weighed over twenty-one stones and his modern coat jacket looked as if it had shrunk onto his frame.

We ordered fresh drinks, and I began to learn about the others. One was a thin-lipped, lethargic importer of French wines. Another who fidgeted incessantly was a breeder of Arabian horses. His ears were sizeable and he sweated profusely. The other gentleman was bespeckled, and I learned that he was a brooding newspaper publisher visiting from Newcastle. Holmes promptly engaged the men in a wide range of topics, converging on the banker's rapid gain in weight, the importer's recent bouts of melancholy, the rising room temperature with the horse breeder, and the newspaperman's digestive issues. I felt a tinge of guilt for admiring the lamb stew more than the general conversation. Normally I'm not fond of mutton, but I nevertheless found the meal to be delicious. This was moments before Holmes elected to thrust me center-stage as his conscripted ruse. In a few moments, I would find the club members' full attentions directed towards me.

"Gentlemen, allow me to confide in you a most vexatious challenge, involving a close acquaintance of Dr. Watson's. The long and the short of it is that some rogue has been writing anonymous letters accusing this individual egregious behavior and threatening him if he doesn't meet the blackmailer's demands. There are supposedly flashlight photographs of him involved in extramarital activities."

The men stirred and the effusive banker was the first to comment. "Don't have your friend go to Scotland Yard, Doctor. Their priorities are murders, kidnappings, and stabbings. What is the amount of the blackmailer's demand?"

With the members raptly staring at me, I looked at Holmes, who put his hand to his face and spread apart his five fingers and then folded in four, exposing just his index finger.

"Six gold sovereigns, gentlemen," I responded, looking at each of their eager faces.

"There seems to be a rash of this sort of thing," the importer said, his face flushing.

"Agreed," said the gloomy publisher, his voice rising. "Such misfortune increases readership of my paper, but I would hate to be the target."

"It would cost you," the importer offered slowly, "more in time and labor to locate this rascal than to just acquiesce and pay it. If your friend can get away with paying this amount and the problem stops, it's worth trying."

"I'm inclined to agree with the advice," the horse breeder said, wiping his forehead with his dinner napkin.

"Have any of you gentlemen experienced such matters?" Holmes asked. "Or know of anyone else similarly affected? Anything you share will remain *completely* anonymous."

The men paused, looked towards one another, as if seeking each's approval, and then scrutinized Holmes and me. The overweight banker chimed in first, placing his hand to his mouth.

"I haven't experienced it personally, no," he coughed. "That said, I have encountered a few who've been in similar situations. Gentlemen of repute. Gentlemen appreciated by society. Individuals with personal fortunes at stake. Gentlemen who could be harmed by such besmirchment. As a banker, I am often brought into the confidences of such people. In my experience, one should pay the piper and get this matter into the past."

The other club members nodded slowly in agreement.

Holmes turned to the men and said, "Let us change the subject to something brighter, shall we? What we need counsel upon most at this juncture is dessert. What would you recommend?"

The men offered their suggestions, and we finished our meal with Bramley apple crumble and spiced cider. Afterwards, as we walked out together, we went through a tall hallway of juxtaposed mirrors. Our figures seem to stream endlessly down opposing corridors.

"We've nicknamed this the 'Infinite Corridor', and you can see why," the wine importer confided. The other men chuckled.

On the way out, Holmes excused himself, saying that he had left his gloves at the bar. We shook hands with the three men and exited down to the street. Once inside the cab and underway, Holmes turned to me and smiled slightly.

"Of course, they're all lying. My suspicions are confirmed."

Chapter V – Sandown Park

The following day I found Holmes slowly and absentmindedly turning his calling card over in his fingers. As it flipped, I noticed narrow lines of handwriting on it.

"Is that the calling card you retrieved from O'Donnell?"

"It is. There are three names on the back. One of a wine importer, one of a banker – both of whom we met yesterday at dinner – and one other. Next to the first two names are the words '*nervous*' and '*agitated*,' respectively."

"So they're up to no good? Blackmailers? It seems the stakes of the game are beneath them."

"I'm beginning to get a sense of the line."

"The line?"

"The line from the fisherman to the fish."

"I see," I responded, not making heads or tails out of his statement.

"There's a third man listed – an employee of The Elivas who wasn't present during our visit: Jackie Dobbs. I invite you to read the words beside Mr. Dobbs."

"'*New gold watch and signet ring.*' Doesn't seem that out of the ordinary."

"If an aristocrat comes into a windfall, what might he do to place himself above others of his station?"

"An affluent aristocrat? Buy a larger estate in the country or a bigger home in town, I suppose?"

"Certainly alternatives for the well-to-do. And what about an individual from a much lower station?"

"Jewelry or personal effects, I take it," I answered, disinterestedly.

"Exactly. These are a trifling most gentlemen would take for granted. But for a cook, barkeep, or steward, they would make a statement."

"The man received a payment of substance but didn't have the wisdom to bury it in a sock."

"They rarely do. And men of his type aren't going to use such funds to purchase books."

"No, they wouldn't, I suppose . . . ."

"Let us pay Dobbs a visit, shall we? This morning, I followed him a bit and did some research on his activities, and now hope to make his acquaintance. Today happens to be the man's day off, and so we are off to Sandown Park."

"To the horse races?"

"Indeed. Dobbs isn't one we'll find at the library or museum. Any advice on wagering?"

"Yes. My advice is to stay away from wagering."

"Watson, you are a man who gets along well with his fellows, has been in service to his country, and continues to exhibit the rarest of qualities."

"What would that be?" I asked.

"Why, sound judgment!"

"Thank you."

Most know that Sandown Park racing course in Surrey is an excursion, well on London's outskirts. Home to the Eclipse Stakes, it requires an entire day to visit properly. We took a train and then boarded a horse-drawn carriage once closer to our destination. Holmes kept his gaze out the window. The morning brightened as we dashed under tree-covered lanes, along the perimeter of small pastures and past country houses.

"Heave, ho!" Holmes said as he stepped out of the carriage and walked towards the main entrance. The fields were bustling with activity. I could smell the racetrack straw, burning tobacco, and wood smoke.

Sandown Park is a flat course, but it also features the National Hunt races. Barely twenty years old at that time, having opened in 1875, the grounds still retained much of their freshness. I had read of its reputation – for good food, well-dressed ladies, and stirring races. Try as I might to look at the spectacle about me coldly, I could feel a quickening of my circulation and breathing. Such was the impact of the race bells, hooves upon the turf, high stakes of the derbies, and raised voices – all pressed upon me. Though my medical work had provided stability since the days of being limited to a modest Army pension, I vowed to keep my wallet well-pocketed.

We went to our seats in the wooden stadium. Holmes manifested a pair of binoculars and turned the glasses upon the field, looking from one side to the other.

"It's easy to study the animals. Handicapping a horse for age is one thing, but it's difficult knowing which jockey has been induced to throw a race. Most are trustworthy, but a slight easing up on the reins or less aggressive whip influences the results. It makes for a sucker's bet, no matter what the good Admiral may espouse in *The Laws and Practices of Horse Racing*."

"I see you're eyeing the front runner."

"Yes, but I'm also looking at the periphery. Our man Dobbs is along the rail, third from the right. Top hat. Medium brown coat. Black lapels and trim. Boyish face. Let's take a walk in his direction, shall we?"

We made our way through the throng. A couple of open carriages were turned at right-angles in defense of the chimerical wind. Many of the younger women wore elaborate, light-colored, multi-ruffled dresses. The older ones seemed to be more practical, dressed in black. A gentleman in fox-hunting attire, red coat, and black riding boots stood over a portable, sporting table. Picnic blankets lay upon the ground in spots. One visitor had an enormous meat pie dish and a lobster set in front of a wicker basket.

Holmes found the youthful-looking man still leaning at the rail. The enthusiast watched the riders guide their horses to take slow strides, limbering up the animals ahead of the race. Holmes began chatting affably with his adopted friend. The detective moved his arms about with some animation. After a moment, he said, "Watson, let me introduce you two." He looked at the man. "Mister – your name sir?"

"Dobbs."

"Mr. Dobbs seems to think that Percy's Prize is a long shot. I believe the horse is ready for his due. Sir, would you be amenable to a side wager,

326

just to keep it interesting? How about five shillings? Or do you not have the stomach for it?"

"Well, sir, I guess if anyone's going to school you on horses, it might as well be me. You're on!"

Holmes and Dobbs shook on the wager. We watched the horses fall into line, dance with anticipation, ready to chug at the air. The starter dropped his flag and the beasts leapt forward. The jockeys perched ahead of their stirrups, reins and whips high on the animals' necks. As the horses passed 'round, hooves chopped at the turf, fetlocks angled, almost a blur, such was their speed. Rounding the final turn, the audience rose. I observed Percy's Prize four horses back from the lead.

"It seems, Mr. Dobbs, that you were right!" Holmes announced, passing the young man his winnings. The racing fan appeared to be shaking slightly, as if the event produced a state of fever, or he had been given a stimulant.

"On a day like today, with the clouds clearing, we all join one another in the winner's circle. Gentlemen, let me treat each of you to a beverage!"

Time passed, with Holmes buying Dobb's additional drinks and regaling us with stories of horse racing. I was once again reminded of Holmes astonishing diversity of knowledge. Tobacco ash, soil composition, martial arts. And today derbies. As the afternoon light receded, field tents were being folded and carriage drivers began to form lines.

Holmes offhandedly asked Dobbs the time. The young man pulled a gold watch from his pocket and stated the hour. Holmes advised that we should take our leave of Sandown, inviting Dobbs to join us on our carriage ride back.

"Why, that would be handy," the man responded. "We can split the fare three ways."

After Dobbs and I entered the carriage, Holmes had a quiet word with the driver before joining us. Then we set off, riding in silence. Several miles from Sandown Park, the carriage stopped suddenly. I noticed that we were on an isolated road.

Dobbs looked out his window. "I don't recognize this lane."

"Mr. Dobbs," said Holmes coldly, "we know why you came into a small fortune about a month ago. We'll keep your secret safe, but it's time to share with us the details."

"Why, why . . . ." he stammered. "I don't know what you're talking about – "

"This is no time for tricks, Mr. Dobbs. You're presently among friends, and we'd willing to have it to stay that way with your cooperation."

327

Holmes put his hands together and studied the tips of his fingers.

"Unless you would prefer that Scotland Yard become involved . . . ."

"I could lose my job at the club," Dobbs said quietly.

"We know that, of course," Holmes responded. "So let's have out with it."

"I – I found an envelope in my coat."

"Yes?"

"Inside was a letter which offered me a tidy sum for a roster of the club's members and their addresses."

"Written with a shaky hand."

"How did you know that?" Dobbs blurted.

"I know more than you can imagine. So you produced the roster of members, whose privacy is normally strictly maintained. Such information would normally be kept locked in the manager's office."

"It would," the boyish faced man responded, "but I'm given the responsibility of closing The Elivas on Friday and Saturday evenings."

"Giving the manager time to get home earlier to his wife and family," Holmes said, "and allowing you plenty of time to copy the information."

"It took me several weeks."

"You were well paid for your disloyalty."

"True," the man replied, looking at the carriage floor.

"Where did you leave the roster once you completed it?"

"The Encomium Hotel desk. The letter in my coat had me address the package to a '*Mr. Ishmael*'."

"The pariah," Holmes responded thoughtfully.

"At which bench in Hyde Park did you retrieve your payment?"

"You seem to know everything. I guess the person who paid me has turned against me. The bench is on the southwest corner."

Holmes opened the door to the carriage. "Mr. Dobbs, it's time for you to exit," he instructed, pointing to the country road.

"You don't expect me to walk all the way back, do you? It's almost nightfall!"

"I invite you to think about your actions," Holmes responded. "Considering the harm you've caused others, it's a rather lenient penalty."

Dobbs stepped down from the carriage and surmised from Holmes's tone of voice that there would be no negotiation.

Chapter VI – Face-to-Face with a Rapier

Over the next few days, I had a series of patients to attend to and, with time passing, I looked forward to seeing what progress Holmes had made. I arrived after lunch to find Holmes with his violin. He played with

328

competence, and I recognized the piece as one of Mendelssohn's. Holmes set the instrument down and rested the bow next to it.

I sat and began a conversation. "I've been wondering: Have your Irregulars caught anyone retrieving Sir Everett's ransom under the park bench?"

"No. They haven't seen anyone make a move. They've watched tourists with their children, locals eat their lunches and read their papers, couples courting hand-in-hand, geese squawking for pieces of bread, and of course, dogs of all shapes and sizes darting in and out of the pathways."

"It's been several days. This is truly one patient blackmailer."

"More elusive than patient. Despite my Irregulars' round-the-clock vigilance, the ransom has vanished."

"By what feat of magic? Without being able to trail the blackmailer or his courier, your efforts are surely doomed. The blackmailer will remain cloaked in anonymity – at least until his next victim."

"It's true that I don't know the exact identity of the blackmailer."

"You mentioned after our dinner with members of The Elivas that they were lying. Are they involved in the blackmailing?"

"They are. Without a doubt."

"Why not press upon them and get the truth out of them, then!"

"Such actions would bring me no closer to finding the culprit, I'm afraid," Holmes replied, as he selected a pipe and began scooping tobacco into its bowl from the Persian slipper.

Perplexed, I persisted.

"But why? They seem to be your best leads yet!"

"Because they're not the blackmailers. Remember their traits? The rapid weight gain. The sweating. The melancholy. The digestive troubles. One or two of these could be discounted, but together, it tells us that they are all suffering from states of acute nervousness."

"The gain in weight? How can you deduce it's rapid?"

"We can deduce the speed of his weight gain by his jacket size and its being of the latest fashion. The man can certainly afford a new jacket, but he hasn't quite adjusted to the reality of weight. At some point in the near future, driven by discomfort, he will concede and modify his wardrobe accordingly."

"Holmes, I am forever awed by your powers of observation."

"The cues of what we seek to unravel are more often than not right in front of us."

"So you were able to determine that they are the victims."

"Indeed. And, from the advice given to you, we can assume that each has paid the blackmailer in exchange for the hope his reputation is left intact. But such is an uneasy bargain. If I'm not mistaken, I hear Lestrade's familiar footsteps, along with Constable MacPherson." Holmes opened the door, saying, "Inspector. Constable."

"Mr. Holmes," Lestrade replied, squinting like a ferret as he adjusted to the light. "I see that you've convinced Sir Everett that you're ready to catch one of London's most prolific blackmailers."

"Only with your help, Inspector."

"I have a couple of extra men, ready to monitor the exits of Hyde Park."

"I don't think they'll be necessary, but I appreciate your precaution."

Lestrade cleared his throat and said, "Well, just what does the man look like?"

"I can't say, just yet."

"Most unusual. As you've requested, I've asked my men to stay at least twenty paces from the park entrances."

"Wonderful, Inspector. Watson, shall we catch a hansom? It's time to take a walk in the park."

Holmes bid the inspector and constable a hearty goodbye and we collected our coats. There were still a few good hours of daylight as we disembarked and entered Hyde Park. Holmes and I followed the footpath along the southern bank of the Serpentine. We passed London plane trees, sweet chestnuts, and common lime trees. I did my best to study the faces of passersby, but began to tire of the exercise.

"This is a large space, comprising many acres. How do you expect to locate the blackmailer? You mentioned that he's unconventional. Should I be on the lookout for an eccentric?"

"London is filled with them. I have a simpler strategy. Come, let us find a comfortable spot and let our blackmailer come to us. Here's a lovely bench with a view of Park Lane."

"You've situated us halfway up the lane, I see."

"True. I appreciate your observation."

I redoubled my efforts to scrutinize those walking the park. Leaves in the trees near us were turning. I could see hints of crimson and gold.

Holmes crossed his legs and began reading a small book. I glanced over. It was in French, written by Lavoisier on the topic of chemistry.

A few hours passed and dusk was nearly upon us. It seemed as if Holmes's plan, whatever it might be, was not unfolding.

"Watson, I may need your help."

Holmes removed a small coil of stout rope from his jacket and set it down on the bench between us.

"We're going to use this for restraint?"

"Correct," he said.

For a moment, I became distracted by a black terrier sniffing in zigzag pattern in the grass. The animal had its ears back and began bounding towards us. To my surprise, it leapt into my lap and began dancing excitedly.

"Well, it seems you've made a new friend."

"Apparently! The dog seems quite smitten."

"Would you be kind enough to run the rope through the dog's collar and hold on to it?"

"I'll do my best. If I can get the animal to settle down."

"This may help," Holmes said. He extended a piece of sailor's hard tack to me.

I gave the dog the biscuit and, while the animal was preoccupied with it, I quickly ran the rope through a ring in its collar.

"Gentlemen!" a man shouted out to us, waving a thin cane above his hat. "Forgive my dog's behavior!"

As he got closer, I could see he had a Maltese beard and wore a blue suit with a red bow tie.

"Sir, I must ask you to release my dog immediately!" he said, his tone suddenly curt.

The man closed his distance to about ten paces and Holmes stepped in front of me. I rose from the bench and held the animal by the makeshift leash.

"We would enjoy a visit with its owner," Holmes replied, casually.

"That would be me, and I'm in no mood to visit," the bearded man replied, his voice becoming quieter.

Holmes removed his hat and held it in front of himself. "You've been resourceful, I must say," he said.

"I'll show you resourcefulness!" the man replied, pulling at his cane.

"Holmes!" I shouted. "He has a rapier!"

Holmes stood his ground, just a few feet from the blackmailer's gleaming blade.

"Surely you don't think I would walk in such a park without being prepared for the likes of you two?" he said, bending at his knees and taking the stance of a fencer.

"You've caught me with just my hat in hand, sir" Holmes responded, "but I must insist that you drop your weapon."

"Why would I do that?" the man responded, taking a half-step forward with the blade pointed at Holmes's torso.

"I have a .450 Short Barreled Metropolitan Police Revolver aimed directly at you – precisely for this occasion. The game is up. We have men stationed at all the park exits."

The man tilted his head and began reassessing his choices.

"You're bluffing!" he shouted.

"Put the sword cane and sheath down and raise your hands, or I will cut you down where you stand. Do it now!"

"Very well," the man spat, eyeing Holmes's hat. He placed his sword and scabbard on the ground and raised his hands. His knees were still bent as he eyed Holmes.

My friend took a step forward, closed the distance between them, and kicked the rapier away from them.

"I congratulate you on making the right choice. Now, I suggest for your sake that you step back. We're going to have a walk together."

Holmes showed the man that he was holding a short-barreled revolver after all and covered it again with his hat.

"Now turn around and walk in front of us"

I grabbed the cane and sheathed the weapon. The terrier trotted eagerly beside me. I could see Lestrade and two constables walking quickly towards us.

"Well, Mr. Holmes, you've captured your elusive quarry," Lestrade said as the constables handcuffed the man "but I'm going to need a lot more explaining from you at Scotland Yard tomorrow." The rogue flashed a scowl at us before being frog-marched toward Piccadilly.

Before accompanying his men, the inspector turned to Holmes and asked, "How did you convince this fellow to walk so peaceably with you?"

"I wish we could say that our visit was congenial, Inspector. Watson has his dog, as well as his sword cane."

Holmes placed his hat back upon his head, and then held his palms open at his sides and shrugged his shoulders. He had re-pocketed the weapon with a magician's finesse.

"I suppose Watson gets the credit. After all, he retrieved the rapier."

"I see," said Lestrade, raising an eyebrow. "We'll see you at Scotland Yard tomorrow. I need you to unravel this repugnant mess."

"Certainly, Inspector."

Chapter VII – Cloves and Curiosity

Lestrade paced the floor of his office with his hands behind his back and then turned to Holmes and me, giving us new information about the blackmailer, a man named Friedlander. "He's a man of vast wealth," explained the inspector, "and he has no need for the ransom money he was extracting."

"Correct," Holmes responded. "I've done some further research as well. He's one of the most successful merchants in central London."

"I'm still at a loss why the man would risk his station for such foolhardy antics," Lestrade stated, scratching his head.

"We'll get to his motive shortly," Holmes answered.

"Yes, yes," Lestrade said impatiently, "but you plucked this culprit from out of the ether is beyond me," Lestrade continued. "How would you know that you'd capture him in Hyde Park?"

The great detective placed a forefinger to the palm of his hand and readied his points.

"As we know, Hyde Park served as his drop off and pickup location. Despite knowing this, the blackmailer remained elusive."

"And yet, you identified him with ease."

"The extraordinary rat problem at The Elivas Club raised my level of suspicions. And, with its members being targeted for blackmail, I began to consider that the concurrent phenomena were not a coincidence. But it was our spiced cider at The Elivas which aided my strategy for capturing the culprit."

"Spiced cider?" I said. "I'm not following."

"Made with cloves. I kept asking myself. 'Why require cloves to be included in the coin purse?' Did they have some symbolism? Did the blackmailer simply want his victim to be more frustrated? Did he get a peculiar delight in making a man assemble strange bits and pieces in addition to a simple ransom?"

"I found it odd at the least," I said.

"Odd indeed."

"And so?" the Inspector asked. "Was this rogue doing it for sport? What is the purpose of the spice?"

"Scent, gentlemen."

"Scent?" I questioned.

Holmes's grey eyes surveyed Lestrade's' office, taking in the papers on his desk. "I had the park bench watched round the clock," He continued. "Despite the watchfulness of my Irregulars, no one was spied reaching under the bench to retrieve the coin pouch. If a man or woman wasn't seen nabbing the pouch, then I had to change my perspective. It would have to be an entirely different accomplice."

"A terrier retriever!" I blurted. "Who would have thought? Just as hunters might use a German wirehair to retrieve pheasants!"

"Exactly. The animal was trained to locate the coin purse by scent and retrieve it. Since the dog is black in color, could be released nearby, under the cloak of darkness, and complete its task unseen."

"A retriever schooled with cloves," Lestrade said, tapping his forehead. "Who would have thought of such a thing?"

"To us, a pungent spice, but to a trained animal with acute senses, the covers provide a strong scent."

"I saw the terrier zig-zag towards us. I take it you baited the animal."

"Precisely. I dropped a trail of cloves and I hoped to lead the animal to us. I invite you to check your left coat pocket," Holmes smiled.

"Goodness!" I responded, pulling out a handful of cloves. "No wonder the terrier made such a fuss over me!"

"You mentioned that the man acquired a roster of Elivas' members," said Lestrade, "but how did he ensnare his victims? Did he have a network of spies digging into their activities?"

"Think of it as using scattershot rather than a rifle on a flock. Friedlander preyed upon their conscience and their predilections, hoping that some would take the bait. In fact, in checking Friedlander's premises last night, I can tell you that he took no photographs and had no evidence of any indiscretions."

"Bluffing with a worthless hand," I said.

"He was a man who enjoyed games. But with Sir Everett, he encountered a prey who was willing to turn the tables on him."

"What made him decide on The Elivas Club?" Lestrade asked. "The affluence of the members?"

"Another reason, Inspector. If you make an inquiry at The Elivas, you'll find that despite Friedlander's success and wealth, his membership application was denied. I confirmed this with the club's manager. Apparently, the club's board concluded that a merchant's path to such a recent fortune didn't entitle him to join."

"Old money versus new money," Lestrade offered.

Holmes nodded, signaling to me that he was ready for us to take our leave.

"Few more powerful forces act on the human psyche than being shunned," I said, shaking my head at the turn of events.

"When treated unjustly," Holmes mused, "some turn to despair. Some turn to violence. Others turn to drink. In this instance, Friedlander turned to blackmail."

"It was effective," Lestrade said.

"For a time, Inspector," Holmes said. "For a time."

NOTE

* There was an actual "Rat King" in Victorian times by the name of "Jack Black". According to Wikipedia, "*Jack Black was a rat catcher and mole destroyer from Battersea, England during the middle of the nineteenth century. Black cut a striking figure in his self-made 'uniform' of a green topcoat, scarlet waistcoat, and breeches, with a huge leather sash inset with cast-iron rats. Black promoted himself as the Queen's Official Rat Catcher, but he never held a royal warrant.*"

The author's reference to his son ("Jack Black, Jr.") and his taking up the father's line of business as the "Rat Prince" is fictional.

The Adventure of the Counterfeit Uncle
by Michael Mallory

I confess that over the decade-and-half that I have spent in the company of Mr. Sherlock Holmes, there have been times when I wondered if he was somehow more than a mortal man. It was not simply his brilliance of mind, which was extraordinary, or his tenacity in pursuing a goal, which was remarkable. It was also his propensity to see what others could not, as though he possessed a special kind of vision that was alien to the rest of us. All of those characteristics converged to create the very model of a man who had achieved a heightened state of humanity. Such did I regard his singular intellect, though in the summer of 1896 I learned that his body was as mortal as anyone's. While attempting to leap out of the way of a speeding brougham, which was being driven by a miscreant he had been tailing for the better part of a week, Holmes mistimed his move, resulting in the steed's front hoof connecting with his shin bone.

It proved to be a somewhat superficial injury that was more painful than damaging, and his full recovery was assured. Yet his convalescence required him to remain off of his feet for a fortnight while the bone took it upon itself to reknit, during which time I was able to provide draughts to ease his discomfort. There was, however, nothing I could do to alleviate the indignity he felt about being injured not simply by an escaping criminal, but by the criminal's horse.

For the first few days he berated himself for the mishap. When he became tired of that, he took to berating the police for not having apprehended the criminal in question in the first place, and then the laws governing the operation of vehicles and coaches in the city of London, and finally the horse itself. After the first week he turned his scornful frustration toward me, the man who refused to let him be up and about.

On a particular morning in August, I entered our sitting room to find him already up and clad in his mouse-coloured dressing gown, his right leg resting on an ottoman whose top was softened further by a cushion. The crutches he used within the confines of our flat were leaning carelessly against the mantel. I couldn't tell at first if he was awake or asleep, and then one eye cracked open. "How are we today, Holmes?" I asked.

"How are *we*, Watson?" he replied, languidly opening the other eye. "I shall take you first. Since it is twenty-one minutes past your normal time of emergence from your bedroom, I would say that you are still rather tired from lying awake, no doubt worrying about my condition, as though such worry will have any effect on its improvement whatsoever. As for me, my leg continues to throb more than it causes actual pain, annoyance being only a partial remedy for agony, while my other joints are sore from having to remain confined in this position and not be allowed to move about. Furthermore, from the cinch of my trouser waistline, I would judge I have gained one-and-three-quarter pounds as a result of the inactivity. But those are trifles, Watson. My mind and my spirit are so thoroughly, numbingly bored that I shall soon be forced to return to the needle to alleviate this soul-crushing *ennui*."

"That is not a sound idea," I told him. "In another day or two, you may try putting your entire weight on that leg to see if it has healed enough to support you without a sharp relapse of pain. Until then, I'm afraid you must continue to be still and rest."

"Rest, rest, rest . . . The world is going on out there without me, and yet you insist I remain here exhibiting less life and movement than Nelson's Column."

While I will always regard Sherlock Holmes as the finest man I have ever known, and the best friend I have ever had, he was by no means the easiest patient I ever treated. Clearly this was to be a trying day for both of us.

The reprieve, as it were, arrived later that morning in the form of a young woman who was ushered into our rooms by our landlady, Mrs. Hudson. "This lass wishes to see you, Mr. Holmes," she announced on behalf of an auburn-haired young woman who was clad in green velvet dress and matching hat.

"Please come in," I said, rising to greet the woman as Mrs. Hudson discreetly retreated into the hall, closing the door behind her.

"Tell the young lady in the emerald dress to come closer," Holmes called, which amazed me, since he was facing the opposite direction.

"How on earth did you know our visitor was a young lady in a green dress?" I asked.

"Come now, Watson. Mrs. Hudson referred to her as a 'lass' which indicated a young woman, and unless she has come straight from a theatrical production of *As You Like It* and is outfitted like an Elizabethan boy, she is wearing a dress. As for its green hue, would you believe me if I told you that during my forced convalescence I have acquired the ability to smell colour?"

"I would not," I replied.

"Stout fellow," he said, craning his head around the side of the wicker chair to face us. "Because the truth of the matter is that I saw her reflection in the mirror over there."

The fact that he said it with a slight grin – his first in more than a week – made me smile as well, since it indicated his mind was becoming engaged enough to make a joke.

"Do please come in, Miss – ?"

"Clayden," the woman responded. "Violet Clayden."

"Forgive me for not rising," Holmes said, "but at the moment I am incapacitated by a leg injury."

"Oh, oh dear."

"It is nothing serious," I assured her.

"But how can he help me if he isn't able to move?"

"If you are seeking a solution to your problem provided by one's feet, I suggest you try the Metropolitan Police, whose feet are as productive as anyone's, even if their brains are not," Holmes said. "I, on the other hand, make it a practise to solve problems with my mind, which works perfectly well even in a stationary position. Now, please sit down, Miss Clayden and tell me what it is that troubles you."

The woman took a seat on the sofa and began. "It is all quite simple, Mr. Holmes. I don't believe that a man who is presenting himself as my mother's brother is, in fact, my uncle."

While keeping his leg on the ottoman, Holmes leaned forward slightly. "What has brought you to this conclusion?" he asked.

"Call it a feeling, augmented by circumstantial evidence."

"I prefer facts to feelings, Madam. Please start at the beginning and tell me what you mean. Leave nothing out."

"Very well. I suppose I should first tell you that my Uncle Ralph and I are not close. My mother disowned him, after the two had been estranged most of their lives. She was a very moral woman, and Uncle Ralph . . . Well, he followed his own path. He spent much of his life in Tasmania, where he made his fortune in some sort of mining operation. When he returned to England, and in what state, I cannot say. All I know is that my brother Geoffrey and I both received letters some weeks ago telling us that Ralph was ailing and feared the end was approaching, and that he wished to make amends with his only living relatives."

"Meaning you and your brother?"

"Yes. Our parents are deceased."

"Who was it that sent this letter?"

"My uncle engaged an attorney named Amos Griggs to help him with his will, and it was he who contacted us."

"How long has it been since you last saw your uncle?"

"I had never actually met him in the flesh prior to this," Violet Clayden said.

"So you cannot know conclusively that this man is not he."

"By the testimony of my eyes, no. However, in the course of speaking with him, we got on the subject of my mother. While he claims to feel great regret over his treatment of her, his recollections of her weren't accurate. When pressed about details of her life as a girl, he grew vague, and in some cases, he was outright wrong. He might have learned enough about our family to fool the lawyer, but he couldn't fool me."

Holmes now leaned back in his chair and tented his fingers. "What sort of facts did he get wrong?" he asked.

"Her full name, for one thing," Miss Clayden answered. "No matter how long one has been away from a sister, it is inconceivable that he would forget her middle name. My mother was born Harriet Marguerite Dandridge. But the best this man could come up with for her middle name was 'Margaret'. Not the same thing at all."

"What does your brother say to all this?"

"I haven't been able to convince him of my suspicion. I fear he is falling for the charlatan's act."

"Who do you think this man is, if not your uncle?" I asked.

"I can only assume he was an associate of Ralph's in Tasmania who learned about our family through him. My real uncle, I fear, is dead, perhaps even murdered by this same blackguard who is taking his place. I believe this fellow has convinced the lawyer of his identity, and plans to stake a claim on my real uncle's estate, leaving Geoffrey and me high and dry."

While I don't possess the sort of brilliant brain of which Holmes can boast, my intelligence was sufficient enough to question what the young woman was saying. Quite frankly, her story as she related it didn't make sense. "Forgive me, Miss Clayden," I said, "but you say that your uncle – or at least the man claiming to be him – is dying, and that is why he has summoned you and your brother to him. Yet you further claim that it is all a ploy for the imposter to gain that wealth for himself. What does a dying man need of wealth?"

"If he really is dying," she replied.

"I see. But if he is merely pretending to be ill and wants the money for himself, why would he have bothered to send for you in the first place?"

"I wondered that myself," she said. "Now I believe that this man learned about the two of us from my real uncle and knew he would have to deal with us, sooner or later, so he chose sooner."

"Could he not simply omit you from the will?" I persisted.

"Not if an earlier will exists somewhere."

Turning to my friend, I said, "I must admit, Holmes, that all of this is beyond me."

"Perhaps so, Watson," he replied, "though I cannot fault the logic behind your questioning." Then turning to Miss Clayden, he said, "Would I be inaccurate if I were to deduce that the man presenting himself to you as your Uncle Ralph is attempting to 'deal' with you, as you put it, by imposing some sort of condition on your inheritance?"

"You would be very astute by deducing so," she said. "The man pretending to be my uncle wishes to legally adopt us."

"Adopt you?" I cried.

She nodded. "And if we don't agree, we will see no penny of his wealth. Were he truly my uncle, the inheritance would be assured in any court of law. But with the condition he wishes to impose, we must renounce our mother and become his children to inherit. Since I have no intention of doing so, the estate of Ralph Dandridge is destined to be bequeathed elsewhere. Somewhere outside of the family."

"How does your brother feel about the prospect of adoption?" Holmes asked.

"He is less adamant than I about rejecting it."

"Which means if he agrees, he becomes the sole heir?"

"No. The plan is that both of us must agree, or neither of us inherits."

"I see," Holmes replied, leaning back in the chair and tenting his fingers over his chest. "Exactly what is it you wish me to do for you, Miss Clayden?"

"I had rather hoped that you would find conclusive evidence that this man isn't my uncle and shed light upon this appalling scheme. I had hoped you could see him and speak with him, but in your current situation, that seems impossible. And since my counterfeit uncle professes to be bedridden, he cannot come to you."

"I could pay a call on the man," I offered. "If he is genuinely faking a serious illness, I should be able to detect that in short order."

"Thank you, Watson," Holmes said, "but I don't believe encountering him in person will be necessary. I would, however, like to meet your brother, Geoffrey. Could it be arranged for him to come to Baker Street?"

"If you think it is necessary."

"I do. I would also like to see the letter you were sent."

"That request is even easier," she said, opening her handbag and withdrawing a piece of paper, which she handed to Holmes.

Holmes opened and examined the missive, and afterwards he asked, "What are your plans if I do, in fact, prove that your alleged uncle is a fraud?"

340

"Investigate what happened to my real uncle," Miss Clayden replied. "If he is, as I suspect, dead, his money will go to Geoffrey and me as his legal heirs."

"It still might require a court case."

"I am prepared."

"I see. Very well, Miss Clayden, I will investigate this for you. Please ask your brother to see me at his earliest convenience."

"I shall. Thank you, Mr. Holmes."

I escorted the young woman to the door as Holmes returned to his deep-in-thought position: Perfectly still with his hands folded as though in prayer, his two index fingers touching his upper lip. After a long, silent pause, he asked, "What sense do you have of this case, Watson?"

"Frankly," I replied, "it strikes me as a Dickens novel playing out in real life."

He smiled. "My thoughts precisely, complete with a heroine destined to spend years languishing in the court of chancery. The only thing it lacks is a missing family member suddenly turning up, perhaps a twin to the dying man."

"She seemed disappointed that you couldn't go see him. Are you certain it wouldn't help if I paid him a professional visit on your behalf, to assess his medical condition?"

"I am confident what you would find is a man who is indeed ailing, if not quite ready to shake off the mortal coil. Instead, tell me what you make of this letter."

He handed me the letter from the lawyer and I perused it, finding nothing particularly noteworthy. It was simply a missive that requested the presence of Violet Clayden as an heir to the estate of Ralph Dandridge, to discuss the inheritance, signed by one Arthur Griggs, Esq. "Nothing leaps out," I said. "I'm not an expert on penmanship, you know."

"Penmanship is not a factor in this case." He shifted his weight in the chair again and grimaced slightly before adding, "I am very much looking forward to meeting Mr. Geoffrey Clayden."

The opportunity arose the next day, when a tall, solidly built young man appeared at our door. He wore a country tweed suit whose buttons struggled to contain his girth and a flat cap, and peered at us through small, round eyeglasses. "Mr. Holmes, I am Geoffrey Clayden," he said, extending his hand to my seated friend.

"Forgive me if I don't rise," Holmes said, taking his hand, and seeming to examine it quickly before letting it go.

"Violet told me you were chair-ridden," Clayden said. "Frankly, Mr. Holmes, I am confused as to why you wished to see me."

"Your sister explained the problem she is having regarding your uncle, but I should like to hear it from you as well."

"Violet told me she informed you of everything."

"Even so, there might be an important fact your sister left out."

"Very well," the young man grumbled. "Approximately three weeks ago, we each received a letter from a solicitor named Arthur Griggs, Esquire, informing us that our uncle was in his final days, and that we were his sole heirs."

"Because your parents are dead?" Holmes interjected.

"Well, Violet . . . Her statement to you should have revealed that."

"Quite. Please go on."

"The letters asked us to come and see him – the solicitor, I mean – which we did. Upon doing so, we were informed by Mr. Griggs that there was a condition to the inheritance, that being we must become the legal wards of Uncle Ralph. It wasn't a proposition that upset me unduly, yet it seemed to do so to Violet. She has since become convinced that the man we are dealing with is not, in fact, our uncle."

"Do you and your sister share a home, Mr. Clayden?"

"Share a home?"

"Live together."

"Not yet. I mean, once the inheritance has cleared we are considering purchasing a home large enough for both of us."

"In London?"

"We live in Tunbridge Wells. Kent may not be far from London, but it is a world away, if you know what I mean."

"And what do you do in Tunbridge Wells?"

"What has this to do with Uncle Ralph?"

"I like to have all the facts regarding any case in which I am engaged," Holmes replied.

"I work as a schoolteacher."

"I see," Holmes said. "And your sister?"

"Violet?"

"Do you have another sister?"

"Oh, no. Violet works as a governess. She lives within the household employing her, also in Tunbridge Wells."

"Interesting. Now, then, Mr. Clayden, setting aside your sister's suspicions, do you have any personal reason to suspect that your uncle is an impostor?"

"Honestly, Mr. Holmes, I wouldn't know one way or the other. Violet says there are discrepancies in the way he speaks and remembers things that are suspect, but I couldn't swear to any of that. We were both very young the last time we even heard the name Ralph Dandridge."

"Your sister requested that I find evidence that this man purporting to be your uncle is not in fact he, and if possible, find out who he is. Is that also what you want?"

"I want what Violet wants," Geoffrey Clayden replied.

"I see. One thing I forgot to mention to your sister is that I will require a retainer for my involvement, particularly now that I have to hire out tasks which I could previously do myself on my own two feet." Holmes quoted a price, and quite a reasonable one, though I had never heard him ask for a retainer in the past. "A cheque will be sufficient," he told the man.

"Oh, well, I . . . I'm afraid I haven't brought my checkbook," Geoffrey Clayden said, appearing rather flustered.

"Writing a promissory note to me stating the amount I quoted you will serve adequately. Watson, would you please produce a sheet of paper and a pen for our friend?"

I did so from my desk, and watched as Geoffrey Clayden wrote out such a note. When he was finished, he handed it to Holmes, who glanced at it, and then said, "Excellent. I shall be in touch, Mr. Clayden. Please give my best to your sister."

"I shall. Thank you, Mr. Holmes."

After the man left, I commented, "I must say, I have never known you to ask for payment ahead of a case before."

"And I haven't received such, merely this promise of payment, which is quite enough for our purposes."

"If you say so, though I cannot see how the visit of that young man was in any way helpful."

"On the contrary, Watson, his visit was crucial. In fact, through his appearance here, I have solved the case."

"You've what?"

"The entire matter is as clear as the sunlight through which I cannot at present walk. Did you not notice something about Clayden's speech, in particular the way he said the word 'sister'?"

"I cannot say I did."

"That is because he never actually *said* the word 'sister'. He referred to Violet only by her Christian name."

"What does that tell you?"

"That he is totally unaccustomed to thinking of Violet Clayden as his sister. Then there was the matter of his clothes. His waistcoat and jacket were tightfitting almost to the point of being a size too small."

"You think he borrowed the suit from someone else?"

"No, I believe them to be his garments, though ones he hasn't worn for some time, during which time he has added a bit of weight."

"None of this makes any sense to me," I admitted.

"No matter, all will be revealed soon. Now, if you will excuse me, I should like to rest for a bit." He leaned back and closed his eyes, though the slight smile remained on his face.

I had patients to attend to for the rest of the afternoon. When I returned shortly before dinner, I found Holmes up and out of his chair. "Really, you shouldn't be putting weight on that leg quite yet."

"I am on the mend," he replied. "In fact, I feel better than I have in days. I would like to be upright when our guests arrive tomorrow afternoon."

"What guests are those?"

"Violet, Geoffrey, and the lawyer Griggs, all of whom I have summoned and expect to see at two o'clock. I asked Mrs. Hudson to send a telegram to the solicitor, requesting their attendance, and promising a solution to this matter. I intend to deliver one, and since I would prefer not delivering it from a position of weakness, I am practising my stance."

"All right, but don't overtax yourself," I cautioned. I then asked what Holmes had deduced regarding the case from the relative comfort of his chair, but he refused to disclose his solution. I took it as a sly way of exacting revenge upon me for keeping him restrained for days on end, but since no amount of cajoling could release the information from his satisfied lips, I resigned myself to waiting until two o'clock on the morrow.

The lawyer, Amos Griggs, was the first to arrive, five minutes early. He was a short, dour-looking man with greying hair and, in my opinion, an imperious manner, who indicated that his presence here at Baker Street was something of an inconvenience. "You will not be here long, Mr. Griggs," Holmes told him, cryptically.

Violet and Geoffrey Clayden arrived together promptly at two, and now that I had the opportunity for a second look, I could see what Holmes meant about the man's suit being a size too small. By contrast, Violet's dress fit her perfectly, though instead of the green one she wore previously, this one was wine-coloured. "Please sit down," Holmes bade them, directing them to the sofa. Amos Griggs remained standing.

"Don't keep us in suspense, man," the lawyer said. "Tell us why you have summoned us and do it quickly."

"Very well," Holmes began. "I have deduced to my complete satisfaction the identity of the man you know as Ralph Dandridge."

"How can you do so without seeing him?" Violet asked.

"As I told you before, seeing him in the flesh wasn't necessary."

"So you too are endeavouring to convince me that Ralph Dandridge is not Ralph Dandridge?" Griggs sneered.

"On the contrary," Holmes replied, "I am telling you that he is indeed Ralph Dandridge. Mr. and Miss Clayden, on the other hand, aren't who they profess to be."

Violet Clayden rose to her feet. "What do you mean by that?" she demanded.

"Precisely what I said, Madam. Your name may be Violet Clayden, though I doubt it, but I am confident that you are of no actual relation to Ralph Dandridge."

"Geoffrey, say something!" Violet demanded.

"Go ahead, Mr. Clayden, rejoin in support of your sister . . . or is she your wife?"

Geoffrey looked up, his face having gone pale.

"I see no need to listen to any more of this," Griggs declared. "If, as you say, they aren't the true heirs of Dandridge, then there is no reason for me to continue with the matter of inheritance."

"Do not go yet, for I suspect you are involved in this as deeply as those two," Holmes said. The lawyer opened his mouth to speak, but then opted not to.

Focusing his attention now on Geoffrey, Holmes said, "You were the key to solving this little conundrum, Mr. Clayden. You *are* Mr. Clayden, are you not, or is that an alias?"

"I am Geoffrey Clayden," he uttered.

"To pass yourself off as a provincial schoolteacher, you donned the outfit that you now wear, one that you have clearly not worn for quite a while, probably since you moved from the country to the city. Why would you do so? The obvious answer is so that you could avoid wearing your regular suit of clothing which might have identified your true occupation, that of a law clerk . . . and unless I am mistaken, a law clerk in the employ of Amos Griggs."

Once again, the lawyer made a motion as though he were about to object, but remained silent.

"How did you know?" Geoffrey asked.

"Be quiet, Geoffrey," Violet cautioned.

"Ah, a good wife always knows how to keep her husband in line," Holmes remarked with a smile.

"We are betrothed, but not yet married," Geoffrey uttered, as Violet turned and walked away from him, visibly annoyed. "But how did you figure out that I am a law clerk?"

"Your hand gave you away, Mr. Clayden," Holmes explained. "When I first met you, I noticed a small ink stain on the middle finger of your right hand, meaning you are given to writing on a regular basis, such as would a clerk. Or an author."

Holmes glanced in my direction and I instinctively looked down at my own hand and saw that the ink stain on my finger was very nearly washed away since my last literary effort.

"But what put me on the scent prior to that was the letter purportedly sent to you and Violet, which she produced for my examination." Turning to the now-livid young woman, Holmes added, "I would address you more formally, but I don't know your last name, which is not yet Clayden."

"It is Aldershot," she said.

"Thank you. The letter Miss Aldershot presented to me was signed by '*Arthur Griggs, Esquire,*' – *Esquire* being a legal term used mostly between one lawyer and another rather than to the public at large. An actual solicitor would not write *Esq.* after his name as part of his signature. But for his law clerk, penning such an amendment would be a matter of course, if not habit, given the volume of correspondence he wrote to other lawyers. Then you reinforced my supposition in our first meeting when you spoke the word as though it was part of Mr. Griggs's name. The final piece of evidence came when I asked you to write a retainer cheque for me, a request with which you complied by instead writing a promissory note. My objective wasn't to receive payment, or even the promise of it, but to compare your handwriting with that on the note. Need I say they are identical?"

"You young fool!" Griggs cried, glaring at Clayden. "I told you I would handle things."

"But sir, Violet thought you might get cold feet," Geoffrey replied.

"Oh, of course, this is *my* fault entirely!" the woman cried.

"Be silent, everyone!" Holmes cried. "I am in no mood to witness a public argument in my own home, so let me lay out what I believe to be the facts of the case, and if any of you has an objection, you may indicate so when I am finished." Limping his way to center stage, as it were, in front of the cold fireplace, Holmes continued. "I believe Ralph Dandridge is, in fact, ill, and I also believe him to be wealthy. I believe that you, Mr. Griggs, are indeed his solicitor, though I question his judgment."

Griggs said nothing, and merely sneered at Holmes.

"Mr. Clayden, it has been established that you work for Mr. Griggs and that you intend to marry Miss Aldershot, so I am left to surmise that you don't have what you, or perhaps she, considers enough money to enter into matrimony. Therefore, I presume you went to your employer to ask for a raise, or possibly a loan, but instead he offered you a proposition: He knew his wealthy client was dying and also knew the man had no heirs. This is merely speculation, but I am confident that further investigation would show that the will Dandridge was asking Mr. Griggs to prepare would bequeath his wealth to charitable concerns, in hopes of atoning for his improvident life. Did you conclude, sir, that that would be a waste of good wealth? Did you realize that if heirs to the estate were to suddenly appear, the will could be rewritten so that the money went to them? Did you further decide that in the absence of genuine heirs, you had to create them? Is that the way your scheme was planned, Mr. Griggs?"

No one spoke in response, so Holmes went on. "For an experienced solicitor, it would have been easy to submit adoption paperwork without Dandridge's knowledge and rewrite the will so that the three of you became his beneficiaries. I imagine he convinced you, Mr. Clayden, to pose as the long-lost nephew, perhaps even on threat of dismissal were you to refuse. But unless my reading of your character is faulty, the crime of embezzlement didn't lie easy with you, making you the scheme's weak link – hence the involvement of Violet Aldershot, who was more than willing to play out the game for the prize. As Griggs was good enough to announce a minute ago, he was prepared to handle every aspect of the plan. But that didn't satisfy you, did it, Miss Aldershot? You began to worry that Griggs would either not go through with the scheme, or would somehow legally cut the two of you out of it and obtain the inheritance for himself. That was why you coerced your fiancé to forge a letter from his employer to use as proof, should Griggs, to use Geoffrey's turn of phrase, get cold feet. Now, then – Do I hear any objections?"

None were raised.

"Excellent. I feel that I must congratulate you, Miss Aldershot, on how well you played the game. That business of the middle name and the using it as a clue to your suspicions regarding Dandridge was well-devised, and calculated to pique my interest in the case. Having deduced the truth, however, I remained puzzled about one aspect to all of this, which is why you came to me in the first place. Had you not, your scheme would very likely have worked without anyone's knowledge otherwise. Can it be because you *wanted* me to arrive at the conclusion that Ralph Dandridge was indeed he? Were you seeking unimpeachable testimony, if I may say so, that Dandridge was *not* an imposter – testimony that the police and the courts would trust implicitly?"

Violet Aldershot faced him directly and defiantly. "There was more to it than that," she said. "I wanted to find out if there was any flaw with this plan that might be detected – which would complicate, or even prevent the result, which we could take action to correct. I figured if anyone could spot such a flaw, it would be the great Sherlock Holmes. I did not count on you being able to see through our entire plan so quickly."

"Aided by my friend Watson, I must add, since it was he who first poked holes in your story."

"I confess some of his questions gave me pause and forced me to think quickly," the woman said, "but those were holes I could have plugged." Then turning her gaze toward Geoffrey, she added, "My darling fiancé, however, has excavated a crater that is now impossible to fill."

"See here, Holmes," Amos Griggs said. "We have broken no laws. Dandridge is still alive – at least he was when I last saw him – and we haven't relieved him of any of his wealth. We cannot be charged with anything."

"That is quite true, Mr. Griggs, which is why I have no intention of calling the Yard."

"What do you plan to do then?" Geoffrey asked.

"Nothing for the time being. If Dandridge is as ill as you say, I will erelong be reading his obituary in the newspaper. If he leaves a large sum to a charity or a foundation, I will likely read of that as well. However, should I hear of the late Ralph Dandridge's fortune being inherited by a niece and nephew, or willed to his solicitor, I will inform the police of everything I know regarding this case. I am well connected within the City of London, and have sources of information that extend to court proceedings. Do not think, any of you, that you can deceive me at this point in time. Now, then, despite my promise to my friend and doctor that I would not, I am afraid I have overtaxed my leg a bit, so I will bid the three of you goodbye. Show them out, Watson."

They were nearly through the door when Holmes called, "Oh, since it was you who engaged me, Miss Aldershot, let me offer you one piece of advice."

"And what would that be?" she asked.

"If you are foolish enough to attempt to carry off this charade despite my warning, find clothing more befitting the persona of a governess."

It was Violet Aldershot who slammed the door so violently behind her it caused dust to filter down from the upper shelves of our rooms.

"Once I am completely mobile again, Watson," Holmes said, "we must vacate these rooms to allow Mrs. Hudson to do a comprehensive cleaning . . . Everything but my desk, of course." He then sat back down in his chair and rested his leg on the cushioned footstool.

The Adventure of the
Seven Sins
by Tracy J. Revels

"**I** am here on my dear Lisa's behalf," Mr. Leonard Oliver Rhodes explained as he settled onto the sofa at Baker Street. He was a sleek, elegant man of some forty years, his blonde hair combed neatly to his head, his garments proclaiming a comfortable income and a life of leisure. Despite the warmth of the early summer's day, Rhodes carried himself briskly, with an almost icy demeanor. His card gave no indication of his employment, only of his residence in the dignified suburban neighborhood where a tragedy had occurred, just two days previous. "Lisa is quite distraught," Rhodes continued. "Any woman would be, of course, to lose her precious child in such a terrible fashion. Before I came here, I spoke with Inspector Lestrade of Scotland Yard. Everyone claims he is a master of detection, and yet he says there isn't enough evidence for an arrest and recommended that I speak to you. And so that wretched – " Here the gentleman's fair face turned muddy with emotion. " – *foreigner* resides among us, his filthy brown hands dripping with poor Bennie's blood."

I shot a side-long glance at my friend. Only that morning, we had been discussing the murder of the young boy at Crestwood House, and Holmes had been bemoaning the fact that he hadn't been called in to examine the matter. Every newspaper had dubbed it an "impossible case" with a proverbial "'locked room'". Holmes leaned forward in his chair, rubbing his hands together.

"Before we jump to any conclusions, either of a culprit's guilt or the shortcomings of the official forces, let us have the story from your perspective, Mr. Rhodes. You appear to be an intimate of the family."

"Indeed, Mr. Holmes, I have known Lisa – Mrs. Branch, the general's widow – since we were children. Her maternal family is distantly related to mine, and we were thrown together a good bit at school holidays. I was delighted when Lisa made such a distinguished match, and even more gratified when the old general chose to make his home nearby. Of course, his loss, three years ago, was a tragedy to all of us."

"General Martin Branch died of cancer, if I recall," Holmes said.

Forbes nodded. "Yes, poor man. Imagine surviving all those battles and charges, fighting the bloody Indian mutineers hand-to-hand, and then succumbing to your own body. When the doctor informed him there was

349

no hope, the general begged Lisa not to remarry until his son came of age. He feared the influence of a stepfather, you see. And Lisa, always an angel, agreed to this condition, sealing it with a kiss as her husband slipped away.

"For two years after her husband's passing, Lisa lived a very quiet life and observed all the proprieties of mourning. Of late, however, she has begun to socialize again, to attend teas and parties."

"You know a great deal about her social calendar," Holmes noted. The man's clear skin again took color.

"As I have said, we are distantly related, and as I am a bachelor with no family to claim my time, I can put myself at her disposal as an escort, when propriety demands one." The man crossed his legs and took out a thin cigarette. "But I am not here to gossip, sir. Let me explain what happened to poor little Bennie, as we called him in the family. Since the inspector can do nothing, perhaps you can throw some light on matters. Anything I could tell Lisa would greatly relieve her mind."

Holmes signaled for the man to continue. Rhodes drew deeply upon his cigarette.

"To economize during her widowhood, Lisa reduced her household to only three servants – Neville, the butler, Mrs. Neville, the cook and housekeeper, and Miss Wilma Lewis, a young woman who serves as a maid-of-all work. There was previously a governess, but she was dismissed late last year, when Bennie began to attend classes at St. Matilda's School. Wilma lives in the attic, and the married pair occupy a small cottage behind the house. The Nevilles are in their late sixties. He is almost completely deaf, though still capable enough in his duties. Wilma is a rather simple, straightforward, pious girl. There is one other concerned party, not a part of the household but . . . ."

Mr. Rhodes squirmed in his chair, looking decidedly uncomfortable. He coughed several times and put out his cigarette. "This is a rather delicate matter."

"The foreigner," Holmes prompted. "Mr. Darsh Kohli. I do read the newspapers."

"And it is shameful how they put people's most private concerns in the street! Very well, then, let me speak with utter frankness. A year ago, Kohli moved into the neighborhood and took a lease on Chicora House, which stands across the street from Crestwood House. Kohli had served General Branch as a spy among the mutineers, but he was just a boy at the time of that service, so his heroics may have been exaggerated. Kohli was newly widowed and arrived with his young daughter. Naturally, he paid his respects to the lady of his former commander." Rhodes sniffed. "Bennie was most alarmed."

"What do you mean?" I asked.

"The little chap worshipped the memory of his father," Rhodes said curtly, as if that should be obvious to me. "He didn't appreciate an interloper, especially one of a dusky race."

Holmes scowled. "Kohli is mentioned several times in Branch's memoirs. If the man himself bears any resemblance to his portrayal, I am surprised the youth was opposed to him. Most young boys are impressed by spies, soldiers, and native rogues."

Rhodes shook his head. "Perhaps it was only the timing, sir. Bennie had just turned nine and was beginning his studies at St. Matilda's – the plan was for him to matriculate there until he could take his place at a military academy, as his late father had directed. He continued to live at home, for the school is less than a mile from his front door, though most of the lads who attend St. Matilda's also board there. Perhaps Bennie was coddled a bit. Lisa always indulged and rarely chastised him. But whatever the reason, he immediately bristled at the man. It didn't matter how many stirring stories were told of Kohli's service – the lad refused to be friendly, or even decent, toward him."

"And how did Mrs. Branch act toward the newcomer?"

Rhodes sighed. "Lisa was only thirty when her husband died, and after mourning him for so long, she had begun to feel the pangs of loneliness. Like Desdemona with Othello, she was swayed by the stories of Kohli's adventures, and she was naturally drawn on maternal strings toward the motherless girl in his household. Lisa began to be seen in Kohli's company, far more often than was truly proper."

"How long has this affair been known?"

"Some eight months have passed since they began to gad about openly. Bennie continued to express his displeasure, even when Kohli became a fixture of the household. The child spoke rudely whenever he was in Kohli's presence. Bennie threw eggs at Chicora House and was vile to Santosh, Kohli's daughter, at a church treat, yanking her braids and tripping her into a fishpond. I encouraged Lisa to send Bennie to the military academy early, but she wouldn't hear of it. To make matters worse, some of the lads at school began to tease Bennie about his mother being in love with a Sepoy. There were fights, though Bennie was a bold little lad, the very image of his father, and he usually got the better of his opponents."

"How did Kohli react?" Holmes asked.

"He tried to ignore Bennie's actions at first, but his temper flared some two months ago. He shook the boy rather roughly, and Lisa ordered Kohli out of the house for this offense. Since that time Kohli has made several remarks to the locals – you may ask the grocer and the chemist –

to the effect that if Bennie were his son, he could soon put 'the fear of the tiger' into him."

"Had Kohli proposed marriage to the lady?"

"I have asked Lisa that very question, and she refuses to answer. I think, however, that Kohli did beg for her hand, and she told him she wouldn't marry until Bennie reached manhood." Rhodes puffed up, his eyes flashing with sudden anger. "And that, sir, is what sealed poor Bennie's fate."

Holmes leaned back in his chair. "Tell us what you believe happened."

"It is more than belief, sir – it is fact! Two days ago, the boys of St. Matilda's were dismissed from their books early for a half-holiday, and Bennie came home at two. Old Neville let him in at five past the hour and brought him tea and cakes in the study. Lisa and Mrs. Neville had gone into London, to buy some new curtains for the parlor, so the child was alone in the house except for Neville and Wilma. Neville returned to the kitchen to polish the silver – as I have said, he is quite deaf, and heard nothing. Wilma was upstairs in her attic room, attending to some sewing, but she heard Odin – that is the child's wolfhound – barking, and Bennie shouting for him to hush, very shortly before three. She then came down from her room to attend to other chores. The late general's study is on the ground floor of the home, and as Wilma passed it, she noted that the door – usually open – was closed. She also heard muffled sounds, a conversation which seemed to be growing more agitated, but she ignored it and went back up to the first-floor parlor. She had barely entered the room when she heard a bloodcurdling scream, followed by a heavy thud. Wilma hurried down to the study. She knocked and called out to Bennie. As she stood there, she heard the bolt on the door being thrown. She continued to knock and call, but, getting no answer, she fled to the kitchen to seek assistance from Neville."

"What time did this occur?" Holmes asked.

"We are in luck, for there is a clock in the hall and the girl glanced at it as she ran. It was precisely five past three. She went into the kitchen and roused Neville, who had dozed off at the table. Together, they returned to the study. The lock turned smoothly, but the deadbolt prevented entry and there was no other way into the room, which is a small chamber without windows. Neville was not strong enough to break down the door, but he ran outside, saw Kohli on the steps of Chicora House, and alerted him that some misfortune had occurred. Together, the men were able to break down the study door. A horror greeted them.

"Bennie was laid upon the floor, his forehead shattered by the large marble bust of General Branch, which had previously graced the mantel.

Books and papers were scattered about, as if the lad had been attacked while attending to his studies. The tea and cakes were also spilled. A doctor was quickly summoned, but there was no hope. The poor child expired instantly in that room. A sweet, innocent boy – "

Holmes interrupted. "Was there anything in lad's hand? Or any writing on his books or papers?"

"None, sir. The papers contained nothing more than an unfinished essay on King Henry VIII."

"What happened next?"

"The police were summoned. Scotland Yard was alerted, and Inspector Lestrade came out. He made a careful inspection of the room, but concluded that the boy was alone when he died. There is a fireplace, but it is a small one. No man could climb through it."

"The examination of the body found no traces of poison?"

"None, sir. The child was perfectly healthy until he was savagely struck."

Holmes placed his palms together. "Intriguing. What has been the reaction of the community?"

"Grief and horror, sir. Poor Lisa has taken to her bed. The servants are all downcast. Wilma blames herself for not realizing that something was amiss in the study. And none of us are satisfied with the solution proposed by Inspector Lestrade."

"Which was?"

"An accident, sir. He argues that the lad was dancing about the study – acting out some scene from a play, perhaps, to account for the different tenor of the voices and the scream that Wilma heard. Somehow the bust tumbled down upon his head."

"Hmm – one wonders how a child with a shattered skull then secured a bolt on the study door," Holmes said dryly.

Rhodes ignored the jab of logic and lowered his head.

"It was Kohli who did this terrible deed, Mr. Holmes. Everyone in our neighborhood knows his passion for Lisa. It's a scandal, though one that could be forgiven in the fullness of time. But the lad hated Kohli, and more than once I have witnessed an angry exchange between them when Lisa wasn't in the room. I have heard Kohli opine that a flogging, such as administered to rebellious Sepoys, would vastly improve the lad's demeanor. On the afternoon of Bennie's death, Kohli claims to have been puttering about in the rear garden of his house. He says he had just finished washing up and was about to run errands when Neville saw him. But Neville testified that Kohli appeared sweaty and flushed when Neville alerted him to the emergency."

"And *how* do you think Kohli committed the murder?"

"Kohli knew Bennie would be home with only the two servants, and that Neville was old and nearly helpless. Kohli waited until Lisa departed with her housekeeper, then slipped inside and hid in the study. After Neville brought in the tea and cakes, he revealed himself to Bennie, perhaps thinking to have a more manly discussion of their differences. But Bennie provoked him, and in his anger, he seized the bust and brought death to the child."

"And then became a puff of smoke?" Holmes asked. "I have heard of magical Indian fakirs, but this man's talent surpasses them all."

Rhodes scowled. "The death of a child is hardly amusing."

"Neither is an unfounded accusation of murder. Leave off for a moment the difficulties of escaping from a locked room and tell me if Kohli's daughter was at their home when the event occurred?"

"Yes, his daughter says she looked out of her bedroom window and noted her father in the rear garden of the home at about two-thirty. She isn't certain of the time he came inside the home, but she heard him walking downstairs at just past three. Inspector Lestrade made a point of asking her why her father would have been sweaty and in disarray when Neville called to him, if Kohli had just cleaned himself from working in the gardens. It was a question she couldn't answer." Rhodes wrinkled his nose. "I have no doubt Kohli coached her in what to say to the police. Her statement means nothing."

"No further action has been taken?"

"None. The family is waiting for the arrival of some kinsmen from Germany. Bennie's funeral is in two days." Rhodes rose and gathered up his cane and hat. "What should I tell my dear cousin?"

"I shall look into the matter," Holmes said, "for there is nothing sadder than the death of a child. I will do everything to see that justice is done for Master Benjamin."

Rhodes nodded solemnly. "That is all we can ask."

An hour later, we were seated in Inspector Lestrade's office in Scotland Yard. It was a small room, more like a prisoner's cell than a place of business. Lestrade's walls were covered with maps, photographs of criminals, and posters advertising rewards for information about crimes. In one corner was a collection of headlines proclaiming Lestrade's triumphs. Holmes had drawn my attention to it with a wave of his cane and a smile, just before the inspector joined us.

"That Crestwood House business. Nasty, yes. Give me two fellows cutting each other's throats, or a jealous husband pushing his wife out the window – anything but the death of a little boy."

"Do you truly think it was an accident?"

Lestrade sneered. "Of course not! But it was all I could offer since clearly no one was in the room with the boy when he died."

"What about suicide?" I asked

"Suicide! Well, I suppose he could have done this." Lestrade picked up a small bronze bust of the Queen and waved it over his head. "Lifted it high and then dropped it – *Ouch!*"

"A rather unlikely way to commit self-destruction," Holmes agreed, reclaiming the bust from where it had tumbled to the carpet after bouncing on the inspector's scalp. "You tested the room thoroughly?"

"Yes. I found nothing. The house isn't some gothic mansion filled with trap doors, hidden staircases, or revolving bookshelves."

"And you judged the witnesses reliable?"

"Neville was useless – you have to shout every question at him. The girl refuses to be dislodged from the idea that she heard the bolt being thrown *after* the heavy thud which alerted her to violence. But she must be wrong about that. She is just a woman, and we know how women are prone to let their hysterics lead them astray."

"And the dog's bark? She is clear on when that occurred?"

Lestrade laughed snidely. "You are obsessed with dogs! Yes, she says she heard the bark and the young master shushing him."

"Which means the dog was alerting the household to an intruder or outsider. However, this newcomer was welcomed. The boy called off the dog." Holmes arched an eyebrow. "What do you make of Mr. Rhodes?"

Lestrade shook his head. "That one thinks he's clever. He'd like to see Kohli in handcuffs." The inspector leaned over his desk, dropping his voice to a whisper. "The maid told me that Rhodes is in love with the widow, had been squiring her around and whimpering at her feet, but then she threw him over for the brown fellow who is younger, better-looking, and served her first husband loyally. So there's no love lost there!"

Holmes nodded. "If the child could be done away with, as well as the romantic rival, the field would be cleared for his wooing."

"Does Rhodes have an alibi?" I asked.

Lestrade slumped in his seat. "He does, an impeccable one. He was meeting with the parish vicar from one until almost four. Rhodes didn't kill Benjamin Branch. Quite frankly, we'll never know who did."

"Lestrade gives up far too easily," Holmes said the next morning as we stepped off the train. "I shall not be critical, for his plate is rather filled with the Judson forgery case and the Whitestone jewel heist. That business with the Bank of Holyrood could be cleared up easily enough, however, if he just had the sense to talk to the one-legged newsboy who works outside the institution. Ah, what a lovely suburb this is. We could almost forget how close we are to London."

Indeed, our destination was a delightful place, with large homes built in graceful, sinuous styles, all of them comfortably set back from the roadway and shielded by stoat oak and elm trees. The spires of St. Matilda's School rose just above the treetops, and we heard bells signaling the start of a school day.

"Lestrade has missed a significant avenue for investigation," Holmes said. "Let us see if we can still follow the trail. To Crestwood House first, to see where the tragedy occurred."

The late general's residence was among the finest on the street, a substantial red brick home of three stories that projected modern efficiency. Much to my surprise, the wolfhound that had been described to us as fierce and protective didn't even bother to lift its head, but only whimpered as we came up the flagstones to ring the bell.

"The beast is broken-hearted," I said.

"So it appears," Holmes agreed, reaching down to give the dog a gentle pat on its neck. "Whatever the nature of the late child, he was clearly Odin's best friend."

The door was opened by a young maidservant in a black dress. Holmes explained our mission, and we learned that Mrs. Branch had been collected earlier that morning by her sister, to be comforted at that lady's house. The Nevilles had also departed, to tend to necessary shopping. Holmes assured her that he merely wished to see the room where the tragedy had occurred.

"Your statement to Inspector Lestrade was clear and helpful," Holmes said to the girl as she obliged us by leading us to the study. "Let me ask you only a few more particulars. Did Master Benjamin entertain his little friends at home?"

"No, sir, he did not." The girl hesitated, but after a moment swallowed her emotion and spoke firmly. "Bennie was once a happy child, but over the past year he had turned grim and sullen. He told me last week that he had no friends, and that he hated all his schoolmates."

"A very sad situation," Holmes said. "And what is your opinion of Mr. Kohli?"

"It isn't my place to comment sir, though . . . I saw the gentleman lose his temper with Bennie once and grab him roughly by the arm. That was when Mrs. Branch sent Mr. Kohli away, but – I shouldn't gossip."

The maid opened the study door. The room was in startling disarray. Papers and schoolbooks were scattered across a desk, a table was overturned, and a tea pot was broken upon the floor. Cakes were stomped into sugary powder. Several leather-bound tomes had been removed from shelves and cast down wildly, perhaps while the police had searched for some secret passage in the walls.

"A man was called in to fix the door, but Inspector Lestrade insisted that I not clean the room until he is certain the case is closed. And, of course, Mrs. Branch cannot bear the sight."

"Quite understandable," Holmes said. He had already pulled his lens from his pocket, and his eyes were glittering. "If you will give us a few minutes? I see a bell rope there in the corner – I presume it works? Thank you. And now it will be a great help to us if you will go to the room you were in when you heard the cry."

"Why does a bell rope matter?" I asked after the maid closed the door.

Holmes gestured to a circular, silken rug on the highly polished floor. It was crumpled from the struggle. In its center was a bloodstain, and resting beside the stain, still smeared with dried gore, was the marble bust of General Branch, the instrument which had ended the life of his son. Holmes examined it, and then lifted it a few inches from the floor. I could see by the tensing of his hands and arms that the item was extremely heavy. Holmes put it down and directed my attention around the room.

"Watson, imagine yourself a young boy. You have been tricked by an enemy and are now inside this room with him. What do you do?"

"I run to the corner, and I pull the bell rope to summon help! Or – " My eyes took in an array of weapons on the wall near the rope. Knives, scimitars, and the general's ceremonial sword hung within reach. "I might grab a weapon to defend myself."

"Of course you would, especially if you were the son of a military hero facing the man who betrayed your father, who caused your schoolmates to torment you, and who you feared might become a hated stepfather."

"The maid said she heard voices rising."

"Though not rising enough to alarm her until she heard the scream and then the thud. Allow me to test a theory." He was walking around the room as he spoke, examining every detail. He knelt by the small fireplace, looking up the chimney. "Hurl abuse at me, Watson."

"What?"

"Abuse. Epithets. Foul language. Surely you have some choice names in reserve for me, the man who always owes you a thousand apologies. Go on – give voice!"

Awkwardly, I spat out some phrases, none of them complimentary to my friend. Holmes signaled for me to be louder. I quickly exhausted my old army expletives.

"Really, Holmes!"

He rose from an inspection of the floor beneath the desk. "All for a noble cause, Watson." He tugged upon the bell rope, and not a minute later the maid appeared, her face shiny with embarrassment.

"Ah, I perceive that you have unwittingly overheard some of my friend's impolite words," Holmes said. "He is rather unguarded when annoyed with me."

The maid favored me with a sour look.

"But you didn't hear distinct words on the afternoon that young master Benjamin was slain?" Holmes asked.

"No sir. There were voices, much muffled, and then a wild, angry scream. I couldn't say if it was Bennie I heard or someone else, but it was shrill. Immediately afterward . . . I presume that was when Bennie was struck and fell."

"The door was locked when you came to it?"

"I didn't try it, sir. I merely knocked, but as I did so, I heard the deadbolt being thrown. That sound sent me running for Neville."

"And nothing was heard afterward?"

"No sir."

"Thank you – and do forgive my friend his rudeness. It was purely an experiment, to see how sound travelled in the house."

The maid saw us out, though from the expression on her face, I doubted that she believed Holmes's explanation.

"On to Mr. Kohli's for an interview," Holmes said as we crossed the street. A trio of loiterers were clumped at the corner, jaundiced eyes fixed upon the residence, but Holmes ignored them. A lovely Indian girl in a white dress admitted us and led us to a modest chamber that held only books, a desk, two well-worn chairs, and a small display of Indian artifacts. The gentleman who rose to greet us was dark, handsome, and broad-shouldered, with a neat mustache. He was immaculately dressed, as if primed to depart for London to conduct important business.

"I am glad that you have come, Mr. Holmes and Doctor Watson. I have read the newspaper stories about you, and I know you care only for the truth. But I must prepare for the worst, and for justice to be miscarried. You see, when they drag me out to hang me, I shall at least be nicely dressed."

My friend shook his head. "Unless you are a magical creature, one who can turn his body into vapors, you couldn't have murdered Master Benjamin and then bolted the door behind you. I don't wish to discomfort you – a few honest words and we will depart. You care for Mrs. Branch?"

"Deeply, sir. When I came to England, I thought it only proper to pay my respects to the wife of my leader. They married after his return to this country, so I had never known her before she was widowed. When I met her, I understood at once why General Branch had given his heart to her, for no man could see her and not admire her." He gestured to his desk, and a photograph of an exceptionally beautiful woman. "She took an interest in me because I had served her late husband, and because of my poor motherless girl. In turn, I vowed to serve her."

"Do you also love her?"

Kohli put a hand to his chest. "Only here, sir, in my heart. She told me of her vow to the general, and I would never ask her to break it, as certain others have. We were happy to be good friends, to wait and see where our feelings might lead in the proper course of time."

"How does your daughter feel about Mrs. Branch?"

"She is fond of her."

"And how did Mrs. Branch's son react to you?"

Pain distorted his features. "Benjamin hated me from the start. He misbehaved, he was rude, he was irksome. I know that such is the nature of a boy who feels he must keep his mother's love all to himself. We made it clear to Benjamin that he had nothing to fear – but when the other boys taunted him at school, he grew more intransigent.

"Were you ever rough with the lad?"

Kohli hung his head. "Yes – and I regret it, but one afternoon his rudeness taxed me beyond my patience, and I shook him. He cried for his mother. It was that act which led to our separation." The man wiped a hand across his face. "And I admit that I have, more than once, made comments about Benjamin's need for discipline. I said that in my native village such foolish behavior would never be tolerated. I meant no harm, but I realize now how it must have sounded to others, since I am a stranger here, and not of your race. It doesn't matter that I had only the boy's best interests at heart."

Holmes nodded. "You were working in your garden that afternoon. Did you hear the dog bark next door?"

"Yes, but only briefly. I thought nothing of it, for Odin often yaps at passing strangers."

"And you came upstairs to refresh yourself and change?"

"Yes. I washed quickly in the basin in the bathroom. I noted that it was three when I put my watch in my pocket, as I finished dressing."

Holmes asked Kohli to call his daughter back into the room. She returned, her eyes downcast, a doll clasped in her arms.

"Miss Santosh," Holmes said. "You are a brave girl to come with your papa to this country. You know there are people who dislike you and your father for no reason other than their own ignorance. But now I must ask you a question, and you and your father must answer truthfully. Will you do this? Both of you?"

They each nodded. Holmes leaned forward, studying the child's innocent face.

"What did you and your father quarrel about on the day Master Benjamin died, just before Mr. Neville ran over and called to your father?"

Two identical pairs of eyes went wide. The girl hesitated. The father frowned, but then spoke to the child.

"Tell Mr. Holmes the truth, *Bitya*."

The girl's delicate voice quivered. "Papa told me I should be nicer to Bennie. I said Bennie was a mean and stupid boy, that he hurt me when he pulled my hair and that he pushed me into the water! But Papa said Bennie liked me. I said I hated Bennie and I wished he was dead!"

Tears trickled down Kohli's cheeks. "She speaks the truth, sir. I thought that Bennie was smitten with her in a childish fashion, and if she would be nice to him, all the troubles between our families would be mended. I lost my temper with my dear girl – and in my rage I slapped her face. I am sorry. I was wrong to do it. Neither one of us wanted the police to know we had argued."

The girl threw her arms around her father's neck. Holmes motioned to me.

"Our investigation takes us elsewhere. We shall leave these two to make amends."

Much to my surprise, Holmes turned west, toward the spires of St. Mathilda's. I asked him why we were heading to the school.

"It should be obvious, Watson. Benjamin Branch admitted someone to the house, someone unknown to the family – recall that he silenced the dog."

"So you think the boy let his killer in."

"Yes. His willingness to collar Odin indicates this was someone who was unfamiliar in the home, but not perceived as a threat by the boy. Perhaps it was someone he wanted to see."

I halted in my tracks. "Holmes – my God – *Kohli's daughter!*"

"Is a prim and proper young lady likely to have the skills to scamper up a chimney?" my friend countered.

"What?"

"The only means of egress, Watson. Once you eliminate the impossible – Hello, what's this?"

A carriage had nearly run us over and was clattering through the gates of the school. We dashed after it, and some ten minutes later we were witnesses to a new tragedy.

In a classroom where the names of the English kings were written on a blackboard, a schoolboy's body was sprawled upon the floor. The man who had nearly crashed into us was identified as a Doctor Powers, and when Holmes announced my qualifications, Powers instantly drew me to his side.

"Poison," he whispered. I could only nod, for the evidence of bloody foam and violent convulsions was clear. I knelt beside the poor little chap. He was no more than ten, with soft legs and arms, a protruding belly, a chubby face covered in freckles, and a crown of wiry ginger hair. A handful of his classmates were cowering in a corner, but the rest of the boys had been sent back to their rooms. A gray-haired schoolmaster in an antique robe, his mortarboard long since lost in the excitement, stood next to my friend. His voice was wane and ghostly.

"We had just begun our lesson on the Plantagenets. I had called upon Hurley for a recitation of the career of Henry III when I noticed Tubby – forgive me, Master Thomas – was eating candies from a handkerchief. That is strictly forbidden in class, of course. I was primed to chastise him when he fell from his chair and began having a fit, I thought it was a prank at first, as did some of the lads who laughed at him . . . and then . . . Oh God! I saw what was happening. The doctor was sent for but . . . ."

"There was nothing you could have done," I said. "This was a strong and terrible poison."

"Are there any remaining candies?" Holmes asked, looking around the chairs and desks.

One of the boys inched forward. "No sir. I'm Ewell, sir. When Professor Morris pointed at Tubby, he swallowed the sweets all at once."

Holmes knelt and retrieved a handkerchief from the floor. "The candies were wrapped in this cloth?"

"Yes, sir," another lad offered. "He probably stole them." The master tried to shove the boy back, but Holmes insisted the child be allowed to speak. The young fellow tugged nervously at his jacket.

"Tubby wasn't allowed treats, sir. The headmaster said he needed to slim down. But Tubby would steal from us. If you had even a ginger snap in your pocket, he would find it and he'd grab it and gulp it down."

Holmes rose and looked at the schoolmaster. "Tell me, do you have an exceptionally thin and small boy among your scholars?"

Reggie Tigerson had quarters in the attic of the dormitory. The headmaster explained that his was the chamber where the "charity boys" lived, and at present Tigerson was the only resident. Holmes told the headmaster to wait downstairs while we went up. He knocked on the door, then tried it. Holmes called out to the youth, but there was no answer.

"Watson, quickly. We must break it down!"

We put our shoulders to it, and the door gave way. A horrible tableau was before us.

At the far end of the room, a young lad, so small and emaciated he could have been a collection of twigs, not flesh, stood on a cot. He had thrown his school tie over the beam above him and was struggling to fix it into a knot. Holmes raced forward before the deed could be completed, lifting the boy down, and settling him on the opposite bunk.

"You should have let me finish," the boy said, dropping his face into his skeletal hands. "They'll hang me anyway, for what happened to Tubby."

"They will not," Holmes said. "For you did not kill him. Nor did you kill Benjamin Branch."

The boy blinked, drawing back. He gasped for air and stared at my friend in utter astonishment. At last, tears filled his eyes, and he slowly nodded. "Why . . . that's true, sir, I swear it on my mother's soul. I never meant for any of this to happen. But who will believe me?"

"Sherlock Holmes will," I said. "If you tell him the truth."

"I've never been a liar, sir. This the God's honest way of it. I'm an orphan. I came here from London, where I was a chimney sweep, apprenticed out to my uncle. But he got in trouble with the coppers, and some church ladies took up a collection to send me to school. No one likes me here. They say I'm poor and dirty. Bennie was the worst. He used to lead them in teasing me. I told the masters, but what did they care? Bennie was the general's son. Everyone said we had to be nice to him because his father died." The child wiped his nose on his sleeve. "Both my mother and father died, but no one was ever kind to me." He frowned, then shook his head. "At least, not until a few days ago."

"What happened then?" Holmes asked.

"I like to sit under the oak tree, at the corner of the yard. Nobody ever goes there, so I can read and do my studying. A nice man came up to me and said he could help me. I thought maybe he had been sent by the church ladies, but instead, he told me he hated Bennie as much as I did and that we could make Bennie pay for being cruel. This man gave me a handkerchief filled with candy. Yes, that very handkerchief I see you holding, sir. He told me the candy had castor oil in it, and it would make Bennie's belly hurt. It seemed like a good lark. Then he gave me two shillings and said that was more when the trick was done, but I must never tell anyone that he had helped me.

362

"The next day was our half-holiday because exams were beginning. That morning, I told Bennie I needed help to study for Professor Morris's test. Bennie was very good at history. At first, he said no, but I told him if he would help me in history, I would tutor him in mathematics, and then he said yes. I thought I would offer him the candy while we studied. I followed him home, but I had to wait for him to call off his dog. We went into the study and shut the door.

"I saw some tea and cakes there, on a little table. Because I'm on charity, I'm only allowed one meal a day, sir, and nothing on half days. For a moment, I forgot the prank because I was so very hungry. I took a cake and stuffed it in my mouth, not asking Bennie's permission to eat it. Bennie grew angry with me. I told him not to yell, I was sorry for eating his cake. Bennie's face turned red. He said I was a thief and then he grabbed the big marble bust of his father from the mantel. It was heavy, but he lifted it over his head like a rock to hurl it at me. He screamed at me, he took a step, and then – the floor was just polished, and the rug twisted tight, and he slipped! The bust went flying up in the air as he lost his balance and . . . oh sir . . . *the blood!*"

The boy wept hysterically. Holmes waited as I opened my bag and diluted a bit of calming medication. The child drank it down and, after a moment, continued with his tale.

"There was a knock at the door. A lady asked if Bennie was alright. I knew it would look like I had killed him. I slid the bolt into place, then went up the chimney and came out over the roof and climbed down a tree.

"I ran back here, sir, and changed my dirty clothes. I bundled up my soiled togs, stuffing them in a satchel I keep under my bed. By the time I was all cleaned up, the news had come to us, and everyone was upset about Bennie's death. Somehow, no one noticed that I had ever been gone.

"The candies were still wrapped up in the handkerchief in my grimy shirt. I was so upset that I didn't think about anybody nosing about in my satchel. I knew Tubby stole sweets, and I should have thrown them out when I was running home, but it slipped my mind. I forgot, and now it's my fault that he's dead."

"No," Holmes said sternly. "The fault rests with an evil man who schemed and lied to trick an innocent boy into doing murder for him."

"Good Heavens!" I murmured, seeing the whole thing clearly. As a "charity lad" who had been abused by Benjamin in the past, who would believe Reggie's protests of innocence or his accusation of some outstanding adult?

"The man who gave you the tainted candy intended, via his plot, to have you legally murdered by The Crown," Holmes told the child. "But he will not go unpunished."

363

"What is his name?" I asked the boy.

"Sir, he never told me."

Holmes unfolded the handkerchief and pointed to the elaborately embroidered initials in one corner.

"So it was a murder? Accident?" Lestrade scratched his head. "Act of God?"

Holmes smiled grimly. The inspector had joined us within the hour, and Holmes told him the story as we walked from the station.

"It was villainy. Our culprit wanted Benjamin Branch dead, so that his way would be cleared to woo the boy's lovely mother and avoid delaying their marriage for another decade. Imagine this fiend's delight at finding Bennie done away with by an even more mysterious means than the one he had planned. The child's death was now one that he could further use to his advantage by casting suspicion on a romantic rival." Holmes began counting on his fingers. "What a fine demonstration of the seven deadly sins this case has been! Wrath carried young Benjamin away, as his undisciplined fury led to his fatal wounding. Greed and gluttony were the downfall of poor Tubby, who ate the poison intended for another. Envy perhaps ensnared the unwitting Reggie in the plot. Lust motivated our villain – and pride allowed him to think he could engage my services and outwit me! Here is Mr. Leonard Oliver Rhodes's home – be sure to keep this handkerchief as evidence, Lestrade, and I would suggest you speak to the local chemist, who will surely recall selling the man a substantial amount of arsenic. Congratulations on another triumph, Inspector! Do come by our quarters soon, and we shall drink a toast to you."

"Holmes," I said, as we left the Lestrade preparing to charge inside and arrest his man, "you have made an omission. Where is sloth?"

My friend yawned. "It has been a long day, and I intend to commit that sin as soon as we return to Baker Street."

The Adventure of the Fourth Key
by Carlos Orsi

"My dear Watson, you are perfectly right: The people flocking to sponsor Mme. Houret's so-called 'cause' are behaving with the utmost foolishness."

I let *The Times* slip from my hands but offered only a half-smile to the tall, thin man who smoked a briar pipe in front of the fire, the remains of our breakfast still scattered upon the battlefield of the side table.

It was a morose summer Saturday, and I had been an associate of Mr. Sherlock Holmes for too long to feel astounded by this exhibition.

"Ah, I see," he said genially. "Familiarity breeds contempt, indeed."

"It hardly befits you, Holmes," I replied, wryly, "to claim credit for deducing that I was thinking about the foolishness of those who fall for Mme. Houret's 'investment'. It's almost the only thing of note in the papers nowadays."

"In the more sensational press, it even displaced the disappearance of Adams, the forlorn jeweler!" Holmes answered, with a chuckle. "Astonishing!"

"Oh, come. A young man 'goes missing' with a briefcase full of jewels after his fiancée runs away with another beau . . . ."

"On their wedding day, Watson! Their very wedding day!"

"Whatever. It's the shallowest of melodramas."

Holmes's chin trembled with mirth.

"I don't know what it says about the future of our present civilization, when the promise of riches mobilizes more public attention than the breaking of hearts."

"Indeed," I said, affecting a gravity I didn't feel.

"The respectable newspapers, at least those who'd like to be seen as such, ignored poor Adams' plight, as they now make every effort to downplay the locked safe-room charade."

"As they very well should."

At this, Holmes gave a sharp, short nod, as if I had just conceded his point. He went on to elaborate.

"Your absorption in the lower left-hand corner of the last pages of the morning papers, to where the material considered most unfit for serious attention is usually consigned, was enough to allow anyone to deduce that you had Mme. Houret's claim to the Yates fortune on your mind. I will give you that," he said, humorously. "You know my methods, and you see right through them. But to deduce that your train of thought moved on the direction of a verdict of 'foolishness' required something a little more sophisticated on my part, if I may say so," he teased.

"Oh, yes?" I rose to the bait. "What, then?"

"Horses, Watson! Horses! Your eyes wandered from the printed page to that little memento of the Silver Blaze affair we keep on the mantelpiece. You were thinking that it would be easier for a man to attain wealth by betting on horses than by investing in the contents of Yates' safe-room."

I felt myself blush, only so slightly. Holmes was right. On the mantelpiece was a small trophy, a miniature of the cup won by the horse Silver Blaze so many years ago, thanks to the intervention of my friend.

Madame Sophie Houret was a middle-aged French widow, quite a handsome woman, who had arrived in England bringing two sons and the most astonishing claims – she said she was the legal heiress of an obscure, misanthropic American millionaire, Stuart Yates, originally from Louisiana, who had died in British soil, leaving behind a large house in an upscale London district, a house distinguished by an apparently impregnable safe-room – steel doors, three strong locks and, it was rumored, steel-lined walls.

If one were to believe what the sensationalist papers printed, the insides of the room would look like the riveted hull of an ironclad. But it seemed that no one had really been there in recent memory.

Despite Mme. Houret taking possession of the house – called Sunset Manor – without facing any opposition, it seemed that other presumptive heirs objected to the opening of the fortified room, where, the tale went, the monies, jewels, shares and bonds of the late millionaire were all preserved.

Madame's opponents did obtain a court order demanding that the safe-room should be kept locked – the three keys that she'd brought with herself from France had been confiscated and entrusted to a magistrate.

To support the house, herself, and her sons in a perhaps not too frugal lifestyle, and to pay the legal fees of the ongoing litigation, she began to sell "shares" against the contents of the room. Her first advertisements appeared in the press soon after the start of the court proceedings.

It was Holmes's opinion – and mine – that the safe-room was, in all probability, empty, and that the mysterious and never properly identified other claimants to the fortune, who supposedly kept Mme. Houret tied in knots in the courts, were simply nonexistent or, perhaps, her paid accomplices.

366

Scotland Yard, however, couldn't do much without positive evidence of fraud. Inquiries made across the Atlantic showed that a Mr. Stuart Yates, a reclusive Yank of few friends or acquaintances but, apparently, ample means, had lived in New Orleans for a few years before liquidating his considerable state there and vanishing without a trace. It was as likely as not that he'd moved to England.

No one had approached Holmes to investigate the issue, and it was even doubtful that he would deign to touch it if offered the opportunity. Sometimes I'd hear him musing about the capital invested in the swindle, and the identity the original owner or builder of the house, but that was all. His interests clearly rested elsewhere.

Our almost-Olympic indifference towards the Yates "treasure" case was about to change, however.

Mrs. Hudson came to clean up our breakfast. She was usually quite efficient about it, coming and going almost unnoticed, and then coming back with the first client of the day. Now, however, it didn't take a Sherlock Holmes to notice that she lingered, deliberately.

Much have been said about Holmes apparent lack of emotion – how, in words I have registered elsewhere, he seemed capable of poisoning a friend just to observe how the organism would react. But this ultimate ratiocinator had an ample heart, and profound was his capacity for compassion.

"Is there anything you would like to talk to me about, Mrs. Hudson?" he asked, with a gentle voice. "Or perhaps it is a medical problem . . . ?" he added, nodding towards me.

"Oh, no, no Mr. Holmes, it is nothing," she replied, surprised and, it seemed to me, grateful. "It's just . . . ."

"Pray, be seated," encouraged my friend.

And so it came to pass that Martha Hudson sat on the client's chair.

"It is about my son, James Junior," she said, barely containing a sob.

A son! For a moment, I was taken aback. Of course, a widowed Mrs. Hudson presupposed a late Mr. Hudson – I had a vague remembrance of her mentioning, years ago, that he had been struck down quite suddenly, due to a hereditary heart condition –and children are just the natural fruit of most marriages. Even so, I caught myself pondering how little we – I – knew about this long-suffering woman, who worked so hard to make these rooms a home.

If my friend too was surprised, he gave no sign. His eyes softened, and his smile was reassuring.

"And what seems to be the trouble with young Mr. James Hudson Jr?" he asked.

"He has a small business, a locksmith shop by the Thames," she explained. "Captains of foreign ships come to him so he can properly appoint their cabins' doors and put proper locks on their safes. He says his work is so specialized, he is almost an engineer," she raised her head, proudly.

"I am sure of it," Holmes reassured her. "Did anything ill befall him?"

"Oh, that's just the question, sir." She took a small white handkerchief to the eye. "I am afraid it did. I haven't heard from him in days. Bart, his young apprentice, is taking care of the shop all by himself since Tuesday. It isn't like him. It isn't. Young Bart says he left word that 'a big job' had come, without giving details. But he wouldn't leave for so long without saying anything more to anyone, would he?"

Holmes raised himself.

"Never fear, Mrs. Hudson," he said. "Leave, please, your boy's address, and that of his shop and of his apprentice as well. Watson and I will look into the matter immediately. Won't we?"

"But of course!" I agreed, jumping from my chair. "At once!"

Mrs. Hudson took a piece of paper from the desk and scribbled a few lines. She also described to us, in painstaking detail, the appearance of her son and of "young Bart". Then she left, tray in hand, looking relieved and proffering a veritable flood of thanks.

The three addresses Holmes asked for were only two: James' living quarters and workplace shared the same location, with the store and workshop at the ground level, and rooms upstairs. As for young Bart, he lived with an elderly aunt, not too far from the shop.

"*Jack Hudson Locksmith: Specialty Locks and Safes*", as the sign read, occupied a squat red-brick building near the docks. The thoroughfare was quite lively, noisy, and busy. We found Bart – it was impossible not to recognize him from the picture painted by Mrs. Hudson's words – at the store, behind a fragrant, well-waxed oaken counter.

While we were entering the shop, Holmes whispered to me, "Did you notice the sign on the front?"

"Seems to describe the place quite well," I answered, looking around.

"Nothing else caught your attention?"

"Can't say it did." I tried to sound noncommittal, but my curiosity, of course, was piqued.

"The young Mr. Hudson has taken to call himself 'Jack', but his dear mother still refers to him as 'James'."

"Meaning?"

Holmes sighed. "Meaning, perhaps, that to our dear, long-suffering mothers, we'll always be children playing with fire in a hostile world."

"G'day, sirs, how can I help you today?" asked Bart, a freckled, blonde lad of perhaps sixteen, wearing a blue shirt with rolled-over sleeves and a green vest.

"We'd like a word with Mr. Hudson," Holmes said.

"Oh, sorry, sir, but I'm afraid it won't be possible. Mr. Hudson is otherwise engaged."

Holmes insisted. "Is he in the workshop? There is a workshop at the back of the premises, isn't?" He began to move as if to go around the counter and into the workshop, but Bart planted himself firmly in Holmes's way.

"Really sorry sir, thousand pardons, but Master Hudson isn't here. He's doing outside work. And he doesn't like strangers going through his things."

Holmes chuckled. "Well said, young Bart, very well said indeed!"

The boy looked puzzled. "How do you?"

"Know your name? I am Sherlock Holmes, and this is my friend and colleague, Dr. Watson. Mrs. Hudson, Master Hudson's mother, asked us to come here and check on her son. She hasn't had word from him since last Tuesday."

"Oh, Mister Holmes!" Bart was flabbergasted. "How nice to make your acquaintance! And yours too, Doctor Watson!"

"Same here, lad," I answered, politely.

"What can you tell us that will help to assuage Mrs. Hudson's fears?" Holmes pressed.

"I . . . I don't know," the boy blurted. "I mean, I don't even know if there's any reason for her to be worried. Mrs. Hudson was here yesterday, bringing fresh-baked cakes for the weekend, as she always does on Fridays, but Master Hudson wasn't here, and when she asked me when he'd be around, I said I didn't know, because he'd been out on a special service since Tuesday and hadn't come back or sent word since."

"Is it unusual for him?" I asked. "To be away for so long on a job?"

"It happens, sometimes, when he has to work on a ship that can't remain moored on a pier, for instance. Then he depends on a launch or longboat to take him on and to bring him in, and sometimes Master Hudson stays onboard overnight. But these jobs never keep him away for more than two days at a time. And he is always here on Fridays, to get the cakes from his mother."

"Are you worried about your Master, Bart?" Holmes asked.

The boy blinked before answering.

"Well, I . . . No. Not yet, Mr. Holmes. This job is taking longer than usual, it's true, but things don't always go as planned, and Captain French's second desk is quite a nuisance."

369

"Captain French?"

"Yes, that's the client who sent for Master Hudson on Tuesday morning. It seems that he has two desks, and the second one has a special lock that is always giving him trouble. He has Master Hudson on beck and call because of the contraption."

"This captain – What does he look like?"

Bart scratched his nose. "I don't think I've ever seen him. He usually sends his people to fetch Master Hudson."

"And 'his people', as you call them – How do they identify themselves?"

"They just say they come from Captain French, and then leave a note. That's all. Usually, Master Hudson takes the note to the workshop to read and then leaves sometime later."

"I see." Holmes let his chin fall to his chest and took a deep breath. I was very close and heard him mutter to himself, "This is going to be very amusing, or very dangerous."

Suddenly, he raised the head and said to Bart, "I'm quite sure there's nothing for Mrs. Hudson to be worried about, but can we take a look at Master Hudson's quarters and workshop, to make our report to her more complete?"

The apprentice looked doubtful. "I know of your reputation, sir, and both the Master and his mother speak highly of you. But the Master is also a very private person. I have instructions to never let anyone go beyond this counter without his permission."

"Which is very laudable, and you dedication commends you highly. But to put Mrs. Hudson's fears to rest . . . ."

Bart raised the eyebrows and cocked his head in a show of indecision, but eventually smiled.

"Well, you are both well-respected gentlemen, and friends of the family. Please. Come."

Our search of Jack Hudson's workshop revealed very little. His toolbox wasn't there, which was consistent with him being out on a job.

The backdoor had been locked, Holmes ascertained, from the outside. There were some burnt papers in the workshop fireplace, but Bart told us it was a common occurrence – Hudson had the habit of destroying most of his copies of schematics after the completion of every job, for security reasons. Holmes rummaged through the ashes for clues but found nothing of interest.

Hudson's living quarters were clean and tidy, with no sign of struggle or hasty departure.

370

"You don't look satisfied," I remarked, once we were back on the street.

"It's because I am not," he answered. "We're treading on thin ice, over what could be very deep waters indeed."

"Then shouldn't we go to the Lloyd's to locate this Captain French's ship?"

"Watson, I am quite sure that this 'ship' is very well grounded on *terra firma*. Are you familiar with the expression *Deuxième Bureau*?"

"Why, it is French for – "

"'*Second Desk*'. It is also the informal name of the French government's intelligence service, headed by Mycroft's counterpart in the Continent. I'm very much inclined to think that the 'Captain French's second desk' that kept, and is keeping, Jack Hudson so busy really is – "

"Holmes!"

"This is one of those crossroads in which we have to decide if our interference will be wanted, needed, or even beneficial. As I said, thin ice over deep waters. If we break it, how many more will be plunged into the cold darkness with us?"

On our way to Baker Street, Holmes stopped to send two telegrams. Once we were back, my friend did his best to soothe Mrs. Hudson, telling her that everything seemed in order at her son's home and workshop, without any sign of trouble or foul play (which was true), and that Bart had said to us that sometimes his Master got stranded on client's ships, waiting for an available launch to bring him back.

The answer to his first telegram brought us an invitation for dinner at the Diogenes Club. Waiting for us in the Stranger's Room – the only place in the club where it is allowed to entertain conversation – was the answer to his second, in the person of François Le Villard, Holmes's friend and disciple in the Parisian police force. Besides Mycroft Holmes and Le Villard, we were met by two other men. One was our old friend, Inspector Lestrade of Scotland Yard, and – a face I recognized immediately from the numerous sketches in the newspapers – Mr. Edward Adams, the abandoned groom and missing jeweler!

As I stood there dumbfounded, Holmes narrowed his eyes. "You are playing a funny game this time, Mycroft."

"Not so funny as you may think, Sherlock, but the stakes are high nonetheless – both for Her Majesty's Government and the French Republic. Now, please gentlemen, pray be seated."

"I always knew this affair would land right on your lap, Mr. Holmes," Lestrade said, with a nod of resignation. "It's all too bizarre."

"The only bizarre affair that concerns me, so far, is the disappearance of Mr. Jack Hudson, Jr.," Holmes answered. "I wasn't aware that the case had been referred to the Yard, nor to Whitehall. I had, however, some inklings that it might fall into the purview of – " He then nodded towards Le Villard. " – the Deuxième Bureau."

"Jack was a talented and discreet artificer that Her Majesty's government was good enough to share with us in certain situations," the French policeman – or, as it was becoming quite clear, secret agent – told us. "Our countries may be rivals and even adversaries in many spheres, but we have our share of us common causes, too."

Holmes's eyes shone with a cold, terrible light. "I find myself rather upset by your choice of verbal tense. What do you mean by Jack '*was*' a talented artificer?"

"We don't know if he's dead, Sherlock," Mycroft interposed, sounding slightly annoyed. "He disappeared on his way to render to us, and to our French friends, an invaluable service. He is missing, but no body has been found so far. As to the nature of the problem, I believe it will all become clear after Mr. Adams here tells his story."

"Mr. Adams." Holmes looked pointedly at him. "The newspapers described you as a jeweler, but you are more of a gem-cutter, I perceive."

Adams had a powerful frame, with the shoulders and arms of a rugby player, but the impression of great strength was undone by his short stature and delicate, almost childish facial features. He was clean-shaven, with a thin, tiny nose, small, delicate mouth, and green liquid eyes behind a somewhat incongruous *pince-nez*. This all-too-meek countenance was topped by a diaphanous shock of grey-yellow, almost-transparent hair.

He stared at the younger Holmes. "How did you – ?"

"He noticed the shining callus between your left thumb and index finger, caused by the constant contact and friction with emery," Mycroft explained. Then, turning to his brother. "Really, such a meretricious showmanship at this time."

"I am sorry. You are absolutely right, Brother. Please tell us your tale, Mr. Adams."

He cleared his throat, then began.

"The truth, sir, is that I am, or was, both a jeweler and a gem-cutter. For years, I have been a cutter in my late father's jewelry business, an artisan in the workshop, and I never dreamed of taking over the business.

"But it finally happened two years ago, and I must say that I was astonished to find out that father had left so many debts. I only got the business back on its feet about six months ago, and that was when I met Ethel – Miss Reynard – who became my fiancée. She had a cousin, Firmin, who lived in France. Last month he appeared suddenly, in a sort of surprise visit, and I could tell Ethel wasn't happy about it.

372

"Well, this Firmin Reynard had a friend called Poligny who crossed the Channel with him. They very much forced themselves upon us and, due to the relation, we were quite powerless to avoid them."

"Why would you want to avoid them?" Lestrade asked. "Were they unpleasant company? Uncouth?"

"Quite the opposite," said Adams, ignoring Lestrade and answering directly to Holmes. "They were charming and ingratiating – very much so. And quite fond of gambling."

There was a meaningful silence in the room.

"Against Ethel's best advice, I fell in with them," Adams confessed, crestfallen, "and suddenly, as my father before me, I saw myself sinking in debt.

"My situation wasn't desperate, yet, but I could see the writing on the wall. Then one night, I was brooding over my predicament before the fire, thinking about liquidating a good portion of my stock, paying up what I owned, how it would force me to postpone my marriage, and how it would affect poor Ethel. Then I raised my eyes from the flames, looked at my chamber's door, and saw Reynard there. It startled me."

Holmes's eyes shone. "Where were you living then?"

"After putting the family business in order, I had rented a suite of furnished rooms near here – in Pall Mall," the jeweler answered. "But I was afraid I'd have to move back to the small cottage behind the store in a very short time."

"Did your future brother-in-law have the keys to your rooms?"

"No."

"Then how do you account for his sudden presence at the threshold of your private chamber?"

"Later, the police were to find that the front door of the house had been jimmied. But it didn't occur to me to question his presence right then. My need for funds, my anxiety, my insomnia, and the brute fact of his presence were all that occupied my mind."

Holmes sighed. "Pray continue."

"The witching hour was well passed and, as I said, his presence startled me. I even dropped my glass of port on the carpet. Seeing that I had noticed him, Reynard smiled. I haven't described him to you. He's very tall and thin, slightly stooped, with small eyes, and a straight nose. His mouth and chin are both quite large. When he smiles, one can see big, square, yellowed teeth. He has black hair, shaggy around jug ears.

"'I may have a means for all your troubles to go away', he said.

"'What?' His words made me hopeful. 'How do you mean?'

"'Poligny and I have a transaction occurring tonight, and we need some expert advice on a question of gems and jewels', he answered. 'If all goes well, we'll be flush enough to pluck you out of trouble.'

"'Tonight?' I asked, my heart leaping in my chest like a scared rabbit.

"'At this very moment.'"

"I knew they were serious gamblers. It occurred to me that someone might be trying to pay a debt with a family heirloom, and they needed me to ascertain it's value. The late hour could be explained by the seller feeling ashamed, something I could understand. I agreed. I changed into street clothes, put on a heavy woolen coat, and we went out."

"To Sunset Manor," Mycroft interjected.

"That was the night Mr. Stuart Yates passed from the sight of mortals, I gather," Holmes commented dryly.

"You are most right, sir," Adams said, his voice trembling as he recounted the rest of his story.

They went, first, by hansom, but Reynard had them to alight at an empty street, and from there they proceeded on foot. Then they were at the house.

"Did you go in through the main door?" Holmes interrupted suddenly.

"No. Through the back – the tradesmen's entrance."

"No servants?"

"None that I saw. I don't believe there were any."

In a large room of Sunset Manor, a horrible tableau waited, multiplied by the score of golden-framed mirrors of all sizes that were the main decoration on three of the four walls.

Adams saw a man – Stuart Yates, as he was to know later – tied to a strong chair. One of his eyelids was hideously swollen. There were gashes on his scalp and cheeks. Nose and lips were burst. Blood covered his mouth and chin, dripping from his beard to the floor. Teeth, very white, shone among the purple-and-crimson mess of his face. The man was virtually naked. His undershirt and outer garments were behind his chair, laid open, shredded, and with the pockets turned inside-out.

Poligny was standing in front of the victim, looking at Yates with eyes full of hatred. When Reynard and Adams entered, his attention was diverted to them. He smiled before returning his gaze to Yates and saying, "Ah! See here, Stéphane? It's almost over."

The tortured man remained silent.

"What are you two doing with this man?" he demanded. "Why did you bring me here?"

The gem-cutter had recovered from his shock and was indignant. Poligny took a step toward him, raising the revolver he had in his right

374

hand – he carried it by the muzzle, and the stock, which he'd been using as a club, was bloody.

"We demand that you tell us what that is, 'Cousin'." His voice was pregnant with menace.

Adams might have been weak-willed, but he wasn't a fool. These were dangerous men, and they'd brought him to the location of a crime. He knew that neither he nor the poor man tied to the chair would live to see another day.

Poligny was pointing to a shining object, the size of a peach stone, poised on a nearby desk. That, a grand piano (with a velvet-pillowed bench for the pianist), and the chair occupied by the prisoner were the only pieces of furniture in the room, which was lit by a huge silver chandelier was hanging from the ceiling. There were no windows.

The desk, Adams noticed, was made of ebony and had intricate ivory inlays. It was covered with drawers of every size. Several had tiny keyholes. An unmarked side drawer – a secret panel – was open, and empty.

The bright object was very red, a jewel cut in a modified Briolette, or teardrop, style – and modified so that the general shape guarded an uncanny resemblance with the contours of the human skull.

Examining it, the gem-cutter knew that it was a piece of glass made to look like an exquisite ruby.

"So?"

He heard Reynard moving behind him.

"So what?" Adams demanded.

"Is it real?"

He took a deep breath. If the men had wanted him there, it was because they needed him. Which meant they didn't know. Which meant he could buy time by lying. Or could he? What if, believing they had what they wanted, the two ruffians were to cover their tracks by killing victim and witness immediately?

"It's glass," he said.

Poligny roared and went for Yates with the gun's stock. One blow to the side of head, one to the body. Adams heard a rib crack.

"No!" The prisoner cried. "I beg you, no more!"

"You know what we want!" his torturer snarled.

"Let me lose and I'll get it to you," Yates said, panting.

"Tell us where it is."

"Combination . . . Difficult. It will be quicker if you let me do it."

"Let him," Reynard said. "But keep him covered."

They untied the man, Reynard unfastening the knots while Poligny watched, gun ready. Adams made a small movement toward the door he'd come in – the servant's door, at a corner of the back of the room – but the gun's muzzle darted in his direction.

The ruffian positioned himself between the gem-cutter and that exit.

Free, Yates staggered. His goal was a huge steel door with three very visible locks – one seemingly gold-plated, one silver, the third, black – that dominated the only wall in the room not covered in mirrors.

He was almost there – his trembling, bloodied hand raised as if to touch the door's frame – when a seizure took hold of him. His naked body spun around, and he collapsed.

Reynard and Poligny were transfixed. The gun muzzle wavered, and Adams saw his chance. He ran for the servant's door. He barged into the armed man, knocking him out of breath, heard a shot that – he surmised – went wild, and kept on running.

There seemed to have been no pursuit. Adams ran out of the house, into the bitter coldness of the night that for him was, suddenly, sweeter than wine, and kept on running until he found a constable.

After calming himself and resting enough to regain his breath, Adams' told the policeman his story. They then went back to the house, finding the back entrance open, the place deserted. The only record of the events of the night was a tumbled chair and an ugly bloodstain on the floor.

"There was a standing order at the Yard, circulated to every police station, that any business involving Sunset Manor should be immediately referred through certain channels that . . . Well, channels that invariably lead to me," Mycroft Holmes added, before his brother could offer more questions. "I then made the proper arrangements with Scotland Yard and called to our friends in France."

Holmes took a deep breath.

"I assume that Mr. Yates' real name was Stéphane?"

"Ives," Le Villard offered.

"That Mr. Stéphane Ives was a person of special interest for both the British Empire and the French Republic. Why?"

Mycroft tossed a golden coin, no larger than the nail of my index finger, onto the table. It had a very small, broken link welded to it. "This was found attached to one of the sleeves of the woolen jacket Mr. Adams' was wearing that night," he said. "What do you make of it, Sherlock?"

The younger Holmes rose to his feet and, producing a magnifying glass from his hip-pocket, went on to examine it.

"There are still a few strands of dyed wool, yes," he said. "The link was an adaptation for use as a charm for a watch chain. It was probably transferred to Mr. Adams' clothes during his violent collision with Mr. Poligny. As for the coin – Hullo! Not something we see every day."

"What is it?" I asked.

"Do you remember the Second Mexican Empire?"

It startled me. "The puppet monarchy set-up in Mexico by Louis Napoleon of France, with an Austrian nobleman – "

"Archduke Ferdinand Maximilian, of the House of Habsburg-Lorraine, as Emperor of Mexico, yes," Holmes replied. "It's his face in one side of this coin – a point of great interest. The other side, however, is even more interesting. See . . . ."

He passed coin and glass to me. The obverse showed the profile of a balding, bearded man, somewhat crudely done, with the word *"Emperador"* written along the side. The reverse had the striking image of a grinning skull. Now looking closely, I could see that the coin wasn't made of ordinary yellow gold, but with a crimson hue.

"That ill-fated Empire ended in a bloody revolt some thirty years ago," Holmes commented. "It was quite short-lived."

"There were many goings-on in the Mexican Empire that the present French Republic would like to forget," Le Villard said. "As soon as it was established, lots of undesirables emigrated there, not only from France, but from all of the Continent. It was almost as far from the peering eyes of European authorities as Île du Diable, and much freer.

"The worst of the worst formed a secret organization, that they called *Le Fantôme – 'The Phantom'*. They took advantage of the chaotic situation in Mexico to establish a network of horror and corruption that extended back to Europe. Their activities probably accelerated the end of Emperor Maximilian's reign. They turned a significant part of their proceeds into gemstones – easy to carry, easy to conceal, more reliable than the coinage of a regime that could collapse at any moment – and when the Empire fell, they dispersed to other French-speaking parts of the Americas."

"Like Louisiana, in the United States," Holmes interposed.

"Exactly."

"The most valuable part of *Le Fantôme* treasure," Le Villard went on to explain, "was 'The Red Death', an enormous ruby shaped like a human skull. Apart from its monetary value, it was a badge of power and authority. But the man charged with its safekeeping, Stéphane Ives, was tired of a life of crime. He faked his own death even before leaving Mexico, and arrived in the United States with a new name and identity. Men from the Deuxième Bureau found him there, however, and, surmising correctly that *Le Fantôme* might be right behind, he negotiated a relocation in exchange for intelligence on his former comrades.

"We agreed to have him in London," Mycroft Holmes said. "This *'Fantôme'* network is pervasive on the Continent, and Special Branch has detected a few tendrils. Its present leader, the self-styled Prince Gaston d'Einsengott, lives in Belgium, but we know that he's been harassed by rivals. The badge of office, 'The Red Death', is missing since the debacle in Mexico."

"You used Ives – Yates – as bait!" I exclaimed, indignant.

"Not at all," Mycroft answered dryly. "We allowed the French Republic to place him among us as a courtesy and received valuable intelligence for our pains. We also placed Jack Hudson at their disposal. As far as we know, it was he who created the Hall of Mirrors at Sunset Manor, and the great safe with the three locks."

"It was," Le Villard confirmed.

"So Mme. Houret's charade," said Holmes, "is part of a plan to flush out D'Eisengott's and Maupertuis' agents in London, of course. Get them at each other's throats, if possible."

I was astonished. "Wait a minute! How – ?"

Holmes's expression was quite intense, but a quick smile touched the corner of his mouth.

"It's painfully obvious." He paused. "They must believe that the ruby is on the other side of that monstrous steel door. By selling 'shares' of the contents in a very public manner, Mycroft is forcing them to show their hands."

I began to grasp the situation. "The lawsuit that forbade Mme. Houret from opening it right way?"

"A ruse," Lestrade cut in. "As was the decision to declare Mr. Yates still 'missing' and to hide the fact that his body had been found."

"Found!"

Lestrade nodded. "Two days later, by the river patrol."

"The men who killed him?" I pressed.

"These are really missing. The last word on them came from the direction of Limehouse, and then, nothing. They may have left England, for all we know. Mr. Adams' broken engagement and disappearance were engineered so we could spirit him and his fiancée away and offer both adequate protection – and especially protect Mrs. Reynard from her murderous cousin, while the case remains open."

"Wouldn't the men from *Le Fantôme* suspect the sudden appearance of an heir to their treasure?" I asked.

"Stéphane Ives had been on the run, with a fortune to his name and at least one false identity, for more than three decades," Holmes said. "Who knows what he might have done all this time? And a suitable track of documents could be produced on demand, I presume."

Le Villard cleared his throat. "Exactly, Mr. Holmes."

"A trail that would only be useful, of course, if the penetration of the French State by *Le Fantôme*'s corrupting influence had been neither too shallow, nor too deep."

The secret agent nodded. "You are right. We gambled that their agents would gain access to the forged papers, not to the forgery. We played it quite close to the chest. And that's why no one – absolutely no one – knew the secret of Sunset Manor steel door beside Stéphane himself and Jack Hudson."

"Pity that they took the precaution of authenticating it *in loco*," Holmes mused.

"Mr. Hudson vanished when he was on his way to open that door for us," Mycroft said. "He'd been summoned to the Manor and never arrived." The older Holmes sighed. "I myself have been there and was unable to puzzle out that game of locks and keys."

"Were you?" asked Holmes. "Unable? I think I will try my hand at it."

I was aghast.

"Holmes, I know that you love puzzles, and that you love even more to show up your brother – " There were chuckles around the table, but I ignored them. " – but shouldn't we concentrate in finding young Hudson?"

"Watson, your heart is, as always, in the right place, but I assure you that puzzling out that door is of the utmost importance. I can formulate seven hypotheses as to what happened to Jack Hudson on his way between his shop and Sunset Manor, and if we are to have any regard for the joint efforts of the Deuxième Bureau, Scotland Yard, and British Intelligence, we can disregard four of them out of hand. The fifth and the sixth are directly connected with the steel door's secret."

"And the last one?" I asked.

"The last one is that he met with foul play and his body has been utterly destroyed, by strong acid or other means."

Except for Edward Adams, we all repaired to Sunset Manor. It was quite late, and the gentlemen of the press were absent from the street. Of course, they didn't represent our main preoccupation. Men from *Le Fantôme* certainly were keeping the place under surveillance.

We went in boldly, through the front door, Lestrade leading the way. Mycroft Holmes had dressed himself in a way that strongly suggested Scotland Yard. Holmes wore a false mustache and side whiskers, and Le Villard and I went as bobbies. The "court order" determining that the big safe shouldn't be opened also demanded a continuous police presence, after all.

The Hall of Mirrors was an astonishing place, with a dream-like quality. The woman known as Sophie Houret and her "sons" – in reality two sturdy French detectives in their early twenties – were there. She had a bun of scarlet hair that likely rivaled The Red Death for fieriness, and very alert, domineering brown eyes.

"We assumed the big door was a decoy, and that the jewel was secreted in the desk or in the piano," she said. "The desk is really made of steel. Ebony and ivory comprise just the external layer.

"Under examination, we determined that the piano is just a piano – or almost. We found small keys hidden inside its black keys. Quite ingenious."

Holmes smiled.

"And these 'keys inside keys' open the drawers of the desk, I presume."

"Yes, but it isn't so straightforward. For instance, if you turn the keys on two of the upper drawers to the right, a spring will release the lower drawer to the left. It's quite intricate."

"But you decoded it."

"Yes. It parallels a song. If you 'play' drawers that represent the right notes in the correct sequence, the next one pops open."

"The song?"

"'Silver Threads Among the Gold'. The sheet music was hidden under the pianist's pillow."

"And the three keys for the large door? The ones you supposedly brought from France?"

"Useless. They were just part of our disguise. But the real three keys were the first thing we found after deciphering the desk. The central drawer opened, and there they were: Black, silver, and gold. A puzzle in itself. If you're going to use three locks, it doesn't make sense to keep all the keys together. If they are together, it makes you no safer than having just one lock and one key."

Holmes's eyes brightened with pleasure. "So it seems. But – "

"After playing around with the desk for a long time, and even after dismantling part of it, we concluded that the ruby wasn't there. Which left us with the big steel door. And then we were stumped."

"How so?"

"The obvious combination – each key in the lock of the corresponding color – doesn't work. Nor does any of the obvious permutations. Then, with the help of your brother, we began to experiment with the non-obvious: Only two keys. The same key on every lock, in different sequences. Nothing. Every key goes in every lock and even begins to turn, but nothing happens."

"Why didn't you call Jack Hudson in the first place?" I asked, bewildered.

"We had to assume that Yates had been betrayed to *Le Fantôme* by someone," Le Villard said. "As soon as we made sure that Mr. Hudson hadn't been betrayed and wasn't under surveillance by the enemy, we called him."

"You 'made sure' he wasn't under surveillance," I said, "and nevertheless he was captured on his way here!"

"Don't get ahead of yourself," Holmes said, approaching the puzzling door. And after a pause, "He had his tools with him. I wonder . . . ." He touched the metal with both palms and went on to feel the casing. He did so for a few minutes, and the others, including me, became distracted. Then there was a distinct click and a thin, sibilant note. We turned: Holmes wasn't there.

The man had vanished without a trace! We ran to where he'd been. There was no sign of him, not even a smudge of shoe polish or a pinch of tobacco-ash on the checkered floor. I banged on the door, to no avail. Lestrade, a cooler hand, began to explore the jambs. "Mr. Holmes must have found a lever, a *fourth* lock – a *secret* lock," said the inspector. "Now – *Here!*"

We heard a click. My heart was booming. We waited. Nothing happened.

Then I tried. Then Le Villard, then Mycroft. Knowing what we were looking for, feeling the lever with the fingertips wasn't too difficult.

But for minutes on end, nothing happened. How many minutes? I'll never know for certain. A slice of eternity.

"Fool!" Mycroft exploded, suddenly, barking with laughter. "What a fool I've been! Of course! It's more than a vault, it's . . . But then, there must be an exit! A way out. We must . . . ."

I was close to believing that Mycroft Holmes was deranged, his great mind destroyed by the loss of his brother, when the safe door swung open, and I heard Holmes's cry: "Watson! Quickly! Brandy! This poor man has been here for days, barely conscious, without food or water."

Years of medical and military training took hold instantly, and I was well into my ministrations when a certain family resemblance told me that my patient was James "Jack" Hudson, Jr.

"It wasn't a *safe* room, it was a *safety* room," Holmes said as he reached the gasogene. I thanked him as he topped my glass with soda. "Designed first and foremost to protect anyone who took refuge inside. Unfortunately, the ruffians surprised and dominated their victim before Mr. Ives – or Yates – could avail himself of those facilities that, we now know, Jack Hudson's ingenuity had created for him."

381

We were in Baker Street. Jack Hudson was recovering well under the watchful eye of his mother. I made a point of checking on him. He'd had a close call – a heart attack, not strong enough to kill him, but because of it he fell hard and broke a kneecap, badly. My opinion was that he'd have to walk with a cane for the rest of his life.

"The three keys were an ingenious decoy," added Mycroft, who had left his usual orbit to join us in our rooms and discuss the case. "Of course, once the true nature of the door and the chambers behind it become clear, a lot follows. The door should open and close again very rapidly, to allow for a quick escape – "

" – And, once used, it should become impervious to new attempts to open it from the outside, in order to avoid pursuit," Holmes added. "I conjectured about the true nature of the 'safe' after listening to Mr. Adams' narrative of the last moments of the late Stéphane Ives, moving naked toward the door, reaching for the head jamb . . . ."

"Why is 'naked' important?" I asked.

"It showed he had no key or any other tool with him. It suggested that the safe could be opened by a button or a lever somewhere on the door itself, or in its frame. When I hit the right place, the door and a section of the floor pivoted quite rapidly. I must confess that the suddenness of the movement took me by surprise."

"All quite pedestrian, really," Mycroft grumbled. "I would have realized all of it, were it not for the infinite distractions offered by the small and, in the end, irrelevant puzzles, but the *camera obscura* inside was a touch of genius."

Several of the mirrors in the hall of Sunset Manor were, in reality, semi-transparent, part of a system that I can only describe as "conductor of light". With the help of prisms hidden inside the very walls, they projected a real-life image of the room on a screen inside the first chamber of the safe. Anyone there could see everything that happened on the outside.

"It entertained me for a moment, that silent projection of you all grasping at the door," Holmes remembered, "but I soon recovered and, finding a dark lantern, began to explore my whereabouts. I knew the safety room must needs have another exit. No man would allow himself to be starved there, while his enemies waited on the other side.

"What I found was a short corridor and a stairway that went deep into the earth. On the first landing, I found Mrs. Hudson's son."

"He'd been climbing the stairs in a hurry when the pain in his chest made him lose consciousness and fall," I said. "The weak heart is as an hereditary condition in the Hudson male line as, I am told, is the cavalier attitude toward it."

"Lestrade has since explored the full extent of the stairway," Holmes continued. "It leads to an abandoned mews house, outside the walls of the property. The secret door there is quite easy to open from the inside, but devilishly hard to move – or even to see – from the outside, unless one knows exactly where it is and has a special key."

"Hudson told me he decided to enter that way in case Sunset Manor was under observation," I said. "It was well thought. If he only hadn't tried to run all the way up the stairs!"

Holmes came to the defense. "He knew we'd need him and his tools to crack open the strongbox inside the safety chamber, where The Red Death and assorted documents concerning *Le Fantôme* were kept. That combination had really died with Ives."

"What about the shares?" I exclaimed. "I know the whole case has been kept out of the papers, but – "

"We have a tight lid on it," explained Mycroft Holmes. "As far as anyone outside of our circle knows, the steel chamber remains inviolate and its contents a mystery. We also have people following the trail of the shares – there are primary buyers, and buyers who buy from them, and then there are hoarders. And we begin to see it all converge. It's tantalizing. But we will flush *Le Fantôme* out in the end."

"These men combine ruthlessness and cunning, a volatile mixture. I'm afraid that neutralizing their organization will be a little harder than you or our friends in the Continent may expect," said Sherlock Holmes, using a forceps to pick an ember from the fire and light his pipe. And but for the crackle of the coal, the room fell silent, as the pungent smoke filled the air.

The Adventure of the
Deathstalker
by Susan Knight

Early on a dull morning in late October, Holmes and I were just about to tuck into the usual substantial breakfast, as provided by the inestimable Mrs. Hudson, when that lady herself reappeared clutching the morning mail. For once there was nothing for Holmes, and only the most recent copy of *The Lancet* for me, along with a letter addressed in a hand I failed to recognise.

"Well, well," I remarked, having perused it. "Here's a surprise – an invitation from an old colleague of mine, Major Blunt, to visit him the weekend after next. Good Lord, I don't think I have seen Blunt since Afghanistan! Or maybe at that reunion – ? Let me think . . . ."

"Pass the butter dish, Watson, would you. It is in imminent danger from your elbow."

I slid it across to him, adding, "He extends the invitation to you, Holmes."

My friend laughed.

"Now why would I wish to travel all the way to Wales at this dreary time of year?"

"How the devil did you – ? Oh, I suppose your eagle eye spotted the postmark." I consulted the envelope. "St. Asaph."

I recognised his methods.

"Elementary," he agreed, nodding. "St. Asaph in the county of Flintshire – the second smallest city in Great Britain, with a cathedral and little else. Not a place I have ever felt inclined to visit."

"All the same, listen to what Major Blunt has to say before you dismiss the offer completely."

"Well?" He formed a steeple with his fingers and gave me a quizzical look.

"Since his retirement, he has apparently taken up a rather strange hobby – namely . . ." I paused. ". . . collecting scorpions."

I sensed a subtle change in Holmes, a slight stiffening in his demeanour, a new alertness.

"He has, he says," I continued, "recently acquired a rather interesting specimen, an *Omdurman*."

"Has he indeed?" Holmes said, now truly engaged. "The little devil also known as the *Deathstalker*."

"Ah, you have heard of it."

"Do you not recall my paper on arachnids? No? Ah well, wasted on the desert air as usual, with you, Watson."

"*I* may not have read it, but Major Blunt no doubt has, and that is why, recognising a fellow enthusiast, nay a specialist, he has invited you in particular down to stay."

Holmes chopped the top off his boiled egg with a degree of smug satisfaction.

"In that case, please inform your friend that I should be delighted to accept his generous offer."

Ten days later, however, it was a highly disgruntled Holmes I found unpacking his bags when I joined him in his bedroom, having just arrived at Major Blunt's establishment in Wales.

"I had not realised, Watson," he stated in accusatory tones, as though it were my fault, "that we should land ourselves into the middle of a veritable house party. I had assumed that we were invited for a quiet stay with someone who shared my zoological interests. Instead, I find myself in Bedlam."

To tell the truth, I had been taken aback myself, first at the grandeur of the Major's mansion – thanks, as it turned out, to an inheritance from Mrs. Blunt's father, who had made his money in soap – and then at the sheer number of people presently in occupation. Hoards, it seemed, of noisy young folk in particular who had the run of the place, the daughters of the house and their friends. In addition, our host proved no longer to be the trim young man of my memory. He had quite gone to flesh, with the hair that had once graced his head now descended to his chin in the abundance of a reddish beard. Furthermore, John Blunt, rather than living up to his name, displayed the vague geniality of one devoted to an obsession, to whom the practical concerns of daily life were mere distractions, and he seemed quite oblivious of the present hullaballoo. In vain, I looked for the disciplined soldier he had once been, and then had to ask myself if he had ever truly been that soldier. Had he not always chased butterflies, so to speak, even on the battlefield?

That he was delighted to see us, there could be no question. No sooner had we stepped through the door than he would have carried us off then and there to view his collection, had his wife not stepped forward and demurred.

"The gentlemen will surely wish to go to their rooms and rest, John, after their long journey." She turned to us with a warm smile. "Don't let

John bully you. Tea will be served in the drawing room, when you are quite ready for it"

Angharad Blunt was a Welsh woman in her forties, plain of countenance, it must be said, and possessed, in particular, of an unfortunately long nose, but with an amiable manner that offset these deficiencies.

"Speaking for myself, Mrs. Blunt," I replied, "I should greatly appreciate a cup of tea now, if that is at all possible. There was little enough in the way of refreshments on the train, and the coach trip from Rhyl has left me quite parched."

Rather to my surprise, Holmes nodded in agreement, since he is usually indifferent to such bodily needs as liquid refreshment.

"Well then, gentlemen, this way. Jenkins can arrange for your bags to be taken to your rooms."

Jenkins turned out to be the butler, very properly clad in black, and sporting spotless white gloves, a long, thin lugubrious individual of considerable age, with a Welsh accent so pronounced that, at first, I thought him to be speaking that unfamiliar Celtic language itself. (In my account, I have rendered his speech into the Queen's English for the convenience of my readers.) He had come with the house, as Major Blunt told me later, a devoted old retainer.

Mrs. Blunt led the way into a large and comfortably furnished parlour, at which point a tiny but noisy dog rushed over to us and fastened its teeth onto Holmes's leg. He kicked it away with such force that the creature let out a loud squeak of protest.

"Oh, my poor Emperor Tzu! What has the nasty man done to you? Come to mamma, my poppet!" These words boomed from a lady of advanced years and considerable girth, seated on a chaise longue. She presented a formidable sight, decked out in a huge dress of bright turquoise silk in a style harking back many decades, her wide crinoline skirt bedecked with so many frills and flounces that she called to my frivolous mind the vision of an elderly Thetis rising from the sea. Her hair, surely coloured in some way to achieve that unnatural look of tarnished brass, was similarly old-fashioned in style, parted in the middle, with ringlets of curls cascading down each side of her craggy face. A many-stranded necklace of pearls hung around the double chins of her neck, along with a lorgnette.

She glared at us, clutching the dog to her bosom.

"The thing bit me," Holmes said, in a cold voice.

"The *thing*! The *thing*!" Now she was become a veritable Lady Bracknell.

386

"Oh dear, Mr. Holmes," said Mrs. Blunt. "I hope you aren't badly hurt."

"I don't suppose I will die of it, unless the dog is rabid."

"The Emperor Tzu himself might have died of that kick, sir," the lady said angrily. "Poor little darling!"

She cuddled the pampered creature, letting it lick her face. Holmes, beside me, scowled in disgust.

All in all, not an auspicious start to our visit, and Mrs. Blunt tried her best to calm tempers down.

"Well, well" she said. "Neither party badly hurt, so not too much harm done. Gentlemen, may I introduce Lady Manning, a relation of my husband's. Lady Manning – Dr. Watson and Mr. Sherlock Holmes."

I am afraid mention of my friend's name made no impression at all on the lady. However, she raised her lorgnette to her eyes and looked upon me with interest.

"A doctor!" she said. "Well, now – "

Before she could launch into a list of her ailments, which intention I discerned, from bitter experience, in her eager expression, Mrs. Blunt hastily added, "Dr. Watson served with John in the East, you know."

"Come and sit next to me, Doctor," Lady Manning said, patting the narrow area of the chaise longue that she herself did not occupy.

It was an order rather than a request and, although I was reluctant, given the proximity of the wretched dog's sharp little teeth, courtesy overcame my misgivings and I sat myself beside her.

The antipathy The Emperor Tzu had shown towards Holmes was not, I am relieved to say, displayed towards me. I was encouraged by Lady Manning to pet him, which I did, and in return he licked my hand and wagged a fluffy tail.

"He likes you, Doctor!" she said, her smile revealing long yellow teeth, stained and notched – Could it be? – by clay pipe smoking. Surely not? I had observed such signs before among people living in the slums of the East End of London, yet I could hardly think it of a woman of the upper class.

I couldn't puzzle the mystery for long, since at that point a maid arrived with the tea, followed by Major Blunt, two big, ruddy-cheeked girls of about fourteen or fifteen hanging off either side of him. These were introduced to us as Blodwen and Gwen.

"Our daughters," the Major announced proudly, while the two maidens collapsed in giggles.

More girls, the friends, tumbled in after, and descended on the plates of sandwiches and buns with a ferocity that left little or nothing for Holmes and myself. Even The Emperor consumed more than I did, her Ladyship

387

feeding rich titbits into his ever-open muzzle. No matter, for at least we could enjoy cup after cup of strong and reviving tea, which was all I really wanted.

The house party, as it turned out, was being held to celebrate a Celtic festival marking the end of summer.

"I was quite cross with John for inviting you this particular weekend, since I am sure you weren't expecting such mayhem," Mrs. Blunt said, smiling indulgently at her husband. "He can be so thoughtless, sometimes."

"Not at all," I felt I had to reply, since Holmes was scowling the more. "It will be most interesting to experience your Welsh customs."

"Welsh poppycock!" exclaimed Lady Manning. "A pagan excuse for all sorts of goings-on. The Emperor and I shall play no part in it, as I am sure, Dr. Wilson, you will not, when you see the nature of things. No, indeed, Angharad." She turned to Mrs. Blunt. "Try as you might, you shall not persuade me."

Judging from the expression on the latter's face, she had no intention of so doing. It was all rather discomfiting, and I couldn't help but wonder into what exactly we had landed ourselves.

Holmes and I soon made our excuses and departed to our rooms, conducted thither by the same maidservant, Polly, who had served the tea.

"What is this festival exactly?" I asked her as we climbed the stairs.

"'Tis *Nos Calan Gaeaf*, of course," she replied in a tone which suggested that surely everyone knew of it. "When the speerits go wandering and the *Yr Hwch Ddu Gwta* comes a-looking for souls to eat."

I nodded, but wasn't much the wiser.

"Three whole days of this!" exclaimed Holmes, once Polly had departed. "Good Heavens, Watson, how will I bear it?"

"Remember the Deathstalker," I said. "And the rest of Major Blunt's collection, which I am sure will divert you."

"Ah yes. I suppose I can hide away with those predatory arachnids. They will no doubt prove better company than that below. And who, the deuce, is Lady Manning?"

I confessed that I had no better knowledge than himself. Major Blunt and I had never been close enough to exchange personal histories.

"It is you he wanted to see," I added.

"Clearly, although apparently no one else in this backwater has heard of me."

The Major was lurking in the hall when we descended the stairs a while later, agog to carry us off instantly to what he called his menagerie. This proved to be a stone-built outhouse in the garden, with a stove constantly fired up to keep the heat high enough for his tropical pets. The walls were lined with terrariums, some containing sand, some stones and peaty soil. Holmes stared into them appreciatively.

"Ah," he said, "*Pandimus imperator, Heterometrus.* Yes, I have seen these specimens before. But can these be . . . ." Peering into another case. "Yes, indeed. A pair of the genus *Androctonus?*"

"Ha! Trust an expert like yourself to know all the Latin names." Major Blunt rubbed his hands together in pleasure. "Big fellows, aren't they?"

I gazed at the horrid looking things and wondered that anyone could feel enthusiasm for them.

"See the slender *pedipalps,* Watson?" Holmes went on. "And the distinctive thick tail."

"The *pedipalps?*"

"The *pincers,*" explained Major Blunt. "As for its rear end, that's why in English those particular chappies are dubbed 'Fattails'. Get a sting from them and you'll soon know about it!" He laughed merrily, though I failed to appreciate the humour.

Holmes had already moved on.

"Now where is this famous *Leiurus quinquestriatus* of yours?" he asked.

"Over here," the Major replied, moving to another sand-lined case. "Here she is. All by herself, for I'd be afraid of her eating her friends and relations otherwise. As well as her husband," he added. "Beware the female of the species, gentlemen. Much more aggressive, don't you know." He gave a little grin. "Naughty of me, perhaps, but I call this one 'Lady Manning'."

The scorpion in question, yellow with a striped back, seemed to be staring back at us balefully, as if longing to grab us with its *pedipalps* and sink the sting in its curled tail into our flesh. Holmes, however, was enchanted. I trusted that this would make up for the other disappointments of the trip.

"Exactly how poisonous is it?" I asked.

"Not as deadly to humans as her Ladyship's nickname suggests," Blunt replied. "Unless you are old or sick or very young. Her prey is usually insects or small mammals, like mice. However, I'd strongly advise against getting bitten by Lady Manning. Very painful, what, Holmes?"

"So I understand."

"Who is Lady Manning exactly?" I asked, while my friend continued to study the Deathstalker, and it him. "The real one, not the scorpion."

Major Blunt looked doleful.

"That's a very good question, Watson," he replied.

"You must know, surely."

"She's some distant relation of mine, fallen on hard times. That is to say, her late husband blew the lot . . . ." He lowered his voice for some reason. "Gambling dens, vice, that sort of thing. She only found out after he died. Nothing left of her fortune."

"Good Heavens! The poor woman."

"Poor us, rather. She landed on us for a short stay – seven months ago. Not a penny to her name, but the way she carries on – well, you'd think she was Lady of the Manor. She's a great trial to us, never mind the expense. Eats like a horse. And drinks . . . ."

I thought him rather indiscreet, talking in that way to us whom, in truth, he hardly knew. However, I felt I had to ask why he didn't simply send her on her way.

"That's what Angharad says. But Aunt Hermione is a frail old woman. I just haven't the heart."

She hadn't looked at all frail to me.

"She must surely have other relations she could go to."

"They won't take her."

There seemed no more to be said on the subject. Holmes called Major Blunt over to another of his collection, and they embarked on an intense discussion which held no interest for me. I excused myself then and took myself out into the garden, rejoicing in the fresh autumn air after the stifling atmosphere within the menagerie.

That part of North Wales is pleasant, rolling hills without the grandeur of the mountains of Snowdonia further west. In fact, a gentleman I found out strolling, like myself, was able to inform me that the city of St. Asaph – it still felt strange to me to give such a grandiose designation to such a tiny place – lay in the Vale of Clwyd on the River Elwy, and that, if I was interested in historic remains, I should certainly visit both the cathedral and the ruined castle in the nearby town of Rhuddlan.

This Mr. Broderick Williams, as he introduced himself, was a distinguished-looking, sleekly clean-shaven man in his early fifties. He proved to be half-brother to Angharad on the maternal side. I should soon have guessed a relationship, for he possessed the same long nose that she did, giving him, together with his leanness, something of the appearance of a greyhound.

"You are here for the festival?" I asked.

"For my sins," he replied with a smile, "being father to a young lady who wouldn't miss the party for the world. My wiser wife has stayed home with our two boys, judging them to be too young for the excitement. That is her excuse, at least."

"Please tell me more of what to expect," I said. "My friend and I had no idea we would be attending such an event."

"No?" He sounded surprised. *Why are you here, then?* was quite clearly the question in his mind.

"Major Blunt invited myself and Mr. Holmes down from London to view his collection of scorpions."

The other laughed. "Oh dear. You poor things. John is a renowned bore on the subject."

"For my part, I should be happy never to see a scorpion again, but my friend is quite fascinated. He has written on the subject, do you see, and was especially keen to see the Deathstalker."

Mr. Williams shot me an astonished glance.

"The what?"

"It seems to be a rare-enough specimen and highly poisonous."

"Indeed. Well, good luck to them both. I have to say I prefer more harmless pets. Dogs for instance – Lady Manning's over-indulged little tyke excepted." He shook his head in repugnance. "But you wished me to tell you about the festival of *Nos Calan Gaeaf.*"

I nodded.

"It's full of superstition, as you might expect. A night when spirits walk abroad. For your own good, Doctor, tomorrow evening please avoid churchyards, stiles, and crossroads."

"Why?"

"Because that's where the spirits gather, of course."

"So it is really just a Welsh name for Hallowe'en."

"Well, of course the origins are the same, but there are specific traditions and beliefs associated with *Calan Gaeaf* that you won't find in that festival. For instance, on the eve, a bonfire is lit and only the women and children dance round it. Everyone writes their name upon a stone and throws it into the fire. Then, when the blaze dies down, we all run home as fast as we can."

"It sounds very energetic," I said. "Especially for the ladies."

"If you were to linger by the dying fire," Mr. Williams informed me in ominous tones, "your very soul would be in danger of being devoured by *Yr Hwch Ddu Gwta.*"

"I heard that nonsense before from the maid. What does it mean?"

"It's an evil spirit – a black sow without a tail. Even worse if it is accompanied by *Y Ladi Wen*, the headless white lady."

"I shall endeavour to avoid the pair of them at all costs. So is that the end of it, then?"

"By no means. The following morning, the stones in the fire are checked. If your own stone is clean, your name burned off, then that signifies good luck. However, woe to you if your stone is missing. You will be sure to die a short time afterwards."

On that grim note – although, as Mr. Williams said, there was much more to the festival – by then, we had completed a circuit of the grounds, and since it was getting late, bade each other a cordial farewell for the present and went our separate ways to dress for dinner.

This repast, although good and plentiful, was marred by the domineering presence of Lady Manning: Her demands, her complaints, her loudness, her sheer greed. I was made sit beside her, as the new favourite. Holmes, for his part, facing me across the table, cast reproachful looks my way, and winced every time the woman opened her mouth to speak, which was almost constantly. Our only respite, in truth, was when she opened that same orifice to insert food within it, and even then she didn't always keep quiet while masticating. Her chief grievances were directed at our hostess who, it seemed, could do nothing right. Mrs. Blunt's dress (too youthful for a matron), her hair (not frizzed enough, her Ladyship touching her own bright locks with satisfaction), her demeanour (so sulky) all came in for comment over the bone-marrow toast.

"Sometimes, indeed," she said self-pityingly, "I think you don't want me here, any of you."

Angharad Blunt cast her eyes down, while the Major protested, "Not at all, Aunt Hermione."

"For if that were the case – you know, if I was no longer welcome – well, there is always the workhouse for the likes of a poor abandoned widow."

Here Lady Manning lifted a lacy kerchief to dab at an eye which to me looked to be quite dry.

"Goodness, Aunt, we would never turn you out! Would we, my dear?"

Angharad, head still down, shook her head.

"All the same," the Major continued, "you might – you . . . might, well, er – "

"What might I, pray?"

The Major quailed under the gimlet gaze, the hardened tones.

"Excuse me, Madam." The butler had noiselessly approached her Ladyship from behind, making her start. "Would your doggie like the bones?"

"Bones, Jenks!" she screeched. "Do you want to kill the poor innocent creature? Cause him to choke to death? Well, I suppose you do, at that. I know how much you hate him." She turned to me. "The sensitive little thing can tell, you see, who are his enemies, Dr. Wilson. That is why sometimes he has to defend himself against those who wish him harm." She glared across at Holmes. "He cannot abide Jenks."

The butler, expressionless, was meanwhile removing the plate from in front of her, the bones sucked clean.

"Give them to the yard dogs, Jenkins," said Mrs. Blunt, adding pointedly. "*They* will enjoy the treat."

"Yes, by all means throw them to those barbarians," Lady Manning said, as though giving her permission. "The Emperor Tzu has a delicate palate, Dr. Wilson." (I had given up correcting her regarding my name.) "My poppet would appreciate some marrow, if there is any remaining."

She had saved none of her own, but now looked at my plate accusingly, as if I might have thought to leave something for her pet. As Jenkins left the room with the bones, she remarked, "Can you believe it, Dr. Wilson, that horrid man is the reason my dear sweet innocent pup is forbidden to sit at table with me? Jenks has refused point blank to serve if The Emperor be present, on the pretext that he has been nipped a couple of times." She turned to Mrs. Blunt. "I am astonished, Angharad, how you let yourself be bullied by a mere underling. I am sure, Dr. Wilson," she addressed me again, "you would never countenance your staff making so free."

Thoughts of the excellent Mrs. Hudson brought a smile to my lips. "I am afraid I could hardly claim to have staff. We live very modestly, you know."

"You wife surely has help."

"My wife – " But I wasn't about to discuss my dear late Mary with this woman, nor to explain my current living arrangements. In any case, Lady Manning had moved on to another subject.

"I suppose I should, in all honesty, Angharad," quoth she, and even I could hear how she mangled the pronunciation of the mellifluous Welsh name, "bequeath *you* my pearls." Here she toyed with her necklace. "They are all I have to leave, since Reginald abandoned me to my sorry fate." Another recourse to the lace handkerchief. "However, I fear that you wouldn't appreciate them as you should, and so . . . ." Now she lifted the lorgnette that lay, with the pearls, across her vast bosom, and studied Gwen and Blodwen at the far end of the table, "I have decided that one of your girls shall inherit these priceless gems. Which of them, I haven't yet chosen. Whoever shall prove herself the more deserving." After which speech, and leaving the girls gaping at her, and the friends giggling, she dropped her lorgnette and focussed her attention on the dish just placed in front of her. This proved to be *cawl*, a traditional Welsh soup, substantial in nature, which, though her Ladyship pronounced it to be unsatisfactory – "It is overly salted as usual, Angharad." – she consumed to the last drop.

If every meal was to be like this, it must prove quite an ordeal. Of course, Holmes and I were here for the weekend only, but the Major and his poor wife had to put up with her Ladyship, day in and day out. I wondered that they could.

This sentiment was echoed by Williams, when the ladies had withdrawn, allowing us men to partake in the traditional way of port or brandy and cigars.

"Really, John," he said to our host. "I cannot understand how you let that dreadful woman bully my sister so. It makes me rage."

Major Blunt looked sheepish.

"I know," he replied, "and I have tried. But you see, the poor woman has come down so far in the world. She is used to a much more splendid way of life than we can supply. In any case, she behaves much better without an audience, when we are alone with her."

Holmes, who had remained largely silent during the meal and subsequently, leaned back in his chair, and drew on his cigar before speaking.

"I rather doubt that," he said.

"No, no. I can assure you. She can even be almost quiet sometimes."

"I didn't mean that," Holmes replied. "I meant that I doubt she was used to a much more splendid way of life, as you put it."

"Oh yes. She has told us all about it."

Holmes put on the superior expression that I recognised so well of one who knows better.

"I grant perhaps many decades ago, that might possibly have been the case, but her dress is outmoded and shabby – the silk quite rotten in fact. And as for those renowned pearls, I am convinced they are paste."

"My dear fellow," I said. "Surely – "

"Before dinner, I took advantage of some moments of calm to visit your library," he informed Major Blunt. "I was fairly sure no loud young person would break in on me there. However, what I did find was a *Burke's Peerage*, alongside a volume of *Burke's Landed Gentry*."

"Did you, indeed?" replied the Major. "Well bless my soul, I had no idea we owned such things. We inherited the library, and in fact, the house itself, do you see, from Angharad's father. And I am afraid I'm not much of a reader – Unless, of course, it be works like your own most excellent paper on scorpions, Mr. Holmes."

"Well," my friend replied, brushing aside the compliment, "had you investigated, you would have found no mention of Reginald Manning in either volume."

"You mean," said Williams eagerly, the greyhound sniffing the hare, "she isn't who she says she is? She has been pulling the wool over our eyes all this time?"

"As to that," Holmes continued. "I have no means of knowing. Perhaps she fell prey to a scoundrel who led her to believe he was of noble birth."

"Or perhaps there never was a Reginald at all!" Williams was chasing the hare now. "Perhaps she isn't even related to you, John."

"I am sure she is," the Major replied, though quite evidently the new intelligence had shaken him. "She arrived with excellent credentials, you know, as some sort of a cousin of my late mother. Used to play with her as a child. Best friends. Knew all about her."

"The cook's daughter, perhaps." Williams sank his teeth into the hare with vast satisfaction. "I have always thought that though she has pretensions to class, she displays low habits."

"Like the pipe smoking," Holmes said, pre-empting me as usual. "And the rum drinking. Her breath stinks of pineapple."

That I hadn't particularly noticed, or at least had thought her Ladyship was wearing a rather stale and pungent perfume.

"Well, well." The poor Major was quite distressed. "Yes, indeed, she likes her pipe, but told us it was a habit she developed on the Continent. As for the pineapple rum – she says it settles her stomach"

Both Holmes and Williams snorted in derision.

We were all agreed, however, that nothing should mar the forthcoming festivities. Afterwards, it would be up to the Major and his wife to decide whether or not to challenge the lady in question regarding her identity.

The following day was *Nos Calan Caeaf*, that on which the spirits were said to walk. Holmes and I, feeling somewhat superfluous amid the bustle of preparations, headed out with Broderick Williams to walk the few miles to Rhuddlan to view the castle there, a handsome-though-ruined pile dating from the Thirteenth Century. In truth, Holmes was soon bored by the history of the place, as recounted in considerable detail by Williams, and took himself off to sit upon a piece of tumbled masonry, while we two explored further. Since I fear my readers might well share the indifference of my friend, I shall not burden them with repeating the history of the place, which, if they are interested, can be found by consulting a *Baedeker* or an encyclopaedia.

Having fully admired the ruins and the pleasing prospect of the river than ran beside it, we took refreshments in the adjacent Castle Inn before heading back to St. Asaph.

There we found the construction of the bonfire almost completed. It rose high over a patch of rough ground away from the well-kept lawn, the young ladies flitting like butterflies around it and quite getting in the way of the workers. On spotting us, a decidedly pretty maiden of thirteen or thereabouts rushed up to Williams.

"Oh, Papa," she said. "I cannot wait for night to fall! Gwen says that if I make my room dark and then look in the mirror, I might see the face of my future husband, but if I see a skull I shall die within the year. Imagine! Oh, Heavens, I cannot bear it!"

"I think, my dear Sophy," he replied, caressing her curls, "that if you look in a mirror in the dark, you are likely to see nothing at all."

"Well, in that case, Gwen says I must throw the peel of an apple over my shoulder, and how it falls will form the initials of my future husband."

She flew off as quickly as she had arrived, having been summoned in peremptory fashion by the self-same Gwen. Williams smiled at us and shook his head.

"Girls and their fancies," he said.

"She is quite charming," I remarked.

Luckily, I thought, Sophy hadn't inherited the long Williams nose, her own snubby one sitting in perfect harmony with the rest of her face.

What to do next? Holmes had been dragged away willingly by Major Blunt back to the menagerie. Williams and I betook ourselves to the nearby Cathedral of St. Asaph, a saint of whom I knew nothing until enlightened at some length by my companion. We spent an hour or more exploring that Gothic construction and surrounding graveyard, Williams reassuring me that it was quite safe, even given the day that we were in it, to linger there *before* sunset, though – with a wink – to be sure to avoid it once darkness fell.

"You don't really believe the superstitions, do you?" I asked.

"Not a jot," he replied, "although I should rather prefer to be safe than sorry. Now, come and look at this most interesting inscription, Watson."

He proved rather more intrigued by the gravestones than I, but finally, his commentary on the subject faltering, we addressed more personal matters. I discovered, hardly to my surprise, that he was a school teacher with a particular specialisation in history.

"So what exactly does your friend do?" he asked me, as we made our way out through the lychgate.

"Do?" I asked, somewhat bewildered.

"Well, I assume from his interest in scorpions and the fact that he has written a paper on the subject, that he is either a learned arachnologist, or at least an entomologist."

"Good Heavens!" I exclaimed, astounded. "That is just one of his many hobbies. Really, Williams, have you never heard of Sherlock Holmes?"

He shook his head. Not heard of the greatest detective of our time! What a backwater we found ourselves in! I soon corrected his ignorance.

"A policeman?" said he. "I should never have guessed it."

"Not a policeman, Williams. A private detective."

"I see." He became thoughtful, and we spent the rest of the walk back in silence.

Upon entering the house, I was immediately waylaid by Polly, who said that Lady Manning particularly wished to speak to me. I received the news with, I am afraid, extremely muted enthusiasm, but again felt that courtesy required me to attend the lady. I found her, as before, on the chaise longue, in the self-same turquoise dress, The Emperor scampering at her feet and showing great delight at my presence, wagging his tail furiously and licking the hand I stretched out to pet him. His mistress looked on approvingly. There was a cloyingly sweet smell in the place that, now I had been apprised of the lady's habits, I recognised to be that of pineapple rum.

"You wished to talk to me, your Ladyship," I said.

Of course, it concerned her health. She was soon describing, in vivid and disconcertingly grisly detail, various symptoms, the which, I rather felt, could be put down simply to a daily overindulgence in rich foods, combined with a total lack of exercise. However, opining to myself that Lady Manning wouldn't appreciate such a forthright diagnosis, and knowing how sufferers often prefer to treat themselves with medication rather than change the way they live, I suggested she might try papaya tablets, which should aid her digestion, and certainly do her no harm.

"It has proved efficacious in a number of my patients," I told her.

She nodded graciously, as I wrote her a prescription, then frowned.

"But you know, I am sure that my affliction is partly the fault of the Blunts. The way they vary mealtimes, you know. Regular ingestion is so important, is it not? No wonder I suffer, given the inconsistency of arrangements in this establishment. It wouldn't be borne for a moment, Dr. Wilson, if I had the running of the place."

Her chief grievance, as it emerged, was that on this same night she would be required to wait for her supper until after the festivities.

"My stomach will hardly support the delay," she said. "I am sure that if you speak to them as a doctor, you can convince them that I must not wait, and that dinner must be at the usual hour."

I hardly thought that the timetable of events would be changed on a whim of hers, but suggested a compromise.

"Perhaps dinner could be brought to you earlier, your Ladyship."

"You mean that I should eat by myself, alone?" In her displeasure at the suggestion, she was turned to Lady Bracknell again. "Why should I be discommoded for their sport? Why should I be dismissed from their table? A personage of my breeding treated like a poor relation!" (Which is what she was, of course.) "It is too cruel, Doctor. But I know their game. They want to drive me away."

In vain I tried to sooth her, even though, again, it was naught but the truth.

"No, no. You cannot understand what I suffer here. How constantly *she* plots to get rid of me." She struck a tragic note. "I shall be in the workhouse before another year is out. There, or in the grave, you mark my words, Doctor. And it will be all *her* fault. That soap-maker's daughter! Blunt, you see, is quite under her thumb. Shameful in a man, but the hussy winds him round her little finger!" Lady Manning was working herself to a frenzy of self-pity, The Emperor leaping up and down betimes in excitement, and contributing to the general commotion with his yelps.

"Perhaps," I said, "I can ask Jenkins, or," in response to her dark look, "Polly to bring you a little snack – to fill the gap, so to speak before you join us all later for supper."

"Dr. Wilson," she said, instantly calm, "you have saved my life."

She could, of course, quietly have requested the same from Polly earlier, but I understood her. She had to be the centre of attention, and resented it greatly when she was not.

Now she begged me to stay with her, patting the space remaining on the chaise longue with a fat, beringed hand, and – Good Lord! – a flirtatious fluttering of her eyelashes.

"For I am sure," said she, "an educated man like yourself has no interest in such silly superstitious antics, the like of which will be indulged in tonight. Let you stay here and enjoy some civilised conversation with me."

Courtesy to an elderly lady was all very well, but I wasn't prepared to forgo the festivities – especially given the alternative she offered – and, as politely as possible, informed her that, on the contrary, I was most interested in observing local customs.

"As you please," she replied coldly.

At that moment, Gwen burst into the room, a rock in her hand.

"Good Heavens, girl, whatever have you there?" Lady Manning exclaimed. "Have you been sent to stone me to death?"

"Not at all, Aunt Hermione. Everyone is writing their names on rocks to throw into the fire. We thought you might like to do so as well."

"I? Have I not made it perfectly clear that I wish to take no part in these tomfooleries?"

"But it's for good luck!"

The girl looked at me. Her expression wasn't quite pleasant, sly in fact, and I wondered what she was up to. Then she smiled at her aunt, holding out the rock.

"Should I, Doctor?" Lady Manning appealed to me. "What do you think?"

I was about to make a non-committal reply when Gwen forestalled me.

"Dr. Watson will, I am sure, be wanting to put his name on a rock, too," She pulled another out of her pocket.

I laughed. "Well, I can always do with some good luck." I took the proffered rock and signed it.

"As you know," Lady Manning remarked, "The Emperor and I will not be attending the bonfire, but perhaps you, Doctor, would be so kind as to do the necessary on my behalf."

I bowed assent, and thereupon she took the other rock and inscribed her name upon it.

"Only for you, Gwen," she said, fingering her pearls. "You're a good girl, aren't you?"

"I hope so, Auntie." Gwen smiled winningly.

"Give your Auntie a kiss then."

The girl did so and then turned away, an expression on her face I can only describe as triumphant. What exactly was she up to?

"But how," I asked, "if the names are burned off in the fire, will you be able to tell whose is whose?"

"That's easy," the girl replied. "We count up the ones with no names on them."

It sounded random to me, but after all, it was just a silly childish game, wasn't it?

Having asked Polly to bring a sandwich and glass of milk to her Ladyship, I dressed myself in my overcoat and muffler and made for the garden where the rest of the party was already gathered. Rather to my surprise, Holmes had also deigned to attend the bonfire, although he resisted attempts to throw a stone bearing his name into it.

"I make my own luck," he said dismissively as the rest of us merrily cast our stones into the flames, Lady Manning's among them.

Holmes and I then stood for a short while, observing the flickering fire and the people dancing around it, but my companion had soon had enough of what seemed to me a rather charming spectacle, claiming that he had no intention of catching a chill on this autumn night.

"That's surely unlikely," I replied. "For my part, I am almost too hot."

"Will you not accompany me then?" he asked.

"I will follow shortly," I replied, and with a shrug he started back to the house.

Call me fanciful, but the sight of the girls and women dancing, silhouettes against the fierce blaze, or, as they reached the far side, their Maenad faces illuminated across it, aroused in me a sense of the primitive forces that lie beneath our veneer of civilisation. Over how many centuries had this same ritual been performed, and what pagan gods to appease? It was both a disturbing and pleasurable notion, and when the fire finally died down, I ran back to the house with the others, quite as though believing I was being chased by a horde of evil spirits.

Alas, all good humour was dispelled by the row that ensued over supper. In her enforced solitude, alone but for the company of Emperor Tzu and – eschewing the milk – a bottle of pineapple rum, Lady Manning had clearly been brooding over what she considered her unjust treatment at the hands of a soap maker's daughter and her lily-livered spouse. Without reporting further the language employed (and that of a fishwife might have been rather less expressive), I can reveal that the result was Angharad Blunt leaving the table in tears, the Major staring at the tablecloth in distress, Williams seething, the girls exchanging glances and suppressing giggles, Jenkins looking daggers, and Lady Manning sitting back in her chair, exulting at the chaos she had caused.

We finished the meal in silence. Her Ladyship, to everyone's relief, then expressed her intention of retiring early – the company, as she remarked, having turned so dull. Polly and Jenkins had to support her as she banked, rather like a great galleon about to keel over, while The Emperor, who had somehow escaped from confinement, snapped and growled at Holmes. Then he chased the procession up the stairs, likely to cause disaster by making a beeline for Jenkins's ankles.

"She is an absolute monster," quoth Williams a few moments later, over the port. "John, I demand that you get rid of the woman forthwith for the sake of your wife's sanity."

"Yes, yes, yes – although you know, I am sure she didn't mean all the things she said." The Major looked appealingly at us. "So unpleasant, don't you know. Drink taken . . . ."

"It's no excuse," his brother-in-law continued. "Pay for her to go away if you must. Put her on a slow boat to China, or something or the sort."

"Yes, yes," the Major repeated. "Certainly."

"You say yes, and yet do nothing!" The other struck the table with his fist. "It has gone on long enough, Blunt! The woman must be got rid of!"

While Williams sat seething and shaking his head in exasperation, I advised the Major to go to his wife. "She must need comforting," I said.

Blunt looked at me astounded then, as if the idea hadn't occurred to him before. Then he gathered himself together, and replied, "Yes, yes," again. And was gone.

Holmes, so uncommunicative that I was sure he still bore a grudge against me for landing him in this madhouse, excused himself soon after, but Broderick Williams and I remained talking until well after midnight. While trying to calm him down, I'm afraid that, in the process, the two of us consumed the greater part of a bottle of brandy before we finally retired.

After that, I slept heavily, although at a certain point was roused by what might have been the persistent ringing of a bell, followed soon after by the clamour of a barking dog.

"That d----d Emperor Tzu!" I thought to myself, burying my head in my pillow to drown out the racket, which in any case soon stopped.

I was late going down to breakfast, but in that respect wasn't alone. Lady Manning had failed yet to make an appearance – no doubt, as I reckoned, nursing a head as sore as my own. The others of the household, Holmes included, were already helping themselves from chafing dishes set on the mahogany sideboards to a huge spread of porridge, sausages, eggs, hams, venison pies, and all manner of other tasty comestibles. My poor stomach, however, could only face a round of buttered toast and blackberry jam – made, as I was told, by Angharad Blunt herself.

I complimented that lady.

"A regular taste of the countryside," I said.

She smiled wanly, her plain face made even more so by the evidence of hours of weeping, her long nose quite red.

"You must take a pot of it home with you," she said.

I rather suspected she hoped our departure was imminent, so that she might soon be excused from the duties of a hostess. For his part, Holmes, doubtless would concur enthusiastically with the notion of an early exit.

At that moment, Gwen, Blodwen, Sophy, and the other girls burst in excitedly, bearing some heavy items in their aprons.

"There's a stone missing," Blodwen cried out.

"Really, girls, it isn't the thing, you know, to come in shouting like that," Mrs. Blunt chided them. "Whatever will our guests think of you?"

"It's *hers*!" Gwen said, ignoring her mother. "We looked and looked, but hers isn't there."

"Whose?" asked the Major.

"*Hers*! The Queen Wasp."

"Do you mean your aunt, Gwen? That's no way to talk."

"What do you think, Doctor," the girl asked me. "You took her rock. Can you see it here?"

Despite Mrs. Blunt's protests, the girls spread their sooty collection on the floor for me to inspect. The names written upon them were burnt off but I had particularly remarked on the rock passed to Lady Manning by Gwen, which was of a distinctively irregular shape. Certainly, none of those in front of me resembled it. As I examined them, shaking my head, the girls around me giggled.

"You are right. It doesn't seem to be there," I said.

"Hooray!" cried Gwen. "She'll be dead soon, then, like she's always saying she will be."

"And you'll get the pearls, Gwen," said Blodwen, good-humouredly.

Her sister made a face.

The girls were instantly soundly rebuked, with Gwen in particular sent off to clean her mouth out with soap before being allowed any breakfast. Their parting giggles, however, didn't indicate any remorse.

"Well," said Major Blunt, after they had skipped off, "I wonder where is Aunt Hermione? It's late even for her."

He sent Polly to find out if Lady Manning would like breakfast sent up to her.

Did I have a presentiment then that something terrible had happened? I cannot say for certain, although I'm sure Holmes did, for he sat alert, listening.

The scream wasn't long in coming, and with a bound he was out the door and up the stairs, closely followed by Broderick Williams and the Major. I went after, first advising Angharad to stay where she was.

Polly stood shivering outside Lady Manning's bedroom, the door closed.

She muttered, "Oh, do take care, sirs!" as we entered.

I shall never forget the horrific sight that greeted us: A mountain of soiled white on the bedroom floor, that soon revealed itself to be Lady Manning in a voluminous night dress, her eyes wide and staring, her fists clutched tight across her belly, her big dead face distorted by terror. At first, I thought that, in her final agonies, she must have torn out her hair, for it lay on the carpet beside her. Then I realised it was a wig, and that, under it, she had been almost completely bald. However, now her head was crowned with a new hideous embellishment, as over it crawled a yellow scorpion, the Deathstalker itself, waving *pedipalps* in our direction as if warning us, *This is mine! Stay away!*

Stunned into silence and immobility as initially we were, it was Major Blunt, displaying at last the soldierly qualities of his rank, who

402

grabbed a dry glass from the bedside table and placed it over the creature, sliding a card underneath, thereby trapping it inside.

"I'll return her to her terrarium," he said grimly. And left to do so.

Meanwhile, Holmes was crouching down, examining the body, and then the floor around it.

"What a frightful accident," exclaimed Williams.

Holmes raised his head.

"Hardly." he replied. "Someone else must have brought the scorpion here, for I doubt very much that Lady Manning fetched it or that it found its way here by itself."

"A deliberate act!" Williams exclaimed. "My God! Who would do such a terrible thing?"

You might, I thought to myself, remembering his rage of the night before, and how the brandy could have fired him up further to a drastic and irrevocable action. And had I myself not told him how poisonous the thing was?

"Have a look at the body, Watson," Holmes said, "and tell me what you think?"

I knelt down and gently examined what I could see, mindful that the police would no doubt prefer that little was disturbed.

"There's a redness and swelling on her neck," I told him. "And a puncture mark, I think, though it is difficult to tell."

"Exactly what I found myself."

"So it was indeed the scorpion that killed her," Williams said.

"Strange, all the same," Holmes remarked. "Scorpion stings are seldom fatal."

"But the Major told us," I reminded him, "that it could happen in the case of an elderly or sick person. If Lady Manning's heart happened to be weak . . . ."

"I don't like 'if's', Watson. But you're perhaps right."

He looked thoughtful.

"But where is The Emperor?" I suddenly realised the little dog was nowhere to be seen. Or heard.

A further search – I am sorry to say, even though the creature had been difficult to like – found him where he had crawled under the bed to die. Presumably, I remarked, another victim of the scorpion.

"Not possible," Holmes said. "The stinger would have to grow back, and that couldn't have happened instantly.

"Good Lord! Then perhaps there are other scorpions here!"

We looked around ourselves anxiously. Unfortunately, the intricate pattern on the carpet provided the perfect camouflage for the darker species, and none could be easily discerned. The Major, returning as we

403

searched, announced gravely that yes indeed several others of his collection were missing.

"We should secure this room," he said. "The last thing we need is for the whole house to be overrun. I shall return properly protected and look for the runaways."

"We must inform the police," I said.

"The police?"

"Well, it's murder, isn't it?"

"Oh! I suppose." A blankness passed over his face. "Of course, you know," he said, "whoever did it might well not have intended to kill her. Only to give her a nasty jolt."

He suspects who it is, I thought. And he doesn't like it.

"Of course," Holmes said, "the police must be informed. However, in the meantime, if you will permit it, I should like to interview certain people, Major, starting with yourself."

"Me!" He looked aghast.

"Only regarding who might have had access to the menagerie."

"Oh!" His relief was evident. "That's easy. Anyone."

"You mean the place isn't locked."

"No. At least, yes – " (Holmes made an exasperated gesture.) " – in that the door is locked, but that everyone knows where the key is kept. It hangs in the kitchen."

"And was the door locked just now when you went back?"

"Er . . . no."

"So who, in this household, would know how to handle the scorpions without getting stung?"

"Everyone again, I'm afraid. You see, with such dangerous creatures around, I felt it necessary to give a demonstration."

"Would that include Williams here?"

"I say, Holmes – !" The schoolteacher reared up. "What the devil are you suggesting?"

"I am suggesting nothing. I am asking merely in order to eliminate."

"Well, I can't be eliminated, because John showed me what to do, along with everyone else, including Sophy. I hope you don't intend to cast suspicion on her as well."

Holmes smiled. "We'll see," he said, which hardly calmed the man down.

"This is preposterous!" he raged. "Some fool of an amateur detective meddling in something too big for him. Call the police, John, and send this charlatan packing."

Now I was angry on Holmes's account.

404

"You should know that Holmes is constantly called in by Scotland Yard when a case baffles them," I declared. "And he always solves it!"

"I have noticed before that you have a very short fuse, Williams," Holmes said calmly. "You really must try and control your temper."

I thought the man might have struck him then, but – luckily for him, Holmes being adept in the martial art of baritsu – Major Blunt intervened.

"Now, now, gentlemen, a woman lies before us dead. Some decorum, if you please. Mr. Holmes, you are welcome to question anyone here, but only if they are willing to talk to you."

"What do you think, Holmes?" I asked as we walked away. "Was it the brother-in-law? Last night he made threats, you know."

"Well, it could be. On the other hand, it might not."

How frustrating he was!

"The Major," Holmes continued, "suspects his wife."

"Good Heavens, surely not!"

"Could you not tell from his demeanour? His words? He thinks his wife released the scorpions to frighten Lady Manning, not to kill her. To frighten her to such an extent that she would leave of her own volition."

"Do you believe that?"

"I should first like to talk to some others. Ah, here they are."

We had entered the parlour where Angharad sat sewing, her daughters, cousin and friends huddled together on the chaise longue, no longer ebullient, but silent and shocked, their eyes red from crying. Had they then loved their aunt after all?

"Gwen and Blodwen." Holmes went up to the girls, talking in gentle tones. "I wonder could I have a little chat with you."

He looked at Angharad for permission. She nodded, somewhat surprised, and the girls most reluctantly got up. Sophy, too.

"We can go to the library," he said.

"Well, girls," he continued, once we had established ourselves in that cosy little room, "what have you to tell me?"

"Nothing." That was Gwen, ever the spokeswoman.

"Now, that isn't quite true, is it?"

He looked at them keenly, but not unkindly. Time passed. The girls fidgeted. Finally, Blodwen blurted out, "We didn't mean it!" For which outburst she was given a sharp nudge by her sister.

"I'm sure you didn't," Holmes continued in the same calm tone. "Just a silly prank that went wrong, wasn't it?"

I was aghast. These little girls killed their aunt! And her dog!

"We just thought they would give her a sting." This was Sophy. Also involved, then.

"She deserved it. She's always so horrid to Mama," said Gwen, adding defiantly. "I'm not sorry she's dead."

"Hmm, I see. But what do you think the police will say to that?"

Now they looked wide-eyed at him. Blodwen and Sophy burst into tears. Gwen, however, was of stronger stuff.

"I don't care!"

"Even when you go to prison?"

Now even Gwen looked chastened.

"However," Holmes said, ringing the bell, "there may be more to it, after all."

The ensuing silence was broken only by the occasional sob.

"We didn't know the dog would die, either," said Sophy.

Gwen sniffed. She clearly didn't care about The Emperor.

The door opened, and the butler came in, looking questioningly from Holmes and myself to the girls.

"Ah, Jenkins," Holmes said. "The police will be coming soon to arrest these girls for killing Lady Manning. What do you have to say to that?"

The man's mouth hung open.

"The girls!" he finally spluttered. "Miss Gwen and Miss Blodwen, is it?"

"And Miss Sophy. You see, they have just confessed to taking scorpions to her Ladyship's bedroom, intending to give her a fright. Instead of which, she died."

"No, that isn't right," the butler said. "No, sir."

"I agree. That isn't quite how it happened, is it, Jenkins?"

The man continued to stare at him.

"Let me tell you what I think transpired." Holmes sat back, his fingers making the customary steeple. "Lady Manning discovers the scorpions in her bed. One stings her on the neck. In a panic, she rings the bell. You respond. Meanwhile, and before you arrive, she has got up to go to the door for help. However, the agonising pain of the poison overcomes her and she sinks to the floor. You enter and find her there."

We were riveted, the girls staring wide-eyed at Holmes.

"And that," he continued, "is when you kill her. You simply hold her down, your gloved hand over her nose and mouth, until she runs out of breath."

Jenkins looked at Holmes as though he were clairvoyant. Then he broke down, the words bursting out of him.

"I didn't see the scorpions. I just saw her lying there, sir – nasty drunken old woman – and it came over me, she might die like that. I reckoned you'd all think she had a heart attack. Natural causes, you know."

He looked across at the girls. "I would have said, sir. I wouldn't have let the little girls suffer for what I did."

"I know that," Holmes replied, still in that calm voice. "You are devoted to the family, and especially to Mrs. Blunt, aren't you, Jenkins."

"I've been with Miss Angharad since she was a baby," the man said. "I hated what that woman was doing to her, sir. The life she made her lead. I saw it more than most. More even than the Major."

"How ever did you know it was the girls who let loose the scorpions?" I asked Holmes later, after the police had taken Jenkins away.

"Once I learned there was more than one of the arachnids in the bedroom, it was a simple deduction. No single person could easily transport so many. And those girls both knew how to handle the scorpions, and quite evidently were up to some mischief. I imagine it was they who removed Lady Manning's stone from the bonfire and disposed of it. To give her yet another fright."

"Very well, but how did you guess that it was the butler who killed her?"

"How did I *guess*, Watson? Really – I was reading late and heard the bell, and then the dog barking. Of course, at the time I had no idea what had transpired, but remember thinking to myself, it would only bark like that at a perceived enemy, which meant either Jenkins or myself, and knowing it wasn't me, reckoned it had to be Jenkins going to see what her Ladyship wanted."

"Then you knew all along that he did it."

"Not quite. I had to make sure it wasn't the sting after all that killed her. Luckily, Jenkins confessed."

"And the girls? What will happen to them now?"

Holmes leant back in his chair.

"They have assuredly learned their lesson, which is enough for the present. No need to complicate the issue further. But I shall impress on Major Blunt that he must keep the menagerie locked from now on and the key safely about his person."

"So it was a case of the dog that barked in the night," I said. "And the butler that did it."

"Precisely."

We left shortly afterwards to return to Baker Street (and civilisation, according to Holmes), on good terms with everyone, including even Williams, who had quite come round to the advantages of a discreet private detective. As for Lady Manning's pearls, she left no will, despite her threats, and so they went to the Major, as her closest relation. (He was. She hadn't lied after all). When he had them valued, to everyone's surprise and delight, they turned out to be genuine and worth a pretty penny to boot. Which just goes to show that even Sherlock Holmes isn't always right.

The Keeper of the
Eddystone Light
by Tim Newton Anderson

The following pages were amongst many found in Dr. Watson's dispatch box in the vaults of the bank of Cox and Company in Charing Cross. On reading it, it will be obvious why Watson never shared the case with the public, and only obliquely referred to it by a title which obscured some of the key facts. However, as all of the principles are long dead and the political issues it unveils are no longer relevant, it seems appropriate to publish it now.

The gale force winds from the west were dispersing the London Particular fog from the streets and blowing the autumn leaves from the trees along The Mall as Holmes and I walked towards the Diogenes Club. We would normally have taken a hansom, but Mycroft's summons had arrived as we were finishing our meal in Simpsons, so we supped the rest of our ale and strolled to meet Holmes's older brother.

I was worried about Holmes's health. Even if his long brisk stride suggested a man in the peak of health, it had been an extraordinarily busy year and it was only two years since he had returned after his fight with Moriarty at Reichenbach Falls. His travels and studies in Tibet had given him a deep resilience, but I was still concerned that his busy schedule would burn out that febrile intelligence and cause him to again seek support in the needle. The case of Laughing Corpse and the affair of the Pentstone Pearls had been particularly trying, and had certainly adversely affected my own constitution. The biting wind was creeping inside my clothes, and my old war wound throbbed with the cold.

It was with a grateful heart, therefore, that I entered the warmth of the Diogenes Club and handed my top coat to the unspeaking uniformed doorman. We found Mycroft nestling in a red leather armchair in front of the fire in the Stranger's Room, tapping ash from his Cuban cigar. I felt a pang of jealousy, as they had been hard to obtain since the start of the revolutionary war on the Island, but no doubt Mycroft had his own suppliers. I would not have been surprised to learn that it had come from Generalissimo Maximo Gomez himself for secret services rendered by a man Holmes said sometimes "*is* the British Government".

Mycroft waved Holmes and me to the two other chairs beside the roaring blaze in the hearth. Never one for small talk, he immediately launched into the reason for his summons.

"You will no doubt be aware of the tragic death of a keeper on the Eddystone Lighthouse," he said. "I know you have an obsessive interest in the daily newspapers, despite their tendency to exaggerate the sensational and ignore the reality behind the news."

Without having been summoned, a waiter appeared with three glasses of fine brandy. I hoped they would ease the chill in my bones, as the fire had already commenced to do.

"I have seen it, and it contains some elements of interest," said Holmes. "However, as you are aware, I have a full caseload at present."

"Paltry matters of larceny and murder, no doubt," said Mycroft. "I am sure they keep that mind of yours occupied, but they are scarcely as important as this affair."

"I confess you pique my interest," said Holmes. "I wasn't aware that the case was of sufficient weight to make you miss your evening meal and break your daily meeting with Matthew Ridley."

"This is too important for your parlour tricks, Sherlock," said Mycroft. "No doubt you reasoned that I missed the meeting because today's briefing papers are on the table next to me, and you know I would normally leave them in the office after my meeting with the Home Secretary."

"That, and the plate on top of those papers which still has some sandwich crumbs. As the evening meals are sumptuous in this establishment, you would never have had such a snack if you had enjoyed one. You had better tell us why the death of a lighthouse keeper is of such importance."

There was a glint I recognised in Holmes's eye which was only partly due to his enjoyment of the verbal sparring with his brother. I could see he was excited about the potential case. The weariness I'd seen in his shoulders – a sign no doubt everyone else would miss – had evaporated like the dew on our clothes.

"I am sure you're aware that nothing I tell you should be repeated outside of this room," Mycroft said. Holmes nodded. "And you, Doctor, must never be tempted to use this as the basis of one of potboilers about my brother." I nodded also.

"You're aware of the tensions between ourselves and Russia over the Indian Subcontinent?" he continued.

"I had been led to believe they had reduced of late after the signing of the Pamir Protocols," said Holmes, "and our joint activity to restrict Japan's expansionist activities."

"So we had hoped," said Mycroft, " but there are many people within the government who believe Russia is merely seeking to buy itself time to deal with its problems at home before moving again to expand through Afghanistan into India. Therefore, those of us who seek a lasting accord between our two nations have to operate quietly to develop a lasting agreement. A top official from the Russian state was sent in secret to Britain, far away from Whitehall, to meet with one of my representatives to work on a new accord. It was important to not only carry out these negotiations away from the watchful eyes of my colleagues, but without them being spied on by agents from other nations who would stir up trouble between ourselves and the Tsar to distract us from their own military ambitions."

"I am aware that since Bismarck's departure, the Kaiser's ambitions in Europe and South Asia have increased," said Holmes. "I don't have your knowledge of the inside machinations of international politics but, as you say, I read these papers. I also surmise that the man who died at the Eddystone Light was either the Russian negotiator or our own."

"The Russian, Ivan Lentov," said Mycroft. "My agent arrived at the lighthouse to meet him and found him dead on the rocks at its foot. Stabbed, but with the other keepers still upstairs, having never left each other's sight while the crime was committed."

"Couldn't someone else have rowed to the lighthouse, killed Lentov, and then travelled back to shore?" I asked.

"Impossible," said Mycroft. "Heavy winds prevented anyone from setting out to sea, and my man was only able to get there in a brief lull in the gale. Even then, the conditions were so bad he was forced to turn back several times before he eventually managed to arrive."

Holmes sank back into his chair and steepled his fingers.

"I see – an interesting puzzle indeed, although I think not an impossible one to solve," he said. "Why did the other keepers not discover the body?"

"They had no reason to think the man was outside in the storm," said Mycroft. "They operate in shifts, and both believed he was sleeping on another floor, as he had been the last time they had seen him."

"Of course," I said, "they could all be complicit in his murder. Perhaps they *all* stabbed him."

"I believe it would be more sensible to examine the facts before jumping to wild conclusions," Holmes said. "No doubt both the police and Mycroft's men have interrogated them. The chances of multiple murderers managing to maintain consistent stories in the face of questioning are slim. Inconsistencies would be spotted immediately, even by the average British Bobby."

411

"I've had some of my best men looking into it," said Mycroft. "I would like you to investigate and tell me not only who committed the murder and how, but if there is evidence of the Prussian State being involved. I was able to take the body brought to the morgue at Barts, so you're able to examine it tomorrow before travelling to the West Country."

Holmes and I examined Lentov's corpse early the following morning. The cold conditions meant there had been little deterioration en route to London. He had been a short, stocky, clean-shaven man. The night before, Holmes had researched his history, learning that he had grown up on the family farm before joining the civil service in St. Petersburg, and quickly working his way upwards through the ranks. He still had the muscles and calluses from a childhood on the farm, although his fingernails were clean and well-trimmed, which I was surprised hadn't aroused the suspicion of his colleagues. There was no evidence of the oil which stains the fingers of lighthouse keepers, so he couldn't have been there long.

As we had been told, the cause of death was a single stab wound to the neck, piercing deeply into his spine. There was also considerable discoloration around the wound, suggesting that the hand wielding the weapon had slammed it into place with some force. I told Holmes my findings.

"That much is obvious," he said. "What you failed to mention is the lack of defensive wounds on the hands and arms. Lentov was obviously surprised by the fatal blow and had no time to fight back against his assailant."

"Surely it's obvious from the fact that the blow was to the back of the neck that his attacker sneaked up on him," I said. "He was found outside the lighthouse, and the high winds and the noise of the waves would have masked the sound."

"That is certainly one theory, but we will not be able to test your hypothesis until we examine the lighthouse," Holmes said. "I can only hope that wind and sea haven't obscured too much of the evidence, which is why we must leave immediately for Cornwall to examine it in person."

We set off to Paddington Station by cab, and arrived with just a few moments to spare before the Cornishman Express departed for its non-stop journey to Exeter, and them on to Plymouth. From there, we took a boat to the lighthouse. During the journey, Holmes told me a little of its history. The original was completed in 1698, and was the first off-shore open-ocean lighthouse. It was destroyed in a storm, along with its creator, in 1703, and two further towers were built or modified on the site before the present structure was opened in 1882.

After the comfort of the train, the twelve-mile sea journey to the rock was torture. The gale force westerly's were still whipping up the waves, and it was only by using Mycroft's name that we were able to persuade the captain to make the trip. I'm well used to boats and love to row, but this was beyond any previous experience I have endured on the water. Our vessel was thrown up and down and from side to side as if a giant's hand was playing ball with us. My doubts about Holmes's current constitution were somewhat dispelled as he showed no signs of the seasickness I was feeling. It was only his example that prevented me from calling on the captain to turn back to shore.

We were escorted on our journey by a flight of seagulls, holding stationary against the wind before swooping down on our boat, no doubt in the hope we were a trawler which would have scraps of fish on its deck. As the lighthouse came into view on the horizon, I could see more gulls circling it, and a few more waddling on the rocks at its base, which was whitened by their droppings. This far off the coast, it must be a welcome haven, and I was certainly looking forward to enjoying its warmth and stability. The sun was setting over the ocean before us, and the light was already sweeping across the waves, reddening their crests. The structure stretched up from the rocks like a dark finger pointing to the sky, with the dying sun haloing its white granite body and the red lantern structure at its apex. By its side was the forlorn stub of the previous tower.

As we'd embarked, Holmes asked the captain to wait for us, but he refused, saying that the storm was predicted to become even worse and he couldn't risk his vessel being dashed against the rocks if he moored up. He promised to come back in a day's time, unless the weather prevented it.

"A gloomy place to be marooned," I said to my companion as we clambered on the rocks.

"On the contrary," he replied. "It's a place of safety from the storm for us and the ships that rely on it to prevent their foundering. With a few essentials, I could spend a happy time here in contemplation."

"Surely you would miss the bustle of London?" I said.

"After a while, no doubt," he said. "But as you will have observed, there are times when I prefer my own company and need little in the way of creature comforts."

As we picked our way across the rock, the door to the lighthouse opened and a tall man dressed in a pea coat and woolen cap came out and pushed against the wind in our direction, while beckoning us towards the structure. Fortunately the wind was behind us, which made our trip easier, despite the wet uneven ground beneath our feet. As I walked, I spotted a white shape on the rocks just above the sea line.

"I see even the birds have problems in this wind," I said, pointing. "Is that a dead cormorant?"

"I believe it is a gannet," he said. "I know you question my knowledge of anything that doesn't pertain to the solving of crimes, but I'm surprised you don't recognise such a common seabird."

"In the poor state it's in, it could be anything," I said. I was a little annoyed not to correctly identify the bird, having spent my childhood near the port in Stranraer.

Inside the base of the lighthouse it was at least dry, even if the temperature was only a few degrees above that outside. However, as we silently ascended the steps behind the keeper, it became warmer, and the common room was heated by a paraffin stove that gave up a welcome glow. There were two other men on wooden seats warming themselves by it.

The first man hung up his coat and hat at the back of the stove to dry and then introduced himself as Magnus Kettering, the head lighthouse keeper.

"These are my colleagues, William Rogerson and Charles Williams," he said in an accent I recognised as Cornish. Kettering was almost Holmes's height, somewhat over six feet, and had a weather-beaten face which betrayed years of exposure to the elements. Although I estimated his age to be in the late forties, his hair and full beard were snowy white. Rogerson, by contrast, was only about five-foot-three, stocky, and ruddy-faced. His red hair and side whiskers suggested Celtic heritage, confirmed when he said hello with a soft Irish accent. The birthplace of the third man, Williams, was harder to pin down, as he spoke in the universal accent of the Southern English middle classes. He was about five-foot-ten in height with broad shoulders and long dark hair. He was clean-shaven and his eyes were blue, rather than the brown I would have expected from his colouring, and shone intelligently behind thick round glasses.

"The man who discovered the body told us there would be an investigator arriving," said Kettering, "although we weren't expecting one so soon in this d----d weather."

"My name is Sherlock Holmes," he said, "and this is my colleague, Dr. Watson."

"The famous detective," said Rogerson. "Even in this outpost we get the newspapers and read of your exploits. I suppose we should be honoured."

"I don't care who you are as long as you clear up this d----d mystery," said Williams. "We have to live at close quarters, and the suggestion that one of us is a murderer makes that impossible to bear. The killer can't be one of us. I was at the top of the tower tending the light and Kettering and

Rogerson were asleep in bed. Even in this wind, this place magnifies every sound, and one of us would have heard if someone had sneaked out and back in again."

"And yet Lentov managed to go outside without being noticed," said Holmes. "I understand he wasn't missed by anyone until the government agent arrived and found his body."

"True enough," grunted Kettering. "We thought he was asleep on a lower level – although we also thought his name was Ian Leonard, and none of us suspected he wasn't from Bristol as he had claimed,"

"Are you suggesting someone came over to the island in these winds, killed Lentov, and then returned to the shore?" I asked.

"The weather was slightly calmer the night he was murdered," said Williams. "In fact, it was still enough for thick fog, which meant I had to sound the bells."

"I can see that this is upsetting in such a tight-knit group," said Holmes. "How long have you all been stationed here?"

"Williams and I have manned the lighthouse for two years," said Kettering. "Rogerson arrived a few days before Lentov."

"Surely you must have thought two new keepers in a short period unusual?" I said.

"Not at all," said Williams. "This life isn't for everyone. We have seen lots of keepers come and go in our time at Eddystone. Some have families and decide one of the onshore lights is a better posting so they can spend more time at home."

I could see by the glint in his eye that Holmes had the same thought as me. Perhaps the Germans had placed Rogerson here a few days in advance, knowing Lentov was due to arrive. I also surmised that with the bells sounding, the sound of any movement inside would be hidden. The three men were sticking to the same story, which could also support my theory they were all involved and covering for each other.

"It is too dark to see the site of the murder clearly," said Holmes, "so I would be grateful for a tour of the lighthouse so you can show me where you all were."

Kettering led the way up the stairs, followed by Holmes and me and then the other two keepers. The first bedrooms, occupied normally by Williams and Lentov, were one flight up. As I expected, Holmes got down on his hands and knees to inspect every inch of the floor before standing up and pulling out the sparse furniture – only two single beds, one chair, and a chest of drawers on which an oil lamp sat. Each of the drawers were taken out in turn and examined.

"Have any one of you touched Lentov's belongings?" he asked.

"We were told not to by the other investigator," Kettering said. "In any case, it would be bad luck to interfere with a dead man's things. We would normally wait until the supply boat arrives, and the boatman would take them to the mainland to be given to his relatives."

Holmes nodded and waved Kettering to take us further up the tower. The next floor was the bedroom he shared with Rogerson. Holmes repeated the search in a room that was identically furnished, except for some drawings of seabirds pinned to the wall.

"Whose are these?" he asked.

"Kettering's," said Rogerson. "Charles and I see enough of the d--n things swooping about every time we go out onto the rock to have any enthusiasm about sharing our room with their image."

"They are good likenesses," said Holmes. "You may wish to share your knowledge with Dr. Watson, as he has difficulty telling one gull from another."

I reddened slightly at the jibe, despite being used to the barbs Holmes often threw in my direction.

"Rogerson and Williams have little appreciation of nature," said Kettering. "They see our location as a necessary evil to be endured, while I relish in the opportunity to learn more about this small corner of the world. Seabirds are fascinating creatures – each species with its unique characteristics. My companions don't even know the difference between birds that are surface fishers and those that dive onto their prey from a height. To them they are all just gulls that make the rock treacherous with their guano."

I was about to share some of the knowledge I have of seabirds from my childhood, but Holmes strode briskly towards the stairs leading up to the tower.

"And now you can show us what you were doing the night of Lentov's death," he said to Williams.

I knew from Holmes's lecture during our journey what a miracle of engineering the light was. We passed the eighth story with its fixed light, and ended at the summit where the great flint glass lenses stood on their rotating platform. Apparently they were the largest lenses in the world, with a calorific engine to ease the keepers' efforts when winding the mechanism that powered the lenses and the bells which hung outside the tower. Williams walked over to the engine and switched it on as he began the winding process.

"We have to do this every few hours, as well as watch that the fuel for the lamp doesn't go too low, and start the bells if visibility drops," he said. "We each take a night in turn, and the others carry out maintenance on the lighthouse during the day."

"We cannot risk leaving the light," said Kettering. "If you observe the rope by the wall, that rings a bell in or sleeping quarters in the event the man on duty needs assistance."

"Very good," said Holmes. "Would it not be easier if more than one person manned the light and assisted with the winding?"

"That's the normal practise," said Rogerson. "But Kettering, who normally shares his shift with Williams, had fallen and injured himself during the day, and Leonard and I were tired from our maintenance tasks, so Williams volunteered to do a solo shift. With the engine to help us, it's a lot easier than working on other lights."

"Perhaps we should leave Mr. Williams to his duties," said Holmes. "Watson and I are tired from our journey and would appreciate some sleep. If we could share the upper bedroom and you the lower, that would be splendid."

It was unlike Holmes to admit to fatigue. Perhaps I had been right in discerning signs of strain.

When Rogerson and Kettering had continued down to their chamber, I started to take off my boots to prepare for bed. I planned to sleep in the rest of my clothes, as the room was freezing.

"Please leave you footwear on," Holmes whispered. "And take your Bulldog revolver from your pocket, ready for action. I discovered a number of hidden weapons in my search, and I'm sure they aren't here in case of an attack by wreckers. If we leave Williams to his own devices for a few minutes, we should be able to confirm my suspicions."

I wanted to know more, but Holmes put a finger to his lips for quiet. He lay back on his bed in silence with his arms folded over his chest and open eyes. I could hear the wind still howling outside, making false the keeper's claim they would be able to hear clearly any internal movement. Wind makes eerie noises in the most comfortable of buildings, but in this thin needle in the middle of the sea it was even more unnerving. It seemed like some angry beast roaring around the lighthouse in an attempt to breach its defences.

After a full thirty minutes, Holmes sat up and gestured for me to do the same. As requested, I had remained ready and stood up off the wooden cot, prepared to follow him. My pistol was held in my hand, cocked and ready.

We moved as silently as possible to the stairs leading up to the light and began to ascend, Holmes in the lead. Above, I could hear the rumble of the lenses as they turned to sweep the light across the night sky and the clicking of their gears. Holmes and made elongated shadows against the wall as we ascended from the subdued oil lamp of the bedroom to the brighter illumination in the light chamber.

Holmes was almost fully in the upper chamber as my head cleared the entrance. Williams was on the opposite side of the chamber, looking outwards to the open Atlantic, and didn't seem to have heard us.

"I would recommend you cease your signals to your colleagues on the boat," said Holmes. "Watson and I are armed."

Williams spun round, dropping a signal lamp to the floor and reaching in his pocket for his own weapon. His face was a mask of fury, but when he saw Holmes and me standing, guns in hand, he checked himself.

"I was simply answering a question about the sea conditions from a passing fishing vessel," he said. "We often have Morse conversations with boat crews. It helps alleviate the boredom of the night shift."

"That boat is no more a fishing vessel than you are an Englishman," said Holmes.

"Why do you say that?" asked Williams.

"The reason for Lentov's death was scarcely in doubt, nor the nationality of his killer," said Holmes. "The question I needed to answer was the identity of that assassin. My search of everyone's belongings provided the answer."

"That is ridiculous," said Williams. "You are clutching at straws in an attempt to frame one of us for Lentov's murder, instead of looking for the real killer. We've already told you how none of us could have committed the crime."

"You may believe you have been clever," Holmes said, "but the truth of the matter is obvious to a trained observer."

"What do you mean?" Williams protested.

"Lentov was clean-shaven, as are you," said Holmes. "Yet there was no shaving equipment in Lentov's possessions, but two razors and soaps amongst yours – one blunt from years of use, and one sharp. I deemed it unlikely you had brought a spare set, and decided that you helped yourself to his new one, rather than sharpen your own."

"What if I did?" said Williams. "He had no further use for it, and I was in need of it."

"I was aware of the sea superstition about the effects of the dead," Holmes said. "A real sailor would never have taken the razor. I assume Lentov found out you were signaling to the Germans to pass on the secrets your colleagues operating undercover within the government had discovered and provided in coded correspondence in the mail. It would be less likely to be intercepted than a letter sent directly to Berlin."

The bravado seemed to leach out of Williams, to be replaced by defiance.

"He never discovered my secret," said Williams "I found out his. One of the ciphers informed me of his identity and your brother's planned negotiations. We could not allow that to take place."

"So you followed him outside and killed him," I said. "You will hang for this."

"Not so," said Holmes. "As Williams told us, it would have been dangerous for him to leave the light unattended. If such dereliction had been discovered, he would have been removed from his post and the German plan threatened. And of course, the identity of the killer would have been obvious. Williams' partner had designed what they assumed would be the perfect plan."

"And what was that, Detective?" asked a voice from behind us. I looked over to the stairs and saw Kettering standing there with a gun in his hand. "Please place your weapons on the floor."

"You couldn't kill both of us before the other fired," I said.

"Possibly," Kettering said. "But that would give my colleague time to pick up his weapon and shoot the other."

"And how would you explain two more dead bodies?" I asked.

"Three, as Rogerson will also have to die," said Kettering. "That will not be necessary, however. As you observed, there's a German ship a few miles away, and Williams – Burgholz, to give him his real name – would escape on it. I can place all the blame on him and claim I managed to hide before he fled. We cannot risk capture and our comrades within government being exposed. After the government wastes its time chasing my colleague, I can continue as before."

"Put down your gun, Watson," Holmes said. "It seems we are at a disadvantage."

"But they'll kill us anyway!" I protested.

"Perhaps, but I would like the satisfaction first of testing whether my theory about Lentov's murder was correct."

I reluctantly placed my pistol on the floor, as Holmes did the same. Williams retrieved his weapon and we now faced two armed spies.

"And what is this theory?" asked Kettering.

"One I formulated the moment Watson and I landed on the rock," said Holmes. "Do you remember the dead bird, Watson?"

I nodded. "What significance was that? Surely there are scores of dead birds within a mile of here?"

"True," he said. "But what you failed to notice was the red mark on its beak. As Kettering told us, he's very familiar with the habits of seabirds, and would be aware of the feeding habits of the gannet. It hovers above the ocean until it spots its prey and then plummets at great speed, piercing the water and the body of the fish with its beak. It reaches speeds of sixty miles-per-hour in its plunge. Kettering undoubtedly trained several birds to dive for pieces of fish he scattered on the surface of the sea over several weeks. Perhaps it was merely a pastime at first – something to alleviate the boredom and pursue his interest in ornithology. When he found out Lentov's true identity, it provided a perfect and untraceable weapon with which to kill him. He didn't even need to leave the bedroom. He must have sent Lentov outside on some pretext and then thrown a scrap of fish down to land on his collar. The gannet's dive would have pierced his neck and resulted in instant death, for both him and the bird. If it hadn't succeeded, Lentov would be none the wiser about the attempt, and would assume the bird had attacked for no reason. It was his bad luck that the waves hadn't yet washed the bird off the rock."

"Congratulations on solving the case, Mr. Holmes," said Kettering. "It's a shame you will not be able to tell anyone of your superior reasoning skills."

"That's where you are wrong. Please drop your weapons."

Rogerson was standing in the stairwell which Kettering had recently vacated. There was a pistol in each of his hands.

"Apologies for not properly introducing myself earlier, Mr. Holmes," he said. "Your brother sent me here to pave the way for Lentov's arrival. I obviously failed to keep him safe. I was anticipating a less-subtle attack."

Before Holmes and I could retrieve our guns, Kettering launched himself at Rogerson, taking Mycroft's agent by surprise and knocking him backwards. They both tumbled down the stairs. Williams was startled by the turn of events, which gave Holmes the opportunity to bound across the lamp room and grasp the German's hand, forcing him to release his weapon. I picked up my own pistol and ran across to the stairwell. Looking down I could see Kettering and Rogerson were both lying at the bottom of the stairs. I lost no time in descending. Rogerson was slowly regaining his feet, but Kettering was unmoving. I could see at a glance that his neck had been broken in the fall. Quickly returning to the lamp room, I found Holmes holding Williams at gunpoint. We marched him down the stairs and tied his hands behind his back.

"Stay here, Watson," said Holmes. "The German ship must be wondering what is happening. I'll return to the lamp room and send them a signal. Mycroft has made me familiar with the most likely code, and a simple Morse message saying they should return after you and I have left should be enough to allow Rogerson and his colleagues to begin feeding them false information."

The next day, the supply boat arrived and took Holmes, Williams, and me ashore, leaving one of its crew to help Rogerson man the light until replacement keepers could be sent. I had little doubt that Mycroft would have arranged for some of his men to be standing by in anticipation of the denouement of our investigation.

Two days later, we joined Mycroft again in the Stranger's Room at the Diogenes Club. We found him in exactly the same position we had left him, relaxing in front of the fire. Although the winds had dropped since our return, the night air was still chilly, and I for one was recovering from the icy journey back to London and welcomed the warmth.

"Well done, Brother," he said as we sat in matching armchairs. "You'll be pleased to hear that scrutiny of shipping records enabled us to identify the German ship involved and track the letters to the conspirators back to their source within the Government."

"Have you arrested them?" I asked.

"By no means," said Mycroft. "They're far more useful staying in post, where we can feed them false information to throw the Germans off track."

"But they were complicit in murder!" I protested.

"There are more important matters at stake than the death of one man, however unfortunate," said Mycroft. "Burgholz is, of course, in custody and will remain there. As he is to be arraigned for spying, he will not face a public trial so that the details of what happened will not tip off the Kaiser's men. He is being kept well away from other prisoners to ensure he cannot pass on any messages."

"There are times I am grateful I operate in a simpler world of guilt and innocence," said Holmes. "Although even there, I sometimes face moral conundrums where the lines of justice and the law are blurred and may even be at odds."

"That is why I only call you in to assist with the simpler matters, Sherlock," Mycroft said. "Not everything in life is susceptible to logic alone."

Holmes's elder brother leaned back into his chair and took a sip of his brandy.

"It goes without saying," he said, "that none of this is ever to appear in any of your sensationalised scribblings, Doctor. My job is to prevent speculation in the press, not encourage it, and suppressing their questions following the initial reports of Lentov's death has been challenge enough. I have had to have a serious word with some Fleet Street editors."

"I am aware of my duty," I said stiffly.

"And no doubt you would wish to conceal your lack of knowledge of the difference between a cormorant and a gannet," smiled Holmes. "I shall remember that if you tease me again about the narrow boundaries of my knowledge."

As he sat in the chair and ordered a dozen oysters from the omnipresent waiter, I observed that the challenge of the case had dispelled the exhaustion I'd seen in my friend a few days before. It was good to see him back on form, and even if he would receive no public acclaim for his work, that was reward enough.

About the Contributors

The following contributors appear in this volume:
The MX Book of New Sherlock Holmes Stories
Part XXXVIII – 2023 Annual (1890-1896)

Ian Ableson is an ecologist by training and a writer by choice. When not reading or writing, he can reliably be found scowling at a clipboard while ankle-deep in a marsh somewhere in Michigan. His love for the stories of Arthur Conan Doyle started when his grandfather gave him a copy of *The Original Illustrated Sherlock Holmes* when he was in high school, and he's proud to have been able to contribute to the continuation of the tales of Sherlock Holmes and Dr. Watson.

Tim Newton Anderson is a former senior daily newspaper journalist and PR manager who has recently started writing fiction. In the past six months, he has placed fourteen stories in publications including *Parsec Magazine*, *Tales of the Shadowmen*, *SF Writers Guild*, *Zoetic Press*, *Dark Lane Books*, *Dark Horses Magazine*, *Emanations*, and *Planet Bizarro*.

Brian Belanger, PSI, is a publisher, illustrator, graphic designer, editor, and author. In 2015, he co-founded Belanger Books publishing company along with his brother, author Derrick Belanger. His illustrations have appeared in *The Essential Sherlock Holmes* and *Sherlock Holmes: A Three-Pipe Christmas*, and in children's books such as *The MacDougall Twins with Sherlock Holmes* series, *Dragonella*, and *Scones and Bones on Baker Street*. Brian has published a number of Sherlock Holmes anthologies and novels through Belanger Books, as well as new editions of August Derleth's classic Solar Pons mysteries. Brian continues to design all of the covers for Belanger Books, and since 2016 he has designed the majority of book covers for MX Publishing. In 2019, Brian received his investiture in the PSI as "Sir Ronald Duveen." More recently, he illustrated a comic book featuring the band The Moonlight Initiative, created the logo for the Arthur Conan Doyle Society and designed *The Great Game of Sherlock Holmes* card game. Find him online at:
www.belangerbooks.com and
www.redbubble.com/people/zhahadun and
zhahadun.wixsite.com/221b

Sir Arthur Conan Doyle (1859-1930) *Holmes Chronicler Emeritus*. If not for him, this anthology would not exist. Author, physician, patriot, sportsman, spiritualist, husband and father, and advocate for the oppressed. He is remembered and honored for the purposes of this collection by being the man who introduced Sherlock Holmes to the world. Through fifty-six Holmes short stories, four novels, and additional Apocryphal entries, Doyle revolutionized mystery stories and also greatly influenced and improved police forensic methods and techniques for the betterment of all. *Steel True Blade Straight*.

Danica Dvorak is a multimedia freelance artist and first year architecture student. This is her first commissioned work, though she is now currently hard at work on new projects. She enjoys visiting museums, traveling, and reading

Anna Elliott is an author of historical fiction and fantasy. Her first series, *The Twilight of Avalon* trilogy, is a retelling of the Trystan and Isolde legend. She wrote her second series,

The Pride and Prejudice Chronicles, chiefly to satisfy her own curiosity about what might have happened to Elizabeth Bennet, Mr. Darcy, and all the other wonderful cast of characters after the official end of Jane Austen's classic work. She enjoys stories about strong women, and loves exploring the multitude of ways women can find their unique strengths. She was delighted to lend a hand with the "Sherlock and Lucy" series, and this story, firstly because she loves Sherlock Holmes as much as her father, co-author Charles Veley, does, and second because it almost never happens that someone with a dilemma shouts, "Quick, we need an author of historical fiction!" Anna lives in the Washington, D.C. area with her husband and three children.

Steve Emecz's main field is technology, in which he has been working for about twenty-five years. Steve is a regular speaker at trade shows and his tech career has taken him to more than fifty countries – so he's no stranger to planes and airports. In 2008, MX published its first Sherlock Holmes book, and MX has gone on to become the largest specialist Holmes publisher in the world with over 500 books. MX is a social enterprise and supports three main causes. The first is Happy Life, a children's rescue project in Nairobi, Kenya, where he and his wife, Sharon, spend every Christmas at the rescue centre in Kasarani. They have written two editions of a short book about the project, *The Happy Life Story*. The second is Undershaw, Sir Arthur Conan Doyle's former home, which is a school for children with learning disabilities for which Steve is a patron. Steve has been a mentor for the World Food Programme for several years, and was part of the Nobel Peace Prize winning team in 2020.

Mark A. Gagen BSI is co-founder of Wessex Press, sponsor of the popular *From Gillette to Brett* conferences, and publisher of *The Sherlock Holmes Reference Library* and many other fine Sherlockian titles. A life-long Holmes enthusiast, he is a member of *The Baker Street Irregulars* and *The Illustrious Clients of Indianapolis*. A graphic artist by profession, his work is often seen on the covers of *The Baker Street Journal* and various BSI books.

John Atkinson Grimshaw (1836-1893) was born in Leeds, England. His amazing paintings, usually featuring twilight or night scenes illuminated by gas-lamps or moonlight, are easily recognizable, and are often used on the covers of books about The Great Detective to set the mood, as shadowy figures move in the distance through misty mysterious settings and over rain-slicked streets.

Arthur Hall was born in Aston, Birmingham, UK, in 1944. He discovered his interest in writing during his schooldays, along with a love of fictional adventure and suspense. His first novel, *Sole Contact*, was an espionage story about an ultra-secret government department known as "Sector Three", and was followed, to date, by three sequels. Other works include seven Sherlock Holmes novels, *The Demon of the Dusk*, *The One Hundred Percent Society*, *The Secret Assassin*, *The Phantom Killer*, *In Pursuit of the Dead*, *The Justice Master*, and *The Experience Club* as well as three collections of Holmes *Further Little-Known Cases of Sherlock* Holmes, *Tales from the Annals of Sherlock* Holmes, and *The Additional Investigations of Sherlock Holmes*. He has also written other short stories and a modern detective novel. He lives in the West Midlands, United Kingdom.

In the year 1998 **Craig Janacek** took his degree of Doctor of Medicine at Vanderbilt University, and proceeded to Stanford to go through the training prescribed for pediatricians in practice. Having completed his studies there, he was duly attached to the University of California, San Francisco as a Professor. The author of over two-hundred medical monographs upon a variety of obscure lesions, his travel-worn and battered tin dispatch-box is crammed with papers, most of which are records of his fictional works. These include several collections of *The Further Adventures of Sherlock Holmes*: *Light in the Darkness*, *The Gathering Gloom*, *The Treasury of Sherlock Holmes*, *The Travels of Sherlock Holmes*, *The Chronicles of Sherlock Holmes*, *The Histories of Sherlock Holmes*, *The Acts of Sherlock Holmes*, and *The Assassination of Sherlock Holmes* – as well as two Dr. Watson novels (*The Isle of Devils* and *The Gate of Gold*), the complete and expanded *Adventures* and *Exploits of Brigadier Gerard* (*Set Europe Shaking* and *A Mighty Shadow*), and two non-Holmes novels (*The Oxford Deception* and *The Anger of Achilles Peterson*). His short stories have been published in several editions of *The MX Book of New Sherlock Holmes Stories, Part I: 1881-1889* (2015), *Part IV: 2016 Annual* (2016), *Part VI: 2017 Annual* (2017), *Part VIII: Eliminate the Impossible* (2017), *Part XI: Some Untold Cases* (2018), *Part XVIII: Whatever Remains Must be the Truth* (2019), *Part XXIII: Some More Untold Cases* (2020), *Part XXV: 2021 Annual* (2021), *Part XXXII: 2022 Annual* (2022), *Part XXXVI: However Improbable . . . .* (2022), and *Part XXXVIII: 2023 Annual* (2023). Other stories have appeared in *Holmes Away From Home: Tales of the Great Hiatus* (2016), *Tales from the Stranger's Room 3* (2017), *Sherlock Holmes: Adventures Beyond the Canon* (2018), *Sherlock Holmes, A Year of Mysteries – 1881* (2021), and *Sherlock Holmes: Stranger than Fiction* (2021). He lives near San Francisco, California with his wife and two children, where he is at work on his next story. Craig Janacek is a *nom-de-plume*.

Roger Johnson, BSI, ASH, PSI, etc, is a member of more Holmesian societies than he can remember, thanks to his (so far) 16 years as editor of *The Sherlock Holmes Journal*, and thirty-two years as editor of *The District Messenger*. The latter, the newsletter of *The Sherlock Holmes Society of London*, is now in the safe hands of Jean Upton, with whom he collaborated on the well-received book, *The Sherlock Holmes Miscellany*. Roger is resigned to the fact that he will never match the Duke of Holdernesse, whose name was followed by "*half the alphabet*".

Susan Knight's newest novel, *Death in the Garden of England*, from MX publishing, is the latest in a series which began with her collection of stories, *Mrs. Hudson Investigates* (2019), the novel *Mrs. Hudson goes to Ireland* (2020), and *Mrs. Hudson goes to Paris* (2022). She has contributed to several of the MX anthologies of new Sherlock Holmes short stories and enjoys writing as Dr. Watson as much as she does Mrs. Hudson. Susan is the author of two other non-Sherlockian story collections, as well as three novels, a book of non-fiction, and several plays, and has won several prizes for her writing. Susan lives in Dublin.

Sonya Kudei is a writer, illustrator and former web developer with degrees in English Literature and Cognitive Linguistics. Originally from Croatia, she lived in London for over twelve years and currently resides in the Netherlands.

Gordon Linzner is founder and former editor of *Space and Time Magazine*, and author of four published novels and dozens of short stories in *F&SF*, *Twilight Zone*, *Sherlock Holmes Mystery Magazine*, and numerous other magazines and anthologies. He is a full member of the *Horror Writers Association* and a lifetime member of *Science Fiction and Fantasy Writers Association*.

David MacGregor is a playwright, screenwriter, novelist, and nonfiction writer. He is a resident artist at The Purple Rose Theatre in Michigan, where a number of his plays have been produced. His plays have been performed from New York to Tasmania, and his work

427

has been published by Dramatic Publishing, Playscripts, Smith & Kraus, Applause, Heuer Publishing, and Theatrical Rights Worldwide (TRW). He adapted his dark comedy, *Vino Veritas*, for the silver screen, and it stars Carrie Preston (Emmy-winner for *The Good Wife*). Several of his short plays have also been adapted into films. He is the author of three Sherlock Holmes plays: *Sherlock Holmes and the Adventure of the Elusive Ear*, *Sherlock Holmes and the Adventure of the Fallen Soufflé*, and *Sherlock Holmes and the Adventure of the Ghost Machine*. He adapted all three plays into novels for Orange Pip Books, and also wrote the two-volume nonfiction *Sherlock Holmes: The Hero with a Thousand Faces* for MX Publishing. He teaches writing at Wayne State University in Detroit and is inordinately fond of cheese and terriers.

Michael Mallory is the author of the *Amelia Watson* series and twenty other books, both fiction and nonfiction. His story "What the Cat Dragged In," published in *The Strand Magazine*, has been selected for inclusion in *The Best Mystery Stories of the Year*, 2023 edition. By day he is a Los Angeles-based entertainment journalist who works with the Academy of Motion Picture Arts and Sciences' Visual History Program as a researcher and interviewer. He can also tell you where to find the best British pubs in Southern California.

David Marcum plays *The Game* with deadly seriousness. He first discovered Sherlock Holmes in 1975 at the age of ten, and since that time, he has collected, read, and chronologicized literally thousands of traditional Holmes pastiches in the form of novels, short stories, radio and television episodes, movies and scripts, comics, fan-fiction, and unpublished manuscripts. He is the author of over one-hundred Sherlockian pastiches, some published in anthologies and magazines such as *The Best Mystery Stories of the Year 2021* and *The Strand*, and others collected in his own books, *The Papers of Sherlock Holmes*, *Sherlock Holmes and A Quantity of Debt*, *Sherlock Holmes – Tangled Skeins*, *Sherlock Holmes and The Eye of Heka*, and *The Collected Papers of Sherlock Holmes*. He has won first place fiction awards from *The Arthur Conan Doyle Society* and the Nero Wolfe *Wolfe Pack*. He has edited over eighty books, including several dozen traditional Sherlockian anthologies, such as the ongoing series *The MX Book of New Sherlock Holmes Stories*, which he created in 2015. This collection is now at thirty-nine volumes, with more in preparation. He was responsible for bringing back August Derleth's Solar Pons for a new generation with his collection of authorized Pons stories, *The Papers of Solar Pons* and *The Further Papers of Solar Pons*. Pons's return was further assisted by his editing of the reissued authorized versions of the original Pons books, and then several volumes of new Pons adventures. He has done the same for the adventures of Dr. Thorndyke, and has plans for similar projects in the future. He has contributed numerous essays to various publications, and is a member of a number of Sherlockian groups and Scions, as well as *The Mystery Writers of America*. His irregular Sherlockian blog, *A Seventeen Step Program*, addresses various topics related to his favorite book friends (as his son used to call them when he was small), and can be found at *http://17stepprogram.blogspot.com/* He is a licensed Civil Engineer, living in Tennessee with his wife and son. Since the age of nineteen, he has worn a deerstalker as his regular-and-only hat. In 2013, he and his deerstalker were finally able make his first trip-of-a-lifetime Holmes Pilgrimage to England, with return Pilgrimages in 2015 and 2016, where you may have spotted him. If you ever run into him and his deerstalker out and about, feel free to say hello!

Jen Matteis is a professional writer and editor who lives in Silicon Valley. Her writing has appeared in a dozen community and alt-weekly newspapers on both coasts of the U.S., magazines, fiction anthologies, and countless other publications. When not writing for work, she writes for fun: mystery, sci-fi, horror, and fantasy. Find her online at: *www.jenmatteis.com*

Carlos Orsi is a Brazilian writer of mystery, science fiction, and fantasy, and an award-winning science journalist. He coedited the first anthology of original Sherlock Holmes stories by Brazilian authors, Aventuras Secretas, in 2012. His mystery stories have appeared in Ellery Queen Mystery Magazine, Mystery Weekly, and Needle. His Sherlockian musings have been published in The Baker Street Journal and The Watsonian.

Sidney Paget (1860-1908), a few of whose illustrations are used within this anthology, was born in London, and like his two older brothers, became a famed illustrator and painter. He completed over three-hundred-and-fifty drawings for the Sherlock Holmes stories that were first published in *The Strand* magazine, defining Holmes's image forever after in the public mind.

Tracy J. Revels, a Sherlockian from the age of eleven, is a professor of history at Wofford College in Spartanburg, South Carolina. She is a member of *The Survivors of the Gloria Scott* and *The Studious Scarlets Society*, and is a past recipient of the Beacon Society Award. Almost every semester, she teaches a class that covers The Canon, either to college students or to senior citizens. She is also the author of three supernatural Sherlockian pastiches with MX (*Shadowfall*, *Shadowblood*, and *Shadowwraith*), and a regular contributor to her scion's newsletter. She also has some notoriety as an author of very silly skits: For proof, see "The Adventure of the Adversarial Adventuress" and "Occupy Baker Street" on YouTube. When not studying Sherlock, she can be found researching the history of her native state, and has written books on Florida in the Civil War and on the development of Florida's tourism industry.

Geri Schear is a novelist and short story writer. Her work has been published in literary journals in the U.S. and Ireland. Her first novel, *A Biased Judgement: The Diaries of Sherlock Holmes 1897* was released to critical acclaim in 2014. The sequel, *Sherlock Holmes and the Other Woman* was published in 2015, and *Return to Reichenbach* in 2016. She lives in Kells, Ireland.

Michael Sims's nonfiction books include *Arthur and Sherlock*, which was a finalist for the Edgar of the *Mystery Writers of America*, the Gold Dagger of the *Crime Writers Association of Great Britain*, and the H. R. F. Keating Award of *the International Crime Writers Association*; *Adam's Navel*, which was a *New York Times* Notable Book; and *The Story of Charlotte's Web*, which was chosen by the *Washington Post*, *Boston Globe*, and other venues as a *Best Book of the Year*. His many anthologies include *The Penguin Book of Murder Mysteries*. His Sherlockian pastiche "The Memoirs of Silver Blaze" appears in the Anthony-winning anthology *In the Footsteps of Sherlock Holmes*, edited by Leslie Klinger and Laurie King. His work is widely translated around the world.

Award winning poet and author **Joseph W. Svec III** enjoys writing, poetry, and stories, and creating new adventures for Holmes and Watson that take them into the worlds of famous literary authors and scientists. His *Missing Authors* trilogy introduced Holmes to Lewis Carroll, Jules Verne, H.G. Wells, and Alfred Lord Tennyson, as well as many of their characters. His transitional story *Sherlock Holmes and the Mystery of the First Unicorn* involved several historical figures, besides a Unicorn or two. He has also written the rhymed and metered Sherlock Holmes Christmas adventure, *The Night Before Christmas in 221b*, sure to be a delight for Sherlock Holmes enthusiasts of all ages. Joseph

429

won the Amador Arts Council 2021 Original Poetry Contest, with his Rhymed and metered story poem, "The Homecoming". Joseph has presented a literary paper on Sherlock Holmes/Alice in Wonderland crossover literature to the Lewis Carroll Society of North America, as well as given several presentations to the Amador County Holmes Hounds, Sherlockian Society. He is currently working on his first book in the *Missing Scientist Trilogy, Sherlock Holmes and the Adventure of the Demonstrative Dinosaur*, in which Sherlock meets Professor George Edward Challenger. Joseph has Masters Degrees in Systems Engineering and Human Organization Management, and has written numerous technical papers on Aerospace Testing. In addition to writing, Joseph enjoys creating miniature dioramas based on music, literature, and history from many different eras. His dioramas have been featured in magazine articles and many different blogs, including the North American Jules Verne society newsletter. He currently has 57 dioramas set up in his display area, and has written a reference book on toy castles and knights from around the world. An avid tea enthusiast, his tea cabinet contains over five-hundred different varieties, and he delights in sharing afternoon tea with his childhood sweetheart and wonderful wife, who has inspired and coauthored several books with him.

Charles Veley has loved Sherlock Holmes since boyhood. As a father, he read the entire Canon to his then-ten-year-old daughter at evening story time. Now, this very same daughter, grown up to become acclaimed historical novelist Anna Elliott, has worked with him to develop new adventures in the *Sherlock Holmes and Lucy James Mystery Series*. Charles is also a fan of Gilbert & Sullivan, and wrote *The Pirates of Finance*, a new musical in the G&S tradition that won an award at the New York Musical Theatre Festival in 2013. Other than the Sherlock and Lucy series, all of the books on his Amazon Author Page were written when he was a full-time author during the late Seventies and early Eighties. He currently works for United Technologies Corporation, where his main focus is on creating sustainability and value for the company's large real estate development projects.

Peter Coe Verbica grew up on a commercial cattle ranch in Northern California, where he learned the value of a strong work ethic. He works for the Wealth Management Group of a global investment bank, and is an Adjunct Professor in the Economics Department at SJSU. He is the author of numerous books, including *Left at the Gate and Other Poems, Hard-Won Cowboy Wisdom (Not Necessarily in Order of Importance), A Key to the Grove and Other Poems*, and two volumes of *The Missing Tales of Sherlock Holmes* (as Compiled by Peter Coe Verbica, JD). Mr. Verbica obtained a JD from Santa Clara University School of Law, an MS from Massachusetts Institute of Technology, and a BA in English from Santa Clara University. He is the co-inventor on a number of patents, has served as a Managing Member of three venture capital firms, and the CFO of one of the portfolio companies. He is an unabashed advocate of cowboy culture and enjoys creative writing, hiking, and tennis. He is married with four daughters. For more information, or to contact the author, please go to *www.hardwoncowboywisdom.com*

Margaret Walsh was born Auckland, New Zealand and now lives in Melbourne, Australia. She is the author of *Sherlock Holmes and the Molly-Boy Murders, Sherlock Holmes and the Case of the Perplexed Politician, Sherlock Holmes and the Case of the London Dock Deaths, The Adventure of the Bloody Duck and Other Tales of Sherlock Holmes* and *Sherlock Holmes and the Curse of Neb-Heka-Ra*, all published by MX Publishing. She is currently working on her sixth book, *Sherlock Holmes and the Hellfire Heirs*. Margaret has been a devotee of Sherlock Holmes since childhood and has had several Holmesian related essays printed in anthologies, and is a member of the online society *Doyle's Rotary Coffin, as well as being a member of Sisters of Crime Australia.*

She has an ongoing love affair with the city of London. When she's not working or planning trips to London. Margaret can be found frequenting the many and varied bookshops of Melbourne.

I.A. Watson, great-grand-nephew of Dr. John H. Watson, has been intrigued by the notorious "black sheep" of the family since childhood, and was fascinated to inherit from his grandmother a number of unedited manuscripts removed circa 1956 from a rather larger collection reposing at Lloyds Bank Ltd (which acquired Cox & Co Bank in 1923). Upon discovering the published corpus of accounts regarding the detective Sherlock Holmes from which a censorious upbringing had shielded him, he felt obliged to allow an interested public access to these additional memoranda, and is gradually undertaking the task of transcribing them for admirers of Mr. Holmes and Dr. Watson's works. In the meantime, I.A. Watson continues to pen other books, the latest of which is *The Incunabulum of Sherlock Holmes*. A full list of his seventy or so published works are available at: *http://www.chillwater.org.uk/writing/iawatsonhome.htm*

Emma West joined Undershaw in April 2021 as the Director of Education with a brief to ensure that qualifications formed the bedrock of our provision, whilst facilitating a positive balance between academia, pastoral care, and well-being. She quickly took on the role of Acting Headteacher from early summer 2021. Under her leadership, Undershaw has embraced its new name, new vision, and consequently we have seen an exponential increase in demand for places. There is a buzz in the air as we invite prospective students and families through the doors. Emma has overseen a strategic review, re-cemented relationships with Local Authorities, and positioned Undershaw at the helm of SEND education in Surrey and beyond. Undershaw has a wide appeal: Our students present to us with mild to moderate learning needs and therefore may have some very recent memories of poor experiences in their previous schools. Emma's background as a senior leader within the independent school sector has meant she is well-versed in brokering relationships between the key stakeholders, our many interdependences, local businesses, families, and staff, and all this whilst ensuring Undershaw remains relentlessly child-centric in its approach. Emma's energetic smile and boundless enthusiasm for Undershaw is inspiring.

The following contributors appear
in the companion volumes:
The MX Book of New Sherlock Holmes Stories
Part XXXVII – 2023 Annual (1875-1889)
Part XXXIX – 2023 Annual (1897-1823)

Hugh Ashton was born in the U.K., and moved to Japan in 1988, where he remained until 2016, living with his wife Yoshiko in the historic city of Kamakura, a little to the south of Yokohama. He and Yoshiko have now moved to Lichfield, a small cathedral city in the Midlands of the U.K., the birthplace of Samuel Johnson, and one-time home of Erasmus Darwin. In the past, he has worked in the technology and financial services industries, which have provided him with material for some of his books set in the 21st century. He currently works as a writer: Novelist, freelance editor, and copywriter, (his work for large Japanese corporations has appeared in international business journals), and journalist, as well as producing industry reports on various aspects of the financial services industry. However, his lifelong interest in Sherlock Holmes has developed into an acclaimed series of adventures featuring the world's most famous detective, written in the style of the originals. In addition to these, he has also published historical and alternate historical novels, short stories, and thrillers. Together with artist Andy Boerger, he has produced the *Sherlock Ferret* series of stories for children, featuring the world's cutest detective.

Donald I. Baxter has practiced medicine for over forty years. He resides in Erie Pennsylvania with his wife and their dog. His family and his friends are for the most part lawyers who have given him the ability to make stuff up just as they do.

Bob Byrne was a columnist for *Sherlock Magazine* and has contributed to *Sherlock Holmes Mystery Magazine* and the Sherlock Holmes short story collection *Curious Incidents*. He publishes two free online newsletters: *Baker Street Essays* and *The Solar Pons Gazette*, both of which can be found at *www.SolarPons.com*, the only website dedicated to August Derleth's successor to the Great Detective. Bob's column, *The Public Life of Sherlock Holmes*, appears at *www.BlackGate.com* and explores Holmes, hard boiled, and other mystery matters, and whatever other topics come to mind by the deadline. His mystery-themed blog is *Almost Holmes*.

Chris Chan is a writer, educator, and historian. He works as a researcher and "International Goodwill Ambassador" for Agatha Christie Ltd. His true crime articles, reviews, and short fiction have appeared (or will soon appear) in *The Strand*, *The Wisconsin Magazine of History*, *Mystery Weekly*, *Gilbert!*, *Nerd HQ*, Akashic Books' *Mondays are Murder* web series, *The Baker Street Journal*, *The MX Book of New Sherlock Holmes Stories*, *Masthead: The Best New England Crime Stories*, *Sherlock Holmes Mystery Magazine*, and multiple Belanger Books anthologies. He is the creator of the Funderburke mysteries, a series featuring a private investigator who works for a school and helps students during times of crisis. The Funderburke short story "The Six-Year-Old Serial Killer" was nominated for a Derringer Award. His first book, *Sherlock & Irene: The Secret Truth Behind "A Scandal in Bohemia"*, was published in 2020 by MX Publishing. His second book, *Murder Most Grotesque: The Comedic Crime Fiction of Joyce Porter* will be released by Level Best Books in 2021, and his first novel, *Sherlock's Secretary*, was published by MX Publishing in 2021. *Murder Most Grotesque* was nominated for the Agatha and Silver Falchion Awards for Nonfiction Writing, and *Sherlock's Secretary* was nominated for the Silver Falchion for Best Comedy. He is also the author of the anthology of Sherlock Holmes stories *Of Course He Pushed Him*.

Leslie Charteris was born in Singapore on May 12th, 1907. With his mother and brother, he moved to England in 1919 and attended Rossall School in Lancashire before moving on to Cambridge University to study law. His studies there came to a halt when a publisher accepted his first novel. His third one, entitled *Meet the Tiger*, was written when he was twenty years old and published in September 1928. It introduced the world to Simon Templar, *aka* The Saint. He continued to write about The Saint until 1983 when the last book, *Salvage for The Saint*, was published. The books, which have been translated into over thirty languages, number nearly a hundred and have sold over forty-million copies around the world. They've inspired, to date, fifteen feature films, three television series, ten radio series, and a comic strip that was written by Charteris and syndicated around the world for over a decade. He enjoyed travelling, but settled for long periods in Hollywood, Florida, and finally in Surrey, England. He was awarded the Cartier Diamond Dagger by the *Crime Writers' Association* in 1992, in recognition of a lifetime of achievement. He died the following year.

Barry Clay is a graduate of Shippensburg University with a BA in English. He's dug ditches, stocked grocery shelves, tutored for room and board, cleaned restrooms, mopped

432

floors, taught cartooning, worked in a bank, asked if you'd like fries with that (and cooked the fries to boot), ordered carpet for cars, and worked commission sales at Sears, and most recently a long-time veteran of the Federal employee workforce. He has been writing all his life, in different genres, and he has written thirteen books ranging from Christian theology, anthologies, speculative fiction, horror, science fiction, and humor. He volunteers as conductor of a local student orchestra and has been commissioned to write music. His first two musicals were locally produced. He is the husband of one wife, father of four children, and "Opa" to one granddaughter.

Martin Daley was born in Carlisle, Cumbria in 1964. His thirty-year writing career has seen over twenty books and numerous short stories published. Inevitably, Holmes and Watson remain his favourite literary characters, and they continue to inspire his own detective writing. In 2010, Martin created Inspector Cornelius Armstrong, who carries out his police work against the backdrop of Edwardian Carlisle. With the publication of the first Inspector Armstrong Casebook (published by MX Publishing), Martin became a member of the Crime Writers' Association. He lives with his wife Wendy, in Kirkcudbrightshire, in Southwest.

Ian Dickerson was just nine years old when he discovered The Saint. Shortly after that, he discovered Sherlock Holmes. The Saint won, for a while anyway. He struck up a friendship with The Saint's creator, Leslie Charteris, and his family. With their permission, he spent six weeks studying the Leslie Charteris collection at Boston University and went on to write, direct, and produce documentaries on the making of *The Saint* and *Return of The Saint,* which have been released on DVD. He oversaw the recent reprints of almost fifty of the original Saint books in both the US and UK, and was a co-producer on the 2017 TV movie of *The Saint.* When he discovered that Charteris had written Sherlock Holmes stories as well – well, there was the excuse he needed to revisit The Canon. He's consequently written and edited three books on Holmes' radio adventures. For the sake of what little sanity he has, Ian has also written about a wide range of subjects, none of which come with a halo, including talking mashed potatoes, Lord Grade, and satellite links. Ian lives in Hampshire with his wife and two children. And an awful lot of books by Leslie Charteris. Not quite so many by Conan Doyle, though.

Alan Dimes was born in Northwest London and graduated from Sussex University with a BA in English Literature. He has spent most of his working life teaching English. Living in the Czech Republic since 2003, he is now semi-retired and divides his time between Prague and his country cottage. He has also written some fifty stories of horror and fantasy and thirty stories about his husband-and-wife detectives, Peter and Deirdre Creighton, set in the 1930's.

Brett Fawcett is a humanities and Latin teacher at the Chesterton Academy of St. Isidore in Sherwood Park, Alberta. He lives with his wife and son in Edmonton, where he is a member of The Wisteria Lodgers (The Sherlock Holmes Society of Edmonton). He vividly remembers the first time he finished reading the Sherlock Holmes stories in Grade 6, and has been a student of Holmesian literature and scholarship since then. He is also a frequent author of columns and articles on topics like theology, education, and mental health, as well as the occasional mystery story.

James Gelter is a director and playwright living in Brattleboro, VT. His produced written works for the stage include adaptations of *Frankenstein* and *A Christmas Carol,* several children's plays for the New England Youth Theatre, as well as seven outdoor plays co-written with his wife, Jessica, in their *Forest of Mystery* series. In 2018, he founded The Baker Street Readers, a group of performers that present dramatic readings of Arthur Conan Doyle's original Canon of Sherlock Holmes stories, featuring Gelter as Holmes, his longtime collaborator Tony Grobe as Dr. Watson, and a rotating list of guests. When the COVID-19 pandemic stopped their live performances, Gelter transformed the show into The Baker Street Readers Podcast. Some episodes are available for free on Apple Podcasts and Stitcher, with many more available to patrons at *patreon.com/bakerstreetreaders*.

Denis Green was born in London, England in April 1905. He grew up mostly in London's Savoy Theatre where his father, Richard Green, was a principal in many Gilbert and Sullivan productions, A Flying Officer with RAF until 1924, he then spent four years managing a tea estate in North India before making his stage debut in *Hamlet* with Leslie Howard in 1928. He made his first visit to America in 1931 and established a respectable stage career before appearing in films – including minor roles in the first two Rathbone and Bruce Holmes films – and developing a career in front of and behind the microphone during the golden age of radio. Green and Leslie Charteris met in 1938 and struck up a lifelong friendship. Always busy, be it on stage, radio, film or television, Green passed away at the age of fifty in New York.

Arthur Hall *also has stories in Parts XXXVII and XXXIX*

Paula Hammond has written over sixty fiction and non-fiction books, as well as short stories, comics, poetry, and scripts for educational DVD's. When not glued to the keyboard, she can usually be found prowling round second-hand books shops or hunkered down in a hide, soaking up the joys of the natural world.

Paul Hiscock is an author of crime, fantasy, horror, and science fiction tales. His short stories have appeared in a variety of anthologies, and include a seventeenth-century whodunnit, a science fiction western, a clockpunk fairytale, and numerous Sherlock Holmes pastiches. He lives with his family in Kent (England) and spends his days taking care of his two children. He mainly does his writing in coffee shops with members of the local NaNoWriMo group, or in the middle of the night when his family has gone to sleep. Consequently, his stories tend to be fuelled by large amounts of black coffee. You can find out more about Paul's writing at *www.detectivesanddragons.uk*.

Kelvin I. Jones is the author of six books about Sherlock Holmes and the definitive biography of Conan Doyle as a spiritualist, *Conan Doyle and The Spirits*. A member of *The Sherlock Holmes Society of London*, he has published numerous short occult and ghost stories in British anthologies over the last thirty years. His work has appeared on BBC Radio, and in 1984 he won the Mason Hall Literary Award for his poem cycle about the survivors of Hiroshima and Nagasaki, recently reprinted as "Omega". (Oakmagic Publications) A one-time teacher of creative writing at the University of East Anglia, he is also the author of four crime novels featuring his ex-met sleuth John Bottrell, who first appeared in *Stone Dead*. He has over fifty titles on Kindle, and is also the author of several novellas and short story collections featuring a Norwich based detective, DCI Ketch, an intrepid sleuth who investigates East Anglian murder cases. He also published a series of short stories about an Edwardian psychic detective, Dr. John Carter (*Carter's Occult Casebook*). Ramsey Campbell, the British horror writer, and Francis King, the renowned novelist, have both compared his supernatural stories to those of M. R. James. He has also published children's fiction, namely *Odin's Eye*, and, in collaboration with his wife

Debbie, *The Dark Entry*. Since 1995, he has been the proprietor of Oakmagic Publications, publishers of British folklore and of his fiction titles.

Steven Philip Jones has written fiction novels for adults and young adults, comic books, graphic novels, radio scripts, non-fiction, and advertising pieces. His Sherlock Holmes pastiches include the novel *The Adventure of the Coal-Tar Derivative* from MX Publishing and the radio dramas "The Adventure of the Petty Curses" and "A Case of Unfinished Business" for Jim French Productions' *Imagination Theatre*. He currently makes his home with his family in northern Utah.

Naching T. Kassa is a wife, mother, and writer. She's created short stories, novellas, poems, and co-created three children. She resides in Eastern Washington State with her husband, Dan Kassa. Naching is a member of *The Horror Writers Association*, *Mystery Writers of America*, *The Sound of the Baskervilles*, *The ACD Society*, *The Crew of the Barque Lone Star*, and *The Sherlock Holmes Society of London*. She works in Talent Relations at Crystal Lake Publishing and was a recipient of the 2022 HWA Diversity Grant. You can find her work on Amazon.
https://www.amazon.com/Naching-T-Kassa/e/B005ZGHTI0

Sonya Kudei *also has a story in Part XXXVII*

John Lawrence served for thirty-eight years on personal, committee, and leadership staffs in the U.S. House of Representatives. A visiting professor at the University of California's Washington Center since 2013, he is the author of *The Class of '74: Congress After Watergate and the Roots of Partisanship* (Johns-Hopkins, 2018) and *Arc of Power: Inside the Pelosi Speakership 2005-2010* (Kansas, 2022). His collected "history mystery" Sherlock Holmes pastiches have been published in *The Undiscovered Archives of Sherlock Holmes* (MX Publishing, 2022), in numerous volumes of *The MX Book of New Sherlock Holmes Stories*, and in Belanger Books' *After the East Wind Blows*. *Sherlock Holmes: The Affair at Mayerling Lodge* will be published in 2023. He blogs at DOMEocracy (johnalawrence.wordpress.com). He is a graduate of Oberlin College and has a Ph.D. in history from the University of California (Berkeley).

David Marcum *also has stories in Parts XXXVII and XXXIX*

Kevin Patrick McCann has published eight collections of poems for adults, one for children (*Diary of a Shapeshifter*, Beul Aithris), a book of ghost stories (*It's Gone Dark*, The Otherside Books), *Teach Yourself Self-Publishing* (Hodder) co-written with the playwright Tom Green, and *Ov* (Beul Aithris Publications) a fantasy novel for children.

Will Murray has built a career on writing classic pulp characters, ranging from Tarzan of the Apes to Doc Savage. He has penned several milestone crossover novels in his acclaimed *Wild Adventures* series. *Skull Island* pitted Doc Savage against King Kong, which was followed by *King Kong Vs. Tarzan*. *Tarzan, Conquerer of Mars* costarred John Carter of Mars. His 2015 Doc Savage novel, *The Sinister Shadow*, revived the famous radio and pulp mystery man. Murray reunited them for *Empire of Doom*. His first Spider novel, *The Doom Legion*, resurrected that infamous crime buster, as well as James Christopher, AKA Operator 5, and the renowned G-8. His second Spider, *Fury in Steel*, guest-stars the FBI's Suicide Squad. The Spider clashed with The Skull Killer and his Nemesis, the Scorpion, in Scourge of the Scorpion. Twenty of Murray's Sherlock Holmes short stories have been collected as *The Wild Adventures of Sherlock Holmes*, Volumes 1 and 2. He is the author of the non-fiction book, *Master of Mystery: The Rise of The Shadow*, which is an exploration of the famous radio and magazine character, and a sequel, *Dark Avenger: The Strange Saga of The Shadow*. *The Wild Adventures of Cthulhu* Volumes 1 & 2 collect Murray's Lovecraftian short stories.

Ember Pepper was born and raised in San Diego, CA. She has an M.F.A. degree in Creative Fiction Writing. She has been a fan of The Great Detective since she was a pre-teen and her greatest artistic enjoyment is challenging herself to write quality pastiches of Sherlock Holmes and his stalwart biographer and friend, John Watson.

Tracy J. Revels *also has stories in Parts XXXVII and XXXIX*

Roger Riccard's family history has Scottish roots, which trace his lineage back to Highland Scotland. This British Isles ancestry encouraged his interest in the writings of Sir Arthur Conan Doyle at an early age. He has authored the novels, *Sherlock Holmes & The Case of the Poisoned Lilly*, and *Sherlock Holmes & The Case of the Twain Papers*. In addition he has produced several short stories in *Sherlock Holmes Adventures for the Twelve Days of Christmas* and the series *A Sherlock Holmes Alphabet of Cases*. A new series will begin publishing in the Autumn of 2022, and his has another novel in the works. All of his books have been published by Baker Street Studios. His Bachelor of Arts Degrees in both Journalism and History from California State University, Northridge, have proven valuable to his writing historical fiction, as well as the encouragement of his wife/editor/inspiration and Sherlock Holmes fan, Rosilyn. She passed in 2021, and it is in her memory that he continues to contribute to the legacy of the "*man who never lived and will never die*".

Dan Rowley practiced law for over forty years in private practice and with a large international corporation. He is retired and lives in Erie, Pennsylvania, with his wife Judy, who puts her artistic eye to his transcription of Watson's manuscripts. He inherited his writing ability and creativity from his children, Jim and Katy, and his love of mysteries from his parents, Jim and Ruth.

Jane Rubino is the author of *A Jersey Shore* mystery series, featuring a Jane Austen-loving amateur sleuth and a Sherlock Holmes-quoting detective, *Knight Errant*, *Lady Vernon and Her Daughter*, (a novel-length adaptation of Jane Austen's novella *Lady Susan*, co-authored with her daughter Caitlen Rubino-Bradway, *What Would Austen Do?*, also co-authored with her daughter, a short story in the anthology *Jane Austen Made Me Do It*, *The Rucastles' Pawn*, *The Copper Beeches from Violet Turner's POV*, and, of course, there's the Sherlockian novel in the drawer – who doesn't have one? Jane lives on a barrier island at the New Jersey shore.

Fifteen of **Brenda Seabrooke**'s Sherlock Holmes pastiches have been anthologized in MX Publishing and Belanger Books, six in *Best Crime Stories of New England*, one in *Destination: Mystery* and *Mystery Tribune*, and twelve in literary reviews such as *Yemassee*, *Confrontation*, and one in *Redbook*. Twenty-two of her books for young readers have been published at Penguin, Clarion, etc., and won awards such as a Notable from the National Council of Social Studies, Junior Literary Guild, Hornbook Honor, an Edgar finalist, etc. She received a grant from the National Endowment for the Arts, and The Robie Macauley Award from Emerson College. In 2022, MX published her collection, *Sherlock Holmes: The Persian Slipper and Other Stories*.

Shane Simmons is the author of the occult detective novels *Necropolis* and *Epitaph*, and the crime collection *Raw and Other Stories*. An award-winning screenwriter and graphic novelist, his work has appeared in international film festivals, museums, and lectures about design and structure. He was born in Lachine, a suburb of Montreal best known for being massacred in 1689 and having a joke name. Visit Shane's homepage at *eyestrainproductions.com* for more.

Kevin P. Thornton was shortlisted six times for the Crime Writers of Canada best unpublished novel. He never won – they are all still unpublished, and now he writes short stories. He lives in Canada, north enough that ringing Santa Claus is a local call and winter is a way of life. He has contributed numerous short stories to The MX Book of New Sherlock Holmes Stories. By the time you next hear from him, he hopes to have written more.

William Todd has been a Holmes fan his entire life, and credits *The Hound of the Baskervilles* as the impetus for his love of both reading and writing. He began to delve into fan fiction a few years ago when he decided to take a break from writing his usual Victorian/Gothic horror stories. He was surprised how well-received they were, and has tried to put out a couple of Holmes stories a year since then. When not writing, Mr. Todd is a pathology supervisor at a local hospital in Northwestern Pennsylvania. He is the husband of a terrific lady and father to two great kids, one with special needs, so the benefactor of these anthologies is close to his heart.

Thomas A. (Tom) Turley has been "hooked on Holmes" since finishing *The Hound of the Baskervilles* at about the age of twelve. However, his interest in Sherlockian pastiches didn't take off until he wrote one. *Sherlock Holmes and the Adventure of the Tainted Canister* (2014) is available as an e-book and an audiobook from MX Publishing. It also appeared in *The Art of Sherlock Holmes – USA Edition 1*. Tom's collection of historical pastiches entitled *Sherlock Holmes and the Crowned Heads of Europe*, was published in 2021. Although he has a Ph.D. in British history, Tom spent most of his professional career as an archivist with the State of Alabama. He and his wife Paula (an aspiring science fiction novelist) live in Montgomery, Alabama. Interested readers may contact Tom through MX Publishing or his Goodreads author's page.

DJ Tyrer is the person behind Atlantean Publishing and has had fiction featuring Sherlock Holmes published in volumes from MX Publishing and Belanger Books, and an issue of *Awesome Tales*, and has a forthcoming story in *Sherlock Holmes Mystery Magazine*. DJ's non-Sherlockian mysteries can be found in anthologies such as *Mardi Gras Mysteries* (Mystery and Horror LLC) and *The Trench Coat Chronicles* (Celestial Echo Press), and on *Mystery Tribune*.
DJ Tyrer's website is at *https://djtyrer.blogspot.co.uk/*
DJ's Facebook page is at *https://www.facebook.com/DJTyrerwriter/*
The Atlantean Publishing website is at *https://atlanteanpublishing.wordpress.com/*

Peter Coe Verbica *also has a story in Part XXXIX*

Mark Wardecker has contributed Sherlockian pastiches to *Sherlock Holmes Mystery Magazine* and the *MX Book of New Sherlock Holmes Stories – Parts XIII* and *XXXIII,* and has contributed Solar Pons pastiches to *The New Adventures of Solar Pons*. These stories and others can be found in his book, *The Endeavours of Sherlock Holmes* (MX Publishing, 2022). He is also the editor and annotator of *The Arrival of Solar Pons: Early Manuscripts* *and Pulp Magazine Appearances of the Sherlock Holmes of Praed Street* (Belanger Books, 2023) and has contributed articles to *The Baker Street Journal* and *The Sherlock Holmes Journal* (forthcoming). He is an instructional technologist at Colby College.

Matthew White is an up-and-coming author from Richmond, Virginia in the USA. He has been a passionate devotee of Sherlock Holmes since childhood. He can be reached at *matthewwhite.writer@gmail.com*

The MX Book of New Sherlock Holmes Stories
Edited by David Marcum
((MX Publishing, 2015-   )

"This is the finest volume of Sherlockian fiction I have ever read, and I have read, literally, thousands." – Philip K. Jones

"Beyond Impressive . . . This is a splendid venture for a great cause!"
– Roger Johnson, Editor, *The Sherlock Holmes Journal,*
The Sherlock Holmes Society of London

Part I: 1881-1889; Part II: 1890-1895; Part III: 1896-1929

Part IV: 2016 Annual

Part V: Christmas Adventures

Part VI: 2017 Annual

Eliminate the Impossible
Part VII: (1880-1891); Part VIII: (1892-1905)

2018 Annual
Part IX: (1879-1895); Part X: (1896-1916)

Some Untold Cases
Part XI: (1880-1891); Part XII: (1894-1902)

2019 Annual
Part XIII: (1881-1890); Part XIV: (1891-1897); Part XV: (1898-1917)

Whatever Remains . . . Must be the Truth
Part XVI: (1881-1890); Part XVII: (1891-1898); Part XVIII: (1898-1925)

2020 Annual
Part XIX: (1882-1890); Part XX: (1891-1897); Part XXI: (1898-1923)·

Some More Untold Cases
Part XXII: (1877-1887); Part XXIII: (1888-1894); Part XXIV: (1895-1903)

2021 Annual
Part XXV: (1881-1888); Part XXVI: (1889-1897); Part XXVII: (1898-1928)

More Christmas Adventures
Part XXVIII: (1869-1888); Part XXIX: (1889-1896); Part XXX: (1897-1928)

2022 Annual
Part XXXI: (1875-1887); Part XXXII: (1888-1895); Part XXXIII: (1896-1919)

"However Improbable . . . ."
Part XXXIV: (1878-1888); Part XXXV: (1889-1896); Part XXXVI: (1897-1919)

2023 Annual
Parts XXXVII (1875-1889), XXXVIII (1889-1896), and XXXIX (1897-1923)

In Preparation
Further Untold Cases (Part XL – and XLI and XLII as well?)
. . . and more to come!

The MX Book of New Sherlock Holmes Stories
Edited by David Marcum
(MX Publishing, 2015-)

Publishers Weekly says:

Part VI: *The traditional pastiche is alive and well . . . .*

Part VII: *Sherlockians eager for faithful-to-the-canon plots and characters will be delighted.*

Part VIII: *The imagination of the contributors in coming up
with variations on the volume's theme is matched by their ingenious resolutions.*

Part IX: *The 18 stories . . . will satisfy fans of Conan Doyle's
originals. Sherlockians will rejoice that more volumes are on the way.*

Part X: *. . . new Sherlock Holmes adventures of consistently high quality.*

Part XI: *. . . an essential volume for Sherlock Holmes fans.*

Part XII: *. . . continues to amaze with the number of high-quality pastiches.*

Part XIII: *. . . Amazingly, Marcum has found 22 superb pastiches . . .
his is more catnip for fans of stories faithful to Conan Doyle's original*

Part XIV: *. . . this standout anthology of 21 short stories written
in the spirit of Conan Doyle's originals.*

Part XV: *Stories pitting Sherlock Holmes against seemingly supernatural phenomena highlight
Marcum's 15th anthology of superior short pastiches.*

Part XVI: *Marcum has once again done fans of Conan Doyle's originals a service.*

Part XVII: *This is yet another impressive array of new but traditional Holmes stories.*

Part XVIII: *Sherlockians will again be grateful to Marcum and
MX for high-quality new Holmes tales.*

Part XIX: *Inventive plots and intriguing explorations of aspects of Dr. Watson's
life and beliefs lift the 24 pastiches in Marcum's impressive 19th Sherlock Holmes anthology*

Part XX: *Marcum's reserve of high-quality new Holmes exploits seems endless.*

Part XXI: *This is another must-have for Sherlockians.*

Part XXII: *Marcum's superlative 22nd Sherlock Holmes pastiche anthology features 21 short stories
that successfully emulate the spirit of Conan Doyle's originals while expanding on the canon's
tantalizing references to mysteries Dr. Watson never got around to chronicling.*

Part XXIII: *Marcum's well of talented authors able to mimic the
feel of The Canon seems bottomless.*

Part XXIV: *Marcum's expertise at selecting high-quality pastiches remains impressive.*

Part XXVIII: *All entries adhere to the spirit, language, and characterizations of
Conan Doyle's originals, evincing the deep pool of talent Marcum has access to.
Against the odds, this series remains strong, hundreds of stories in.*

Part XXXI: *. . . yet another stellar anthology of 21 short pastiches that
effectively mimic the originals . . . Marcum's diligent searches for high-quality
stories has again paid off for Sherlockians.*

Part XXXIV: *Mind-bending puzzles are the highlight of Marcum's fully satisfying 34th anthology,
which again demonstrates that multiple authors are capable of giving Sherlock Holmes and
Watson innovative mysteries to tackle while staying in character. Marcum's inventory of canonical
pastiches shows no signs of being exhausted any time soon.*

The MX Book of New Sherlock Holmes Stories
Edited by David Marcum
(MX Publishing, 2015-   )

An Investees' Anthology
Edited by David Marcum
(MX Publishing, 2022   )

Selected Contributions to
The MX Book of New Sherlock Holmes Stories
by Members of
The Baker Street Irregulars

*All royalties from this collection are being donated
for the benefit of the preservation of Undershaw,
a school for special needs students located at
one of the former homes of Sir Arthur Conan Doyle*

Stories, Forewords, and Poems in this volume
have previously appeared in Parts I – XXXVI of
The MX Book of New Sherlock Holmes Stories

Featuring Contributions by:

Mark Alberstat, Marino C. Alvarez, Peter Calamai, Catherine Cooke, Carla Coupe, David Stuart Davies, John Farrell, Lyndsay Faye, Sonia Fetherston, Jayantika Ganguly, Jeffrey Hatcher, Roger Johnson, Leslie S. Klinger, Ann Margaret Lewis, Bonnie MacBird, Stephen Mason, Julie McKuras Nicholas Meyer, Jacquelynn Morris, Otto Penzler, Christopher Redmond, Tracy J. Revels, Steven Rothman, Nancy Holder, Mark Levy (and Arlene Mantin Levy), Nicholas Utechin, and Sean M. Wright (and DeForeest B. Wright, III)

MX Publishing

MX Publishing is the world's largest specialist Sherlock Holmes publisher, with over five-hundred titles and over two-hundred authors creating the latest in Sherlock Holmes fiction and non-fiction

The catalogue includes several award winning books, and over two-hundred-and-fifty have been converted into audio.

MX Publishing also has one of the largest communities of Holmes fans on Facebook, with regular contributions from dozens of authors.

www.mxpublishing.com

@mxpublishing on Facebook, Twitter, and Instagram

445